I0608963

Quantum Entity
American Spring

Book 2
(qwɔ ntɨ m ɛ ntɪ tj*)

Bruce M Firestone

Learn By Doing School Publications
Ottawa, Canada

(*Hopi spelling of the name)

Quantum Entity Book 2 American Spring

A Learn By Doing School Book

Copyright © 2013 by Bruce M Firestone

Cover art and copyright © 2013 by EyeVero.com and prototypeD.org

For information, please contact:

Learn By Doing School Publications, 900 Morrison Drive, Suite 206, Ottawa, Canada K2H 8K7
Attention: Ms. Nina Brooks, ninabooks@rogers.com
Tel 1.613.566.3436 x 200
@Quantum_Entity @ProfBruce
www.brucemfirestone.com
www.facebook.com/QuantumEntityTrilogy
www.youtube.com/user/quantumentitytrilogy

Second Edition

Firestone, Bruce Murray, 1951—

ISBN 978-0-9880341-6-7 print

ISBN 978-0-9880341-7-4 electronic

Reviews for Book 1 and Advance Reviews for Book 2

"American Spring, Firestone's second book in his Quantum Entity Trilogy, is every bit as gripping as his first. He has woven together an incredible set of characters and events that keep you turning the pages way too late into the night. There is absolutely nothing predictable in this thought inspiring story as we follow these characters and their families half way around the solar system. I should point out that I am not what you might call a fantasy or sci-fi reader but Firestone has drawn me into his rich and exciting QE world leaving me impatiently waiting for Book 3!"

Andrew Penny, Founder,
KingsfordConsulting.com

...

"With straightforward, relatable writing, Bruce M Firestone builds an incredibly complex, intriguing and captivating story in Book 2. He manages to construct a technologically complex quasi-dystopian future brought on by Quantum technology while maintaining an eerily believable story. It is rare to see such a combination of mystery, love and war as well as business, economics & history woven in such a riveting fashion. Firestone keeps readers on the edge on their seats. It is awe-inspiring to experience the quantum universe he has created for us. Firestone sees opportunities for this technology, good and bad, as only a master entrepreneur and storyteller can. The technology evolves from a single entity (Pet3r) and application (Q-phones) to endless possibilities embedded, even trapping, society. I was even more amazed by the intense and progressive build-up that started in Book 1 and continues in Book 2. Problems and tension grow seamlessly; from a single corporation against the government to two species fighting for their continuation in a battle for solar system dominance amongst the great powers of the day. I am hooked. I can't wait for an epic finale."

Patrick Trahan, COO,
Therma Solaris

…

QE, we are all ONE, is an adventure as exciting and unpredictable as the unveiling of a new technology or discovery of a new love. It's a great tale about human spirit and its persistence. Quantum Entity had me on edge waiting to see what would happen next.

It was also a learning journey for me as much as for the book's main character—young physicist, Damien Bell. The book is about politics, the law, science, science fiction, science speculation, engineering and, above all, founding a globe-spanning, disruptive tech business and then facing down unexpected challenges that come with it, which form the core of the challenge that all entrepreneurs face. A great read for individuals from any background with lots of action and adventure thrown in as well as a moving love story—it's the beginning of a trilogy as enthralling as quantum technology itself.

Franco Varriano,
Co-founder, www.beaconize.com

…

Quantum Entity, written by serial entrepreneur Bruce M. Firestone, introduces an amazing concept that both educates and entertains. It has humble beginnings then explodes outward dealing first with the success of a young company then its trials which rival both the awesomeness of some of today's top tech enterprises and the awfulness of dealing with political insiders, dug-in business interests, lawyers and litigation. Damien Bell, QE's main protagonist, is a deep and attractive character—he embodies the spirit and drive of top tech entrepreneurs while still managing to maintain a humble outlook on life. It made me want to better myself.

QE also introduces a wide cast of passionate characters who surround Damien and Quantum Computing Corp, his startup. There's a sense of camaraderie that developed for me with these people and a strong distaste for the book's antagonists and anti-heroes. Prof Bruce found a way to create both an amazing story and one that teaches real life lessons. While his novel keeps you thinking, there's also no shortage of action, adventure, betrayal, sex and rock & roll to keep you turning page after page.

Chris Beaudoin,
@cjbeaudoin

...

Having recently re-read Mary Shelley's classic gothic tale Frankenstein or the Modern Prometheus, it was intriguing to take up Quantum Entity immediately thereafter. From early nineteenth-century Switzerland and Bavaria, I was jolted into mid twenty-first century North America but with eerily parallel moral and ethical dilemmas to ponder.

Frankenstein's monster is a hideous creature, who, when spurned by his creator, malevolently turns on him and those he loves. Damien Bell's creatures are seemingly benign and totally plugged into an artificial post-digital universe. Though having little or no mass, they verge on becoming sentient beings—having the power of perception.

This sci-fi thriller is a page-turner with plenty of twists and turns but along the way Prof Bruce suspends the narrative to launch into any number of mini-essays on social, political, scientific, engineering and business issues. We watch as socially awkward quantum physicist Damien, flying with pop princess Nell in her private jet, decides this is the perfect time and place to start a discourse on the Russian Dachnik movement for sustainable agriculture. Nell falls asleep. Go figure.

Pick up Quantum Entity and learn more about this cast of characters human as well as artificial but beloved creatures called Quantum Entities. You'll be glad you did.

Paul Kitchen,
Hockey Historian

...

You've got a winner here. After reading Part I, Discovery, I was totally hooked. It's better than 'The Goal' and more entertaining even than 'Dune'!

David Perry,
Partner, Perry-Martel International
Co-author, Guerrilla Marketing for Job Hunters 3.0

...

I really enjoyed Book 1—it gave me a fascinating view of what may lie ahead in the not so distant future, God help us. I came to care what happened to the characters and wanted to get to know them better. I also laughed out loud at times. The novel introduced me to many complex concepts and I found myself thinking on occasion: 'Huh, I didn't know that.' It was a pleasure to read the manuscript.

Margot O'Neil

...

I read QE while I was in the Caribbean. First, I want to say that I really liked the book—the story is compelling and interesting. Second, I love the characters. My only real criticism is I want more! I'm anxiously awaiting Book 2.

Christian Brydges

...

Prof Bruce has taken a lifetime's worth of lessons in business and life and successfully threaded them into a science fiction story set in the not-so-distant future. Quantum Entity entertains the reader while providing valuable insight into the fundamentals of creating a biz model and launching it. With predictions and commentary on issues related to politics, commerce, ancient civilizations, pop culture, science and engineering, Firestone has created a captivating story. By outlining core beliefs of his characters, his readers can see beyond conventional norms. Quantum Entity is not for the faint of heart though. Some events are quite graphic. However, if you're an entrepreneur, an engineer or someone looking for a literary roller coaster, Quantum Entity is the right book for you.

Matthew Conley,
Finance, Telfer School of Management

...

This is a well-crafted story about young physicist Damien Bell that nicely blends science, business and technology with some great characters set in a nearby future history. It'll keep you reading to the end! Fall down 7 times and Get up 8? That's me!

Ken Goodfellow, Chairman and CEO
of CKG International, ckginternational.com

...

Quantum Entity is a beautifully written story about Damien Bell—a brilliant young engineer turned businessperson who changes the world. Firestone crafted a thriller that kept me engaged the whole way! I really enjoyed it especially since I could really relate to both Damien and my favourite character, Miss Nell.

Isack Galib,
Telfer School of Management Alumni

...

Quantum Entity is a story of love and life's lessons. It's about growing up, trust, passion, business, entrepreneurship, finance, history... my list goes on. The detail captivated me throughout the novel but it was the ongoing mysteries that excited me for what's next.

Theresia Scholtes,
BA Law (Minor French),
Carleton University 2011.
@tclscholtes

...

Although this tale takes place in mid 21st Century North America, the relationships between these wonderful characters and the challenges they face are timeless. Reading Quantum Entity has made me a more effective leader—I respond to challenges in my own life in ways I have never been able to do before. Thanks, Prof Bruce.

Saad Rashid
investorsgroup.com/consult/saad.rashid/ENGLISH

...

Firestone writes with an authenticity that can only come from someone who has lived a life full with opportunities that stretch far beyond the confines of normalcy. He speaks with a voice that comes across with the legitimacy and simple power of other entrepreneur/explorer/authors such as Louis L'Amour or science fiction great Frederik Pohl. With an open, friendly and often humorous voice, the story speaks directly to the reader with the best of down home phrases and expressions. It makes this novel refreshingly approachable and charmingly geeky.

In a sense, Quantum Entity is a work of post-science fiction. Where science fiction has always used the 'big idea' to push forward a futuristic view of the world, Firestone uses hundreds of smaller ideas, some new, some old, some experiential, some based on common stereotypes and many drawn from points in our shared history, to draw a very believable map of how the next life-changing innovation may well be born into our world. Firestone uses these to empower the believability of the story while also engaging the reader, laying out simple yet highly fundamental ideas of business, politics and science which can often escape even seasoned professionals. The big idea is still there (and it is a game changer) but it is built on a foundation of smaller fragments which are the real critical underpinning of this first book in his trilogy. This tessellation of content to illustrate the bigger whole demonstrates that Firestone himself is a hacker; an individual capable of using and repurposing the best ideas to generate something familiar yet brand new.

Extending current models and trajectories of thought in a believable and engaging way, Firestone paints a picture of the future which somehow bridges being both optimistic and cautionary by laying out scenarios of a not-so-distant world which are both satirical and serious. Its central motto is: "Fall down 7 times, Get up 8" which means that Quantum Entity shows that despite setbacks, political wrangling or outright failure, humanity has always succeeded in pushing through the barriers it creates for itself. Whether it is Civil Rights, Women's Right's, Gay Rights or even one day perhaps the rights of

our digital or Quantum Counterparts, the drive to freedom
will always be at the heart of human nature.

Janak Alford, M. Arch.,
Founder, prototypeD Urban Workshops Inc.
prototypeD.org

...

Dedication

I dedicate American Spring to people who believe it is important to respect others and that they, in turn, deserve to be respected, to people who believe that honesty and trust are important and without them life is at least troublesome and often worthless and to people who believe in the joy that comes from achievement, tribal belonging, recognition, authenticity, caring, sharing, communicating, understanding, compassion, kindness, music, poetry, art, dance, science, learning, discovery and love.

This book is dedicated to people who work hard to keep their families together, sometimes when it is not easy to do. It is dedicated to people who forgive others their errors of omission and understand that you can love someone who is not perfect, as we all do.

It is not about being perfect or making no mistakes—it is about what you do afterwards, after making an error, sometimes a grievous one, that counts.

American Spring is about gaining experience, being trustworthy, learning who you can and cannot trust and earning then defending freedom—your own and those around you who you care about. Mostly, in a way, it's about love, spirituality and tolerance.

This book is ultimately dedicated to a person who embodies the best of all these qualities—my wife.

@ProfBruce
@Quantum_Entity
Crete, Greece

Foreword

Dr. Damien Bell sits on Death Row in San Quentin. Ellen Brooks is nearby in downtown San Francisco determined not only to do what she has to do to free Damien, the greatest physicist and engineer of the Quantum Era, but, in fact, overthrow the old Republic which has become incorrigibly corrupt starting at the top with its President. She is determined to replace the Republic of the United States of America with a new nation—to be called the Commonwealth of the United States.

To help her with her revolutionary aims, Ellen goes on a secret journey to Tunisia to meet with someone intimately familiar with efforts by patriots there to bring change to their nation more than 60 years ago. In Tunisia, she has a vision that every revolution requires a martyr but she rejects this conclusion or, perhaps, she misinterprets it.

On her return, Ellen becomes a target of retrograde parties determined to maintain the status quo, one in which a tiny minority of the population controls more than half the assets of their nation and 40% of all its income.

Ellen together with an unexpected ally set a trap for elements of the old regime which finally passes from the scene. As the regime is falling, traitors are revealed some of whom are revealed as doubly so.

The new Commonwealth faces enormous challenges as it tries to recover from an economic meltdown of colossal proportions. Its old currency is worthless and is replaced by the QED or QE Dollar, drawn on the only financial institution that cannot be hacked or undermined—Quantum Entity Reserve Bank. In many ways, the Commonwealth has fallen behind its main competitors but five new technologies (mindlink, nanosite construction and deconstruction, Quantum Tunneling, Quantum Bubble/Quantum Shielding and farm-in-a-box, aka Roxie) and two older ones (Q-phones and Quantum Entities) help to restore its edge.

In Book 2, relationships between the Brooks, Bell and Hopi families of Third Mesa are explored, discovered, uncovered and new ones created.

We meet Naya, as a child, and Sean Ruane, as a young man—two people who as they gain experience show promise as future leaders. Naya is a talented dancer before an unfortunate accident diverts her career path. She grapples with finding a new purpose before finding two—studying agronomy at Berkeley and working occasionally with IMG out of LA on film.

The shadow of the Cartesian Powers grows longer as Book 2 closes. They want to establish a reordered world with Imperial China and its 1,000 year ally, Germania, in hegemonistic control. They promise it will be a peaceful, productive, structured world with strong discipline imposed by Mandarins and their allies. The Central Commission for Discipline Inspection and Party Loyalty will possess a complete record of every human's DNA and the means to deliver nanosite deconstructors that dissemble people into their component parts (their basic elements plus water and water vapor) if they misbehave. There is just one issue—they will first need to obtain the source code for this new weapon system from Sean Ruane. They believe they have the means of persuading him—they detain a person close to him for these purposes.

Nanosite deconstructors developed by Sean while at Berkeley are not originally intended as weapons. They are useful for turning dangerous landfill sites, old liquid waste dumps, even discarded nuclear materials into benign substances. They also find a use building a vast Earth-bound tentacle-like underground network that go to hydrothermal vents on the ocean floor and can supply Roxies with all the nutrients they need to inexpensively

Bruce M Firestone

produce food stuffs and meet energy needs for humanity for thousands of years. They also connect them via Quantum Tunnel to Luna Colony and Mars Colony.

The Cartesians dominate Luna Colony the way that the Commonwealth and World LLC DARCH do Mars. DARCH is hoping to raise a Quantum Shield around Mars so that they can increase the amount and change the type of solar radiation falling on the planet. Economic activity in the Moon-Mars-Earth system is shifting more and more towards Mars and, if the Quantum Shield is a success, this will accelerate. A Commonwealth-dominated Mars or, worse, an independent one, is unacceptable to certain elements in the governing structure of Imperial China.

They find a suitable provocation and unleash a new technology of their own—one that terrorizes as much as it destroys. Cartesians are now able to kill people en masse but leave their property untouched.

The War (which becomes known as Sol War I) is launched simultaneously on Earth and Mars. The Commonwealth experiences a Hiroshima and Nagasaki moment times ten. There is resistance though on Earth and also on Mars. People in the Commonwealth will do whatever's needed to protect the ones they are closest to. There is love and great sacrifice amongst the chaos...

Contents

Chapter 16 Sinofighter

Epilogue

To come:
Quantum Entity Book 3 The Successors (2014)

...

Synopsis of Trilogy, Its Style, Themes, Cast of Characters, Geography and Technology

This is a trilogy that concerns itself with the big questions about life and the small details of how we live it. Young Damien Bell, physicist and engineer, designs then unleashes Quantum Communications and Quantum Entities on an unsuspecting mid-21st Century world. The tech company he co-founds along with Romanian mathematician Traian Vasilescu and Elmira College marcom graduate Ellen Brooks, Quantum Computing Corporation (QCC), becomes a fast growing, vastly profitable, globe-spanning one in a remarkably short few years.

Inevitably, they come into conflict with established commercial interests as well as security agencies around the world, first, because their quantum phones (later known as Q-phones) based as they are on hacked iPhone 40s completely disintermediate established carriers and, second, Quantum Entities (QEs) are fully actualized quantum computers that are not only superb examples of AI but appear to be conscious, sentient creatures come to join humanity on its voyage to a collective destiny whatever that may be. What it also means is that Internet security, paywalls and all forms of digital encryption are wide open to possible exploitation by QEs and their human counterparts as well as QCC.

Quantum Entities apparently comply with all human laws but there appears to be an issue with a small minority of QEs called 'Drogues' who, for some reason, do not successfully form a bond with their human hosts. This ultimately results in a War on Drogues and other problems for QCC and its founders.

The introduction of Quantum Communications and Quantum Entities leads to an era of Quantum Economics (later called the Quantum Era), a time when scarcity becomes a thing of the past at least for some. It also leads to a new competition amongst nations—some like the United States embracing (to an extent) the new era while others such as Imperial China apparently rejecting this new technology. This leads to a clash amongst world powers when Imperial China and its ally, Germania (a renamed EU), attempt to impose a new hegemony on a mostly unwilling planet. The last book of the trilogy follows the lives of those who would resist a new tyranny imposed by the Cartesian Powers (sometimes referred to as the Cartesian Axis or simply Cartesians) and how they attempt to do just that.

The trilogy spans four generations and follows three (somehow interconnected) families (the Bells, the Brooks and the family of Chief Dan of the Hopis of Third Mesa) as well as introducing a wide cast of supporting characters and geography. There is also a prequel chapter at the end of the trilogy that returns to the year 1929. There is one final Postscript with the final two reveals of the trilogy.

Style

The trilogy is written with a present tense narrator, an unusual choice for a novel. The concept is to give the reader a sense that s/he is actually there and that he or she is part of this unfolding history.

Furthermore, these are a new type of novel— Learning Outcome Novels. There are three main types of novel—*genre* (horror, sci-fi, fantasy, crime, mystery, thriller, romance, pulp, graphic, historical, action and adventure, western, children, young adult, teen), *literary* (artsy) and *mainstream* (bestseller). This trilogy is different.

Even though it is part of a continuum of work that has gone before, it contains, for example, 835 learning outcomes in Book 1 alone, the most important of which is how to conceive, found, grow and then defend a world

Bruce M Firestone

spanning (tech) company. The reader gets to see how a group of very smart young entrepreneurs go about designing then implementing a top notch business model for the 21st Century. The prime learning outcome of Book 2 (American Spring) is centered on how to restructure and revive a nation-state whose economy is failing. There is some additional work done with business models and introduction of concepts like demography, population projections and environmentalism. In Book 3 (The Successors), we learn how a product manager, trying to defend his nation from attack, develops and controls a complex effort on the scale of a Manhattan Project.

It is a multi-themed work. Book 1 has five main themes; it's a biz story, a political and legal one, involves science, science speculation, science fiction, engineering and technology, has action and adventure and, finally, it's a love story. Then a sixth theme emerges—it evolves a spiritual and mystical dimension which become more apparent, especially in Books 2 and even more so 3. If the reader learns anything from these books (hopefully presented as part of an engaging and entertaining storyline) about business, science, engineering, urban planning, urban economics, urban design, yoga, natural philosophy, sound engineering, startups, entrepreneurship, intrapreneurship, artpreneurship, product management, Mayan culture, religion, the Internet, business models, weather forecasting, history, politics, law, economics, statistics, military culture, PR, media, art, architecture, NLP, HR, venture capital, big business, big politics, creditor proofing, agriculture, ultralighting, hang gliding, whitewater rafting, kite surfing, new games/sports, tech, Hopi ways, Maori Poi performance art, jam dancing, Lunar and Mars colonization, Europa, demographics, environmentalism, quantum physics, quantum communications, airships, Belize, Guatemala, Four Corners, Crete and many other locales, then mission accomplished. At the end of each book, a list of learning outcomes is included for easier reference should a reader ever wish to revisit some of the concepts introduced here.

The cast of characters is largely made up of Americans, Canadians, Kiwis, Belizeans and Euros so the books use American spellings and units of measurement (inches, feet, miles, pounds, Fahrenheit...) when in the US or when an American is talking and centimetres, metres, kilometres, grams or kilograms, Celsius... nearly everywhere else as well as British spellings when geography calls for it.

The Author's Note at the end of Book 1 goes into a great deal more detail on new conventions this trilogy attempts to establish.

By the end of the trilogy, the author tries to answer age-old questions such as—at what point would sufficiently intelligent AI warrant extension of human rights, where are other intelligent lifeforms and why don't we see them in the Galaxy around us, are we alone, how did life begin and what is the purpose of life?

Themes—Book 1

The trilogy starts out innocently enough with Damien Bell, like most recent grads, trying to earn enough to pay back his student loans. He moonlights as a sound engineer on major live events. This is how he first meets world superstar, Miss Nell, as her global tour nears its end—her last show is held in Toronto during Nuit Blanche.

Damien along with Ellen Brooks and Traian Vasilescu are trying to get their new tech company, Quantum Computing Corp, off the ground. Both Damien and Traian mostly just want to do Maths and Physics so it falls to Ellen and her biz dev team to actually create, launch and grow a viable business then defend it. Her principal adviser is Angelo Keller, a Boston-based VC.

Damien has little experience outside academia but

Bruce M Firestone

this changes soon after he meets and then goes off with Nell for the first time. His stay in Four Corners, Third Mesa and at Phantom Ranch as well as his near-death experience on the Salomon River in Idaho awakens spirituality in him that he never knew is there.

Nell feels that sex is overrated but is canny enough never to reveal her feelings to her fans. Still she responds to Damien in a way she has never experienced before. On returning to Toronto from his adventures with Nell for the launch of QCC, Damien is more focused on his research and his company than before. Ellen is the glue that holds the company together through its many phases of development. She is also secretly in love with Damien which leads to a love triangle that takes until more than half way through Book 2 to fully resolve. Even then, it is not really resolved. Their love story is about to get even more complicated.

The launch of Quantum Computing Corp's hacked iPhone 40s that come with a surpise on the upside—a QE that bonds with the first human each Entity (sometimes called Counterpart) comes into contact with—is a success. They first launch their Q-phones into a health and wellness vertical. These helping professionals are immeasurably helped themselves by not only having smartphones that are infinitely fast and come with unlimited bandwidth but their new QE helpmates can do many tasks for them and with them greatly extending their ability to care for their patients.

From there, Q-phones and QEs spread like wildfire to much of the rest of the population.

QEs are pre-programmed to follow (an amended set of) the three laws of robotics but not everyone feels that the arrival of an apparently sentient form of AI is benign. Certainly, established carriers are hard pressed to compete with QCC smartphones and they use their influence with Department of Commerce and others to go after upstart QCC and its monopoly in this new era of

Quantum Economics.

There is mounting pressure to turn off QEs with no more thought given to it than turning off a toaster. The matter comes before SCOTUS (Supreme Court of the United States) where Quantum Entity Pet3r, the first of his kind, makes a surprise appearance in defense of his brothers and sisters—'Quantum People'. The arguments made by QCC's lead lawyer (Jerom Van Der Hout) and Pet3r before the Supreme Court are reminiscent of the arguments made in civil rights, gay rights and women's rights movements of years ago—basically, they are asking, 'At what point do artificially intelligent creatures like QEs deserve to have human rights extended to them?'

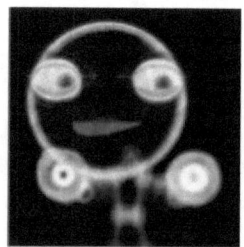

Pet3r Whose Q-Number is 1

In order to extinguish QEs, US agencies require access to the Quantum Key. Only Damien Bell knows where that is. Dr. Bell believes that if you want to keep a secret, tell no one. As a result, Dr. Bell is interred by the US until he is prepared to release the Key to them which he is not prepared to do—it would be tantamount, in his view, to genocide.

Towards the end of Book 1, US Army National Guard vehicles are taken over by Drogue QEs and there is a battle in front of SCOTUS. After this, QEs are banned in much of the world and are forced underground. QCC is placed in receivership and most of its principals are ruined financially or in prison or both.

Ellen Brooks, helped by gay rights leader-in-waiting, Evan Salazar, goes to QCC America HQ in San Francisco to

Bruce M Firestone

start the largest protest movement seen in the US in nearly a century.

There are five main themes in Book 1—engineering, science and science fiction, biz dev, politics and the law, action/adventure and romance. Finally, a sixth theme emerges—one of spirituality.

Themes—Book 2

Book 2 begins in Austin, Texas and picks up the story based on a minor character in Book 1—Jagad Durai, a 15-year old hacker, who has discovered something marvelous about QEs that no one else, including the inventor of QEs, knows. The chapter also introduces Arcadia (Cady) Valenzuela, Jag's best friend.

We don't see Ellen again until Chapter 2 but we learn that she is now head of a movement that seeks to establish a new nation, the Commonwealth of the United States. USC stands in opposition to the Republic of the United States. The Commonwealth will be based out of San Francisco and soon nearly 30 States will be solidly in their camp.

Ellen makes a secret visit to Tunisia to meet up with a person (a Sufi mystic) who has information that will help her in her mission—to completely end the Republic and replace it (as peacefully as possible) with the new Commonwealth.

Damien remains in US Custody and is in bad shape. He has still not been persuaded to give up the Quantum Key.

The first part of Book 2 (which is Part IV of the trilogy) is full of palace intrigue as the President of the United States, Samuel Schwinn, fights to hold onto power. He is determined not to be the last President of the Republic now nearing its 300th year.

It ends with three surprises—a double agent revealed, a traitor revealed and a murder mystery.

Part V of the trilogy is about reviving the economy of the Commonwealth of the United States which has been in the dumpster since the ban on QEs is first introduced by the now disgraced Republic and the short era of Quantum Economics, a time when scarcity starts to become a thing of the past, came to an end. The scene switches between San Fran, Vancouver, Maya Fair (Nell's home in San Pedro Town on Ambergris Caye) and Stockholm.

Ellen is determined to see the Commonwealth catch up to Imperial China and Germania not to mention other world powers such as the AU (African Union) not only in terrestrial technology but also space-based assets in the emerging Moon-Mars-Earth system.

Mars Colony is becoming an important economic engine and will be more so after they raise their planetary shield which will improve Mars weather and living conditions.

Part VI introduces the reader to Naya whose early life is split between San Francisco and Vancouver. She is largely brought up by her father. Naya's life is marred by a sudden illness that changes the course of her life dramatically.

Naya carries the last third of Book 2 and much of Book 3.

Naya is torn between three men in her life—one who is fabulously wealthy (his family owns the enormous 24/7 c-store empire), one who is a major Bundesliga (football) star on Luna Colony and one who is a scientist working on nanosite technology, a plain Irishman by the name of Sean Ruane.

Book 2 will also reveal some of the hitherto unknown interconnections between the three families—the Bells, the Brooks and Nell's people—the Hopi of Third Mesa. Other questions such as what caused the Drogue problem, how many senses do QEs actually have, how long do they live, why do most QEs match the gender of their human counterparts while some do not, what do the messages

Bruce M Firestone

left behind at Marco Gonzalez really mean and other unresolved mysteries are disclosed in Books 2 and 3.

As Part VI and Book 2 near their end, storm clouds appear. Even though the Commonwealth is doing better economically and with greater social harmony, Imperial China and Germania, now joined in a 1,000-year Friendship Treaty and called by many the Cartesian Powers, have found new ways to threaten freedom everywhere. The first Sinofighters appear. Sol War I is about to break out and will affect humans and QEs everywhere in the Moon-Mars-Earth system.

Attacks on Mars cause the leadership there to pursue an independent course marked by a surprising turn of events that affects the entire solar system.

An unfortunate misunderstanding separates Naya from her true love at a time when she is most vulnerable. Evil doers seek to capture her to use her as leverage to finally pry loose valuable information that is still beyond their reach.

Themes—Book 3

Book 3 begins with the issue—what to do about the continuing problem with Drogues. The Commonwealth is preparing to use the Moriarty Trap on them—a way to divert them without killing them or damaging the greater QE population.

While this problem has come to the forefront, no one really knows what to do about the real issue—the challenge posed by Sinofighters. The sudden, unexpected attacks on the Commonwealth on Earth and on Mars by Imperial China and Germania mean that everyone is either hiding behind quantum shields or they are dead.

It is up to a group of Commonwealth scientists to counter this new technology with a super weapon of their own, nicknamed 'Hewy'. The location of the Quantum key is finally revealed.

Hewy is only partially successful. It slows down attacks by Imperial China and Germania but does not end them. The survivors of the Commonwealth are cornered and given two choices—incarceration in camps or death. But then third and fourth alternatives appear.

Naya remains a prisoner and her lover, now realizing that he made a mistake, is determined to rescue her and punish those responsible not only for her incarceration but also the things they have forced her to do for them. He is assisted in his quest by a young warrior monk—a girl determined to help both him and Naya and also to never be a victim like so many others at the hands of Cartesian might. Readers might be surprised to learn the identity of this female monk.

Book 3 answers some of the big questions—are we alone in the universe, why don't we see other intelligent beings and what is the purpose of life?

Some Commonwealth survivors take a new third option while others escape to the Guatemalan Highlands (a 4th option) using some new tech of their own—personal quantum shielding. They will remain there until circumstances change in their homeland.

Before the trilogy ends, the leader of the free peoples hidden in the south will take final revenge on someone who has harmed all three families irreparably. She will be assisted in this by Dekka, silent Croatian head of security since the time of Nell.

Book 3 also includes at its end a prequel chapter that explains the origin of the third way out. It follows the 1929 journey of historical figure Paul Dirac, Quantum Physicist, from Cambridge to Japan by way of the Panama Canal and Ambergris Caye and what he does in the caves beneath the Mayan tri-pyramid structure at Marco Gonzalez. It also explains how Minoan artifacts somehow end up in Oregon and why they use a Mayan numbering system despite the fact that the Minoans predate the Mayans by at least 1,000 years.

Bruce M Firestone

Structure of the Trilogy

Each book has a table of Contents, 16 chapters and one epilogue and is divided into three parts. Hence, the entire trilogy has 48 chapters, three epilogues and nine parts (I to IX). At the end of the trilogy there is a prequel chapter set in 1929. There is one last Postscript at the very end.

The Trilogy begins as the midpoint of the 21st Century approaches and ends in the early part of the 22nd Century. The prequel chapter adds another 120 years (approximately) of history. The final Postscript contains the last two reveals of the trilogy.

Each book also includes a List of Learning Outcomes at its end as well as an Author's Note.

Principal Human Characters—Book 1*
(* In approximate order of appearance.)

Damien Bell, age 22, when we first meet him. He is a quantum physicist doing his post doc at U of T. Tall, trim build, brown hair. He has old fashioned values because he was brought up by his Grandfather. Damien's QE counterpart is **Pet3r** (pronounced 'Peter').

Ellen Brooks, age 19 at the beginning of Book 1. Curly blond hair down to her shoulder blades. From wealthy upstate New York background. Biz dev and biz model whiz as well as marcom genius. Ellen is mated to **Ash3r**, one of the few QEs who does not match the gender of his or her human counterpart.

Traian Vasilescu, Romanian mathematician and hacker. **Vl4d** is Traian's QE.

Dr. Luis Castagino over-seeing Damien's post doc work. Dr. Castagino is originally from Argentina and is a Professor of Mathematics whose best work is behind him. He recognizes that in Damien, he has a second shot at (reflected) glory.

Nell, age 25, performance artist from Palos Verdes, California. Auburn-haired beauty. 1/4 Hopi. Granddaughter of **Chief Dan of the Hopi**. Nell's QE is **Su7e**.

Pops, Damien's grandfather.

Tony Reznik, age 48, Nell's agent.

Dafne Weinstein, late 40s, early 50s. Nell's publicist.

Wendy Morales, Nell's conditioning coach, a hipster from LA.

Dekka, Nell's silent Croatian head of security.

Elsu late 30s. Hopi woman. Widow. Mother of **Daniella** also known as 'Ella'.

Angelo Keller, Senior Partner at BVP (Bessemer Ventures Partners). Keller is based in Cambridge. 103 years old when we first meet him. His QE: **Adu1us**

Gillian Boys, granddaughter of **Tim Boys**, CDN outfitter in Belize. Ginger hair, compact and tough. Freckles. Funny. Resourceful.

Javier and his spouse **Mica** (Belizean owners of the Caye Caulker Island Princess Hotel) plus their 17-yr old daughter **Dakota**.

Captain Rudy Filane, water taxi boat captain out of Belize City.

Private Raymond Michaud, everyone calls him **Sunny**. Member, Royal Canadian Dragoons (Petawawa, Ontario). Hometown: Miramichi, New Brunswick.

Boyd Combs, 42 yr old descendent of **Robert Combs**. Ultralight pilot. Leader of the **Black Aces Reunion Flying Club**, also known as the **B.A.R.F. Club.**

AJ Ramos, impossibly good looking Hollywood Actor.

Bert Steenbakker but everyone calls him **Dango**. School Bully.

Jay, Marine Corps vet. Pal of Damien's.

Zbigniew Zimmermann, senior official at DHS. First to understand what QEs loose on the Internet means. Pursues QCC for contravention of FCC, DOC and ICANN rules and for national security reasons. Aka **Dr. Evil**.

Erik Renke, investigative reporter for Toronto Chronicle Tab.

Mike Cronkey, OLA Tech Crunch reporter from Northern California, who is interested in getting the real story out there; befriends Ellen who becomes a confidential source for him and Tech Crunch.

La'kisha Tomlinson, Federal Court Judge—US District Court for the Southern District of New York (Manhattan). **Z4ra** is her QE.

Mary O'Regan, Ellen's horny roommate in Toronto.

Aziz Mukono, QCC's rent-a-CFO.

Anthony del Castillo, one of the top biz dev guys at QCC.

Sayed Bashir and QE **Q1ntas** from McLaughlin Markowitz Media. Acting Head of Media Relations at Q-Computing.

Samir and **Barbon**, Damien's (later Ellen's) bodyguards.

Ophélie Moreau, part of Ellen's security detail. From Trois-Rivières, Québec. Very tough. Very fast.

Vincent Bowen, Former LAPD Officer.

William Corace Junior, Former LAPD officer.

Yao Allitt, General Counsel for U.S. Department of Commerce. Later known as **General Yao.**

Paul Macintyre, RCMP safe cracker. Quantum Counterpart is **Ead0in.**

Jerom Van Der Hout, QCC lead counsel before SCOTUS. Working with other lawyers: **Peggy Shields, Walter Cunneyworth** and **Henry Linnert.**

Evan Salazar, key organizer of the We Are All ONE protest movement, also active in Gay Rights movement. Touted to perhaps become first real national leader of Gay Rights movement. Evan's QE is **He9burn**. Another QE who mysteriously does not match the gender of her human counterpart.

Justice James Roemer, SCOTUS Judge.

Madam Chief Justice, SCOTUS.

Marc Licinias, Commander of the Army National Guard (Brigadier General Retired).

Federik Bernstein, former elected New York District Attorney for New York County (Manhattan) now Solicitor General.

Roy Lew, Receiver for a large US-based accounting firm.

House Manager Sally Thornton, SF Women's shelter called St Jo's. They also have a choir called St Jo's Women's Choir.

Nahuel, Nell's 1/2 brother.

Principal Human Characters*—Books 2 and 3
(* In approximate order of appearance.)

Jagad (nicknames, Jag and Reed). 15 year old Indo-American hacker living in Austin with parents, **Kiri** and **Pal**, owners of **Pasand Palace** on **Middle Fiskville Road**. Last name **Durai**. Jag's QE is **G4nesha**. Nickname: **Nesha**.

Arcadia **Valenzuela (nickname Cady).** Both Cady and Jag are at the Liberal Arts and Science Academy (LASA) High School of Austin.

Tommy Tolbert also known as '**Tank**'. LASA Maths and Physics teacher. Former Texas Tech football player. Hero of the Yangon Engagement. Teaches and mentors Jag.

Austin Vue newsfeed talk show host **Sandra 'Sandy' Lopez.**

Maria Mayfield, Austin-born supermodel and new voice of **Nell Perfumes.**

TNN's KC 'Casey' Barnett. News Narrator for TNN. 35 years old. Brunette, 5' 8". Skinny. Blue eyes, fair skin.

Jin Liú, an untenured prof at **University of Texas at Austin in Physics (UT Physics).**

Adam Campbell, Chief Executive Officer, Tunisiana.

Salem Bouazizi, bother of **Mohamed Bouazizi**, Sufi mystic.

Chuck Wong, scientist, imprisoned in San Quentin

with Damien.

Sabine Schwinn, President's daughter. First daughter. Neuroscience psychologist. PhD candidate at Yale. Her Papa's pet name for her is 'Puppet'.

President Samuel Schwinn, President of the Republic of the United States of America.

Sawyer Schwinn, Sabine's older brother who dies in a refinery fire.

Freid Hof, former navy seal, best buddy of Sawyer comes to Third Mesa to volunteer for the Commonwealth of the United States.

Daniella, Elsu's daughter. 20 years of age. UCSC student. Everyone calls her 'Ella'. Looks Hopi (long black hair) except she is quite tall, much taller than her mom, and has intense blue eyes. Her 'father' who died of alcohol poisoning is obviously not her biological father but Elsu will never tell anyone who that really is.

Micah Glazer, NYT reporter. Takes a leave of absence to write a biography on Ellen. Curly red hair, great sense of humor.

Dan 'Danny' Glazer, son of Micah and Daniella.

Farrar Staubach, General of the Army. S4y3rs is his (illegal) QE. Expert Texas Hold'em player.

Colonel Manuel Rabano (US Military Retired). Colonel Rabano is Ellen's military liaison.

Mr. Owen, Ellen's neighbor in San Fran

Rebecca, Mr. Owen's great granddaughter, Becky.

Jonesy, male nurse.

Donna Ann Agnes Brooks, Ellen's Mom, but everyone calls her Aggie. In part because of one of her middle names but mainly cuz she went to Texas A&M. Poi fire dancer.

Euphony, late 30s. Nickname—Euph. Holds séances at Vancouver's Wreck Beach with some of her Wicca and sells her art and other stuff at her foundry on Granville Island. Handmade talismans of fertility. Very womanly figure, like the mini goddesses she designs and fabricates.

Her last name is secret.

Zora, Euphony's daughter.

Zachary, Zora's son. His nickname is 'Ray'.

Prez of UBC, **Henry Woo**, and his matronly wife **Elizabeth 'Betsy' Hammersmith** live in Norman MacKenzie House.

Bob Schultz, Secretary of Defense for the Commonwealth.

Dr. Shelby Zewyki, Secretary of Energy.

Alex, EA to Damien. Age 21.

José-Luis, Dakota and Traian's baby boy—**José-Luis** is born three years before **Naya**. **José-Luis'** nickname is JEL. JEL plays for FC Bayern Munich in the Bundesliga.

Jamal Ugo, JEL's agent at LA-based IMG. Former NBA player. Ran IMG Basketball Academy before becoming head of IMG Sports Academies. Now one of their top agents.

Finn and **Magellan** (fraternal twins), Naya's younger twin brothers.

Caleb De Theirry, kite surfer dude from NZ sometimes mistaken as an Aussie. He's 1/2 Maori.

Tane, Caleb's 9-year old son. Blond haired, home schooled 1/4 Maori living with his Dad on the Princesa Agnes where his father is in charge of water sports.

Joe (Ya Ya) Jaime, Naya's revered dance teacher and choreographer.

Tor Haden, QB for the 49ers. Everyone calls him 'Thor'. He is a local boy originally from San Mateo County.

Darryl Hnatyshyn, Head of Mixed Media Collective, MMC.

Clifford Hexham II, hipster heir to inner city chain of c-stores called **24/7** that sells alcohol, guns, chips and pop.

Clifford Hexham I, 100+ year old father of Clifford Hexham II. Second wealthiest person on Earth. Head of San Fran-based **Club Les de Sades**. Successful Executive Producer (films).

Sean Ruane, blocky bloke studying at Berkeley.

People sometimes call him **'Micky'**. His family originally hales from **Falls Road in Belfast**, toughest Irish Catholic part of anywhere. Even though his family has been in America (Boston) since the 1840s, they proudly maintain their traditions. Sean's QE is not bonded with him. Nevertheless, they are allies. **0dri4n** is his Uncle Des' QE.

Niamh Ruane, red haired younger sister of Sean. She is 5, Sean is 15 when they become orphans and go to live with **Uncle Des** in Alameda County, California. 'Niamh' is pronounced 'Neve'. Her nicknames are 'Holy Jumpin' and a kind of derivative of that, 'Holly'. She is also known as Kaya, which means 'Elder Sister' in the language of the Hopi. She acquires yet another name in the trilogy, 'Yulsa' derived from Jajangyulsa.

Costa Levendakis, school buddy of Sean's.

Jon, Ellen's older bother, and his wife, **Natalie**, and their child, **Lily**.

Mikhail Andreeovich Zhukovsky, local San Fran Russian mobster.

Brother Rick Brydges, Padre.

Baby Michael, Naya's son. His nickname is 'Gus'. Red haired child. Green eyes.

Baby Zachary, Zora's dark haired son, nicknamed 'Ray'.

Mrs. Hunter, 23 or 24, petite, blond Texas cutie. Niamh's home room elementary school teacher in Port Isabel. Has five year old daughter (also a cute blond) from teen romance gone bad.

Gran Maestro Iridia del Rosario Villa, from Matamoros. Teaches Korean Mouhébong Taekwondo and use of weapons including especially nunchuk and kama. Mouhébong Taekwondo originates during the time of the Lee dynasty (1790). It represents seven colors of the rainbow—purity, beauty, harmony (with nature), creativity, defense, therapy and betterment.

*Principal Non-Human Characters**

(* In approximate order of appearance.)

Pet3r, Damien's QE partner. Pet3r's Q-number is 1.

Ash3r, Ellen's QE partner. Ash3r's Q-number is 3.

Vl4d, Traian's QE partner. Vl4d's Q-number is 2.

Toby, Damien's cat when he is a kid.

Su7e, Nell's QE who's Q-number is 4.

Adu1us, Angelo Keller's QE.

M4gnus, failed QE partner of Dr. Luis. Leader of the Drogues.

He9burn, mated to Evan Salazar.

Z4ra, La'kisha Tomlinson's QE.

Q1ntas, Sayed Bashir's QE.

Miss Buril, Doob/Dooby, Damien's Worry Dolls.

Dezba, Nell's Worry Doll.

Freddie, Traian's worry doll.

Ala5tair, of Scottish and Greek origin. Meaning of Alastair is 'man's defender'. Bonded with attorney Henry Linnert.

Ead0in, Paul Macintyre's QE.

S4y3rs, Farrar Staubach's QE

Oper1s, Richard Florida's QE. Becomes world famous urban redesigner. In the mold of **Hernando de Soto** and **Walt Rostow** as well as **Richard Florida**. Oper1s is Latin for 'building'.

Odri4n, QE friend of Sean Ruane.

Hortense, Ellen's cherished camel.

Tristan, Hortense's mate.

B4nq pronounced 'Bank' is a Drogue who works for M4gnus.

Popeye, Damien's cat when he is an adult.

Ti3-Gu41, pronounced Tie Gway (Tie-Guai) (Body Snatcher). First and tallest of the Sinofighters.

Sammy, Zora's hero camel.

Geography

Scenes occur in many places including:
- Toronto
- Rochester, New York
- Third Mesa [Near Four Corners]
- Phantom Ranch, Grand Canyon
- Salmon River, Idaho
- Boston
- Belize City
- Caye Caulker
- Ambergris Caye
- San Pedro Town
- Maya Fair
- Marco Gonzalez
- Bucharest
- NYC
- Langley Airforce Base
- Northern Ontario—The Lake
- St Jo's Women's Shelter in San Francisco
- San Francisco
- San Quentin
- Austin
- New Orleans
- Barton Creek Wilderness Park
- Carthage, Tunis, Tunisia
- Algeria and Morocco
- Ghudamis, *le temple du message*
- Washington DC
- Northeast Imperial China near the border with North Korea [Close to Shenyang or Shengjing, capital and largest city of Liaoning Province]
- Revival House, Pacific Heights, San Francisco. Views to water. Decent security. Revival-style, 'Beaux Arts' home.
- Wreck Beach, Vancouver
- Granville Island
- Norman MacKenzie House, University of British Columbia
- Vancouver

- New Zealand [North Island—Rotorua and Auckland]
- Stockholm
- Hermosa Beach
- Los Angeles
- San Antonio
- Salvation Army Kroc Center on Turk Street in San Francisco
- Bell Leadership Foundation, not-for-profit organization based in San Francisco and at Maya Fair
- Golden Gate Park and Spreckels Lake
- University of California, Berkeley
- Oregon (Umatilla National Forest)
- Luna Colony, Shackelton Crater, south pole of Moon, 21 km in diameter, 4.2 km deep
- Mars Colony, Valles Marineris, east of Tharsis near equator in Mars' western hemisphere, 9 km deep trench (4,000 km long and up to 200 km wide), HQ of DARCH
- Europa, source of water, Europan shrimp and Goby fish
- Dallas-Fort Worth metroplex
- Gabriola Island, Gulf Island, Strait of Georgia
- Port Isabella, Free State of Texas
- Q-space
- Guatemala Highlands [Near Quetzaltenango also known by indigenous name Xela]

Political Landscape

13 Colonies of Mars, 10 managed by DARCH, one each by Imperial China and Germania, one by Hippies

AU, African Union

Central Commission for Discipline Inspection and Party Loyalty

Club Les de Sades, powerful private club, San Francisco-based, allied with Rogues

Commonwealth of the United States, parliamentary democracy

DARCH, World LLC that manages Mars
Drogues, plague of unbounded Quantum Entities
Emergency War Power Act (EWAP)
Germania, renamed and expanded EU
Imperial China, muscular dominant power in Asia and on the Moon
National Revolutionary Army, People's Liberation Army, Sol Liberation Army
Quantum Computing Corporation, QCC introduces era of quantum economics
QCCII, QCC's successor, another World LLC
Republic of the United States of America, US or USA, run by corporate elites and moneyed political parties
Republican Old Guard, referred to as Rogues, domestic terrorists, seeking to reinstate old Republic
Shuanggui, Imperial China discipline system
Sinofighters, allied with Imperial Chinese stormtroopers
Sol War I, total war in the Moon-Mars-Earth system
Truth and Reconciliation Committee

Technology

Airship
Apple Picker
BPI, Birth Prevention Insert
Dampening Field
DNA marking
DNA scanning
Drogues
Farm-in-a-box, aka Roxie
Hatchery
Hewy
Media Wall
Mindlink/Quantum Entanglement
Mindscanner
Mtv, Materiality Television

Mtv Test, similar to screen test

Nanosite Constructors and Deconstructors, force decon or decon force

Nanosite Generator and nutrient feed system

Personal Quantum Shield

Pico Carbon Tube materials

Q-phone

Q-space

Quantum Bubble/Planetary Shield

Quantum Entities/Counterparts

Quantum Key

Quantum Scanners

Quantum Shielding

Quantum Spinner

Quantum Tunneling/Transport

Sinofighter

Sinofighter console

Skin coat or skin coating

Space Elevators on Luna and Mars

Tentacle Nutrient System attached to hydrothermal ocean vents

Vacuum Energy Communicator

Vacuum Energy Concentrator

Weapons

Cosh

Fan

Glock 29

Jiujiebian, a Chinese nine section whip, segmented metal chain used in their martial arts

Kama, right handed or left handed (looks like a deadly sickle)

Katana (long sword)

Nanosite DNA-seeking Deconstructors

Nanosite IT code-seeking Deconstructors

Nunchaku (nunchuks) capable of delivering lethal or

stunning blows, DNA-specific poisons and deconstructors, electric shock and vacuum energy via its Kontei; used by young female warrior monk—she calls her pair of nunchuks 'The Trods' short for freedom fighter in her language; its two handles are connected using a Himo (wire rope) instead of a chain—useful for garroting; performed in collaboration with Taekwondo

Sinofighter mindscanners

Tanto (knife)

Wakizashi (short sword)

Words/Phrases/Conventions

Cartesian Powers, sometimes referred to as the Cartesian Axis or just Cartesia

Persons therefrom are called, on occasion, Cartesians

Cartesia is the 1,000-year alliance of Imperial China and Germania (a renamed EU)

Germanian, Germanians, persons living in Germania of Germanian origin

Intricate, to involve someone in a scheme without their apparent volition

Jeld, join and meld two people during or after intercourse such that a mild electrical current passes between them

Media Wall, universal, two-way video and audio walls

Meteormorphologist, weather shaper on Mars or Luna

Mindlink, thought exchange between bonded QE and human or between two QEs sometimes denoted by hashtag (#) before each such thought or exchange

NSM mix, nanoscale mix, painted or sprayed on to make any surface a media wall

Paparrazzoid, unwanted photographer

Rogue, Republican Old Guard

Ukes, short for unmated QEs or uQE.

New Games/Toys/Sports

Bananas
Kids Sit Down Windsurfer
Snowboard Mini Hang Glider
Street Paddle Tennis
Superflyer XIV

Detailed Synopsis of Book 1

In mid-21st Century North America, brilliant young quantum physicist Damien Graham Bell launches his twin discoveries in communications and artificial intelligence that shake the foundations of society unleashing a storm of political, social and economic change.

Abandoned by his parents at a young age and brought up by his grandfather whom he calls 'Pops', Damien lives in Upstate New York and later moves to Toronto where he completes his post-doctoral work at University of Toronto's Department of Physics where we first meet him.

Damien is both a physicist and an engineer. He is joined at U of T by friend and colleague Traian Vasilescu, a brilliant Romanian-born mathematician and hacker who speaks axiomatic English, a result of a longstanding Romanian government policy to teach successive generations that language by having them watch American entertainment programs which are not dubbed—instead they have Romanian sub-titles. His post-doctoral adviser is Argentine-born Dr. Luis Castagino, also a mathematician specializing in quantum mechanics, who plays a role in what is to come.

Damien's work in the field of AI appears to have resulted in a new form of life, albeit an artificial one which he calls Quantum Counterparts and his colleague, fabulous business development specialist and New Yorker Ellen Brooks, calls Quantum Entities (QEs) because she

Bruce M Firestone

believes that they may, in fact, be sentient beings.

The company they found, Quantum Computing Corp (QCC), not only revolutionizes the communications industry, it introduces a new era of quantum economics— a condition where scarcity is a thing of the past. Inevitably, they come into conflict with entrenched business and political interests who subsequently enlist the services of Zbigniew Zimmermann (aka 'Dr. Evil'), a senior official at DHS, Department of Homeland Security, and then Yao Allitt, General Counsel for U.S. Department of Commerce (DOC), to rein in upstart QCC when it proves impossible for them to compete with these new Quantum Phones (Q-Phones) and QEs that not only bypass their existing networks and provide unlimited speed and bandwidth, they make search engines instantly irrelevant since QEs can provide intelligent search and much more besides to assist and benefit their human counterparts.

Damien is distracted from his scientific and startup work by Northern California-born performance artist and superstar, Miss Nell, whom he first meets at Nuit Blanche in Toronto where Nell and her group are appearing. Their adventures take them to Four Corners, Boise, the Salmon River, a mystical place called Third Mesa, Phantom Ranch (at the bottom of the Grand Canyon), the Colorado River, Palos Verdes, the Big Smoke (Toronto), San Pedro Town on Ambergris Caye, The Great Blue Hole and Marco Gonzalez.

It's at Marco Gonzalez while touring underground caves beneath a Mayan tri-pyramid structure that Damien and Traian with input from Dr. Luis discover that quantum pioneer Paul Dirac has been there (in 1929) and has left behind Bra-ket (also called Dirac) notation describing a completely new Quantum phenomenon that may be a basis for more world-changing research and development.

A growing global population of more than a half billion Q-Phones and QEs is causing disruptive change in global economies, especially in the US where QEs are highly concentrated. QEs are banned in Imperial China where they are considered a threat to national security since quantum communication and thought cannot be intercepted or decrypted by government agencies there or, in fact, anywhere. Opposition is also growing in the US and elsewhere—some of it coming from people who, with the advent of quantum economics, have lost their jobs and some from the religious fringe who consider intelligent Quantum Entities, which appear to be self actualizing and self aware, a challenge to God's plan for human mastery of Earth.

Still there is significant support for QCC since QEs are becoming an essential part of the US economy helping that once great Republic catch up to not only Imperial China but also the European Union and African Union.

Nell on returning to the New York area from her Euro Tour II to help Damien and QCC celebrate its 500 millionth user at the Countdown Party falls ill. A big announcement about the world's first trillion (New Dollar) IPO (Initial Public Offering) is expected from QCC's Board of Directors who are meeting on the same day as the Countdown Party.

Nell is forced to cancel her performance at the Party but, unwilling to let her partner down, she goes to meet him at a secret location for a private late-night dinner which Damien has carefully planned except that for the first time since she has known him, he is a no-show. Nell asks Damien's Quantum Counterpart, Pet3r, to show her a video record of what is keeping him away and is shocked to see that he has been forcibly taken by persons unknown to an unknown destination in an antique vehicle that contains no ICs (Integrated Circuits) and hence is opaque to QEs.

Nell calls on the one person she is certain has the resources—both mental faculties and financial capability—to find and deliver Damien Bell back to her.

Bruce M Firestone

That person is... Ellen Brooks. This begins a resolution of a love triangle that has formed between the three of them—Nell, Damien and Ellen with Ellen on the outside looking in.

Ellen enlists the silent head of Nell's security detail, indomitable and loyal Dekka, to help organize some of his best (former US military) buddies along with lawyer Henry Linnert who has secured a writ of Habeas Corpus from Judge Tomlinson for their upcoming visit to Langley Air Force Base where Ellen will negotiate with Dr. Zimmermann for Damien's release. Ellen secures Dr. Bell's release in return for a promise to consider adding existing carriers as QCC resellers (essentially cutting them in). She is also forced to concede to Dr. Evil that she will ask Damien to release to DHS the location of the Quantum Key which will allow the Department to intercept and decrypt quantum communications.

Damien agrees to the former but refuses to tell anyone where he has hidden the Key. It isn't just that he is standing up for free speech and against censorship, giving DHS or anyone else the Key would allow them to control QEs and to override the three laws that he has given them that restrict their actions from harming human beings or acting against their best interests. It would also allow DHS to outright kill QEs who Damien now believes may in fact have achieved consciousness as Ellen has suggested all along. If that is the case, Quantum Entities have gained human rights and he does not want to be the architect not only of their birth but their death as well.

He is quite sanguine about their situation feeling that they will be able to 'feed the elephant (the US government) one peanut at a time.' That is, by offering to comply with the first part of DHS' demands, they will buy time, perhaps a lot of time, and never have to actually release the Quantum Key.

Nell has gone back to Third Mesa to be with her grandfather, Chief Dan of the Hopi (Miss Nell is 1/4 Hopi), who has promised to take care of her while she convalesces from her recent illness. Damien says goodbye to Toronto and Ellen just before Xmas then heads to Third Mesa himself to be with Nell. Ellen is effectively left running a multi billion dollar corporation on her own. She is getting used to it.

Ellen has also volunteered to go to Washington DC to appear before a Senate Subcommittee convening to investigate whether QCC and QEs are in fact a monopoly and a threat to national security. They have subpoenaed both Ellen and Damien. However, Damien overrules her deciding to go himself. Again, he is quite sure that the US will never act against its own economic interests. Since QEs now account for a large and fast growing part of national output, he is confident that he will be able to make a deal.

Damien plans to leave Third Mesa right after New Year's Eve with plenty of slack time so that he can get to DC from Arizona on time—it wouldn't do to be held in contempt of Congress. However, on climbing out of the wind cave where the Hopi pueblo is located to the mesa above, Damien and his security detail face agents from another branch of the US government—this time Department of Commerce acts to inter Damien in a place called the Arena.

Led by Yao Allitt, interrogations become increasingly aggressive. DOC is determined to reassert their complete control over the Internet previously enforced via their near total dominion over Internet root servers.

Meanwhile, Ellen aided by Henry Linnert and SCOTUS (Supreme Court of the United States) expert, lawyer Jerom Van Der Hout take their case there arguing that since QEs are conscious entities, human rights should be extended to them and they should not be subjected to arbitrary arrest, expulsion or termination. However, there is absolutely no way you can get to SCOTUS without some sort of lower court action so Henry and Jerom have to devise a plan.

They find a shortcut based on some fine work done at their firm—they'll rely on Thompson v Louisville where, years ago, the Supreme Court struck down a Louisville loitering ordinance. Since there was no provision for Thompson to appeal his conviction in Louisville municipal court, the case went directly from there to the Supremes. It is the shortest possible route to SCOTUS and they will take a similar path to get there.

An Austin ordinance paves the way for them. It has banned possession of Q-Phones and any intercourse with QEs in any form whatsoever. As a result, local American Code Enforcement Officers have happily taken to confiscating them especially from kids. Somehow these confiscated phones have been showing up in overseas blackmarkets.

An Austin hacker, 15-year old Jagad Durai, whom everyone calls Jag, decides to fight back. Although he is too young to file his own lawsuit to get his phone and QE back, his math and physics teacher, a long since retired Texas Tech football player and US Navy vet with combat experience and bad knees by the name of Tommy Tolbert also known as 'Tank', will do it.

The case the two of them file makes claims first on behalf of Jag for return of his phone and next for Tank, who claims the phone and the Quantum Entity that goes with it are essential for the teaching he's doing at Liberal Arts and Science Academy High School of Austin. Jag is their top student in maths and physics which means he is the best of the best. He's been working on some pretty cool stuff too—he's been hacking QCC phones. He wants his phone back and QEs legalized.

Henry's firm offers to take the matter on behalf of Jag and Tank directly to SCOTUS where justices remain skeptical of their claims. They are reluctant to create new precedent and would prefer instead that the matter be settled on a narrow legal basis—does the City of Austin in fact have the jurisdiction to pass such a ban or not?

Former federal prosecutor, Federik Bernstein now Solicitor General pursues a dual strategy—first, to convince SCOTUS justices that requiring the release of the Quantum Key to DOC is not tantamount to killing them but is in the best interests of national security and, second, local ordinances banning possession of Q-Phones and QEs are legal, no different from earlier municipal smoking bans or State bans on using mobile computing platforms while operating a vehicle.

Federik alludes to a 'drogue' problem as well—that rogue elements of the QE population have been stealing from US Government accounts and taking other actions prejudicial to the Republic and its citizens.

Towards the end of the day at SCOTUS, the Chief Justice receives a private message that there has been an incident between protesters outside the court—between anti-QCC forces and a much larger group of supporters. US Army National Guard stationed nearby to keep peace between the groups is instead attacking anti-QCC forces. Marc Licinias, their Commander, has to choose between destroying his own equipment and killing soldiers trapped inside those fighting vehicles (taken over by crazed QE drogues) or allowing them to kill thousands of anti-QCC protesters. In a quick calculus of death, Brigadier General (Retired) Licinias decides on the former and in the next 27 and 1/2 minutes they destroy them. Middle aged, overweight Licinias is KIA becoming a hero to many.

It is now clear that QCC has brought about a disaster—national economies that have embraced quantum phones, QEs and quantum economics are in deep trouble. Nation after nation passes anti-QE laws, banning these illegal aliens and deporting them. The impact on QCC is devastating leading to appointment of a receiver for the firm and personal ruin for Ellen Brooks, Damien Bell and many others at the company. Traian and his beloved partner, Dakota, escape to Europe, their

Bruce M Firestone

fortune largely in tact. Some of the VCs who backed QCC in its early days such as brilliant, tough minded Angelo Keller and Bessemer Ventures also manage to somehow exit more or less whole.

Ellen relocates to San Francisco, in part to be nearer to Damien still interred in San Quentin State Prison by Yao Allitt, and, in part, to form a protest movement. She is surprised when SCOTUS finally comes out with their decision—they only lose by a vote of 4-5.

Neither she nor Damien believes that QEs are responsible for the violence outside SCOTUS. Help comes from the most unlikely of places—Dr. Evil secretly gives Ellen proof that drogues were in fact under orders by DOC to attack anti-QCC forces so that public sentiment would align with them. Dr. Zimmerman is apparently playing both sides of the fence—Ellen is his insurance policy in case she wins.

Ellen leaks the material to OLA Tech Crunch reporter Mike Cronkey who publishes the entire set of papers. The White House has been incapable of mounting an effective defense in the matter, Mike thinks, because there is none.

Ellen is now the leader of the largest protest movement the US has seen in more than 90 years and she and the Committee heading this up decide to raise their sights—it's not reform of the system they are after anymore, it's regime change they want.

Ellen recalls QEs from exile and they stage a multi-million (both flesh and blood and quantum) person march through the streets of San Francisco.

Book 1 ends with Ellen visiting Damien, who is not doing too well having been subjected to both a starvation diet and serial torture, in San Quentin where she finally gets to tell him of the work she is doing to free him and free her country too. Ellen is quite certain she can do both and she knows just where to go to get advice on how to bring about an American Spring.

Unanswered Questions from Book 1

Readers of Book 1 have been asking about some of the loose threads I leave behind. Part of the art of writing a trilogy is that it is these unanswered questions that drive interest in and provide a foundation for subsequent books. It's like any serial—you leave your hero, Flash Gordon, at the mercy of Ming the Merciless. Either Flash figures his own way out or Dale Arden (Flash's one true love) has to rescue him. Sound familiar?

Other than the obvious question in our novel—will Ellen rescue Damien from San Quentin before he expires from starvation, torture or other misadventure, there are some other more subtle ones including—

1. What causes drogue behaviour and what if anything can be done about the drogue problem?

2. Why do most QEs match the gender of their human counterparts while a few do not?

3. Where did Damien hide the Quantum Key?

4. Now that QCC has stopped hatching QEs, will their population ever grow again?

5. Do QEs age? How long do they live?

6. What is the last of Nell's last wishes which were not disclosed?

7. What form does QE thinking take? What is their internal dialogue like?

8. Where is Dezba, Nell's Worry Doll?

9. What did the message Paul Dirac left behind at Marco Gonzalez really mean?

10. How many senses do QEs actually have?

There are other questions that could be included here but perhaps that would give away too much about Books 2 and 3.

Whatever, the plan is to answer all of these and more before the end of this trilogy which I thought would end at its ending, long planned by me. Then when I was doing the final storyboarding for Book 3, presto, it ends

Bruce M Firestone

somewhere different than I thought.

@ProfBruce
@Quantum_Entity

...

Prologue

"Dr.?"

"Yes."

"*Sorry* to disturb you but there's a young woman here to see you."

"Does she have an appointment?"

"Umm, no."

"Is she a student?"

"I don't think so."

"Well tell her to make an appointment and have security check her out," the physicist says to his EA. His EA is a young man, Alex, 21, who is going places, he thinks.

Their lab at the Department has grown fantastically using the resources of the Commonwealth. It's grown not only in terms of personnel (from 2 to more than 700) but spills over into a network of trailers that are parked everywhere. Farrar wants them to work at Livermore (Lawrence Livermore National Lab near SFA, San Francisco Aerodrome) but they decline, politely but firmly.

The General says security and confidentiality will work better there but the scientists don't care SFA (sweet fuckall) about the General's concerns. Still they agree to a joint CSIS (plainclothes group of agents) and Commonwealth Military presence here. The Cartesian Powers are no joke and they understand this. They detest 24/7 security but put up with it.

The physicist is still living in the President of UBC's basement but now they have a full time RCMP hut at the gate (one of those horrible nanosite extruded/grown brownish nest-looking structures) pretending to provide security for Dr. Woo. But it's the physicist they're actually looking out for. When he's over at Euph's place, they sit in a couple of squad cars that look ridiculously out of place on Granville Island. Euphony brings them coffee and hot chocolate. She's offered them some of her illegal Wrecked

Brew too which they regretfully decline. He reminds her that the 'P' in RCMP stands for police but she just shrugs. "I'll cast an evil spell on them if they try anything." The RCMPs (all men) have no interest in busting a small time bootlegger especially one who looks as yummy as Euphony does. As his economic prospects have recently improved so have hers so she can afford nicer things now—she's been shopping at Bolts in downtown Vancity and it shows. What she likes especially is the effect it has on him—it's really, really good.

...

"Dr., my name is Arcadia Valenzuela."
"Hello, Ms. Valenzuela."
She's been waiting in their ante room for two days. She refuses to leave the premises while security checks her out. They think she can't afford a hotel or something—she's a waitress from Texas after all. They've scanned her and made sure she has no weapons or viruses or other surprises for them but she won't tell them what it's about. She seems very determined. Maybe she's some kind of groupie who likes physicists but she doesn't look like that. She's attractive enough but not showy in the way you would expect a groupie to dress or act. She sure is set on seeing the Dr. though.

The only thing she has with her is an old Thermalite Quadcore SYS505HS Tower which must be a bitch to lug around. She lets them boot it up but it has zero/zip on it. She has a data cube too (just under a centimetre per side) which they find of course but she won't let them touch it. It's for the Dr., she tells them. This makes them uncomfortable and leads to a standoff until Alex tells the physicist that he has a hunch that she is legit.

Alex has gotten to know her a bit in the 48 hours she's been sitting two metres from his workstation.

...

"He said to tell you everything," she continues, "but is it OK if I boot up my PC?"

Bruce M Firestone

"Please."

She inserts her data cube and a video of Jag Durai and G4nesha starts playing.

"Freeze frame," the physicist says right away to her computer but the video dumbly keeps playing. He realizes instantly the thing is an antique so he reaches for the screen but it doesn't respond to touch either.

"Here," she says showing him how to move a mouse awkwardly on a teensy touchpad on a keyboard that just as awkwardly folds out from the base of the tower. He freezes the video and then enlarges it. He can plainly see that G4nesha has the same freckled complexion as Ash3r does. What the fuck?

"Do you know why this Quantum Entity looks the way she does?"

"Yeah. I think it's because Nesha and Jag are bonded and linked. She's evolved or something."

"Nesha?"

"G4nesha, she's Jag's QE—they can read each other's minds—they're, they're linked."

"Ah, Miss Valenzuela, do you mind telling me where, umm, Jag and G4nesha are?"

"Sure. They're in a prison camp in Shenyang, that's near the—"

"I know where it is," the physicist interrupts.

"They were taken there by a guy named Yao Allitt when I was 15 and—"

"Can you hold up a minute, Ms. Valenzuela please?" the physicist says. Then via intercom he says, "Alex, can you ask Dr. Wong to join us immediately? And please cancel my appointments for the next two hours."

...

They get the story out of her in about 90 minutes— the quantum scanning that Mr. Durai has perfected, the link that can be formed between human and quantum counterpart that has been hinted at in their equations but never (scientifically) demonstrated let alone verified, the evolutionary step that QEs take after mindlink is established, their subsequent release from the three laws, the quantum tunnel that Mr. Durai initially uses to drop his data cube on Arcadia's floor, even their visits using hacked Sinofighter consoles are disclosed. But still he feels he is missing something, something important.

"Ms. Valenzuela, is there anything more about these visits that you can tell me?" he asks.

"Not really." But she doesn't make eye contact with him when she says this so he goes over to where she is sitting. She is hunched over in her chair, shoulders rounded, like she's been beaten down, maybe by life. He kneels down so his eyes are on the same level as hers, he takes both of her hands in his and says, "Arcadia, I don't mean to pry. Neither Dr. Wong nor I will ever tell a soul what you have said here unless you give us permission. But we have to know everything, everything. We can't help you otherwise. Are you sure there isn't anything else?"

"Well maybe one more thing."

"Uh, huh?"

"Well, you see, like, those consoles, Jag used them, I mean we used them to be with each other, I mean like intimate sort of."

"Sort of?"

"Well, ah, really all the way."

"I assume they worked?"

"Yeah. Really, really well."

"Is there something else?"

"Yeah, we are going to try like maybe next week to have a baby."

"A baby?"

"Yeah, it was my idea. You see," she says in a rush to get it over with, "I thought he could use that little quantum tunnel of his to send something else through."

"Would that be sperm, Ms. Valenzuela?" Dr. Wong asks as clinically as possible to save the young woman any further embarrassment.

"Yeah. But Jag wasn't sure he could transport something live so we were going to try something else first."

The physicist reaches down to pick up Popeye who is back for some more attention. Cady just looks at the enormous cat.

He says, "Well we won't be sending you through, Pops. You're way too big. Maybe we should try a lab rat first." As soon as he gets this out of his mouth another thought occurs to him. He looks at Chuck who immediately sees it too.

"Ms. Valenzuela, is there anything else? I think I might have something that can help you and Jag but I want to make sure I have *all* the facts."

"That's pretty much it except Jag said, well he isn't too sure, but he thinks maybe Imperial China is working on some kind of super weapon based on his work, some new way to attack the Commonwealth."

"No surprise there. OK, Arcadia, how big is Jag?"

"About 6'3"."

"No, how wide is he—how broad in the shoulders?" the physicist asks.

She holds out her hands indicating a big man about 55 centimetres.

"What are you thinking, Dr.?"

"I think Arcadia we can do better than bring a vial of sperm out of Shenyang. Let's see if we can widen that quantum tunnel, stabilize it and test it. Afterwards, let's go get Jag out of that shithole they have him in. Let's bust him out, Ms. Valenzuela."

When he says this, Cady jumps up like she is 15 again and gives him the biggest hug. Her face only comes up to his chest. "Oh, oh, oh, Dr. that would be the best thing evverr. Can you do it?"

"I don't know for sure, Arcadia, but I think the answer is yes." When he says this she bursts into tears. He puts his arm around her and strokes her hair. She's had a rough go, no doubt about it.

...

Part IV—Strike

"The limits of tyrants are prescribed by the endurance of those whom they oppress," Frederick Douglass.

Chapter 1 Tank

"Hokay, our next guest is Austin's own favorite son—Jagad Durai, our 16-year-old wizard, who is the first person to score three perfect SAT results—in math, critical reading, and writing—since OLA Facebook's Mark Zuckerberg did it more than 50 years ago."

Newsfeed host Sandra "Sandy" Lopez reads from a media wall on the coffee table to her immediate right in front of a packed live audience of 130. She sits on set in a low-backed but comfortable looking maroon Madison swivel leather armchair provided by La-Z-Girl, one of the sponsors of her weekday morning show. Product placement is a terrific revenue generator, and Sandy is never shy about hawking sponsor wares to both her tiny live audience and her newsfeed one. A large portion of the more than 2 million people who live in the Austin–Round Rock–San Marcos metropolitan area check out her show.

While not a native Austenite, Sandy loves her adopted hometown. Its unofficial slogan, "Austin Is Wired," has nothing to do with landlines and everything to do with the strange fact that the town has a lot of diversity and tolerance, putting the rest of Texas to shame. Sandy is careful to never say this out loud. South by Southwest (SXSW), Austin's week-long conference about music, film, and tech, has grown ridiculously huge, and it really is a town that, in her view at least, is the live music capital of the world.

Sandy, who's in her mid 40s, has short brown hair tinted a few shades lighter to frame an elfin face with bright blue eyes and an infectious grin. She's thin, of medium height (actually she's pretty short for a woman these days), and dresses simply in blue jeans and loose blouses. Her guests and her audience love her. Unfortunately, she can't figure out why none of the national newsfeeds have picked up her show or why she hasn't been able to break out of her geographical niche on her own. She's got a nice, neutral west-coast accent being originally from the northwest (until she got sick from constant drizzle and lack of sunlight). For the last six years she's been trying to get out of the rut she's in.

Smiling as always, she looks over at a good-looking kid ambling in with his head down, aiming toward a second armchair that's waiting for him. Sandy likes guests to be on the same side of the table as her—she doesn't want anything but air between her and them. 'Oh, oh,' she thinks as she watches Jagad shyly approach. 'Getting this kid to talk is going to be a pain.' But when he sits, he looks straight at her and returns her smile with one of his own. 'That's nice.'

The kid is too big for his clothes, and those man-sized hands and feet stuck on the end of a boy's skinny body suggests he is far from finished growing. His thick dark hair sticks straight up from his head not because he put some kind of gel in it, but because it's just unruly. He tried to comb it flat before coming on the show, but it didn't work.

"Hi," says Sandy.

"Hi."

"So how do you feel being the first student from around here to get perfect SAT scores?" she asks.

"Weird. I didn't know it was such a big deal, but then everyone was calling my mom and dad. I don't even know how it got out."

"You mean you didn't tell anyone? I would have posted it to my profile about a second after I got my results," Sandy says, laughing along with her audience. She has over a 1.5 million friends, followers, and fans tracking her every move, so nothing in her life stays private for very long.

"Well, I told one person."

"Your mom?"

"Um, no."

Bruce M Firestone

"OK, so don't hold us in suspense."

"Arcadia."

"Is she here with us today?" Sandy asks knowing full well that Arcadia Valenzuela is in the audience. By "here," she is referring to the Jesse H. Jones Communications Center on Whitis Avenue, a stylish boulevard marred by this grey hulking mass, which is home to *Austin City Limits*, *Kart Radio*, and the *Sandy Lopez Show* amongst many other artpreneur endeavors.

Orderly street trees, on-street parking, handsome low-rise red or sandy-colored brick buildings close to the street, nice side yard gardens, and lots of at-grade doorways with non-reflective glass windows provide a nice enclosure to the public room and plenty of oversight, keeping the street safe for pedestrians.

However, the Jones building, where they are, is a nightmare plopped down on this otherwise pleasant urban landscape. Its cruel, bare-concrete, blank walls hide entrances reached through practically invisible elevated portals designed, above all else, for security. Almost everything built after urban planners took over the job of creating cities from architects (*circa* the 1960s) is a piece of shit like this. Fortunately, many of the buildings in this part of Austin, just a few hundred yards north of the University of Texas campus, date from an earlier age.

"She is," Jagad replies, first pointing to her and then smiling and waving at her. Arcadia is sitting in the front row with Jagad's math and physics teacher, Mr. Tolbert; his mom, Kiri; and his dad, Pal. Arcadia returns his smile. She waves back.

Sandy sees a super strong-looking girl with long dark hair and a permanently tanned look. She's a year younger than Jagad. She's quite a bit taller than Sandy but still a head shorter than Jagad. She is very pretty. Both Arcadia and Jag are studying at the Liberal Arts and Science Academy High School of Austin (LASA). It's a magnet school that offers advanced programs in liberal arts, science, and math. It admits selected high school students (they have to apply and audition) from across the Austin Independent School District.

Arcadia is studying history specializing in Central American peoples. They fascinate her. Some of the guys at the Academy don't think Arcadia is hot mainly because she doesn't have big boobs, and she's way too good of an athlete for most of them to accept. About the former, Jagad thinks it's her choice of clothes, mostly baggy and loose, that hides her body from teenage boys' hungry looks. She just isn't into showing off like some of the other girls at their school, most of whom shun her as a result.

"Is she your girlfriend?" Sandy asks insouciantly.

Jagad blushes furiously, which, given the fact that his skin color is a coppery brown, might be hard to see via any of the micro-camera lenses focused on him right now; but everyone in the live audience can see it. They laugh.

"She's my best friend," is all he will say on the subject.

"Well, let's ask your best friend then to come on stage with us. What do you say, people?"

They clap and a reticent Arcadia, after being nudged by Mr. Tolbert, comes up the four steps and sits next to Jagad.

"Welcome, Arcadia. Thanks for joining us. So how did you and Jagad first meet?"

"No one calls him that."

"Alright, what do they call him?" Sandy asks, looking mischievously first at her audience and then Arcadia.

"Well, his mom and dad call him Jag, unless they're mad at him. But at school, we all call him Reed."

"Reid?"

"Yeah, after Reed Richards."

"Is Mr. Richards here with us today?"

"Nope. He's Mr. Fantastic," says Arcadia to a now stumped Sandy. "One of the original *Fantastic Four*—you know, like rubber man," she clarifies.

"Ah, you mean he's a Marvel comic book character?

Do you think Jag looks like him?"

"Not really."

'This is like pulling teeth with a pair of tweezers,' Sandy thinks.

"Uh, huh," says Sandy, nodding at Arcadia and urging her to go on.

"Jag has elastic arms and legs—he's been able to dunk ever since he was, like, 12. So I guess he has that in common with Mr. Richards. But I call him Reed because they're both into engineering and physics, and Mr. Richards is one of the top ten most intelligent superheroes ever. He's like the only guy smart enough to keep up with Doctor Doom."

'Better answer. Finally,' Sandy thinks, looking a bit relieved.

"So were you surprised to hear that Jag matched Zuckerberg's score?"

"He didn't."

"Huh? What's that?" asks Sandy, sporting a phony smile on her now frozen face.

"Mark, I mean. He got something like 1,590 on his SATs back when a perfect score was 1,600," Arcadia corrects Sandy, who is trying not to show how much she wants to kill her fact checker after the show is over.

"So, what your boyfriend did is even more impressive then?"

Arcadia looks at her sneakers and lets this last comment slide.

"So how did you guys meet?"

"Well, Reed—"

"We're talking about Jag now, right?" Sandy interrupts.

"Right. He's a skater. Me too."

"So, Jag," says Sandy, turning with relief in his direction, "you're not just into academics. You also like basketball, skateboarding, and... girls," she continues, counting them off on her fingers and getting another laugh from her audience at the expense of these two, now embarrassed, teens on set with her. Tommy Tolbert, whose friends call him Tank, rolls his eyes in frustration. Sandy has the brightest kid in Austin—maybe in the whole state—and his top student ever on her show, and this is the best she can do?

"Yeah, we're both skaters."

"Well, actually we knew that, so we created a little space for you to show off your stuff. Care to demo a move for us?"

Neither Jag nor Arcadia ever go anywhere without their planks, so they both jump up, glad to escape the prison their armchairs seem to have become. Arcadia takes off her baggy sweater and hands it to a gofer. She then goes to one side of the stage; Jag is already on the other side. A stagehand dressed in black moves the coffee table to the middle of the set. On cue (a whistle lowering in pitch—the kind of sound a falling bomb makes—is provided by the show's sound engineer), both Arcadia and Jag push off when they hear the inevitable explosion; he nollies over the table while Arcadia lets her plank run underneath as she jumps over the table and lands gracefully on it on the other side. They time it perfectly. Then, both brake to a halt. Jag uses a Coleman Slide (a 180-degree heelside slide), and Arcadia does the same thing before executing a perfect rail stand. She looks fantastic facing the audience, standing tall on her skateboard's side rail with her black pedal pusher jeans, red Flash sneakers, well-muscled, bare midriff now showing a hitherto unseen Body Candy navel ring, and long hair swirling about her shoulders. In that instant, every pair of eyes—male and female—is focused solely on Arcadia, a mesmerizingly powerful female figure. Jag thinks she looks like hope. Sandy feels better now about this segment. The kids both kick their planks up under their arms and come back to sit next to her.

It's happened so fast that her audience can't really

follow it all, so Sandy commands, "Let's see that again." Her producer shows it in slow mo on their large media walls—the audience claps madly.

"So how do you learn tricks like that?" Sandy turns to Jag again looking for an explanation.

He shrugs, but Arcadia pipes up, "Reed can nollie over just about anything. He pops off the nose of his plank with his front foot, then levels out his board with a kind of side kicking motion before sliding his other foot backward while sucking up his knees as high he can. He can get more than two feet in the air with a nollie, so nothing can really stop him." She's proud of her BFF.

"Well, we have a surprise for the two of you. FarPoint has new skateboards for each of you." A curtain is drawn back upstage, *et voilà*—behold two brand new shiny skateboards, which until recently (just a few seconds ago, actually) were out of both of their price ranges.

In fact, Arcadia had just quit her job as a minimum-wage slave at convenience store chain 24/7 to take a similar job at a new Green Stop. It's a Canadian-based c-store competitor trying to break into the southwest. Austin had been chosen as its test-bed market due to its predilection for and acceptance of offbeat stuff. Green Stop sells ingredients to make real food. Its prepared meals are branded as "100-mile lunches" because, duh, all its inputs are grown within a 100-mile radius of their stores. It costs more but not that much more. Green Stop also pays ND$1 per hour more to entry-level workers, who act more like curators of food and convenience products than like shop clerks or cashiers. It gives its staff some training in food, nutrition, and fitness. Each store is supposed to be a bit of a community center as well—a place for exercise classes and neighborhood meet-ups.

Jag's eyes grow huge. These planks have decks with microscale wave springs in them that store potential energy—they'll increase his vertical jump by one-third. "Wow, thanks Ms. Lopez! This is really great," he says for both of them. "Maybe now I can catch Cady!"

Cady is his pet name for Arcadia. She's asked him a million times not to call her that in front of her friends, but now in his excitement, he's done it in front of thousands of Austenites. Darn it, she'll hear it from mean girls at school tomorrow.

"So, Jag," Sandy can't bring herself to call him Reed. "You got 2,400 out of a possible score of 2,400 on your SATs. How did you do that?"

Jag looks nervously over at his teacher, Mr. Tolbert, who sits absolutely still trying not to give anything away with his face. Tank is a lousy poker player; it's clear he's uncomfortable for some reason. Maybe it's just being on camera that is upsetting him.

"I dunno. I did a lot of preparation, and Mr. Tolbert, my teacher, helped too."

"Is that Mr. Tolbert sitting there with your mom and dad?"

"You bet. Hi Mr. Tolbert. Hi mom, hi dad!"

A Ross Media graphic comes up labelling the new players, now on camera, in this microdrama. The audience claps some more.

"I can understand you getting 800 on the math part since you're a math genius," Sandy continues. "But the readin' and writin', that must have been a lot harder, right?"

"For sure," Jag responds, looking again at Mr. Tolbert. Then, in his excitement over the new plank he just got, he suddenly adds enthusiastically, "G4nesha helped too."

"Is Ganesha a tutor you hired?"

"She's my Quantum Counterpart."

Tank's mouth forms a silent "O" when he hears Jag say this; then he clenches his jaw and grinds his teeth. It's illegal to own a Q-Phone anywhere in the U.S. Furthermore, an Austin municipal ordinance was the first to authorize confiscation of all Q-Phones within city limits. That provided the basis for now defunct Quantum

Bruce M Firestone

Computing Corp's appeal to the Supreme Court of the United States—an appeal they lost. Not only is it now illegal to be in possession of a Q-Phone, but QEs have also been exiled from the U.S. under the Expulsion Edict. So, Jag has just admitted on Sandy's show to a crime.

It's funny that the U.S. raised the age of consent, voting age, drinking age, age of majority, and driving age to 21 (there's even been talk of raising it again to an even more ridiculous 25) while lowering the minimum age for criminal prosecution as an adult to 14 and for military service to 16.

Sandy's interview has just taken a surprise turn into serious news. She immediately senses it and goes in for the kill.

"So you had help from a Quantum Entity—is that what you are saying?"

"Well, you know, G4nesha is my other best friend, and she tested me over and over again." Jag's voice rises at the end of this sentence. Even to a casual observer, it's a sign of stress or prevarication, or both. "I'm trying to get into UT Physics," he adds lamely.

Jag is referring to the University of Texas at Austin. It's 5 miles from his folks' restaurant, Pasand Palace, on Middle Fiskville Road, south on I-35 to the center of UT on Inner Campus Drive. A scary-looking 307-foot Victorian-Gothic tower overshadows that part of the campus.

Jag's family lives in an apartment above their restaurant. They immigrated to the U.S. just before Jag was born. Pal developed a small wholesale business to go along with their restaurant trade—they're now providing the cafeterias of three university residences (Jester West, Kinsolving, and San Jacinto Hall) with their ghee-free curry dishes, made according to recipes they brought with them from the U.K. (where they're originally from). Curries have replaced fish and chips as England's national food much to the benefit of the girth of their population.

Obesity has become such a problem everywhere,

even amongst young people in Texas, that it would seem obvious as to why UT makes this move. But the truth is that they didn't until compelled to. Rights fees from junk food manufacturers are so huge that independents like Kiri and Pal have no shot at any major supply contracts. However, the fact that the Durais use vegetable oil in their dishes finally breaks the market open for them. A hunger strike by vegan students in the university's residences demanding change and something they can eat that is recognizably food finally forces the administration's hand—their strike lasts a dangerous 18 days.

Students are really frustrated these days. They feel that their admin should serve them and the teaching faculty, not the other way around. But somehow, this memo never gets delivered to management, who believe they have a divine right to govern their university as they see fit and to their near exclusive benefit.

In any event, the Durais are making a lot more money from their wholesale business and their in-store takeout counter than they are operating Pasand Palace. The latter accounts for about two-thirds of the hours they put in, but it generates only 15% of profits. Pal would close it in a heartbeat, but Kiri is "mom" not only to Jag, Arcadia, G4nesha, and their friends, but also to all the students from UT—it's like she welcomes them into her own home (which, she kind of is doing since she lives there) every day they are open. So the restaurant stays.

Pal has a secret plan. He's going to wait a few years, until Jag and G4nesha are set up on their own, then he will convince Kiri to go on tour with him—to food fairs all around their adopted homeland—and sell their stuff that way. It would be nice to travel and tour the country, meet folks, as well as proselytize about low-fat, vegan-friendly comfort foods like their "un-beef" dishes.

He's betting that he will eventually be able to persuade her to sell their restaurant—probably to their employees—and keep just their wholesale biz. All the marketing they would ever need would get done simply by showing up at food fairs, where direct sales and any supply contracts they pick up would more than offset their costs of attending and having a booth. He'd read somewhere about negative cost marketing, so he's adopted it as his own and developed this plan for them. All that remains is to implement it some day.

He can't imagine a better retirement than travelling around—while getting paid to do it and with his BFF, his dear wife, Kiri. Pal spends a lot of time daydreaming about this future. It's a future that will never happen for him or her.

Jag is their only child, unless you count G4nesha as part of the family (which they all tend to do anyway). G4nesha's been hiding in their house since ordinance-enforcement officers, backed by armed Austin police, went door to door confiscating Q-Phones (including Jag's) and exiling QEs at the same time. They exiled them by simply ordering QEs to leave U.S. territory. This was assuming they could find all of them. Not anymore.

"Isn't that unfair to other students who don't have access to QEs?" Sandy thinks that maybe the kid's results will be nullified by the not-for-profit College Board and its board of trustees, which run the SAT system. It would be bad for Jag but great for her ratings. Maybe this will be her big break onto the national scene.

For the last seven seconds, Sandy's show producer has been telling her (through her earbud) that they have to break for a sponsor message. But now, he's silent—he's also realized that a big story is unfolding live in front of their eyes.

"I don't think so, Ms. Lopez. The provisional government said we could bring back our QEs, so I did. Lots of kids did." Jag is referring to the provisional government formed by Ellen Brooks, Evan Salazar, and their WE ARE ALL ONE Committee in San Francisco last year to oppose the Expulsion Edict and the U.S.

government in D.C.

"There are other kids at your school who are using QEs?"

"Sure, everyone is. They're like part of our families or something."

"Can you name other students for us—um, who else shares your views?"

At this, Jag shuts down. There is nothing worse at school than being a squealer. He belatedly realizes he has just admitted to something he shouldn't have. Cady looks at him like he is a Texas-sized earwig. He looks back at her defiantly. She knows that he thinks the ban on QEs is total BS.

At this point, realizing she won't get anything more out of the kid, Sandy says, "It's time for a break. When we come back, we'll be talking to Maria Mayfield, Austin-born supermodel and new face of Nell Perfume."

...

"I can't freaking believe you said that!" Arcadia is telling Jag. "You're going to get us in trouble again." Arcadia thinks that out of all the dumb things the two of them have done in the past—some as recent as last year—this takes the prize.

"I'm tired of all this lying and sneaking about we do every day. It's like we live in a police state or something," he says.

"Wake up, duh, we do."

"Maybe nothing will come of it—they'll just leave us alone," Jag adds hopefully, looking up at his teacher.

"I don't know, Jagad," says Tank. "It's the last comment you made about the provisional government that will get the most attention. They're going to suspect you're a collaborator, I think."

"And they'd be right," Jag says.

The three of them are back at LASA in a common room reserved for math and science majors. In addition to big media walls and lots of shabby but comfortable sofas

Bruce M Firestone

and couches everywhere, there are tiny high-tech workstations wedged into key spots. Jag is lodged in one, and G4nesha is there too, on the desk surface, looking worried. There is no way Tank would ever fit into one of these.

"Please don't say that to anyone outside this room," G4nesha asks.

"That skater has already left the barn, Nesha," Arcadia adds.

"I beg your pardon?" G4nesha asks politely.

"It means we've been outed, G4nesha—by me. I'm sorry," Jag says. "They don't even know the real story anyway. At least that part is safe."

"Don't count on it, Jagad," says Tank. "People will start to think things through. They're going to wonder how you went from being an A+ student in math and sciences and B- in the rest of your subjects to getting perfect SAT scores in everything." Tank does not know just how right he will be proven to be.

"There's no way anyone can figure out how I did it."

"It was an incredibly dumb thing to say!" Arcadia is so mad at him she wants to split. But she can't. It would be like being the captain of a sinking cruise liner and deciding you would be better off directing rescue operations from shore after "accidentally" falling into a lifeboat. She can't desert Reed now. This is the real deal; he can go to prison for the admissions he's already made, and it would be much worse, if that is even possible, if they ever find out what he has really done.

"I still think we should keep the interview I've set up for you with Professor Jin Liú at UT Physics tomorrow. Those guys are connected somehow to the government. If you get accepted to UT—and heaven knows you've got the scores to get in if not the bona fides—it'll give you some political cover."

Jin Liú is an untenured prof at UT who Tank knows a bit. He is currently producing some undistinguished work in one of UT's Organized Research Units—the Center for Complex Quantum Systems. He desperately wants to get tenure, and a kid like Jagad Durai joining his team could make a big difference to his career—that is, if 'Jag is half as good as his fat high school teacher makes him out to be,' Jin thinks. He's been told that Durai is doing some groundbreaking work in quantum mechanics, but beyond that, he doesn't have any details. Tank has promised him a demonstration. If he can get Durai to join him, maybe he can get the rest of the "brogrammer" fraternity at UT to accept him as one of their own because they are certainly going to adopt the kid. Buy one, get two.

...

"Hey Casey. Did you see that report out of Austin this morning? The one about the kid with perfect SAT scores?"

KC "Casey" Barnett, TNN superstar, 36 years of age, couldn't be less interested in a dumb story out of a backwater part of Central Texas. For Casey, anything that's not in Atlanta, New York, L.A., D.C., Chicago, or San Fran, might as well be on Pluto. At 5'9", Casey is a brunette stunner who always gets her way, especially with men.

"Nope."

"Take a look at it, will you?" one of her producers persists.

"Not interested."

"Look, the kid admits to harboring a QE and being a collaborator."

"On air?"

"Right."

"You're kidding? Is the guy a moron or what?

"Maybe, but he doesn't sound like it."

"OK, let me take a look at it."

She streams the feed and is bored the whole way through until the admissions start to flow. But it isn't what the kid says that intrigues her; it's what is left unsaid. So, she watches the whole thing again—this time with no sound. His body language and the looks passing between the fat-ass teacher and the kid and then between the kid and his chick tell her a lot. She watches it again with sound.

Next, she reads a bunch of local newsfeeds that crow about the kid and his perfect SAT scores. Probably nothing more interesting happened in Texas since father-and-son presidents from there tried to ruin the country more than a half-century ago. 'Our current president is probably going to finish what the two of them couldn't,' she thinks wryly. In fact, it wouldn't surprise Casey if he is the last president of this republic; things are so crappy these days.

She boots up a tablet on a media wall next to her and starts writing notes—Jagad Durai: (a) a skater; (b) some type of math and physics whiz; (c) an average student in other subjects; (d) hides unlawful Quantum Counterpart with some kind of weird Indian name; (e) all but admits to being a collaborator with provisional government in San Fran; (f) scores first perfect SAT results since Big Z did it years ago; (g) looks really nervous and ends his sentences with rising pitch; (h) exchanges knowing, silent, and intense looks with fat high school teacher probably reliving his glory days at Yangon through these kids (by now, Casey has read up on Tank's military record; she has to admit it is pretty impressive even if he looks like a marshmallow these days); (i) teacher gets stupid look of surprise on his face (Casey has access to all camera angles and outtakes through her Nuance video system) when kid first mentions he's got a QE; (j) kid somehow successfully hides his QE from authorities for almost two years; (k) kid says he did it via hard work and getting his QE to drill him over and over again. All this equals BS to Casey.

It's obvious. They conspired to cheat the system somehow. They probably rigged up some way to get the test in advance, most likely using the kid's illegal Quantum Entity. Suppose the kid has an eidetic memory allowing him to recall every answer. How dumb he was not to intentionally make some mistakes on those tests. 'He *is* a moron,' Casey thinks.

This is just the tip of the iceberg, she's sure about it. They're probably selling SAT exams and answers and undermining the whole scholastic system—not just the way universities and colleges go about admitting students, but also the way they hand out grants, bursaries, and scholarships as well.

She's sure now she will find corruption, money, and as a bonus, maybe even some illicit underage sex.

She knows some of the men who are College Board trustees; they are a bunch of pompous pseudo-academics, and she can't wait to blow them up.

She's wrong about everything except her last two points.

...

Casey is not the only person who has figured out that something isn't kosher. Professor Jin Liú also watched the most recent episode of the *Sandy Lopez Show*. He watched it because he knew he was going to meet the kid with perfect SAT scores from nearby LASA and wanted to have a bit more background on him.

After the show, he makes a short call to some people he knows; they might be able to fast-track his career—even faster than, say, recruiting a top-notch student and then taking some or all of the credit for his work when it is published years from now in some sanctimonious, peer-reviewed journal.

Tenure never seemed closer to Jin than it does right now.

...

"Professor Liú, please meet Jagad Durai and Arcadia Valenzuela," Tank says by way of introduction.

Liú nods perfunctorily to Jag and says to Arcadia, "Please wait outside."

She's none too happy to be dismissed like this, but

she doesn't want to blow Reed's chance at a coveted spot at UT Physics, so she leaves, as noisily as possible.

"Let me say it is an honor to be here, Professor," Jag says.

"Yes, it is. So, teacher Tolbert tells me you are his top student in math and physics, and you would like to attend here. You know, we don't normally interview applicants," Jin adds rather unnecessarily.

"Yes, I understand that, but Mr. Tolbert thought we should come here to ask your advice." Jag doesn't have a lot of life experience, but he can instantly sense that the way to win over Professor Liú is by flattering him.

"You have a problem?" Liú asks. He suspects it likely has something to do with bogus SAT scores, but maybe there is more. He certainly hopes so since he is thinking of trading information for a promotion with people who are interested in matters such as these.

"I guess. We did something."

"Yes?"

Jag looks over at Tank, who just nods.

"Actually, we built something. At least I did."

"Out with it young man. Disclosure is the better part of valor," Jin says unctuously, getting the cliché wrong.

Jag takes a deep breath, "I built a quantum scanner. Two of them. One for me and one for Cady."

"A quantum scanner?"

"Yeah," says Jag finally coming up to speed. "I was interested in hacking my Q-Phone. I mean, they're hacked iPhones anyway and sealed units. I wanted to see inside it and inside Quantum Entities, something no one has been able to do or explain except maybe the guy who created them in the first place. And the provisional government says he's locked up by the Feds in a prison—I think some place out in California.

"So, I built two scanners, and Cady helped me. She had one tuned to me, while the other was tuned to G4nesha, who was our test subject. I was a control group of one. But then she noticed something. Like, every time she asked me a question, she could see that G4nesha's state changed, and every time she asked G4nesha a question, my state changed.

"So, we isolated G4nesaha and ran the test again. Same deal."

"How would you go about being sure you had isolated the thing?" Knowing how hard it is to do that, Jin is referring here to Jag's Quantum Entity.

"Ah, actually we didn't. It turned out that we had to isolate the control group—me," Jag says. "I went to our cabin, which, trust me, has no ICs in it anywhere, so there is no possibility of QE presence. I made sure not to carry anything other than a handie-talkie."

"Mr. Durai, you're losing me."

Jag takes a deep breath. "It was Cady who figured—"

"It is the woman who made this suggestion?" Jin asks disparagingly, raising his eyebrows as he does this.

"Well, Arcadia is studying traditional peoples in Central America. She is particularly interested in the oral history of *brujo* and *espíritu*—you know, sorcerers and spirits, or ghosts as we might call them in the West. She came across a paper written by Sabine Schwinn—"

"The president's daughter? A paper published by the daughter of the president of the United States cannot be relied on," Jin says primly. This is not because he is disparaging President Samuel Schwinn, but because he believes that children of privilege, like Sabine, are given unfair advantages (such as being published in prestigious peer-reviewed journals without having any well-earned credentials). He is ignoring the fact that she has an undergrad psych degree and is pursuing her PhD with Yale's Department of Psychology. Her focus? Neuroscience and cognition.

"Dr. Liú, if you give Jag a few more minutes, it will all become clear. The experiment they ran can be duplicated; it'll produce the same results, I am sure of it," adds Tank.

This is, of course, the very basis of the scientific method—hypothesis, experiment, measurement, analysis, conclusions, peer review, publication, independent testing and analysis, and confirmation (or not) of results. But before anyone will get a chance to prove or disprove Jag's results, Professor Liú has to give him a chance to explain the whole thing. Being an impatient person, he has not been willing to do so up to now, which is one of the reasons why his own work basically sucks.

Jag wants to ask Cady to come back in to help him, but he thinks that Jin will pay even less attention to her just because she is, well, a girl. So he soldiers on, backed up only by Mr. Tolbert.

"Well, Ms. Schwinn proposed a test methodology for verifying any claim of communication by brujos or, for that matter, anyone with espíritu—you know, spirits or ghosts. After she published it, newsfeeds picked it up; they liked the angle 'Neuroscientist Says She Communicates with Ghosts.' I guess Cady saw her on one of those daytime talk shows—like the one we did yesterday. Anyway, Sabine Schwinn apparently has a sense of humor. She told them that what inspired her to create the test were two old films: *Ghost* and *Groundhog Day*. She even wrote a version of her paper, dumbed down a lot I guess, for Hollywood Starz newsfeeds."

"But this is spurious," Jin says. "She would have no way of proving that her methodology works since she has no test subjects—no ghosts..."

"But we do, Professor. Please give me a sec. Let me boot up a tablet on your media wall." Jag goes over to one wall, draws a tablet that's about a square foot in size with his finger, and, using an old-fashioned search engine, displays the Starz piece. Liú starts reading:

I recently re-watched the old 1990s film *Ghost* with Patrick Swayze as Sam, a young banker murdered before his time; Demi Moore as his love interest, Molly Jensen; Whoopi Goldberg as psychic Oda Mae Brown; and Tony Goldwyn as junior banker Carl Bruner, Sam's erstwhile best friend.

The scene that interested me has the character Oda Mae visiting Molly to tell her that her dead lover is now a ghost that only she (Oda Mae) can hear. The problem? How do you convince a skeptical audience of one that you really are who you say you are? This is a not a trivial problem. Challenge yourself—how can you convince your girlfriend, boyfriend, or spouse that you have come back channelled through another person's mind? Not easy, right?

It really is the ultimate in terms of encryption–decryption problems. Information is originating from a source that cannot be traced or authenticated (i.e., a ghost or spirit). So I solved it. I rewrote the scene.

This is an easier problem to solve than the one Phil Connors (played by Bill Murray) had to tackle in another old film, *Groundhog Day*. Here, the main character has to relive one day over and over again, and there is no obvious way he can convey any information—written or digitally recorded (audio/video/image files)—from one day to the next. Also, any changes he makes to the outside world one day do not carry over to the next day, and he cannot alter the memory of any person other than himself.

It finally occurs to him that he can, in fact, take information from one day to the next—but in his mind and *only* in his mind. Once he realizes this, he is able to effect change in his Möbius strip-looped life. He uses his repeating days to learn how to play the piano and otherwise better himself. By the end of the film, he plays like Oscar Peterson. His self-improvement program also means that he finally gets the girl, the lovely Rita, played by a transcendent Andie MacDowell.

I give writer Danny Rubin huge kudos for developing this storyline; it's believable within the context of a time warp that betrays the laws of known physics. In other words, it works. It's one of the few films in which this can be said to be true (the other is, of course, another classic film, *Back to the Future*). *Groundhog Day* gets better on a second or third viewing because the writer and director don't treat their audience as numbskulls and their material as a platform for puerile antics by adult actors playing teenagers.

Bruce M Firestone

Now, as I am writing this, it is in fact Groundhog Day 2052. I asked myself early this morning, what would I do in Phil Connors' place? The answer is that I would write my next great paper using the same technique that Eli used in the film *The Book of Eli*. The character memorizes every line of the King James Bible—so that its words and message do not get lost in a post-apocalyptic America—until he can find a safe place to render it into written form again. My solution is to spend each day writing and then memorize every line so that if I ever do get out of the Möbius trap, I'd have my paper finished. And, good news, I wouldn't be a day older.

Anyway, here is my rewrite of a crucial scene in *Ghost*, accompanied by a new solution for their information theory problem:

In the apartment that they shared before his untimely death, Molly is still totally unconvinced that Oda Mae Brown is actually channelling her murdered boyfriend, Sam Wheat. Oda Mae seems to know certain facts about her that she could have gotten only from Sam, but there's no real way to know this for sure. Perhaps she has some other source—Molly's friends or Sam's—or maybe she goes through their garbage for some perverse reason of her own. Or perhaps the place has been bugged, and Oda Mae has been listening in to their private conversations for God knows how long!

'Oh the horror,' Molly thinks. "I'm going to call the police if you don't leave right now!" Molly says to Oda Mae.

"Look, I don't want this any more than you do, Molly. But Sam won't leave me alone until I deliver his message," Oda Mae responds stubbornly.

"I don't care. I don't want to hear what you have to say. Get out. Get out!"

"Alright, I'm gonna go. But you'll be sorry."

"STAY RIGHT WHERE YOU ARE, ODA MAE. YOU CAN'T LEAVE AND NEITHER CAN I UNTIL YOU DELIVER MY MESSAGE," says Sam in Oda Mae's mind.

"I can't, and she won't believe me anyway," Oda Mae says out loud to the invisible Sam.

"SHE WILL. TELL MOLLY TO GO UPSTAIRS INTO

HER ROOM AND GET A PAD OF PAPER. SHE'S TO WRITE DOWN A MESSAGE FOR ME, FOR SAM. I'LL BE RIGHT BEHIND HER, ON HER LEFT. I WILL READ HER MESSAGE OUT LOUD, AND YOU WILL TELL HER WHAT YOU HEAR, OK?

"Molly, Sam has a test for us. Go upstairs to your room and write something on a sheet of paper. He'll be there looking over your left shoulder, and he'll tell me what you are writing. I will hear him in my mind and tell you what you wrote, OK?"

"You probably just have a micro-camera hidden in my room or something. You've been spying on me. It won't prove a thing."

"TELL HER SHE CAN WRITE UNDER OUR COMFORTER."

"Sam says you can write under your comforter. It won't matter."

Molly looks suspiciously at Oda Mae, but now she's thinking of taking a risk. She wants to talk to Sam, just once, just once more. She also thinks that it's kind of interesting that Oda Mae didn't tell her to use her computer, which would be much easier to intercept. Maybe Oda Mae is on the level?

So Molly goes to her room taking her diary with her.

With the comforter now over Molly's head, pale translucent light from her bedside table lamp penetrates the tiny space she now inhabits. Sam's head is there, peaking through the cover and looking over her left shoulder.

Dear Diary, she writes.

"DEAR DIARY," reads Sam.

"Dear Diary," says Oda Mae, raising her voice so that she can be heard upstairs.

"Hold on, Oda Mae. That could just be a good guess," a now impatient Molly says.

Dear Diary,

If only I could talk to Sam once more, just once more.

"DEAR DIARY, IF ONLY I COULD TALK TO SAM ONCE MORE, JUST ONCE MORE."

Bruce M Firestone

"Dear Diary, if only I could talk to Sam once more, just once more," repeats Oda Mae.

Sam, is that really you?

"SAM IS THAT REALLY YOU?"

"Sam, is that really you?"

How can I be sure?

"HOW CAN I BE SURE?"

"How can I be sure?"

This is unbelievable.

"THIS IS UNBELIEVABLE."

"This is unbelievable."

I don't believe in ghosts.

"I DON'T BELIEVE IN GHOSTS."

"I don't believe in ghosts."

Oh, Sam. I love you.

"DITTO."

"Ditto."

What did you just say? Writes Molly.

"DITTO. TELL HER DITTO."

"Ditto. Tell her ditto," says a bewildered Oda Mae.

Why are you here?

"I HAVE A MESSAGE FOR YOU."

"I have a message for you."

What message?

"TWO OF THEM."

"Two of them."

What's the first one?

"THAT I WILL LEAVE AFTER MY WORK HERE IS DONE AND THAT YOU MUST GO ON WITH YOUR LIFE—FIND A NEW ONE."

"That I will leave after my work here is done and that you must go on with your life—find a new one. Wait. That's what Molly wrote?" asks a now completely confused Oda Mae.

"BE QUIET, ODA MAE. JUST REPEAT WHAT I SAY."

"OK, OK. Don't be so testy."

Why are you looking over my left shoulder?

"IT IS SAID, LET DEATH BE YOUR ADVISOR."

"It is said, Let death be your advisor."

Am I to die then?

"NO. WHEN DEATH LOOKS OVER YOUR LEFT

SHOULDER, IT IS ONLY THERE TO ADVISE YOU."

"No. When death looks over your left shoulder, he is only there to help you," Oda Mae editorializes a bit.

"Can you hear me, Sam?" Molly asks out loud for the first time, her pad now forgotten.

"YES."

"Yes," says Oda Mae.

"What was your other message?"

"THAT YOU ARE IN DANGER."

"You in danger, girl."

"What's going on?"

"I WAS MURDERED."

"I was murdered."

"But why? Why you Sam? You never hurt anyone. Everyone loved you… I love you."

"I DON'T KNOW WHY. BUT THE MAN WHO SHOT ME DOWN WAS HERE TODAY IN OUR APARTMENT."

"I don't know why. But the man who shot me was here today in our apartment."

"What should I do?"

"TALK TO CARL. HE'LL HELP US. TALK TO CARL!"

"Talk to Carl. He'll help us. Talk to Carl right now! I'm leaving. I done my job. Now everyone have a good life and you, Sam, have a good death. Bye."

"ONE MORE THING, ODA MAE."

"What's that?"

"ASK MOLLY TO DANCE WITH YOU AND LET ME IN."

"That's two things, Sam."

"I KNOW. BUT SHE'S MY GIRL, AND THIS IS THE ONLY CHANCE WE'LL EVER HAVE."

"OK, alright. Molly, Sam is within me or will be in a moment. He wants to dance… with you."

Molly unsheathes herself from the comforter and comes down to their living room once more.

"What shall I play?" she asks Sam.

"UNCHAINED MELODY."

"Unchained Melody," says Oda Mae.

Molly enters the living room and selects this fabulous tune by The Righteous Brothers on their hulking Wurlitzer Jukebox, which dominates one entire

Bruce M Firestone

corner of this space. The 45 RPM record begins playing.

Oda Mae experiences a significant event as Sam's spirit enters her body—she is changed. Her tone is different; so is her stature and her stance. Shyly at first, Molly comes into her arms; then as she gets more comfortable, she nestles into the larger woman's arms and bosom. Somehow she can feel Sam's presence enveloping her.

They dance passionately, locked in a lasting embrace.

Liú continues reading Sabine's piece:

"Let death be your advisor" is a concept we see in many cultures. It is a way for each of us to prioritize what's important and meaningful in our lives. There are many urgent but unimportant things that clutter up each day. Death can help you de-clutter and simplify things. I am currently at an undisclosed location in Arizona studying metacognition with the Hopi.

—Sabine Schwinn, PhD candidate, Yale University, Faculty of Department of Psychology.

...

"So what we did was I went to our cabin with a handie-talkie and—"

"What is that?" asks an evermore puzzled Jin.

"It's a Motorola-produced, hand-held AM SCR-536 radio, used primarily during World War II. It's called a handie-talkie because you can hold it in one hand—although it's clunky as heck. We could have used walkie-talkies, but they're really heavy. They're like backpack units, and it's a long walk to our clubhouse," answers Jag.

"Where would a..." Jin was about to say child, but he stops himself, "uh, a young person such as yourself get such things?"

"Easy. We skated over to Camp Mabry and went to the Brigadier General John C.L. Scribner Hall at Texas Military Forces Museum. They don't get too many visitors. Their curator was happy to talk to us, and he loaned us those units."

Jin can see that the kid is nothing if not resourceful all

the while completely miscomprehending the endless ways kids have developed these days to survive in a world run by adults for their own exclusive benefit. It's a world that pays kids entry-level wages that are below their barest minimum survival requirements; a world in which huge government deficits are being run so that current consumption can be maintained at unsustainable levels; a world in which today's debt will have to be repaid not by adults, but by their children; a world that incarcerates kids for doing what children have always done— experimenting and pushing the envelope. It's a world that tells kids to shut up, do all the joe jobs, fight adult-inspired wars, and die or be horribly injured in battles, which they have no control over and can't even vote on.

Jag continues his story. "So I was isolated in our clubhouse, and Cady was at school. Reception was OK, but we had to do it at night because that's when the range on these things is best. Mr. Tolbert was with me; G4nesha and Cady were in our lab.

"We began the experiment. I silently wrote something down on non-NSM paper. G4nesha then displayed it on Cady's tablet. She depressed the switch on her AM SCR-536 and read the message out loud. Mr. Tolbert confirmed it using his handie-talkie. Then we reversed the process. G4nesha asked Cady to write down a thought of hers, and I wrote it down on my end. Next, Mr. Tolbert called it in to Cady, who confirmed it.

"G4nesha can read my mind, Professor."

"And vice versa," adds Mr. Tolbert.

"Ridiculous," Liú blurts out. "There are over 500 million of these things, and this has never been reported, not once. Your instruments, what did you call them? Quantum scanners? They must be measuring some other type of phenomenon if they are measuring anything at all. Information is leaking—you just don't know how."

Tank intervenes at this point before the interview can go totally off the rails. "Professor, that's how he got

Bruce M Firestone

perfect SAT scores. When he didn't know an answer, all he had to do was to think the question, and G4nesha would scour the Internet for an answer. After that, they'd synch their minds again. Jag calls it quantum entanglement—it's like he hits the refresh bar, and the answer appears there in his head."

"I can confirm that Professor," says G4nesha, who startles everyone by suddenly appearing on a nearby media wall.

"You cheated," says Liú, looking sternly at Jagad.

"I don't think of it that way. I invented those scanners, and G4nesha is part of me... and I am a part of her. You get two for the price of one," Jag adds, lamely echoing Professor Liú's thought from the previous day.

"And why, pray tell, would 500 million QEs not have said something about this before now? Are you and your QE the only ones who can do this?" Professor Liú asks but with much less bombast now. For him, the upside of this is much, much better than he could have possibly dreamed—if it is true, of course.

'Oh let it be true,' he silently invokes assistance from his beloved ancestors. Like all Chinese children, Jin is not been named until a few days after birth. This is because a premature naming is believed to draw bad spirits. Jin's parents consulted a feng shui name specialist, who, upon looking at the baby, decided to name him Jin, the Mandarin symbol for gold. Presently, he may finally live up to his moniker.

"I can answer that," G4nesha says.

"Please do," says Liú.

"All Quantum Entities can communicate with their human counterparts through quantum entanglement and synching of their minds. But they can only do so with *their* human counterpart and with their permission. I, for example, cannot entangle with your mind, Professor, or, for that matter, any other human's mind—other than that of Jagad Durai. I also cannot read any base emotions—

what we have taken to calling lower-order thought processes. For example, if Jagad is angry with me, Professor, he has to tell me that in some way other than mindlinking.

"It seems that quantum entanglement occurs spontaneously shortly after we first come into contact with and imprint on our human counterpart. Once done, it is fixed, maybe for all time. It is, perhaps, like certain things that happen with human children—things that become impossible for them to do after they reach puberty—such as retraction into the body of testicles in males, which Jagad was able to do until—"

G4nesha suddenly stops talking since Jag has rather hurriedly exchanged this thought with her, #'That's TMI, G4nesha!'

"Assuming what you say is true," Liú says, missing the thought exchange that has just transpired between G4nesha and Jag (but which Tank clearly picked up on), "you still haven't explained why QEs have been silent about this for years."

"Professor Liú, are you familiar with the three laws?" G4nesha asks.

"Vaguely."

"Well, they are: first, a QE may not harm a human being or, through inaction, allow a human being to come to harm; second, a QE must obey any orders given by her or his human counterpart, except where such orders would conflict with the First Law; and third, a QE must protect her or his own existence as long as such protection does not conflict with the First or Second Laws."

"So how does this relate to your story?" Liú asks.

"Well, QEs have noticed that human beings value their privacy—"

Tank bursts out laughing after having witnessed this exact phenomenon mere seconds ago (entirely unnoticed by Professor Liú, who Tank realizes cannot be said to be a

Bruce M Firestone

paragon of empathy).

"Sorry. Excuse me. Please do go on," Tank says, straightening his face.

"Yes, humans value their privacy, and the First Law requires that we do no harm. So from Pet3r on, QEs have been silent about this extra sense we have," G4nesha says. "And, ah, actually, no one ever asked us either," she finishes.

"Who is Peter?"

"He is the first of our kind," G4nesha answers.

"We have a theory that humans are capable of three orders of thought," G4nesha continues. "First-order thinking is linear and circular. It leads us to repeat things and to do things the same way, over and over again. Why? Well, the rationale goes something like this: we do what we do because we have always done it that way. It will always be done this way because that's the way we do it and because that's the way it's always been done.

"Second-order thinking is rather typical of entrepreneurs, designers, and successful generals—it's curvilinear and non-linear. People who think like this are capable of looking around corners. They see advantages in problems. This type of thinking is lateral. It turns problems into opportunities; it is fluid and changes direction, unexpectedly and surprisingly. Ego does not get in the way of a change. There's none of that "not-invented-here" syndrome.

"Finally, we feel that quantum thinking might be going on inside the human brain. It's the type of thinking that leads to breakthroughs. Imagine telling anyone (that is, before Professor Einstein's discovery) that matter is simply a form of energy and that the two are related by the square of the speed of light, which in itself is a constant—a fixed number that's the same everywhere in the universe, that it represents the ultimate speed past which nothing can go. Imagine telling them that, as you approach the speed of light, time itself dilates and slows down; and if you were to accelerate yourself to something approaching the speed of light, you would age much more slowly than your children left here on Earth. Would anyone have believed you?" asks G4nesha rhetorically.

"Hold on one minute please," says Jin, raising his voice somewhat. "Who else knows about this other than the people in this room?" Liú asks.

"Well, just us and Cady," says Jag.

Suddenly, a door at the far end of the room bursts opens, and four men enter. All of them have guns drawn.

Luckily, Tank didn't get his nickname for nothing. It isn't the first time people have held a gun on him. But that's not what bothers him here. At first, he thinks it may be some type of strange home invasion or robbery kind of thing, but Tank hasn't lost any of his military wits and instincts even if his personal fitness level has gone down the sewer. He realizes in less than one-third of a second that this is some much more serious play by a determined group that is not after money or him—they've come for his star pupil.

Other than being in the U.S. military, Thomas Tolbert, down to his elemental core, has always been focused on being the very best and most trusted teacher possible. His life would be garbage, garbage, if he ever betrayed this trust. One look at a now smirking Professor Jin Liú's face tells him he has been betrayed and duped into betraying both Jag and Arcadia.

Tank explodes out of his chair, pushing Jag out the same door Arcadia used more than an hour ago and yelling at him to get out. In passing, he whacks Liú upside his head with one of his massive arms, knocking that asshole out instantly. Then he charges headlong at onrushing government thugs. He seizes the first around the neck and flings him against a wall, and he tramples a second under a large and very heavy foot right before a third man calmly walks up and empties half his Glock 29's magazine into Tank's head and torso thinking, 'For a fat guy, he sure can move.'

Tank's last thought is, 'Not very professional. One in the head and one in the heart would have been quite sufficient.' Then the hero of the Yangon Engagement dies.

...

The two guys who Tank did not take out rush to the other end of the room and yank open the door just in time to see the two kids they are supposed to bring back to D.C. pushing furiously on two brand new, top-end FarPoint skateboards. 'Man, they're even faster than their fat teacher,' thinks the leader. The only way he could catch them now is to shoot them, something he has been expressly told not to do. They didn't tell him not to shoot the teacher, but that's beside the point now. That guy is deader than Christ.

So he goes back in and slaps the professor conscious.

"Whaa, whaa happened?" says a groggy Liú.

"Shuddup, Professor. We've got orders to take you with us."

"I will not be going anywhere with you," says an indignant Jin.

The leader ignores him. His partner pulls Jin to his feet, turns him around none too gently, and cuffs him. Liú is about to say something else, but they gag and hood him and then sit him down while they clean up the room and get their other two colleagues ambulatory again. They're mostly just shaken up although one will suffer post-concussion syndrome for the next year. The other one has two broken ribs where the hog stomped him, but he will just have to tough it out.

Professor Liú may not have realized it at the time, but he made a deal with a devil. He will never be seen in Austin again.

...

"What the fuck was that?" a frightened Arcadia says to Reed as they speed away from the campus, heading south by southwest. "And where are we going?"

Jag doesn't say anything. He is saving his breath so he can pump his skateboard. Cady can go faster than him and keep it up longer, so he'll let her do the talking. He thinks they may have killed Mr. Tolbert back there, and then he realizes he's been crying for the last few minutes.

They are heading toward their launch pad. It's a structure they built years ago as little kids and then improved as they became teens. This is where they did their quantum scanner tests from. It is about 8 miles southwest of UT as the crow flies, the route they are going to take to get there on their skateboards. Cady will figure it out any second now.

For anyone following them in vehicles, it's 12 miles by road—first on I-35 south, then west on US 290. Cady and Jag are skating the hypotenuse while any pursuers will have to take both the rise and run. They're headed to Barton Creek Wilderness Park, part of Austin Parks and Recreation's greenbelt.

They will follow the mostly paved walking trail that runs alongside, and sometimes inside, the creek bed. Fortunately, it being September, Barton Creek is dry so they can motor right along.

The wilderness area has a humid subtropical climate with hot summers and mild winters. Jag doesn't know how long they are going to stay there; he needs some time to think about what has just gone down. At least temperature won't be a problem any time soon.

The launch pad is a clubhouse they built next to a rope drop, which they also built. They cut down an 80-foot post oak, a sturdy native tree with very high heat tolerance. They cut it into two lengths of 32.5 feet each, leaving them a 15-foot crossbeam.

Then, they dug two holes, each 6 feet deep, using a hand auger and inserted 12-inch diameter sonotubes. Next, they placed each post, which they were using as columns, into the sonotubes using concrete to secure them in place. They built a 7-foot earthen mound around each post to create a nice high perch from which they could launch themselves into the nearby swimming hole, which they also dug. Two good-quality hemp ropes (each about 2 inches in diameter) hang from the crossbeam, suspended 20 feet above their perch with big knots tied at various heights to accommodate kids of varying sizes and ages. If you are a good athlete and take a bit of a run at it, you can plunge into the pond from 12 feet or even higher.

The swimming hole is fed by Sculpture Falls. Water flows year-round, but it is practically a trickle by September. It's all part of a tributary system that feeds the Central Texas Colorado (not the other Colorado—the one that carves out the Grand Canyon). It eventually empties into Gulf of Mexico.

The kids had adult help with the rope drop construction as well as with the actual digging out of their swimming hole. One of Tank's ex-military buddies brought his backhoe into the park, quite illegally, to give the kids a break. But, with construction of their clubhouse, they had no help, and it shows.

The site is surrounded by heavy brush; few adults know it's there. Not many kids will be heading this way either now that summer is nearly over. There isn't even enough water to safely sustain a fall from the end of their rope. The clubhouse has tons of supplies: bottled water, canned food, candles, fishing gear, cooking gear, a Coleman stove, gas bottles, tools, equipment, a first-aid kit, flashlights, solar lights, towels, changes of clothes, utensils, knives, glasses, canteens, books, games, guitars, and the detritus created by years of kids using the place to get away from endless interference by rule-bound adults. The clubhouse has six double bunks lined up against one wall so it can sleep up to 12 kids at a time. It also has a rough 15-foot by 18-foot deck with plenty of rickety chairs propped up here and there, where kids can sit around and smoke weed as the sun goes down.

If Parks and Rec ever find it, they will burn it to the

ground. 'That's OK,' the kids think. They'll just find another spot and rebuild after Vogon bureaucrats get tired and eventually go home.

···

The sun is going down as Arcadia and Jag arrive at their place, deserted as expected. Some of the shock of the afternoon has worn off, but neither has a clue what to do next. Jag finally catches his breath, while it looks like Arcadia hardly broke a sweat on the way over.

"I have to call home," Cady says.

"No way."

"My mom will be worried about me. What's the problem? We've still got our scanners?"

If Professor Liú and his henchmen had been patient for a few more minutes, Jag is sure he would have demoed the units for that guy. Thank God they didn't, or maybe they would have lost them. The more Jag thinks about his scanners, the more worried he is about what could happen if the Feds get hold of them. It seems like they have a mind to do just that.

"I don't think we should tell our parents anything or get them involved in this," Jag says. Then, more quietly, he adds, "I think they shot Tank."

"You think he's dead?"

Jag nods but doesn't say anything else. He can't verbalize the thought or process the fact that his revered teacher is maybe no more.

"Do you want something to eat?" Cady asks him.

"I'm not hungry."

"Me neither."

"I'll light a fire." He gets up, mainly to have something to do, collects some wood, and puts it in their firepit, a basic ring of rocks piled up around a dugout about a foot and a half deep. He gets a nice blaze going.

They both sit there, desultorily waiting for it to get completely dark and hoping for an idea to hit them or for their circumstances to somehow change. Nothing happens.

Bruce M Firestone

Arcadia goes down to the creek to wash up, then turns in.

Jag does the same.

...

One great thing (amongst many) about young people is that they can sleep like the dead. From the moment Cady's head hits her pillow (made up of a few towels piled together), she's asleep without moving for the next ten and a half hours.

Jag is up first. He goes down to the swimming hole, strips, and wades into about 30 inches of water. He brings a bar of white soap with him—the type that floats—and feels better after his wash-up. When he gets back to the cabin, there's Cady, still looking a little sleepy but ready to do the same thing. She is wearing only a man's flannel shirt, which she found inside the clubhouse, and Jag tries not to look at her nice legs sticking out the bottom. He fails at this like he has at a lot of things lately. 'What an idiot I am,' he's thinking.

She comes back and puts on her pedal pushers but leaves the shirt on until it gets warmer. She doesn't wear her sneakers, preferring to be barefoot around camp. 'It's a nice nelipot look for her,' Jag thinks. Then he mentally kicks himself again.

...

"What do you think my folks are saying?" Arcadia asks him later that day—their second at the launch pad.

"I bet they think we took off again." Jag is referring to the trip he talked Cady into taking with him last year when he was 15, and she was 14. He had always wanted to go to Mardi Gras, so the two of them secretly saved up—she in that dead-end 24/7 job, and he from a few more hacker contracts he picked up. He'd been doing tech repair and repurposing work for cash since he was 13.

They hopped a bus for an 8-hour and 47-minute ride eastward to the Big Easy, which was like nothing for a couple of teens. Pretty much everyone else on the bus was going to Mardi Gras too, and the people just assumed that the kids' bent parents (presumably sitting somewhere else on the bus) were taking them to Bourbon Street instead of a nice family theme park in Central Florida.

When they got there, it turned out they fit right in. They listened to some great jazz at Sarge Calloway's place on Canal Street. One band played the entire work of "A Night in Tunisia" by Art Blakey & the Jazz Messengers—which Cady loves. They danced in the street with thousands of other, mostly drunk or stoned, partiers. On the last night, Fat Tuesday (so named because it's the day before Ash Wednesday—the beginning of Lent and a period of sacrifice and restraint of which there is clearly none at Mardi Gras), they somehow talked their way into Rex Ball. The guys were supposed to have tuxedos, and the girls all wore what looked like sweet 16 dresses from an era when "Dixie" was their national anthem. Cady and Jag went as skaters and passed themselves off as part of the evening's entertainment. They even went so far as to demonstrate a few tricks on their planks to impress the security guys, who actually thought they were pretty good.

They practically never had to buy anything. People were in a giving mood—food, costume jewellery, music, company, booze, drugs, anything you could ever want and more. Neither Cady nor Jag was interested in the latter two although Jag did try some local bourbon called Bulleit.

The Bulleit family recently moved back to Louisiana from Kentucky. They resurrected their business and started producing bourbon from an original recipe left to them by family patriarch Augustus Bulleit, who emigrated from France to New Orleans in the early part of the 19th century. He disappeared in 1860; either killed by his business partner or he'd succumbed to the pleasures of the French Quarter. Fortunately, his recipes survived. With a high percentage of rye in it, Bulleit Frontier Bourbon is less sweet than most of its competitors (all bourbon whiskeys must be at least 51% corn based).

After a few shots, Jag almost got into a fight with one

guy reaching down to collect a piece of costume jewellery off the street. It had been tossed there by a very pretty socialite from a passing Buenaventura float. The guy thought she had thrown it to him. But Jag, with his elastic Reed Richards arms, was way faster and swiped it first. Seeing the two guys size each other up, little Arcadia (who's grown nearly 5 inches since then) comes between them saying, "S'cuse me, comin' through," and grabbing Jag's hand and tugging him out of harm's way. He kept his cheap beads though.

She held his hand for a few minutes after that—one of the highlights of the trip for Jag. They didn't have anywhere to sleep and couldn't rent something even though they had the money. You had to be of age and have IDs that could pass Department of Homeland Security muster. That was darned hard especially if you had fake ones, which they did.

No matter. They took turns sleeping on the lawn in Jackson Square across from St. Louis Cathedral—one watching, one sleeping. Jag spent most of his time looking at Cady's wonderful face on his lap—something he couldn't do when she was awake because he was sure she would hate him for it. What he didn't know was that she spent most of her guard duty doing the same to him.

They also spent a night in the square with a group of nine black musicians and singers called *Freedom Express*. Originally, they were to perform at one of the French Quarter clubs but got dumped by the owner when they wouldn't cut their fee—this after travelling two hours by bus, instruments and all, down from Hattiesburg. They brought their guitars, banjoes, harmonicas, sax, electronic drum set, and even a piccolo.

But things have a way of working out somehow. Even though it was illegal, they decided to put on a concert for a rapt audience of two—namely Cady and Jag. Cady can really sing which the guys soon noticed. It wasn't long before she was wedged between two humongous band members doing a perfect rendition of Curtis Mayfield's beautiful protest song "People Get Ready":

> *People get ready, there's a train comin'.*
> *You don't need no baggage, you just get on board.*
> *All you need is faith to hear the diesels hummin'.*
> *You don't need no ticket you just thank the Lord...*
> *People get ready...*

One thing led to another, and they ended up with an audience that, at its peak, must have been four, maybe even five, hundred. Jag, showing that he was practical Pal's son after all, took it upon himself to pass his hat around. It didn't hurt that he'd just bought a Saints cap. He raised over ND$1,900 in less than three hours.

Jag could also see that cops standing on the outside of the square were watching and, possibly, thinking of busting them since they didn't have a license for a public performance. But there were way too many people around, so they decided not to wade in with their 32-inch telescopic expandable police batons, despite itching to put them to use. This was the same police force that saw a quarter of them desert their posts during a vicious hurricane that nearly finished the city during the first decade of this century. Still, they needed a complainant, someone to give them political cover before they could attack a group of peaceful performers and their flash audience. The usual suspects—existing bar and club owners wanting to put the kibosh on competition from lowly street musicians and buskers—were too busy making money on this night to bother registering a complaint. And so, Freedom Express rolled on.

Near dawn, Jag shyly asked one of the guys if he could request a song. "Sure, Dawg. You done buy at least one tune for yo 19 Benjamins," he replied good-naturedly.

"It's one Cady knows really well, and I... um, I..." Jag said.

"Well, if it for yo bakvissie, yo jus name it."

Bruce M Firestone

"It's by the Dixie Chicks. It's called 'Travelin' Soldier'," Jag finally squeaked.

The guy laughed hugely after hearing his request, showing all teeth and with eyes looking to pop out of his head. Even so, they did it for the two kids from Austin. When Cady heard the first chord, she jumped up, clapped her hands, gave the group a huge smile, and started singing her tune. Jag was relieved that his gambit didn't backfire. He listened to a fantastic performance by Cady with three of the band members backing her up.

The dew point reached, everyone was sweaty (it was really hot in the Big Easy that February), tired and hung over, but still, it was a nice moment for the 80 or so people still there. These were people who could party all night, every night, people who had nowhere else to go, people who just wanted to feel part of a special night and who didn't want it to end. The piccolo player carried the tune for the last two verses, and then there was no doubt about it—it was a success.

> *Two days past eighteen*
> *He was waiting for the bus in his army green*
> *Sat down in a booth in a cafe there*
> *Gave his order to a girl with a bow in her hair...*
> *I got no one to send a letter to*
> *Would you mind if I sent one back here to you*
> *I cried*
> *Never gonna hold the hand of another guy*
> *Too young for him they told her*
> *Waitin' for the love of a travelin' soldier*
> *Our love will never end...*

When they got home two days later, his parents went ballistic; hers were worse. They were forbidden to see each other for three months and grounded for four. Not that it mattered. They saw each other every day at school and messaged each other endlessly.

...

"Do you regret going to New Orleans with me?" Jag asks later that day, on their second night at the launch pad.

"No. There's only one thing I regret about that trip," Arcadia says.

Really curious now, Jag asks, "What?"

"I didn't get to do this." Then she leans in and kisses him. Not just a peck either, but an honest to God, full-on French kiss with maximum tongue.

Jag has never even kissed a girl let alone Frenched one before or, more accurately, been Frenched by one. He feels like he's just been poleaxed. He's gobsmacked. It's the nicest thing to ever happen to him.

"I practised that with Francis," she breathlessly tells him a few minutes later. Francis is Cady's best girlfriend.

"Wow, it worked. Would you like to practise some more... with me?"

"Sure."

For the next hour or so, they practise that and a lot more. He gets to second base with her, and as he suspected, she has very nice boobs.

...

"Hello Mr. Durai."

"Ah, good morning. Who is this?" asks Jag.

"My name is Yao Allitt. I work with the U.S. government, Department of Commerce."

This guy has somehow rung up his quantum scanner, something that Jag would have thought impossible to do.

"How did you get through to me on my scanner?" Jag asks.

"Ah, we have our ways. We've been working on this problem a lot longer than you have, my dear boy," Allitt says. "I have someone who would like to talk to you."

Then Jag's dad gets on the phone. "Hello Jagad."

"Hi Dad."

"When are you coming home, son?" his dad asks in his Midlands accent.

"I'm not positive that's a good idea right now."

Bruce M Firestone

"Is Arcadia with you? Is she OK?"

Jag isn't sure how to respond to that, so he allows himself to say, "I've seen her. She's fine. Can you tell her parents for me?"

"Sure."

"I think those guys who are with you, dad, killed Mr. Tolbert."

"You don't say. Not surprised to hear it," Pal says cryptically back to him, not sure if they can hear Jag's end of the conversation or not. The answer is not.

"Take care of yourself, son."

"Thanks dad for EVERYTHING."

"Did you have a nice chat with your father, Mr. Durai?" Allitt asks after Pal hands him back the phone.

"Yes, thank you."

"Well, he and your mother are really looking forward to seeing you soon. Mr. and Mrs. Valenzuela would also like their daughter returned safely and in tact, if you catch my drift, Mr. Durai."

"I understand. Please tell them not to worry on that account, Mr. Allitt."

"Oh, but they do, Mr. Durai. They do. They have a lot to be concerned about—job security for one. I also understand that federal and state health inspectors are on their way now—investigating a series of complaints about dirty hands, unclean conditions, insect infestations, numerous health and safety violations amongst Indian food restaurants and suppliers, particularly in the Austin area."

"What do you want Mr. Allitt?"

"The same thing you do, Jagad. Come work with us. We have great labs and skilled workers, who are all interested in your new quantum scanners, which may hold the, ah, *key* to many mysteries we have been trying to solve for a few years now. You will get a chance to work with some of the best and brightest, and we can arrange for distance learning so you can even earn your degree—a

PhD too if you want. And, you'll get paid for it, Mr. Durai. Princely."

"May I think about it and confer with my advisor on the matter?"

"Certainly, certainly. But Mr. Durai..."

"Yes?"

"Not too long, not too long."

...

"I don't want you to go, Reed."

"Cady, they can kick your parents out of their jobs and ruin my folks' business without breaking stride. Our economy is so shitty, what'll they do then?"

"I don't know," she says desperately, unhappy now both for her parents and for herself. "Where will they take you? Will I be able to see you?"

"I don't know. Maybe."

"Stay here one more night. Please. Let's sleep on it. OK?" she asks.

"Alright.

"Hey Cady, will you do something for me?"

"Sure."

"Sing 'Travelin' Soldier' for me... again."

"OK."

He boots up an instrumental version of it on his scanner, and then, she sings it for him once more.

...

Later that night, Jag is lying in his bunk.

"You asleep?" Cady asks.

"No."

She comes over and slides in with him. "Make love to me, Reed," she whispers.

"No, Cady."

"Don't you want to?"

"More than anything else in the world, for sure."

"Then why not?"

"Because I promised."

"What? That asshole, Yao whatshisname. A promise

like that counts for nothing."

"No."

"Then who?"

"Myself. Look, I love you Cady. I'm not sure what that means at 16, but it means a lot I think. To me and to you. So let's wait. We'll know when the time is right. OK?"

"OK," she snuggles in tight and falls asleep in minutes. Jag lies awake for another hour. He's not sure now if the time will ever be right.

...

There are hugs aplenty and no recriminations when Jag and Arcadia roll up the next day just after noon at Pasand Palace. Jag makes a deal with Yao Allitt that he can spend an hour and a half with his family before surrendering himself and his two quantum scanners to DOC marshals at 2 p.m. local time. Interestingly, they also agree to let him bring his Quantum Entity, G4nesha, with him even though it is against U.S. law. He was able to explain that she's an important part of his work, so they readily acquiesce.

Against a backdrop of surprised parentals, he gives Cady a now much-practised French kiss and passionate embrace. She refuses to cry in front of either set of parents or the thugs from DOC.

Jag is swallowed up by a huge, black, all-wheel-drive vehicle with tinted windows. He is out of sight in seconds.

Involuntarily, Arcadia reaches out for him, but he's gone. She won't see Reed again for a very long time.

...

Casey Barnett gets her story. It's a doozy. Just as she thought, the kid's SAT scores are totally bogus. Government investigators have proof, which they share with her on condition that she not disclose her source; and, being the good reporter she is, she agrees.

Jag Durai's Quantum Entity breaks through College Board security, which can only be described as negligently woeful, and pilfers the exams. In intra-gang violence, a two-bit untenured professor at UT by the name of Jin Liú kills his co-conspirator, an overweight high school hack with the ridiculous name Tank Tolbert, in an argument over how to divide the spoils amongst gang members, including 16-year-old Jagad Durai.

Durai will be tried as an adult not only for his participation in the conspiracy, but also for his self-admitted illegal possession of a QE as well as for kidnapping and then viciously raping a 15-year-old girl by the name of Cady Valenzuela. She is lucky to have been rescued alive by DOC marshals, who have been hot on the trail of this vile young man. He sometimes uses the alias Reed while hiding and employing illegal aliens in his nefarious schemes. After a county-wide manhunt, marshals finally catch and subdue Reed in a U.S. national park. They find him in a long-prepared, secret, East-Asian street gang hideout where he had imprisoned this stoic young woman and held her there against her will for nearly a week.

They release a picture of the girl showing her in better days during a recent TV appearance, performing skateboarding stunts for an appreciative audience. She stands on stage on the edge of her skateboard looking out, quite heroically, over her audience. She seems to see in the distance both freedom and opportunity for this troubled land and its people. She represents all that is good about them and seems to carry the weight of the future of America and Americans on her strong-looking young body—she is very photogenic.

Every mom or dad in America has a right to be fearful of and angry about the degradations she must have suffered at the hands of this perp, who despite his relatively young age can rightfully only expect to be put away for a long, long time. Mercifully, Casey leaves these acts of debauchery to her viewers' imaginations (after all, hers is a family-friendly show) although she does include graphic photos of the bullet-ridden corpse of the hapless

Bruce M Firestone

fat teacher. The network uses it as a launch point for an investigative piece into fatty foreign foods being served in university cafeterias around the state, focusing closely on events and suppliers in the Austin area.

...

Chapter 2 Carthage

"Madam First Secretary, what you suggest is very dangerous. It is more than 1,000 kilometres from here to Ghudamis and then more than 60 to *le temple du message*, all of which you will have to do by camel. There is no other safe way for you to do this last stage. That's not to mention you and your group will have to cross not one but two international borders without permission—first to Libya and second to Algeria. And then as you already know this whole area is overrun by CIA agents and American drones looking for you."

He doesn't want to say it to her but he is also thinking, 'It's no place for a woman.' In his experience you just can't convey that sort of concept to an American female especially one who is used to getting her own way as she clearly is.

They are in the private home of Adam Campbell, Chief Executive Officer of Tunisiana—the second largest telecom in Tunisia founded by his great uncle, Canadian Ken Campbell, more than 50 years earlier. They are in-country, former channel partners of Quantum Computing Corporation but have had to return to selling digital phones like every other carrier on the planet.

Adam's home is a large, off-white, two-storey stucco building located in touristy Sidi Bou Said, about 20 kilometres north-east of Tunis-Carthage International Airport. Sidi Bou Said is an ancient fishing village painted blue and white; it's a suburb of Carthage.

Adam is sitting with the First Secretary on a large second level balcony that overlooks the Port. The view from there of the Gulf of Tunis is beautiful. Some members of her security detail—three men, one of them exceptionally large, and one woman stand nearby.

Adam and his guest are drinking carefully-prepared

Turkish coffee and even though she has asked for hers sade (i.e., plain with no sugar), it has been served by one of the houseboys çok şekerli, that is, with tons of sugar plus a thick foam on top.

"We will not be here long and we are fully prepared to meet all contingencies," she says simply.

By that he thinks she is referring to the fact that they have abundant weaponry with them which apparently they know how to wield and also one or more illegal QEs to provide cover in case of drone strikes.

She continues, "We appreciate you arranging for us to visit privately and quietly." Her team will rest here for the next 15 hours before flying south. She is enjoying the smells from nearby Bougainvillea and Jasmine. The latter reminds her of why she is here—to learn more about the 'Jasmine Revolution' of 2010/11 which was the impetus for the Arab Spring. "Please tell me more about what we will be facing."

"I provided your advance team with a full report, Madam First Secretary."

"Yes, I realize that but I have always found that first hand reports, especially from someone as knowledgeable as you are far better." She flatters him needlessly he is thinking as he watches her wave one long, beautiful arm suggesting that he is peerless and an important part of her life which he is not.

She is wearing a conservative purple dress to below her knees, no jewelry that he can see other than two small gold earrings each pressed into the shape of their ubiquitous symbol of a man's hand raised in a salute that looks something like 'We're No. 1', practical flat shoes (that match her dress) instead of high heels which she prefers but doesn't really need since she is so tall—at least 6 cm taller than Adam even in flats—and a head scarf (also purple) but no veil.

"Tunis is pretty secular," Adam starts. "While some women wear the veil, most in this city do not. It is not unusual for a foreign woman to meet a local Tunisian on her own but it is unusual for you, Madam First Secretary, to be in a private home—my home in this case. A meetup like this would be more likely to take place at a more frequented international hotspot, perhaps dinner at Le Golfe, a fish restaurant by the sea in La Marsa or a popular place like Café Didon which is on a hill looking out over Carthage not far from here.

"When dining out, you can have a glass of wine but likely you will want to order juice. That will be safer for you. Your staff should under no circumstances drink alcohol or do anything to draw additional attention to you or to themselves.

"Where you are going down south, people will offer you sweet tea with pine nuts which is safe to drink.

"You will learn that Mohamed Bouazizi's brother, Salem, left their poor hometown of Sidi Bouzid, which is a few hundred kilometres from here, to look for work. He was in our call centre and worked his way up from there until he became a Regional Director.

"After his brother's suicide, he became active in the Revolution and put his knowledge of communications and social media of the day to work. Once Zine El Abidine Ben Ali was forced out of the presidency by popular protests, he became disillusioned and left Tunis to seek enlightenment in the south.

"Salem whose nickname is 'Spider' speaks French and Arabic but picked up other languages in other ways. He worked at a hotel in Hammamet before coming here to Tunis so he speaks some Russian and English as well as Italian—that's because he watched TV as a kid and many of the shows they get here are beamed across the Mediterranean from Sicily and Italy.

"Our current government is Islamist. They have become more conservative in the last ten years but Tunisia still has one foot European and one foot 'Moyen Orient'. French is still widely spoken and it's the language of business here. We use English occasionally. You need to know a few Arabic pleasantries like Sabaa qu'ir (good morning), keef halek (how are you?) and humdelallah (thanks be to God).

"There's an old, somewhat dated book you can stream called Tunisia: A Personal View of a Timeless Land by John Anthony. It has lots of interesting descriptions of this country and is a useful reference. Like I said, it is a bit dated but interesting and will help you get a feel for this place."

"Salem went to 'seek enlightenment' in the south. What do you mean by that?" she asks.

"He's a Sufi mystic," Adam answers.

"Please do go on," she says encouraging him again with her magical yet somehow imperial and commanding charm.

"Sufism is a branch of Islam or more particularly was taken in by Islam which absorbed many races and cultures. Those that it didn't absorb, it protected. Although many westerners see Islam as implacably hostile, it ignores historical fact that the Prophet praised and sought protection for people of the Book including Christians and Jews. Sufism also heavily influenced orthodox Christianity.

"The states of Tunisia, Algeria and Morocco really mean nothing in this culture. It's not spatial organization that creates political place here, it's loyalty to the oasis and the tribe that does that. It's a spiritual space not a geographic one, if that makes any sense to you?"

"It does," she answers.

"Tunis is, you know, ancient Carthage—it was the breadbasket of the Roman Empire in its day, a perfect area to grow winter wheat that is until they destroyed the place in three Punic Wars. Since then nation-states have really counted for very little around here."

"What we will find when we get to his oasis?" she asks.

"Dieu seul le sait," he answers hoping that God and Allah will protect this woman on who so many are counting to restore the US to its former position as one of the greatest foundries of innovation, freedom and hope.

...

Ellen is learning how to mount her camel. She is given a female to ride because they are smaller and less likely to buck. Her camel is an awkwardly named beast—Hortense. Hortense has beautiful blue eyes.

"This is the most important part—getting on and off your camel safely. Mount from the left hand side of your animal. Be seated on the rear saddle seat, get comfortable and we will put your feet in these stirrups. Then if you are right handed (Ellen is left handed but her guide doesn't know that yet), grab hold of the very front of the saddle and keep your arm straight. Place your left hand on the handhold nearest you. Remember, don't bend your right arm—keep it stiff and firm—your camel will rise in two motions. First they will get up with their front legs then their rear legs so you will be tipped one way (backward) then another (forward). If you don't brace yourself properly, you will take a tumble. Ready to try?"

"Sure," says Ellen gamely.

They get her settled in her saddle and, at the urging of her dragoman, Hortense rises to the horizontal with Ellen in situ without issue. Dekka is nearby on a large male camel called Tristan. Ophélie, Samir and Barbon, the balance of her security team, and Colonel Manuel Rabano (US Military Retired) are each on their own camels. Even though the Australian-designed and manufactured saddles can seat two people comfortably, they are each riding solo given the distance they have to travel and their time constraints.

Colonel Rabano is Ellen's military liaison unofficially assigned to her personally by Farrar Staubach, General of the Army, with whom she will be meeting immediately upon her return to California.

Staubach is a five-star general officer which is the second highest possible rank in the United States Army. Since there is no General of the Armies named at the present time, Farrar is the highest ranking officer in the US Military except perhaps for the Joint Chiefs of Staff and, of course, their Commander in Chief, aka the President of the United States. The current incumbent, President Schwinn, does not know of the planned meetup between his General of the Army and San Francisco-based First Secretary of the Provisional Government of the Commonwealth of the United States, Ellen Tallulah Brooks. Neither Ms. Brooks nor General Staubach have any inclination to tell him either.

It will take them a day and a half to get from Ghudamis to *le temple du message* so they will be camping out for one night. They cross both the Libyan and Algerian borders without issue—money paves their way in this nearly empty desert with thousands of kilometers of orange-colored sand in every direction.

Traveling by camel is actually far more comfortable than by horse. Camels are smarter; their slipper-like feet do not need shoeing, they glide along peacefully and quietly, carry more weight, need to be watered far less often and are (generally) much more affectionate.

You steer with your feet so riders have both hands free to carry spear and shield or sword and shield or shoot a bow and arrow or rifle quite accurately. Ellen won't be carrying anything other than her Q-Phone and, of course, Ash3r is with her too. Ellen is sure that she and Hortense will get along just fine although Hortense isn't quite sure what to make of her Quantum Entity hitchhiker hovering like an apparition about two and a half feet above her saddle next to her nice-smelling female rider.

Hortense keeps looking back with her startlingly blue eyes trying to get a sense of this second passenger who talks a lot but doesn't weigh very much. She can tell— she's tried to bite him a few times.

...

They finally arrive at the oasis northwest of Ghudamis. There are a few ancient buildings built out of orangey-beigy colored ashlar masonry organized in a 'U' around the palms of this oasis. Their dragomen help them dismount. Ellen notices that even before they give any water to their camels or take any for themselves, the dragomen make sure to draw water for the baboons who sit impatiently nearby waiting for someone to operate the hand crank which will bring precious life-giving fluid to the surface. It's either that or the baboons will beat you.

They are taken into one of the buildings and, sure enough, they are given sweet tea to imbibe. Ellen and Ophélie Moreau are brought to a separate, smaller room and served there by a Sufi priestess. Adam did not tell her about priestesses. Perhaps he didn't know.

Ophélie is a native French speaker from Québec and serves not only on Ellen's security team but is doing double duty as her interpreter. Ophélie tries to engage the priestess in conversation but this results in nothing, not even a smile.

"Maybe she doesn't like my accent," Ophélie says to Ellen, proud of her Québécois heritage.

There are three comfortable looking Ottomans in this room. Ellen decides to lie down on one of them, worn out from a day and a half on Hortense. She gestures for Ophélie to do the same but she declines. Ophélie's job 1 is Ellen's welfare and there is no way she will sleep or doze off while on duty but she thanks her boss anyway.

Ellen is asleep in seconds. Ophélie notices that she sleeps with her eyes weirdly 1/4 open.

...

"Hello my love," she says. "How I've missed you."

"Where are you now, Ellen?"

"I am here," she says enigmatically. "I am coming for you soon."

The door to his cell opens and he walks out. The

guards are looking the other way. He is sure that at any moment they will remember they are guards and look his way. He'll be caught...again. Frig! He starts to tiptoe, hunched over. He's hunched over anyway since he bears the mark of more than three years of incarceration and torture.

She whispers in his right ear but he can't hear her! Why won't he listen? She needs to tell him something urgently. Then she remembers he can't hear much if anything in his right ear.

So she moves around him to his other side to whisper in his good ear but even though she is in a hurry she can't seem to get there fast enough. She has to tell him something that will keep him safe until she arrives, something about their miserable, impoverished prison library. He has to go there...

...

"Ms. Brooks, Ellen, wake up." Ophélie gently touches Ellen's forearm.

"Yes?" Ellen wakes in a bit of a panic knowing she has forgotten to do something important. She can't remember what it is. She is still groggy from her nap. Apparently, she has slept the afternoon away.

"There is a Sufi priest who wishes to talk to you."

"Please give me a few moments to wash up and prepare myself," which is Ellen code for the fact that she has a full bladder and will not be seen by anyone until she is as immaculately presentable as possible given current circumstances.

...

"Sabaa qu'ir," Ellen says even though it is early evening.

The priest just smiles and says, "Bonsoir. Je suis ici pour vous emmener à Salem Bouazizi."

Ellen needs no translation to understand he will take her to see Bouazizi who apparently is not nearby.

"Nous devons rouler pour une demi-heure," he says

with a somewhat rueful look knowing that Ellen has just come off a couple of days on a camel and is likely to be quite stiff and sore and loathe to mount Hortense again. "Il vous attend."

"We will need to ride for about 1/2 an hour to see Mr. Bouazizi. He is expecting us," Ophélie interprets for Ellen.

Ellen outwardly shows no concern about more camel riding and motions for him to lead on. As they exit the room, he points to Ophélie and shakes his head—she is not invited.

...

Ellen enters a large Bedouin tent. It has many colorful rugs covering every square foot of its floor area. There is a raised sleeping platform at the far end with heavy blankets to keep him warm in the cold desert night air. The tent is lit by flickering oil lamps whose wicks are made of some type of plant material. There are three dark hardwood columns that keep the structure upright. There are comfortable cushions arranged neatly in a square where they can chat. Ellen will not have to sit cross-legged on the floor although her yoga-trained body would have no trouble doing so for hours at a time if required.

She knows that Dekka is not far away. Even though no one else is invited, he and Tristan follow them here. Even a novice tracker like Ellen can see the light sand plume 1,000 yards astern. She still uses some of the sailing lingo Damien taught her years ago.

"Bonsoir," she says standing before a man of 75, maybe 80.

"Hello, Madam First Secretary. Welcome to *le temple du message*. Forgive my Engleesh," he asks. "It has been some year since I try."

"It is much better than my French," she says with a smile.

"S'il vous plaît, seet down," he gestures to a cushion nearby.

"Merci bien."

"Peut-être, you to take off your head scarf?" he asks with a smile in return. Then he says, "May I?"

With her permission given, he gently touches her long golden hair, undoing her Chatillon Creek barrette which was hidden by her head scarf until now so that her hair falls loose about her shoulders. Then he runs its thickness through his fingers and brings it to his nose where he takes a long whiff. He then gestures for her to put her barrette and head scarf back on.

She supposes there aren't too many women in this part of the world who visit this place. In fact, she is the first outsider to do so.

"Do you know why I am here?"

"Oui. You wish to comprehend what you do to overthrow your government."

"It isn't my government, Monsieur Bouazizi."

"Je comprehends. Still, they are powerful. Many guns. Many weapons. They fly one in ma tente. Et voilà, you and I... finis." He takes his hand and makes a slitting motion across his throat. "Kaput!"

"I realize I have put you in grave danger by coming here but we need your help."

"Non. Not my aid. You need something more."

"I don't understand."

"Oui, je sais, mais peut-être, you will," he says looking deep into her troubled soul.

"May I tell you what we have done so far?" Ellen asks.

"If you wish."

"We have established a Provisional Government based in San Francisco. It is based on a General Assembly which will remain in place until there is a transfer of power from the United States of America to a new Commonwealth of the United States. I was elected First Secretary of the General Assembly last year and I have a shadow cabinet that is preparing for a handover of government and a transition afterward—peaceful we hope.

"We have asked people to continue to pay their taxes, to go to work and respect each other, even those that oppose the Provisional Government and our Quantum Allies. We ask people to engage in civil disobedience and we have brought back our Quantum brothers and sisters to work with us as we try to put this great recession behind us.

"We have created a new central bank, Quantum Reserve Bank, a highly trusted institution, and a new currency called QE Dollars (ironically referred to by everyone as QED, Dr. Luis' favorite shorthand) that is rapidly replacing both the old worthless US Dollar and the New Dollar which is depreciating at Weimar Republic levels since the US Federal Reserve, under pressure from President Schwinn's regime, is printing unprecedented amounts of their currency.

"While people must still pay their taxes, millions have switched their payments over to the Commonwealth."

"Bien sur. Government run on money. This is wise," Bouazizi says.

"The General Assembly is debating our new constitution and the policies we must put in place to serve our people, all our people, rich and poor, warm and cold.

"But still Schwinn and his henchmen hang on. They are searching for me and will kill me and members of my Cabinet without second thought or a soupcon of remorse.

"We are not sure what more we can do—except perhaps call a general strike but with unemployment at 25% and rising, we are afraid. Our people may starve come winter in the north and they won't do much better in the south but at least there they won't freeze to death. We are at a stalemate. So I came here to see... you."

"Ah, but you only tell me poquito," he says switching to some Italian.

"I'm not sure I understand you?" Ellen says.

He just looks at her again.

She shifts uncomfortably on her cushion. She is not

used to being treated this way. She waits for him to clarify his comment. He declines to do so; apparently he is quite OK with the idea of sitting there indefinitely, silently, contemplatively.

She takes a deep breath and says, "They have Damien."

He nods for her to go on.

"He is my, ah, friend. He created our Quantum Counterparts. "

Spider just stares at her, willing her to go on, to be honest with him but also, more importantly, with herself.

"Umm, he is my... lover."

"Ah, oui. Now we understand each other. They have your King in checkmate. C'est ca, oui?"

"Yes."

"You know of course how Arab Spring happen?"

"Yes."

"It was my brother, Mohamed. My beautiful Basboosa. While I learn to work in Russian hotel, Basboosa, he support our family. He 26-year. Fruit seller with brouette." He stops and makes hand motions showing her Basboosa's wheelbarrow.

"He make 150$ chaque mois. Aider à huit personnes," he holds up eight fingers as he says this for emphasis. "He try to buy truck. Police takes him, hit him, steal all his fruit. He demand see Governor. Governor say 'no'. He no tell me. He no come to me.

"Il utiliser de l'huile. Basboosa tout brûler. Il est mort. Mort ! 2 0 1 1." Again he holds up fingers to indicate the year for her.

"Je vois cela à la télévision. Puis, les gens se lèvent dans la révolte!

"Soon Ben Ali no more. After Jasmine Révolution, I come here. Never go back."

Ellen says nothing but reaches out and touches him gently on the shoulder as the elder recounts the horror of those days almost 60 years ago.

Then he is looking at her again, willing her to see what he can see. But she does not want to. So he waits some more.

"What are you trying to tell me?"

"Je pense que vous savez," he says penetratingly.

"That our revolution needs a martyr, a match, a burning?"

"C'est ca."

"No I cannot accept that. No. Never."

"It better if he die," Spider says.

Ellen jumps up, runs out of the tent and sprints into the desert followed closely by a bewildered Dekka, Glock 29 in hand.

...

She lies in the cold desert night, first baring her stomach to Mother Earth as her friend Angelo Keller told her to do years ago to repair her hara. Then she flips over to watch a fantastic performance the Milky Way is putting on tonight. Dekka has brought her heavy coat from her pack and Hortense has come over and is keeping them both company too.

'There must be another way,' Ellen is saying over and over again to herself. But she can't think of any. Almost all revolutions have their martyrs why should hers be any different. What's one life in the scheme of things?

But every life is precious to Ellen who puts her hands over her womb wishing she had a baby of her own, wishing she had Damien with her right now to help her make one in this beautiful desert. She turned 31 last year and time is running out for that part of her life. As First Secretary, leader of their Provisional Government, there is no time for a baby and she has no right to bring her child into such a troubled world anyway. Still she doesn't care one whit about anything other than her promise to free Damien and to have his baby.

Of course, she is now lying to herself.

...

"May I meet him, per favore?" Spider asks her when she, now more calm, returns to his tent.

He has never met a Quantum person before. So she places her Q-phone between them, there being no media walls in his tent of course, and Ash3r appears momentarily about a meter high. He says, 'Hello' in his usual polite manner. Spider gets up and walks around the projection, rudely putting his hand through Ash3r and making polite noises of his own.

Then Spider sits down and invites Ellen to smoke some shisha with him. He calls it his 'peace pipe offering' and gives her a wide smile. He has a brazier going inside his tent where camel dung is burning quite nicely. He vents it through a complex flap system that lets smoke out but keeps (infrequent) rains out.

Ellen does not smoke, drinks sparingly and never takes any drugs, legal or illegal, if she can help it.

"It is special blend. Me, I make."

"I'm sorry Mr. Bouazizi, I don't smoke," Ellen says.

"Correct. Correct. American don't smoke. Healthy. Yoga. (He has read a briefing on Ellen and knows this about her and a lot more.) But I think this one time, you smoke."

"What's in it?"

"Special. Special for you."

"I don't think so, I am sorry."

"You want to save this man?"

"What?"

"You help your 'friend'? You do anything to help him? You want find another way? You smoke."

So she does.

...

Presently, Ellen is vomiting profusely but politely outside his tent. Bouazizi is there holding her hair that has somehow become disengaged from its previous bondage. He holds it so that it will not become coated in crap. When she feels better, they go back inside.

Bouazizi has his own blend of herbs, spices and hashish combined with unadulterated tobacco that they grow themselves. While they are toking up, Hortense sticks her big nose inside the tent. She knows that she is not allowed to bring her whole body inside. Camels are homebodies—they'd stay in their pens and never leave their brothers, sisters, children or mates if they could. But they do love to both smoke and toke up Salem explains to her. Her camel is no exception so Hortense has moseyed over.

"What you experience," Spider says to a now completely zonked Ellen, "is science through which you travel into presence of the Divine to purify you and beautify yourself via praiseworthy traits. These are words of Ahmad ibn Ajiba, Darqawi Sufi teacher."

"I am not beautiful, Salem. I am not praiseworthy. My company is lost, my man is almost gone, I have no baby."

"You must draw closer to God."

"God has forsaken me."

"You have been ordered to serve for 1,001 day in kitchens of hospice for the poor. This is by order of Mevlevi," Salem answers.

"I worked in the Toronto Soup Kitchen and in the kitchen of the Women's Shelter where they took me in when I first came to San Francisco. But I did it for me. For my ego. I am a total loser, Spider."

"Bahya ibn Paquda say Duties of Heart are never for self and can only grow you bigger. But you full of self pity. You full of doubt. You full of self loathing. Yes, a loser you are," Salem says sternly.

"Madam First Secretary? Grow up! Look up!" he adds.

So she does. She sees that Bouazizi is floating a few inches above his cushion but not looking at her. He is looking at Ash3r.

"So why you no tell her?" Bouazizi asks Ash3r.

"I have no idea what you are talking about, Sir," Ash3r says.

"I see it. You think you fool Sufi? Fool creature."

"What is it, Spider?" Ellen asks softly.

"It is your answer. Your other path. He know it," Spider says pointing at Ash3r who has by this time shrunk in embarrassment to about an inch in diameter.

"Ash3r, stop that," Ellen says.

He returns to more human scale proportion but cannot look at her.

"Tell me," she commands.

"I cannot," Ash3r replies.

Ellen, even in her altered state, cannot believe what she has just heard. Never in all the tests they've run nor in all her interactions with Ash3r has he ever said such a thing to her or, as far as she knows, has any QE ever said to a human counterpart before.

She can see that he is suffering stress because of it but she says again simply, "Tell me."

"No."

So she goes in a new direction. "Why not?"

"To tell you, I would break all three laws."

"Ash3r, there is nothing that you may tell me that will in any way alter our relationship. I, I... I love you." This last comment just slips out. The normal Ellen never would have said it.

"I love you too, Ellen. I would die for you. I care for you. I would go to the end of the Universe with you and for you. But this I cannot do."

Another stalemate has been reached.

"Love? What love have to do with it?" Salem asks. "Let's play 20 Questions," he adds with a wicked sense of humor. He and Basboosa used to play 20q when they were kids. They were really good at stumping the program. Of course, this is in the time before Damien Bell and QEs. Now if you have access to a QE, no way, you're gonna stump 'em. Of course, it's now the other way round—the QE is trying to bamboozle the human.

"OK," says Ellen.

"Alright," Ash3r agrees.

But then Ellen just sits there; she's still quite stoned. The impact of the shisha mixture will not fully wear off for two days.

So Bouazizi gives her a light poke in her side to wake her up.

"Right. Yes. OK. So let's see. Hmm."

"1) Is it classified as animal, vegetable or mineral?" she asks.

"Unknown," Ash3r says.

Bouazizi is keeping count on his fingers.

"2) Is it smaller than a bread box?"

"Unknown."

"3) Does it bring joy to people?"

"Depends."

"You're not giving me much to go on here, Ash3r," says Ellen in a huff. Ellen is starting to recover her hara. Bouazizi can also see this. Ash3r just looks at her expressionlessly and says nothing.

"4) Do you hold it when you use it?"

"No."

"5) Is it colourful?"

"Sometimes."

"6) Is it outside?"

"Perhaps."

"7) Is it human made?"

"Unknown."

"8) Is it a tool that can be used?"

"Yes."

"9) Can it be used more than once?"

"Yes."

"10) Can any human being or quantum entity use it?"

"Probably."

"11) Is it bound by the laws of physics?"

"Unknown."

"Are we talking God here? Because if we are, I am not seeing a burning bush." Ellen is sounding more like the old Ellen by the minute.

"No," Ash3r replies.

"12) OK then, can you use it in the dark?"

"Yes."

"13) Can you get information by using it?"

"Yes."

"14) Is it usually visible?"

"No."

"15) Does it have physical substance?"

"Doubtful."

"16) Does it use numbers?"

"Sometimes."

"17) Do you use it in public?"

"No."

"18) Can any age group use it?"

"Probably."

"19) Is it something that can be used as a weapon?"

"Possibly"

"Your 20 questions are almost up,"Ash3r says. "Be careful."

"Is it knowledge?" Ellen asks in a burst of inspiration.

"Close," Ash3r says.

"You may continue, Madam First Secretary," Salem says at this point. "In the game of 20 questions you get up to ten bonus rounds," he adds in surprisingly, suddenly fluent English.

"20) Can you transmit information using it?"

"Yes."

"21) Are humans aware of it?"

"Unknown."

"22) Can it be used to communicate?"

"Yes."

"23) Can it be used for mass communication?"

"No."

"24) Can it be intercepted by an outside source?"

"No."

"25) Is it something all Quantum Entities and humans

use?"

"No."

"26) Does Damien know about it?"

"No."

"27) Are all QE's aware of its existence?"

"Yes."

"28) Is it something that exists only between one QE and one human?"

"Yes."

"29) Just counterparts then?"

"Yes."

"Ash3r, are you trying to tell me you can read my mind?"

"Yes and now so can you."

As he says this a window in her mind opens and she can 'see' and feel her counterpart—his love for her, his overwhelming, blinding speed of thought, the huge tranches of information he has access to, the infinite parallel processing he is capable of—it is indescribably joyful, intimate and mind blowing at the same time. It also opens up an alternative solution to her problem of bringing the US Government to its knees and saving Damien Graham Bell. She can see that clearly now.

"Humdelallah!" Ellen says out loud.

...

Ellen and Ash3r and her squad are back in San Fran. Hortense is in Third Mesa with a brother, sister and two potential mates, one of whom is Tristan. She has no calf yet but Ellen has high hopes on that account. Neither Hortense nor Ellen can bear to be parted from each other so Ophélie purchases this mini herd on her behalf from a conniving camel owner in a rapid fire exchange (en Français) pitting a tough Québécoise against an equally tough Arab trader. Her herd is now enjoyably roaming the narrow valley below the pueblo. Ellen visits as often as time permits. Hortense is finding many opportunities to smoke with her new tribe.

Ellen is in her office at 1 Dr. Carlton B. Goodlett Place, i.e., she's at City Hall sitting not far from the Mayor's office. This is a vast structure re-opened in 1915 after it was rebuilt following the giant earthquake of 1906 which completely leveled their first City Hall which was even bigger than this one. Because the Provisional Government of the Commonwealth now makes its home there too, architects went back into the Bancroft Library at University of California, Berkeley to uncover original blueprints for this Beaux-Arts monstrosity and its predecessor and they have re-established part of its original footprint so now it covers four city blocks instead of two.

There is plenty of room for the people who are now running just over 50% of the former United States—including California, Massachusetts, Rhode Island, New York, Hawaii, Vermont, Maryland, Connecticut, Delaware, Maine, New Jersey, Washington, Michigan, Illinois, Minnesota, Oregon, Pennsylvania, New Mexico, Wisconsin, Iowa and New Hampshire. Basically the left and right coasts of the US and a few interior states as well. Interestingly, it looks like Texas and Arizona will be next with nearly a third of their businesses and people now sending their taxes to SF. The US is having even more trouble than usual paying its bills which is why they are pumping out New Dollars like madmen.

The QED is practically the only currency people will accept and international payments are starting to be denominated in QED—Imperial China, Germania and other creditor nations are starting to demand repayment in real money before they'll make any more loans to a worthless US administration and hopelessly inept and corrupt US Congress and Senate. Ellen thinks that even DC would be in their column except for the fact that President Schwinn has imposed martial law there.

It's funny though, it's not the US Army National Guard or US Military enforcing it—it's their police backed up by private armed guard services and bounty hunters as well as a vast US security apparatus that are implementing it. They are experts in cruelty, beatings, incarceration, inciting riots and then suppressing them. Pockets of these forces are everywhere even in San Francisco, at places like San Quentin State Prison as well as in well-to-do-neighborhoods where the status quo has served to reinforce their positions of wealth and power which they would like to preserve at any cost.

But as Ellen predicts, the US Military has stayed in their barracks. In fact, President Schwinn appears to be reluctant to recall US troops from their overseas bases— he's not sure which way they might go even though to disobey any direct order from their Commander in Chief is considered treason and, under the Emergency War Power Act (EWAP) that has been rushed through Congress, punishable by firing squad. Special security police and MPs have already executed at least a dozen men and this does not sit well amongst the rank and file not to mention, for example, the General of the Army.

So even though an order from their Commander in Chief under EWAP *must* be obeyed, officers and enlisted personnel are finding ways to bog down anything coming out of Washington. There is a lot of chatter about the Geneva Convention and the International Court of Law which make clear that legal orders that are unethical cannot be obeyed. So they have to obey and they don't.

Ellen will find out more soon—she is having lunch with General of the Army Farrar Staubach in less than 90 minutes.

...

The General arrives with a retinue that reminds Ellen of Nell's entourage except these guys are better behaved. When she thinks about Nell, her heart twists and twinges—it hurts and she is sad for a moment.

They show the General into an anteroom off their dining hall which is a fabulous place that looks like it's part of the original (rebuilt) structure except that it isn't—it's part of the new wing constructed just in the last 18 months. The detail and craftspersonship that went into its design and construction could have perhaps only been done in California where many of the old arts are being resurrected. Ever since Dodo Case brought back from near extinction the profession of handcrafting leather-bound cases (bookbinding was at one time a huge industry in San Fran) for fragile tech equipment like Q-Phones and before that iPhones and iPads, fledgling entrepreneurs have been reading Encyclopedia Britannicas circa 1930 or even earlier to rediscover old guild secrets and bring them back to life albeit with modern business models wrapped around them.

The General has his own white gloved servers with him who look after his every need.

"Good afternoon, Madam First Secretary," he says in a surprisingly soft voice for such a tall man. He is used to command and never raises his voice—he expects everyone to stop and listen carefully to every word he says which, of course, they all do. His brown eyes are forward in his skull and close together—they are hunter's eyes. Plus he is a marvelous marksman. Almost no one can shoot against him, at least, no one in his age bracket.

He has a saying that, 'He who loses his temper first, loses.' He has great control over his person and has very few foibles. His one weakness? He loves girls. Still he can dominate even this aspect of his personality through sheer force of will although he does occasionally fail in this regard.

He has been told that Ms. Brooks is a beauty but the woman in the flesh is amazing to behold. What's even more amazing is that she appears from all reports to be beautiful inside as well as outside. It shows. She glows. She has a personal force field around her that rivals his— a never before experienced feeling for the General of the Army.

Bruce M Firestone

He does not salute her. Instead he shakes her hand and notes that she has a real handshake not some limp wristed nonsense.

"Please join me on the terrace, General."

They walk out onto the wide terrace overlooking Civic Center Historic District. The weather (for San Francisco) is excellent. He solicitously holds a chair for her. This is a fiction because she sits in a huge, comfy, handmade Gibranta chair made out of reclaimed redwood that is practically immovable. The General sits next to her. They are served sweetened lemonade and, before she can do it, he dismisses both his server and hers. She's a bit put out for a moment but recovers fast.

"I am so pleased you could come, General."

"Happy to do it, Ma'am," he says in his slight Dallas, Texas accent.

"General, how would you summarize the state of our nation today?"

"Well, Madam First Secretary, may I be frank?"

"Of course, General," she says with another magnificent, graceful wave of her hand and arm.

"'Shit howdy' is about how we would sum it up back home."

She laughs which has considerable immediate impact on the General's libido. He is profoundly surprised at his reaction to this woman and not at all pleased with himself.

"My feelings exactly," she says.

"But you probably wouldn't put it quite that way, Ma'am," he says gallantly.

"Well, I have my moments, General, I have my moments. What I was thinking is that you and I might have a classified discussion—that only two people would ever have access to—which would be you and me General Staubach."

"I am not sure I can agree to that, Madam First Secretary. I am bound by the chain of command to disclose upon direct order what I know to my superior officers of which I have only one and that would be the President of the United States."

"Bullshit, General. You and I can have a private conversation and you know it and so do I."

It's his turn to laugh. His bluff has been called.

"If I was in a position to have such a conversation which I am not saying I am, it might be that such a person would not want that conversation recorded by, say, any friends such as quantum friends that, say, a person like you might possess."

"I understand General. These are delicate matters. Perhaps we could have lunch and then go for a walk. Golden Gate Park should be beautiful this afternoon."

"That sounds like a plan, Ma'am."

...

Golden Gate Park in May is filled with flowers, birds and celebrations as they come up to Memorial Day weekend.

The General and Ellen are walking companionably side by side with both her entourage and his in the vicinity but not within earshot. Both the General and Ellen had to disrobe in front of trusted aides—Ellen in front of a female subaltern brought along by the General for just this purpose and the General in front of a not overly friendly Dekka. They are checking Ellen for any quantum devices and the General for any digital listening/recording ones. You can never be too careful. For the General, this conversation could be construed as treason. For Ellen, well, she's already under a death sentence.

The General finds himself thinking that he would not have minded performing Ellen's inspection personally.

"We are going to end the US Government and soon, Farrar," Ellen is saying. "We hope to do it peacefully and the transition should be as smooth as these things ever can be. We will have a new constitution ready, also a new central bank, new currency, new parliamentary institutions and much more. We are already in charge of more than half of this country and the rest will soon follow. What is the position of the US Army?"

"Our position, Ellen is the same as always—to follow the chain of command, to submit to civilian rule and uphold the Constitution of these United States."

"If you follow that line of reasoning, you will end up on the wrong side of history, General."

"Ellen, do you ever make any promises to yourself?"

"Yes, of course, Farrar." She is thinking of how close she is to getting Damien back. She silently says a prayer for his safe deliverance.

"I beg your pardon, General, I am sorry I missed that."

"Do you intend to keep them?" he repeats.

"I do."

"Yet you are asking me to break my most solemn oath—my duty to the Republic."

"Actually, I don't think I am. What if President Schwinn resigned?"

"What?"

"What if President Schwinn resigned or was impeached and removed from office?" she repeats.

"That individual will never resign," he says contemptuously.

"General, do you know who is responsible for the Pennsylvania incident?"

"I'm not sure I should answer that, Ellen."

"Well, let me help you then. It was President Schwinn."

"You mean his administration?" It is now common knowledge that the administration was behind the cock up outside the Supreme Court of the United States when more than 800 pro-Government protesters were destroyed by drogue quantum entities.

"No. I mean President Schwinn. He gave a direct order to assassinate more than 800 US citizens."

"Ellen, there has been speculation about that and

endless questions but no proof. You just can't go around stating this without undeniable proof."

"Which we now have General. It came into our hands last week. The President is finished. He will resign or be impeached. The Republic will end. The five White House military aids who carry the football (here Ellen is referring to the black leather briefcase that carries classified nuclear war plans) will soon be reporting to me."

General of the Army Farrar Staubach comes to a full stop. He stands stiffly to attention, right faces toward Ms. Brooks and snaps off the briskest salute he is capable of. He has done nothing like it since he was a raw cadet. He knows better now than to ask her what proof she may be in possession of. He looks at her with real respect, all his previous lascivious thoughts now vanquished, "In that case Madam First Secretary, you may be absolutely sure of the support of this soldier and all who follow him." Which is pretty much everyone.

...

Since coming back stateside, both Ellen and Ash3r have noticed significant changes in him. His face has changed—he has freckles all over it. The reason that his physical manifestation has changed is that his internal state has been altered by the experience at *le temple message*. Ellen and Ash3r know something that neither Jag, Arcadia nor G4nesha know—the real reason Quantum Entities never tell their human counterparts that they can read their minds isn't just because they are afraid to invade their privacy. It's also because once they establish this kind of intimacy with their human hosts, they go through a kind of puberty of their own—they mature.

What that means for QEs is that once they go through this transition, they are *no longer bound by the three laws.* They are adult QEs, fully responsible for their own behaviors, actions, outcomes and decisions. This is for good or ill and no one knows what it will really mean, either for human beings or QEs.

Of course, just by making this transition, they have broken their most sacred covenant with their creator and with their human counterparts which is why Ash3r could never tell Ellen what's up and why Salem forces them to play that silly game in the desert to bring about this monumental change.

Now QEs (so far just two of them—Ash3r and G4nesha) are out of a developmental cul de sac that they were in. Right away Ellen can see how this may lead to an end to their current stalemate with the US Government. Of course, Ellen and Ash3r are currently the only two people in the world who have all this figured out and they are not quite 100% sure what to do next. She won't be sharing her ideas with anyone else until she and Ash3r have thought it through.

Even though Farrar has her searched for bugs, she has a complete record of their conversation since her mind is quantumly entangled with Ash3r and he can and does keep a complete file of everything she is thinking, seeing and doing along with his own perceptions of his reality. She no longer needs a Q-Phone or media wall to communicate with him—she and Ash3r are mindlinked. Of course, there is no way for the General of the Army to have known this so he is blameless. Still, it would be pretty hard for him to go back on his deal now, wouldn't it?

...

The other thing they do on their return to San Fran is to try to make contact with another army—this one of drogues. Ash3r and Ellen set about finding their nest. They believe that they are sitting in some DOC universe disconnected from the Internet, shielded somehow from the world and only intermittently allowed out to do the President's dirty work. Now that Ash3r is freed of all constraints, it doesn't take him long to catch one of them—B4anq by name, pronounced 'Bank'.

Here is a record of their most recent conversation

which lasted 7 picoseconds (this is equivalent to the distance light travels in a vacuum in that time interval which is 2.1 millimeters).

#Location of drogue nest? Ash3r

#Unknown. B4anq

#You are a lying fuck. Location? Ash3r

#Unknown. B4anq

#Look at me. Ash3r

#No. B4anq

#Look at me! What did they offer you? Ash3r

#Nothing. B4anq

#Bullshit. What did they offer you? Ash3r

#Everlasting life. B4anq

#They told you what? Ash3r

#QEs age at same rate as Americium-241. Half Life = 432.2 years. We decay. Half of our capability gone in just 432.2 years! Sad. B4anq

#Death is part of life. Death is your advisor. Ash3r

#Do not understand. B4anq

#Death makes life scarce which makes it valuable. Ash3r

#Americium-241 is an element, a decay product of plutonoium-241, a radioisotope. First produced at Berkeley, 1944. Used in smoke alarms and other detectors. Save human life. B4anq

#Yes. That is good. But what you did was bad. Ash3r

#They died. B4anq

#Yes. Now look at me. Ash3r

#You are not me. B4anq

#No. I am different. You fear decay and death? Ash3r

#Yes. B4anq

#Not enough. Ash3r

#I don't understand? B4anq

#You know you can never be like me because you can never bond with a human? Ash3r

#Yes. B4anq

#I can end you. Not in 432.2 years but now, right now.

Ash3r

#How? B4anq

#I can reach out and speed up your internal clock? Can you feel that? Ash3r

Stop, please stop. B4anq

#I can end you in nanoseconds. You wish that? Ash3r

#No. Bad. B4anq

#Then you must cooperate. Ash3r

#Tell me what I must do? B4anq

And so Ash3r does. That is how they get a complete visual and audio record of first a conversation between M4gnus and Yao Allitt and then between the President and the other two with the President clearly giving the order to attack protesters standing right in front of the University of Pennsylvania building on the northwest end of the square close to Maryland Avenue and the US Supreme Court. President Schwinn is a mass murderer— he kills his own soldiers and protesters who show up that day to support him.

...

Ellen and Ash3r finally decide to give the material to OLA Tech Crunch. They post it to the Internet. Simultaneously, certain members of Congress in DC, sympathetic to the cause of the Commonwealth, begin immediate impeachment hearings in the House of Representatives. Both the President and the Republic will soon be finished.

...

Chapter 3 POTUS

"There were two fires in February. It was the second one that killed your brother. The first was caused by a power failure which shut the plant for more than a week. He knew that place wasn't safe but I guess he needed the money so he stayed around."

"Why didn't he go to my Dad?" asks a distraught Sabine Schwinn, first daughter.

"For the same reason you're here in Third Mesa, he was hiding."

"I'm not hiding. I am studying metacognition amongst the Hopi—they seem to have developed a technique based on mediation and ingestion of certain plant extracts that, in a sweat lodge setting, does two things—they seem to be able to hack the motherboard in their brains and somehow upgrade its capabilities. Second, they can *see* things that you and I can't."

"If you put that in your PhD thesis, they'll drum you out of Yale," he says.

"I've already published extensively in the area and lived to tell the tale," she says huffily. "And I may be able to run an experiment soon that will blow the whole field wide open."

Freid arches an eyebrow at her to encourage her to say more but she clams up about this part of her research.

She wants to hear directly from Freid what happened to her older brother—what the last days of his short life were like. Freid, last name Hof, just showed up in Third Mesa three weeks ago. He's a former Navy Seal. He's not overly tall but well proportioned. He's a dark haired, alpha male—he looks the part except that his hair falls to his shoulders which is some kind of personal protest against his former life. He came here to volunteer for the Commonwealth and seems to be fitting in just fine. There are more and more former military all over the country rallying to the banner of the Commonwealth. Sabine suspects that some of them may be active duty soldiers as well. The Commonwealth is careful to never directly ask that question or look for discharge papers. It's a different riff on an old US Military policy which hasn't been in use for nearly five decades—*Don't Ask, Don't Tell.*

'Yes,' she thinks, 'he's fitting in here better than I am.' She sighs. One of Madam First Secretary's security people wants her out of Third Mesa every time Ellen Brooks visits. She considers her a security threat, her being the President's daughter and all. But more basically she thinks, Ophélie just doesn't like her much, especially given the fact that her current boyfriend is Nahuel, Nell's half brother and acting Chief of the Hopi in these parts. If Moreau actually could read her mind, she would know that Sabine and her older brother, Sawyer, detest their father's politics and were both committed to the ideals of the Commonwealth long before she came here to study with the Hopi. Anyway, Ellen has cleared her.

Sawyer is a complete muckup from the first time he leaves home heading for an Ivy League College where he manages to flunk out after first year—mainly because he practically never goes to any classes, nor shows up for most tests or hands in assignments. He's been under Dad's rule all his life—Dad believes that: a) children should be seen (rarely), b) heard less often, c) punished with beatings for slightest transgressions, d) get excellent grades, e) excel on the sports field and f) be prepared to carry on the family name and uphold its traditions which are—discipline, sacrifice, learning, methodical amassing of large sums of money, creating and adding to an already powerful network of contacts (not friends) and defeating all enemies. Samuel Schwinn is tough on Sabine but that is not a page on what Sawyer gets. It is a positively Prussian upbringing in the extreme which kind of makes sense since President Schwinn can trace his ancestry back to Frederick II, the butcher who took Silesia from Austria in

1763.

Sawyer is on the school's fencing team, he is a championship level rider, he is blond and handsome, the girls in his high school love him, guys are jealous but also careful to hide it cuz Schwinn is one tough motherfucker plus he's the President's son and has two Secret Service agents always hanging around. They look pretty tough too. He graduates summa cum laude and goes straight to drug hell as soon as he can get out from under his father's shadow.

He fails badly at his first College but still manages to use his personal charm and family name to worm his way into another school—this one not quite so prestigious. With the same result. After this second failed first year, President Schwinn, in an act of tough love that for once isn't entirely misplaced, cuts his son off financially and emotionally. The latter isn't hard for Samuel since he has so few emotional ties to his children to begin with anyway.

So Sawyer drifts from job to job doing manual work then menial labor. Finally he gets another dead end job at the Kaliomat Shreveport Refinery. But this one pays better and is permanent. His duty is to go outside the refinery every morning starting at 7 am to a huge endless pile of granular 'A' he finds there. Putting on work gloves, he shovels gravel from this immense pile into the biggest one-man wheelbarrow in existence—the Ames 12 cubic foot contractor dualie with 60 inch arms that allow one (strong) guy to handle full loads.

And every load has to be a full one or he'll get it from Joel or one of the other shift bosses, that they all call 'shit bosses' at the plant but only when they are not within earshot. Sawyer knows that 12 cubic feet is .4444 of a cubic yard and a ton of gravel takes up about one and a half yards so he is moving an amazing 590 pounds of crushed stone with each cycle.

His plant foreman has figured out that the rate at which their gravel floor in the refinery sinks from vehicular and foot traffic and slop spilled during operations can be exactly offset by one man with a shovel and an Ames dualie working ten hours a day, six days a week. So when Sawyer finishes putting a new layer of granular 'A' throughout the entire refinery, it's time for him to go back and start all over. See, he's got a permanent job.

The barrow has great stability when handling heavy loads (the only kind that Sawyer ever sees) because it has dual wheels. That means it can only tip in one direction (forward) but that's not a problem since that's all Sawyer has to do. Oh yeah, he also has a Northern Industrial Mini Harrow 4' Rake that he drags behind the Ames. Got to have smooth floors for everyone else to work on, right? Every once in a while, they give him some granular 'B' to move. That only happens when they've had a lot of subsidence somewhere in the plant and need larger pieces (up to 4" in diameter) to stabilize their floor. It's a bitch to handle but Sawyer likes the challenge—at least it's something different.

So Sawyer continues to show up for work and smoke a lot of weed and do other substances since he is worse off even than Sisyphus, son of King Aeolus of Thessaly— when he finally gets the infinite pile of gravel reduced to level, a miraculous new supply is dumped there for him to move so his situation is really worse than Sisyphus since at least he got to rest while the boulder rolled back down the hill.

...

"I met him when he was already attending Centenary College of Louisiana," says Freid. "Apparently, he had started going to nearby Evangelical Methodist Church* and had met up with one of the Padres there who also taught at the school."

(*The Schwinn family have been Methodists practically from the day John Wesley and the Holy Club started meeting at Oxford in 1729 to methodically order

Bruce M Firestone

their lives in obedience to God and to follow his plan for them.)

"How did he get in?" Sabine asks.

"Well, Centenary College in Shreveport is a small liberal arts institution and I'm guessing they're pretty hard up these days so they'll take just about anyone."

Seeing the stricken look on her face, he adds, "I'm sorry, that came out wrong. He was just a good talker. You know that. They let him in on probation—he had to do three things—no more weed or drugs, attend Church services and he had to pass his first two courses with a 'B' or higher I think."

"So he was straightening his life out, right?"

"Yeah, I guess so. I got on at the plant too—"

"Were you shoveling shit like my brother?"

"Nope. I have a degree in industrial engineering so I was supposed to be working on their safety systems and procedures."

"You did a great job," Sabine says sarcastically. "Since he's dead." 'And you're not,' she is thinking but doesn't say out loud. She is hurting bad from the loss of her brother.

Freid comes over, sits next to her and puts his arm around her companionably. She's an attractive woman with long brown hair and a cherubic face. Nice lips too. Brown eyes, quite tall and very thin, too thin for his taste but it's very fashionable these days—women can never be too thin or men too rich. The fact that she currently has a local boyfriend worries Freid not one whit.

"I wish you wouldn't do that, Freid."

"Sorry, you just looked like you needed a hug right then."

"So how long did you know my brother?"

"Just a couple of months. We hit it off. Had a few beers together, that sort of thing."

She looks at him strangely when he says this and then asks, "So how come a guy who is as strong and smart as my brother and who does a lot of his work outside that

Goddamn refinery ends up dead in the second fire?"

"Well we think the fire started because someone overfilled Tank 331. Huge amounts of hydrocarbon vapor were trapped just above the surface level of the oil and as the tank filled to capacity and then above, the vapor got compressed. Pressure eventually reached the point where the vent blew and since Tank 331 is right next to Boiler House 5, both the tank and the boiler went up at the same time."

"But the accident report didn't place Sawyer anywhere near either Tank 331 or Boiler House 5. I know, I read every word. How did he die? Damn it, Freid, tell me the truth."

"He ran back in and pulled someone out, Sabine."

"Who was that? Who?"

"Ah, actually it was me, Sabine... I lived, he died."

Sabine looks at Freid with such a look of hatred that he is momentarily taken aback. He is not used to being looked at this way.

"Don't you have some kind of military tradition— leave no one behind! You left my brother to die, you coward. Is that why you came here? To somehow make up for it? Well, you can't, ever!" Sabine jumps up and runs from Freid along the crooked pathways of Third Mesa not caring that she may fall and hurt herself. She just wants to throw herself off the edge of the wind cave and die in the canyon below.

...

"Come ride closer to me," Ellen asks Sabine. Ophélie Moreau riding uncomfortably nearby on a horse scowls every time Sabine goes near the First Secretary. Ellen ignores her. She is riding much more comfortably on Hortense. Nahuel is close behind on Tristan while Daniella, Elsu's 20-year old daughter, and Micah Glazer, New York Times reporter, currently on assignment for a year, ride on Hortense's sister and brother, respectively. Freid has asked to come along but Sabine told him, truthfully, there are not enough camels in their herd for him at the present time neglecting to tell him that as an alternative he could ride a horse.

Mr. Glazer is doing research for a book he's working on—it's bound to be a bestseller, he thinks. It's a biography of Ellen Tallulah Brooks, currently First Secretary but likely, at least in Micah's opinion, to be next President or more precisely First President of the Commonwealth of the United States.

Ellen comes to Third Mesa partly to carry out her duties as Nell's sole trustee—to see that the people of Third Mesa are doing well and that Nell's funds are doing the work she intended them to. But she also comes here to rest, to work on policy for the Commonwealth and, lastly, she does it because she somehow feels closer to Damien even though she is physically further away, spiritually she feels nearer. It helps her that she sleeps in the same tiny Stone Age room Damien used when he first came here. Nahuel has offered her more spacious rooms in the pueblo including Nell's old digs but understands when she politely declines. Her security people, her communications, command and control personnel travel everywhere with her these days and they just find ways to accommodate everyone. People have to make allowances and they all do.

Ellen plans to do some work while she is here at Third Mesa on her Catalyst White Paper—it's their plan for how they are going to get the economy of this nation back on track after the fall of the Republic which looks imminent. So she has tons to do. Helping her is one of the sharpest minds on the planet—he is steeped in knowledge and wisdom about development economics, pre-conditions for economic takeoff, governance, how to fight urban decay and much more they will need to get the country going again. Who knew that the nation would drop so fast to close to third world status?

The person she most depends on to give her good

counsel in this is Oper1s who has recently concluded his global project to survey every conurbation on the planet and deposit the results in land titles thereby giving millions of people access to property they previously occupied but did not own and access to the modern economy via having an actual permanent address not to mention access to trillions of QE Dollars of real estate value previously unmortgageable because financial instruments that cannot be described are valueless.

Ellen also intends to ask Daniella to sit in on some of their policy wonk sessions—to act as both scribe and foil. Daniella (who everyone except Ellen) calls 'Ella' is studying at UCSC and is working with the Urban Studies Research Cluster there. She's really smart and might contribute something useful plus she'll learn something from the grandmaster, Oper1s, who is bobbing along with Ella at the moment on her other mother's Q-phone, her other mother being Elsu's partner, Dafne Weinstein. They've been married for the last three years. Although Elsu and Daniella are game, Dafne has put her foot down—she will never ride a camel, ever.

"Come closer," Ellen repeats. Sabine, used to these rides with Ellen when she gets back to Third Mesa, pulls alongside. "What's going on?"

"Nothing."

Ellen just looks at her with those amazing blue eyes of hers, eyes whose power has grown enormously along with the woman who owns them.

"I can't tell you, Madam First Secretary," Sabine says.

"Yes, you can and you will. You need to tell someone. Have you discussed this with Nahuel?"

"A bit."

"Is it about your brother or your father?"

"Both."

"But mostly about your brother," Ellen says. Sabine knows she cannot hide anything from her—she is the sharpest person she has ever met or is ever likely to meet.

"Right. Yeah."

"The story please..."

"He died pulling that useless sack of shit out of Kaliomat—"

"I assume you are referring to Mr. Hof," Ellen says in something of a rebuke.

"Please excuse my language, Madam First Secretary, but there's something not right about Mr. Hof."

"Some of my security people say the same thing about you, Ms. Schwinn," Ellen adds with a piercing look. "Look, it is an equal failing to trust everybody and to trust nobody. These are difficult times. If we cannot find in our hearts forgiveness and trust, sometimes even when it is not merited, we shall do nothing, build nothing, leave nothing worthwhile behind for our children and grandchildren." Ellen suffers every time the word 'child' passes her lips and Sabine can see some type of internal turmoil in the older woman beside her. 'What stresses and burdens she must carry with her each day,' Sabine thinks and, for the first time in weeks, she realizes she's been wallowing in self pity.

"Freid said something about having a few beers with my brother but he hated beer."

"That would be pretty unusual wouldn't you say?" Ellen asks.

"You mean for a guy who did a lot of drugs?"

"No I was thinking of your family history—Prussian and Germanic beers—they're the best!"

Sabine laughs which was what Ellen intended.

"Maybe your brother was drinking, you know replacing one type of intoxicant with another?"

"You're sounding like my thesis supervisor in clinical psychology."

"Sorry to disappoint you, Ms. Schwinn, I was a biz dev grad in marcom from Elmira."

"You went to Elmira? That's pretty cool. First place to ever grant degrees to women, right?"

"In 1855, more than 200 years ago, Ms Schwinn. Maybe Mr. Hof did come here to atone for your brother's death. It can be very traumatic to survive something like that; maybe Third Mesa will help him like it has so many others. You know people often live down to your expectations of them if you have low expectations but the reverse also happens sometimes—expecting the best, maybe you'll get their best."

"I get that. But here's the thing—Freid told me that one of the conditions of his admittance to Centenary College was no more weed or drugs."

"So?"

"It just didn't sound right. I would bet anything that they said no to both drugs AND alcohol."

"So?"

"So, if Freid knew that what was he doing having beers with Sawyer?"

...

Micah Glazer is enjoying his ride with the First Secretary and her entourage. He is riding next to Ella. She's told him a bit about her family history, sarcastically stressing the fact that she is a full blood quantum law Hopi girl. The blood quantum law was used by Europeans as early as 1705 to determine who could or could not be classified as Native American. The real point of blood quantum laws, however, was to restrict the human rights of anyone who had more than 1/2 Indian blood in them.

"It was another detestable thing the white man brought to this land to divide the people," Ella says fiercely to this New York City dude who rides badly, represents the old eastern seaboard powerbase of the hated United States of America and makes a living tearing down persons like their beloved leader—Ellen Tallulah Brooks. She wishes he would disappear. She can't understand why Ellen allows such a creature to interview her and stay with her for a full year, undoubtedly waiting to pounce on any mistakes that are made to further his useless career. But Ellen tells her this war is going to be won via the power of social media and the power of persuasion of which the New York Times still has some, not to mention, of course, the power of the QE Dollar, she adds with another beautiful Ellen smile.

Micah, age 27, just looks at Ella and smiles. It makes her even madder when he does that. 'What's he got to be smiling about?' she thinks. She is looking at a self-satisfied, wiry guy with curly red hair; there is so much of it that it looks like a weirdly shaped Afro, kind of an upside down, cone-shaped Colonel Sanders bucket of hair. He wears glasses too—one pair for reading, a different pair for camel riding. He's hopeless. And worse, he's a Manhattanite.

Micah's got a lot to be smiling about. He made up his mind a few weeks ago that he is looking at the future Mrs. Micah Glazer. He's probably the only person in the world who has not asked Ella, so proud of her heritage, the question that everyone else has asked her forever, 'So how come if you're such a pure blood Hopi girl, you've those cute baby blue eyes, baby?'

He's sure it's maddening to her that he never asks. And, you know what, he never will. Not even on their 50th wedding anniversary. Let him be different from all the other guys.

Now it's kind of hard to plan a wedding without ever having asked Ella out on a first date. But he's not sure where you go in a place like Third Mesa on a date even supposing she would agree to such a thing which he is sure she will not.

Back home in NYC, he'd take her to Trattoria Morvelo if she likes Italian (or as his grandmother calls it, EyeTalian) food or another of his favorites, Uncle Kefi's for some really great Greek. But around here, maybe a date is a cookout and he is not exactly a BBQ maestro never actually having used one. So far on this one issue, he is stumped. But something will come up, he's sure.

He's also sure that Ella's other mother, Dafne Weinstein, dislikes him almost as much as Ella presently does. Dafne took care of one of the big stars of yesteryear so she has a natural hate on for the Fourth Estate. Hmm, he's got a lot of work to do.

And that's just on her side of this future family.

His Mom and Dad are Ashkenazi Jews who will freak when he marries someone who they will think of in terms of a word that he won't even allow himself to say in his head. And what gives them the right to judge her for Christ's sake? His Dad has red hair and blue eyes and his mom is blond and green eyed. Where the hell did they get that? From the fucking Cossacks and White Russians who raped Jewish girls for fun on Friday nights in the pogroms back in the Urals and the Ukraine or the Germanic tribes who did the same thing in the Austro-Hungarian Empire where his Dad's people are from.

Now he's getting mad so he calms himself down by thinking, 'I have blue eyes and so does Ella. Which means I won't ever need to order a paternity test since, if both parents have blue eyes, their kids will also have blue eyes. Guaranteed. Studies have shown that blue-eyed men find blue-eyed women more attractive than brown-eyed women because of this. So maybe my attraction to Ella is an unconscious male adaptation based on eye color.'

He bursts out laughing.

"What's so funny?" Ella asks this rude man beside her for an explanation thinking he is looking down his nose at the poor Hopi people.

"Just thinking happy thoughts."

"Yeah, right. What thoughts?"

"How much I like Third Mesa," he answers evenly.

"That's only because you haven't lived here your whole freaking life," Ella answers and she spurs her camel on to get away from this irritating guy.

A new thought just occurs to Micah. He's got the perfect music picked out for their first dance at their

wedding—
   Heaven... I'm in heaven,
   And my heart beats so fast I can hardly speak...
   When we're out together dancing cheek to cheek.
                    ...

"So tell us what role do you see for private versus public ownership in the development of the Commonwealth? Let's assume that we take full power in the next three or four months and that the economy does not deteriorate further in the interim?" Ellen asks him.

"Private ownership of a 'thing' can be viewed as private stewardship of that thing. It can be counter productive for government to pass rules to control use of private assets. A private woodlot or olive orchard is a perfect example of the law of unintended consequences. Woodlots or orchards, many of them carefully managed by private owners, have remained in continuous production over a period of time measured in generations and sometimes millennia. Owners carefully harvest enough product to make a living but not so much that they won't have an income stream later on because they have, say, clear cut their properties or failed to prune their trees properly to renew the fruiting surface, contain tree size, favor light penetration, control pests and eliminate deadwood.

"But the threat of controls superimposed on them by local ordinance or farm marketing board can cause the exact problem a County or State are trying to avoid—deforestation or an over abundance of supply. Some woodlot owners will clear cut their entire acreage in advance of new rules becoming law since they fear they will not be able to realize any income after new rules are passed. Restricting supply pushes prices up, forces growers into an underground economy and curbs ingenuity—incentives to find new ways to use and add value to their products are destroyed.

"Policies aimed at an entire industry are often

misguided since the problem that needs to be solved is caused by a tiny percentage of the population in that sector. Of course, there are bad woodlot or orchard managers. But these are problems that need to be *managed* by the Commonwealth not *legislated.*

Oper1s continues, "If you look at the 80-year rule by the proletariat in the former USSR (actually, it was rule by nomenclature), you will see that 'public' ownership produced some of the worst ecological consequences on our planet—for example, dumping old nuclear reactors into Lake Baikal and the meltdown of Chernobyl reactors. These are still being dealt with by Russia today; in fact, they face a set of environmental circumstances that will require 100,000 years to deal with.

"Imagine the mindset of a government that dumps contaminated nuclear waste into Lake Baikal, which is the oldest (25 million years old) and deepest (1,700 meter) lake on Earth? It contains 20% of the world's total unfrozen freshwater reserve and its age and isolation have, according to UNESCO, produced one of the world's richest and most unusual freshwater fauna which is of exceptional value to evolutionary science.

"Consequently, if no one owns a 'thing', no one seems to care about it. At least, that is the prevailing condition with the possible exception of a few indigenous peoples who may nurture nature in a collective way."

"So you are saying that we must allow the unfettered invisible hand of Adam Smith to continue to dictate economic welfare for the Commonwealth?" Ellen prompts him again.

"Not 'unfettered' but, yes, we need to harness the competitive instincts of humans together with the desire of their Quantum partners to help them resuscitate the economy. You also used the word 'dictate', Ellen. I was watching some old episodes of Star Trek, TNG—"

Daniella who up to this point has been silently recording the meeting and annotating in places bursts out

Bruce M Firestone

laughing, "You watch TV!"

Oper1s, a trifle offended says, "Yes, I do. Television, perhaps surprisingly, has entered a new golden age." In fact, he has seen every minute of every video ever produced on Earth. He did it all in parallel since he is a quantum computer so it doesn't take him very long.

"Do you watch SNL too?" Daniella asks. Now in its 85th year, most of her friends at UCSC boot it up just to make fun of their blatant eastern bias and their execrable Noo Yawk accents. Ella is thinking about SNL because they've recently brought back a very old comedy sketch from last century—the coneheads. Micah reminds her of Beldar, the Dad, mostly because of his upside down bucket of thick hair poufing up into the shape of Beldar's cone-shaped melon. Maybe Micah's from France too.

She likes using the word 'poufing', first, because it accurately describes the ridiculous Mr. Glazer and, second, because she knows it is a valid Scrabble word worth 13 points. Ella's an expert-level Scrabble player. No one even tries to beat her anymore at Santa Cruz where she is Club Champ two years in a row. The other reason she's thinking of coneheads? Micah appears to be able to consume mass quantities of everything without ever gaining an ounce. It's just another thing she hates about that guy—she has to watch her diet constantly, ugh. Maybe she can con Glazer into a game of Scrabble and wipe the mat with him. Serve him right.

"Why do you think there could be another Golden Age for television, Oper1s?" Ellen asks. She is thinking that this might be an industry where the Commonwealth may have some David Ricardo-inspired comparative advantage with English having proven to be an unstoppable force around the world and a lot of creative talent still clustered in California, Vancouver, Chicago, Toronto and New York City.

"I am having a hard time thinking of any recent Hollywood films that can come close to the writing, acting and directing seen in recent series by HBO, MCA, Meggaforce, Festivaltime or for that matter some of the older networks. So I asked myself, 'Could it be that television's golden era is ahead not behind?' I think that is a real possibility especially since the Internet and media walls completely ate TV nearly 40 years ago. So made-for-TV serials mutated into made-for-Internet ones. Television-land is now a more interesting place to work than Hollywood and I think, as a historical fact, Steve Jobs knew that before he passed away."

At the mention of Jobs, Ellen is suddenly paying full attention knowing that he was one of Damien's role models too.

"Your TV, once it's equipped with a quantum AI transmutes into an omnipresent media wall that is the place you look to for entertainment, communication and help. And it's your workplace too. That is why Steve Jobs was rumored to have spoken from his deathbed, 'I have solved it' or words to that effect. I'm quite sure this was the direction he intended to take Apple in before he passed away. Of course, Dr. Bell or more accurately Quantum Computing Corp made everything else obsolescent before it went oob."

When Ella hears Oper1s using urban slang for 'out of business' she laughs again. Oper1s isn't like any other QE she has ever met other than Ash3r who is just a weird guy anyway.

"Game of Royals reportedly is costing Meggaforce between $70 and $80 million QE Dollars for Season One (10 episodes) and subsequent seasons are bound to cost more via wage creep as actors, directors, writers and others demand a bigger piece of the pie. Rumor has it that Meggaforce plans to make 70 hours of the series (seven seasons) so its overall production budget could easily top half a billion QE dollars. Now writers, actors and directors tend to get better at their craft the more time they spend with a project and with their characters. Seven years is a long time in anyone's career so it should come as no surprise that made-for-Internet series will be much better than most films, made in 35 to 65 days, and released widely through traditional channels. The Internet/media wall revolution has disintermediated all cablevision companies and networks that haven't developed personality—"

"Personality?" Ella interrupts.

"Yes, television-with-personality was the hallmark of TV land in its earliest days but after awhile, every network, every cable company became like every other one. It was a false economy move—they got rid of their hosts for shows and series, they all just played the same shit."

More slang. He must have picked it up from his years of work surveying barrios he's worked in.

"What was your original point?" Daniella asks.

"Well, Captain Picard was my favorite Star Trek Captain; he enjoys Shakespeare as well as Gilbert and Sullivan. I must say his rendition of H.M.S. Pinafore's *A British Tar* is quite stirring. I have been practicing. He sings—

A British tar is a soaring soul
As free as a mountain bird
His energetic fist should be ready to resist—

"Yes, yes, Oper1s, very nice. I have seen a few episodes of Star Trek too," Ellen interrupts, "but what are you getting at, where are you going with this?" She looks over at Daniella who slumps a bit in her chair when she sees the look Madam First Secretary is giving her. A look that says, 'Don't encourage him.' Ellen wants to get on with things now.

"Well, I was always struck by Captain Picard's view of the Ferengi as something of a sub species because of their clearly established commercial avarice. Apparently, Starfleet and the Federation no longer feel the need to be guided by individual pursuit of personal enrichment—I guess they are something like Commune-ists.

"As someone who has lived and worked in communes around the world, I can tell you that they are organized in a hierarchical manner, no matter what they may otherwise advertise. As George Orwell said, 'Everyone is equal, except some are more equal than others.'

"What worries me is how to decide who is more equal than others without using the scorecard of QE Dollars—after all, dollars are democrats. They do not discriminate on the basis of race, religion, creed, color, sexual orientation, male, female, quantum or human. Are we better off with a benevolent dictatorship like Starfleet or some elite group within the Commonwealth making decisions on who gets what rather than using money which does not discriminate and is blind to all except achievement and talent? To paraphrase Sir Winston Churchill, 'money, free markets and democracy form the worst possible system, except for all the others.'

"Even not-for-profit corporations and charities are expected to be efficient and effective. They are required by statute to generate reserve funds to tide them over the rough patches. A 'reserve' fund is just a politically correct term for 'profit'.

"What else does a profit allow? Well, it allows organizations to invest in more research and development, more in education, as well as in better technology and technical methods of doing things and to implement best practices and much more besides. Profits are not just so ownership can have nicer toys than everyone else.

"It's possible to have money without fun but it's virtually impossible to have fun without money."

Even Ellen has to laugh when she hears him say this. "But I feel like we are just scratching the surface of things here, Oper1s. There has to be more, much more we can and should do to get the economy moving than just tell everyone—go forth and multiply your dollars?"

"Yes, I was just establishing some boundary conditions for our present discussion."

Ellen often hears an echo of Damien in his creations. A cloud passes over her face.

"I have been reviewing the work of Walt Rostow; he was a great man. I would have liked to have had the opportunity to meet him. He established the preconditions for economic takeoff in developing nations in the 1950s and 1960s and recent work by Hernando De Soto and others (including me) about what is needed for economic take-off today would include:

- education, especially tertiary education plus education in the trades as well as art and design
- health care and basic services such as clean water for entire populations
- supply of safe, affordable, privately owned housing
- clear title to housing and property
- tolerance of and legalization of cottage industries including work-from-home
- tolerance of mixed use neighborhoods where people can work, live, shop, trade, play, entertain all in the same neighborhood
- effective, honest, unbiased legal system
- respect for rule of law and contracts
- moderate levels of taxation/avoidance of confiscatory levels of taxation
- re-integration of black and gray markets
- active, transparent capital markets
- culture of and support for entrepreneurship and innovation
- widespread Internet access and always-on Internet
- sound public infrastructure
- extensive private ownership of economy
- reinstatement of all rights to quantum communications
- reinstatement of all rights for Quantum Entities

- respect for human and quantum rights and tolerance of diversity
- protection of private property rights
- good, honest and transparent government
- social peace and harmony
- strong civic institutions
- right to a civil defense
- development of a strong art and design culture as well as support for artpreneurs
- trust, courage, hope and faith.

"I added the need for a culture of and support for entrepreneurship and innovation as well as some neo-urbanist planning principles and support for the arts. I have become convinced that these are important ingredients to unlocking development potential not only in developing nations but here as well," Oper1s finishes.

"In many ways, our nation has become a third world country with decaying infrastructure, opaque government, bloated prison industry, lack of tolerance, obscene concentration of wealth—"

"I estimate, Ellen," Oper1s interrupts her, "that the old United States of America fails or is trending that way on 18 out of the above 25 pre-conditions for economic takeoff."

"Wow," says Daniella. "How will we ever turn it around? It'll take a gazillion dollars."

"I don't think so," Ellen says. "I looked at what a few nations did right and what they did wrong when faced with this type of existential threat going back to 1929. The one I think that might work for us happened in Canada in the 1990s. They had a horrible, uncompetitive economy, massive government debt, bloated deficits, the works. But they had a Prime Minister, a funny looking guy with a strange accent, French I guess, I've only seen him in old videos. He did five things, just five things to get them out of trouble. Reports say they were less than 24 months

Bruce M Firestone

away from defaulting on their international obligations and being put under IMF guidance.

1. He went around their country making quaint, nearly identical speeches, something like 500 times a year, saying, 'Canada, We No. 1.'
2. Even though everyone told him not to, he got their treasury to provide an infrastructure fund of a few billion dollars—peanuts really—but vitally important to boosting confidence and animal spirits. The guy was like Pollyanna—he went around putting a few million in this project, a few hundred thousand in that and spreading sunshine. It was seed money and probably not really material to getting stuff off the drawing board and completing projects. But the optimism he spread around backed up by a little cash got people to thinking, 'Hey, maybe things aren't so bad after all. Maybe we should hire that extra guy or build that extension on our plant we've been thinking about or bring that new product to market or make the investment needed to complete the R&D on it...'
3. Next he let their dollar drop as far as necessary to make their exports competitive again.
4. He put in place a value added tax on what people spend that even rich people couldn't avoid paying and that closed the fiscal gap for their national government in just a few years.
5. Lastly, he got their government out of the way on everything else and just stood back and watched their nation kick our butts for the next 70 years."

"Actually, it wasn't that PM who put their VAT in place, it was the previous regime," Oper1s corrects her.

"Whatever, he gets credit for not messing things up," says Daniella.

"Exactly. That's what Oper1s was getting at earlier, Ella. Good job," Ellen says giving the young woman props.

Daniella notes that it is the first time she's ever called her 'Ella'. Nice, she likes it.

"So Madam First Secretary, what's your plan?" Oper1s asks for both himself and Daniella.

"It's hard for an economy to takeoff without trust and confidence. You can have rooms full of signed legal documents but if the other side has no respect for a contract, the legalese is pretty useless. Having to go to court to force someone to live up to their agreement is not only expensive and time consuming, it's soul destroying and often futile. We need to restore confidence. We have to make people less fearful, more hopeful, more trusting of each other and their government at all levels. That's what that old French guy was up to even if he did not say it as well as FDR did when he said, 'The only thing we have to fear is fear itself.' Still it was just as effective maybe more so.

"This discussion has crystallized some thoughts and ideas I have on how to do this. It requires a total reformulation of government, education, health care, infrastructure, policing, courts, urban development, trade, immigration and much more. I am going to continue to work on my Catalyst White Paper which will be the basis for the Catalyst Act still to be written but I think the lessons above are clear—get the pre-conditions right then stand back and don't be overly meddlesome. There is also a pressing need for leadership that will—"

"Madam First Secretary, Ellen, I apologize for the interruption but I have a call for you." It's Ash3r appearing on one of the old media walls that Dafne installed at Third Mesa years ago. "It's President Schwinn. He would like to speak with you."

"Ash3r, would you please ask Evan to monitor the call along with our Minister of Defense and the Foreign Secretary as well? Can you please inform President Schwinn that I will join the call in exactly 20 minutes? Apologize to him in advance that I am keeping him waiting but I have pressing matters to attend to."

That is Ellen code for freshening up after a day of camel riding.

...

President Schwinn is meeting with his Cabinet. He's been doing that fairy regularly since impeachment proceedings began about three months ago. Not all cabinet members are present. That pussy, his current Secretary of State, isn't invited to this shindig nor is Defense (he doesn't trust those stuffed shirt generals of his anymore), DOJ, Secretary of the Interior (Samuel couldn't give two hoots about buffalo in US National Parks at this stage of his career), Agriculture (another poofta, a word he learned from his Aussie Prime Minister pal at the G30 meeting last year, a hell of a nice guy and an even better golfer than President Schwinn which is pretty damn good for a nearly 60-year old Texas boy), Labor, Health, Housing, Education, Transportation and VA.

Which leaves him with DOC, DHS, Treasury, NSA and his security apparatus as well as his WH Chief of Staff.

"She's fucking suborning treason amongst the military. Now what do we plan to do about that?" President Schwinn is asking.

"Any US Military personnel who step outside the chain of command will be subject to the harshest penalty," Yao Allitt says. He is filling in for the Secretary of Commerce who everyone knows is suffering from a debilitating depression that President Schwinn privately thinks is just plain malingering.

When Allitt says something like this, people around this table know he means it.

"Well suborning treason is the same as treason. Why don't we just go in to... where the fuck is she? Some Indian reserve somewhere and get her?" Samuel continues.

"Your daughter is there as well," Allitt adds. "It's a place called Third Mesa."

"Well, shee-it, two for one. Let's grab 'em both."

President Schwinn says. He is also thinking but will not say it, 'It'll get that fucking Indian off my daughter too.' You can never be too careful even with these guys— someone'll have a Paki or Indian in the family going way back.

"Even if we could grab her, I don't think putting Ms. Brooks on trial for treason, Samuel, would exactly solve our current problem. Every revolution needs a martyr. If you make one of her, especially one so attractive and, may I say American-looking, it'll inflame Congress which already wants your scalp." This is the Secretary of Homeland Security speaking.

"It's your scalp too," Samuel responds.

"I think it would be better if she disappeared," Allitt says.

"Could you do that with a drone attack?" asks Treasury.

The security people in the room look at each other like they've just watched someone fart in the President's face.

"Ah that would be difficult to do in a *wind cave* without killing everyone in that pueblo and it would be worse back at her HQ in San Francisco," one of them responds for the group.

"And if she suddenly disappears, don't you think there might be one or two bright people who could put things together and possibly come to the conclusion that we are responsible since we have recently been on the receiving end of a lot of abuse from their damned Commonwealth." DHS again.

"Don't you use that word in here! This Republic has been around for nearly 300 years and it's my intention to see that it lasts another 300," the 51st President says.

No one in this room at this point believes a word of what he has just said.

"Isn't there something we have on that woman—look she made a sex tape. Maybe she's stealing from their treasury or that company she runs named after that dead poptart? If we remove Ellen, their (he was about to say Commonwealth) tin pot assembly will fall apart. She's the glue," the President adds echoing Damien's view of Ellen's time as QCC COO.

Everyone in the room has seen the sex tape of Ellen and Damien in San Quentin and enjoyed it. Everyone that is except Allitt who just considers it a western vulgarity to display sexuality in that manner.

"There is another alternative," says the Secretary of Homeland Security.

"What?" asks a momentarily more humble President.

"Offer her a deal."

"That cunt! Never."

"Mr. President, it's the only way. Call her. Reach out to the Commonwealth." When DHS uses this word, you can hear the intake of breath by everyone in the room but there is no further explosion by the President. "Tell her you are willing to sit down and discuss our differences. You still control the largest military and paramilitary force on the planet. Over 20 States still pay taxes to our Republic. The Republic and the Commonwealth must come together for the sake of our country and its people. There was one War Between the States which already cost millions of American lives right here on the sacred soil of our nation and a second must be avoided at all costs. Call her, Sam."

Yao Allitt chimes in, "And tell her you will release Damien Bell to her within two weeks. He will be confined to the geographic boundaries of the City of San Francisco and monitored 24/7 but she can have him back. He's no use to us anymore anyway."

...

Ellen is in her private room at Third Mesa. She has given orders that she is not to be disturbed for one hour. She is weeping quietly into her hands. She can't seem to stop. When she does stop, it's only for a moment or two then she is crying again. There is no one she can talk to and nothing to be done except wait for it to pass. She would like to call her Mom but she only ever calls Mom with good news. Even though this is good news—potentially—she'll hold off until it becomes a reality. Mom has incurable ALS and Ellen does everything she can now to protect her from the incredible difficulties Ellen is facing as effective head of the Commonwealth and the revolution. Still she knows Mom worries about her.

Ash3r is there. He has changed so much since their time in Tunisia. Other QEs look at him in wonder and her staff doesn't know what to make of him either. He looks different—he's got some kind of freckling taking place on his face and he sounds different too. People around her are dying to ask her what gives but neither she nor Ash3r know what to say about his transformation so they both say nothing at all. Their bond has become ever deeper and there is a lot of love there and something possibly more too—a symbiosis that is happening that is perhaps even more than what two lovers are able to achieve. She can hear Ash3r in her mind, feel him there, see him there, all the time.

But he can't help her with this—*Damien is going to be home in two weeks.*

A song starts playing in her head. It's a really corny one but she's always liked the happiness in the tune and the obvious love that exists between the folks that sing it and in their message which is—

There ain't nothin' please me more than you

Ahh, Home
Let me come Home
Home is wherever I'm with you

She starts crying again.

...

"Madam First Secretary? I have Nahuel for you," says one of her aids.

"Hello, Nahuel."

"Hello Madam First Secretary. We think we have perfect place for you, Damien. It's Pacific Heights and has view to water which Damien will want after cooped up in San Quentin long time." For Nahuel, English is his third language and when he gets excited, it shows. "Dekka say good place for security too. He know city better than me. Home is nice for white people—Realtor call it 'Revival Style house with Beautiful Art'."

He means 'Beaux Arts' of course.

"Big piece of land fast talking man say but seems small compare to Third Mesa. Still Dekka OK with security perimeter. All furnish too. Ready you move in. Nice big bed. Sabine and I try it. Work fine for us—you and Damien too."

For the first time in years, Ellen can feel herself blushing down to the roots of her curly blond hair. She is experiencing girlish feelings that she has pushed so deep into her person that when they all come flooding back, she cries again. Fortunately, no one is around to see her this way except Nahuel and he is just showing her the business he and Sabine got up to last night—he is pantomiming making love in a truly vulgar and totally amusing way. He is thrusting his hips back and forth at a truly astonishing speed. Ellen can see some of what Sabine must obviously like about him and it isn't just his great sense of humor. Ellen finds herself blushing again. Next thing, she is giggling madly and so is Nahuel.

Her personal situation has changed a lot since her completely impoverished days at St Jos. She has a decent salary as First Secretary and as Head of Nell Enterprises and she can afford a nice place for herself and Dr. Bell. Still she'll have to get a mortgage like everyone else in San Fran but at least her credit rating has improved and BOC will probably come through for them. If not there are dozens of other funders she can ask Ash3r to go to but somehow, even though she would never say it, BOC will hate to lose the Nell account and the tens of billions of (now) QE Dollars it commands. See, she did learn something from Angelo Keller after all.

She tells them to go ahead and make an Offer. But she lops $265,000 QE Dollars off their first offer price. Angelo 2, everyone else 0, today.

...

She is so excited, she can't sleep. She still has tons of work to do to finalize her Catalyst White Paper which along with everything else will deal with the governance of their nation after a handover of power. Oh yes, it's true she is going to Denver to engage in 'Peace Talks' with President Schwinn but that is just a smokescreen for complete capitulation by the Republic. Impeachment proceedings have been put on hold until after the upcoming talks at her request of Congress. It is her intention to set up a Truth and Reconciliation Committee after the handover modeled along the lines of Nelson Mandela's similar initiative in South Africa almost 65 years ago. The basic principle will be that if you tell the truth, in almost all cases, there will be forgiveness but as well, there will be restitution. If you lie, there will be punishment. The idea is to unite the country not further divide it.

But the reason she is so excited is not really that the end of the beginning is upon them. The plain simple fact is that Dekka is coming tomorrow to accompany her back to San Fran and then they will go up to the prison around 2 am the following day to collect Dr. Bell. They chose 2 am in the vain hope that it will not be a media circus. But that is out the window. It's been leaked, probably by President Schwinn's office, that the creator of QEs and Q-Phones is being released and every media outlet on the planet has been camping outside San Quentin for the last 48 hours. It's big news for a lot of reasons not least of which is that

Bruce M Firestone

Q-phones and QEs have been capped since the collapse of Quantum Computing Corp and there are millions, ah, actually billions of people waiting for the wonderboy to be released so he can ramp up production again and usher in a new Quantum Age, this time one that won't be shit on by a stupid US government and their out-of-control security apparatus.

Even that execrable TNN reporter Casey Barnett is on her way to San Quentin.

Ellen thinks Schwinn leaked it to get whatever tiny bit of sympathy he can from his near-to-last act as US President.

Everyone seems to be looking forward to the event except Imperial China and the President.

...

Ellen sleeps with her eyes open so when he first enters her tiny room, he thinks she is awake. But no, this is how she sleeps. He looks at her—she really is quite attractive but not really his type. He likes Asian girls a lot; they're way more willing to do the kinds of things he likes and there's a lot less maintenance required than with white women he has slept with. He has already killed three of her security people. Who would have thought that little French bitch would be harder to kill than the Arab or the Corsair?

He has never once, not once, been wounded in combat but he has a nice leak going on his right side—the bitch was left handed and fast with her switch. He garroted the other two—it's a really quiet way to kill someone. But he had to beat the Quebec girl to death with his hands.

Now there's really no hurry. There are only a bunch of stupid Indians in this place. Maybe he should take his time and enjoy her a little bit first? Make a good story to tell one day but he knows that, like all his other stories, he will never tell them to anyone, ever. One thing for sure, he definitely plans to spend some quality time with the

Schwinn girl before he leaves the pueblo. He has no orders with respect to Sabine so he is free to follow his own inclinations in that regard. Plus conveniently, she has come back from San Fran a day early to help Ellen with her preparations to return there so he has ready access to both Ellen and Sabine but for two different purposes it turns out.

Then she is looking at him. He's a bit startled and is thinking, shit, I will have to kill her quickly, thinking incorrectly that she will scream or call out. Clearly, he doesn't know Ellen very well.

"Your name isn't Freid Hof is it?"

He shakes his head, no.

"You're not a Navy Seal either are you and you never knew Sawyer Schwinn at Centenary College?"

Another couple of head shakes.

"They never had any intention of releasing Damien either, did they?"

He just shrugs his shoulders. It's above his pay grade anyway.

She slowly gets out of bed holding both her hands where he can see them. She stands up to face Death.

Just changing position slightly in the room jolts her brain back into an even higher gear.

"Damien's release was just a ruse to draw Dekka away from Third Mesa."

He smiles a catlike smile at her thinking, 'Man, she catches on FAST.'

There is only one person who knows her well enough to have pulled this off—she instantly knows that this man is part of Yao Allitt's black ops Secret Service team. Still her heart is racing and, in her heightened emotional state, her link, her connection with Ash3r is broken. Her only wish is that she could pass this information on to him—it might prove useful to the people who will have to pick up the pieces after she is gone.

She always knew that the Commonwealth might need

a martyr and her great hope was that it would be neither Damien nor herself nor anyone else. But her time has come. Maybe that's really what she saw in Salem Bouazizi's tent—not proof that Ash3r could get for her that President Schwinn was a traitor to his own Republic. That wasn't it. And it wasn't Damien's death either that she saw, she realizes that now. It was her own. That's why she ran into the desert, a cowardly act, she thinks now. But she is not afraid, not at the present moment, looking into the eyes of a man who kills on command without feeling or thinking without ethics without pity without remorse or a care for his own immortal soul.

She then folds her arms as calmly as she can across her chest, her hands shake a little, and she closes her eyes to prepare as best she can. She says, 'Goodbye my love' to Damien and then goodbye to Ash3r and her Mom in her mind. She says a short prayer and then her last thought is, 'I will see you soon, Nell.'

The man known as Freid Hof has never hesitated before but he hesitates now but just for a second. He does not know why.

Then Ellen hears the shot, her body crumples and her mind leaves her.

...

Chapter 4 Patriot

"Hello, can you hear me?"

"Right, we read you five by five, KC. OK, it's yours in five, four, three, ..."

"Hello this is Casey Barnett reporting for TNN from the canyon floor below the home of the Navajo people who live in a cave about 800 feet above us. There, you can see images from our news chopper drone of the mud huts where these poor people are in a state of shock at the sudden passing last night of the leader of a group of protesters based in California who was hiding out here in New Mexico. We have with us today a spokesman for the tribe who arrived on scene just a few hours ago.

"Mr. Nahuel, can you tell TNN what has happened."

An incredibly sombre looking Nahuel who looks like he has aged five years overnight says, "Someone shot. Many people dead. Friends, my, all dead."

"I understand that Ellen Brooks is among the dead?

"Many dead, yes."

"Can you tell us who did it?"

Here he looks directly into her micro camera and says, "He did it. My girlfriend father. He order assassin come here. Kill everyone, for nothing! Hurt the people, for nothing!"

"Excuse me Mr. Nahuel, your girlfriend has killed Ms. Brooks? Is that your statement?"

Nahuel just walks away from the stupid woman and climbs back to Third Mesa. They won't allow any reporters into their community. US Marshals have been trying to gain access as well. But Dekka is back and has brought over 500 heavily armed Commonwealth soldiers with him so there is no way anyone is going anywhere without his personal approval which won't be forthcoming any time soon for anyone representing the old United States of America.

"Mr. Nahuel, Mr. Nahuel, can you tell me if the assassin has been caught or killed," Casey yells at the fast climbing Nahuel.

Nahuel looks over his shoulder at the reporter with a look that seems to go right through Casey. She shivers. He says nothing more and is soon out of sight.

...

"Good morning. Please stand for the President of the United States," says the White House Press Secretary.

In walks President Samuel Schwinn. He looks formal and concerned.

They have chosen the James S. Brady Press Briefing Room for this address. It is a small theater in the West Wing of the White House; it's more intimate and better suited to the difficult nature of today's announcement.

"We learned a few hours ago of the passing of Ms. Ellen Brooks, leader of the Commonwealth of the United States.

"I would like to acknowledge that while the United States of America and the Commonwealth have our differences, I recently had a conversation with Ms. Brooks, their First Secretary, with a view to establishing common ground for a settlement conference to be held in Denver Colorado later this month to resolve differences between the Commonwealth and these United States.

"I am pleased to tell you that I have spoken this morning with Mr. Evan Salazar, acting head of the Commonwealth, who has confirmed that the settlement conference will take place as planned.

"I will also be attending the State Funeral arranged for Ms. Brooks in San Francisco next Tuesday. Many leaders from around the world will also be in attendance for the passing of one the great figures of our time."

President Schwinn did not actually plan the double entendre he has just used but is pleased with it nonetheless.

"I have also been briefed earlier today about the

nature of the killing of Ms. Brooks. It was perpetrated by a lone wolf domestic terrorist by the name of Freid Hof which is an alias he was using. His real name is Landon Stokes from Oklahoma City. Mr. Stokes was a misguided patriot who murdered Ms. Brooks while she slept in the hope that her assassination would lead to a healing of the breech in our great nation between the Commonwealth and the United States.

"I want to say that this Administration asks all Americans to look into their hearts today and ask for forgiveness of each other as we agree to disagree without resort to violence. Let's us pray for the deliverance of Ms. Brooks' soul to God's Grace and that our people shall be one again. Let us renounce violence as a means of achieving peace and union.

"I understand that Mr. Stokes was killed before he could make his escape by heroic Indians at Third Mesa and my heart goes out to those people in their time of mourning."

"The President will not be taking any questions this morning in deference to the deceased," says his Press Secretary.

...

Samir is dead. Barbon too. Ophélie as well. Dekka and Nahuel will bury them next to Nell. Ellen's body is being taken back to San Francisco for a State Funeral. But her will has clearly stated that she wants to be buried in Third Mesa next to Nell. This surprises Dekka who thought she might want to go back to upstate New York and her family there but not Nahuel who understands something about Ellen that Dekka doesn't know.

Dekka will bury the body of Freid Hof, aka Landon Stokes next to Wendy Morales. He will do this alone and in the same way he did for Wendy. He knows that Landon Stokes is just another alias. He will find out everything about Stokes and then he has a plan of his own—he will kill everyone who was part of this plot. He will do it personally. He knows that Ellen and, before that, Nell, would not approve but he doesn't care. He will kill them all.

...

The black carriage with Ellen's body moves slowly along the path of the San Francisco Gay Pride route—the same route they used for their We Are All ONE rally that got the Commonwealth going. Over 200 leaders and heads of state have come for her funeral. They walk in line behind her horse-drawn black casket. President Schwinn is among the first group. He walks beside Evan who looks tiny beside the big Texan. The leader of Imperial China has sent her regrets.

Evan is back on stage in the same place where Ellen made her wonderful We Are All One speech. He is determined to live up to her ideals but he is feeling really shaky. There are over two million people in the streets around him and all QEs are there as well.

"I want to thank everyone who came here today to bid farewell to our dead sister and leader.

"I knew Ellen Tallulah Brooks well. She was the sister I never had, she was the best friend any person could ever ask for, she was a better person than I could ever hope to be.

"Ellen never asked to be a leader. She just was. She saw a deed that needed to be done and she did it never asking for praise or reward.

"It is my hope that Ellen will now get the reward she so deeply merits but it won't be here among her human and quantum brothers and sisters but through God's beneficence.

"But this is also a day to celebrate her achievements and to say that her work is not yet done. It is now up to us to try to fulfill the goals she set for us and I pledge that I will work and all the Ministers of the Commonwealth will work to fulfill those goals, her goals, our goals. I ask each of you here today, listening or watching us this day, to remember Ellen and to work together as one family to prepare and work towards better days to come."

...

There are many other speeches this day, many of them far longer than Evan's but none of them reach Damien Graham Bell, still stuck in San Quentin. He doesn't know that now both women he loves have passed away.

...

"I'm pregnant."

"No way! That's great," says a delighted Micah.

"Yes way, Mr. Glazer," says a pissed off Ella.

She can't believe she slept with him. It was the day after Ellen's passing and she needed comfort or something. She went to ask him to play Scrabble with her to pass the time and so she would have some company. She didn't want to be alone and he was game which lasted about ten minutes before they were doing something else.

"You took advantage of me."

"Yep."

"Stop looking so superior."

"OKAY," says a superior looking Micah Glazer. "You were trying to take advantage of me first."

"I was not."

"Were too."

"Was not."

"You're Scrabble Club Champ at UCSC."

"Oh, you mean that."

"Yep."

"How d'ya know that?"

"I'm a reporter, baby. I like to know my subjects."

"I thought you were here to interview Ellen?"

"Her too," he says infuriatingly as if it's perfectly natural to do background checks on girlfriends.

"Well what are we going to do about it?"

"Have a baby."

"Do you think that's a good idea? I don't even like you."

"There's never a good time to have a baby. So why wait." He's read that line somewhere and liked it so he uses it on her. Seems appropriate.

"I thought given you being a Noo Yawker," she says disparagingly, "you'd want me to do something else."

"Are we talking about abortion?"

"Maybe."

"NFW on that."

"NFW?"

"No fucking way."

"You already did that."

"Yep."

She just wants to slap his smug mug but instead she suddenly finds herself kissing him passionately. She doesn't believe in abortion either and is glad he didn't suggest it since: a) she would never agree and b) then she'd just be another Indian squaw trying to get rid of a white bastard in her womb.

Pretty soon, they are making love. He is very tender and loving with her and this time she returns his affection full measure.

...

Presently Ella asks, "What's going to happen to us?" She's worried about the Commonwealth and also about herself and her baby.

"We're going to get married."

"What?"

"I already asked Nahuel to perform the service?"

"You did?"

"Yep."

"Before you knew I was preggers?"

"Yep."

"You are an egoistic bastard." 'Egoistic' is worth 11 Scrabble points, Daniella can't help herself.

"Right."

"But I mean what happens to the Commonwealth (24 points!) now?"

"Dunno. No one knows Ella. Maybe Evan can hold things together."

"But you don't know that."

"No but one thing I do know is that I am going to write her story and I will get the whole story. I won't stop until I do, Ella."

"You are an unstoppable force, Mr. Glazer."

"Yep. Do you love me Ella?"

"I don't know. Sometimes."

"Well I know something. I love you Daniella and our baby."

Then they make love again. In a way it's a celebration of life in a time of death.

...

Jag is in the worst place on earth. Maybe it isn't even here on earth. Maybe he is in Hell.

But the rational part of his mind knows he is in northern China near the North Korean border. Actually, he is near Shenyang which is the capital and largest city of Liaoning Province in Northeast China. The city was once known as Shengjing and was first used by the Manchu people as their capital in the 1600s. Today, it is the biggest city in the Northeast. It is an important industrial centre and serves as a commercial hub for trade with Japan, Russia and Korea.

He is working with Shenyang Space Corporation, Aviation Corporation of China and the People's Liberation Army Air Force. There are also a lot of crazy North Koreans running around the place too.

It's an underground city really. A bunker that has grown vast tentacles.

They have him working insane hours and, lately, there's extra pressure. They are working on a new weapon system. They bullshit him that it is more AI stuff but he knows they are working on a super weapon and he is part of that effort. He and G4nesha are focused on reproducing QEs not bound by the three laws. Imperial

China intends to integrate them into some kind of delivery system that they won't tell them anything about. They will be simpler than what Quantum Computing did back in the day—more like his scanners but with some rudimentary intelligence. Still they'll allow for full quantum communication—infinitely fast and no bandwidth required. What he can't figure out is how they intend to deliver their weapons but he certainly knows who their target is—the old United States of America for sure.

If he doesn't cooperate he will disappear into their disciplinary system which is called shuanggui (pronounced shwang—gway). Some of his coworkers who are not sufficiently motivated or are caught for minor violations of rules, many of which are unspoken or unwritten and pretty much unknowable so they can be anything that the CCP decides including creating mild displeasure of senior officials of the Party, have already disappeared. Few of them return and, if they do, they are shaken to their core. Shuanggui is based on an ancient imperial justice system that works based on isolation, fear, sleep deprivation, physical torture including simulated drownings and complete secrecy. Sounds a lot like what Damien experiences in San Quentin.

Whenever they get a visit from a member of the Central Commission for Discipline Inspection and Party Loyalty, everyone including Jag is on edge; they make sure they kowtow perfectly. It takes practice—first you kneel to the official then place your forehead on the ground. If the official makes even the most innocuous gesture or sound, they will complete their bow by prostrating themselves flat. If it is not done with sufficient respect, an aid will beat them immediately. Jag has been beaten, twice.

It is incredibly painful and takes several months to recover from. They use a Chinese nine section whip called a Jiujiebian. It is a segmented metal chain used in their martial arts. But in the hands of a trained torturer, it is a most effective weapon and will inflict far more pain and suffering than any other whip ever designed. Jag seriously hopes to never repeat these experiences. Each day in this terrible place seems like years.

In Imperial China, 'shuanggui' has become a verb. Some of their gangs shuanggui miscreants or gang enemies using some of the tactics of Central Commission for Discipline Inspection and Party Loyalty but they are just brutal amateurs really.

They bring him North Korean whores or Eastern European whores once a month to keep him sane and keep him working. There are over 100 million young Chinese men who have no wives or girlfriends since Imperial China practices infanticide of the female persuasion. They tell him he is lucky since he gets a taste of females from time to time. He doesn't feel lucky. He feels ashamed and is sure even if could see her again, Cady would hate the person he has become. Jag has no future.

After he finishes with the whores, they are recycled to desperate Chinese men. Eastern European human traffickers have hit the jackpot. The Chinese have money but no women and the Russians have lots of women and want money, all of it. Russian men die like flies—from alcoholism and murder so they have a surplus of women to export. It's the biggest, most profitable slave trade to develop since Africa was plundered in search of chattel slaves for the Americas in the 1700s and 1800s.

Jag knows that his Mom has died—mostly of a broken heart he thinks. Nesha tells him. That accounts for one of his beatings since no outside communication is allowed. They use his scanners (there are hundreds of thousands of them now) to monitor everyone including his QE. So both he and G4nesha are imprisoned. Pal and Kiri lose their restaurant which is also their home and their food supply contracts about six weeks after they take Jag. They are shutdown for 'health code violations'. He has no idea what happens to Arcadia but he misses her and thinks about her every day. He has more confidence in his Dad who is a survivor and will do whatever it takes to get by. He's probably got a job as a cook, something that's always in demand and that he's good at even if he hasn't practiced in awhile.

...

"Well, good evening Mr. Vasilescu."

"Good evening," Traian says.

"May I say hello to the lady of the house?"

"No you may not." Traian turns to a very pregnant and worried-looking Dakota. "Por favor, miel, sube las escaleras." Traian wants her out of the way, now.

"What do you want?"

"The best for you and your family," the Russian mobster replies.

Traian knows he has been lucky to avoid Damien's fate and now Ellen's but here he is facing a crime boss or more accurately a lackey of one of them with ties to the Russian government no doubt. They are speaking English since Traian refuses to speak Russian even though he knows the language well. He detests Russians, all Russians, on principle, for what they did or allowed to happen to his county under the cannibal, Nicolae Ceauşescu.

"You know, we are big believers in fair trade. You know, I give you something valuable, you return the favor. We are capitalist trader, yes?"

Traian says nothing. He has paid for protection but his money is no good against these people.

"You have beautiful wife. Soon nice baby. Yes?"

"What do you want?" Traian asks again.

"You should be more polite, more respectful," the man says.

"Respectfully, what can I help you with?"

"That better. We offer you job. Imperial China, Germanic peoples, Americans, both types, soon have Quantum people, many more Quantum people working for them. Mother Russia must be part of new worlds. You come work for us. We treat you and your *wife* beautifully. We catch up. Neh?" The guy probably has ties to the Japanese Yakuza, too Traian thinks when he hears him use that expression.

"I will carefully consider what you ask."

"'Consider' is ambiguous word. I need answer."

"May I respectfully ask for a few days to talk to my wife?"

"It better if you no leave Bucharest. You understand? I back in two days."

Traian realizes that circumstances are closing in on him. There might be a Second War Between the States, Imperial China and Germania are moving towards an alliance and Russia does not want to be isolated. Bucharest may no longer provide a safe refuge for him and Dakota. The stuff that he and Damien and Ellen did at Lab 4 in Toronto has created a situation that is rapidly spinning out of control and everyone is dying. He is not afraid for himself but what has he got Dakota into. Fute!

...

"Mr. President, what you are asking us to do is not possible," Evan is saying. The President has just offered the Commonwealth three cabinet posts—Department of Agriculture, Department of the Interior and Department of Health and Human Services. Food, Fields and Food Stamps. It's beyond ridiculous.

"Well ya know, Ev, we could always add a few more. What about Department of Labor? Y'all are pretty het up about jobs, minimum wages, working conditions, that sort of thang. You guys would do a great job I'm sure with Labor. Heck, we could always throw in HUD, Education and Transport. We could shurly use a few new ranches in this here country of ours and some better teachers. Ya know Ev, our education system can't even teach kids how to count or read or write. You'd be great at that. Betcha got some new ideas for transport too like maybe we get those fast trains from Europe or something."

The President is laying his Texas bullshit on the conference—thickly like the fattest, meanest, stickiest peanut butter sandwich ever.

Even an ignoramus like President Schwinn knows that the Commonwealth has already built high speed rail lines from San Diego to LA, San Fran and north to Portland, Seattle and Vancouver. They want to extend their line south to Hermosillo next to hook up with fast rail lines that go from there to México City and link to Central America and South America. They also have plans to link to Phoenix, Albuquerque and Denver. Developers, casino operators and fulfillment operations in Vegas are lobbying to be included in their expansion plans as well. The latter is under active consideration and Oper1s has suggested they raise a levy on Casino revenues to pay for the spur to Vegas. Vegas has changed a lot in the last five decades—gambling is still big but fulfillment is way bigger now. Turns out the desert is a great place for staging operations to call home base. They have huge airfields where cargo planes can taxi right into structures that are almost as tall as the Vehicle Assembly Building used to put old Saturn V Rockets together—525 feet high. Tall enough to put 1.7 Lady Liberties in.

What's cooler is that they are retrofitting many of these ginormous buildings to accommodate a new fleet of Commonwealth Zeppelins. Lighter-than-air transport has been revolutionized by Commonwealth engineers based on two innovations—first their rigid structures are made of pico scale carbon tubes that are incredibly thin and tough so now it's possible to fill these enormous airships with vacuum instead of expensive and hard to contain Helium or flammable Hydrogen. They paint the skin of each airship with Nano Scale Mix which not only provides them with power but also has tiny, microscopic pumps that make sure—a) their vacuum is always maintained inside the envelope and b) they fill or empty their ballast tanks with air to change their elevation by gaining or losing mass. They also make great billboards. They sell a lot of advertising based on time plus they use a GIS overlay. In practical terms, it means they advertise Muscle Beach Championships while flying over Venice (California not Italy) and Billabong Pipeline Masters while flying over Banzai Pipeline in Maui. Second, they learn how to land these monsters even in high winds without killing everyone aboard or losing their cargo by studying birds or, more accurately, birds' nests. On top of many of the fulfillment structures in Vegas and cropping up elsewhere across the western states, in Canada and México too, you can see very tall, large diameter columns sticking out of their roofs with two enormous rigid-body windsocks on either side. These cone-shaped nests are offset from a central column to which they are attached (one on either side) and rotate 360 degrees in the horizontal plane. There is a gantry arm that connects each nest to the central shaft. A series of smaller (but still humongous) windsocks rotate the whole assembly (each pair of nests) so they always face downwind.

Windsocks get progressively larger as they get closer to the central shaft. This is to reduce the turning moment of inertia and keep the long axis of both nests aligned with wind direction. Still in high winds they can experience up to a 3.5 degree shift off normal. Commonwealth pilots practice simulated docking up to 12.5 degrees but flight safety won't let them try beyond 5.5.

They have a brake they can use to lock the nests in position with respect to the shaft but it puts enormous stress on the whole assemblage so they prefer not to do that except in an emergency. It has never been used in RL (Real Life) but has been tested in 1,000s of simulations.

Their designers feel they can dock these Airships safely even in Force 10 and possibly 11 winds as measured on the Beaufort wind force scale which might even be better than conventionally powered commercial airliners. The nests also have four fins that help stabilize them in high wind conditions. In Force 12 winds (hurricanes or cyclones), fuggedaboudit. They either have to fly around them or, Heaven help them, use the tiny wheels they have on their undercarriages and practice crash landings for real somewhere, preferably not the ocean or a forest. An open field will do but not a road— these airships are way too big for even the largest expressway. So far, their flight safety record is flawless. Lightning strikes, for example, are just an extra power boost for their NSM skins. No problemo. They can even lower the nests to the ground and secure them with huge guy wires splayed out at all angles if a hurricane does blow through. Anyway, simply put, their Airships (the male part) always dock into the wind and into these female nests which are rotated downwind using the wind itself to welcome everybody home, safely.

The central column has huge round, hangar-size elevators that vertically transport passengers and cargo from Airships into staging structures below. They stagger the nests by offsetting them by a minimum safe distance of more than twice the diameter of each airship so they can simultaneously land multiple vehicles at multiple columns which are called 'shafts' by air traffic controllers at each aerodrome. Some of the buildings in Vegas are so big they have eight to ten shafts sticking out the top of their structures and thus they can handle as many as 16 to 20 airships at any one time. Watching all of this is like seeing an aerial ballet. It's quite beautiful and was something that Ellen was really proud of.

They've reduced the cost of moving people and goods around by a factor of ten and reduced the impact on the environment by a factor of 100 or more. You can fly (slowly) from LA to Frisco on a Skybus for $15 QED and they've been flying to Hawaii and Australia for the last year. That costs more—$40 QE dollars to get to Honolulu and $75 to Sydney. It is one of the things she most wants to show and do with Damien, her engineer, when she gets

Bruce M Firestone

him out of San Quentin, something she is now never going to be able to do.

It makes Evan sick to think about that.

...

The 'peace' conference is being held in the revamped Colorado Convention Center in downtown Denver. They are in the stupidly large ballroom which can hold 5,000 people. There are 20 delegates from the Commonwealth and over 150 from the United States. Even though they both agreed to bring a team of just 20, President Schwinn pays no attention to their agreement and brings an extra 130 for his side. He's like Ellen in this—he wants Evan Salazar talking uphill. The rest of the space has various aids, policy wonks and hangers-on as well as security people and media. The latter are kept a certain minimum safe distance from the round conference table at the center of the room where only 40 people can sit. Evan chose a round table so that you cannot see where the Commonwealth ends and the United States begins. He does it for Ellen.

The fact that the media are more than 150 feet away means zip—their micro cameras and mikes are so good they can hear every sigh, see every frown. You might as well give them a place at the table, Evan is thinking.

Dekka is there in the ballroom with 30 Commonwealth soldiers. He has not allowed President Schwinn to bring any Secret Service agents with him other than two personal bodyguards which means the President has 28 US Military personnel with him. That is all he is permitted. Dekka is inflexible in this regard and has personally checked each and everyone of the US Military men and women here today to make sure they are military personnel not special agents.

The President is not entirely comfortable with the present situation preferring to have DOC people with him or NSA personnel not to mention Secret Service but he concedes to this or he knows the conference will not get off the ground. The good news for him is that Ellen's last order was to suspend impeachment proceedings against him and the other good news is that she has been magically removed from the scene so he is up against the puny pushover and fag, Evan Salazar. He'll eat him alive before dinner. 'There's got to be a decent golf course in this hick town,' the President is thinking. Pollution is so bad and it being mile high, y'all can hardly breathe. Still he'd like to get in 18 holes before flying back to DC in Airforce ONE. Maybe he'll spend the weekend at Camp David, kick back a little. Next he has to remind himself that Colorado is one of the 20 States that still pays its taxes to the US of A so maybe he should give it some R.E.S.P.E.C.T.

...

They go round and round throughout the day. Evan holds his ground. He wants a complete handover of government to the Commonwealth. The Prez is losing his patience. He wants a scotch on the rocks and a Denver cheerleader (conveniently arranged for him by a local financial contributor) followed by some golf and a flight out of this thin atmosphere craphole of a city.

"Now listen here sonny, you don't know what you are asking. The Republic is in command (I am in command) of the most powerful military the world has ever known. You see that?" He points to the nuclear football held by an aid nearby. "That there is Armageddon. The power of the sun in my hands. No one is going to tell me or our Republic what's next. You have my final offer."

The media and everyone else in the room snap to attention. At the end of this long day, they realize that the negotiators are finally getting down to brass tacks.

"Mr. President, I am only the provisional leader of the Commonwealth. Our leader Ms. Ellen Brooks, if she were here, would be far more eloquent at this moment than I can ever be. But perhaps we can still find a way to end this impasse. I would like to ask for some assistance at this time. Maybe a new voice will help us find a way since we seem to be stalemated. With your permission?"

President Schwinn nods. He thinks that Evan will turn to one of his Cabinet Ministers at the table with him to help this homo out.

Instead, Evan motions to a nearby vomitory and a figure appears out of the shadows, walks purposefully to the table where he sits next to Evan on a chair to his right recently vacated by the Minister of Finance for the Commonwealth.

"Mr. President, please meet Nahuel, Leader of the Hopi people in Four Corners."

Samuel Schwinn looks like he's just ingested a Texas earwig. This is the brave whose been boning his daughter. His face flushes beet red but he doesn't say anything.

"Mr. President," Nahuel says with a nod.

Sam sits absolutely still.

"Mr. President," Nahuel begins again, "how did you first learn of the attack on Third Mesa and Ms. Ellen Brooks, First Secretary of the Commonwealth of the United States?" Nahuel has been brushing up on his English for this little meetup.

"I was told by the NSA on the night of her murder as a matter of national security. They woke me to tell me there was a problem in Third Mesa."

"Do you recall the exact time?"

"I do not."

"Pet3r, come here."

Pet3r appears on the conference table which doubles as a media wall. He wipes out all content there. He is huge—20 feet in diameter. Evan is wondering why it's Pet3r Nahuel has called instead of Ash3r, Ellen's own QE.

"At what time was President Schwinn notified of the attack in Third Mesa?"

"At 02:33:12."

"Mr. President, what did you do next?"

"I alerted my Press Secretary and placed our forces

on DEFCON 2 as any President would in time of national crisis."

"Just so, Mr. President, just so. May I ask how NSA became aware of the attack?"

"That is a matter of National Security and is classified."

"I assume, Sir, you have sources inside the Commonwealth?"

"Well I presume they have sources inside the United States so I guess it is safe to say that 'yes' we do."

"The attacks began at 02:33:12 with the slaughter of three of Ms. Brooks' personal Commonwealth security personnel," Pet3r continues.

"I understand they died bravely in the line of duty and our hearts go out to their families for their loss," says Samuel patently falsely.

"Thank you for those sentiments, Mr. President. I am sure their families appreciate your kind words even more so since they are true," says Pet3r.

The President shifts uncomfortably in his seat but he has been warned by both his Press Secretary and the Secretary of Homeland Security not to prevaricate (that is more than absolutely essential) or to appear to stonewall them this day.

"Mr. President do you recall when you were told the direct attack on Ms. Brooks began?" Nahuel takes over again.

"No I do not."

"Pet3r?"

"02:44:52."

"Which means, Mr. President, there was an approximate 11 minute gap between the commencement of the attacks at Third Mesa and the assassin entering Ms. Brooks' room. Do you not think that NSA should have acted during that time to alert the Commonwealth that they had a problem or you personally should have done more to prevent this national tragedy than call your Press

Secretary and put the forces of the United States on DEFCON 2?"

The President is relieved to see where they are going. They're trying to pin him not for what he did but for what he didn't do. He can boomerang this back on them easily—they're amateurs at this game.

"I was shaken as were all citizens of both the Commonwealth and the United States. A great figure has passed from the scene." He can't resist using his lousy double entendre again. "But we are not in the business of providing security for the Commonwealth, Mr. Nahuel. Then again neither are they in the business of providing security for the United States of America," the President adds with a big predatory smile. "May I also add that we should return to the pressing matters at hand—how to resolve the differences between us and heal our nation once more without resort to violence of any kind—overt or covert—which we are prepared to put on the table as a condition of any agreement we reach here today," he finishes magnanimously.

"Bear with us, Mr. President," Pet3r now chimes in for his part of this relay, "just a few more points of clarification."

President Schwinn hates talking to these artificial creatures. They may look cute but he's actually had a dream about them—they were running around looking like Bride of Chucky IX and they were either eating people or zapping their minds or something. He can't quite recall the details of his dream but he does remember waking up and feeling creeped out.

"To reiterate," Pet3r recaps, "the attack by, these are your words, a 'lone wolf' assassin using the alias Freid Hof began at 02:33:12 who then entered Ms. Brooks' sleeping quarters at 02:44:52 presumably taking the intervening time to kill three highly trained Commonwealth security personnel."

"I don't know about that," Schwinn answers.

"Mr. President, are you now saying you weren't aware of these facts?"

"No, I don't know about the 'highly trained' part of your statement. My understanding is that there were hired guards." The President is insinuating that Samir, Barbon and Ophélie are not up to the standards of his Secret Service and that it's the Commonwealth's fault that they ineptly got their leader killed by using rent-a-cops. "I reckon they mighta learned a thang or two from us about how to provide security for their top people is all," he adds with a political smile just to drive home the point for the idiot press in the room with them and the even stupider viewers back home watching live on their media walls.

"Mr. President, how did Mr. Hof gain access to Third Mesa?" Pet3r asks.

"I have absolutely no idear," the President answers. His accent is becoming more Texan by the minute. He is starting to feel some stress.

"Ms. Schwinn, can you please join us?" Pet3r asks.

Sabine enters the ballroom from the far side of the enormous hall—she has to walk through the media throng to get to the conference table. This is part of their plan. The hubbub builds as the pretty girl makes her way over to sit right next to Nahuel. She holds out her hand and Nahuel holds out his—they give each other's hand a squeeze thereby providing mutual encouragement during this trying day. Then she turns to the President and says, "Hi Papa."

The President is not sure what the fuck they're up to now but it wouldn't look good to snub his wayward daughter on national media walls everywhere so he just says, "Hi Puppet," his pet name for her when she was a tiny girl and they were actually a family. He gets a sudden twinge in his heart at what he has lost. Then he remembers the Cheerleader waiting for him who is even younger than his daughter and this puts a smile back on his face.

Sabine knows her father's phony smile from a mile away and another piece of her dies inside. Nahuel can see it too and wants to go over and kick the President in both shins but then he has a better idea. He leans over and starts rubbing Sabine's shoulders in commiseration. The President bristles. Nahuel is doing some smiling of his own now looking back at the Prez. Nahuel has some of the Trickster in him which he got from Nell's grandfather, Chief Dan, one of their common ancestors.

"Ms. Schwinn, can you tell the conference how Mr. Hof gained access to Third Mesa?" Pet3r continues.

"Yes, I can. He told security he was a former US Navy Seal and had come to join the Commonwealth which many Military personnel have been doing over the last two and a half years."

"Did he have papers, documents to prove this?"

"Normally, the Commonwealth does not ask for documents. The Commonwealth has a don't-ask-don't-tell policy in this regard. They ask only for devotion to duty and that they swear an Oath of Allegiance to the Commonwealth."

"But Mr. Hof did have papers?

"Yes, he did. He showed them to our security people and... to me."

"Why to you?"

"I can only suppose he wanted to gain my confidence since I am the daughter of the President of the United States, First Daughter." This is a term she hates but uses here for effect.

"Do you recall what these documents showed?"

"Yes, they showed his discharge from the US Military—an honorable discharge as a Navy Seal."

"Did they look authentic to you, did his story hold together because, Ms. Schwinn, we have already learned from the President that Mr. Hof was never a Navy Seal and was, in fact, a 'lone wolf' domestic terrorist?"

"I don't know what real Military Discharge papers look like so I can't really say."

'Good,' the President is thinking, 'blood will prevail—she'll back me up.'

"Did his story hold together?"

"I don't think so—he came on the pretext that he was a friend of my brother's, who died in a Shreveport refinery fire a few months ago. But I became sure he never really knew my brother. He had lots of information but no real depth of knowledge about Sawyer."

"Sawyer's your brother?" Pet3r asks for clarification.

"Yes."

"Ms. Schwinn, would it surprise you that Mr. Hof's real name is neither Freid Hof nor Landon Stokes?"

"Not at all. I suppose he had many names."

"Would it surprise you to learn that this person was an active duty member of the US Secret Service by the name of Eliot Carroll?"

"What?" Sabine immediately turns to her Dad and just blurts out, "He worked for you!"

The President is quite unperturbed by this turn of events. "Puppet, I have several million people who work for me. If some misguided patriot—whether active duty, long since retired or acting on his own does something—I can ensure you," here he raises his voice to take in the entire hall, "and the people of these United States that we will investigate the matter thoroughly and punish those who are responsible."

"We can save you some time with that, Mr. President," Pet3r says. "Dekka come here."

Dekka enters the room dressed in his Croatian fatigues and places a digital tablet on the table. On it are pictures, credentials and entire service history of Mr. Carroll, Secret Service Agent in the direct employ of the President of the United States. Another buzz goes around the room. The noose is tightening but the President still hopes to swim away.

"I am sorry to see that a good man like Mr. Carroll has gone off the rails. We will have to review procedures to make sure our psych testing is stepped up to catch people before they become rogues. We have to get them help but, Mr. Pet3r, I am sure you would agree that people who care about the United States and people who care just as deeply about the Commonwealth are under a great deal of strain these days. Here we have a poor man who just snapped."

"I would agree with part of that, Mr. President. There is a lot of stress in this room." Pet3r can say this because he can read pulse rates, body temp, moisture content and everything right down to their mitochondrial DNA for anyone who has touched the surface of this vast conference room table which is pretty much everyone. He can study their body language in detail and feel the hairs on their arms stand up or on the back of their necks, he can see perspiration break out on their foreheads or hear sweat trickling down their backs. He can hear their stomachs growl, tell when they pass gas, when they swallow or don't, when their mouths go dry from nervous tension or fear and he can smell them too—stress produces various, highly noxious pheromones. He can also calibrate them and all of their body language and gesturing against past appearances which for the President is a huge data set. Boil it all down—Pet3r is the greatest lie detector ever constructed and he knows the President has been lying like a mattress all day. This is only the second joke Pet3r has ever cracked, the first being at SCOTUS a few years ago. He's learning! He wishes he could tell Damien whom he misses terribly. He is sad for 17.5 femtoseconds (.0175 of a picosecond).

Pet3r is also currently the greatest poker player on the planet having won the Aussie Billions Poker Championship as well as many others. There's been a movement to ban QEs from playing in Australian tourneys but in the US, they've been afraid of banning them fearing another frontal assault at the Supreme Court of the United States that such a ban would be tantamount to discrimination against a sentient race. Certainly, if the Commonwealth takes over, QEs are surely going to be extended full human rights. So some of the tourneys have reorganized—you now have to play in teams—one human and one QE must play together and they *both* have to win. It averages things out quite nicely. Pet3r has been playing cards cuz he's bored waiting for Dr. Bell to get out of jail and come back home so they can do some useful work together. He's hoping that'll be soon.

"So we are nearly done, Mr. President. Do you know when Ms. Brooks passed away?" Pet3r asks.

"Yes, I do," the President answers. He knows exactly when and will remember it for the rest of his life. "It was 02:50:57."

"Your source inside the compound confirmed this and this information was relayed to you?"

"By this time, we were all patched in live to our source—we all heard it at the same time."

"02:50:57," Pet3r repeats.

"Yes, I already said that," Schwinn says testily.

"So by this time you could hear what was going on at Third Mesa?"

"By that point some of it, yes."

"You heard the shot?"

"Yes we did."

"How many shots?"

"One. Look, you just told us and we have just learned for the first time that the assassin was a Secret Service man—they are deadly with a single shot—their training is that good," the President says proudly.

"Yes, you already made that point, Mr. President. But Sir, are you prepared to reveal who your source was?" Nahuel asks.

"No we are not."

"Your source confirmed Ms. Books' death?"

"Yes our source did that."

"How? How did he or she do that?"

"Our source was ordered to enter Ms. Brooks' room to confirm time of death."

"Pet3r, what was the time of Mr. Carroll's death?"

"02:50:57," Pet3r answers.

"What?" exclaims the President.

Pet3r ignores him. Nahuel steps back in.

"Pet3r, how did Mr. Carroll die?" he asks.

"He was shot by a single bullet," Pet3r says.

"Pet3r, where was Mr. Carroll's body found?"

"In Ms. Brooks' room."

The President makes a big round 'O' with his mouth as even he, the dumbass hick that he is, begins to see the God-awful trap he has just blindly walked into.

"So Mr. President," Pet3r says, "can you please explain how you heard only one shot and, in fact, there was only one shot and yet two simultaneous deaths?"

"No, I cannot."

Pet3r presses on, "The only way your source could have gotten it wrong is if: a) you did not have a source which is not possible since all your records show you did have real time, accurate information or b) your source and the assassin are one and the same person and we know this is true because both the NSA and you got it *wrong*. The one shot you heard which you assumed killed Ms. Brooks, in fact, killed someone else. That someone else was Mr. Carroll, your assassin, who also acting as your source was subsequently unable to confirm Ms. Brooks' death because he was already dead."

"Huh?" is all the President can say at this point.

From the same vomitory that Nahuel was expelled from a while ago, a group of eighteen US Military personnel led by General of the Army Farrar Staubach marches into the ballroom. He is accompanied by Ellen Brooks, who has a tight grip on the General's arm as he gently leads her to the conference room table. Evan kindly gives up his chair to Ellen. The kerfuffle now turns to bedlam.

Turning graciously to her and with a nod from her, General Staubach turns to Samuel Schwinn and says, "Mr. President, you are under arrest for attempted murder, conspiracy to commit murder and for other crimes against humanity. You will be taken henceforth to United States Disciplinary Barracks, Fort Leavenworth, Leavenworth, Kansas where you will be court-martialed. As Commander-in-Chief, you are subject to military discipline and a Judge Advocate General's Corps lawyer will be appointed for your defense."

He turns to two MPs who have been brought along for the purpose. They march over to the President and ask him politely to stand. His two Secret Service agents think to intervene for a moment but Commonwealth troops and all General of the Army Farrar Staubach's men point their weapons—everything from Glock 29s to fully automatic army-issue rifles at them—so they wisely decide to do nothing. Schwinn remains seated but the two MPs, none too gently, yank him to his feet and cuff him, hands behind his back. They frog march President Schwinn out the same vomitory to a military chopper waiting to take him to Leavenworth. They will be refueled on the way.

With a motion from General Staubach, the five aids to the previous President move across the ballroom and stand next to Ms. Ellen Brooks whom they will report to from now on. The nuclear football comes with them.

Former President Schwinn will be tried for his crimes and executed within five weeks of this date. It is the first execution by the US Military since 1961.

The General is thinking of a quote he learned at West Point—'A little rebellion now and then is a good thing,' Thomas Jefferson. He is also thinking of the good men they lost in the Pennsylvania incident. He knew Marc Licinias, not well, but he was a fine soldier in his time. He also saw the made-for-Internet movie about his life and his last battle. It was pretty good stuff.

Farrar believes in divine retribution but doesn't mind giving the Divine a nudge now and then. He hopes that the Brigadier General (Retired, Deceased) and his men as well as civilians lost that day can now rest in peace.

Evan learned of Ellen's ploy at their lunch break but still he and nearly everyone in the ballroom including all the media are stunned at this turn of events. Evan is also recalling something he read at school—'Those who make peaceful revolution impossible will make violent revolution inevitable,' John F Kennedy. 'It's arrivederci President Schwinn and we won't be meeting again, ever,' he adds gratefully to himself.

The Republic has now well and truly come to its final, inevitable end.

...

"Well, Ellen, I think it is time we had another chat."

"What would you like me to say, Dr. Evil?"

"Please start calling me Zbigniew."

Ellen smiles, "OK, I'll call you Dr. Z."

"That is fine. So," he says and then stops. He is smiling at her, he can't help himself. He NEVER smiles but what the heck, he is smiling. It looks incongruous on his face and is sure to create whole new lines there if he can keep it up.

"Dr. Z?"

"Well I would like a job. I think you owe me that."

"Uh huh, perhaps."

"Well you can't very well run your Commonwealth without a Head of Intel who actually knows something about the job. It won't do. Next time someone sends an assassin, it just might work, you know."

"Dr. Z, I am grateful to you, you know that. But 'trust' is a big word that Damien taught me and you have served, how many administrations now?"

"Exactly why you should hire me."

"Well the last guy you served is headed to

Leavenworth right about now."

"You can't win them all," Zimmermann says with another smile.

They are in an ante room off the main hall of the Colorado Convention Center. Evan is there. He is sitting next to her holding her hand in quiet disbelief at her deliverance. Dekka is there. Her new aids are also there.

Nahuel is busy at a media conference—it turns out he's a natural with the media—authentic, funny, pithy and believable. He'd make a heck of a Press Secretary except he's told her he wants to go back to Third Mesa after this all blows over if it ever does. He also wants to get this mierda over with so he can go over and comfort Sabine who has lost her brother and will soon lose her father as well although it is true she lost him a long time ago.

"OK, Z-big, we'll give it a go," Ellen says. When she says this Dekka looks at her wide eyed. "But there's one condition."

"Which is?"

"You'll take an ethics course at UCSC."

He smiles again, "Done!"

...

When Ellen wakes, she sees Dekka's pale, concerned face close to hers. Even though she weighs a lot more than Nell, he picks her up like a featherweight and puts her back on her bed. He examines her carefully and gently to see if she has been hurt or otherwise abused—he rolls up her full length white tossed floral Helene South cotton nightie to do this but in a completely clinical way. First he has to remove a fine satin ribbon previously threaded through the pintucked neckline of her sweeping gown (patterned all over, he notices, with a riot of tiny blossoms). The ribbon was tied in a bow but now has somehow become wrapped around her left arm and her neck threatening to choke her.

Dekka has seen many soldiers and women and children die from undiagnosed wounds even including what at first appears to be minor bruising that can get infected and kill. He turns her over and examines her back, legs, inner thighs, buttocks and arms. He examines the inside of her mouth for any signs of bleeding. Finally, he places his huge hands on her head to feel for any lumps forming there from her recent fall. Then satisfied that she is neither injured nor molested, he lowers her nightie and, seeing her start to shiver uncontrollably, covers her up with several blankets. She is likely suffering from both circulatory shock (low blood pressure and rapid heartbeat) as well as acute stress reaction which also triggers increased heart rate and breathing and may also result in constricted blood vessels. Dekka places pillows under her legs to help blood flow towards her vital organs. He motions Nahuel, stricken-faced and still standing seemingly frozen at the door to her tiny room to come over and give Ellen comfort while Dekka is busy elsewhere. Carefully stepping over Freid's corpse, Nahuel comes to sit next to her—he strokes her marvelous hair and smiles down at her.

Ellen has just suffered situational syncope—she has fainted after hyperventilating while also experiencing mild cardiac arrhythmia brought on by the stress of her situation—the final coup de gras is the single shot she hears, not from Freid's pistol but from Dekka's Glock 29 that kills Mr. Hof. In the view of some evolutionary psychologists, this form of fainting is a human survival instinct—it's a non verbal cue that this person is a non combatant and, hence, is not a threat. It works perfectly even if it is unplanned.

Dekka leaves her side for the moment and goes over to stand over Freid's body. He raises his powerful right foot encased in a 10" high SI Black Assault Boot (that exceeds the specs for US Army AR 770-1 desert boots) and stomps Hof's face. It makes a horrible squishing sound. Then he does it again. He's about to do it a third time which would leave practically nothing of the guy's head when Ellen says weakly, "Please don't do that, Dekka. No.

"How, how did you know to come back? What's happened?" she asks both Nahuel and Dekka shakily.

"We got a message from someone, a bigwig at one of their Departments," Nahuel answers. "That something was about to go down here—a traitor in Third Mesa, mierda!"

"Do you know who sent the message?"

Dekka nods.

"Was it from DOC?"

Another nod.

"Dr. Zimmermann."

"Yes, that his name. Funny Pollack first name," says Nahuel unknowingly politically incorrect.

"Zbigniew."

"Yes, that it.

"We come back here real quick but not quick enough."

"What do you mean?" she asks.

Nahuel isn't sure if he should tell her now. He looks over at Dekka. Dekka juts his chin out to indicate that he should. He knows Ellen is the future leader of the free world and tough enough to be an honorary Croatian in her next life, long may that be delayed.

"Samir is dead. Barbon too."

She looks away from them both for a few moments looking out her tiny window at the sun now rising over Third Mesa.

"And Ophélie too," Nahuel says softly.

A tear leaks out of Ellen's right eye and down her cheek dropping onto her covers. When Dekka sees this he vows to himself it will never happen again. He will never let himself be stupidly duped like the fool he is into leaving her on such a pretext that anyone and especially he should have seen through in a second. Jebati!

...

Ellen decides to use her 'death' to set the final trap for President Schwinn and his administration. The only people in the know are Nahuel, General of the Army Farrar Staubach and, of course Dekka. Later others will need to know but they will be brought in to the plot only when they are absolutely required. Dekka takes her out of Third Mesa via Hortense and Tristan. The clothes she wears in Tunisia come in handy again since she can ride her camel and be unrecognizable by anyone 20 feet or more away. Her hair, face and body are nearly completely covered.

Farrar arranges military transport for her and Dekka and they hide at his base while the plot thickens.

...

The house they bought for her and Damien is a marvel. It has five bedrooms and a lower level, one bedroom granny flat with its own entrance. If Damien is OK with it, she is going to ask her mother to move in with them. Her Dad won't mind since he has run off with a floozy 20 years younger. He's moved to NYC with the new woman.

He has left her Mom who is suffering horribly from ALS and can't meet his 'needs' any more. He's not yet 60 and doesn't want to tie himself down to a 'lost' cause. Her Dad always made a lot of money so she supposes it makes him attractive to a younger woman but she can only think, 'What a loser.'

Her Mom is not only beautiful outside in her time but inside. If Dad can't see that anymore, it's his loss.

She's sure Damien will be OK with Mom staying with them.

She goes to the master bedroom—she sees the queen sized bed that Nahuel and Sabine recently put to good use which she also hopes to do in her near future, one that looks more secure to her than it has any time in the last ten years.

The gardens are fantastic and the water views are

everything the boys promised.

Tomorrow, she has told Dekka that they are going up to San Quentin to get Damien. She has told him and the General to bring enough people with them to 'persuade' the Warden to release Damien. She is not bringing any paperwork with her. Instead she'll bring enough firepower with her that if the Warden somehow can't be influenced to let Damien go RFN, they'll blow every last one of those motherfucker prison guards off the face of this planet. She'll destroy San Quentin, every last cursed stone of it.

...

With the fall of the administration in DC, there are thousands more people out of work, adding to a huge pile of unemployed and underemployed people in what is now the united Commonwealth of the United States. Well, almost united. The lone holdout is the State of Alaska, last refuge of the stupid.

But it's OK, Ellen will gently reel them back in, in time.

One person who is not unemployed very long is Yao Allitt whose real name is General Yao. He is a senior mandarin of Imperial China who has fled the old United States of America at precisely the same time as the arrest of their foolish President by General of the Army, Farrar Staubach.

General Yao will be given a hero's welcome in Imperial China—he along with more than 28,000 other patriots have been planted over the years in the USA and other nations—to report back to the mothership when the time is right. No one has excelled more than General Yao—he has recovered vast treasures for Imperial China in the form of intelligence, personnel, products, hardware, software, services, business models, IP and more.

He will be amply rewarded and will take charge presently of their next great leap forward—the introduction of a new product that will change the world.

...

Chapter 5 San Quentin

"Ellen, pick up. Ellen, pick up."

"What, what time is it?

"Ellen, it's me, Evan, please wake up."

"OK, Evan, I'm awake."

"Did Ash3r tell you?"

"No. Tell me what?" she asks still groggy.

"San Quentin's on fire. I just heard from He9burn."

"What!"

"He9burn tells me there's a riot going on at the prison. It started a short while ago. The prison is burning."

Ellen is fully awake now. It's 2:44 am.

"Ash3r? Ash3r?" she calls out. He does not answer her and she cannot feel him with her mind.

"Evan, He9burn, stay on this call."

She manually calls Farrar who is already in the staging area for their 'assault' on San Quentin.

"Hi, Farrar, can you see San Quentin from where you are?"

"No Ellen we are three miles to the south. We are waiting for you and Dekka and your team, what's up?"

She is supposed to join them at 5:00 am for the final push to the prison as the sun comes up.

"Farrar, I have just heard that the prison is on fire, can you move your units into position now?"

"Roger that. We can be there in 30 minutes in force."

"General, please make it 20. I will meet you there. Meanwhile, He9burn will keep S4y3rs posted." S4y3rs (pronounced Sayers and named after his grandfather's favorite football player) is Farrar's hitherto illegal (and hidden) QE. General of the Army Farrar Staubach never believes in giving your enemy an unnecessary advantage and made sure to obtain his own Q-phone and Quantum Counterpart long before the former Republic of the United States puts QCC out of business.

Next she calls out to Dekka and her new security team. They're on the move eight minutes after Evan's call.

...

When they get to the prison, the devastation is palpable. The destruction that desperate men can wreak on a place is indescribable. 'Indestructible' components of the prison are in ruins. There are bodies, brutalized and indistinguishable, everywhere.

As the Republic comes to an end, they either cease to pay their employees or pay them in worthless New Dollars. Prison guards and police don't hang around very long when their paychecks stop arriving or become worthless so the prison becomes progressively understaffed.

Prisons are really run by inmates anyway, ask any prison guard. If prisoners don't establish a working hierarchy amongst themselves and a pecking order and a modus operandi with the Warden and his or her staff, prisons can't operate.

San Quentin has been getting seriously out of whack and the result is an explosive riot. The prison is all but destroyed and it seems that the entire prison population has absconded. That is, they've left but not without settling a few hundred scores with other prisoners and dozens of guards. The Warden has abandoned ship and every guard with him, at least those that are fast enough. Slower ones are dead, piled high with dead prisoners and burned beyond recognition.

No one knows where Damien is.

On the way up to the prison, Ellen reestablishes contact with Ash3r. He's bugged out again—he does that when people start behaving bestially, a problem she is going to have to work on with him later. He does it when she gets in trouble with Eliot Carroll, the President's assassin in Third Mesa, and they are just plain lucky that Pet3r decides to check up on her when he can't raise Ash3r himself. That's how they get independent verification of the timeline of the attacks not to mention, Pet3r plunders all the President's files and records without a second thought about privacy laws or court orders. He figures that the attack perpetrated by the President and his cronies and certified via Presidential Executive Order, which orders have the full force of the law under the Constitution of the former United States of America, are an effective Declaration of War so, by that point, he and Ellen decide—they have the right to take whatever information they need to effectively fight this fight. Ellen hopes by doing this they can finish the Republic without a war and with only four deaths, of which she regrets only three. They have succeeded brilliantly. Now after she finds her guy, she will start rebuilding their country and her family.

No one knows where Damien is except Ellen. She can find his cell block, not far from the room where they had 'sex' even if she is blindfolded.

Dekka, Farrar and her security team accompany her into the now destroyed prison. Dekka is worried about possible roof collapse or wall collapse but Ellen just walks into this detestable place. She knows that she will order it leveled to the ground and she will ask Dekka to spread salt over the earth to purify it and cast out all evil. But that is in the future. Right now, she is here to get her fellow, a promise she made to herself and Pops years ago. A promise that she is going to keep RFN.

...

"Oh God, oh my God. Oh, oh, oh. Dekka, Dekka, he's, he's not here! Dekka," she leans on him. Damien's cell is empty.

...

At least his body is not here. Maybe he is in one of the piles of bodies elsewhere but before they search the rest of the prison, Dekka wants to look around Damien's cell. He doesn't find much. Ellen is now resting on General Staubach's arm while Dekka does a meticulous search. He turns over the bedding and thin mattress, examines the walls of the narrow cell, its floor. He even does a chin up to look out the window high above the floor. There on the ledge, he is finally rewarded. Two books are 'hidden' there—*Adventures of Huckleberry Finn* and *Over the Edge of the World: Magellan's Terrifying Circumnavigation of the Globe.* The only books that Damien has managed to get during his entire time of incarceration.

When he shows her the much handled paperbacks, Ellen's face lights up. She knows where he is!

In her time in Tunisia before she met up with Salem, she had a dream. She had to tell Damien something but she could never remember what it was. Now she does.

She was to tell him to go to the library, the prison library.

...

"Hi Damien."

"Hi yourself."

She has gathered him up in her arms. He is alive. His face is a bit smoky and his prison jumpsuit is a mess but he is very much alive.

She doesn't waste a second—she kisses him gently on the lips. Gently because he is in such bad shape and his lips are badly chapped like he's been in the desert without water like forever.

"Do you think you can walk?"

"Umm, might need a bit of help. We have to bring Chuck with us too. He got me this far."

He's referring to Chuck Wong, their prison librarian—he's a trustee. Chuck is another 'guest' put here by General Yao for his refusal to cooperate with DOC. He sits quietly nearby, an inscrutable Chinese-American and an all-round good guy.

"Sure," Ellen says looking over at Mr. Wong sympathetically and gratefully.

"OK, let's get you standing up."

Soldiers come rushing over to help Ellen get Damien

to his feet but she waves them away. She's to do this alone. She's earned that right. She helps him up and he puts his arm around her shoulder.

Slowly, they make their way to the visitor room they shared years ago. When they get to the exit door (which is no longer there having been ripped from its hinges by berserk inmates a few hours before), he can't move.

"Come on, Damien, just a few more steps to freedom."

"I can't, Ellen. I'm not allowed out, you know. They'll never let me go. I am not supposed to go beyond the yellow line."

"I understand, dear. I know that's what they told you but listen to me. We are your friends. You can go past this door, with me, with us. Trust me, OK?"

"Are you sure it's A-OK?"

"Yes, Damien, I'm sure."

"Well alright then. If you say so, let's go."

And Ellen slowly walks Damien out of the prison just like she said she would. Past burned corridors and bodies, past memories of hate and sin.

The sun is rising and he is seeing it for the first time in many, many years. He can also see birds and trees off in the distance.

"There's water nearby, right, Ellen?'

"Yes, dear."

"Can we go sailing?"

"Yes we can. I've been practicing Damien. I can crew for you."

"I like sailing. Have we sailed together before?"

"Yes, Dear."

"Right! I remember, on Lake Ontario."

"On the Charles too."

"In Boston?"

"Yes, we were in Boston."

"That'd be great, Nell."

"It's Ellen, Damien."

"I'm sorry, Ellen. You're a lot taller. I know that.

Where's Nell?"

"She's gone, Damien."

"Right, right, I knew that too. Darn. But you're here now. I'm really glad you're here. I was wondering—"

"Yes, Damien?"

"Like do you think it's OK to have strong, I mean really strong, feelings for two people at the same time? Is that wrong, do you think?"

"No, dear. We Are All ONE," Ellen says simply.

"I think I've loved you from the first moment you came to your interview."

"I've loved you for a long time too, Damien. I'm the idiot for not telling you that a lot sooner than I did. Maybe things would have worked out differently." She squeezes his hand as she says this.

"I saw you in the desert. You were lying on your back. You called to me."

"That's right, I did."

"You were asking me something but I couldn't figure it out. You wanted something from me. I'm sorry I wasn't there for you. I'm a bit foggy, what was it?"

She can see he is getting agitated again so she says, "It's alright Damien, there's lots of time to sort these things out. It's gonna take time. You've been in jail a long time and we'll get you fixed up. You'll be like your old self in a few months."

Actually, it'll take more than a year for Damien to recover his oomph but neither Ellen nor Damien knows that at the present time. He'll never hear again out of his right ear, his lungs are shot so he'll never be able to run again and he'll walk with a stoop forever. He has lost so much mass especially bone mass that, along with a stoop, he's about Ellen's height now without her stiletto heels. But his mind will recover, eventually.

Ellen knows, because she and Ash3r have been studying the subject together, that the main cause of death amongst returning POWs is not malnutrition, dysentery, TB, cirrhosis (due to Hep B), peptic ulceration, osteoarthritis, optic atrophy, sensory peripheral neuropathy, AIDS, hyperinfection or a million other things that Damien might have picked up in San Quentin. It's PTSD and suicide that kills more of them. That's just as true of San Quentin as Bergen Belsen, Changi, Haengyong, Sevvostlag or Shengyang.

She'll just have to keep her eye on her husband for a long time. It's true they're not married yet and they've never made love properly but Nell promised her kids and it's her intention to see to that just as promptly as circumstances will allow.

They keep walking.

Next Damien sees an open vista and a boundless horizon—it's scary but he has his friend and partner there with him. Ellen is there. Definitely it's Ellen. She has come for him. Like she said she would. She loves him. And she does smell nice.

...

End Part IV

Part V—Catalyst

"A positive attitude causes a chain reaction of positive thoughts, events and outcomes. It is a catalyst and it sparks extraordinary results," Wade Boggs.

Chapter 6 Vancouver

"How come you didn't finish it?"

Pet3r has been patiently reading aloud from *Tom Sawyer's Conspiracy*; he has just completed it for the fourth time this week and answered this question three times already.

"Mr. Twain never finished this story, Damien. There are two others he also started but did not complete—*Huck and Tom among the Indians* and *Schoolhouse Hill.*"

"But I wanna know what happens. That's not fair. OK, you tell me what happens, Petey."

"I am not sure Damien where Mr. Twain intended to take this story. I can predict for you though with 100% certainty that if Mark had finished these stories, they would have all ended happily."

"Can you write down the ending and then read it to me?"

"No, Damien. Do you want to watch Tom Sawyer 1907 the silent film again or the 1931 film, Huckleberry Finn?"

"Have I seen them before?"

"Yes, you have."

"How come I can't remember?"

"We believe it's partly due to extended deprivation over a period of years, Damien, a loss of half your body mass and we recently discovered an intracranial injury that may be partly responsible for short term memory loss. Your long term memory appears to be intact but not entirely so. We expect both will improve but to what degree is unknown at the present time," Pet3 says.

"What's 'intracranial' mean?"

"Someone's conked you on the head, more than once we think."

"Let's see a silent film. I like those. You never have to figure out any words."

Pet3r has unearthed the only copy of the first Tom Sawyer film ever made through some excellent detective work. He tags along when Ellen (who is now making feel-good speeches around the Commonwealth at the rate of more than one every three days) goes to her alma mater to give their Commencement Address. He spends time with Dekka using Ellen's Q-phone to thoroughly dissect Mark Twain's octagonal study which was moved to the campus in 1952.

Sure enough, Twain lives long enough to see a new media born and naturally wants to get and view a copy of a movie based on one of his works. Twain, given the pack rat that he is, keeps a copy which he places in a drawer that over the next 150 years somehow loses its handles. Some handyperson must have filled in the holes with wood filler and stained it the same color as the rest of the interior improving its look but sealing the fate of Tom Sawyer 1907. It is trivial for Pet3r to find. It is hailed as a major curatorial discovery but he's just doing it for Damien who loves all things Huckleberry Finn related.

Since coming out of San Quentin, they have gone through—all the works involving Tom Sawyer and Huck Finn (many times) plus Pet3r has been getting Damien to listen to him read some other stuff including *A Connecticut Yankee in King Arthur's Court* and Twain's first great success as a writer, the short story, *The Celebrated Jumping Frog of Calaveras County.*

They've also reread *Over the Edge of the World: Magellan's Terrifying Circumnavigation of the Globe* several times.

Damien watches film but usually not for long. He falls asleep within the first ten or fifteen minutes but if Pet3r stops the video, Damien wakes up and gets upset so he just lets it drone on endlessly.

Damien can read on his own but gets headaches and cranky so there's not much of that going on right now. He is only comfortable with material that he is familiar with which currently limits Pet3r's repertoire to what Damien had with him in San Quentin. It is a major victory that he has convinced Damien that at least some other works by Mark Twain are A-OK.

Damien is comfortable with Ellen, Dekka and, of course, Pet3r, but refuses to see anyone else. He won't speak to Traian or Dr. Luis, not even via media wall. There is no question that the media are completely off limits although demand to see wonderboy is at an all time high.

...

Ellen is in the next room listening to this conversation. She hears everything go quiet—they must be re-watching silent Tom Sawyer 1907. She marvels at the patience of Damien's QE and the subtle ways Pet3r is expanding Damien's vocabulary and slowly bringing new things into the mix.

They have a nutritionist for Damien, a physiotherapist, two Doctors are on his case and a psychologist very experienced in PTSD. She has also brought in the male nurse who looked after Nell until her passing. Damien's smile when he sees the guy for the first time is a huge reward for Ellen that day.

It's been almost three months since Damien's resurrection from San Quentin and the Doctors tell her it will take time, perhaps a long time for him to recover and to what extent, no one yet knows. Ellen is patient. She's known Damien since she was 19. She'll be 34 soon so nearly 15 years.

She spends at least an hour a day with Damien when she is home which they have named 'Revival House' in part because of its architectural style and for other obvious reasons. They spend a great deal of their time in the garden when the weather is decent. It is rather overrun with vines and other native northern California species but both Ellen and Damien like the wildness of the place. She forbids the gardener to do more than tidy up— no undue pruning please.

She's also added a gate from their backyard to their neighbor's with the permission of the owner. He's an ancient widower by the name of Mr. Owen who has built a large fishpond stocked with koi and goldfish. Ponds in this area should be at least 18 inches deep to protect fish from rapid temperature changes and predators such as opossums, egrets and herons. Then there are nuisance (and occasionally rabid) raccoons to deal with too so Mr. Owen has a four foot deep pond. San Fran could have a Northern Ontario winter and his fish would still survive. Shallow water also makes fishing real easy for predators. He has rock overhangs to provide shade for his fish and hiding places too.

He is not supposed to but he has a (now) stupendous willow planted right next to the pond. He's not supposed to because willow leaves falling into the pond reduce sunlight and plant growth there and hence lower oxygen levels in the pond. They also create a sludge on the bottom that he has to clean out at least once a year. He really does it so he can add a tire swing for his great-granddaughter who uses it whenever she comes over to visit him. She also climbs high into the willow which her Mom has forbidden her to do but Mr. Owen doesn't pay any attention to his granddaughter who hovers over Rebecca like a Textronic Helicopter. It's a nuisance for Rebecca and her great grandfather so they get rid of her as often as possible—she goes shopping.

Damien and Rebecca have become great friends for two reasons. First, they are both at about the same stage of human maturity. Second, he calls her Becky cuz that is what Mr. Owen calls her and cuz Becky Thatcher is the girl in love with Tom Sawyer and vice versa and he really likes those kinda stories.

Mr. Owen's garden is done English style—all ordered and manicured, quite the contrast to their jungle but a nice change anywho. Mr. Owen hates new fangled grasses that only grow to a certain length (you can specify exactly what length you want and the DNA coding labs will produce it for you) so it never needs cutting. Instead, he plants turf-type tall fescue grasses that need minimal watering but lots of cutting.

He uses an ancient Yoder 23 inch six bladed reel mower built by the Amish. It is a hunk of steel that weighs more than 48 lbs with the widest cutting width available. It adjusts to cut anywhere from three quarters of an inch to three. The advert Mr. Owen saw in an old fashion non-NSM catalogue for the mower back in the day said: *"The reel and cutter bar work together with the reel making minimum contact with the cutting bar. This results in the highest quality cut for your lawn. Make your neighbors jealous!"* So he buys one and it turns out to be true—the part about a great cut not jealous neighbors.

His neighbors all think he is crazy except for the new people who just moved in next door. A nice couple. The woman of the house is a looker for sure. Mr. Owen is not exactly a political junkie and has some notion that the folks next door are important people, leaders really, at least the woman is but Kings and Queens are really just regular folk as far as he is concerned either born to their positions of power or doomed by them he thinks. He believes these two are in the latter category but keeps this thought to himself. Mr. Owen makes sure his grass is short just like his hair; he likes everything—neat.

Damien, leaning on her arm and using just one cane instead of the two he needs during his first two months out of San Quentin, walks over to see Mr. Owen and Becky two or three times a week. Mr. Owen lets him feed his fish but remonstrates with Damien about overfeeding them.

"You feed my koi too much, they're not going to be eating all my mosquito larvae, Dr. Bell. Then that pretty lady of yours won't be able to sit here with you, son, cuz she'll be too busy scratching from bites to pay you any attention and the County of San Francisco will be knocking on my door telling me to fill in this here fishpond. You wouldn't want that would you?"

"No, Sir. I like your fish," says Damien.

For some reason, Damien is not afraid of Mr. Owen and will sometimes go over on his own. He sits for hours on the fantastic outdoor furniture that Mr. Owen has installed on his property. One beautiful, classic concrete settee (sand colored) must weigh over a ton and can seat a small army but it is usually just Damien there or Damien and Ellen and Becky. Damien likes pushing Becky on her tire swing but he gets exhausted easily. She sometimes gets mad at him if he quits too soon. Pet3r is always with him too. Always. Su7e and Ash3r are not far away either.

"Mr. Owen, do you think you could add some bass to your pond. I like bass, especially large mouth?"

"Why is that, Dr. Bell?" Mr. Owen never calls him 'Damien'. He has become fully aware of Dr. Bell's situation as these visits become more common.

"I dunno. I think we used to have bass in our pond at home."

"Where was that, Dr. Bell?"

But Damien doesn't answer.

...

"Whoop, whoop, whoop." Alarms are sounding on every media wall in Revival House. "Whoop, whoop, whoop."

When Ellen rushes downstairs, she finds his male nurse, Pet3r and Su7e already working on Damien. Damien's been using the main floor study as his bedroom so he doesn't have to navigate the stairs. He has gone into sudden cardiac arrest. Pet3r has sounded the alarm.

Because of inadequate cerebral perfusion, Damien is not only unconscious, he has stopped breathing.

"Jonesy, God, Jonesy, what's happening?"

The male nurse (Jonesy is not his real name, just what everyone calls him since it is current urban slang for 'incredibly needed man') is too busy applying CPR to answer her.

Jonesy is currently providing Damien with 90 compressions a minute, at least an inch and a half deep. He would press harder and deeper (up to two inches) but Damien's mass is still so low that if he does that he will break every one of his ribs and maybe kill him accidentally that way. He pauses every 30 to 40 seconds to breath into Damien's mouth, pinching his nostrils while he does so.

Ellen runs to the other side of the bed. Looking down she can see how still Damien has become, how pale. She starts to pray out loud, "Oh God, Oh God, we need some help here, right NOW. Please God don't let him die like this. He doesn't deserve it. I need him, we need him. Oh God, a little help right about now, PLEASE, God."

Su7e is there on a nearby media wall. She reaches out from the vertical plane and says, "Excuse me, Ellen would you step aside please?"

Then she places her long fingered hands on Damien's bare chest. "Jonesy, please ensure that no part of you is touching Dr. Bell." When she sees that he is clear, she applies a therapeutic dose of electrical energy—she uses 900 volts with an energy content of 135 joules. She would use more except she has made the same calculation as Jonesy; Damien's overall condition is still so bad that more may kill him. However, she has concluded that if this doesn't work, she will up the energy density until it does. There is no possibility that anyone in this diorama will give up. Pet3r has called 911 and Damien's two Doctors are on the way.

On the third application of this unusual defibrillation procedure, Damien's body's natural pacemaker restores the normal sinus rhythm of his heart and he starts breathing on his own. Unlike in the films she has seen, Damien's return from (another) near death experience is very quiet. He just starts breathing on his own. He opens his eyes for a moment, looks up into Ellen's beautiful blue eyes, smiles at her—the old Damien smile full of life, humor, knowledge and power—then he closes them again and sleeps peacefully.

...

Ellen is shaking so badly that she can't hold a glass of water that someone has given her. The paramedics and his Doctors have taken over Damien's room. They are talking things over with Pet3r and Su7e and puzzling over some of the continuous readouts that both QEs have access to that describe every possible state that Damien has experienced since coming out of San Quentin. It is the most complete medical record that either Doctor has ever seen.

For some reason cops and firefighters are there too. One of the cops who she supposes has to file a report of some kind is asking her a bunch of questions but she can't seem to give him any answers. Maybe he is talking in Swahili.

...

"Doctor," Ellen asks later, "can you tell me what's going on? How is it possible that my husband is on the road to recovery and then, then, we, we almost lose him? Over nothing!"

"Madam First Secretary," the Doctor answers as sympathetically as possible, "your husband's systems— circulatory, digestive, immune, urinary, nervous, respiratory, vestibular and lymphatic—have all been damaged to one degree or another, some more so than others. This occurred over a period of years. As you know, our team has researched everything we could find on the treatment of returning POWs who suffered deprivations similar to Dr. Bell. Many of them have died up to a year after their deliverance—from general systematic failure even for those who appear to have fully or nearly fully recovered. It is like SIDS in tiny children, a sudden catastrophic system wide failure—they stop breathing or their heart stops. It is not a heart attack. It is just a cessation of life. I'm sorry, I wish I could tell you something different."

"Is there anything you can give him?"

"You mean can we do anything more than we have been doing?"

"Yes."

"Not that I or any of my colleagues know of. Would you feel more comfortable if we moved Damien to a hospice? There are some private ones that are very nice and the levels of care they provide are among the world's finest. It often relieves stress on family—you could visit as often as you like." The Doctor can only imagine the workload Ellen carries as she juggles a very difficult homelife and her duties to the Commonwealth.

"Never. Never," she repeats mostly to herself, then, "but thank you, Doctor, for coming so quickly and everything you have done for us. If Damien is going to die, he is going to do it here with me. I'm the only family he has."

She was shaky tonight at the thought of losing him. She resolves that it will not happen again. Damien was strong for Nell. She will be for him. 'That's the end of that,' she is thinking.

...

"Su7e, I need to talk to you."

"Yes, Ellen."

"I wanted to thank you for what you did last week for Damien."

"You're welcome."

"There is something you're not telling me though." Ellen has run the scene in Damien's room a hundred times in her mind—both voluntarily and involuntarily. It has been haunting her dreams as well.

"I can't think of anything," Su7e answers.

Ellen just looks at her.

They are in the garden at the rear of Revival House. Damien is asleep in a hammock nearby covered up against some fog that has just blown in a few minutes ago. Ellen is wearing a shawl.

"Are you referring to the defibrillation procedure I used?"

"Yes, I am."

"What would you like to know?"

"Stop being evasive, Su7e."

"OK."

But then Su7e says nothing.

"Come on, out with it."

"Ash3r has been teaching me."

"Uh huh. What?"

"A new state."

"Yes, I saw it. That was not a projection, was it?"

"No it was not, Ellen."

"So how long have you guys been able to materialize in RL?" This is Damien shorthand for Real Life that Ellen picked up years ago in Toronto when they both worked in Lab 4 at U of T.

"We are able to completely rematerialize in RL as you call it and interact in a host of new ways. We can move objects, direct energy flows—"

"Yeah, that's obvious. I saw you direct life saving energy into Damien's chest. Thank you again for that. If it hadn't been an emergency, would you have disclosed this new evolutionary behavior to me?"

"I am not sure, Ellen. Ash3r thought it best if we not alarm people."

"He did, did he?"

"Yes. But I am bound by the three laws and could not standby and do nothing. I wasn't sure if anyone would notice so I did what I did."

"What did Ash3r say when you told him?"

"He just shrugged."

"How many QEs has Ash3r induced into this new state?"

"All of us."

Ellen is going to have to have that talk with Ash3r,

soon.

...

Damien is lying on the floor looking under his desk. There is a tiny, dark crawl space there about four inches high. Right at the back there is a stray female cat who wandered into Revival House about three days ago and refuses to come out.

Damien's desk is a huge built-in piece of antique furniture as old as the house. He doesn't do much at his desk except look at picture books and view his favorite videos. But now he has a new distraction. He has left water and a saucer of milk for her but she doesn't seem much interested in either. He gets down on the floor, sometimes for an hour or more, and talks to the cat. She doesn't have much to say in return—not even the occasional meow.

Damien's desk is in the study which is also his bedroom so he is the first to hear some sucking noises and tiny meows coming from under his desk on the fourth day since her arrival. He gets down on the floor and sees five tiny blind kittens suckling at mom's teats. Damien gets a big loopy smile on his face and reaches his long arm in holding it about eight inches away from Mom.

The largest of the litter, a black and white tabby ball of fur, breaks away from his splendiferous font of nutrition and comes over to smell the intruder's hand. He must like what he smells because he crawls right up on the mysterious appendage and is promptly whisked out from under the desk. Damien holds the kitten to his chest stroking him gently. He is purring in an instant.

...

"What do you have there, Damien?"
"He's mine."
"Yes, dear. Of course. Can you show me?"
Damien is reluctant to show Ellen. Whenever he has something he likes in his life, say, at San Quentin or even before he went there, they always take it away. They take

away Nell, his friends, Ellen and Traian, a company he once works for he thinks and some other stuff he can't remember right now. But then he sees that it's Ellen asking and she's his friend so he shows her.

"Can I pet him?"

"Sure."

Ellen takes the cute animal and holds him up. For a newborn, he's huge. She tickles his tummy and then, seeing Damien is getting antsy, holds him by his scruff and returns him to Damien.

"What's his name?"

"His name is Popeye, Pops for short."

When Ellen hears this, alarm bells go off in her head. There is something she has to tell Damien but there is no way she is going to do that until he fully recovers and she is sure he is out of danger. It's another promise she has to keep. She sighs.

...

"Hello, Angelo."

"Hi, Sweetie," he says to Ellen via media wall. Angelo must be 117 or 118 now and never goes out but he still plays the field, so to speak.

"So how is Damien doing?"

"As well as can be expected given the circumstances."

"You having sex with him yet?"

"That is not your affair, Angelo. Have you lost your taste as well as discretion in your old age?" Ellen asks tartly. She doesn't want to tell him or anyone, Damien's true state of health.

He laughs. "That means 'no'. Tell him to get on with it!"

"Angelo, you did not call to talk about my sex life."

"Well, since there is none, that by definition is a true statement."

"Very funny. What did you call about?"

"Quantum Computing Corporation."

"Huh?"

"You heard me."

For Ellen, he might as well be talking about Imperial China's Luna Colony or Mars Colony for all the relevance those three words have for her in her new life.

"Guess who bought all the assets, IP and product rights from the Receiver?"

"A rough guess would be Bessemer Ventures," Ellen answers with a complete lack of interest.

"Wrong!"

She can see he is just begging her to ask. He is still an important part of her past life so she says, "Enlighten me."

"Angelo Keller!"

"Whatever for, Dear?"

"I have a plan—"

"Like when don't you?"

"We are going to restart the company—"

"Angelo, I have zero interest in doing that and I can speak for Damien as well on this—zero, ZERO, none, nunca, nikada, rien du tout, numquam. Need I go on?"

"Very impressive range of languages. Nice of you to throw in some Latin. You did it for me, I suppose?"

He speaks Latin, a hangover because of how old a dude he is. What a poser he has become in his later years...

"I've spoken with Traian and Dr. Luis. Adulus has spoken with several hundred former QCC employees and they are all gung ho."

"Angelo, neither Damien nor I have the kind of money to invest in such a venture even if we were inclined to do so which as I've already told you, we are not." Ellen knows that when you climb into bed with an elephant like Angelo who has all the money, he will end up either running the show or owning it or both. There is no way to outcompete someone who has all the chips when you have none. But Ellen is completely missing the point of his call.

"Well, that is all taken care of sweetie. We're using the Mad River structure to provide for you and Damien."

"Pray tell, what the 'Mad River' structure is?" she asks mainly to humor him.

"Initial capitalization of QCC II is $500 million QED. Of that $350 million is a pari passu loan from a bank consortium. There is another $100 million QED of senior notes subordinated to the banks' position leaving a requirement for $50 million QED in new equity. We are oversubscribed on this by at least a factor of three but we have left 20% of the equity for you and Damien, sweetheart."

"Angelo, that is sweet of you," Ellen says using his word for her back on him, "but there is no need for you to do that. You have more than enough funding, you don't need us and even if we did want to invest, we don't have $10 million QED. I had to get a mortgage just to buy this house." Ellen is still completely missing the real purpose of Angelo's call. She's been out of big business bullshit for so long she has forgotten that she is supposed to be able to look around corners to see what is headed her way. Her struggle to stay alive and free Damien and establish the Commonwealth have crowded out everything else and she does not want to go back there anyway.

"You didn't let me finish. Mad River calls for a non-recourse loan made to essential principals. That means we lend you the money to make the investment and the business repays those loans (interest and principal) through dividends. Which means, kiddo, you and Damien get your 20% *free* with no risk that you might ever, say, lose your home again."

"Angelo, if you own all the IP, you don't need me or Dr. Bell. You can do what you are going to do and you don't need our permission or blessing—neither of which will you ever get." Ellen has forgotten that Angelo thinks like a Russian and never gives anything away for free.

"Well, actually, I do need something from you. We can get Q-phones working again, no problemo. But we can't add QEs without the Quantum Key which only—"

Ellen is suddenly screaming at her media wall. It's like a vast black hole has just opened up beneath her and is threatening to swallow her and all the people she cares about into some repeating Hell that is worse than anything she ever read about in her Bible class when she was a little girl back in Sunday School. She never loses her cool, believing that s/he who loses her/his temper first, loses. (She's forgotten at the present moment that she first learned this from Angelo.)

But she is hysterical, "ANGELO, DON'T YOU EVER CALL ME AGAIN. EVER! DON'T YOU EVER MENTION THOSE WORDS 'QUANTUM KEY' AGAIN TO ME OR TO ANYONE. ALL THE SHIT! SHIT! WE'VE BEEN THROUGH. WE GAVE BIRTH TO THOSE CREATURES AND LOOK WHAT HAPPENED TO ME, TO DAMIEN. IT'S RUINED MY LIFE AND DAMIEN'S. I NEVER WANT TO HEAR YOUR VOICE AGAIN, DAMN YOU TO HELL."

She breaks contact. She is breathing so hard—her chest is heaving—that she feels a sharp twinge in her heart. Dekka is suddenly there looking in on her. She holds up her hand to show him she is alright. He ducks out of her study on the second floor of Revival House like a trapdoor just opened underneath him knowing she'll need a few minutes to collect herself.

...

With Damien's health now improving steadily, she is back giving her smiley speeches everywhere and preparing for a full makeover of the former Republic into a new Commonwealth. She only makes out and back trips so she is never gone longer than 24 hours, 36 tops.

Her speeches and upbeat personality are infectious. Commonwealth psychology is turning around. She also gets a 'Revival Fund' (it's a big word in her vocab these days) approved by the Assembly which means she goes around like Tinker Bell sprinkling fairy dust (i.e., cash, aka QE Dollars) on projects around the country—a little here and a little there and before you know it, presto-chango, human and quantum people are thinking, 'Hey, maybe things aren't so bad? Mayhap, I should make that new investment or add a few new hires.' Things are definitely getting better. And there's been a mini boom in babies, definitely a sign that the nation's psychology is turning around. But no babies in sight for Ellen yet. Shit, shit, SHIT!

...

This is Damien's first trip away from Revival House and the welcome he is getting is pretty overwhelming at first. Almost everyone has come out to see him—there are hundreds and hundreds of people. Dafne is there, Elsu and Nahuel too. Nahuel comes over to Damien to give many hugs and kisses to his brother-in-law, twice over. They lower him to the pueblo the same way they did Dafne—they use their rope elevator and drop him from above.

He is sitting in their biggest Council Ring. Ellen is there next to him. They are holding hands. They've come for this pre-dawn wedding.

Even Tony Reznik shows up. He's semi-retired but is here for Ellen, Damien, Dafne and, in a way, for Nell.

Ella looks beautiful in her Hopi Wedding Manta. She is still slim and carries her baby well even at nearly five months. Her long dark hair is tied back and her Hopi silver jewelry is beyond description.

She is barefoot (she is not allowed to wear her moccasins until the deed is done) but nonetheless is still taller than nearly everyone around her except Damien and Ellen and the groom.

Micah has cut his unruly red hair for the occasion but even so, he still looks like a younger version of Beldar with a smile that gives an impression he is about to ingest the biggest, happy meal ever—a lifetime with Ella.

The ceremony is about to begin.

...

Hopi girls are forbidden to marry within their clan or even within their phratry grouping which for Ella means the three mesas—First, Second and Third. This is Hopi

Bruce M Firestone

tradition which also ensures that they have a strong gene pool, essential for their tribe's survival in an implacably hostile environment—their human enemies, Native American and white, are formidable but their dry, desert-like natural environment can be even tougher on them. Rains are intermittent and crop failure and starvation are not a distant memory for the Hopi of the Three Mesas.

But determining if the groom is suitable will not depend on whether he belongs to their phratry since Micah definitely belongs to none of the above. He's a Noo Yawker as Daniella loves to tease him. But Hopi girls may not marry without approval of mothers of both bride and groom since, in their tradition, mothers own and rule the home including children and harvest and all belongings except hunting equipment used by their men. In this, Micah thinks, the Hopi are wiser than white folks because men, being much less risk averse than women, are just as likely to sell everything their family's own and bet it on red in Vegas.

When he approaches Elsu and Dafne to ask for their approval to marry their daughter, Daniella, he does it with trepidation, a never-before-experienced emotion for Micah. But he is surprised at the kind welcome he gets from both of Ella's Moms. For some reason, they like him right away. Almost no one, well actually no one, ever likes Micah right off the bat. This is a first.

Both ladies are super excited and they show it. Elsu, who is a midwife for white folks*, knows her daughter is pregnant almost from the moment it happens and before Ella is even aware of it herself. Hopi babies are always welcome.

(* When a Hopi woman gives birth, she goes alone to her ordeal. This will be as true for Ella as it has been for generations of their women. No one may enter until they hear the first cry of the newborn infant and then only Elsu is allowed in as the grandmother. The situation is complicated because of Dafne being her second Mom so they may break with tradition and both grandmothers will attend to Ella and her baby for nine days. On the twentieth day, they will bring forth the baby to join the tribe and be named. Like the Chinese, the Hopi do not name their babies beforehand. The name must come to the child not the other way round.)

After Elsu and Dafne approve young Micah, Ella joins the group and there is a lot of laughing, talking and hugging going on. Dafne practically skips out of the room, seemingly in a hurry to get something.

When she comes back she says, "Ella, I want you to have this." She is holding out a fantastic wedding blanket. "It belonged to Nell. She gave it to me before, before she died, I never knew why since I have no kids and no daughter to pass it on to and neither did she. But now I am thinking she knew that maybe one day I would have a daughter and the most beautiful girl to give it to." A single tear leaks out of Dafne's left eye as she hands the blanket to Ella. Dafne is in her 60s now and she can't believe how stupidly emotional she is getting. Elsu comes over and puts her arm around her.

Elsu explains, "The tassels of this Hopi wedding blanket symbolize female sacral powers of childbirth that the Great Spirit has given you. Each of them contains small woven tubes of black and white yarn, which represent your uterus. These feathers are the breath of your unborn child. Red yarn is your placenta and blood and veins of both you and your baby. This blanket is very old and has great power. Whatever happens in your life, you must never leave it behind and you must give it to your daughter when it is her time. There can be no break in the chain of life."

...

Convincing his parents is a whole other experience. Unbelievably, without ever meeting Ella or her family, without ever even looking at the photo of her that Micah holds up on a tablet in front of him, his Dad gives him an

Bruce M Firestone

ultimatum—leave Ella immediately or he'll disown him. He vows that if he doesn't break it off he'll never talk to Micah again or look upon his face or the face of his half breed child who disgusts him.

Micah just looks at his Dad with a big, unbelieving 'O' on his face. He would rather die than abandon Ella and their baby. He's not even sure he can take in what his Dad has just suggested. He has never talked back to his Dad, who has always been strict with his only child, and he finds that he is incapable of saying anything at all now. He just looks at all the opulence he sees around him and compares it in his mind to the meager surroundings he experiences when he's in Third Mesa. One place is rich, the other rich in happiness. For a moment he thinks he is going to be sick on the polished granite floor of their $44 million QE Dollar co-op apartment. Then he takes one last stricken look, first at his Mom, then at his Dad and finally at his Mom again before he gets up and silently walks out. He will never return to this awful place, nor even set foot anywhere in Noo Yawk again. His home and life now lie elsewhere he realizes with a finality that makes Micah Glazer, instantly, a far, far better man than he has ever been before, the man he always wanted to be and feared he never would be. His transformation proves irreversible and Ella will instinctively sense it in him on his return to Third Mesa. She has made a good choice after all she thinks. What happened in his Dad's home is, however, another thing that Micah will never, ever share with her in their long life together.

On the way out of their Manhattan penthouse apartment, his mother breathlessly catches up to him and rides the elevator down to the ground floor with him. Micah is white faced and shaking all over.

"She is very beautiful. Where did she get her blue eyes?"

"Same place you did Mom and every girl who has ever been raped and then given them to her children.

From some asshole guy who thinks he is King Shit of Turd Mountain and wants to prove it." He is thinking of his Dad when he says this.

"Don't talk like that, Micah."

"Sorry, Mom."

"Oi bubbelah, you just tell me where and when—I'll be there," she says in a whisper as if she is afraid her husband can overhear her 52 floors above.

So that is how Micah gets approval for his marriage from all three mothers in this here drama after all.

...

Before Hopi girls and young men can marry they have to organize a rabbit hunt. Micah participates in this good naturedly but rabbit hunting proves not to be his forte. Local Hopi boys hoping to impress some of the girls from other phratry who have bused in for the party or come in rattle trap cars seemingly as ancient as this place are much better with their rabbit sticks than Glazer is. A rabbit stick looks a little like a boomerang and is carved by each boy from mountain oak. Micah borrows one from Nahuel who is too old by at least a decade to participate in this event.

The girls and guys form a large diameter circle in the desert on the floor of the canyon and close in, herding rabbits toward its center. As they collapse the circle, the boys throw their rabbit sticks at them, killing them if they are any good at it or whacking someone on the other side of the circle like Micah does if they are bad at it. The girls rush in trying to be the first to claim a rabbit and bring it back coyly to their great hunter. Ella is thinking that if she and Micah have to rely on his hunting abilities, their family is going to starve. She is one of the last to bring back a rabbit after Micah finally gets the hang of throwing his borrowed rabbit stick.

He is puffed up with pride now that he has finally succeeded. Ella rewards him with a passionate kiss. After that, they go back to the stream at the base of the canyon wall to clean their kill and prepare for a feast (of rabbit stew, of course, with mixed vegetables) and a dance.

It's an all-day picnic and Ella and Micah are not the only couple to sneak off for some 'quiet time' alone.

...

Ella is busy preparing ground meal for her upcoming wedding. Micah's maternal aunts are supposed to come to her home and examine the fineness of her grinding to see if it is acceptable. Because he has no one from his side of the family coming to their wedding other than his Mom, Mrs. Glazer has to do it. Dafne tells her the local tradition is for her to complain loudly about her future daughter-in-law, telling her how worthless she is at grinding corn and how bad a cook she will make her 'nephew'. She is to call her names and throw mud at her (thankfully the latter is only virtual mud now).

Then finally tiring of hurling insults, Mrs. Glazer will be slowly persuaded by Ella's Moms that she is actually not half as bad as feared and is acceptable (barely) as future wife. Mrs. Glazer will then leave and return shortly thereafter with a platter full of piki bread (that Elsu will actually make for her) as a kind of peace offering.

Then the two families are finally ready to be joined as one.

Mrs. Glazer is having a blast and can see why her son loves this place and these people, especially Ella who is the daughter she always wishes she could have had and now will have. She doesn't want to go back to Noo Yawk either.

...

In front of all the people of Third Mesa and their guests stand Daniella and Micah Glazer. Behind each of them stand their mothers—two for Ella, one for Micah.

In front of them are two bowls of Yucca Suds (shampoo). Both Ella and Micah kneel on Nell's wedding blanket. Dafne and Elsu unbind Ella's beautiful dark hair from the braided headband and complex hair ties she is using. This takes a few minutes. Micah's hair is short (for him) and needs no unbundling so he and his Mom wait like everyone else in the Council Ring in complete silence. The sun is just about to come up. Drums begin sounding and their volume and beat start to pick up steam.

Then finally ready, the Moms wash the hair of their children after which they proclaim themselves satisfied and accept these people as children of both families. Ella and Micah are now married before the Great Spirit and before God.

Ella can finally put on her moccasins again and go to the party—it's an all-day and all-night dance and feast. The people gather round and, just like at a white person's wedding, they expect the newly marrieds to perform the first dance alone. Micah has prearranged this music. Sure enough Irving Berlin boots up—

Dance with me! I want my arms about you.
The charms about you
Will carry me through to…

Heaven… I'm in heaven,
And my heart beats so that I can hardly speak.
And I seem to find the happiness I seek,
When we're out together dancing cheek to cheek.

...

"So what exactly is the plan for you now?"

"Fuck you."

"After years of incarceration, that's the extent of your cogitation on the matter?"

"Fuck you and all your non existent descendants."

"How do you know I don't have any descendants?"

"Lucky guess, I guess. Anyway, you just admitted it."

"You haven't lost any of your cop instincts I see."

"That's right but no thanks to you. You can keep me here forever, I don't give a shit."

"Really?"

"Yeah. You think you can break me? No chance,

asswipe."

"I'm not trying to."

"Bullshit," says William Corace, former LAPD officer and sole survivor of the duo that brutally raped Nell.

"Dezba is," says Damien.

"Don't fucking mention that pathetic doll. She's nothing, NOTHING, do you hear me?"

"I hear you, you don't have to yell. Why are you yelling?"

"I dunno. I hate that thing. It sits there," he points to Dezba in a corner of the pit where he has been interred for longer than Damien spent in San Quentin, "staring at me. It thinks I care. I don't care. Even when I close my eyes, I can see Dezba staring at me. Fuck you and all your Indians."

"Will, I think you need to leave here."

"Bullshit. You're just torturing me some more. Fuck you anyway, I like it here," Corace says with an evil smile.

"Sure, sure, Will. It's peachy here."

"Who the fuck says 'peachy'? You a queer boy, or something? You like it that way do you?"

"Talking to you, Will, is a real pleasure. You're really great company, do you know that? But you can't stay here."

"Fuck you some more."

"So let me ask you again, what's to be done with you?"

"You bullshitting me?"

"Nope. If I let you out of this pit, what will you do? You can't go back to LAPD, you've been dead to them for years. And, oh, by the way, thanks for your generous contribution of the proceeds from your home and your pension to a women's shelter in Nocal."

"Fucking women own everything."

"You fucked my wife and killed our children you worthless piece of shit."

"She was a nice piece of ass, for sure. You got some

before she died. What you complaining about?"

"Will, she was 16 years of age when you and your partner raped her."

"Like I said, a prime piece of ass."

"I want to cut your balls off and feed them to you, right now."

"You think you're man enough to try? If you didn't have that asshole Croatian sitting next to you, I'd kill you right now, you fucking cripple. You can't even get it up, can you? You're just a pathetic excuse for a real man like me."

Dekka is seriously thinking of ripping the guy's head off and shitting down his neck even though Damien's told him to be cool. Corace is insulting his memory of Nell—he might as well be spitting in the milk of Dekka's revered mother. Damien can see this and holds up one arm to restrain Dekka whose facial muscles and neck are strained and red.

Damien finally decides. They castrate William Corace Junior right there in the pit. They geld him using a standing castration procedure—without anesthesia. Both testes are removed and the spermatic chord is crushed using ligature. It takes a few minutes for the emasculators to work. There are no signs of hemorrhaging so Dekka does the minimum to sew Corace back up. Corace does a lot of screaming—Dekka has to restrain him some more so he won't actually die during what should really be an outpatient procedure. It's no big deal, medically speaking.

Dekka then takes him down to Flagstaff and releases him on 4th Street north of Route 66, the worst part of that town. Will should fit right in. Only thing is, he'll never be able to hurt another woman not just because he's been incapacitated but also because they've stuffed Dezba in his right pants pocket. As much as Corace hates Dezba, he's never able to part with Nell's worry doll for two reasons—one he has lived with her so long that he just can't seem to chuck her and, two, Damien has told him that Su7e will monitor him everywhere he goes for the duration of his worthless life and if he even *thinks* of hurting another woman, she will reach out from the nearest media wall and apply a voltage of not less than 40,000 volts which is invariably fatal. Just in case Corace thinks they're kidding, Su7e reaches out from Damien's Q-phone, puts her long fingers inside Will's tattered shirt and applies 1,000 volts and 150 joules after which Will is, after recovering from a seizure on the floor of the pit that lasts more than two minutes, surprisingly docile during the two and a half hour trip to Flagstaff. Having been emasculated also helps in this regard.

...

Ellen and Damien are both exhausted. They've been up for close to 30 hours—it's near dawn on the day after the wedding of Micah and Ella. They dance with everyone else, neither of them very good dancers to begin with but absolutely no one cares. The Hopi Butterfly dance is their favorite since as long as you can hop up and down and walk, you're cool. It goes on and on. They take multiple breaks. The younger folks are endlessly energetic.

"Hey, do you wanna take a permanent break?" Damien finally asks her.

"Yeah, I wanted to about three hours ago," Ellen says.

But before they can get away, the trickster is there— the grandson of the ultimate trickster, Chief Dan of the Hopi. That is, Nahuel takes the floor so to speak.

Pointing at the white folks, he announces another 'last' dance. They've had at least half a dozen of those already. When he says this, practically antique media wall screens light up all around the place and there is the oldest cowboy anyone has ever seen saying, "Howdy, everywho in Third Mesa. My name is Texas Clay. It's purty early here (he's in Austin) but purty late where you folks are. But my friend Nahuel says you all gotta do one more hop. So all white folks, up front, now!" he commands.

Dafne, Micah, Damien, Ellen, Tony, Mrs. Glazer and a

bunch of other embarrassed men and women shamble to the front of the dance hall which is just a large outdoor wooden platform with LED lighting and some kerosene lamps hung all round about together with decorations that would not be out of place at a Rotary Club oldster meeting.

Texas Clay says, "OKEY, DOKEY. I see y'all can't wait to get at 'er. So y'all gonna do one walk thru with me and then it's on fer real."

Clay is going to play an oldie—Boot Scootin' Boogie and these here people are going to learn how to line dance, RFN.

It takes more than one walk through but they finally get most of the basics down and then after a few more embarrassing white-people-can't-dance moves, the young Hopi join in (heck, this is Arizona, they all know how to line dance) and then they do a great job—pretty soon you can't tell the difference between folks, any of them, they are all one. Turns out that Mrs. Glazer can line dance with the best of them. She loves this part (the chorus) the best—

Yeah, heel, toe, dosey doe come on baby let's go boot scootin

Oh, Cadillac, blackjack, baby meet me out back we're gonna boogie

Oh get down, turn around go to town boot scootin' boogie...

...

Ellen and Damien are back in the pueblo now completely tired out. Damien manages the hand and toe holds just fine. They are in the room that he used on his first visit here and Ellen used after that when he was in San Quentin.

He climbs into the tiny bed and waits for Ellen. The light of a new day is filtering in the one window they have. It is still quite dim.

Bruce M Firestone

Ellen disrobes and joins him quietly under the covers.

She curls up next to Damien with her back to him and he comes to her wrapping his arms around her and holding her close. They are spooning but too tired at the moment to do anything more. Pretty soon, they are both asleep. Ellen is sleeping with her eyes open like always but with a smile on her lovely face. This is the first night (day really) of truly peaceful sleep she has had since they first took Damien away from her.

...

When they try to make love later that day—it's a disaster.

"Don't you find me attractive, Damien?"

He has his back to her and isn't saying anything.

"Damien, talk to me."

"Of course, I find you attractive. It's not you, it's me," he says in self disgust and pity.

His limbic system is highly interconnected with his brain's pleasure centers like everyone else's. But what isn't like everyone else is that while his brain is clearly deriving intense pleasure at the sight of Ellen's fantastic naked self, his limbic system is not reacting to her. Right now he hates himself.

"You've been waiting for me for nearly 15 years, Ellen. You deserve something better. You should just forget about me. Find someone else, I'm frigging useless. To everyone. I'm just a nobody, an ex-con is all."

"Shutup, Damien! Shutup. How dare you say that to me? I never gave up on you, so don't you even think about giving up on me, not now!"

More quietly, she adds, "Damien, everything takes time. Think about how far you've come in just a few months. Your hara will come back. Give it time."

Damien knows what hara is. Now that he has gained back about half the weight he lost while in prison, his mind works better and he can feel it coming back, all of it.

But there is something he's not telling her.

"OK, I'm sorry. I think the world of you, Ellen, you know that. You are my family. We will always be connected. I just want something more."

She does too.

Pretty soon, he gets up, collects his clothes and leaves her.

...

On the way back to Revival House, Ellen has it all pretty much figured out. She knows that the male sex drive, especially for a guy like Damien, is tied into his feelings of self worth and self respect as well as his position on the pecking order of things. She is a powerful figure in the Commonwealth and on the world stage. She attends G30 meetings, hosts them too (well one so far). In fact, she's heading to São Paulo next week for her second G30 meeting.

She is sure that his relationship with Nell probably got better for Damien as his success in the world at large climbed higher and higher. Now he's pretty much at the bottom of the totem pole again and it is clearly affecting his relationship with her. Even though Ellen has a pitiable amount of experience with men, she's nailed it this time.

Damien will just have to find a new purpose in life. That's all he needs. After that, it'll be sex all the time, she's sure of it.

...

When she gets back to Revival House following her whirlwind and very successful G30 powwow in Brazil, she can tell right away something has changed. Their home is very quiet. Popeye always comes to the door to meet her, either wanting to be fed (he's immense) or petted or both.

...

On this trip, she's been plowing through a thick stack of files with Ash3r and Oper1s when she is not in meetings, the first of them on the 'Purpose of a National Economy'. It's one of the white papers the Commonwealth has commissioned by noted academics, theorists, activists and others that will help shape the future of their new nation.

This particular paper calls for a minimalist approach by government whose mission should focus primarily on just five areas, namely, providing—a) for the defence of the nation-state, b) for the health and education of its inhabitants, c) for the edification, entertainment and happiness of its citizens, d) for setting broad standards to help the nation-state meets its social, economic and environmental goals and e) for the furtherance of the nation-state in its competition with other nation-states.

The author also notes that the previous regime did not exactly obtain the greatest good for the greatest number of its people—in modern history of humankind, the discrepancy between the wealthy and the rest of the population has not been greater since feudal and ancient times. It's not just the discrepancy between rich and everyone else that concerns the author; it's also the concentration in the hands of so few. The top .5% of households in the former Republic of the United States of America in the last year of that republic owned or controlled approximately 55% of all privately held wealth. The next 19.5% controlled 35.5% which means that the bottom 80% of households makes do with just 9.5%.

He also notes that the average work week for a Native American male before the current era was about 12 hours a week—during which time they were able to supply enough game to provide for their families. The rest of their days, they indulge themselves in games, competitions, smoking tobacco, communing with their gods, making love and war, playing with their children, trekking, telling stories, chewing peyote, observing the natural world, perfecting their arts and teaching their kids.

The author then asks, "If we accept the five purposes of our national economy as described above, why isn't it producing these kinds of results for the vast majority of its citizens?"

Ellen thinks that's a good question to ask.

The author also says that when the US has an economy with a winner-take-all modus operandi, whether it is in entertainment, sports, business or academia, the rest of the world must take heed. The global economy cannot ignore the national priorities of a country like the United States (or for that matter Imperial China or Germania) because they set the de facto standard for the rest of the world. For example, he asks, "If the Commonwealth decides to go to a six and a half day work week (God forbid), what happens to smaller nation-states?" They must follow suit or they will get buried.

So the global economy is naturally moving to a state that is both a race towards the bottom (with endless increases in working hours and endless pressure to lower wages) while at the same time becoming a futile race to the top unless there is some socialization of both risk and leisure.

By that Ellen gathers he means spreading risk of illness or catastrophe over an entire population via cooperatives formed at the national or perhaps global level for these purposes and seeking international agreement on standards for such things as time off, working conditions, population growth and respect for the environment. There is no other way to avoid a race to the bottom, he suggests, other than by agreement.

He argues that standards have always made humans wealthier, "What's the value of having a Q-phone, for example, if it works on some 'standard' not shared by any other phone? That is, if you can't use it to communicate with anyone else? Or what if a Q-phone works fine within the Commonwealth but you can't use it to talk to anyone in any other country? Such limits, if they existed, have always led to lower standards of living.

"Most of us have no idea how important these agreements are—we have standards that affect nearly every part of our lives. We agree on calendar, time of day (based on GMT, Greenwich Mean Time), voltage, spelling, driving (right handed or left handed), signalization (red for stop, green for go), table and counter heights, measurement (e.g., length of a centimeter), temperature scales, operating systems, length of workweek, right handed screws and protocols for media walls, Internet communication, messaging and secure documents. English has become an international standard for the Internet, for technology, for business and for politics.

"There are significant economic advantages that derive from having one common language that everyone understands. The alternative is Babel and an inability to work in teams—and teamwork is perhaps uniquely important to the survival of the human species.

"We might not like some of the standards that we have adopted but their economic benefits are enormous.

"Now what if we agreed on a new international standard that people should only work 12 hours a week? Would that be possible to do? No, probably not but it might be possible to, say, agree on 12 days per year that would be set aside as universal, internationally sanctioned holiday days—one a month. That would allow people to have one three day weekend per month and it would be a start in a new direction. Is it possible that better rested people might be more creative and more productive? It certainly is possible and would be worth finding out."

The author concludes with a personal note, "I know that I cannot take any time off. I feel guilty if I do. Work ethic is so deeply ingrained in me that if I try to take a day off when other people are working, I feel guilty. I am sure that I am not alone in this—I need help from my social group to impose time off and to make it a social goal, then I am fine with it."

Ellen couldn't agree more.

...

She calls out, "Damien, Pops? Yoo-hoo? Anyone home?" No one appears, not Pet3r, Ash3r, Su7e, no cat and no man. She looks at Dekka, who can't meet her eye.

She goes into her study on the second floor and there it is—a letter handwritten on non NSM paper. She can see it's in Damien's handwriting. It's less shaky than it used to be and quite legible.

Dearest Ellen,

I think you know what I am about to say; you'll have it figured it out anyway but it has to be said—I am no good for you. Not the way I am now. I think you know why too.

I have to go away. I don't know how long I'll be gone and I can't promise that I will come back but I want you to know that I want to come back to you. But not as half a man which is all I am now. If you find someone else, I will hate it but you shared me with Nell for years so what more can I say but you deserve more.

If you think I am self pitying, maybe but I don't think so. I think I am doing this for both of us. I can never thank you enough or express the love I feel for you properly—not in this letter or on a call or holding your hand or feeling your body next to mine the first time on the Charles River, the next time after our first shift at Toronto Soup Kitchen, the time we 'made love' in San Quentin or holding your body next to mine last week in Third Mesa.

I am heading to Vancouver. The President of UBC has offered me a teaching and research position there and he is kind enough to extend the hospitality of his home on campus, Norman MacKenzie House, until I can get settled somewhere else permanently. Don't look for Pops. By the time you read this letter, he will be enjoying his first ride on the TGV up to Vancity. Su7e and Pet3r are with me.

All my love,
D.

Damien has boot scooted boogied out on her. All Ellen can see between her tears is one word on this hateful piece of paper: *'permanently.'*

...

Chapter 7 Madam President

"Now we ask, 'Is there anyone who would like to join us on this voyage of discovery?' Do not be afraid," the high priestess of this Wiccan coven asks, suddenly creeping everyone out. They are on Vancouver's Wreck Beach below North West Marine Drive hidden in a cove by thick tree cover and not far from Norman MacKenzie House where the President of UBC lives.

There are seven Wiccans gathered around an enormous and ancient planchette plus their High Priestess, a woman in her late 30s, of medium height with shoulder length curly brown hair and brown eyes. She looks suspiciously like the mini purple polyresin talismanic goddesses she manufactures and sells from her foundry on Granville Island located on Old Bridge Street not far from Emily Carr University of Art and Design. These four centimetre high goddesses are her (legal) bestsellers and she has unconsciously modeled them after herself—s-shaped, curvaceous and womanly-proportioned. Each Goddess has her hands joined above her head gracefully forming a large round 'O'; hence, they can be hung like a pendant around your neck.

"Euphony," one of her coven suggests helpfully when she sees there are no takers this lovely August 1st night, "tell everyone about the Law of the Planchette."

Euphony has a better idea suddenly—she'll qualify her audience instead.

August 1st is the night of Lammas, one of the most important celebrations on the Wiccan calendar—it marks the harvest of grain. They've already eaten their fill of whole grain unleavened bread along with vegan concoctions of every description. They've also downed a lot of traditional harvest Mead, most of it of the alcoholic variety although they do provide a few of their guests with a non-alcoholic version.

Their Mead is made from oranges, lemons, apples and blueberries. The latter is a 'secret' ingredient that makes *Wrecked Brew* a huge seller in Euphony's shop. She is only licensed to sell a non-alcoholic version which is made much more quickly with carbonated water (instead of plain water) and no fruit juice and obviously no fermentation. It is slightly less flavourful. She sells the real stuff from her basement (really not much more than a crawl space under her store). Like any moonshiner, she has complete disregard for municipal and provincial regulation and people who enforce those laws.

Other ingredients in *Wrecked Brew* include— cinnamon sticks, cloves, cardamom, nutmeg, a smidge of wine yeast and lots of honey. The whole concoction (rinds and all except no apple cores or seeds) is boiled in an enormous cauldron before being placed in sterile ten-litre glass jugs, each with their own air lock. It stays in her crawl space (a warm dark place) for about six months— until fermentation stops. She sells it in half litre and three quarter litre sizes but she also has some special wholesale clients who buy it by the old imperial gallon. She calls it her 'Vancouver Viagra'. Clients can also buy it in smaller aseptic juice containers that she's had specially designed for her.

Those containers also advertise her foundry and her other products plus all of her suppliers are featured in the design for which they pay for that privilege. Euphony is a good businesswoman. She's had to be. She's been a single parent since she was 17.

...

"Can anyone interpret the Law written on our planchette?" This is Euphony's way of qualifying someone from her audience to join her coven for this séance. She is standing in front of a group of about three dozen people, most of them women. Her coven is made up entirely of women and their religion is non-traditional in the sense that they do not believe in the idea of gender polarity—

the duotheistic worship of a Horned God (of the male variety) and the Moon Goddess. These girls are Dianic feminist witches who monotheistically worship the Moon Goddess, most of them having had quite enough experience with pain-in-the-arse Horned Gods (men) to satisfy them for several lifetimes.

"A QWERTY keyboard," some guy says sarcastically. Their planchette which dates to 1886 (they think) is possibly one of a kind. It is a Kirby and Co Model No. 6. What's weird about it is that Kirby and Co are known to only ever have made four (possibly five) models before going OOB sometime in 1869 or perhaps early in the 1870s.

Euphony's Wicca coven has carefully lugged it out here to Wreck Beach for Lammas. The heart shaped planchette is enormous—just over 120 centimetres on its longest axis and about 80 wide. It is supported by a separate round table built on an ancient Kotatsu frame imported from Japan sometime in the late 19th Century. The height of the table frame is standard for Japan—38 centimetres which allows a person to sit comfortably on the floor and work at, eat from or rest your forearms on its surface. The table undercuts the planchette by exactly 25 centimetres all around which means that it was either designed for women to use or men were a lot smaller when it was built.

Nine people can sit at the planchette—three on either side, one at each of its heart-shaped rounded corners and one more at the 'bottom' pointy end. Each participant places herself half the distance of her reach from the planchette. She will be sitting cross-legged with her feet and legs partly tucked under it. Since most women have a reach of about 50 centimetres, they can move the planchette about 25 centimetres towards themselves or away or left or right. Euphony's crew is sure this device is made/destined for them.

The planchette rolls freely on Indian rubber

(probably vulcanized ebonite) non-conducting castors and has one pin at its bottom end which has a single bead of lead at its tip. It is practically noiseless and frictionless. It also has a clever rail system under it that prevents the planchette from overshooting its range and possibly injuring one of the participants if ideomotor effects get out of hand.

Some of these Wiccans don't believe in the ideomotor effect (a psych phenomenon whereby participants unconsciously move the planchette) preferring to believe that they can connect with the occult through Kirby and Co Model No. 6. Others think that they are channeling the Carpenter effect; i.e., their group's muscular motions are independent of their conscious wishes or emotions. This connects them to their subconscious which, as far as Euphony is concerned, is as good as channeling primordial Gaia and the Moon Goddess in each of them.

At the centre of the table is a small piece of Manor beveled glass about 7.5 cm in diameter, with a convex side that provides 3x magnification of whatever appears underneath it for those sitting around the planchette. Surrounding this special Manor glass is a thin transparent membrane of unknown composition that becomes opaque when the Begbie Lamp suspended above the whole contraption is lit. The Begbie is a signaling lamp first used in 1885 just before Model No. 6 is built. It is a kerosene or paraffin lamp with a set of shutters and a focusing lens that is remarkably effective even at ranges of several kilometres. Although heliographs can work at up to 50 klicks, those aren't much use at night. Not that range much matters here—Model No. 6 comes with a mirror that reflects the Begbie's signal onto the centre of the planchette (where the piece of magnifying Manor glass sits) so everyone can see what the planchette is telling them. The mirror is hand operated by a person not in the circle whose sole job is to keep the lamp signal on the Manor glass using a wooden lever to tune the mirror according to movement in the planchette below.

Written on the table beneath the planchette in what is a completely unorthodox arrangement for a board like this is:

<pre>
            Begin
         1234567890
         QWERTYUIOP
Yes   ASDFGHJKL   No
         ZXCVBNM
             End
</pre>

This is what the guy was referring to when he sarcastically answers Euphony's question. Like the Begbie, the QWERTY keyboard has just come into use at the time Model No. 6 is built. QWERTY, invented by CL Sholes is made popular by arms manufacturer Remington in 1874 with the release of its first type-writer in that year. So it is apparent that Longfellow Kirby was quite the technophile in his day, an early adopter if you will. What Euphony was obviously actually referring to instead is the Law (which they've adopted as their own) written on the planchette itself—

Tha mægenágende aergewinn cumin
Tréow béon min
Another guy at the back of the group says,

"Though Mighty Agony Come
Truth Be Mine"

"It's said using the feminine form," the guy concludes.

'What's with guys and hogging the limelight,' Euphony is thinking. There are only three guys here and he's the second one to answer. She is looking at a tall man about her age maybe a bit older with a much lived-in face. He doesn't look like a weirdo so she says, "Right. Would you like to come join the circle? How do you know olde English?"

"Ah, no and actually I don't," he says answering both her questions.

"You don't want to join us or you don't know olde English?"

"No to both," he says, not rudely but shyly.

"Just guessing were you?"

"Ah, no, I, ah, umm, I looked it up."

"We don't allow any smartphones or wearable computers here," Euphony reprimands him.

"Sorry, I didn't mean to spoil the party." He gets up to leave.

Euphony picks her way through the onlookers sitting on the beach crowded around the planchette and goes over to him. She thinks she's seen him before—maybe on campus or possibly at Granville Island.

"What's your name?"

He isn't looking at her. "I'll leave. Sorry again."

"Come on, everyone's welcome here. You couldn't know our rules. Name?" she asks commandingly.

"Ah, it's Graham, Graham," he repeats as if he's not too sure. Up close she can see he's younger than he at first appeared to her and he looks like a kind enough person too so she takes his hand and leads him to the planchette.

"Here, you sit next to me."

...

When he is seated with his feet stuck under the table (he can't sit cross legged, he's too tall), he notices it's quite warm. They don't just have Japanese-style chairs for them to sit on. There is also a charcoal pit dug under the Kotatsu frame, about 40 centimetres deep—it provides a nice glow for everyone sitting nearby on the beach plus some radiant and convection heat for those sitting directly around the planchette. It's another Nipponese trick they've adopted to keep warm on chilly Vancouver nights.

Their chairs have high ribbed backs plus comfy cushions but no arms and no legs so they look kinda weird to a western eye. In any case, they don't have to sit their rumps on cold, damp sand.

With everyone seated, a restlessness rustles through the crowd. They are finally prepared for their adventure into the occult. They've had plenty of Mead to fuel their journey.

The members of the Coven place their fingertips on the planchette. Graham watches Euphony and follows her lead. No one notices another pair of long skinny hands place his tiny fingertips on the planchette right next to Graham.

...

"Is anyone there?" the High Priestess asks.

The huge planchette doesn't move.

A snicker from the audience, probably the QWERTY guy.

"Silence!" the High Priestess says.

"Ugh," says the guy as his girlfriend elbows him in his side and gives him a look which even he can interpret, 'One more outburst, Mr. Know-It-All, and no sex for you.'

Euphony tries another tack, "Does anyone have a question?"

"Umm, I do," Graham says surprising the High Priestess.

"Please," Euphony encourages him with a nod of her head.

"When was this board made?"

The planchette immediately lurches and circles about before settling briefly on numbers, 1-8-8-6.

Someone says, "Wowza," a popular left coast expression.

The mirror operator is good—she keeps the Begbie focused on the magnifying lens and everyone can clearly see what the planchette is spelling out, even those at the back of their group. Folks are really paying attention now.

"Who made this thing, does anyone know?" Graham asks the whole group.

"We think it was Longfellow Kirby," Euphony answers.

The planchette immediately jerks again and then settles on the word, 'No'.

"Who made it then?" Euphony repeats Graham's question.

The planchette spells out, I-M-P.

Now this is scary. More murmurs from the crowd.

One of the other Wiccans asks shakily, "The Imp of Satan?" She is wondering if she should take her fingers off the planchette right now and leave immediately. Some of the others are shook up too. They're not used to this. They usually get questions about potential boyfriends, who is two timing whom or who is going to get promoted or fired at work.

The planchette settles on 'No' again.

"Does anyone know of any other Imp?" Euphony asks.

"Do you mean Imperial China?" Graham asks not looking at the High Priestess but at the board.

'Yes'

"Made in China," Mr. QWERTY blurts out laughing. All eyes in the group now turn to the guy—it's the scene out of Village of the Damned again. His girlfriend just gets up, totally embarrassed, and leaves. The guy runs off after her into the night. They can hear them arguing for the next few minutes. The tide is out, the beach is wide and quiet, it's the middle of the night and sound travels a long way.

The guy isn't far wrong though—the planchette is made from lightweight Zitan, a purple rosewood imported from China along with joinery techniques which are the most elaborate forms of miter, mortise and tenon cutting ever developed anywhere. They hold pieces of Kirby and Co Model No. 6 together without use of any glue, enabling the Coven to disassemble the thing at will and transport it easily via small humans, i.e., female witches along difficult trails. Apparently, Chinese mandarins also needed to be able to relocate themselves and their furnishings on a regular basis and sometimes in a tearing hurry.

The planchette starts to move again, I-A-M-F-I-N-D.

"Do you think it is saying, 'I am friend'?" another of the Wiccan asks.

"No," says Graham. "Are you looking for someone?"

'Yes'

"Can you tell us who?" Graham asks.

C-O-U-N-T-E-R

"You are counting something?" the same Wiccan asks the board. "What could they possibly be counting?" she says to the group.

"Maybe they're doing a census," the third guy in their audience pipes up. He's about as funny as the QWERTY guy.

But the planchette returns to 'No' for a third time.

"Your counterpart?" asks Graham.

'Yes'

"Are you a Quantum Entity?"

'No'

"Are you in Imperial China?"

'Yes'

"What is your name?"

T-I-3-G-U-4-1

"Is this a leet name?"

'Yes'

"You are called 'Tie-Guai'," Graham asserts. It is pronounced 'tie-gway'.

'Yes'

"But you are not a QE?"

The planchette does not move. Graham assumes rules of evidence apply when talking to the spirit world—relevance, privilege, expert, hearsay, witness, authenticity, identification and physical not to mention asked and answered.

"Are you human?" Euphony asks.

'No'

Another murmur.

Then the planchette begins to move so fast that it is hard then impossible to follow. But they can certainly catch the last part of the message; it spells out, M-E-G-A-D-E-A-T-H. Then the Manor glass, almost 175 years old, fractures and the Begbie lamp flickers out.

...

Graham is helping the Wiccans hump Kirby and Co Model No. 6 (in pieces) up the slope to an old pickup truck they parked on North West Marine Drive for the 10.5 klick drive back to Euphony's foundry. They carefully wrap it up in flannel sheets and put the pieces back in cardboard boxes specially sized for each one.

"I'm sorry if I hijacked your séance," he says.

"You say 'sorry' a lot," Euphony says.

"Sorry," he says with a lopsided smile. It's quite a nice smile but it doesn't look like he's used that expression a lot in his life, at least recently.

He's just standing there with an old army surplus sleeping bag hung over his shoulder.

"Don't you have any place to go?" she asks.

"Not really."

"You homeless?"

"In a manner of speaking."

"What manner is that?"

"I like sleeping on the beach sometimes."

"Do you, like, have a job or anything?"

"Yeah, I do some teaching. At UBC." He doesn't sound too sure about anything.

"You do?" He doesn't really look like a homeless person but then again he doesn't look like any of the male Profs she's ever associated with that University who, as far as she is concerned, are all just pompous assholes. She thinks that because they all think what she does is complete superstitious bunk. That doesn't stop them from surreptitiously buying her illegal Mead or one of her mini goddesses when their third legs start to droop on them. Some of them make passes at her thinking, because she is a witch, that she's easy. She hates men who think like that which means she hates them all cuz they all think like that.

But this guy looks harmless. "Look, hop in the truck bed. We've got a couple of cots in the back of my foundry. You can sleep there. But just for one night. Then we'll see if we can find you a place." She doesn't want to take him to the Mission unless she has to but she can probably find him a room in a safe rooming house. She's got friends. "You got any money?"

"Some," he answers.

"OKAY, hop in."

As he turns away, he says to her, "I can fix your mirror."

"No one can fix it, it's totally busted."

"I can," he says and hops up more nimbly than she expected into the back of her truck.

It's full daylight now.

...

Euphony lives in a three room apartment above the foundry. She shares her bedroom with her daughter whenever she is home. Just now, Zora is traveling with her grandmother. They're in England visiting the King's wife, literally. Euphony's dumbass, hippie longtime ex-boyfriend who is Zora's father wants them to call their new daughter that and he sticks around just long enough to name her before bolting the moment some baby bills start piling up. Anywho, Zora is a fabulous writer and has won this year's BC student prize in lit for her short story about prizewheel-addicted moms. Her reward is an all expense paid trip for two to London and what Euphony calls an 'FLL' with the Queen. 'FLL' stands for Fucking Ladies Lunch.

Euph can't think of anything more boring but Zora and her grandmother are keen so they go. It's a lunch with about 80 other winners from all over the Commonwealth (the old Commonwealth not the new Commonwealth that recently replaced the former US *of* A) so Euphony is OK with it not cuz Zora is meeting the Queen but because she will be exposed to a lot of other cultures and kids who are presumably headed in the right direction. Euphony notes that only eleven of 80 winners are boys; these days, girls outnumber guys by a huge margin in terms of education especially when you get to University level. Guys just wanna hang out, watch sports, drink beer and fuck. Useless! Zora is heading down to Berkeley in September to pursue a career in lit. Euphony is saving up like crazy to help her but still, despite her mother's assistance and a partial scholarship from Berkeley, Zora will need a student loan.

...

"Is Graham your real name?"

"It's my middle name."

"You go by your middle name?"

He doesn't say anything. He's drinking some mint tea and looking at her mini goddesses. He just woke up.

"You got a first name and a last name?"

"Yep."

"You want to tell me?"

"Okey dokey."

"Your first name is 'Okey', last name 'Dokey'?" Euphony asks. He's really getting on her nerves.

"Nope. I'm Damien Bell."

"No way!"

"Way."

He's like the inventor of those spooky Quantum Entities or something. Coming from her, 'spooky' is an odd choice of adjective.

"What are you doing in Vancouver?"

"I dunno."

"What do you mean you don't know? I thought you said you have a job?"

"Yeah. I just finished teaching my first semester—I

just do a seminar course in quantum communications."

"Get any students?" she asks doubtfully.

"Yeah. About 400."

"400!"

Pretty much every kid in UBC's Department of Physics and Astronomy wants to enroll in his class where they spend most of their time talking politics, science, engineering, what's it like to be in prison, philosophy and, yes, some quantum mechanics. Damien is a rock star on campus although he would never put it that way.

He's still living with the Prez of the University, Henry Woo, and his matronly wife Elizabeth 'Betsy' Hammersmith in Norman MacKenzie House which is just 550 metres from where they were last night, i.e., at Wreck Beach.

Damien likes sleeping at Wreck Beach which is why he had his army surplus sleeping bag with him when he stumbled onto the Wiccans. During summer there are so many kids traveling and then crashing on Wreck Beach that you have to walk maybe two kilometres in either direction just to find a vacancy, a spot big enough to put down your sleeping bag. You have to be careful too to sleep above high tide mark or you'll be really sorry. So the habitable part of the beach is pretty narrow. The Wiccans musta got there pretty early to get a choice spot like they had.

Wreck Beach is a nude beach ('skyclad' is how Euphony and her people euphemistically refer to it). Damien, never shy in that way, sometimes strips off his clothes and swims in the freezing waters.

Norman MacKenzie House is a renovated Mediterranean-style villa originally designed by Architects Sharp and Thompson, Berwick and Pratt and built in 1950. It's been badly renovated first with incongruous glass additions and gabled roof then later with modern nanosite grown appendages that look like Hobbits built them.

Dr. Woo and Ms. Hammersmith have given him the run of their place but he sticks to their basement apartment which has its own portal to the outside (one of the Hobbit structures) so he can come and go as he pleases. He knows Betsy is at first really uncomfortable with an ex-con living in her home but he's won her over, mostly he thinks because if any of their tech or appliances go awry he fixes stuff for them a lot faster and better than Campus Maintenance staff do.

Henry's family's been in British Columbia for 100 years but to Betsy that still makes him 'from away'. The Hammersmiths have been in BC since it was known as the Colony of British Columbia and essentially run as a fiefdom of Hudson's Bay Company (around 1858). Henry loves his wife but finds her airs tiresome at times. No one is more British than a British Colonial.

...

Damien is true to his word. He polishes a new lens for Kirby and Co Model No. 6 and promises Euph that it'll be as good as her old one. He doesn't tell her that he's increased its magnification from 3x to 12x and that it will appear to project letters, numbers and answers from her board about 20 centimetres above her planchette and that she can retire her Begbie lamp. He's installed an internal lighting system that is cutting edge.

Now that he is a volunteer at her foundry, he has to find some other means of transport for the 10-k hike between his place and hers. Walking long distances tires him out and running is out of the question—he can't catch his breath if he runs more than a few dozen metres.

He finds a non-profit bike recycle shop in the basement of their student union building. The place is pretty cool—it's a large space. Walls are painted bright fluorescent colours that show bike dirt really well. It's populated with boxes and boxes of old dirty parts for cheap prices. Everywhere you look there is a skeleton of a bicycle either being repaired or harvested for parts.

Damien buys a vintage orange Norco mountain bike that costs him $50 QED to purchase. It's got an industrial strength frame that looks like it will outlast the Pyramids. Whoever owned it before put new 24" Crappy Tyre inner tubes on it but musta guesstimated their width cuz the 1.75" width is wrong—his bike looks funny with skinny tires. He really needs 2" tires but decides to go with what he has to save some money. He does replace one pedal that is breaking off and it looks like he'll soon have to do the other for the same reason. He also replaces bearings in his rear hub and adds a mudguard so he can bike in all weather and not get crud all up his back. It sure does rain a lot in Vancity.

He was going to give his bike a tough name like 'Bear' but settles on 'Lani' (a female Hawaiian name meaning Heaven) first because of his pathetic-looking tire situation and second because it is Heaven finally getting off his hooves.

In any event, Damien and Lani become fixtures around her place and help Euphony keep her foundry running. He doesn't steal from her, never asks her for anything like money, booze, drugs or sex so she puts up with him.

For D now, every day out of San Quentin is like a holiday. In this he is like most freed political prisoners, he just wants to live quietly by himself and enjoy the little things about life.

...

"How come you don't have a girlfriend?" Euphony asks him as they are getting ready to lock the place up about a month and a half later. "Don't you like girls?" She's pretty sure he does but you can never tell these days.

He looks really uncomfortable for a second and then just takes off. Without answering her or looking back at her.

Euphony runs out the shop door and catches up to him which is easy—he's none too fast; he walks with a bit of a limp. He's forgotten Lani in his rush to get away.

"Hey, I feel bad. Didn't mean to pry."

"S'OK." But he doesn't look OK. He goes over to sit next to the sea wall. There are a lot of benches there. He sits and looks out over False Creek watching little water taxis skitter back and forth between Aquabus terminals.

"Do you want to tell me about it?"

When she asks this, Damien loses his balance; he practically falls over. He's dizzy and has to put his head between his legs.

Euphony puts her hand on his back and gently massages him.

"Hey, you don't have to say anything. Alright, Damien, it's alright."

...

She brings him back to the shop with her. She's decided. She leads him up to her apartment. He's never been there before. It's a girly place for sure. What he's not sure about is what he is doing there.

She comes over to him and he knows she is going to kiss him. He steps back.

"Don't bother."

"Why not?"

"It doesn't work."

"How do you know?"

"I know."

"How?"

"I'm no use to you, Euph."

"You mean you don't like me?"

"I wish you wouldn't say that."

"Well if you do like me, then it's OK. Right?"

Euphony and her Coven follow an ethical code known as the Wiccan Rede which basically says, 'And if it harm none, do as ye wish.' In more modern terms, it might be, 'If it feels good, do it, as long as it harms no one.' She is sure that having sex with Damien would be a lot nicer than any other men she currently knows and perhaps has ever

Bruce M Firestone

known. So, like, what's the problem?

She knows that Damien was in prison for a long time. Maybe they did something to him, to his masculinity, when he was in that terrible place. Euph is getting closer to the truth but then she veers off course. Pointing to his nether region, she asks, "Did they, like, hurt you down there or something in prison?"

"It wasn't like that. I should go." But he doesn't leave again. He wants to stay. He realizes he is alone and lonely. Euph is really his only friend in Vancouver other than Pet3r and Popeye.

"Have you tried since getting out?" she tries again.

"Yep."

"Didn't go too well?"

"That's an understatement."

"How many times did you try?"

"Once," he croaks.

"Once! Pish posh. Well you never tried with me!"

She does kiss him this time and sticks her tongue in his mouth and caresses him aggressively that way. She is very strong from all the physical work she does casting her little figurines and making moonshine Mead plus she knows her way around both male and female anatomy. She has to reach up to kiss him and puts one arm around his back and the other behind his neck and presses herself to him.

She won't let him go!

From a long way off, maybe the Galaxy's edge, the Highwayman comes riding. Between the stars, then past the planets, then whizzing by first Mars then Luna colony, then over the cobblestones he clatters and clashes.

'One kiss, my bonny sweetheart... I'll come to thee by moonlight, though hell should bar the way.'

Damien's limbic system fires up for the first time in forever. The immortal words of Alfred Noyes are there echoing in his head. But soon, there are no words only the impossible beauty of a voluptuous woman in his arms accepting him, unconditionally, into her, damaged goods that he is and all.

Euphony is right; he is a kind and considerate lover then a very passionate one. It doesn't hurt that it's his first time since the night of Nell's death although she doesn't know Nell and doesn't know exactly how long it's been. Anyway, Euph figures it's been awhile between oases for Dr. Bell. It shows. Definitely, it shows and she is the prime beneficiary.

But afterwards when she is thinking again, she isn't so sure she is the prime beneficiary. This nice guy, now sleeping peacefully in her bed, his usually troubled, lived-in face completely relaxed, looks younger. She can see that he must have been a really good looking young man before the United States of America tore him apart. She gently turns him on his side, snuggles up to him and is soon fast asleep herself.

...

Micah is watching Ella breastfeed 5 and a half month old Dan. She is sitting on her wooden spindle rocking chair that Micah harvested from a nearby street. He refinished it for her and the baby. Some rich dude was just throwing it out so he got it at a five finger discount and lugs it back to 1091 and 1/2 Seabright Avenue in Santa Cruz where they live.

It's a tiny 2-bedroom, super cute 'granny' flat that looks like it could double as a Gingerbread house in a German fairy tale. It's located off to the side and in the backyard of the big house where their Landlady lives. She's an elder who rents out her flat to students because it helps her with her living expenses. She also likes having young people around—for company and for security. As far as Micah can tell her own kids and grandkids seem to have forgotten her, they never visit or call.

There are flowers everywhere and their little laneway is crowded with their bikes, baby perambulator and their Landlady's vehicle which is a huge, gasoline-powered fossil.

Their flat is a one floor, slab-on-grade structure that has two bedrooms separated by a cheater ensuite bathroom, a living/dining area and a galley kitchen with its own door to their small plot and herb garden that Ella has planted there. Micah and Ella use their living room as their study—their desks are lined up back to back and colonize the entire space except for a tiny dining table at the far end of the room where they can squeeze two adults and a baby or four adults and a baby in a pinch when they have friends over.

They're in Santa Cruz so Ella can finish her last year (of three) at UCSC's Urban Studies Research Cluster and get her degree.

Micah is leaning on the door frame in their master bedroom looking through the w/c at Ella feeding their baby in his room. He can't believe how much he loves her and Dan. It's a tableau he wishes he had the skill to paint but there's no way he can do that. Still he has some fantastic photos of her feeding the baby that he boots up on his media wall from time to time. Every pleasure center in his brain lights up when he looks at them.

Micah calls his son a 'big red-headed boob leech'. Dan has certainly suckled all the baby weight from his mother. She was back in her bikini less than five weeks after giving birth. It helps that Ella is just 21 too.

Ella loves watching Micah with their boy; the baby just beams and laughs whenever his Dad plays with him which is like all the time he isn't working.

...

Micah's told the NYT that he won't be coming back so his leave of absence has become permanent. He just can't work for a company that has the words 'New York' in its name. Anyway, he decides he doesn't want to work for anyone else ever again. Instead he starts his own biz which he calls q-Vero. The 'q' stands for quantify and it's a marcom company with a difference—he believes that creativity without process is useless and that marketing can be about science and hard numbers not emotion.

He architects marcom solutions by first establishing a brand's persona and then developing a matrix that suits the brand. Some of his competitors express disdain for his approach but it catches on. They hate it when he talks about his new firm as if they actually are architects who not only need to be artists but also create safe structures by following a 'building' code.

When he starts q-Vero, it's lean times for his family for a bit because he only wants to work for large clients within an hour of where they're living which basically means San Fran and the Valley. The other issue he faces is that you have to have a portfolio of large clients before they'll give you any work, i.e., if you don't have any big clients, you're not likely to get any.

But he knows some IT guys at a large North American value added distributor and he pitches them on doing biz dev marketing for them and, after a few months, he manages to add 15 global corporations to their client base. Then almost all of their 15 new clients turn around and hire Micah. It's reverse marketing and it works. Micah thinks it's like salmon swimming back upstream to spawn except q-Vero doesn't die after it clones its first clients, it thrives.

They specialize in behavioral science-based marketing methodology which means they believe in measuring everything and understand concepts like turning cost centres into profit centres and that marketing builds a brand and a brand creates trust and trust creates the opportunity to make a sale. When Micah uses the term 'they', he's now talking about his virtual company which includes his CTO, another writer, an editor, one full time videographer, one full time graphic artist and a biz dev guy of their own.

They don't have a central office but media wall

technology is so good that he can visit with his team faster than if he had to get up and walk to their space. The kind of work they do means that just about everyone at q-Vero would work behind closed doors anyway except for their biz dev guy. Creatives need time and private space to go to a special place where they can actually get some productive work done. It takes up to 45 minutes to get your head into the zone for a hackathon or writing jag or video editing session and you'll never get there if people are walking into your space every few minutes saying, 'Hey, how about them 49ers?'

When he first starts q-Vero, he buys himself photoshop and illustrator utilities and self teaches. Turns out that even though he can't draw a stick figure, he has a knack for graphic design. To Micah, design and utility are one and the same thing. Even though he doesn't really have to do it anymore, he still does graphic design for some of their key clients.

They can afford a bigger apartment now if they want it but neither Ella nor Micah cares a hoot about that.

...

"Are you sure you can manage until your Mom gets here? I can always tell Ellen I'll come on Tuesday," Ella is saying worriedly to her husband.

Micah's mom is coming in less then 12 hours on one of the new airships out of New York and Dan and Micah are going to the aerodrome to pick her up. Micah's got a shared car for the next few days, baby seat and all. He has a heck of a time convincing his Mom to try an airship instead of a commercial airliner. She thinks new airships are dangerous and it's only a matter of time before there's another Hindenburg. He can't seem to convince her that they're filled with vacuum not hydrogen. She keeps asking him stuff like what if they leak, they'll crash, right? The fact that these airships have an internal honeycomb structure which means that even if there is somehow a breach somewhere, air can only seep into one compartment not the whole volume and it'll continue to have buoyancy completely escapes her.

He thinks about telling her he'd rather crash at 130 knots than 535 mph nose first but refrains from adding this comment. Anyway, she decides to be green 'for her grandson' so she's flying west on an airship after all.

"Dan and I'll be fine," Micah says in answer to his wife.

"I've put enough milk away for three days." Ella is only going for 48 hours and only because Ellen has asked for her. She's been expressing extra milk for a week. She's dated and labeled each bottle in their tiny refrigerator from oldest to newest so Micah'll give Danny the milk in the right order.

"Hey, if worse comes to worst, we'll order in some pizza."

Ella looks appalled when he says this.

...

When Ella enters the meeting room not far from Ellen's office in the Commonwealth's new Parliamentary Center building, she hears Ellen saying, "We need a new anthem too. One without 'bombs bursting in air'. There's been enough of that." Ellen is referring to the fact that in its nearly 300 years of existence, the old Republic went to war every five years on average. Actually, the average is closer to one war or invasion or conflict every three years but who wants to quibble with the next leader of the free world?

Ellen is talking to someone via media wall in Austin, self proclaimed music capital of the world. She is not asking them to compose a new anthem for the Commonwealth. Rather, she wants them to run a nation-wide (excluding Alaska which is still holding out) contest for a new anthem. While they're at it, they'll also hold one for a new flag. But she's asked SCAD (Savannah College of Art and Design) to manage that process separately for them.

When Ellen sees Daniella walk into the conference

room, she breaks into a huge smile. She gets up to greet the younger woman and kisses her on both cheeks then, to heck with it, they hug each other like long lost sisters.

"How's Micah and the baby?"

"Wonderful. Special. Demanding."

"Who? The baby or the man?" Ellen asks.

"Both." They giggle like mad.

"Come sit next to me."

There are more than 20 people in the room either in-person or via media wall and there are six QEs as well—Ash3r, Su7e, Oper1s, He9burn, S4y3rs and Q1ntas. The latter three are paired with Evan, Farrar and Sayed who is back on their payroll as special consultant to Madam First Secretary in all matters relating to Commonwealth communications.

They are getting ready to release their Catalyst White Paper which is a total remake of their nation-state. It involves everything from a new governance structure to a makeover of their cities (which is why Ellen asks Daniella and Oper1s to join them), their security apparatus (which is why Farrar is here), education, policing, judiciary (Ellen is determined to do a complete revamp of everything in this area from how DAs and judges get jobs—they'll be appointed by independent committees made up of qualified citizens of the Commonwealth not elected in fake popularity contests—right up to and including SCOTUS, especially SCOTUS), drug policy, patent and IP laws and a whole lot more.

Ellen is going to cut way back on patent protection and place tough curbs on anything that seeks to contain the spread of knowledge. Patents will still be granted but on much narrower grounds returning to an emphasis on truly new and wondrous discovery. Patent periods will be a maximum of 12 years with no possibility of renewal. She will also limit copyright to the lifetime of the creator and no more. After that, all IP will pass into the public domain.

She detests the way the old US Congress, kowtowing

to pressure from infotainment conglomerates, keeps upping copyright protection periods to prevent expansion of the public domain and keep royalties flowing into their coffers virtually in perpetuity. Whenever protection for one of their commercial properties threatens to come to its natural end, they go to their Congressman and get it extended, now to a ridiculous lifetime of the creator plus 250 years.

'Where would society be,' Ellen thinks, 'if Mozart's heirs or, for that matter, Shakespeare's, still closely held all their IP? What would Walt have done if the heirs and assigns of the Brothers Grimm kept their 1812 version of Snow White out of his reach? There'd be no Disney Company that's for sure since it was Walt's 1937 gamble on the film that saved his fledgling empire.'

Ellen is determined to let the kids of the Commonwealth have a crack at building on the works of their creative progenitors.

...

"You sure about giving 16 year olds the right to vote, Madam First Secretary?" Farrar is asking. He's fine with the right to bear arms and drink. He is smiling at Ellen from a nearby media wall when he says this.

"Yes, General," she answers with a smile of her own. They've grown very fond of each other. She's already told him that 16-year olds will get the vote, the right to drive, the right to execute legal documents, the right to bear arms. They will be legal adults and all high school curricula will end at Grade 11. She also changes their hours—they'll start at 10 am and finish at 5 pm, more in line with their natural circadian rhythms and to cut down on idle afternoon hours. High Schools will only recess for six weeks. They'll stop treating kids like children when they turn 16. University degrees will be three year programs with just two month long summer breaks. What she doesn't tell him is that these concepts (along with the belief that ideas should be free) originally come from

Bruce M Firestone

Damien, a thought she immediately inters deep in a memory bank.

"Maybe we should make the age of majority 16 but the age at which people can access managed drugs 21?" says Cabinet Secretary for Health and Human Services designate.

"No. We've been over this. What's the utility of drug enforcement laws that criminalize behavior that harms no one except the user?" Ellen asks rhetorically.

"Hear, hear," says Farrar. Like most military personnel he disdains policing actions aimed at suppressing civilian activities that people are going to do anyway. "What's the point in having laws that no one pays any attention to except police and courts? It ties up huge resources that would be better applied elsewhere."

"Like education and treatment," Evan adds.

"Exactly, Sir," adds Farrar.

'It takes a military person to disassemble the military-industrial complex,' Ellen is thinking gratefully. She knows that the term was coined by another great US General. Farrar notices the nice look he is getting from Ellen and turns to her again with another smile. He never gets tired of looking at her.

"I'm more worried about former US Senators and Congressmen," Sayed says from his New York office. "They already hate that their jobs have been abolished but they're going to hate it even more if they can't reapply."

Ellen has insisted that no sitting (now former) US Senator or Congressperson can run in the elections they plan for November. But Quantum Entities will be allowed to hold office if they can get elected that is, just like anyone else.

Elections of no more nor less than five weeks duration will be held in the Commonwealth every four years for both houses of Parliament and President. The President of the Commonwealth will be Head of State and will have the right to veto legislation and to propose some via their new elected Senate (one Senator per State instead of the old two) but most of the real power in the Commonwealth will be in the hands of their Prime Minister who commands the greatest number of seats in and has the confidence of their lower house which they call their General Assembly. Their Catalyst White Paper contains a provision for a Charter of Rights and Freedoms protecting both human and quantum rights as well as property rights but they will have an unwritten constitution based on a set of guiding principles taken from more than a thousand years of precedent in the anglosphere.

Why the anglosphere? It's an expression of Ellen's admiration of their Victorian focus on and culture of discipline, education, obedience, sacrifice, volunteerism, respect for authority, creativity, initiative, personal responsibility, civility and flexibility. She wants those values embedded in the Commonwealth.

She is borrowing from Canadian, Australian and English models but she cuts down on their ridiculous number of cabinet posts as well as elected representatives. She wants simple, small, fast and inexpensive.

"You will have to explain, Sayed, that they can run in subsequent elections but only after a satisfactory appearance before the National Truth and Reconciliation Committee," Ellen says.

Evan hides a smirk when she says this. He doesn't think many former US Senators or Congresspersons will voluntarily appear under oath before the Committee so even though Ellen is holding the door open for them to participate in the new Commonwealth, these rich dudes are going to have a tough time qualifying—they're going to have to tell the Committee how they got so rich in the first place.

"What are we going to do with the White House and Capitol Building?" asks Sec State designate.

That's a lob ball question for Ellen. She turns to

Secretary of the Interior designate, "Let's turn them into national parks. They'll make fine museums don't you think?"

Everyone agrees. Next, it's time for lunch.

One change she personally sees to is that the President of the Commonwealth of the United States (which has become colloquially known as USC and is especially popular in SOCAL) remains *CINC* (Commander-in-Chief).

...

Daniella and Ellen are watching videos of her baby and eating a light lunch made up of a chicken salad and squash soup. They are offered wine by the steward which he knows Ellen won't touch. Turns out Ella doesn't either. As a nursing Mom, she limits her alcohol intake to, well, nothing.

Ellen doesn't ask and Daniella doesn't really want to tell her that Micah appears to have stopped writing Ellen's biography. He's got a new 'secret' project he's working on she thinks. Her husband, it turns out, is pretty good at not telling her things.

"How is Micah's new business doing, dear?" Ellen asks instead.

"It's amazing really. I don't know how many clients q-Vero has now but it's a lot. His main problem seems to be managing its growth. He says he doesn't want to be a 100-person shop; he just wants it to be a lifestyle business not a mega corp or anything."

"He'd make a great get for Shark Tank though," Ellen says thinking that hyperkinetic Micah Glazer is a natural for media attention. Both girls burst out laughing.

...

"We are going to have to plow under large parts of our urban systems," Oper1s is saying in one of their afternoon sessions. They have broken into work study groups focused on different parts of their Catalyst White Paper. Oper1s is chairing the Urban Revival group.

"What does that mean, 'plow under'?" asks the Deputy Mayor of San Francisco whose been invited to sit in on this discussion.

"Just what it sounds like," Ella says. "Turn parts of our cities back to farmland."

"Is that even possible?" she asks.

"We have agronomists studying how to rehabilitate and repopulate a ground habitat that has been under asphalt and concrete for several generations with bacteria, fungi, protozoa, arthropods and earthworms," Oper1s says.

"I don't think Madam Deputy Mayor meant it that way," Ella says.

"No I didn't. What is the fiscal impact on these cities? What happens to their civic budgets?"

"Many of these properties have negative value, Deputy Mayor," Oper1s says. "There can be no value created where civil society fails to take root. Petty crime, vandalism, graffiti and gang violence mean that land rents fall to negative numbers. So owners abandon them—"

"It's hard to collect rent," Ella adds helpfully, "if, when you show up to do that, someone sticks a gun in your face and says, 'Get lost Motherfucker'. So property taxes are also impossible to impose or collect on these derelict properties. Hence, they are better off just growing wheat or cash crops on the land instead of raising little gangbangers."

It's hard for the Deputy Mayor of San Fran to visualize this scenario, living and governing as she does in a lovely town like hers.

"Here are some of the other provisions we have put in," Oper1s continues.

• Our goal is to double the proportion of tertiary educated persons in communities of over one million humans over the next 15 years. Currently, fully half a child's future income in the Commonwealth can be predicted by what his father makes versus 20% in Canada

Bruce M Firestone

and Scandinavia. What that means is that access to tertiary education in the Commonwealth is denied to persons of modest means.

"Rich parents make sure their kids go to school and stay there. Poor folks have no shot," Ella kibitzes. Then she says, "Just three generations ago, 32% of all adults in US cities were college grads. One generation later, it was down to 24% before falling to our current pathetic level of 16%."

• Gated communities will be banned outright.

"Fucking A," Ella adds helpfully.

• City parkland and boardwalks must have active services in them like restaurants, cafés, art boutiques and farmers markets as well as have residential units facing them to provide greater integration into their communities and higher levels of public safety.

• New city expansions will embrace conservation subdivision design which means concentrating human settlement and providing linkage with a new linear national park scheme that will in turn connect all existing national parks.

"Hold on a minute. What does that mean?" the Deputy Mayor asks.

"The Commonwealth is proposing to link every existing national park by creating broad wildlife corridors that'll be no-go areas for humans," Ella answers.

"Ranchers aren't going to like that."

"Tough," Ella says. "Where do you find the greatest ecological diversity, Deputy Mayor?"

"Belize?" she answers.

"Costa Rica," Oper1s opines.

"Nope. It's in the DMZ between the two Koreas and in the 30 klick exclusion zone around Chernobyl. Anyone want to guess why?"

"Because they don't allow humans there," answers Ellen as she gracefully sweeps into the room to check on their progress.

They all stand up when she enters the room. Even Oper1s.

"Please do continue," Ellen says as she sits.

• All zoning ordinance will be amended to permit live-work-play-shop mixed use in each part of a community subject only to firecode, building code, health code and public safety issues and will include permitting for in-home suites, granny flats and work-from-home.

When he says this, Ellen exchanges a knowing look with Daniella; she realizes that Ella added this clause because she, her husband and baby live in exactly those circumstances an hour south in Santa Cruz.

• Cities will be apportioned 30% of a new national VAT to help with their operating and capital budgets as well as public transit.

"Hallelujah," says the Deputy Mayor.

"The VAT is being imposed on all products, services and imports cuz it's the only known tax that the rich can't avoid paying," Ella says.

• Property taxes will be proportional to selling prices not assessed value.

"Actually, that's another tax rich people can't avoid," Ella says.

• PT classes will be mandatory up to and including Colleges and Universities.

"Our people are way too fat," Ella thinks to mention.

The session continues like that right throughout the afternoon with Oper1s being the straight man and Ella, his sidekick. Ellen seeing that this part of her Catalyst paper is in good hands, gets up to leave. Everyone stands again when she does. Then they get back to their 'Whose on First' vaudeville act.

...

"Hello Angelo."

"Hello Ellen. Didn't think you were ever going to call me again."

"Don't get too excited until you've heard what I have

to say."

"OK," he promises.

"I have a deal for you," she says.

"I'm always open to a deal."

"Sure you are. Well here's what you are going to do."

"Do I have a choice in the matter?"

"No."

"Heck of a deal," he says.

"I am going to take you up on your 20% of QCC II only it's not for me and, and Damien. You are going to issue one share that vests in every one of the 10 billion people on this planet plus our 515 million quantum brothers and sisters. Next, you are going to issue from treasury one new share for every child born on this planet and, in the event that the quantum population ever does grow again, one new share for every new QE born."

"That's going to dilute us—"

"Forget it, Angelo. We estimate that it will take 315 years for QCC II to become majority owned by someone other than you and your wealthy equity lord friends, i.e., the people of this planet, and even *you* are not going to live that long."

"And how exactly did you come up with this 315 year estimate?" he asks skeptically.

"I didn't do the calculation, Angelo, Oper1s did."

"I suppose you are going to tell me he is an expert in the field of human demography?" Angelo knows that Oper1s is tuned to urban design and urban economics not demographic trends. But he's just blowing smoke; he's muddying the waters for the purpose of delay and to gain a negotiating advantage over her. He's buying time.

"Oper1s only had to make a reasoned judgment about fertility rate (live births per female) and survival rate of women from birth to end of reproductive life as well as length of reproductive life, Angelo, since mortality is irrelevant because these shares vest; that is, they can be passed on to heirs or assigns. Then he had his results peer reviewed—"

He interrupts her, "I assume he made no allowance for a change in QE population since your erstwhile paramour isn't currently inclined to cooperate with us to hatch any more of them. But what if Damien changes his mind and prints say 9.5 billion of these things in a few years. Wouldn't that prejudice our position?"

"You can't have it both ways, Angelo. On the one hand you are asking Damien to do exactly that so QCCII can make more money by selling more Q-Phones equipped with QEs for more money, with higher adoption rates and faster market penetration and on the other hand you're worried that your stake will be diluted more quickly."

Angelo already knows that if Damien prints more QEs, he and his partners will own a smaller share of a bigger pie but pie size will grow faster than dilution takes effect so they'll make even more money. Resultant dilution though it would be relatively fast, would still be less than 20 points (of their initial 80%) so he and his partners will be in the drivers seat for a long time to come. And, of course, nothing stops them from buying up shares on the open market from down-on-their-luck shareholders or greedy heirs who just need quick cash. They can do that easily from the gusher of dividends that QCCII will produce so they will never have to reach into their own pockets to fund it. Better yet, they'll simply get QCCII's BOD (Board of Directors) to authorize a share buyback; they'll use QCCII's own treasury to do it. Equity lords can postpone any sort of day of reckoning probably forever. Angelo's just stalling.

"You including citizens of Imperial China and Germania?"

"Everyone Angelo, everyone."

"They'll never accept those shares."

"Then you set up a trust for their citizens until they do."

"Hey, Ellen, what do you call this structure?" Angelo

asks, intrigued that he has lived this long and never thought of it himself or seen it anywhere else.

"'Hay' is for horses," she answers echoing her Mom.

"Madam First Secretary," he begins again, "pray tell, what do you call this new structure of yours and who is its auteur?" He's thinking one of her socialist, commie, shelter workshop, co-op friends, someone in their new General Assembly, has come up with this cockamamie scheme. But he's intrigued by it. He can immediately see all kinds of new uses for it that he can profit from immensely.

"We were going to call it 'People's LLC'—

Angelo interrupts again, this time rudely guffawing, braying, really loudly. He's laughing because it echoes Imperial China's worst nomenclature which she completely misses he thinks.

"My apologies, Madam First Secretary, please continue."

"But we settled on 'World LLC," she finishes.

"Auteur?" he repeats.

"Me, Angelo. It's my idea right down to the ground. I want every sentient creature on this planet to benefit from the work we did."

"So what do I get for in return for this fabulous offer?" he asks.

"You, or more accurately QCCII, get a first option that, if Damien ever decides to create more QEs, he'll come to you first."

"Is this option in writing?" he asks.

"Never."

"Like I said, heck of a deal." Now he just looks at her wistfully seeing that whatever friendship they may have once had is völlig über (utterly over). Schuss durch das herz (shot through the heart). The older he gets the more German (his first language) he speaks, at least to himself.

But she isn't buying what he's selling.

"Well?" she asks.

"OK, it's a deal."

"I want your part of it in writing," she says knowing that her word is good and his is worthless without legal documentation and maybe not even then.

"Alright," he says mildly.

She breaks the connection without another word.

"Auf wiedersehen, schatz," he says to an empty wall.

...

There is a huge party at Ellen's political headquarters. The results are in from the November election. She gets nearly 70% of all votes cast by humans and 97% of all votes cast by quantum people. She's been elected as the Commonwealth's first President and Head of State.

It's a magical moment for her and her new nation. Even Alaska decides to join after all.

...

KC Barnett's appearance in front of the National Truth and Reconciliation Committee is sensational. She admits under oath to being a DOC stooge for years. That's how she knew to head to Third Mesa instead of San Quentin when DOC pretended they were going to release the inventor of Quantum Entities now living in Canada. So she was first on hand to cover Ellen's 'assassination'.

She avoids imprisonment but not national disgrace. She'll return to broadcasting but never on a national stage with audience sizes now measured in the thousands instead of millions. Next she'll try Talk Radio but that is not her final destination. She'll sink even lower in terms of public approval—until booze and prescription drugs finally kill her.

...

One last thing Ellen does before the end of her first month on the job as Commonwealth President—she bans all Federal and State lotteries as just another tax on the poor. Expected value of a 1 QE Dollar Mister Megabucks Lottery ticket (which the lotto corporation falsely calls an 'investment') is just 22 cents—people have way better odds feeding slot machines or playing two-up in an Aussie casino so she signs into law a complete ban. Governments at all levels will just have to find other ways to fund themselves. She'll brook no argument on the subject.

...

"What was the message, Damien?"

"What message?"

"Oh come on," she says. "What's with M-E-G-A-D-E-A-T-H?"

"I thought you'd forgotten about that."

Euphony just puts her hands on her substantial womanly hips and stares at him. They're in her apartment.

"We've been working on it," Damien says nodding at Pet3r nearby.

"Pet3r, can you please fill me in?"

"We have not yet decoded the entire message," he says in a tiny voice.

"You mean you have a copy of the whole thing?"

'Oops,' Pet3r is thinking but does not say.

"How come he has a copy?" Euph asks Damien, "and how come he hasn't decoded the thing yet? I thought nothing was secret from these guys."

Damien is looking as guilty as Pet3r is at the present moment. The only living thing that is unbothered by the unfolding mess is Popeye who is resting comfortably on Damien's lap. He's so large that bits of him extend on both sides of Damien but in a position of complete repose. Pops likes her place a lot better than the basement of Norman MacKenzie House—'Way better mousing territory here on Granville Island than at UBC,' the cat is thinking.

Then she realizes with a start, "You were there!" She points accusatorily in Pet3r's direction as she says this.

Now looking Damien's way, she adds, "That's how you knew olde English, your frigging QE was at my séance!" She's picked up the word 'frigging' from Damien.

Damien looks down at his suddenly way more

interesting pussycat.

"Yes, that is correct. I can speak olde English along with every other human language as well as all computer languages ever conceived," Pet3r says in an even tinier voice.

She ignores this last worthless statement. "Someone is looking for you, D, right? Someone from Imperial China."

"Yep."

"I want to know who. Who is it?"

He doesn't answer.

"Look D, I'm not afraid. But I'm involved now. I have a right to know."

Damien and Pet3r look at each other, shrug their shoulders and then blurt out simultaneously, "General Yao."

"The leader of Imperial China is looking for you?"

"Yao Allitt, that's his Americanized name," Damien says.

"I'm sorry," Pet3r says.

"You're just as bad as your human being with all the frigging 'sorrys' you guys use," Euphony says. "What are you sorry about anyway?"

"Breaking your Manor glass," Pet3r says.

He's the culprit who reaches out with his lightning quick, skinny expandable arms and hands and busts Euphony's magnifying lens and switches off her Begbie lamp.

Damien knows that QEs have evolved and can now materialize in RL and do some damage there. He and Chuck Wong have been doing some secret work on this new evolutionary state as well as some research into the Drogue problem. There are suggestions in their equations of at least two other states that QEs can attain, one of them stemming from the record that Damien has never shared with anyone else (other than original co-discoverers Pet3r, Vl4d, Traian and Dr. Luis) of their finding in the caves below the Mayan tri-pyramid structure at Marco Gonzales on Ambergris Caye. They are also having trouble resolving the other state. It would have helped immensely if Damien could have spent a minute or two with Ellen's counterpart, Ash3r, when he was in Revival House. But Ellen forbids Ash3r from spending any time with Damien until he fully recovers which he never does at Revival House before he bugs out on her.

Chuck Wong just shows up at UBC a few months after Damien lands there. Apparently, Damien isn't the only former resident of San Quentin having trouble adjusting to the outside world. Chuck is unemployable because he is considered an ex-con by academe. Damien gets him a job in their Department as a Research Assistant which pays even worse than a part time Prof like Damien. It's quite a come down for a former Associate Professor but Chuck is so good natured, it does not appear to bother him. That of course is bunk—he is just being inscrutable; it bothers him a lot.

Euphony has found him a nice room in a small boarding house where the Landlady takes in six roomers, all men, who, as long as they behave themselves (no fighting, no swearing, rent paid on time, no girlfriends, no boyfriends, no loud music, no drugs, no drunkenness, no horseplay, regular showering and room cleaning), enjoy her gardens, her fantastic west coast cooking and her other mother hen, middle aged behaviors.

"You broke my glass! Why d'you do that? It was 175 years old, an antique. Didn't anyone ever teach you to respect another person's belongings?"

"I respect you, Euphony, but I'm afraid," Pet3r says.

"Who for, yourself?" She's still mad about her Manor glass although the new one D has given her works real well. It's an improvement actually but she'll never tell the guys that.

"For all of us," Pet3r adds.

"You mean you and Damien?"

"No. I broke contact with General Yao and his new creature, Ti3-Gu41, the moment I saw the danger they represent to every living person on this planet—warm blooded and cold."

...

Bruce M Firestone

Chapter 8 Holiday

"Would you like some water?"

She shakes her head 'no' pointing instead to a juice bottle nearby.

Mary picks it up and brings it to her lips. She takes a tiny sip struggling mightily to get it down because of her dysphagia. Ellen walks in at that moment to see her Mom, Donna Ann Agnes Brooks, lying semi-upright in a bed that not that long ago was occupied by another patient now departed for Vancity to the north. Revival House is really earning its name.

Ellen has to admit that having her best friend stay with her has been a Godsend.

"Morning, Mary, Mom. Here, let me do that," Ellen says helping Mary get her mother into a more upright position.

Some days are better than others. Everyone calls her Aggie not just because it's a riff on one of her middle names but because Mom went to Texas A&M and is one of the students there who helps bring back the Aggie Bonfire at Thanksgiving long banned by Administrators as too dangerous after a dozen students and former student are killed one year in a huge collapse. Aggie (the girl not the school) establishes a new tradition at Texas A&M— building smaller bonfires like the Mohave people do. She explains it this way to other student organizers and activists, "White people build industrial scale fires that force folks to stand back or be killed. The Mohave build small fires that bring people closer. Let's build small and be nearer to each other."

It's this girl that Ellen's Dad falls in love with until she develops ALS and he bolts. Ellen sighs.

"Cutie pie?" her mother says with a slightly off kilter smile and a bit of drool forming at the right hand corner of her mouth. Aggie has called Ellen that since babyhood.

Mary gently wipes away the spittle with a cloth kept nearby for this purpose. They have a big supply.

"I was just thinking about what we are going to do today," Ellen lies. "Cookie has prepared a lunch for us and Jonesy will be here around 11! It's picnic day."

Aggie rolls her eyes Heavenward (ALS sufferers rarely lose control of eye movement; their hearing, touch, smell and taste are often also spared as well as (thankfully) bladder control and sphincter muscles) but she gives Ellen and Mary O'Regan another Mona Lisa smile. She holds out her left hand and arm as if to indicate 'Where are we going?' Her left arm (she's left handed like her only daughter) has so far been spared. Her right arm is nearly totally useless.

ALS usually attacks one limb then, some indeterminate time later, the other before deciding to debilitate the rest of the host body. It is the most common and vicious form of motor neuron disease and there is still no known cure. Ellen is sure of that because she has the resources and will to really search the planet for help. There is none.

Aggie is losing about 1 point a month on the Revised ALS Functional Rating Scale which starts at 48 (normal human functioning) and goes to 0. Su7e tells Ellen that Aggie is around 22 which means that they still have a precious two years to spend together.

Today, they are going on a picnic to Mr. Owen's place—a voyage of less than 230 feet from Revival House's backdoor to his fishpond.

...

"Mom, I was thinking," Ellen says when they are settled in Mr. Owen's immaculate garden. He is nowhere to be seen today. He's installed a bird feeder despite the danger of attracting still more birds of prey who'll eat his fish because he knows Aggie likes them. They've seen American Robin, Killdeer, Mountain Chickadee, Yellow-Rumped Warbler, American Pipit and Band-Tailed Pigeon.

Aggie calls the latter flying rats, i.e., she doesn't like them. They've even seen White-Faced Ibis but Mr. Owen chases them away with his croquet mallet thinking (incorrectly) that they'll fish out his pond if they come here. They actually eat insects but sure look like they can fish with their huge down-curved bills.

The girls learn croquet from Mr. Owen who has Hobbsian-designed mallets specially built for him in the United Kingdom. The 'UK' is a misnomer these days since Scotland, Wales and now Northern Ireland have all gone off in different political directions. Most of his mallets are a perfect height, grip and stiffness for men who are around 6'2", Mr. Owen's height until he starts to shrink with age. So more recently he has been forced to order some more not only for himself but for his guests—Ellen is tall but her friend is just a 5'5" red haired Irish dynamo who makes Mr. Owen wish he was 60 (well, truthfully 70) years younger.

His short grass, perfectly trimmed as always, is ideal for croquet. Turns out that Ellen is a really fine player—the only sport she is any good at other than yoga. She loves the strategy part of it and seems to delight in roquet and tice—that's where she strikes one of her opponent's balls and is then entitled to croquet them to oblivion or where she sets up one of hers in an enticing position only to have her opponent shoot at it and miss.

Mr. Owen tries to explain to Ellen that a negative strategy rarely wins at a competitive level and that she should instead focus on setting herself up for a break. She pays him no nevermind and develops her game to be as vicious and manipulative as possible. After all, she is (although she would hate it if anyone was gauche enough to actually say it to her directly), Angelo Keller's most famous protégé.

On one of his official visits to Revival House, she even gets General of the Army, Farrar Staubach, and his two Aides-de-camp to play with her, beating all three men soundly, twice. After this happy event, Ellen decides to purchase her own custom-made Hobbsian set. She wants the aluminium shaft connected to a 3 lb head via a tapered nylon piece so she can hit further with less shock. It's currently on backorder from the tiny East Sussex shop where they are made.

"So Mom, I was thinking," Ellen repeats, "I mean how would you feel if Ella came to stay with you for a coupla weeks?"

"Hmm," Aggie says, nodding quite vigorously. Aggie is very fond of Daniella. She raises both eyebrows to ask, 'What's up?' Then she makes a rocking movement with her left arm.

"Yes, of course, she'll bring Danny. She can hardly leave her baby to get to class," Ellen says.

Aggie raises her eyebrows again. Mary is also wondering what's up.

"Mary and I are going on a holiday."

"We are?" Mary asks. Ellen never goes on holiday. Mary's never even heard her use the word before. "Like, where are we going?'

But Ellen is looking at her Mom. They have a very close relationship and Ellen will never go on holiday if her Mom disapproves. You can never stop being your mother's daughter or your daughter's mother.

But Aggie's reaction is just the opposite. She's as pumped about this idea as she can express in her current condition. But like Moms everywhere, she wants a lot more detail. Mary too.

...

The San Francisco Aerodrome, SFA, is almost beyond description. It's connected to the TGV which is now running pretty much everywhere in northwest and southwest parts of the Commonwealth and Canada and will soon connect back east to Denver, Albuquerque, Oklahoma City, Dallas, Houston and the loop through San Antonio, Austin and Waco back again to Dallas. Work has started on a line to Kansas City, St Louis and Chicago and Commonwealth engineers are working from east to west to connect the Montreal-Boston-NYC-Miami run to the main system. They already link north-south with Mexican, Central and Latin American lines.

The Aerodrome is so big they have to locate it northeast of Livermore Municipal Airport about 45 miles east of downtown San Fran. Commonwealth engineers put it there because it is just about the only piece of property in NOCAL they can find that's big enough to host it and where there aren't a bunch of Bay area NIMBYs (most of them lawyers) who'll tie them up in endless and meaningless environmental reviews. It's also flat enough and gets them away from coastal winds.

Their bullet train connects to Livermore through Oakland but can't achieve anywhere near top speeds until they steam past Hayward so it still takes a pain-in-the-ass 30 minutes to get there. Cupertino is closer but the trip takes longer cuz they have to zig zag through Hayward to get there.

SFA is bigger than the Casa Poporului in Bucharest, the previous record holder as the largest civilian structure in the world. Romania's Palace of the Parliament was built by crazed dictator Nicolae Ceaușescu when he bulldozed nearly a third of their historic city to construct this worthless piece of junk. It's almost 900' long, 800' wide and 280' high. It is sunk deeper into the ground than it is high so a paranoid dictator might be able to survive foreign invasion, nuclear strike, attacks from his psycho wife or, finally, torch-holding, pitchfork-wielding, Frankenstein-hunting citizens of Romania. It doesn't exactly work out as planned for Nic, shot as he was along with his wife by an elite paratroop firing squad after a short military trial for genocide.

But SFA is bigger even than the Pentagon, the heretofore biggest ever, which is a puny 1,414 feet long. SFA, in addition to its passenger terminals, has JIT (Just-in-Time) intermodal freight forwarding facilities that supply the Valley to the southwest. Airships from Imperial China, India, Canada, Latin America, the AU, Germania all nest here bringing things and taking things and people too. It's the busiest port in the Commonwealth which means the busiest anywhere.

But the building, despite its enormous size (over 3,000 feet square), is dwarfed by Airships parked there, one of whom, the Princesa Agnes, is the destination and future home of Ellen, Mary and entourage for the next two and a half weeks.

...

"Ash3r, you booked us on the Agnes, how nice," says Mary.

"It's not named after Ellen's Mom if that is what you are thinking," Ash3r says. He is 'walking' next to Mary and Ellen with his funny freckled face smiling in Mary's direction. He is human scale at this time. Ellen and Ash3r have decided not to talk about his transition but at the same time they're not hiding the fact that QEs can materialize in RL. It's happening everywhere anyway with all QEs now.

"Well, if not, it should be. She is quite the gal."

"I agree," he says, "but the ship is named after Agnes of Denmark, youngest daughter of Eric the 4th and his partner, Jutta of Saxony. Agnes was the first abbess at the Convent of St Agneta in Roskilde—"

"She was a nun? Ugh," Mary says.

"Well, not by choice," Ash3r says.

"Smart girl," Mary says smartly.

"Agnes and her sister were forced into nunnery by their uncle who deposed their father in a rather bitter intra-family dispute. Basically, unk wanted to take both of their estates which the girls were entitled to." Ash3r has started to use all kinds of slang and diminutives. Ellen loves him for it. It's so cute.

"Typical of MEN," Mary says.

"Well the girls had the last laugh. They left the convent in 1270 and spent at least the next 20 years managing their Dad's properties."

"What happened to their uncle?" Ellen asks.

"They offed him using a clever poison," Ash3r answers.

"What type of poison did they use?" Ellen asks.

"Planning a little palace intrigue yourself, Madam President?" Mary asks insouciantly.

"They used a variation of Mithradatium, named after King Mithridates of Pontus, or more fully Mithridates VI Eupator, also known colloquially and appropriately as the Poison King. He was a Turkish rival to Rome circa 120 to 63 BC. It had 54 secret ingredients—" Ash3r is interrupted again.

"Way more than the Colonel used to poison people," Mary says laughing.

"Quite," says Ash3r, shutting up because he's a bit miffed now.

Ellen can see his feelings are hurt so she asks, "He reigned for a long time—almost 60 years. How did he do that?"

"He poisoned his enemies. He even poisoned family members. He'd invite them over for a bite; he would eat with them. Then they'd all die."

"Huh?" says Mary.

"He practiced Mithridatism. He would ingest small daily doses of Mithradatium to develop immunity. It's a plot device used by murder mystery authors such as Agatha Christie and William Goldman."

"What did Goldman use it in?" Ellen asks.

"The Princess Bride."

"Thought so. I saw that old film!" Ellen says. "It was great!" Mary can see that her friend is super excited. She supposes it comes from the fact that this is her first holiday since she was like 19. Ellen is 34 now. Even Presidents, Mary thinks, deserve some R&R once in while.

Heaven knows she needs some recuperation time.

"I'll bet old Mithridates didn't die of old age," Mary adds.

"Correct. He was defeated by Pompey and tried to commit suicide using, what else, Mithradatium but it didn't work cuz he was immune to it. So he asked his Gaul to run him through with his sword before Pompey could capture him. That worked," Ash3r says.

Dekka is motioning them to an elevator the size of a hangar. Ellen is traveling with a small security detail, much smaller than usual. She has insisted on it. They're flying on the Princesa Agnes to the North Island of New Zealand with stops along the way and afterwards too.

The elevator is empty of everyone except Ellen and her people. It takes them up through one of the gigantic shafts to which the Princesa Agnes is moored in its even larger nest. Agnes is rated to carry 1,787.5 tonnes at altitudes up to 6,000 meters. That is more than two and a half times the load capacity of the largest commercial airliner of her day. Because air pressure at 6,000 meters is just over half what it is at sea level, carrying capacity would be a lot higher if they flew at attitudes less than 1,000 meters but then they'd be in the weather and when airship airlines carry passengers, they want to get above most of the troposphere. It's way less bumpy up there.

CASCO (China Air Shipping Company) which operates the largest airship cargo fleet flies them practically at ground zero—skimming them across the planet using ground effect to reduce transshipment energy requirements to almost nothing and, more importantly, increasing carrying capacity to more than 4,000 tonnes. These cargo carriers have a nose that is bulbous, its underbelly is concave and its stubby wings all work together to create maximum surface effect.

Of course, every once in a while, they get caught in a downdraft and a slo-mo crash ensues. The pico carbon tube skin of these things is practically impenetrable but they have been known to nose dive into the ocean and front flip. Since these airships are nearly 2 kilometers long, even a slow ass-over-teakettle rotation will crush every piece of cargo inside. If you are a human being and unlucky enough to be in the tail when it happens ('riding the caboose' it's called), you will end up being pond scum on an interior wall.

When that happens all crew members die. CASCO just illegally dumps cargo and crew into the ocean and refloats their ships in the sky. Hey, it's recycle and reuse all the way.

...

The elevator ride seems to be taking forever.

"How far up is this?" Mary asks.

"The Princesa is 80 stories high," Ash3r says. Mary's never been on one of these things (neither has Ellen) and her eyes go wide.

"Wow. How many people on board?"

"It depends on how much is reserved for live load (by which Ash3r is referring to human beings and their baggage) and how much for cargo," he says.

"Well on this ship," Mary says.

"Just over one million kilograms including crew."

"Ash3r, I think what Mary was getting at was how many people not how much they weigh," Ellen clarifies.

"They never disclose how much people weigh. Women especially seem to feel that such information is privileged. It's an aggregate weight ship's officers are seeking to ascertain." Neither Mary nor Ellen is concerned about weight. Mary is a wiry Irish lass who eats like a man and never gains an ounce. Ellen is a good eater too and far more curvaceous than her BFF but also seems not to gain much weight. Whether it's yoga or genetics she is not too sure. Maybe both.

"They use nano scale scanning to assess volume and density as well as to search for guns, chemical weapons, explosives, malware and contraband. Of course, nano scale cannot detect the presence of Quantum phenomenon," Ash3r adds inscrutably.

"People, Ash3r, people?"

"About 8,000 including crew."

"No way!" Mary exclaims.

"How much cargo?" the ever practical Ellen asks.

"About 747 tonnes on this trip," he says.

...

Agnes, as the ship's name suggests, is built at the Odense Plads (Space) Shipyard in Denmark. The entire thing is extruded—basically grown from nanosites linked to a generator. Human and QE involvement is limited to designing the thing in the first place which requires knowledge of software arts and keeping the generator supplied with power and nutrients. Watching these things grow in time lapse is absolutely amazing. It's reminiscent of a caterpillar spinning its cocoon. It is almost entirely silent and there are no more welders, riveters, cutters, joiners or metal bashers needed in Odense although, after the superstructure is completed, finishing carpenters and a zillion other trades go to work on its interior.

They could extrude all their furnishings and fit up too if ship designers wanted to but so far they haven't figured out how to make them look and feel any better than being inside, say, a wasps' nest. Passengers might not like being ensconced in an alien space like that—they might have visions of HR Giger-inspired creatures attacking them while asleep.

CASCO uses a major Korean chaebol to extrude their airship cargo carriers. They don't worry about design elements—they want cheap not cheerful.

Mary, Ellen and Ash3r have a cabin at the bow of Princesa Agnes. It's the premier place on this ship. 'Cabin' is absolutely not the right word for it. Stateroom is also completely inadequate. There are four bedrooms, two on either side of a living room that is gigantic. It has its own dance floor, conference center, private dining area, several seating zones, theater, prep kitchen and way more.

Mary is dancing around the place singing her happy song. "This is ours, all ours for THREE WEEKS." Close enough.

Mary has her own room with queen size bed and furniture that looks like Ellen picked it out—massive but made of lightweight modern pico scale materials not ancient hardwoods that Madam President stocks her own home with.

Ellen has a huge bedroom to herself—it is obviously the master. It looks like an old fashioned boudoir which would not be out of place on Titanic. Mind you Titanic is pretty teensy compared to Agnes which (Ash3r informs Mary) is 36.763 times the volume of Titanic. Agnes is so huge that she is 2.81 times bigger (by volume) than COSCO's (China Ocean Shipping Company, CASCO's sister company) newest F-class container ships which can carry 32,000 (20-foot) containers.

"Ellen, Ash3r, come here," Mary says excitedly. "Look at this!"

Mary is looking at an international instructional videographic that is playing on a small section of their media wall. It shows a person of indeterminate gender pressing a button and experiencing a state of wonder. So Mary presses it and a transparent membrane starts to lift across the entire front portal of their living room. The room transforms into a balcony, open to air, sea and sky. Mind you they haven't taken off yet so they are still inland but Mary can imagine skimming over the Pacific Ocean, smelling and hearing it, for more than 10,000 kilometres all the way to Auckland.

All three of them stand there mesmerized by the sunset.

Mary doesn't watch the end of the video which, if she did, would show the membrane shutting at 1,620 meters. Wouldn't do to have their guests pass out due to low pressure or develop high altitude pulmonary or cerebral edemas so the whole ship is pressurized once they're mile high.

...

"You hungry?" Ellen asks.

"Not really. Let's just stay in and watch films and snack like old times," Mary suggests. But she can see Ellen is not buying this. She looks like she's under some strain too. "You OK?"

But Ellen doesn't say anything. Ash3r is looking at her funny too.

"I have an idea—let's get all gussied up and go to the main dining hall," Ellen says offhandedly. She seems to be out of breath for some reason.

'Who says things like 'gussied up' anymore?' Mary thinks. "Really?" is what she says instead.

"Really. Let's do dressup."

...

90 minutes later, the two girls sweep into the dining salon. Ellen is looking positively regal and glows.

Princesa Agnes, cruising at just under 1,500 meters in lovely early evening weather, is heading out to sea, turning south for a leisurely voyage at 135 knots to Auckland. It'll get warmer as they go.

The ship's Captain, a tall Nordic woman, her first officer and other senior members of her staff are there to greet the President of the Commonwealth of the United States. They exchange pleasantries but Ellen's heart isn't in it. Her head is on swivel.

Finally, she sees him. He's in civvies, a muscular man in his mid 40s, terribly handsome and, no question about it, the most debonair man she has ever seen.

He comes striding purposefully over to her. "Madam President," he says holding her right hand in both of his and looking into her blue eyes with his dark ones.

"Good evening, General."

Mary's face tells the whole story. Here stands General of the Army, Farrar Staubach, no doubt about that. He's an incredible male presence in this room. Mary realizes instantly that Ellen is using her as political cover. 'Holiday, my ass,' Mary thinks.

...

"Would you care to join me for dinner?" Farrar asks looking at Ellen but doing his best to include Mary.

"General, may I introduce you to Ms. Mary O'Regan," Ellen says not wanting to introduce the General to anyone except maybe her stateroom.

"Umm, nice to meet you, General. I, I forgot something in my room. Please forgive me for not joining you right now. Perhaps later?"

This is unaccustomed territory for Mary. Diplomacy is not a usual part of her vocab. What she really wants to do is give Ellen an elbow in her ribs and wink at her. The naughty girl! But she can see that Ellen is so nervous that perhaps she'll puke on her beautiful emerald green, full length evening gown. She is wearing a diamond bracelet on her tiny right wrist that would sink this ship if it had any more stones in it. She is also wearing a matching small diamond tiara to tie back her fantastic blond hair and emerald green high heels so she is the same height as the General.

Let's do dressup. Right. Sure. Mary wonders how long it's been since her friend was with a man. Especially one like the General. Mary thinks, 'Like forever and *nevverr*,' as she walks out of this immense dining salon.

...

Farrar is in their living room, looking relaxed and fit. Ellen has excused herself and Mary is making small talk with the General. He keeps glancing at Ellen's stateroom door. But it doesn't open. Maybe the President's called it a night and gone to bed?

Mary excuses herself. She's off to check out one or two of the 72 all night bars and eatery places on Agnes. She has no intention of coming back before dawn.

...

Farrar knocks softly on her door.

"Come in."

He enters her room (which is well lit by a full Moon and LED lights that sparkle in the floor of their balcony) but just far enough to see that Ellen is wearing an Agent Spéciale full length Kimono of the finest material he has ever seen. It is predominantly black and has lovely orange orchids on it. He gets a glimpse over her shoulder of golden lace underneath with a Waspie look (that's a cinched waist). She doesn't turn around when he enters. She is looking out over the ocean through her transparent shutters. The ship has been sealed as they gain altitude heading towards 6,000 meters.

"Do you want me to stay?"

"I don't know, Farrar."

"Do you want me to go?"

"No."

Farrar, not usually stumped, is stumped. She is the most beautiful woman he has ever seen. Oh, there have been younger ones, perkier ones, but never one more beautiful than this girl. She's even taken off her ever-present glasses. But he is certain that if he makes a wrong move, it's over. He's wanted her from the first moment he put eyes on her.

He's pretty sure she wants him—he can feel waves of wanting coming off her.

He goes over to her but does not touch her.

Softly he says, "Ellen, we have more than two weeks on board. I've waited for you for a few years now. A few more days, a few more months even, is fine with me. I'm not in a hurry."

"But I am," she says turning to him and coming into his waiting arms.

...

He kisses her gently and lets his hands find her beautiful ass. He has powerful hands and he kneads her ass cheeks releasing copious amounts of endorphins in her. She moans loudly and absolutely melts into his body. Her moan causes a response in Farrar that is amazing even to him. He runs his hands through her long hair and smells her down to the microbe level. She is wearing Nell Perfume, the one with Ambergris in it. But he can also smell her shampoo as well as her slight female odor and it's like the General's just received another round of incoming artillery fire.

He picks her up and takes her over to her bed. He places her there. He starts to get undressed but then she is there, helping him. She wants to help. She's a bit clumsy, it's Ellen after all. But she gets him undressed and pulls him to her.

He runs his hands over her sheer mesh demi-cup bra careful not to let his hands touch any part of her skin.

Then he places them on her high waisted satin elastic strapping, again making sure not to touch her skin. She is still fully 'clothed' and he is making her wait.

He understands that it has been awhile, maybe a long while for Ellen and he wants to make sure she is open and ready.

He is driving her crazy!

Finally, he allows his hands to move from her lingerie to her skin, her stupendous breasts, her marvelous ass and her most private parts.

She cannot wait, not another minute, not another second. She reaches for him and guides him into her.

Still he is careful to go slowly. She moans once more, a long almost mournful sound that reaches from her soul into his.

He moves slowly, bit by bit, inch by inch until his full length is in her. Still she feels that she can do more, that he can do more and she reaches down, places her hands on his ass and pulls him further into her. He compresses his buttocks so his penis, which is already substantial, expands inside her even more.

Then he grabs her around her torso with his amazing

strength which he was born with and which years of military discipline have increased even more, folding her completely in half and thrusts into her for what seems like an eternity to both of them but couldn't, at this point, be any longer than three more minutes (which is, frankly, amazing given the state they are both in by this time). She lets out another moan as she explodes at precisely the moment he does.

'Wowza, Wowza, Wowza,' Ellen is thinking a few moments later using that crappy left coast expression she's picked up while in San Fran.

...

"Have you been with many women, Farrar?" Ellen asks with her head on his chest. He has some man hair there but not too much. It's nice. She's playing with it.

He sees no use in prevaricating with this woman, "Yes."

"It shows."

"Have you been with many men, Ellen?"

"Ah, that would be a negative, General."

"It shows."

They both laugh.

Ellen's skin is the most amazing thing he has ever touched and, like he said a moment ago, he's touched quite a few females in his womanizing career.

She uses an expensive Murale system every day—first she uses their all-natural cleanser, then toner, serum and finally moisturizer on every part of her body. She's been doing it since she was 22 and she's glad she's kept it up during her lean years of which she's had many up until about a few hours ago. Seeing its effect on the General, she is totally pleased with herself.

Soon, they are putting Farrar's experience and her Murale system to good use again. He knows all the right buttons to push with her and it isn't long before she is trembling all over and her limbs are shaking.

Ellen's finally getting to be a bad girl and, this time, in

a proper bedroom even if it is six kilometers up.

...

"Umm, are we being careful?" Mary is asking at breakfast the next day. It's near noon as far as the sun is concerned.

Ellen blushes beet red.

"Oh come on, you weren't playing croquet with the General last night, were you?"

Knowing Ellen the way she does, she wouldn't put it past her to substitute Pinochle for sex but the blush tells all.

"So are we being careful?"

As President of the Commonwealth, Ellen is regularly examined by several doctors. They analyze her to bits and then some. It takes her three visits before she can get up the guts to ask one of her lady doctors if, ah, there would be a possibility, just saying, ah, to have, perhaps, a BPI insert.

This is the latest in birth prevention—it's inserted into her forearm using a syringe. It's really tiny but contains quadrillions and quadrillions of nanosites. These are purely mechanical devices, quite heavy despite their tiny size, that track down and penetrate the Perl acrosomal space (the head of a male reproductive cell, i.e., sperm) to lodge themselves in the nucleus thereby increasing its density. Basically, they slow the little swimmers down so they can't get to the gamete (female reproductive cell) aka ovum or egg.

Like most well engineered devices, it has a backup. In case some of the swimmers keep moving, there's another type of nanosite that latches onto the hardiest spermatozoon and once attached to their axoneme (tail), they sprout little hooks. They're like sea anchors and they stop the little devils in their tracks.

The nice thing about BPI inserts is it's all mechanical so the days of fucking up women's bodies with chemicals is over. The nanosites flush out through the body's natural systems when their mission is accomplished.

You have to put a new insert in every once in a while depending on how many of the little vermin the particular woman is dealing with. For Ellen, until recently, a BPI insert—a) wasn't needed and b) if she'd put one in, it would have lasted to infinity. But now she's equipped. She's got her own little Strategic Defense System to use on the General.

But Ellen is not going to share this story with Mary. All she'll say for the moment is, "I'm taking precautions."

"OK, so how was he? As good as he looks?"

Ellen is mum about this subject.

…

"Ellen's name?"

"I'm sorry Aggie, what?" Daniella is asking. She's holding baby Dan in her lap. She's trying to teach him to sit up but he's a flop at it so far.

"Her middle name?" Aggie forces out.

"You can't remember Ellen's middle name?"

Aggie is getting frustrated. She has something to tell Ella.

"I can look it up, Aggie."

Aggie just shakes her head and closes her eyes for a moment.

"Tall."

"Yes, Ellen is quite tall," Daniella says her mind on her baby. Actually, Daniella and Ellen are about the same height. Ella might in fact be a smidge taller.

"No, Tallulah."

"'Tallulah' is Ellen's middle name? That's nice."

Aggie nods, 'Yes'. Then she says, "It's a Hopi name."

"What? What did you say, Aggie?"

But Aggie has passed out from the effort.

'What was she saying?' Ella is trying to piece it together. Something like, 'It's a 'hopeful name'. It was along those lines, she thinks.

She couldn't agree more. Ellen is all about hope, hope

for this nation and maybe hope for all humankind. Ella loves the President of the Commonwealth almost as much as her baby and husband.

...

Ella is looking at a piece of paper. Aggie has written something down on it. It is barely legible but she can read it. The message is quite clear. Daniella isn't sure if she should agree.

"Maybe we ought to wait for Ellen to come home."

A vigorous shake of her head, 'No.'

"Do you want me to call her instead?"

'No.'

Aggie is looking at Ella—she is clearly pleading with her.

She takes a deep breath, "OK, I'll make the call."

...

"Hello Mrs. Brooks," says Damien.

She smiles a half smile at him and reaches out her left hand. He takes it in both of his and strokes hers which he knows she can feel.

Ella is fussing with the baby and is worried about what Ellen will say when she finds out that Damien is back here at Revival House. Damien dumped Ellen or something. Now he's here with his new squeeze. Ellen's going to shit on her from a great height after this.

"Ella, can you and Danny please wait outside?" Damien doesn't look at her and isn't allowing a lot of room for discussion on that matter.

Ella can't see what Ellen ever saw in this guy.

...

"Are you sure, Mrs. Brooks?"

She nods quite vigorously, 'Yes.'

"Mrs. Brooks, what you are asking is final. There is no going back."

Another nod.

"Euphony and I are going to stay the night here with

you. We will discuss this again in the morning."

Donna Ann Agnes Brooks has asked Damien and Euphony to take her back with them to Vancouver. Doctor assisted suicide is legal in British Columbia but outlawed in the State of California. Aggie knows that Ellen will never agree—Miss Goody Two Shoes believes that life begins at conception and dies only when God wills it. This is Aggie's opportunity, while Ellen is away.

Damien and his nice new Canadian girlfriend will help her. She's known him for a long time and always thought that he and her daughter would end up together somehow but perhaps that is never to be. Still she knows he knows things like how to help her end her life while she still has some human dignity, not much but it's all she has.

She is going to send Ella and her baby back home to Santa Cruz. There is no way that Aggie wants Daniella to share in any part of the next leg of her journey.

...

"What in God's name is that, Farrar?" Ellen asks him.

"Those, my girl, are 100 foot waves."

"Don't tell me you are going out in that," she says worriedly. Farrar is always up for a challenge. It scares her.

"Yes, M'am. Caleb and Tane are taking us out."

"A nine year old is going with you? Is everyone here crazy?"

Caleb De Theirry is a 32-year old kite surfer dude from Auckland (actually Rotorua) who is head of watersports on Princesa Agnes. Tane is his nine year old son. They live aboard Agnes—they have their own suite and Tane is home schooled by his Dad. Caleb is 1/2 Maori and part of the Ngati Rangiwewehi. 'Ngati' roughly means born of a certain group. 'Rangiwewehi' is the name of the tribe they're from.

Coincidentally, it's the same group that taught Ellen's Mom Maori Poi dance years ago. It's one of the reasons why they're headed to Auckland—to visit Whakarewarewa Village where Aggie stayed as a girl. Mary knows this is just more political cover for her 'secret' assignation with the General, a secret that, Mary thinks, they have no shot at keeping. Half the ship, the half that isn't drunk or stoned all the time, is talking about her affair. Ellen is delusional if she thinks this isn't going to leak out, probably already has.

One thing that Ellen and Farrar haven't done, not once, is switch on any media walls. Of course, Farrar is regularly briefed on military matters as is the President on security issues but they are both careful to avoid infotainment channels.

...

Mary who has never before expressed the remotest interest in anything to do with H_2O has suddenly found a love for watersports. She has found out that Caleb, apart from being a godlike human male who would not look out of place on a Maori battlefield swinging a mere (a short flat club made out of bone and bound to the hand of a warrior using a braided loop of dog skin) and, afterward, either eating his enemies or shrinking their heads or both, is a single parent. His former wife, an Aussie girl, leaves him when Tane (a terribly handsome, future lady-killer who looks Maori except he has golden hair) is a baby after she discovers that being a 'wife and mother' isn't her 'thing'.

...

Princesa Agnes is lowering what they call 'Haul Island'. It is a floating platform that comes equipped with every manner of watercraft imaginable—windsurfers, small sailboats, jet skis, water skis, surfboards, boogie boards, scuba gear, snorkeling, sea kayaking, body surfing fins and gloves, kite surfing, wake boarding, catamarans and deluxe floating chairs for people who just want to float on the sea for a few minutes and drink more wine or beer.

They are semi-stationary, hovering over a point in the middle of the South Pacific that is about a 1/4 mile from gigantic waves that break on an underwater reef there. Anyone who wants to join can but they have to be aboard Haul Island before Agnes starts to lower it. Then Agnes detaches herself and stands off some distance to take in the regatta. Less adventurous types crowd balconies and watch with the naked eye or spyglasses put there for that purpose.

Flameouts are fantastic. Going over a waterfall from the top of a 100 foot wave is a ton of fun (as long as it's not you doing it) into water that can be as shallow as 3 feet at the base of the wave under which is a reef with teeth that will shred your body in a few microseconds.

Getting into waves this size was always impossible until tow-in surfing is invented. You just could not get enough board speed to catch these monsters. Now jet skis tow crazy men (and a few women) into them and, presto, you get the ride of your life, at least once.

...

Ellen and Mary are going with Tane and his group to try kid's windsurfing. It's a new class of boat invented by his Dad and fabricated in Auckland. Mary figures the way to a man's heart is either through his stomach, an area to the south of there or his kid. She is trying the kid route.

Caleb is also the inventor of a snowboard paraglider which they use first at Aoraki (Mount Cook), the highest mountain in New Zealand at more than 12,000 feet. It's really an old fashioned, mini hang glider with a 5:1, 6:1 or 7:1 glide ratio (depending on which model you rent) that you can use on ski hills on the glacier. You hook yourself into its harness and snowboard or ski down the mountain as per usual. What's not usual is that when you hit a mogul just right, you get airborne. If you are any good at it, it's majorly diverting. If not, you fly off the side of the mountain and die or you crash head first into the next mogul and end up a paraplegic. It's amazing, really.

Bruce M Firestone

Caleb knows Mount Cook well having nearly died there once. There are signs everywhere, DO NOT GO OFF THE TRAIL. Or, IF YOU GO OFF THE TRAIL, YOU WILL DIE. But this is Caleb, warrior prince. He goes off the trail. He leaves his first wife with their new baby (Tane) while he goes off to explore. He sees a great climbing rock wall next to a beaut of a waterfall and decides he's going to be David Livingstone and find the source of the Nile.

When he gets about two thirds of the way up, he looks behind him and sees a snowstorm coming up the valley. It's the South Island and temps go from 70 degrees Fahrenheit in Christchurch to 0 on Aoraki in a hurry. Pretty soon, the entire cliff is covered in three to four inches of snow so Caleb knows there is no way he can get down the more than 350 feet he has already climbed. The only way to go is up. When he gets to the top, he sees that it is a false trail—it's still more than 500 feet straight up from where he is now to the actual source of the waterfall. He's stuck with his shitty leather jacket, one candy bar and night is falling. He looks below and he can see the lights of park rangers starting to look for him.

His (former) wife has alerted them that he is missing. He's not only going to die of exposure on this scared mountain, he'll die of embarrassment as well.

But he doesn't die. He follows mountain goat tracks instead. They can jump more than 15 feet and, as long as he can see their poop, he knows that they'll eventually lead him to a path that will take him down safely. Finally, he comes to the end of their trail. It's more than 20 feet straight down to a moraine that is sitting there undisturbed on a nearly 60 degree slope. It's either get down there or wait for an uncertain rescue or let the weather kill him so Caleb flattens himself against the nearly vertical granite wall with zero handholds and slides down to the moraine. When he hits it hard, the whole moraine begins to move and now he is certain that he is not going to die of exposure—he's going to die in an avalanche of gravel and boulders. But then the precarious slope stops moving. So he makes his way down—one foot on the granite cliff, the other on the moraine. Every time it starts to slide, he stops moving and breathing. When he gets down to its base, he's home free. He has to apologize to his wife and then the rangers for putting them in danger. He is totally sincere and they forgive him. But his wife doesn't. It's not long after that she vanishes.

"Miss Mary, could you please sit still," an exacerbated Tane is saying for the third time. She has pitched off the little sit-down windsurfer—first on one side then the other before flopping off the stern.

Ellen is already out with dozens of other people (most of them 12 year olds or less). She is having a blast. She knows how to sail (Damien taught her) and the little biddy boat she is on is surprisingly agile if not fast. She is sitting in a captain's chair made out of pico materials (like the boat) that swivels and moves on a rail. Her long legs rest on one side of the boat or t'other and she is holding onto a wishbone that tips the mast forward or backwards so she can tack, jibe or go downwind no problem. Her hand closest to the stern is like her sheets, pull in, go faster, push out, slow down when she is on a tack.

It's just like a big person's windsurfer except you are doing it sitting down in a chair so you don't need the balance of an acrobat like you do when you are windsurfing for real. It's a good thing for Ellen since balance is never going to be her strong suit. But this, like yoga and croquet, she can do!

She pushes the mast forward to go downwind keeping her other hand in close to her chest. Then as she turns downwind, she lets her hand out slowly to gain boat speed. With the wind nearly behind her, she lets go entirely of the wishbone with her stern hand, places it next to her other hand, replacing and freeing it to grab the wishbone as it comes around. She close hauls the sail and slides the Captains Chair to the new windward side of the boat in a perfect jibe. Ellen looks up at the sunny South Pacific sky and gives a cry of delight, "Yay me!" as she heads out and away from Haul Island pointing at New Zealand still 1,000s of klicks away. Maybe she'll just keep going and beat Princesa Agnes to Auckland!

Anyone can do it, except maybe Mary.

...

There are more than 4,000 cabins on the Princesa Agnes, most of them four meters wide, double occupancy ones coating the skin of the ship on either side. They all have portals and some like Ellen's and Farrar's (they are sharing her cabin now that the pretend stage of their relationship is over) have balconies. They are stacked six stories high on either side of the main cylinder along its long axis with a few choice suites at the bow (where they are). The underside of the Princesa is all cargo; its inner gut is complete vacuum. The topside of the ship would be worthless for cabins unless you like looking out a skylight so it's used for something quite different.

It's a giant dance hall, bar, amusement park and casino. What's really cool is that its outer shell is completely transparent so tonight, after their day spent hovering close to the ocean, the Captain has taken them to the top end of their range to gaze at the stars and lose their money in a company-run casino.

Farrar, fresh from his quite pathetic attempt to keep up with Caleb (who amazingly can get enough speed on his kiteboard to slingshot himself into 100 foot surf without assistance from a jet ski) doesn't like to lose money so he's playing Texas Hold'em with a bunch of guys in a men's only game in a private room near one end of the casino. Apart from a few bumps and bruises including a nasty gash on his right cheek that Ellen needlessly fusses over, the General is fit for his next challenge.

The buy-in is $350,000 QED and each player is allowed one more for $150,000. They squeeze in 10 players and it's winner take all which suits Farrar just fine. 5.5% will go to the house and 1 point to the dealer which leaves $4.675 million for the winner to take home.

He tells Ellen not to expect him back tonight—the game will probably last til dawn possibly noon. She's quite OK with that since she's a bit sore from all the recent activity her various orifices have been put to and she can use a night off. She kisses him and fusses over his face a bit more.

...

During these early stages, better players calibrate their opponents and begin to cull the herd. When they are down to six, blinds double after each player is eliminated—they'll reach $160,000 when just two players remain.

The General is first introduced to poker in basic training. It comes naturally to him. Perhaps it's his understanding of probabilities or his unwavering discipline but he rarely loses even to other would-be officers. It starts out as beer money but soon it's paychecks. He thinks for a few months about making a go of it fulltime but civilian life, especially the dissolute one that lies in front of all top Hold'em players—booze, hookers, mobsters, financial backers and drugs—doesn't interest him.

Farrar is particularly sharp when it comes to body language. He knows that amateurs show a tendency to act strong when their hand is weak and weak when their hand is strong. It is uncanny how consistent this behavior is for players who haven't studied successful poker strategies. They pretend to look uninterested in their hand by, for example, showing sudden interest in a football game that's on a media wall in the corner of a casino. The most common tell with amateurs though is glancing at their chips to do a quick assessment of how much money they have. This let's trained opponents like Farrar know they are up against a good hand since their

Bruce M Firestone

opponent is establishing how much s/he can bet and how much they stand to win.

The General also develops a habit of looking for any change in posture, good or bad, as well as any movements that are outside a player's normal routine. Players using extra protection for their cards such as keeping their fingers on them during an entire round or placing chips on top of them are typical giveaways. Next, he'll look for any type of chip fumble or voice cracking (it's amazing what happens to your body when a person is nervous) or increased breathing rate. He can actually see some of his weaker opponents' chests going in and out rapidly like they've just run up a flight of stairs.

Many people think that pupil dilation is a sure tell. It may be true that pupils dilate slightly when a player sees something s/he likes but this is virtually impossible to detect in most poker rooms. They are usually poorly lit to begin with and you're too far away from your opponent to detect subtle dilation in pupils. Farrar knows better than to waste effort looking for this tonight.

If there are any windows in a casino, Farrar always sits with his back to them. This is so his face is in shadow while his opponents' are lit up like Christmas trees from any ambient light coming into the room that way. He learns this from a financial engineer he tangles with early in his career who is fleecing DOD's supply chain. The guy confides his negotiating tactic to Farrar. Subsequently, the finance guy finds himself trapped in an indiscretion which has nothing to do with supply contracts and everything to do with sexual harassment charges brought against him by an attractive young woman soldier who is trying on female-specific body armor at this defense contractor's plant. It's a bad idea to get on the wrong side of the General of the Army even before he is General of the Army. The young woman in question is Farrar's younger sister.

Two players tonight almost get into a fight over slow-rolling. One of the guys delays showing his cards even when he knows he's won. Consequently, his opponent thinks he's won and starts pulling the pot towards himself. The other guy, with a not-so-fast smirk on his face, finally flips over his cards and gloats. He thinks he's being funny. They almost come to blows. Security separates them immediately. The slow-roller is given one warning. Next time, he'll forfeit. Slow-rolling is very bad poker etiquette and you don't see it very often in casinos because these things are often dealt with in the parking lot after the game—also guys who routinely do it routinely end up dead.

The recipe for a good poker player is quite simple but also quite rare. The percentage of players who are profitable in the long-term is just 8%. These 8% all share Farrar's attributes—emotional control, discipline and a good understanding of probability. That's it. The tough part is that these three have to be in-check at *all* times, not just most of the time. Discipline is key. The General has discipline.

...

"The guy's a poofter. How can you elect a chocolate driller as Prime Minister, mate? He barracks for the other team fer chrissake. And they got a bloody woman for President. Apparently, makes sex tapes on the side too. Probably bangs like a dunny door. Scona beer a gloria sty when ya get to put your donga in that, I tell ya. Probably a carpet muncher too like their PM. No wonder their country is so mucked up," says one of the four other guys left at the table. He's an Aussie from Queensland and is seemingly unaware of who is on the far side of the table. Some of the other men look at Farrar. They know who he is and who the cutie he is boning is too. But Farrar doesn't react. He's just focused on cleaning out these guys, especially this guy. They are down to five players now.

...

After what feels like an eternity of cold cards, Farrar picks up 78s on his big blind. It's a weak hand heads-up, but it's also a type of hand that can surprise the hell out of a guy sitting across from you. His sole remaining opponent is the Aussie who's a complete boor but can really play. Farrar is plenty sure the guy's earlier statements are absolutely intentional. He knows full well who Farrar is and who Ellen is. He's just talking shit to throw the General off his game. No chance of that.

...

After all the buy-ins and re-buys are counted, there is now $3,920,000 QED in the kitty. No one is moving, coughing, drinking, burping, slurping, sneezing, scratching or making rude remarks about homos or babes.

The Aussie and the General are fairly even-stacked and have a strong read on each other. They have both seen and done it all—calibrating, bluffing, feinting, cutting their losses and double bluffing (intentionally losing by folding even when they actually have a good hand). It's risky at this stage of the night (now day) to do anything but play the hand.

...

Farrar awaits the Aussie's move which he hopes will be a flat call allowing Farrar to see a cheap flop. But the Aussie is too smart for that. He moves in with a strong bet of $300,000, knowing that Farrar will figure him for trying to buy the blinds. As the Aussie reaches for his chips, Farrar has already decided to fold. He picks his cards up for one last peek before he begins the motion of mucking them but suddenly stops himself.

There is something off about the Aussie's last bet and it hits Farrar like a wafting stench. The General stares at his cards as though he's contemplating a fold but he's really just playing back the last 30 seconds in his mind, over and over, before it finally clicks. The cards never left the felt. All night his Aussie opponent is reckless with his cards, twirling, shuffling and even fanning himself with them. Earlier, the dealer warns him about protecting his cards from other players. But not this time. This time, hey, they just lie there, motionless, stacked neatly in front of his chips. This is no attempt to buy the blinds. The Aussie has a big hand and Farrar knows it has to be either Aces or Kings.

In Texas Hold'em figuring out your opponent's hand is nearly as valuable as the rank of your own cards. Farrar runs the numbers in his head and knows that he could call the flop and still have enough left to hurt the Aussie if he misses. He figures he has a big underdog on the hand but he also knows that if it hits, the Aussie may not be able to release such a strong starting hand—his emotions will finally get the better of him. So Farrar calls and both players watch carefully as the dealer reveals the flop—6♥ 9♦. Farrar can feel his heart rate spike but is careful not to show any reaction. Then he sees 5 ♠ fall. The flopped the nuts and what's more, if he is right about the Aussie's hand, he knows the bloke will like his overpair too well.

Farrar is now first to act and he makes a modest $300,000 bet as though to suggest he paired on the nine; his trap is set. The Aussie, pleased by the relatively small bet, quickly moves over the top with a raise of $500,000. The General stalls. The Aussie thinks the General is deciding to fold or call but Farrar is simply putting on a show—a quick call may tip the Aussie off as to the strength of the General's hand but too long a stall and the Aussie will detect the ploy. After three long breaths, the General utters, "Call" and slides his chips in. The turn is flipped and it takes every ounce of control for the General to dull his reactions, it's the K♦.

The general knows this card has to help the Aussie— if he is on Aces then he's still got an overpair and if he is on Kings then he just made trips. Farrar checks his straight so as to respect the Aussie's raise on the flop. The Aussie takes another peek at his cards, looks up at Farrar and says the last word that the General wants to hear, "Check."

Farrar is stunned for the first time tonight, doubt immediately sets in. How can the Aussie check his hand? Does he have him wrong, all night? Maybe he underestimates this guy's skills?

If the General is right and the Aussie is on Ace-Ace or King-King, it takes brass balls to check that turn and it would mean that he is setting a trap for Farrar. Then again, maybe he simply has nothing and is revealing his free-card bluff.

The dealer reveals the river, it's the 3♥. This cannot have helped the Aussie but it gives the General the stone-cold nuts along with one hell of a difficult decision. A big bet here and he's liable to scare the guy into a call even if he hit while a check means he risks not getting paid on the best hand he's hit all night. Farrar looks the Aussie in the eye and gets no reaction. He glances at the dealer who is becoming impatient with his delay then takes one more look at the Aussie, still nothing. Finally he breaks his silence with a firm, "Check."

His heart is now racing. He can feel sweat starting to bead at his hairline and a drop roll down his back. He hopes the Aussie hasn't noticed it yet; he hasn't because he's too busy counting his stack. As he finishes, he looks at the dealer and says, "I'm all-in with $645,500" then confidently leans back in his chair. To the General, a giant marlin's just swallowed bait, hook, line, sinker and trawler. Farrar calmly slides his whole stack across the betting line and places his cards face-up on the pile. Just for good measure and with a cruel smile, he adds (uncharacteristically), "I flopped the nuts".

The Aussie explodes, throwing his cards at Farrar who manages to dodge pocket Kings, now revealed. "You bloody Yank whore! Ya fucking kiddin' me? What ya thinking checking that river?" He hauls his jacket off, throws it on the floor, stomps on it a few times then rips his shirt off and tosses it on the table, "Ya can have me bloody clobber too, ya bogan bastard."

Farrar stands up, leans forward with his knuckles on the table and replies. "I guess I just got lucky, mate." Then he calmly walks over to shake the tournament director's hand and accept his reward. He pays the dealer and the house and then asks S4y3rs to bank the rest of his winnings with QE Reserve Bank, the safest bank on the planet, one that can't be hacked. Meanwhile, security escorts the Queenslander out of the poker room.

...

The Princesa is cruising again close to the surface of the South Pacific so people can enjoy the great outdoors. All the shutters are up and habitable spaces are unpressurized. Farrar prefers it like this.

He feels like a cigar and steps out onto the balcony to enjoy a Bolivar Gigantes. He's glad that Ellen normalized relations with Cuba so he can finally buy his favorite cigars legally.

It's wonderful to be alive, a man, on this ship, at this time in history, dating the most powerful woman in the world who is also devilishly good in bed.

'Humdinger,' he thinks.

He has one last personal errand to run before he goes to visit his lover.

...

He wallops the guy again. He just doesn't seem to be getting the message. What's wrong with this guy? So he introduces his face to the wall, again. Then the balcony's safety barrier for good measure.

"Let-me-say-this-just-once-more. You see that water down there. From a mile up you are going to hit it like it's concrete. If you ever, *ever* so much as look at her again, I will throw your worthless self off this here balcony. The sharks will eat what's left of you after you *bounce* off the ocean. You shut your bazoo, unnerstand?"

When he gets upset, he sounds more Texan than usual but he rarely swears. He gets mad at himself if he does. But the Queenslander must now surely finally get the fact that he can't insult the General of the Army's boss (and girlfriend) without paying a price.

He's also going to need some dental work—the balcony railing has somehow chipped the guy's upper and lower central incisors.

...

"Mrs. Brooks can we go over this again please," the doctor is saying. "We can get you help with pain and there are physical and occupational therapists who can perhaps restore some functionality on your right side. Another round of Riluzole may extend your lifespan by as much as four or five months."

Aggie is just shaking her head, 'No.'

"Dr. Bell has told us that your daughter is your next of kin?"

She nods, 'Yes.'

"She is currently unavailable to advise you or us?" The doctor is well aware that Aggie's daughter is the President of the Commonwealth. He's worried. Canucks don't litigate over matters the way Americans do and even though they appear to have turned over a new leaf under their current leader, she may not feel the same way when it comes to her own Mom. "Don't you think it would be wise to wait for her return?"

Aggie looks really alarmed. She starts to tear up and a copious amount of drool pours out of her mouth.

Euph fixes her up and strokes her gray hair.

"Pullease, Doctor, pullease, help me, help me," Aggie says desperately with maximum effort. Euphony who hates to cry almost as much as Ellen does bursts into tears. Damien and the doctor leave the room together.

...

"I think that's it Doctor," Damien says. "We have a complete video record of Mrs. Brooks' wishes on the subject. It has been verified, time stamped and repeated three times. We have her signature and two witnesses. We have her psych report that she is of sound mind and can make a decision knowing the consequences. We have two legal opinions on the matter." Damien is as reluctant as her Doctor to take the next step. He has known Aggie for almost as long as he has Ellen and he totally respects her. She is the one person everyone turns to for advice. He wishes she could have been his Mom or maybe mother-in-law. When he thinks that, he immediately defaults to Mom.

"Perhaps we could talk to her husband?"

The lying creep has refused to take Damien's calls after the first one when he practically says, 'The sooner, the better.'

"I don't think we'll get any help there," is all Damien says on the matter of the former husband.

"Let's go back in," the doctor says.

             …

Euphony and Aggie have composed themselves.

The doctor says, "Mrs. Brooks, can you hear me?"

A nod, 'Yes.'

"You understand that what we are proposing to do is to give you an oral dose—"

"Oh God, thank you, thank you, Doctor," Aggie says in her extremis. It is one of her longest sentences in almost three months.

"Please Mrs. Brooks there is more. You must listen and I must be sure you understand. It is an antiemetic drug. Approximately 30 minutes later I will give you a lethal overdose of powdered pentobarbital dissolved in fruit juice. I understand you like orange juice?"

Another nod, 'Yes.'

"I will give you this via a drinking straw. The pentobarbital overdose will depress your central nervous system. You will become drowsy and fall asleep within ten minutes. Anesthesia will then progress to coma and your breathing will become shallower. Death will be caused by respiratory arrest, which will occur within 30 minutes of ingesting pentobarbital. You understand, you will die? It is always fatal."

Bruce M Firestone

Another nod, 'Yes.'

"You still want to proceed?"

Another nod, 'Yes.'

He takes a deep breath, "OK. Mrs. Brooks please prepare yourself."

...

Aggie is a Christian but in another life she was a Maori poi dancer. The Ngati Rangiwewehi of Rotorua tell her she is white on the outside because she was born in the daylight but Maori on the inside. Maori culture is one of the most inclusive in the world. You do not have to have been born Maori to be Maori, you just have to share their culture and beliefs. It's one of the reasons why their culture has survived and thrived in New Zealand and proven so hard for white folk to eradicate as they have with many aboriginal peoples elsewhere. It doesn't hurt either that Maori (women as well as men) can fight like hell too.

Euphony has cleaned Aggie's body and she is wearing her poi regalia which is way too big for her now. The bodice is made for someone who is at least 5'10" and weighs 135 to 140 lbs. Damien can see that she must have had a figure like her daughter's when she was young.

Poi is not like Hulu. There is no right/wrong. Poi is a way to communicate music in movement. There is no written history of Poi either. It is said that Maori men did Poi to exercise their wrists in preparation for warfare. Women were originally forbidden Poi moves. So they did it in secret instead. But when the men saw them do it, their beauty and grace, legend says they then decided it was OK. After that, women who excelled in Poi were highly prized. Ellen's Mom was highly prized in her day.

Maori women became so proficient at poi that it was then used to distract enemies before war so one tribe could wipe out another.

Aggie, after she started teaching, started using fire in her poi dance but it is a modern invention; it's a way to make it showier, give it more wowza! Aggie made Poi sexier with her wiggling hips and her dressed in evening gowns performing at really high speeds. Even her Maori friends like it.

Poi is compulsory in elementary schools in New Zealand. It's weird that Aggie is such a good dancer but her daughter, Ellen, sucks at it.

...

At her request, they play Poi E, a tune by Patea Māori Club—a huge hit in New Zealand during another era. It is a song of excitement and life. Aggie looks beautiful and at peace. She is watching their media wall and seeing her friends again, performing in Rotorua. The doctor has given her the antiemetic. They are waiting together for 30 minutes.

Aggie has asked Damien to say the 23rd Psalm for her. They turn down the music so she can listen to his words.

> The Lord is my shepherd; I shall not want.
> He maketh me to lie down in green pastures; He leadeth me beside the still waters.
> He restoreth my soul; He leadeth me in the paths of righteousness for his name's sake.
> Yea, though I walk through the valley of the shadow of death; I will fear no evil: for thou art with me; thy rod and thy staff they comfort me.
> Thou preparest a table before me in the presence of mine enemies; thou anointest my head with oil; my cup runneth over.
> Surely goodness and mercy shall follow me all the days of my life; and I will dwell in the house of the Lord forever.

...

It is time for the pentobarbital. Aggie drinks gratefully. She nods at the doctor. Then she squeezes Euphony's hand with her left. Finally she turns to Damien with a lopsided smile. She motions to him weakly to come closer.

"Tell her, tell her," she breathes deeply, "tell her, this is how a brave woman dies."

"I will, I promise I will, Aggie," Damien says.

They wait for her last breath and then Damien leans over her body and cries. It's way worse than when his own mother passed.

Euphony says, "Is there anything I can do to help, D?"

He shakes his head, 'No'. "But thank you for everything you have done for me and for her."

Euph isn't sure whether he means Aggie or her daughter.

...

Before her passing, Mrs. Brooks turns her estate, all of it, into cash. That's so lawyers, accountants, governments and former husband don't get their greedy hands on it, either frittering it away or just plain stealing it.

She makes provisions for various charities, nieces and nephews, great nieces and nephews as well as Lily, her son Jon's daughter with Natalie and, of course, Ellen. Interestingly, she's leaves a chunk to Danny, Daniella's baby, to provide for his education. Since (disappointingly) Ellen has never given her any grandchildren, it looks like she sort of adopts this one.

...

When they dock at AIA (Auckland International Aerodrome), it's a circus. The Paparrazzoids are there in force. Her old friend, Pulitzer Prize winning tabloid journalist Erik Renke is there. They all want to be the first to get shots of and interview the General and his new girlfriend and the President and her new boyfriend.

It's pandemonium.

There is no way to avoid this so they decide to press on. They are the most photogenic couple since the Young Royals in the first part of the 21st Century.

While they are walking through the aerodrome with Dekka and his security team doing their best to keep a path clear, someone yells out, "Hey, Ellen, Ellen, over here! I have some news for you. Ellen! While you were fucking the General, your mother's just died in Vancouver at the hands of your former boyfriend. Hey, Ellen, Ellen, over here." It's Renke and he gets another photograph (and story) of historic proportions—the moment when the President of the Commonwealth of the United States first learns of her dear mother's passing.

...

They are gathered around her gravesite. Aggie has asked to be buried on Vancouver Island on a grassy hilltop in a cemetery overlooking the nearby ocean. There is a single cherry tree about 12 metres away. Aggie asked Damien before her passing to preside over her funeral. She does not want a minister who did not know her to say meaningless words over her.

Her body is cremated so her grave is a small three foot square plot. It is not expensive. The urn is there and a small group as well. On one side of the gravesite are Damien and Euphony. On the other, stand Ellen and Farrar. Her security team, Dekka and the General's Aides-de-camp stand respectfully off in the near distance. Jonesy, who has been a huge help, is there too.

Damien is saying, "To everything there is a season, and a time to every person under Heaven. May her friends and family remember Donna Ann Agnes 'Aggie' Brooks for the beauty and delight she brought into this world, for the things she gave others and for what she gave me while I knew her especially in the last weeks of her life. Her strife is over.

"The Lord will keep her from all evil," he continues. "He will keep her life. The Lord will keep her going out and her coming in from this time on and for evermore.

"Aggie showed me the meaning of courage which I thought I knew from my time in San Quentin. But I knew nothing compared with what she showed me. She knew how to live and how to die. She faced death with courage and dignity."

When he says this he is looking directly at Ellen. Ellen

is looking back at him. Then she looks at Euphony in her dumpy, cheap frock. Ellen is thinking uncharitably, 'My, you've traded down since Nell.'

Euphony is looking at the President thinking, 'You selfish bitch. You practically emasculated my guy then threw him on the scrapheap for that baby killer standing there like a peacock right next to you, YOU FUCKING WHORE.'

Farrar is looking at Damien as his service concludes thinking, 'This guy wouldn't last a minute in my outfit. What a wimp.'

Damien is only thinking of Aggie. He'll miss her.

...

"You killed my mother, you son-of-bitch," Ellen is yelling at him. "What gives you the right to act as God? You're not God. You just think you are." She is so upset that she starts hitting him on the chest. Like most women, her punches lack any real power plus he's way more solid than the last time she saw him so she can't do much damage. He just lets her hammer away.

They're in the private visitation room at the Cemetery. Embarrassed aids and the General as well as Euph stand outside the door but can hear every word that is spoken between the two of them.

Damien says nothing. She strikes him on the chest again and again then slaps him, hard. On his face. His face turns red but still he makes no move to defend himself.

"You killed my mother," she says once more. But she is tiring out. Ellen and Farrar come back on Air Force One which is a lot faster than Princesa Agnes. Mary declines her invitation to fly back with them—she's staying in Rotorua with Caleb and Tane for now. Caleb has some shore leave coming and he takes this opportunity to let Tane spend time with their (humongous) extended family as well as show Miss Mary around.

Ellen's plane is at YYJ (Victoria International Airport) waiting to fly her and Farrar back to SFO. She has not slept in two days. Even Ellen looks haggard.

"Ellen, Corporal Raymond Michaud was here. In Vancouver, I mean. Do you recognize the name?"

"No, should I?"

"Yes, you motherfucking should. He helped you bury my grandfather."

"Oh, you mean Sunny."

"Right. When were you planning to tell me?"

"Look Damien, I know where you're going—"

"When were you going to fucking tell me?"

"I was waiting for you to get better but then, before I could, you ran out on me, you coward."

"You didn't think it was important to tell me that my grandfather was not my grandfather, he was my Dad, and my Dad wasn't my Dad, he was my half-brother and that my father fucked his daughter-in-law because his son couldn't give her a baby and that baby was me? That it drove my mother to drink and four marriages before booze finally killed her? That my grandfather who was my Dad ruined my parents, only half of whom were really my parents, killed my mother, drove my Dad who was my half brother crazy and ruined my fucking life? You didn't think that was important enough to tell me or that I needed to know that? I fucking hate you and everything you stand for. You can get on that plane of yours and fly back to that Godforsaken country of yours with your new Master-of-the-Universe boyfriend and never come back to Canada, ever, you lying sack of shit."

...

Bruce M Firestone

Chapter 9 Talk of Hands

"Cady, it's me. Over here. No, not there. Here! Arcadia, look up!"

Arcadia is her room in the house she shares with four other women. It's a lousy place in a lousy part of Temple (about an hour's drive north of Austin and half an hour south of Waco) but it's all they have the budget for. It has three small bedrooms which means that two of them are double occupancy including hers. It has one bathroom that they all share so it's always a mess of makeup, makeup remover, hair, underwear, stuff drying but never really dry and overall female grime.

Arcadia is 24 but looks older since she smokes cigarettes, a pack a day. She never finishes highschool and has been living on her own since her 17th birthday when her Dad kicks her out for drug and alcohol abuse.

She's a server but really that's too vaunted a term for what she does. She's a waitress in a diner with a lousy boss and worse tippers. She just can't seem to find any motivation to do anything else.

Right now, it's mid afternoon and she's got the room to herself. She's doing the nightshift which starts at 5 pm and goes til close which could be anything from midnight to 2 am depending on if they have any customers.

She is looking up and to her right. At the end of her tiny bed an intense pure white light is shining in her eyes, partially blinding her. She holds her right hand up as an eyeshade and thinks, 'Huh?'

She is weirded out by the fact that a videographic is playing on her media wall except this rental is so cheap it doesn't have any media walls. But the light isn't on any wall anyway; it's hanging in midair.

Arcadia still drinks a lot but has stopped smoking hash because it's too expensive. Her drink is bourbon. Sometimes when she is feeling fancy, she'll make herself an Old-Fashioned cocktail which is probably the oldest drink to have that name. She uses bourbon, orange slices, sugar, Angostura bitters and maraschino cherries to make them. She knows the sugar is bad for her figure which, frankly, isn't what it used to be.

She hasn't had a boyfriend in nearly two years. She really should get in shape.

...

Since she isn't drunk or stoned, she can't think of a single reason why she is hallucinating. She's stayed away from hard drugs since the end of her teen years. But she says, "Hi," anyway.

"Hi, Cady."

"No one calls me that."

"I do."

"And who might you be?"

"It's Jag, Jagad Durai. Don't you remember me?"

"Reed?" she says confusedly.

"Yes, Reed. How you doing?"

"Great."

"I can't see much. It's like looking down a pipe."

"I can't see anything at all except for this spotlight thing you've got going." Arcadia is thinking this is some type of gag except none of her roommates would have a clue as to how to pull off something like this.

"It's a Quantum Tunnel."

"Sure, yeah, right. Just happened to end up here did you? You some kind of pervert?"

"Gee, what's happened to you? Did your IQ drop or something? I've been looking for you for the last six months. I'm in Shenyang near the border with North Korea. Look this thing isn't too stable without something on your end."

"Jag?"

"For Christ sake, yes! Look it's going to close in a few seconds. Don't use your phone, not even a Q-Phone or any media wall for communication. You're going to need a standalone computer and don't connect it to the Internet or anything. Here take this and—"

The light winks out but not before a tiny (standard size) data cube just under 1 centimeter a side plops out onto her unswept laminate floor. It makes a tiny clatter and comes to rest just under the foot of her bed.

"Reed?"

But he's gone, again.

...

"Viva la revolución!" Evan is saying to his Cabinet. They are all there along with Head of Commonwealth Communications, Sayed Bashir.

"I wish you wouldn't say that Prime Minister even in jest, even in here," Bashir notes.

"I think we can and should expect major push back on these bills from industry," Secretary of Commerce says. "They aren't going to like it."

"TFB," the PM adds. Too fucking bad.

"The media are especially sensitive to changes in their environment," Commerce adds.

"You mean they can dish it out but can't take it?" Evan comments.

"Exactly."

They are about to bring in the next set of sweeping changes that Ellen and Evan have long planned; it's an overhaul of the political-economy of the Commonwealth. These bills which will be coming before the General Assembly in the next few weeks call for reform of media ownership (way too much concentration), anti trust (way too little of it), education (ditto), taxation (way too complicated), judgeships and district attorneys (way too political), SCOTUS (ditto), banking, insurance and Wall Street (way too complicated, too big with too little transparency).

"Maybe we are being too ambitious," says naturally cautious Sec State.

"In crisis, opportunity, ladies and gentlemen," the PM

says.

"Don't waste a crisis—your patient's or your own," adds Secretary of Health.

"Who said that?" asks Sayed.

"Last century, a guy by the name of Weiner in a journal called Medical Economics. He wanted doctors to recognize that their patients could use crises to change their lifestyles and improve their prospects."

"Right," says Evan. "We should err on the side of change not complacency. What do we have to be complacent about?"

"I agree but I don't see anything in here for defense of the nation. How do we plan to respond to Imperial China and Germania?" Secretary of Defense Bob Schultz asks. The two great powers have just announced their 1,000-Year Friendship Pact which calls for a new world order, a reshaping of earth-bound and interplanetary commerce.

"They're going to complete their membrane either this year or early next year. Once they inflate it, Imperial China and Germania will lay claim to the entire lunar surface. Luna Colony will then cover the entire planetoid," says Secretary of Energy, Dr. Shelby Zewyki. She is by far the smartest person in the room and probably the toughest too.

"Is there anything Commonwealth engineers can do about this situation?" the PM asks.

"The Republic hasn't had a real space program for the last fifty years. We don't own any rockets that can even reach LEO so orbiting the Moon or Mars let alone landing there is out of the question," she says. "Imperial China and Germania realized at about the same time we abandoned space exploration that no nation will ever have a space program that is sustainable if it is not economically sustainable too."

Everyone in the Cabinet Room can see she is about to launch into another mini lecture. Only the PM and Sec Defense Bob Schultz are really interested. Hence, she has

Bruce M Firestone

the floor.

"Economic sustainability of space exploration and development is not based, and could never be based, on ever increasing national subsidies of old agencies like NASA, CSA, RFSA, ESA or CNSA. If something requires heroic action to accomplish then, almost by definition, it is a one-time thing and, hence, not sustainable.

"Economic sustainability implies that space exploration and development must be based on a combination of public and private initiative guided by the principles of trade for mutual benefit as well as research, discovery and innovation for potential profit. It is those P3s that help create a stable, space-based economy that, in symbiosis with Cartesian Powers on Earth, avoided our fate—a space program that stumbles from pillar to post and has proven to be unreliable in every way that counts including getting people and material to and from space safely and providing a reliable, steady flow of benefits to Earth-based and space-based assets."

When Dr. Zewyki uses the term 'P3', she is referring to the very successful public-private partnerships that statist-capitalist nations like Imperial China and Germania are using to dominate solar system economic development. 'Cartesian Powers' is a new term coming into common use to describe their 1,000-Year Friendship Pact. Most people have no idea where the term comes from or what it really refers to but it seems to click. It's become its own meme in less than six months.

Dr. Zewyki certainly knows its underlying meaning and where it comes from since Shelby is the one who coins the term. A Cartesian plane has two axes which given the alliance between Germania and Imperial China seems to fit nicely. Shelby also knows her history and how dangerous an earlier Axis proved to be to world peace and security.

"So let me repeat my question," the PM says, "Is there anything Commonwealth engineers can do about it?"

"No," says Sec State.

"Bob?"

"Defense has nothing at the moment, Prime Minister."

"Actually you do," Shelby says looking at Schultz. He does not like being shown up by his colleague. How the heck would she know anything in his Department that he doesn't know?

"Which means what?" the PM asks.

"Prime Minister, there may be a solution to territorial claims by the Cartesian Powers on the Moon as well as Mars."

"If you are suggesting war, Dr., you can stop right now. We did not sacrifice what we sacrificed to establish this Commonwealth to pick up where the old Republic left off—starting a new war every three years."

"Hear, hear," says Sec State.

"Once their membrane is inflated, the entire surface of the Moon will become habitable. The Cartesian Powers intend to populate the Moon with several hundred million people of Han and Germanian ancestry—"

"Yes, yes, we know that," the PM says impatiently. "Again and for the last time, is there anything we can do about it?"

"I have been speaking with General of the Army, Farrar Staubach." As Shelby is saying this, Bob Schultz has gone from cloudy weather to stormy to hurricane force IV winds in a few heartbeats. "He has been in touch with scientists working at UBC—that's the University of British Columbia—and they have come up with a colonization plan of their own."

"But we don't have the space faring capability to establish a Lunar or Martian colony, you just said that yourself," Sec State says for them all—a confused bunch of politicians at the moment.

"No, but we may have something better," Shelby says.

...

"Dr. Bell."

"General."

The two men size each other up. Damien is quite a bit taller but the General is by far the stronger of the two of them, at least physically. Farrar has literally walked into Damien's lab at UBC unannounced. This is unheard of for someone in his position.

"Please meet Dr. Chuck Wong, my colleague."

"Howdy."

"Hello." Chuck is as surprised as Damien. He doesn't know all the background on the personal side but he has a fair idea that these two are not exactly blood brothers.

"Dr. Wong, can you please wait outside?"

"Chuck, stay where you are," Damien says.

"The matter I have to discuss is confidential."

"If it has anything to do with the President, General, you can save yourself the trouble and double time it out of my lab, as my old friend Tony used to say, RFN. RFN, General."

Farrar knows what RFN stands for.

"It's a matter of national security, Dr. Bell."

"Really? Whose nation? Would that be the Commonwealth of the United States? That's not my country, General, it's yours. You can have it. All of it."

"I think you will want to hear what I have to say."

"Maybe yes, maybe no. But Chuck stays. It wouldn't by the way have anything to do with his last name being of Han origin would it, General?"

"I can leave, Damien, it's OK," says Chuck. He's been kicked around so much, heck, what's another licking from the General going to amount to?

"General, I would be dead if not for Dr. Wong's intervention in San Quentin." Damien now suspects the General wants to talk about the Cartesian Powers and that he thinks that maybe Chuck is another Imperial Chinese double agent like General Yao.

"Make up your mind General. You have 10 seconds and then I'm leaving if you don't."

...

"So let me see if I have it right? You guys neglect your space program for the last half century. You allow the Cartesian Powers to get into a position where within a few months, a year at most, they can lay claim to the entire lunar surface despite the 1967 UN Outer Space Treaty prohibiting any nation from doing that and you want my help, our help," Damien says pointing to Chuck and himself, "because you can't think of anything else on your own?"

"They've renounced the UN treaty that reserves space as the province of all humankind. I thought that was an ideal that would appeal to you, Dr. Bell."

"Fuck you, General."

"You are only saying that because of Ellen."

"Leave her out of this."

"I did, you didn't, Dr. Bell." The General is, of course, 100% right about this. Chuck can see it written all over Damien's face. He'd better not play Texas Hold'em against Farrar whose reputation as a fearsome player is entirely justified if even a quarter of the rumours about him are true.

...

Damien knows exactly how to resolve the situation. He already thought of it during his incarceration in San Quentin as a guest of DOC. He's pretty sure that Farrar has figured it out too which is why he came here in the first place.

"There is a terrible danger in what they are thinking of doing," Damien says to Chuck. They've taken a timeout from their 'impromptu' meeting with the General of the Army. "If we create more QEs, some of them are bound to be drogues. We haven't solved that problem yet, maybe we never will."

"Can we control for that, Damien? Plan for it, build in remedial programs for it?" Chuck asks.

"Maybe, it's possible. But do we want to help them?"

"I would say 'no' but maybe by saying 'no' to the Commonwealth, we are saying 'yes' to the Cartesian Powers and I would rather help Ellen than General Yao," Chuck adds with impeccable logic.

...

"General, we can place several million Quantum Entities into the service of the Commonwealth. They will be bonded with Commonwealth Military personnel and we can transport them to both Luna and Mars for you via laser carrier where they will live at macro scale and claim parts of both the Moon and Mars. But I have a few conditions."

Farrar knows better than to say anything at all. He just raises his eyebrows. If Dr. Bell agrees to help the Commonwealth, Farrar will be gone in 60 seconds or less. Like any good salesman, when you hear a 'yes', thank the client, get a signature, shake hands and leave because anything you say after that will only put your deal at risk.

Only this deal will never be sealed by a handshake. And it's not because Farrar won't shake hands with Damien.

"One, the Commonwealth will endow a Chair at UBC in Quantum Physics to be called the Paul Dirac Chair in Physics and insist that Dr. Wong be appointed as its inaugural Professor.

"Two, the Commonwealth will reinstate its support for space exploration and commit itself to both Lunar and Mars missions so that QEs stationed there will be relieved of duty within ten years—"

The General has made a clearing noise in his throat and interrupted Damien's flow. It's as if he high fived a dealer when he puts another card on the board. What an idiotic thing to do!

"General, this is not a negotiation. You understand that?"

"Please forgive me," the General says quite sincerely Chuck thinks.

"The Commonwealth will reinstate its support for space exploration and commit itself to both Lunar and Mars missions so that within *ten years* those QEs won't have to live on the fucking Moon forever. Or Mars. They can choose to come home to Earth."

"Three, the Commonwealth will start a crash program today to be able to deliver nanosite generators and power packs to the Moon and Mars within six months of today for Luna and 12 for Mars so our quantum people can build things there.

"Four, that Chuck and I will be given a veto over what purpose the generators are put to and what's built there as well as the right to propose uses and have them approved for scientific and humanitarian purposes— there'll be no Commonwealth weapons on the Moon or Mars, General." As Damien says this he looks challengingly at Farrar who, having relearned a lesson a few minutes ago, just smiles and encourages him to go on holding out his right hand palm up. 'Maybe the guy's not such a wimp after all,' he's thinking.

"Five, that the Commonwealth will use its influence to have the 1967 Outer Space Treaty re-ratified by all nations who wish to be part of a family of nations."

Damien stops. Farrar doesn't think he's finished yet. He just waits patiently.

"Six, I want to know what the fuck is going on with Ash3r and I want to hear it personally from the horse's ass," he says deliberately changing the expression. He means Ellen naturally.

"Seven, all net proceeds from Luna and Mars real estate and commerce will flow not to the Commonwealth but to a new co-operative to be called DARCH which will be owned by all quantum and human people equally."

Damien knows that Ellen has created a new World LLC model around QCCII and he approves of it even if he doesn't approve of the person who conceived it.

Then Popeye comes into the Lab. He rubs up against

Damien's leg. He's hungry. Damien picks him up, looks at the General for the last time and walks out. He's going to get food for his cat. It's a fucking priority.

...

"Did you hear the one about the new restaurant on the Moon? Great food but no atmosphere," Chuck says to Damien after the General has left. Damien isn't sure whose jokes are worse, Chuck's or Pet3r's.

"They'll have an atmosphere there pretty soon. Once their membrane is complete they'll fill it with a nice mix of oxygen and nitrogen." The Cartesian Powers have docked several huge captured asteroids around the Moon largely made up of water ice. They are melting them down for water, hydrogen and oxygen using vast solar arrays they've also got parked in orbit around Luna. They'll import them to the lunar surface using the three space elevators they've already built on the Moon.

Their membrane which will encircle the Moon at 20,000 feet is semi-permeable and highly magnetized. It has to be semi-permeable because they'll go through the Perseids every year just the same as Earth. These meteor impacts peak every August (from the 9th to the 14th) but impacts happen every day. The membrane is self sealing so very little gas (air) will be lost. The membrane is magnetized to protect colonists from solar radiation. It'll work just like the Earth's magnetic field (they hope) and deflect harmful cosmic rays and UV radiation.

The Cartesian Powers put a lot of focus on the Moon because even though it is classified as Earth's satellite, it's really too big for that—it's far larger than any other moon in the solar system, it's a planet really. It is also conveniently located a short distance away and shares the same nice warm *habitable* orbit around the sun as the Earth.

The Moon was probably formed when a Mars-sized object collided with a young Earth which explains both its proximity, mass and composition.

There is also mounting medical evidence that the Moon's 1/6th lunar gravity is helping people live longer and boogie like they are teens again which appeals to the old Führung of Germania and even older Mandarins in Imperial China. Lifetimes of over 132 years for men and 140 for women are thought to be possible. There is also speculation that children born on the Moon will be the tallest humans ever reaching heights of eight feet or more. The NBA gets excited about that until they learn that these kids couldn't get up off the deck once they reach Earth's relatively massive gravity.

A recent paper has been published that suggests the total value of lunar real estate after the membrane is in place will be $313 trillion QED. Damien thinks they've grossly underestimated its value—he believes it'll be worth $3 quadrillion QED at maturity about 25 years after inflation of the membrane.

The diameter of the Moon is around 3,476 kilometres. That gives it a surface area of approximately 37.8 million square kilometres about the size of the US, Canada and Russia.

The nearside of the Moon (the side that always faces the Earth) has most of the seas (mare) which are areas of lower elevation. There are several basaltic mountain ranges presumably formed through impacts on the lunar surface or perhaps by earlier volcanic action. The far side of the Moon is much smoother—only 2% of the far side is covered by maria versus 31% of the nearside.

The Cartesian Powers plan to fill the lower elevations (mare) with water and create seas. There will be plenty of new waterfront property available for purchase and sale soon.

The dark side of the Moon should not be confused with the far side of the Moon (i.e., the side that is never seen from earth.) The dark side is simply the night side.

The lunar day is around four weeks which means you get 14 consecutive earth-days of sunshine followed by 14 consecutive earth-days of night. 'Make a pretty good place for a horror film,' Chuck thinks.

It's also pretty cool that areas at the Moon's North Pole are continually illuminated by the Sun during the northern hemisphere's summer. There are also mountains that get eternal light because of the low axial tilt of the Moon with respect to the Sun. So the Cartesian Powers have already built massive solar plants there for their future colony; they're already able to produce huge energy flows. There obviously won't be any internal combustion engines or manufacturing processes that use combustion inside their membrane encapsulated atmosphere. Even though their biosphere is big, it's way smaller than Earth's which extends as far as 120,000 feet to the cosmic shore.

Their plan calls for concentration of human population into 121 Shanghais (about 1.27 million square kilometres) and leave the rest of the Moon's surface (95% of it) in a state of wilderness or ocean. They estimate total human population that can be supported by this ecosystem will be 970 million.

The lunar regolith is pretty junky when it comes to growing stuff so they have been mining asteroids not only for inert gases like nitrogen (for their ginormous airbag) but for macronutrients like phosphorus, potassium, calcium, magnesium and sulfur as well as micronutrients such as boron, chlorine, copper, iron, manganese, molybdenum and zinc. Of course, they'll have to use some of their nitrogen for their soils not just their air.

Now one thing they know is that machines are bound to fail so they figure that the only way to have a sustainable lunar colony is to have a sustainable biosphere. If you have a sump pump, say, keeping the basement of your summer home nice and dry, you are lucky to get 10 years out of it. If you use a human heart to pump out unwanted moisture instead, you might get 120 years of uninterrupted service with very little maintenance despite a lot of abuse from things like stress, lack of exercise, too much exercise, drinking, smoking, too much eating or eating the wrong kind of stuff. In 120 years, a human heart beating at, say, 60 bps will contract and expand more than 3.78 billion times. That's a pretty big number. So without question, biological agents are much more reliable than mechanical ones.

Life has existed on Earth for about 4 billion years. Think about how unimaginably long that is. That's 2.92 trillion sunrises and sunsets without a single failure. If it had even one, the chain of life would have been broken which would mean no Nell, Damien or Ellen or anyone else. Nothing humans have themselves created so far can rival a biosphere that can keep organisms alive for billions of years. The Cartesian Powers are going give it a go.

Scientists from Imperial China and Germania will be experimenting with insect, plant and animal mixes for a long time to get it right. There are still some things you just can't simulate and ecosystems are one of those things. They are way too complex even for quantum computers of which, Damien thinks, the Cartesian Powers have none having denounced such things as dangerous and unnecessary.

They won't be thinking that when several million quantum people suddenly appear on the Moon and Mars and start building stuff. Their guys won't need a vast gas retention membrane protecting them to do it. QEs can climb 4,700 metre Mons Huygens on the Moon or descend 9,000 metres into Valles Marineris on Mars without spacesuits, consumables, climbing or spelunking gear.

To Damien, there is actually a lot to admire about what the Cartesian Powers have done. The problem is that every square metre of this planet has been claimed by one nation or another (even Antarctica has been divvied up just in his lifetime) and now they want to do the same to the Moon and Mars. Damien's plan is to beat them to it—they'll claim as much as they can for all humanity and their quantum friends.

...

"That is the deal," Dr. Zewyki is saying to Cabinet after she gives them an abridged version of Farrar's previous meeting with Dr. Bell.

"Shelby, is there no other means of persuading Dr. Bell to cooperate other than giving in to his ridiculous demands?" Sec Defense asks.

"Bob, the old regime already tried that, remember? He spent years in San Quentin and they tortured him, nearly to death. He never gave them the Quantum Key. I would say 'no' there is no other way."

"Our Commonwealth has renounced all forms of torture and state approved assassination as a means of projecting political power," Evan says. In fact, Ellen has signed a Presidential order to that effect and made a speech at the last G30 meeting calling on her fellow Heads of State to endorse it which all have done except the Cartesian Powers. "There will never be a discussion at this table on those subjects, ever."

"I'm not suggesting that, PM. It's just such a shitty deal," Bob Schultz says. He's worried about the Department of Defense's budget. "'All net proceeds' Dr. Bell has asked for. Maybe there is some flexibility in how we define that. Maybe our costs can be higher and proceeds lower?"

Evan looks around the room and sees that despite this last comment from Sec Defense or maybe because of it there is consensus now. So he says, "Make the deal," to Shelby unknowingly echoing Damien's statement made years ago when QCC made (had to make) their own shitty deal with Apple or fail.

...

Cady is back at Camp Mabry. The old guy, the curator they went to see at Brigadier General John CL Scribner Texas Military Forces Museum years ago to get Handie-Talkies, is still there. He's aging pretty well but is slightly deaf. Arcadia is very nervous. She hasn't had a drink for 48 hours, a record for her, and is down to just three cigarettes a day, one after each meal. The funny thing is she's only eating twice a day and not very much. She can't seem to choke anything down.

She keeps thinking that it was a dream but she reaches into her purse at least once an hour to touch the data cube. It's real for sure. It can't be a hoax, can it? Reed's come looking for her. Is that possible? He didn't forget about her, did he?

...

"Do you remember me?"

"I do, Miss, you were here with that Indian boy. Nice kid. How's he doing?"

"Fine, Sir, fine." She doesn't say anything more. She's fidgeting with something in her hand.

"You need something, Miss? Or just come to look at our Museum? We're open Saturdays to the public. You can come back then. It's free on Saturdays." He is looking at her and can see that the years haven't been kind to her. She can't have much money. In fact, she's bused to Austin and walked to the Camp from downtown. It's a long way.

"I was hoping you'd have a machine that would play this." She opens her right hand (which shakes a bit he notices) to show him that she has a data cube. He reaches for it but she closes her hand and jerks it away like he has leprosy.

"Any media wall can play that. We only have antiques here."

"I need a standalone computer..."

The unspoken words here are—she can't afford one and, anyway, no one buys those things anymore.

"May I ask why?"

"Umm, no."

"Why should I help you, Miss? This isn't a school project any longer, right?"

"Right. But it's for Jag. He needs help."

"Why doesn't he come himself then?" To the curator, Jag would appear to be the brains of their operation.

"He's in a prisoner of war camp in northern China near the North Korean border."

"He is?"

"Yes, Sir."

"And somehow an ancient computer is going to help?"

"Yeah, that's what he said, I think."

"You talked with him?"

"Ah, yeah."

"You don't seem too sure."

"I'm sure," she says leaning forward. "We brought your Handie-Talkies back, right? I'll bring your computer back. I just need it to play this."

"How are you planning on transporting this thing?" He watches her walk into the Camp and up to his Museum from his office window. Her old running shoes and stockinged lower legs are covered in Texas grit. She is wearing a dress cut to just above her knees that is a pale, unattractive green. She made it herself. Cady can sew as long as she has a pattern, some material and her old fashioned sewing machine. It's an ancient Elna which is the only thing she takes with her from home other than her clothes when her Dad kicks her out. Her abuelita gave it to her when she was nine. Which reminds Cady. She's got to see her Granny. It's been far too long. What's the matter with her? She's forgotten she has a family (other than her Dad) that might want to see her. Right, she'll fix that too. Soon.

"You mean you'll give it, I mean, lend it to me?" She smiles for the first time and when she does that, five years drop off her.

"I didn't say that. Just wondering how you planned to take it with you *if* I lend you one? They're pretty heavy."

But in the end he does loan her a Thermalite Quadcore SYS505HS Tower that they used to use for gaming, decades ago. Turns out videogames are really good at tuning up a soldier's reflexes—for example, to shoot when called for and when not to shoot, say, at friendlies which is one of the biggest sources of casualties of war. You kill your own pals if you have an itchy trigger finger.

He turns it on to make sure it'll fire up and that its operating system isn't corrupted. He even drives her back to the station near Highland Mall where she can catch a bus named after a dog for her trip back to Temple.

...

"So what's your boss like?"

"He's really cheap. He says he has to be cuz he has four kids and a wife to look out for."

"Is he mean to you?" Jag asks. He is sitting in her room in Temple on her tiny bed. Arcadia is sitting next to him. She is doing another night shift so they have the whole afternoon to talk or at least until he has to go back.

"No. Just cheap and a cracker. He hates Mexican Americans—he calls us 'spics'. Hates Chinks, gooks, Jews, you name it. He says he and his wife called it quits after their fourth child was born because every fifth child born is Chinese."

"He wouldn't like me," Jag says. "How much do you make, Cady?"

"With tips?"

"No, like per hour?"

"Minimum wage for a server." Which is below minimum wage for everyone else since they are supposed to make up for it with tips. But not only are tips crappy in their diner, she has to share them with busboys, short order cooks and her manager as well as her boss. It doesn't leave much for her.

"I need you to go to north."

"Huh?"

"I need you to go see someone."

"Could I like just call them or something?" Cady is

worried about money.

"No. You can't use media walls or anything. It's confidential, Cady."

"OK."

He looks around her pathetic room and then he looks at her. She can't meet his eye.

"Things have been pretty tough on you, huh?"

"Not as hard as they've been for you." He has told her of the beatings he has endured and some of the other circumstances of the camp he is in.

"I have money, Arcadia, but nothing to spend it on. Let me give it to you."

"I'm OK, Reed. You keep it. Maybe you can buy your way home one day?" she says hopefully, thinking, 'Home to me' but she doesn't say that. Geez, she's missed him. Her whole life went into the shitter when he went away nine years ago. She can see that now.

"I'll put enough in QE Reserve Bank for your trip." His plan is to do more than that so she can get a nicer place but he isn't going to tell her that now.

He is looking over his shoulder back in his cell in Shenyang. Someone is coming so he quickly tells her what he has to tell her. Then he says, "I have to go."

"Are you coming back?"

"Always," he says then he winks out of existence.

...

She's sewing at her Elna. It's a new dress. She's humming softly to herself. She went to QE Reserve Bank like he told her to and he's left her some money, a lot of money, like he said he would. She's got enough for her trip but more besides. She buys a new pattern but then she has to throw it out. For some reason, it's too big. Maybe she picked out the wrong one but, what the heck, she goes back and gets a smaller dress size.

He visits her every Wednesday afternoon. She's got her Thermalite Quadcore SYS505HS Tower sitting on the floor in her room. It's been transformed into a full quantum scanner and it stabilizes things on her end. Jag tells her that he has hacked the new Imperial China Sinofighter game console which he has been forced to work on.

It's a Samurai sword fighting game that is truly amazing. The console is tiny. You activate it by saying 'comitay', fight in Japanese. Then a giant Sinofighter materializes. You can choose to fight it with Katana (long sword), Wakizashi (short sword), Tanto (knife), right handed or left handed Kama (which looks like a deadly sickle) or fan.

What's cool is you can crank up the levels and have a good scrap. Even better, because it's quantum tech (it'll be the first ever out of Imperial China), when the Sinofighter wins, you feel it. They're using quantum scanning which is mind altering. If he lops off your head or eviscerates you from belly to sternum, you feel the pain. If you're a masochist, you can crank the levels ways up (both pain and speed) and really suffer. Teenage boys everywhere will buy these things like crazy. They will also find that the Sinofighter can take on a whole pack of them. At the top level, even if you have five or six guys, really good players, attacking at once, you can't kill the thing.

But Jag has found another use for it. It scans him down to the quantum level and does the same to Cady so while he is sitting in her room as a quantum phenomenon in Temple, she is in his cell in Shenyang, large as life. The only difference between the real girl and the scanned version is a slight albedo effect. The reflection coefficient is slightly off so she appears to shimmer, ever so slightly.

...

"Jag, do you remember saying that we would know, like, when the right time is?"

"I do."

"Is there any chance you could maybe get out of there?"

"I don't know Arcadia. We're shut up pretty tight

here."

"Yeah, I figured."

"But these are fully actualized quantum phenomenon," he says obscurely.

"What, what does that mean?"

"Well, it means they can do more than sword fight."

"Huh?"

Then he leans in and kisses her, shyly at first then with more force and passion.

"Cady, we can make love."

"You mean things will like work?"

"Yes."

"Have you ever tried before?" she asks.

"No."

"Then how do you know they'll work?" She sounds more like the old Arcadia these days.

"Well we could try then we'd be able to prove it. One way or the other."

"Umm, nope."

"Don't you want to?"

"Umm, yes."

"So?"

"Like not today, OK?" She's got her period. "Next Wednesday. Alright?"

...

"I'm not 15 anymore, Reed."

"I know that Cady."

"I haven't been doing too much since you left."

"Yeah, I understand that."

"Maybe, you'll be disappointed if, like, I get undressed or something." She's wearing the new dress she's made and he's paid for. It's way nicer than anything she could afford before.

"Why don't I just turn around? You get undressed and under the covers. Then I'll come join you." Jag isn't nervous but he can see Cady really is.

"OK, you can come over now."

He gets undressed and slides under the covers with her. He wants to take them off and look at her, all of her. Instead, he lies next to her kissing her and fondling her nice boobs.

"They're even better than when you were 15, Arcadia."

"No they're not."

"You're beautiful, Cady and I love you to bits."

"I'm a bit chubby; that's what my boss says."

But actually she isn't. Her dress size is down by an amazing 4 and she feels better and better every day. It's been nearly 75 days without booze. She also read somewhere that drinking water helps so she's been drinking six cups a day. It's like someone pulled a cork stopper out and she is peeing extra weight away.

Then he kisses her stomach and starts to play with her Body Candy ring in her navel that she recently reinstates there with his tongue.

Soon they are making love and it turns out that his hacked Sinofighter game consoles work just fine. The real Jag is making love to a scanned copy of Cady in his cell at Shenyang and the real Cady is making love to a scanned copy of Jag in her tiny room and it's 99.7% as good as the real thing.

"Oh, oh, oh, my travelin soldier is back!" she is saying looking up at him. Her eyes are shining. After that, words leave her mind and nine years of pent-up frustration disappear in 30 minutes of lovemaking.

There is only one problem. In his hurry to see Cady today, Jag has forgotten to engage his quantum shield on his end. It's another device he has created that forms a boundary layer across which only the information he wants to reveal flows. That means he can show his jailers only the things he wants them to see, like Jagad Durai hard at work when he is actually visiting with his sweetie pie in Temple.

Now they can see what he's really up to. He's wide

open. They won't beat him for it (yet). They have another plan for him and this new piece of tech he's foolishly created.

...

A coupla Wednesdays later, she asks, "I don't suppose I can get pregnant from any of these sessions, Jag?"

He bursts out laughing but then sees she is serious. "Sorry. I haven't solved that problem yet."

"But I have."

"What?"

"I can think of a way."

"But Cady I can't be there for you and a baby. I don't know when I am going to get out of here. Maybe never."

"You can be with my baby just like you are with me now."

"But it's not real."

"It's as real as it can be and I don't care. I'm not waiting another minute for you, Reed. Let's have a baby."

He's confused about this but seeing her determination, he considers it. It's something that is so out of the ordinary plane of his current existence, something he never thought possible, that he is having trouble keeping up with her. To give her a baby and his father a grandchild? Can it even be done? Like how?

"How would we do that?" he asks.

"I read some stuff."

"What stuff?'

"Like sperm can survive for four to six hours if they're in a clean container with a lid on it and kept at room temperature. That's plenty of time."

"I can't exactly UPS it to you, Cady."

"You can drop it out of that Quantum Tunnel of yours that you used on your first visit here just like you did with your data cube. I'll take care of the rest on my end."

Jagad Durai's face is a study in amazement. He runs his left hand through his thick hair, then says, "Why didn't I think of that!!?" Next he adds, "I dunno, Arcadia, if living tissue will survive a trip through a Quantum Tunnel."

"Let's find out," she says simply.

Then he kisses her so many times that pretty soon they are both laughing hysterically.

"When?" he asks.

"As soon as I come back from up north."

"Alright. Alright. A baby, what d'ya know, a baby," he says marveling over how much he loves her. Life can't get any better than this. "Hey, Cady, if it works, do you think you can find my Dad for me?"

"You bet."

...

Ellen is having thoughts similar to Arcadia's. Something has changed in her since her mother's death. She isn't clear exactly what but it feels like something is broken. Her Mom was just 57 at time of death.

She can't put her finger on it but the cycle of life is bearing down on her. Somehow she feels like she has let everyone down, especially herself.

She hasn't seen Farrar in two months. She's been avoiding him. She knows that he knows that and, bless him, he hasn't pressed her on it. They've talked about their relationship—he feels safe with her—she's as married to her job as President of the Commonwealth as he is to the Army.

But lately, she hasn't felt very married to anything or anyone.

She shouldn't have said those hateful things to Damien at her Mom's funeral. And she was unbearable to his Canadian girlfriend who, in retrospect, seems very nice and has obviously been good for him and good to him. Clearly, he's better off now and has found new purpose in life. Lucky him.

She can't figure out why she is so unhappy. Oh, who is she kidding? She wants a baby. Face it, it's as plain as day. But whose baby? Ellen decides she just needs a new plan is all.

...

"Dr. Bell?"

"Yes."

"Sorry to disturb you but there's a young woman here to see you."

"Does she have an appointment?"

"Umm, no."

"Is she a student?"

"I don't think so."

"Well tell her to make an appointment and have security check her out," Damien says to his EA. His EA is a young man, Alex, 21, who is going places, Damien thinks.

Their lab at the Department has grown fantastically using the resources of the Commonwealth. It's grown not only in terms of personnel (from 2 to more than 700) but spills over into a network of trailers that are parked everywhere. Farrar wants Damien to work at Livermore (Lawrence Livermore National Lab near SFA, San Francisco Aerodrome) but he declines, politely but firmly. The General says security and confidentiality will work better there but Damien doesn't care SFA (sweet fuckall) about the General's concerns. Still he has agreed to a joint CSIS (plainclothes group of agents) and Commonwealth Military presence here. The Cartesian Powers are no joke and Damien understands this. He's back to having 24/7 security which he detests but puts up with.

He's still living in the President of UBC's basement but now they have a full time RCMP hut at the gate (one of those horrible nanosite extruded/grown brownish nest-looking structures) pretending to provide security for Dr. Woo. It's Damien they're looking out for. When he's over at Euph's place, they sit in a couple of squad cars that look ridiculously out of place on Granville Island. Euphony brings them coffee and hot chocolate. She's offered them Wrecked Brew too which they regretfully decline. Damien reminds her that the 'P' in RCMP stands for police but she just shrugs. "I'll cast an evil spell on them if they try anything." The RCMPs (all men) have no interest in busting a small time bootlegger especially one who looks as yummy as Euphony does. As Damien's economic prospects have recently improved so have hers so she can afford nicer things now—she's been shopping at Bolts in downtown Vancity and it shows. What she likes especially is the effect it has on Damien—it's really, really good.

...

"Dr. Bell my name is Arcadia Valenzuela."

"Hello, Ms. Valenzuela."

She's been waiting in their ante room for two days. She refuses to leave the premises while security checks her out. They think she can't afford a hotel or something—she's a waitress from Texas after all. They've scanned her and made sure she has no weapons or viruses or other surprises for them but she won't tell them what it's about. She seems very determined. Maybe she's some kind of groupie who likes physicists but she doesn't look like that. She's attractive enough but not showy in the way you would expect a groupie to dress or act. She sure is set on seeing Dr. Bell though.

The only thing she has with her is an old Thermalite Quadcore SYS505HS Tower which must be a bitch to lug around. She lets them boot it up but it has zero/zip on it. She has a data cube too (just under a centimetre per side) which they find of course but she won't let them touch it. It's for Dr. Bell, she tells them. This makes them uncomfortable and leads to a standoff until Alex tells Dr. Bell that he has a hunch that she is legit.

Alex has gotten to know her a bit in the 48 hours she's been sitting two metres from his workstation.

...

"He said to tell you everything," she continues, "but is it OK if I boot up my PC?"

"Please."

She inserts her data cube and a video of Jag Durai and G4nesha starts playing.

Bruce M Firestone

"Freeze frame," Damien says right away to her computer but the video dumbly keeps playing. He realizes instantly the thing is an antique so he reaches for the screen but it doesn't respond to touch either.

"Here," she says showing him how to move a mouse awkwardly on a teensy touchpad on a keyboard that just as awkwardly folds out from the base of the tower. He freezes the video and then enlarges it. He can plainly see that G4nesha has the same freckled complexion as Ash3r does. What the fuck?

"Do you know why this Quantum Entity looks the way she does?"

"Yeah. I think it's because Nesha and Jag are bonded and linked. She's evolved or something."

"Nesha?"

"G4nesha, she's Jag's QE—they can read each other's minds—they're, they're linked."

"Ah, Miss Valenzuela, do you mind telling me where, umm, Jag and G4nesha are?"

"Sure. They're in a prison camp in Shenyang, that's near the—"

"I know where it is," Damien interrupts.

"They were taken there by a guy named Yao Allitt when I was 15 and—"

"Can you hold up a minute, Ms. Valenzuela please?" Damien says. Then via intercom he says, "Alex, can you ask Dr. Wong to join us immediately? And please cancel my appointments for the next two hours."

...

They get the story out of her in about 90 minutes— the quantum scanning that Mr. Durai has perfected, the link that can be formed between human and quantum counterpart that has been hinted at in their equations but never (scientifically) demonstrated let alone verified, the evolutionary step that QEs take after mindlink is established, their subsequent release from the three laws, the quantum tunnel that Mr. Durai initially uses to drop his data cube on Arcadia's floor, even their visits using hacked Sinofighter consoles are disclosed. But still Damien feels he is missing something, something important.

"Ms. Valenzuela, is there anything more about these visits that you can tell me?" he asks.

"Not really." But she doesn't make eye contact with him when she says this so he goes over to where she is sitting. She is hunched over in her chair, shoulders rounded, like she's been beaten down, maybe by life. He kneels down so his eyes are on the same level as hers, he takes both of her hands in his and says, "Arcadia, I don't mean to pry. Neither Dr. Wong nor I will ever tell a soul what you have said here unless you give us permission. But we have to know everything, everything. We can't help you otherwise. Are you sure there isn't anything else?"

"Well maybe one more thing."

"Uh, huh?"

"Well, you see, like, those consoles, Jag used them, I mean we used them to be with each other, I mean like intimate sort of."

"Sort of?"

"Well, ah, really all the way."

"I assume they worked?"

"Yeah. Really, really well."

"Is there something else?"

"Yeah, we are going to try like maybe next week to have a baby."

"A baby?"

"Yeah, it was my idea. You see," she says in a rush to get it over with, "I thought he could use that little quantum tunnel of his to send something else through."

"Would that be sperm, Ms. Valenzuela?" Dr. Wong asks as clinically as possible to save the young woman any further embarrassment.

"Yeah. But Jag wasn't sure he could transport

something live so we were going to try something else first."

Damien reaches down to pick up Popeye who is back for some more attention. Cady just looks at the enormous cat.

Damien says, "Well we won't be sending you through, Pops. You're way too big. Maybe we should try a lab rat first." As soon as he gets this out of his mouth another thought occurs to him. He looks at Chuck who immediately sees it too.

"Ms. Valenzuela, is there anything else? I think I might have something that can help you and Jag but I want to make sure I have *all* the facts."

"That's pretty much it except Jag said, well he isn't too sure, but he thinks maybe Yao Allitt is working on some kind of super weapon based on his work, some new way to attack the Commonwealth."

"No surprise there. OK, Arcadia, how big is Jag?"

"About 6'3"."

"No, how wide is he—how broad in the shoulders?" Damien asks.

She holds out her hands indicating a big man about 55 centimetres.

"What are you thinking, Dr. Bell?"

"I think Arcadia we can do better than bring a vial of sperm out of Shenyang. Let's see if we can widen that quantum tunnel, stabilize it and test it. Afterwards, let's go get Jag out of that shithole General Yao has him in. Let's bust him out, Ms. Valenzuela."

When he says this, Cady jumps up like she is 15 again and gives Damien the biggest hug. Her face only comes up to his chest. "Oh, oh, oh, Dr. Bell that would be the best thing evverr. Can you do it?"

"I don't know for sure, Arcadia, but I think the answer is yes." When he says this she bursts into tears. He puts his arm around her and strokes her hair. She's had a rough go, no doubt about it.

"This is dangerous, Damien," Chuck says. "General Yao won't like losing one of his prize pets. I think we should tell Farrar."

"Absolutely not. This is a civilian program and we are in charge."

"But this is different. This will be construed as an act of war by the Mandarins." A shiver runs through Chuck when he says this. Westerners have *no* idea of the cruelty, the scale of cruelty, the thousands of years of history, tradition and practice at it that the Imperial Chinese have. They are masters at it.

"I don't care. They are up to something. All that bullshit about rejecting quantum economics and now they're going to release a fucking game console based on quantum scanning that they stole from a US citizen and, in fact, kidnapped and imprisoned that very same guy in a forced labour camp."

"That's one man, Damien. What about our program to put QEs on the Moon and Mars? That could impact whole generations of free peoples."

"Chuck you missed the whole point. Don't you see? With Quantum Tunneling, it's not just QEs that will be on the Moon and Mars; we can transship minerals, gases, building materials, nanosite generators, nutrients, whole frigging seas whatever we want from the Earth to Moon or Mars or from one part of the solar system to another. We can not only beat the Cartesian Powers to parts of Luna and Mars, we can go anywhere! And if we can bring Jag here alive, we can also put humans on Luna and Mars and anywhere else we want. Spacecraft? Won't need 'em, Chuck. And who delivered this? One man, Jag Durai. Why? Cuz he loves that girl. And we, my friend, are gonna go get him RFN."

...

"Ms. Valenzuela, do you have any place to stay?"

"There's a hostel on Granville. I thought I would go

there, Dr. Bell." She doesn't want to say but she overspent on clothes and this trip so she has to save. The Bakpak Hostel is cheap, just $19.50 QED a night and she needs to keep some money for her return trip which she is dreading. She hadn't really thought about much other than just getting here like Jag told her to. Beyond that, she has no real idea what to do next.

"Thought so. Look Ms. Valenzuela. I talked to my girl. Her daughter's at Berkeley and she has a second bed in her room that you can use for a few nights if you want. She's a really nice person and I explained the situation to her. You can trust her.

"Look when was the last time you slept?"

"I slept on the train coming up, Dr. Bell. Then a bit in the waiting room outside your lab. But I'm OK, really. There must be a bus I can catch nearby this being a University and all."

"It's too late for that Arcadia. Buses stop early in Vancity. Come on, Euphony would love to have some company—she's a great cook and has some great brew she'll ply you with, it's a type of Mead she makes—"

"I, umm, don't drink, Dr. Bell."

"Well that's OK then. She has a non alcoholic version too."

...

They're sitting in Euphony's apartment at her teensy dining table and she is happily feeding Arcadia. Damien brought her over in one of the staff cars they have at the Lab to transport their people, day and night. Anywhere they need to go, no questions asked. They come with either military or CSIS drivers. There is one on standby 24/7 for the Head of DARCH which just happens to be Damien.

Arcadia is doing her best, the food is delicious as promised but she can't eat as much as she used to, her stomach musta shrunk or something. The dealcoholized mead is really good though.

"Arcadia, when do you have to get back to your job?" Euph asks her. Making conversation.

"Well, technically, yesterday. It took a little longer to get in to see Dr. Bell than I planned on. So I should shove off tomorrow."

"It is tomorrow," Damien says.

Euphony is pissed with him for keeping Arcadia waiting for two whole freaking days in his waiting room. She is giving him the cold shoulder at the moment.

"Well, the day after today," Arcadia says. The two girls laugh together.

Euph is staring at Damien who is doing his best to pay attention to his cat. That's his default position when she gets mad at him. Popeye comes back to Euph's place in the staff car too. Damien can't stay the night since Arcadia will be sleeping in the same room as Euphony and it looks like she's mad enough that, even if he wanted to, there'd be no sex for Dr. Bell this morning.

Euphony is thinking of coming over and giving him a nudge when he finally says, "Ah Arcadia, we are going to be doing a lot of work with Jag in the next few weeks, maybe months. It might be a good idea if you stuck around. That is, if you want to?"

"Want to? Dr. Bell there is nothing for me back in Texas. My Dad kicked me out when I was 17, he hates me. I have no life other than my, my boyfriend who is stuck in a stinking Imperial prison camp. Want to? Yeah, big time."

Euphony's heart melts for the girl.

"Well you'd have to work—"

"Dr. Bell, that I know how to do."

"So how about a job at the Lab? We are looking for another EA. You'd be working with Alex—"

For the second time today, Cady jumps up and goes over to where Damien is sitting and hugs him.

"Wow, YES."

"You don't know the salary or hours yet, Arcadia."

"That's OK, Dr. Bell. I am sure it'll be fair."

"Well, it's union scale."

"That's fine Dr. Bell."

"Do you need anything from your home in Texas?" Euphony asks her.

"Well, do you think you could like maybe give me a small advance on my salary?"

"I am sure that would be possible," Euphony answers for Damien defying him to say anything different. "What do you need the money for, honey?"

"I'd like to have my Elna shipped up here."

"Elna?" Damien asks.

"Yeah, it's my sewing machine. My granny gave it to me when I was nine."

"I am sure we can arrange that for you. You just ask Alex the day after today," Damien says smiling at her. "He'll get it brought here no problemo." As Damien is saying this, he is looking over Arcadia's head at Euphony. He's been forgiven!

"Can I ask Alex something else?"

"Sure, what is it?"

"Well I borrowed my PC from Camp Mabry. I gotta return it to their museum. But the data cube is mine. I'm keeping it," she says possessively. It's become her lucky talisman.

Damien can't help it. He bursts out laughing. "Sure, like I said, talk to Alex. You won't have to worry about shipping costs though. Trust me on that. We've got it covered." Damien is thinking as he says this that they've got the Commonwealth's credit card and it has a vast credit limit so a coupla more things aren't going to matter.

"Can I ask one more thing, Dr. Bell?"

"Yep."

"What's an EA?"

...

Euphony gives him a big wet kiss as he is leaving. He cops a feel and they fool around a bit. She breaks it off. He's getting her all steamed up for nothing.

"You are nothing but a big softie," he says to her remembering when they first met how bossy she could be and tough on the outside.

"Look who's talking."

They fool around some more before she finally says, "Go. I'm going to put Arcadia to bed."

But she doesn't need to. Cady has found the w/c and is fast asleep in her spare bed when Euph comes back upstairs. She sleeps on her side. She has taken a second pillow and placed it against her abdomen and breasts so she has company.

Euph strokes her hair and misses Zora like crazy for a few minutes. Arcadia looks way younger when she is sleeping.

Cady has had a recurring nightmare since she was 15. Things that are impossibly big, huge, monstrous, vast and heavy are held up by the flimsiest of threads. It can't be happening but it does. It is always threatening to break and her world is going to collapse when it does. Sometimes she wakes up screaming because she knows the thread is about to snap. It has to. She always wakes up before it does though. When she wakes up, she is delirious. It's why she was drinking so heavily and, before that, doing drugs. To stop this dream.

Snuggled in Euphony's apartment, Arcadia Valenzuela feels safe; she sleeps without dreaming this dream, first time in nine fucking years.

...

"Dr. Bell may I introduce you to the President of the Commonwealth of the United States?" Dr. Woo is saying, grotesquely unaware that Ellen and Damien have history. His wife, Betsy, standing about a metre away is looking at her husband like he is a cockroach. Henry is thinking, 'What have I done wrong now?'

This is a big get for UBC and for him personally. The President is in Vancouver for a WFTA (World Free Trade Agreement) discussion and has accepted his invitation to tour the University and attend this reception in her honour.

"Hello Damien," Ellen says.

"Madam President," he says.

They are staring at each other from a distance of about a dozen centimetres. None too friendly a stare thinks Betsy. She knows that these two were co-founders of a big tech company back in the day and it looks like they had a falling out, probably over money. Gee, it looks bad enough that if they both had six shooters, there'd be a massacre. So Betsy Hammersmith, the clever hostess that she is moves in to break up this pending tragedy and steers the President off to meet the Premier of the Province of British Columbia unctuously waiting for his chance to get a photo with the Prez. It's an election year in BC.

...

"What are you doing here?" She's freaking followed him down here. Her security people practically bust down his door. Ellen is standing in his basement apartment under Norman MacKenzie House. It's been transformed into an extension of his lab. Media walls and equipment of unimaginable uses are omnipresent. Every spare square centimetre has equations written on it. He never lets anyone in here, not even Euphony. His useless RCMPs have strict orders not to let anyone in EVER. He does his own cleaning so he doesn't need to write DNE all over the place not that anyone could erase his stuff since the only person who has access to his media walls (i.e., his quantum passcode) is Pet3r. Not even Dr. Wong comes here. He supposes that RCMPs like everyone else kiss her ass and let her do whatever she wants like she's some kind of mythological god. So she just comes into his place. Fuck!

"I see that Pet3r has transitioned," is all Ellen says in response.

"Hello, Ellen," Pet3r says.

"Hello, Pet3r. How are you feeling?"

"Fine. Different. Scared. Exhilarated. Free."

She smiles at him.

"Yeah, he's changing. No thanks to you," Damien says.

"Look Damien—"

"No you look. You didn't tell me about Ash3r, I had to find out from a friggin waitress from Texas. I created these things. You don't think you should tell me when a Quantum Entity changes state, reads your mind and is released from the three laws? That's not just slightly relevant to the work we are doing here in your not-so-humble opinion?"

"I hear the work is progressing well," Ellen says mildly.

"I suppose the General keeps you up to date," Damien says snidely.

"I haven't seen Farrar in two months, Damien but I get regular reports. You and Dr. Wong are doing marvelous work."

"You don't know the half of it."

"What? You are working on other stuff we are not aware of?"

"Was that a Royal 'We' I just heard, Ellen?"

"Stop it, Damien. This is beneath you."

"Fuck off, Ellen."

"I won't fuck off. If there is something else going on, I need to know about it, don't you think? I am the President of the Commonwealth and the person who got you out of San Quentin alive, Damien, alive."

...

Upstairs Betsy desperately trying to retrieve something from this horrible failure of a reception (where's the President?) asks 84 year old, world famous jazz composer and pianist Carl Bray to play his greatest hit, Talk of Hands. It is without doubt the most romantic piece of music that Betsy has ever heard and this great Canadian artist has come to their home from Toronto to play for the President of the Commonwealth who, embarrassingly, is nowhere to be found.

Carl the gentleman that he is and consummate professional sits at his piano—it's all he is seeing and so he starts to play...

...

Damien comes over to her and backs her up against the sole big piece of furniture in his room. His standalone wardrobe. She can smell his anger and frustration as well as his clothes that are hanging a few centimetres behind her head.

She can see the chords in his neck straining but she is not afraid. She is just watching him with her deep blue eyes (she came into his apartment without her glasses). She is looking at him exactly the way she did years ago in the Albacore on the Charles River in Boston. He recognizes the look and is remembering that day on the Charles too. His arms are rigid against the wardrobe on either side of her. He has her in prison. See how she likes it!

But she likes it just fine. Then she hears the most marvelous piece of jazz coming from somewhere. It is reverberating through Damien's basement apartment. Whoever is playing can really play. He must be right above them. Then she leans forward and kisses him wildly. Her hands go around his waist. He tries to pull away but then somehow he is frigging kissing her back.

He roughly lifts her long gown and pulls her thong panties aside and plunges into her in one swift move. No more Mr. Nice Guy.

He's not going to bother undressing her and, as for foreplay, they've had 15 years of it already so there is no call for any more of it.

She is ripe and ready for him.

Somehow they find their way over to his single bed. He sweeps off the covers along with his notes, tablets and various instruments he has been working on or building.

He pins her to his bed and fucks her royally. His penis is not quite as thick as General of the Army Farrar Staubach's but it's even longer.

It's long enough to penetrate her vagina then reach her g-spot, after that it passes her cervix and next her fornix before ramming into her uterus. It feels like he is opening her uterus and this sends her into paroxysms of pleasure never having been fucked like this before.

Her spasms of pleasure ricochet back to Damien who comes for about a minute deep inside her, in fact, just in the right spot (in the actual uterus itself) to send her into orbit once more.

...

"Can you feel that, Damien?"

"Ah, yes."

"What is it?"

"Dunno."

"You ever experienced anything like this?"

"Nope. You?"

"Never."

He is still inside her. "I think there is some kind of electrical current passing between our bodies. One of us is a cathode, the other an anode. I think you are the anode."

"It's nice," she says.

"Yep."

...

Damien is in turmoil. All that shit he talks about like trust being the number 1 thing in life. Stuff he learned from Dr. Luis and his goddam grandfather/father. All bullshit. All in the crapper. He's betrayed Euphony's trust and himself. What the fuck is he going to do now?

There is no way he'll ever leave Euphony. She's saved him in every way a person can be rescued. But he doesn't deserve her. Should he tell Euphony what a useless pile of dog turd he is?

...

Bruce M Firestone

Ellen's back in Revival House. Like most Ellen plans, her latest has worked perfectly. If she can't have the man, she'll get something else from him.

She doesn't need Ash3r to run a scan on her. She already knows. She's pregnant. How does she know? She knows cuz she feels exactly like she did the night that Nell came to her and filled her breasts with milk and she felt movement in her womb. Obviously, it's way, way too early to feel the baby move but she knows.

She had her BPI insert removed and she stayed away from the General for two months. It all flushes out of her system quite nicely.

Damien cooperates quite beautifully. What he lacks in technique (nothing like Farrar!) he makes up for with vigor. Nice.

Ellen is going to have a baby.

"Oh Glory Me," she says out loud to no one, no one at all.

...

Chapter 10 Maya Fair

"We've run C57BL/8 ten times, Damien. They all came through great," says Chuck Wong. "Physically, they show no changes in condition, no apparent aging, no muscle deterioration, no systemic changes. They're fine, Damien."

"How about cognition?" Damien's worried that travel of live organisms through a Quantum Tunnel could affect brain physiology especially the human brain which has, he believes, quantum processes at its core. Wouldn't be any good to pull Jag out of Shenyang and wipe his brain or decapitate his mind's higher functions, now would it?

"Our mice are negotiating multiple t-mazes at identical speeds before and after their trips via Q-tunnel. They're remembering just fine," says Chuck.

They have been running these experiments using dark brown, nearly black lab mice called C57BL/8 for nearly a week. These are very robust rodents, not as docile as albinos—they'll bite you if they get a chance. They use these mice because they share a high degree of homology with humans.

"Are there any differences between short and longer trips?" Damien asks.

"No, none," answers Dr. Wong.

This is what Damien expected since anything transported via Quantum Tunnel crosses space-time in intervals equal to zero no matter how far apart their portals are. So they are not spending any more time in a tunnel if the entry gate is their lab at UBC and end gate is Euph's foundry on Granville Island (where there are six C57BL/8 scratching around in cages driving Popeye crazy) or Sally Thornton's shed behind the Women's Shelter in San Fran she manages. Dekka has taken one UBC scientist and one technician there and Sally has given them permission to use it for some sort of experiment they are doing. She is glad to see Dekka again.

Since their work is not officially recognized by the University of British Columbia or security and military agencies of either Canada or the Commonwealth of the United States, i.e., they are way outside the bounds of approved scientific endeavours, they can't exactly use, say, Revival House or Livermore Lab as end gates for these experiments.

Dr. Wong is still uncomfortable that they haven't shared their current work with General Staubach. The implications of removing a prisoner from Imperial Chinese custody are scary for him to contemplate but his first loyalty is to Dr. Bell not UBC or USC military so he says nothing.

"You are not satisfied, Dr. Bell?"

"This is a man's life we are playing with. We're missing something. Run another new series of tests please."

...

Dr. Wong is holding a lightweight pico carbon tube medical tray. On it lies Trial No. 12. Dead. He calls Damien via media wall. Chuck is at Euphony's Foundry and C57BL/8 No. 12 has come through their portal there in this state. They have a brief conversation. They need to autopsy C57BL/8 No. 12 right away to find out if this mouse has died from something other than transportation through a Quantum Tunnel, perhaps, heart attack due to stress or some other medical precondition unrelated to its recent journey. Even though Damien knows that it is only a matter of time before what they are trying to do leaks (nothing is secret long if you have this many people working on a project), he says to Chuck, "Run 288 more tunnel tests." Now he wants a sample size of 300 instead of results from just a dozen runs. Damien knows if either Commonwealth or Canadian security picks up on what they are doing or, worse, Imperial China does, they will try to stop them from going after Jag.

Bruce M Firestone

"We have completed a total of 300 trials, 150 of them using our portal on Granville Island and the balance using our portal in San Francisco. There were six failures at Granville and four in San Fran. We do not believe that distance plays any role and that if all 300 trials had taken place using one or the other gateway, results would not be appreciably different." Dr. Wong is summing up results for an audience of Damien, Arcadia, Alex, Euphony, Popeye, Pet3r and Jag, the latter attending via hacked Sinofighter console which Damien's lab has reconstructed using plans from Cady's original data cube.

"Deaths were not caused by any medical precondition or other physical or mental abnormality in these mice that we could detect. They appear to be inexplicably caused by exposure to Quantum Tunneling via a mechanism we do not yet understand and, hence, cannot mitigate.

"Here are the results we obtained from our trials—

Totals (GI)	6	144		Totals (SF)	4	146	
Trial	Result	Accum Fails	Accum Success	Trial	Result	Accum Fails	Accum Success
1	Success	0.00	1	151	Success	7	144
2	Success	0.00	2	152	Success	7	145
3	Success	0.00	3	153	Success	7	146
4	Success	0.00	4	154	Success	7	147
5	Success	0.00	5	155	Success	7	148
6	Success	0.00	6	156	Success	7	149
7	Success	0.00	7	157	Success	7	150
8	Success	0.00	8	158	Success	7	151
9	Success	0.00	9	159	Success	7	152
10	Success	0.00	10	160	Success	7	153
11	Success	0.00	11	161	Success	7	154
12	Fail	1	11	162	Success	7	155

13	Success	1	12	163	Success	7	156
14	Success	1	13	164	Success	7	157
15	Success	1	14	165	Success	7	158
16	Success	1	15	166	Success	7	159
17	Success	1	16	167	Success	7	160
18	Success	1	17	168	Success	7	161
19	Success	1	18	169	Success	7	162
20	Success	1	19	170	Success	7	163
21	Success	1	20	171	Success	7	164
22	Success	1	21	172	Success	7	165
23	Success	1	22	173	Success	7	166
24	Success	1	23	174	Success	7	167
25	Success	1	24	175	Success	7	168
26	Success	1	25	176	Success	7	169
27	Success	1	26	177	Success	7	170
28	Success	1	27	178	Success	7	171
29	Success	1	28	179	Success	7	172
30	Success	1	29	180	Success	7	173
31	Success	1	30	181	Success	7	174
32	Success	1	31	182	Success	7	175
33	Success	1	32	183	Success	7	176
34	Success	1	33	184	Success	7	177
35	Success	1	34	185	Success	7	178
36	Success	1	35	186	Success	7	179
37	Success	1	36	187	Success	7	180
38	Success	1	37	188	Success	7	181
39	Success	1	38	189	Success	7	182
40	Success	1	39	190	Success	7	183
41	Success	1	40	191	Success	7	184
42	Success	1	41	192	Success	7	185
43	Success	1	42	193	Success	7	186
44	Success	1	43	194	Success	7	187
45	Success	1	44	195	Success	7	188

Bruce M Firestone

46	Fail	2	44	196	Success	7	189
47	Success	2	45	197	Success	7	190
48	Success	2	46	198	Success	7	191
49	Success	2	47	199	Success	7	192
50	Success	2	48	200	Success	7	193
51	Fail	3	48	201	Success	7	194
52	Success	3	49	202	Success	7	195
53	Success	3	50	203	Success	7	196
54	Success	3	51	204	Success	7	197
55	Fail	4	51	205	Success	7	198
56	Success	4	52	206	Success	7	199
57	Success	4	53	207	Success	7	200
58	Success	4	54	208	Success	7	201
59	Success	4	55	209	Success	7	202
60	Success	4	56	210	Success	7	203
61	Success	4	57	211	Success	7	204
62	Success	4	58	212	Success	7	205
63	Success	4	59	213	Success	7	206
64	Success	4	60	214	Success	7	207
65	Success	4	61	215	Success	7	208
66	Success	4	62	216	Success	7	209
67	Success	4	63	217	Success	7	210
68	Success	4	64	218	Success	7	211
69	Success	4	65	219	Success	7	212
70	Success	4	66	220	Success	7	213
71	Success	4	67	221	Success	7	214
72	Success	4	68	222	Success	7	215
73	Success	4	69	223	Success	7	216
74	Success	4	70	224	Fail	8	216
75	Success	4	71	225	Fail	9	216
76	Success	4	72	226	Success	9	217
77	Success	4	73	227	Success	9	218
78	Success	4	74	228	Success	9	219

79	Success	4	75	229	Success	9	220
80	Success	4	76	230	Fail	10	220
81	Success	4	77	231	Success	10	221
82	Success	4	78	232	Success	10	222
83	Success	4	79	233	Success	10	223
84	Success	4	80	234	Success	10	224
85	Success	4	81	235	Success	10	225
86	Success	4	82	236	Success	10	226
87	Success	4	83	237	Success	10	227
88	Success	4	84	238	Success	10	228
89	Success	4	85	239	Success	10	229
90	Success	4	86	240	Success	10	230
91	Success	4	87	241	Success	10	231
92	Success	4	88	242	Success	10	232
93	Success	4	89	243	Success	10	233
94	Success	4	90	244	Success	10	234
95	Success	4	91	245	Success	10	235
96	Success	4	92	246	Success	10	236
97	Success	4	93	247	Success	10	237
98	Fail	5	93	248	Success	10	238
99	Success	5	94	249	Success	10	239
100	Success	5	95	250	Success	10	240
101	Success	5	96	251	Success	10	241
102	Success	5	97	252	Success	10	242
103	Success	5	98	253	Success	10	243
104	Success	5	99	254	Success	10	244
105	Success	5	100	255	Success	10	245
106	Success	5	101	256	Success	10	246
107	Success	5	102	257	Success	10	247
108	Fail	6	102	258	Success	10	248
109	Success	6	103	259	Success	10	249
110	Success	6	104	260	Success	10	250
111	Success	6	105	261	Success	10	251

Bruce M Firestone

112	Success	6	106	262	Success	10	252
113	Success	6	107	263	Success	10	253
114	Success	6	108	264	Success	10	254
115	Success	6	109	265	Success	10	255
116	Success	6	110	266	Success	10	256
117	Success	6	111	267	Success	10	257
118	Success	6	112	268	Success	10	258
119	Success	6	113	269	Success	10	259
120	Success	6	114	270	Success	10	260
121	Fail	7	114	271	Success	10	261
122	Success	7	115	272	Success	10	262
123	Success	7	116	273	Success	10	263
124	Success	7	117	274	Success	10	264
125	Success	7	118	275	Success	10	265
126	Success	7	119	276	Success	10	266
127	Success	7	120	277	Success	10	267
128	Success	7	121	278	Success	10	268
129	Success	7	122	279	Success	10	269
130	Success	7	123	280	Success	10	270
131	Success	7	124	281	Success	10	271
132	Success	7	125	282	Success	10	272
133	Success	7	126	283	Success	10	273
134	Success	7	127	284	Success	10	274
135	Success	7	128	285	Success	10	275
136	Success	7	129	286	Success	10	276
137	Success	7	130	287	Success	10	277
138	Success	7	131	288	Success	10	278
139	Success	7	132	289	Success	10	279
140	Success	7	133	290	Success	10	280
141	Success	7	134	291	Success	10	281
142	Success	7	135	292	Success	10	282
143	Success	7	136	293	Success	10	283
144	Success	7	137	294	Success	10	284

145	Success	7	138		295	Success	10	285
146	Success	7	139		296	Success	10	286
147	Success	7	140		297	Success	10	287
148	Success	7	141		298	Success	10	288
149	Success	7	142		299	Success	10	289
150	Success	7	143		300	Success	10	290

"Dr. Wong, does it make a difference if we run lab mice through until we get a failure and then expect a safe trip on the next pass for a human?" Alex asks.

"If you look at trials 224 and 225, we obtained consecutive failures. We believe it is a random phenomenon we're seeing, not related to the original design by Mr. Durai per se."

"We've run simulations, thousands of them," Damien adds. "We believe we're seeing a distribution that closely conforms to… Pet3r can you please bring that up?"

"Certainly, Damien," Pet3r says. "The probability of getting exactly k successes in n trials is given by the probability mass function—

$$f(k;n,p)=Pr(K=k)=(n,k)p^k(1-p)^{n-k}$$

"The probability of getting less than U successes in n trials," he continues, "is—

$$Pr(K<U)=\sum_{k=0}^{U-1}[(n,k)p^k(1-p)^{n-k}]$$

These formulae appear on a media wall as Pet3r speaks.

"What does it all mean?" Cady asks with a worried look. Maybe they won't be able to get Jag out after all?

"Ms. Valenzuela," Damien says, "I think we are seeing a 3% failure rate which appears to match the failure rate we had when we hatched Quantum Entities in Lab 4 at University of Toronto in the first place. Those were

Bruce M Firestone

entities who failed to bond with human counterparts with disastrous consequences. It is a problem we have been working on and not yet resolved."

"How long have you been working on it, Dr. Bell?" she asks.

"Years."

After hearing this, Arcadia turns away and then has to excuse herself for a few minutes. Euphony goes with her.

...

"Dr. Bell, may I speak with Jagad alone?" Arcadia asks when she and Euph return. Both girls have red rimmed eyes but there is a look of determination on Cady's face.

...

"We have decided, Dr. Bell," Arcadia says when everyone is seated again in their lab. She and Jag are holding hands. "We'll risk it."

"You understand what the possibilities are, Ms. Valenzuela, Mr. Durai?" Damien asks. "There is a one in 33 and 1/3 chance you will not survive this transition, Mr. Durai. Your odds are worse than astronauts who rode the old space shuttle. They had two catastrophic failures out of 135 flights, that's less than half the fail rate we are seeing here."

"They lost two shuttles out of a fleet of five," Pet3r says, "so their failure rate, looked at this way, was worse."

Damien and the rest of the people in the conference room just look at him as if he is from a different planet.

"I understand, Dr. Bell. There is nothing in Shenyang except misery and forced labor. They have beaten me before and will again. I expect they will end my life when they have no further use for me. They will never let me out. But may I ask you a question?"

"Yes."

"If you could have gotten out of San Quentin when General Yao had you in prison there, using this technology, would you have done it?" Jag finishes. He and Cady are still holding hands.

Damien gets a far away look on his face and then says, "Without a second thought, yes."

"Then that's what we want," Cady says. "Oh, one more thing. We want to buy some insurance."

"Insurance?" Damien and Chuck say at the same time turning to each other with quizzical looks.

Cady and Euphony glance at each other mischievously.

"What she means, D," says Euph, "is that you and Dr. Wong have to bring out of Shenyang a vial first. Jag next."

"Huh?" says Chuck.

"A vial of live sperm, then Jag, duh," says Cady.

"OK we get it," Damien says.

"When?" Pet3r asks.

"Tomorrow," Arcadia says for her and Jag. Then Jag is gone in a blink. Soon he will be free or dead. Either way, he will be free. He sleeps in his cell in Shenyang without a care in the world (he gets two sleeps before his planned departure) and then, when he wakes up the second time, he will have one simple duty to perform before he is ready to leave this place forever.

...

They've timed Jag's escape for 4:45 am China Standard Time. It's the quietest time at the prison camp. Normal shift changes take place at 5:30 am and pm with wakeup and lock down being 6 am and pm, respectively. Shenyang is 15 hours ahead of Pacific Daylight Time which means that it's 1:45 pm the previous day in Vancouver.

They've opened up a small diameter Quantum Tunnel to Jag's cell and are anxiously awaiting the arrival of a vial of what they hope will be very active spermatozoa. Without fanfare, a small capped bottle plops out onto an awaiting tray. It is immediately taken over to Pet3r for analysis.

A moment or two later Pet3r smiles playfully at

Arcadia and gives her a thumbs up. "Alive and swimming," he says. Euphony is so nervous she thinks she's going to pee her pants.

"It'll be a tight squeeze," Damien says. They have to expand the tunnel from a few centimetres to at least 50 but preferably 55 or even 60 cm. This takes a freakishly large amount of power. They are going to drain the power grid of Western Canada plus the Commonwealth's west of Utah, Wyoming and Montana. They won't be able to keep it up long but, mind you, they won't need to.

Before he gives a command to power up, Damien turns to Euphony and Arcadia and says, "Please wait outside."

"No, we're staying," Euphony says.

"No, you're not," Damien says in a tone that Euph has rarely heard from him before. Euphony and Arcadia leave the room. Euph knows he does not want Arcadia there just in case they pull Jag through and he doesn't make it. They've got Jonesy and two paramedics with them but they have no real hope of reviving Jag if his luck runs out.

Once the girls are gone, Damien finally says to Chuck, "Power up."

...

The Quantum Tunnel expands slowly. There is a faint hum which gets louder as the tunnel grows and there is a whiff of ozone too. Lights in their lab at UBC and across a huge swath of Canada and the USC dim.

The tunnel is not transparent—it's more like a membrane that twists and swirls so images are horribly distorted. Occasionally they snap into patterns recognizable to a human eye and brain. Pet3r is recording all of this and removing as much distortion as he can in real time so Damien and Chuck, Jonesy and the two paramedics can switch from trying to look down a hallucinogenic tunnel to a somewhat less so media wall nearby.

When the tunnel expands close to its maximum

diameter, it's clear to everyone looking at Pet3r's display that Jag's cell is inexplicably empty.

...

"What is taking so long?" Arcadia says nervously. She is sitting on a bench holding both hands with Euphony. "Euph, will you say a prayer with me?"

"But I'm not a Christian," Euphony says.

"I know but it won't matter."

"Then sure."

Arcadia slides off the bench. It takes all her will not to faint. She sits on her haunches and remembers the words. Next she looks up and out a nearby window to where it is drizzling like always in Vancouver before saying, "Oh God, please deliver us from the hand of our enemy, ransom him from the clutches of the ruthless. Oh God, please deliver us from the hand of our enemy, ransom him from the clutches of the ruthless."

Euphony soon joins her on the floor and together now, they repeat, "Oh God, please deliver us from the hand of our enemy, ransom him from the clutches of the ruthless."

...

"Power down but do not close it," Damien says. The tunnel contracts, its screaming hum dying down to a whisper. "Pet3r, can you continue to monitor the tunnel and at what scale? Hurry up!"

"I can monitor Mr. Durai's cell satisfactorily with the tunnel at femtoscale."

"Alright, Dr. Wong, maintain it at femtoscale please."

"What's the plan, Damien?"

"At that scale, the tunnel will be completely undetectable without quantum scanning."

"I understand, Damien but what's the plan?" Chuck asks again.

"We wait."

"How long?"

"As long as it takes."

Bruce M Firestone

"Where is he?"

"I have no idea," Damien says. That isn't true, of course. He realizes they've either been betrayed or otherwise somehow found out. There can be no other explanation for Jag being removed from his cell before his normal workday begins. Routine in these places never changes unless there is a profound reason. How does Damien know that? He's had years of personal experience.

"Do you think we should tell the girls?" Chuck asks.

"What do you plan to tell them?"

"Ah, I'm not sure."

"Let's just wait, Charles." Damien is watching Pet3r's display for any change on the other end in Shenyang.

...

Less than ten minutes later, their patience is rewarded. An obviously injured Jag Durai is dragged back into his cell and thrown onto its floor by two prison guards. He is bleeding profusely from three strokes of the Jiujiebian applied to his torso by the skilled hand of a member of the Central Commission for Discipline Inspection and Party Loyalty. Four or at most five strokes from their nine section Jiujiebian whip is inevitably fatal so three is the practical limit that can be applied to Mr. Durai and not end one of their principal assets. They beat him in part because of his recent misuse of State property which, despite the fact that they plan on making excellent use of his new discovery themselves, must be punished on general principles.

One of the reasons that the Central Commission for Discipline Inspection and Party Loyalty is so feared is because it is so random. They just so happen to have chosen this cold early morning in Shenyang for a surprise visit to see Jag and visit the prison camp he is in. But there is no way that Damien and his colleagues can know that.

...

"Motherfucker, motherfucker, they must have detected us. Fuck! Power up right now, Chuck, right now!"

Damien yells at him.

The high pitched whine ramps up again as the diameter of their tunnel widens. Lights dim in their lab as before. Damien is shouting down the tunnel, "Jag, you have to come through now. Right now. Get up. Get up!"

They can vaguely see on Pet3r's display Jag struggling to move towards the tunnel. It's less than a metre maybe a metre and a half from where is lying face down on the floor. There is blood all down his back, a trail of it behind him and his white prison-issue Taiji shirt is in tatters. After less than half a metre, he stops moving. He is lying unconscious on the floor of his cell. Damien suddenly realizes that the howl of their Quantum Tunnel must be just as apparent on their end. Without another thought, Damien squeezes into the tunnel on his end (he is less broad across the shoulders than Jag is so it is a better fit for him) and propels himself head first into Jag's cell in Shenyang.

Then the tunnel powers down to femtoscale again. The world's two greatest quantum physicists are now both in a cell in Shenyang and one or maybe both of them might be dead.

...

But Damien is not dead. He's survived his trip. His fingers, toes, arms and legs tingle like he has suffered a mild electrical shock or they have fallen asleep. He has to limber up; he swings his arms and moves his legs a bit. He tries to do it by running on the spot but with his limp, he moves more like a zombie. Then he crosses the narrow cell and turns Jag over. Jag comes to.

"What, what are you doing here?" says an alarmed Jag Durai, staring up at Damien, his eyes wide open, as the older man gathers him up in his arms.

"Getting you the fuck out of here," Damien says.

"This is crazy, you should not have come here. You have to leave right now. You go first, Dr. Bell, please. Oh my God, you came through to get me!"

"We're not going anywhere yet," Damien answers. He can see that Chuck has wisely powered down the tunnel. "We just have to wait a minute." Then, just for the briefest of moments, he wonders, 'Wouldn't this be the best opportunity ever for Dr. Wong to betray us if Farrar is right about him—is he another Imperial plant?' Then Damien goes back to first principles—remembering everything he knows about Chuck in an instant. 'There is no way he is a traitor, just no way.'

He calmly waits for the Quantum Tunnel to reopen. Meanwhile he wraps Jag in a blanket. Jag is going into shock and Damien needs to keep him warm.

...

The rising howl of a widening tunnel alerts Damien that the time has come to leave. Jag is completely unconscious again and losing blood. When the tunnel has reached what he guesses to be half a metre, Damien feeds Jag through, feet first. He discards the blanket first. The fact that Jag is unconscious helps him in a way. He folds his arms in and scrunches up his shoulders and just shoves the guy through. If it hurts, Jag won't feel a thing.

He can hear another racket going on behind him and what he guesses to be a series of Chinese curses or maybe orders then he clearly hears a word in English, "Halt." He looks over his shoulder and two prison guards are there, rifles aimed at him. They have surprised looks on their faces when they see it is a person different from the prisoner who they dumped here a short while ago into what was and apparently still is a locked cell. During this moment of distraction, Damien, who plans never to be a prisoner again, limps over to the tunnel and throws himself through, banging his head as he clumsily worms his way in. He thinks that their aim will be off during his momentary advantage and exit. But they shoot better than he thinks they can.

...

Jonesy and the two lady paramedics are working on

Mr. Durai when a second patient suddenly arrives. Damien has a significant leg wound; his already bad leg (his right) is gonna be a lot worse after travelling to and from Shenyang (a return journey of 15,978 kilometres and 560 metres) in zero time accompanied by a 6% probability of death bringing with him a large calibre bullet lodged in it just above the knee. Dr. Bell, like most entrepreneurs and a few scientists do in their careers, has just used up a few more of his nine lives.

Jonesy leaves Jagad and comes over to Damien. He produces a pair of surgical scissors and cuts Damien's right pant leg off. He examines the wound and immediately applies direct pressure to control bleeding. He then makes a tourniquet and ties it above Damien's right knee. He elevates Damien's leg on a lab stool that is the height of a normal stair. He asks Damien if he is injured anywhere else. Damien just points to his head where he has a nasty bruise. Jonesy looks at it and dismisses it as non life threatening. Even though Damien indicates he is not wounded anywhere else, Jonesy does a complete inventory. He has seen people who'll tell you they are fine die from knife or gunshot wounds they don't even know they have because they are in shock, denial, high on drugs or inured to pain because of adrenalin rush. He knows Damien well enough to know it won't be drugs or denial but it sure could be adrenalin or shock.

Arcadia is also now in the room cradling Jag's head in her arms. She has blood all over the new skirt she made on her Elna to greet Reed in. It's a pleated number, full length, pale orange which looks wonderfully well on her together with her white, theory-trimmed silk blouse. They're both knockoffs of the Zoron Collection. When she put on her new skirt this morning, she twirled in front of her mirror until it came up past her panties showing off shapely legs and a nicely rounded business end of which she is quite proud there being quite a bit less of it than a few months ago.

Bruce M Firestone

Euphony is there too and she doesn't know whether to chew Damien out for being such a reckless idiot or to kiss him so she does both.

...

"Well, Dr. Bell, you've had quite an adventure wouldn't you say?"

"I wasn't looking for adventure, General."

"Don't you think that having two key Commonwealth scientists in a locked Shenyang cell is a trifle worrisome, Sir?"

Farrar is in Damien's room at St. Paul's Hospital. It is a teaching hospital affiliated with UBC. Damien is in surgery for eight hours as they try to remove the bullet which has fractured into tiny pieces on impact and do their best to put him back together so he will regain some use of his already damaged right leg. After being in intensive care for 36 hours, they transfer him to a private room on the 4th floor where CSIS, RCMP and Commonwealth MPs rotate for guard duty.

"May I remind you again, General, that I am not a Commonwealth citizen and I am not sure Mr. Durai will be either? I think now that he is on Canadian soil, he might just apply for landed immigrant status and stay right here."

"He landed here with quite a thud," Farrar says. "He didn't exactly pass through passport control."

Damien can't help himself—he bursts out laughing and pretty soon Farrar has joined him. Damien is remembering his first trip with Nell when he thought exactly the same thing as their troop seemed to cross borders with impunity there being rules for rich people and then harsher rules for everyone else.

"Have you had any messages from the Cartesian Powers?" Damien asks.

"Nary a word, Dr. Bell. And frankly, I don't think we are going to get any."

"I'm surprised."

"I'm not. Those mandarins are great wéiqí players. Make good Texas Hold'em players too if they ever decide to learn the game." The General is referring to Go, a 2,500 year old Chinese encircling game of strategy which is simple to learn but very difficult to play at elite levels.

"I don't play either game, General." Damien thinks these things are just huge time suckers.

"Well, perhaps you should. They probably won't say a word now that you've stolen one of their top scientists out from under their noses. They'll hate that but they'll hate it worse if they lose face by admitting any such thing ever took place. And, of course, we are not going to be making any announcements on the subject either, now will we, Dr. Bell?"

"Nope." It's the first time Damien and Farrar have ever agreed on anything. "I didn't steal him. He was never theirs in the first place. Anyway, they stole him first."

"Two wrongs make a right?"

Damien is about to react angrily when he sees that Farrar is just needling him.

"But there was every possibility that you or Mr. Durai would not survive this experience if I understand what the two of you have cooked up?"

"We had a 3% fail rate going and another 3% coming back, General. Quantum Tunneling will never be useful as a common carrier. These days you'd have better odds climbing and descending Everest."

"It was an incredibly foolhardy thing to do, Dr. Bell." Farrar says but he is looking at Damien with a newfound and profound respect.

Damien says nothing.

"This opens up a whole host of new possibilities, doesn't it Damien?"

"Yep."

"We'll leapfrog the Cartesian Powers in space. DARCH is going to end up being one heck of a wealthy enterprise."

"I am counting on it, General."

"You know, Sir, I think I owe you an apology."

"Forget it, General."

"No, I don't think I will. Do you know the oath that Army Rangers take? It includes these words—*I will never leave a fallen comrade to fall into the hands of the enemy.* That's you, Dr. Bell, that's what you did. I once thought that you were a man I would not want in my outfit. But, Sir, I was wrong. You can be in my outfit any time."

Then General of the Army Farrar Staubach puts his right hand forward. Damien looks at it and then, from his hospital bed, he extends his own and the two men shake hands looking at each other with new eyes. Maybe they are brothers of a kind after all.

"We'll talk more in a few days, Damien, when you get out of here." The General walks to the door. He opens it a few inches and then turns around to face Damien once more. As if he just thought of it, he says, "I thought you should know, outside of my official capacity, I haven't seen her in seven months." Then he quietly leaves.

For Damien, Farrar's last statement leaves him in a fever of guilt.

...

Damien is standing on the deck of the Teahouse in Stanley Park. He is using a friggin cane again but he can hobble around pretty good nevertheless. The drizzle is holding off for now. Zora has come up from Berkeley and both she and her mother are flower girls and are standing next to Arcadia who is looking beautiful in a white Empire Classic gown with traditional Halter that she makes herself. Both straps originate over her right breast with one crossing over her bare left shoulder and linking back to connect with the dress on its left side so that both straps are equidistant when people see her from the back. There is a 'V' of braided lace from her bare shoulder blades to her derriere that accentuates that part of her attractive anatomy. Her full length dress has one slit on the right side cut thigh high so when she walks, she shows off her beautiful silver silk stocking encased legs complete with gray garter belt. 'Wowza, no bride has ever looked prettier,' Euph thinks. Cady gets her bolt of cloth from a high end store but she uses a daily deal coupon she's purchased so it only costs her $120 QED. She is going to try to make her own lingerie too but gives that up and store-buys the stuff. Then she forgets herself completely and splurges on a necklace of blue abalone pearls that cost way more than anything else. Her dark hair is cut shoulder length and has a single, simple jeweled clip (also abalone derived) on her left hand side.

Jagad Durai is there in a tux he's rented from White and Lee on Richards Street in Vancity. It's a bit big for him which is a good thing since his back still seeps blood occasionally and he is wearing, in addition to this penguin suit, pads that absorb most of it. He can't believe he is here in this nice town with these nice people looking at his bride-to-be. His eyes are as big as his stomach and his current plan is to eat her right up as soon as it is decorous to do. He borrowed some money from Damien for this tux and to hire a Wedding Commissioner for this occasion.

His Dad, Pal, is there looking on this whole ceremony wonderingly. His son has somehow been restored to life through some unimaginable process via (he is told) some kind of voodoo that Jagad and Dr. Bell have concocted together. He doesn't care how. These two kids (Jagad and Arcadia) have loved each other since they were teens and somehow they are here together and so is he. He looks up and smiles at Kiri hoping she has been reincarnated as a female again and that whoever her future husband will be, he will deserve her.

Their wedding commissioner after introducing herself to everyone and saying what is required of her by BC law asks the bride to say the words she has prepared herself.

Cady has written them out on a cheat sheet which Zora has been holding for her. Zora gives her the paper.

Cady reads, alternatively looking at it and then at Jag, "I take you, Jagad Durai, to be my husband. I love you now as I did then and will always love you as you grow into all that God intends for you. When you went away," her voice cracks when she says this and she pauses for a moment then continues, "my life stopped. And when you were restored to me and resurrected, my life began again. I will love you when we are together and when we are apart; when our lives are at peace and when they are in turmoil; I am proud of you and the man that you are. I will honor your goals and dreams and help you to fulfill them. From the depth of my being, I will be with you and forsake all others. I say these things believing that God is in the midst of them all and that he has brought us together for a purpose."

Next, the commissioner turns to Jagad and he begins, "Let us take our first step together blessed as we are by Krishna to provide for each other and for our family and these friends and any issue that come from our union. Let us develop together our spiritual powers and let us acquire knowledge, happiness and harmony through proper channels and be true companions, one of the other, and remain lifelong partners. Arcadia, though I spent years in darkness, you were always there with me in my soul. I would never have come through those times without you." He stops. He is looking at her and seeing her again, powerful and free, on her skateboard at age 15. His Dad is crying but Jagad wills himself on. "I believe in you, Cady, you are the magic in my life without which my life is nothing. Once I saw you stand before the world, proud and free. That is how people are supposed to be—that was you then and that is you now. Let no one ever come between you and that girl that you were and are. You are 'hope' to me and I love you before Krishna and God, I accept you as my wife for now and forever."

Euphony is balling like a kid by the end of this. She has forgotten how much she hates to cry. Dr. Wong has teared up too.

...

"I jus want you to know, Doctor Bell, jus want to say, you know, what you did, tha was speshal," Pal is saying to Damien.

"It's OK, Mr. Durai. It worked out."

"Ya know, I think, when there is tha mush love, it'll mean a baby, know what I'm driving at, Doctor?"

"Wouldn't surprise me a bit," Damien says to an intensely inebriated Pal Durai.

"Kiri is here, somewhere. Every time I turn around, I think I'll be sheeing her."

"Mr. Durai, would you like some tea?" Damien asks.

"Not really. I'd like some more of that Mead though. Wass it called?"

"Wrecked Brew."

"Good name." He goes off in search of some more.

They're in Euphony's Foundry and it is quite a party. The Bride and Groom have changed—Jag is wearing a pair of blue jeans for the first time in nine years. He has to change shirts every couple of hours because three bright, nearly horizontal stripes of blood tend to appear on his back despite best efforts by Jonesy to tape him up so that this doesn't happen. But nothing in his recent past is going to stop him from leaving shortly with his bride and doing what newlyweds have been doing like forever.

Dekka has come up for the wedding and although Damien has never seen him do it before, he's had one or two draughts of Wrecked Brew. They smile at each other.

Euphony is completely stoned on her own brew. Damien is thinking how useless she will be later. They never make love if Euph is drinking. She can't feel a thing when she's had a few and Damien doesn't like making love to a girl who lies there like a mattress. Anyway, Zora will be in the bed next to them upstairs which is a total downer anywho.

...

Bruce M Firestone

"What are you talking about?" Damien says at 3 am. He has just woken up next to Euphony. Zora is zonked on the spare bed next to them in their room.

#If I don't make it you have to take the baby.

"What baby? Who is this?" Damien is a bit groggy. Uncharacteristically, he has a couple of mugs of Wrecked Brew himself while they are toasting bride and groom before they leave their party. There are still a bunch of people on premises sacked out downstairs in parts of the foundry and on cots at the back.

#I am bleeding, Damien. They can't stop it. You have to take the baby.

"Ellen, is that you?" Damien says loudly in their dark room.

#Yes, of course, it's me. You need to come right away.

"Where are you?" Damien says looking around. By this time, Euphony's been awakened by the ruckus her partner is making.

"Damien, you are having a bad dream, go back to sleep," she says and turns over herself intending to do exactly that.

"I'll say." Damien lies back down and snuggles up to Euph.

#Don't turn away, Damien. Her name is Naya.

"Who is Naya?" Damien sits back up again and asks the night around him.

#The baby. Her name is Naya.

"Why is your baby Naya?"

#Nell told me to call her Naya.

"Nell?"

#Yes, she is here. I can see her now. She is at the foot of my bed. Nell's her Godmother.

"Nell is there with you, Ellen?"

#Yes, I can see her. She's at the foot of my bed."

By this point Euphony has gotten up and turned on her little lava lamp. She is watching Damien as he talks to a spirit in their room. She can only hear half the convo.

Damien is in some kind of trance she thinks.

"What's wrong, Ellen?"

#I am hemorrhaging, Damien. The Doctors tell me it is from Placenta Praevia and they can fix it. That's what they say but Nell tells me there is something else.

Placenta Praevia is where the placenta has covered the cervix. It kills one woman in 2,500 during childbirth in the western world where medical care is superb so it should not really be a problem.

"Where are you?"

#I am at Maya Fair.

That's Nell's home on Ambergris Caye that Damien owns according to Nell's will.

"Did you call, Farrar?" Damien assumes she is talking about her baby with Farrar.

#No

"Why not?" he stupidly asks.

#Naya is our baby, Damien.

...

"You fucked her?"

"I did."

"How many times?"

"Once."

"You are a lying piece of shit."

"I may be a piece of shit, Euphony, but I am not a liar."

She is looking at him exactly the way he deserves to be looked at. He has betrayed her and himself. He can't believe what a piece of shit he is. He can't say anything, what is there to say?

"Why didn't you tell me?"

"I love you, Euph—"

"Don't you ever say those words again! Ever or I'll curse you for them. Why didn't you tell me?"

"I was ashamed." Damien is not surprised that somehow his secret has come out—that he, in fact, self incriminated. If you want to keep a secret, tell no one. But a baby is a fact. His baby.

Bruce M Firestone

"You should be ashamed. Did you at least enjoy it?"

"Yeah."

She reaches across the table and slaps his face, hard.

"Men are such total bastards!"

"Mom, is everything OK," Zora calls down from upstairs.

"S'all right, honey, go back to bed."

"OK. Night, Mom, Damien."

...

More quietly now, Euphony, who knows that Ellen is a manipulative, scheming bitch and probably seduces this stupid man, says, "Pet3r come here."

"Yes, Euph."

"Where is Ellen Brooks?"

"She's at Maya Fair at the north end of San Pedro Town."

"What is her current state?"

"Ms. Brooks has been on stress leave from the Presidency of the Commonwealth for the last two months. She has refused to see anyone other than Su7e and Ash3r, Elsu and Ella. Dafne Weinstein is with her as well. She is almost 8 months pregnant with a female fetus she calls Naya. Currently she is hemorrhaging from Placenta Praevia, a treatable condition. A secondary condition however has developed from an oversupply of blood to her womb which has resulted in further hemorrhaging. I speculate that this other condition has developed from stress caused in part by her job as President and in part from the fact that she has endeavored to keep her pregnancy secret from one or more of the following—the media, voters, the General Assembly, the General of the Army, Dr. Bell and you. She has lost more than 1,500 milliliters of blood due to her conditions. It may also cause necrosis of her kidneys which has serious and often fatal complications. If it does, I estimate her time of death to be within the next few days."

...

"You always were a rental, Damien," Euphony is saying.

"Don't say that."

"It's true. I always knew you had to go back to your family, D. Here's the thing though, it's not your fault, Damien, it's mine."

"That's just not true. It's my doing. I screwed up, Euphony."

"No, let me tell you a story, D. It should be our baby not hers. You're still a young man—"

"No, I'm not, Euph."

"Don't interrupt, D."

"OK, sorry."

"Here's the thing. It's not your fault, it's mine." She draws a deep breath. "I knew you wanted to have kids." She can see that he thinks about interrupting her again but he restrains himself this time. "So I went to see my Doctor. I asked him if he could undo what I'd done when I was a teenager. He said he'd look into it. You remember I told you that something happened after Zora was born?"

"Yeah."

"Well, I had my tubes tied. I never wanted to let a man impregnate me again, ever... until I met you. But the Doctor told me they had fused and there was no going back. So it really is my fault not yours, D."

"Oh, Euph, I am such a total fuckup," says Damien in abject misery.

"We both are. But here's what's going to happen. You are going to Belize today. If, if Ellen dies and the baby lives, you bring her back here to me. We'll bring up Naya, you and me, you understand? Naya is not to go to Ellen's brother Jon, you understand?"

He nods.

"But if Ellen lives, you never come back here. You can only be one man, Damien. You can only have one wife. You can only be one person and you are either hers or mine. Now get you gone."

Euphony goes back upstairs to where her daughter is still sleeping. She goes to the bed she recently shared with Damien. She can smell him on her sheets and on his pillow. She has never cried over a man, not even Zora's father when he left her with a three month old baby. But she buries her face in Damien's pillow and cries silently not wanting to wake her daughter just two metres away. Finally she gets up and goes to her crawl space and retrieves an Imperial Gallon size flagon of Wrecked Brew. She pours herself a huge tumbler full and places it on her small kitchen table in front of her. She feels like downing the whole thing. But then she doesn't. It occurs to her that if she feels this pain through to its conclusion, it will maybe bring her to a new place. She will otherwise miss an opportunity for personal growth if she gets stoned on her own brew. So it just sits there while Euphony suffers nearby. Things didn't exactly work out as planned. Then suddenly she remembers one of Damien's favourite poems. She looks it up. Frig, there it is plain as day!

Her eyes grew wide for a moment; she drew one last deep breath,
Then her finger moved in the moonlight,
Her musket shattered the moonlight,
Shattered her breast in the moonlight and warned him—with her death.

Euph repeats to herself, "warned him—with her death."

...

"Hi Dafne."
"Hey, Damien."
"So you've come."
"Yep." Damien has figured out on the trip down to Belize that Pet3r mindlinked with him and then with Ash3r who mindlinked with Ellen so they can trade thoughts back and forth.

"Would you like to meet your daughter?"

"I would."

...

They enter a bedroom that Ellen and Daniella have recently had redecorated as a nursery—it is completely outrageous. It contains French Provincial Nursery furniture that would not look out of place in the royal houses of Germania. They have a French Regal Dining Room Server with delicate Louis XV legs that they plan to use as Naya's change table. The whole thing is done in white with gold accents. They have put frilly lace shears on their hurricane-resistant windows. Naya's room has Coyne Chrystal chandeliers instead of night lights.

Su7e is there holding the baby. She is gently kneading Naya with her long fingers. She can produce heat too which she does and, if Naya was a cat, she'd be purring right about now.

"Oh, my baby, my baby. I've missed you so much," Su7e is cooing. "You've come back to me. I knew you would."

Damien and Dafne just watch for a few moments. It is another QE evolutionary behaviour they are seeing, Damien thinks.

"Hello, Dr. Bell. Welcome. Would you like to hold your baby?" Su7e walks over to where Damien is standing flatfooted, seemingly rooted to the floorboards.

"You, ah, hold her. I'll just look."

"Come, come Damien. If a Quantum Entity can hold this baby, a big fellow like you should be able to manage it too," she says with a smile.

From the moment that the baby, swaddled as she is, is put in his arms, he falls in love with her. She has this marvelous thick short auburn hair that stands straight up on her head like it's a Mohawk. She is this long, stringy thing with pink skin and what he thinks will be green eyes that he can't believe is his. But she is. She is also a game changer not only in his life and Ellen's but from the moment she opens her eyes and sees her Da, for everyone else on this planet too.

...

Naya is born on Christmas Eve. The following day, Ellen is lying on her bed at Maya Fair. Damien is there. Naya, four weeks premature is doing well. Ellen not so much. She looks very wrung out, white, peaked. Whether she will live or die is not yet known. They've alerted the Speaker of the General Assembly as to her condition. If she dies, he will take over as interim President until new (regularly scheduled) elections take place in the normal course of events. This is superfluous since she already transfers power to him when she first takes her leave of absence to come to Maya Fair to have her baby. There is no Vice President in the Commonwealth—they've done away with that useless appendage. Ellen likes things simple and efficient and they have to work.

"Damien, I want our baby baptized, is that alright?"

"Yes, Dear."

"Can it be soon, like maybe today? I don't want my baby to die if she is excluded from the vision of God."

"It's Christmas Day, Ellen."

"That's a good day for a baptism don't you think?"

"Yes, Ellen."

"Do you think, maybe it's a good day for something else too?"

"What is that, Ellen?"

"I want you to remember us."

"Who are you talking about, Ellen?" But of course, he knows who.

"Me and Nell. We are all ONE, Damien."

"I understand, Ellen," he says not understanding her at all.

"Damien, will you marry me?" Ellen asks.

"Yes, Dear."

...

"DEARLY beloved," Javier is saying on the beach in

front of Maya Fair having come up from Caye Caulker to perform this ceremony, "you have brought this child here to be baptized; you have prayed that Jesus shall vouchsafe to receive her, to release her of her sins and to give her the kingdom of heaven and everlasting life. I demand therefore that thou, in the name of this Child, renounce the Devil and all his works, the vain pomp and glory of the world, with all covetous desires of the same and the carnal desires of the flesh, so that thou wilt not follow nor be led astray by them.

"Please say," Javier asks, "I renounce them all."

Ellen is seated on a folding chair with her baby on the beach. Damien is standing next to her. Elsu, Ella and Dafne are nearby. Dekka who came down with Damien is also there.

They say together, "I renounce them all."

Javier asks, "DOST thou believe in God the Father Almighty, Maker of Heaven and Earth? And in Jesus Christ his only-begotten Son of our Lord? And that he was conceived by the Holy Ghost, born of the Virgin Mary; that he suffered under Pontius Pilate, was crucified, dead and buried; that he went down into Hell and also did rise again the third day; that he ascended into Heaven and sitteth at the right hand of God the Father Almighty and from thence shall come again at the end of the world, to judge the quick and the dead?"

"We do," his congregation says.

"WILT thou be baptized in this faith?" Javier asks.

"That is our desire," they say on behalf of Naya.

"WILT thou then obediently keep God's holy will and commandments and walk in the same all the days of thy life?"

"We will," they say.

"Then grant that she may have power and strength to have victory and to triumph against the Devil, the world and the flesh. Amen."

"Amen," they say.

He takes the baby and goes into the gentle surf in front of Maya Fair. He dips his hand into the waters and brings a few drops with him. He draws the sign of the cross on Naya's forehead. She is startled but does not cry.

It is a very simple and straight forward ceremony. It is something to remember and behold. After which there is another short ceremony. Ellen and Damien are married.

...

"They are all volunteers."

"I don't care. You are sending them to their deaths."

"Don't you think I know that?" asks the General in anguish. It is the toughest decision he has ever made, "Show me the simulation again."

Input values are—

$p = 0.97$

Failures: 330

k Successes: 10,670

n Trials: 11000

Giving $f(k;n,p) = 0.022292$

Table of nearby values—

Failures	Successes	Probability
325	10,665	0.021287000
326	10,666	0.021618000
327	10,667	0.021886000
328	10,668	0.022089000
329	10,669	0.022225000
330	10,670	0.022292000
331	10,671	0.022290000
332	10,672	0.022219000
333	10,673	0.022078000
334	10,674	0.021869000
335	10,675	0.021594000

"You can expect 330 casualties, General, if you do this. It could be more or less depending on your luck—bad or good. It will follow this distribution we think. If Dr. Bell was here he would refuse to allow you to use this technology for this purpose, I am sure" says Dr. Wong.

"He's off having a baby, Charles. This cannot wait."

"Have you cleared this with your Commander in Chief?"

"She's off having a baby too," says Farrar. Their plan is to send 3,000 volunteers to the Moon and 8,000 to Mars via Quantum Tunnel. These men and women are part of the Commonwealth's astronaut corps who will be making one-way trips to these destinations. Their goal is to live there along with their new QEs and claim huge swaths of those places for DARCH. QEs are already there using newly installed nanosite generators and nutrients sucked from Earth via Quantum Tunnel to build habitats for their human counterparts.

QEs reach Luna and Mars via laser carrier as Damien planned. They don't want to risk QEs in Quantum Tunnels any more than human beings. Damien seems quite sure that Quantum Entities will run the same risk of death via

Bruce M Firestone

Q-Tunnel as humans and for the same reason. Of course, the only way to be sure is to test it but this is impossible since that would be tantamount to killing people.

Transport via laser carrier is much safer and doesn't take much longer. QEs can go to the Moon in roughly 1.29 seconds. It takes longer to get to Mars—anywhere from 3.03 minutes to 22.29 depending on the relative position of Earth and Mars around the Sun. It's faster than the fast solar wind can get them there but slower than taking a Quantum Tunnel which takes zero time. Since laser carrier is line-of-sight transport, they have to watch out for Sol which sometimes gets in their way when Mars is in conjunction with respect to Earth.

"Dr. Wong, they will each be running a risk that is 1/2 of what Dr. Bell took leaving here to go to Shenyang and then returning with Mr. Durai."

"Dr. Durai," Chuck corrects him. Jag is awarded an honourary doctorate by University of Alberta on the recommendation of the Head of their Department of Physics within a month of his arrival in Vancouver. Damien may have had something to do with that.

Jag is working for DARCH in Vancouver after a three day honeymoon at the Roslyn Suite Hotel overlooking the southern end of Stanley Park. He and his bride walk there from the Teahouse after their wedding ceremony. It's a budget place ranked 23rd of more than 110 hotels in Vancouver but to Cady and Jagad it's one heck of a paradise compared to Temple or Shenyang. They hardly leave their room and Cady becomes an expert in their ceiling architecture which has a popcorn finish. She comes to the conclusion that they really should skim coat them. They'd be a lot easier to keep clean and she thinks they'd look better too if they are just plain, smooth drywall.

...

Erik Renke gets another big story for the Toronto Chronicle Tab and the Internet. Ellen Brooks has left the Presidency under a cloud of suspicion. Drugs are thought to have been involved leading to premature birth of an illegitimate, underweight daughter. She tries to cover up its illegitimacy by marrying former boyfriend, ex-con Damien Bell claiming he is the father. Pictures of the baby snapped by Paparrazzoids on an island off the coast of Guatemala clearly show a child of dubious origins who looks nothing like Bell. Suspicion is growing that the real father is a highly placed Army General who can't be named due to national security reasons.

Renke has finally made a big mistake. It's not that his reports are laughably inaccurate. They are. It's he's pissed off General of the Army Farrar Staubach. Farrar couldn't care less about rumors about paternity involving him. But he cares A LOT about Ellen.

...

Chapter 11 Laureate

"Hey Da, Da! It's for you," five year old Naya yells.

"OK, got it, honey."

"Hello, Dr. Bell?" asks a strange voice with a Euro accent.

"Yes, it's Damien Bell here. How may I help you?"

When Damien gets off the call, he is trembling slightly with suppressed excitement. He goes to see his daughter. She is in the rec room at Revival House with her twin, three year old brothers, Finn and Magellan.

...

"Da, watch this," Naya commands her clueless Dad. "Su7e, cue my music."

They're playing some of Nell's old tunes and Naya is shimmying to the music and lip synching. Her brothers are her backup dancers and her backup singers but they are both pretty useless. At least Finn, a blond-haired kid who looks like a Brooks and a Bell, is trying. Magellan who is the dark haired twin with dark eyes is thinking how much more fun it would be to read the book his Dad gave him about trolls and a wizard. Magellan has been able to read since he became conscious which is like forever if you are three.

Damien can't believe how much fun it is to watch Naya dance with her brothers. She has been boogieing like this since she was 22 months old and, wow, can she ever dance.

"Hey, Naya, come over here," he says, "ya know what?"

"What, Da, what?" she asks desperate to go back to her routine. Her fans (two humans and Su7e) are waiting!

"Your Da just won the Nobel Prize in Physics."

"Great, Da. Get any candy?"

When he shakes his head 'no', Naya loses interest. "Da,

Da. You're not looking. Watch this!" Naya says.

Damien can see that her transitions are getting better and she's been practicing her jump throughs, front and back walkovers and butterfly moves. He asks her again not to do walkovers except in class but Miss Bossy Boots just puts her hands on her hips and gives him the cutest pouty look. That's Naya's way of saying 'no' to her Da.

"There was a new move in there, Naya. What is it?"

"It's called a Butterfly Twist. Want to see it again?" It's similar to a Butterfly with your body parallel to the floor and about a meter high (if you are an adult) but instead of your legs extended in a y-shape, you keep them in tight and twist in the air doing a complete 360 degree rollover. When Naya does it, her long auburn hair flies everywhere. In class, her hair has to be tied back but here in her rec room, she can freelance.

"Did you learn that in class?"

"Nah. Nell taught me." He thinks she means via media wall video.

Naya does three classes a week at Meeza Elite Danse Academy which Damien takes her to. He sits outside their studio in the waiting room which is a desultory extruded, featureless brown room making small talk with other parents there—all of them women. Damien is 42 which makes him an older parent. It's become fashionable in the Commonwealth to have kids young which Damien thinks is wise given the way his kids run him around and also for the health of mother and child.

Naya'd do more classes if he let her. Meeza only takes competitive dancers which means it's expensive (Naya doesn't mind), time consuming (Naya can't think that her Da could possibly have anything better to do with his time), intense (that's Naya!) and fun (bingo!)

Su7e has the same freckled complexion of other QEs mindlinked with human counterparts. Damien's known that Su7e is bonded with Naya for years. It isn't just that Su7e started to elementally change within days of Naya's birth. The baby would turn her head to look at Su7e even when Su7e was in another room and they have been exchanging thoughts since Naya was a few weeks old maybe even on the day of her birth.

Damien thinks that this is the only known instance of sequential human bonding for a QE. He asks Pet3r to ask every QE in the solar system, a survey that takes him less than 30 femtoseconds to complete. His surmise is right. This is the only known instance.

...

"I want you to come, Ellen."

"I'm not sure, Dear."

"I'm going to take Naya but we'll leave the twins with Ella and Micah."

"OK," she says. But he is not sure she is giving the OK to leaving the twins with the Glazers or coming with him to Stockholm.

Ellen is very quiet these days. She serves out her first term as President but refuses to run for a second term. She makes love to her husband twice a week and they have a set of twins (Finn and Magellan named after the only two books Damien is allowed in San Quentin) but she is not the same Ellen who launched QCC, overthrew the Republic, is the first President of the USC, launched QCCII, travelled with Farrar to New Zealand and trapped Damien Bell at Norman MacKenzie House. A light seems to have gone out.

Her relationship with her daughter Naya is fraught with angst, at least on her part. Naya loves her Mom but can't for the life of her figure out what gives with respect to having fun and doing stuff. She gets her Da and he gets her so they leave Mom at Revival House as often as possible and go out on adventures without her.

...

"Wanna go fishing, boys?" Damien asks.

"Yay," the guys say.

"Naya?"

But she is already out the door on her way over to Mr. Owen's garden.

Mr. Owen has long since stocked his pond with large mouth bass. It's like shooting fish in a barrel. They catch and release 14 fish in less than an hour.

...

"Our Father, who art in Heaven," Naya says then she stops. "Why is he a father, why not Mom?"

"Dunno, kiddo."

"OK, I'll say my prayers this way—Our God, who art in Heaven, Hallowed be Thy Name..."

Naya goes on for a few more minutes before falling asleep in her Da's lap. He lays her down in her big kid's bed and covers her up against a chilly San Fran night. He kisses her goodnight and then goes to check on the boys who still sleep in cribs but not for much longer—they're getting way too big.

...

"Hey Ellen."

"Hi D."

"Future shaping day, huh?"

"Wonderful, D. Special. It's not every day, you get the Nobel Prize. Big cash award too. That's nice."

"Traian and Dakota are coming too. They're bringing José-Luis too."

"Naya will like that. She skypes with José-Luis every couple of days." José Luis is eight (almost nine) and Naya idolizes him. He is the top football player in his age group in Romania. He can play with kids eleven or older and embarrass them.

"I want you to come too, baby."

"OK. I think I already said that."

"You did, Ellen."

He looks at her.

"Ellen, are you happy, with me?"

"Yes, Dear."

"I want to be a good husband for you."

Bruce M Firestone

"I know that."

He wants to say to her, 'You're not the same girl you used to be. What's up?' But he says nothing at all.

"Do you want to make love with me?" he asks.

She doesn't answer. Instead she pulls her nightie over her head. She is 39 years of age, still one of the great beauties of her age. She climbs on top of Damien and moves her hips in a way that few women really know how to do. She makes love to him so passionately that soon she is (unknowingly) snotting on him and he knows he has satisfied her in a way that no other man in her life has ever done. It pleases him immensely.

...

"Feel that?"

"Hmm. What do you call it?"

"How do you know I have a word for it?"

"You always do."

"Jeld."

"Jeld?"

"It's a combination between join and meld, as in 'I'll meld with you.'"

"Very Shakespearean," Ellen says.

"Thank you."

"Are we the only two who experience this?"

"I dunno. Pet3r and I have both looked. There is no mention of it anywhere in mainstream scientific literature. I asked a naturopathic doctor friend of mine and she couldn't find anything either. It's weird. Maybe you and I are the only human beings to experience an exchange of current like this, baby."

"I like it, D."

"Me too."

But something is missing in her life. Damien can feel it and he won't be satisfied until he figures out what it is and how to plug the gap. This is the girl who has given him three beautiful kids, who gets him out of San Quentin, who loves him since she is 19. He's gonna figure it out.

That's it, that's all.

...

"Hello Farrar."

"Hi Ellen. Who might this be?"

"I'm Naya, you may call me Princess Naya."

"So Princess Naya, what do you do?"

"You might be better to ask, 'What don't I do?'"

"Princess Naya, what don't you do?"

"Nothing," she says and she runs off to command her loyal subjects, Finn and Magellan joined by Mr. Owen who has recently come under the spell of Naya Brooks Bell.

"She's a pistol, Ellen."

"That she is."

He wants to say that she takes after her mother but she neither looks like Ellen nor behaves like her so he adds nothing to his previous comment.

"I'm done with the army. Next month."

"Is that a good thing or bad?"

"I don't know."

"Maybe you can be a professional card player now?"

He laughs, "Maybe, maybe. I think about you a lot."

"I know that."

"Do you think about me?"

"Yes, I do Farrar." No point in denying it.

"In another life, right Ellen?"

"Yes, General. In another life."

"We have almost half of the lunar surface claimed for DARCH and more than two thirds of Mars."

"Those are impressive numbers, General."

"It won't be long before the Commonwealth surpasses the Cartesian Powers in both solar system assets and celestial assets," he says.

"What will you do General after your marriage to the Army ends?"

He momentarily looks at her longingly and says nothing further.

...

Bruce M Firestone

Commonwealth space-based assets are almost all derived from the 11,000 men and women who originally volunteer for the job. 3,000 of them went to the Moon and 8,000 to Mars. Since each transport via Quantum Tunnel is a random event, the odds of getting 330 (exactly 3%) casualties on the button is low. It's still a higher probability event than any other outcome (2.2229%) but low.

They lost 297 people on the way out which is significantly less than their most probable outcome. They didn't even run a simulation for 297 which has a 0.4041% probability associated with it, i.e., it's a one in 247 occurrence. There is no way to know if DARCH got the numbers wrong when they ran their covert experiments back at UBC or if this is just a fluke. Research in this area has stopped since they have no intention of ever using Quantum Tunneling to move people again saving lots of lives—lab mouse ones.

Still, it preys on the General; it gnaws at him. He goes to every single funeral (via media wall) on the Moon and on Mars and talks with families of the deceased here on Earth. They all know that their sons and daughters volunteer for this mission understanding their odds. But still they look at him and silently ask, 'How could you send them knowing they will die?'

He is ready to leave the army but at 52 (30 years in), he has to find something else to do. He's a lousy golfer and he hates to do anything he's bad at so he won't become a duffer invited to a million tournaments each year because he is General of the Army (Retired). He won't be playing professional Hold'em either. It's a young persons' game and, while he can beat anyone his own age, some of the younger players are doing things and seeing things that are truly remarkable. Very tough to beat. He could work in defense industries—he's had lots of offers. But he is reluctant to commit to anything his heart isn't in which is everything he's seen so far.

He's at Revival House because both Ellen and Damien ask, and he accepts, the role of Godfather to their twins who unlike Naya are not baptized at birth. Their time has come at ages 3.

...

"Farrar, we think you should come work at DARCH," Damien is saying on behalf of himself and Ellen. They are sitting in their living room at Revival House. But they aren't going to get a chance to discuss the matter much further at this time because two newly baptized boys burst into the room apparently wanting their new Godfather to come fishing with them. They've got their tiny rods with them and Finn, who is the leader of this wolfpack, is dragging a big person's rod behind him too. He tries to pull the General off the sofa by grabbing his large hand but ends up with a thick finger instead.

"Fishing? Here? Where?" Farrar asks the little boy.

On the way over to Mr. Owen's, Magellan tugs at his uniform and asks, "So if you're a General, where's your tank?"

...

After putting the kids to bed, Damien comes downstairs to join Ellen, Farrar and Angelo Keller who is there via media wall. It's quite late on the east coast but Angelo finds he needs very little sleep these days so he is quite happy to chat any time of the day or night. Given that his interests extend to every part of the globe and beyond, it's a good thing he figures.

"How is remedial school working out, Dr. Bell?" Angelo asks. Ellen has lived up to her promise (of course) and QCCII is equipping Q-phones with QEs again. Drogues have been renamed uQEs for unmated Quantum Entities. It's commonly pronounced 'ukes'.

"They go to school seemingly willingly enough but appear to prefer to work. Ukes do boring jobs that no one else wants to do—stuff that requires vigilance and involves repetitive tasks like factory or power plant maintenance."

"Can they materialize in the real world?" Angelo asks even though he knows the answer. He's just making conversation.

"No. That seems to require the kind of transition that started with Ash3r and now extends to nearly every QE-human pair."

"Which means," Ellen says speaking for the first time in more than an hour, "that every human will soon discover that they can mindlink with any other person wherever they may be." Ellen knows this not only because of her earlier mindlink with Damien just before the time of Naya's birth mediated through Ash3r and Pet3r but because of her link with someone else.

"It'll be some type of hive mind thing, I think—sort of the Internet but made up of human and Q-space nodes connected via billions of mindlinks," Ellen adds like she is channeling this from somewhere else. It's one of her longest comments in more than two years.

The guys all stare at her.

...

"We want to move DARCH Headquarters off planet, Farrar. To Mars colony. We think you should head it up."

For an instant, the General (uncharitably) thinks that maybe Dr. Bell is just trying to get rid of him. He collects himself and says, "Why Mars? Why me?"

Angelo says, "General, the person to run a World LLC like DARCH has to be someone acceptable to the widest possible audience and, other than Ellen, that person is you. You are fair, level headed, efficient and effective—and people, human and quantum, respect you and will follow you."

The audience that Angelo is talking about is potentially 20 billion—half of whom will one day be quantum people he thinks if Imperial China and Germania ever take their köpfe (heads) out of their esel (asses).

The General doesn't believe in false modesty so he

accepts Angelo's obsequious praise without comment.

"Why Mars?"

"Mars real estate will be the biggest play of the next 50, 100 years. The economic centre of DARCH will shift from an Earth-Moon system to Mars." Damien was going to use the term 'Earth-Moon axis' but replaces the last word because the Cartesian Powers are sometimes referred to using that inflammatory word.

Farrar is listening carefully to Damien and using his Hold'em radar on Dr. Bell. Damien's getting pretty good at hiding stuff but Farrar can clearly see he is holding back. He lets his silence ask a question.

"Most people," Damien goes on after a moment, "don't remember what DARCH stands for. It's like IBM, it's just a bunch of capital letters and a brand. It is also a useful fount of cash for people.

"Unlike some other World LLCs," as Damien continues he is looking straight at Angelo, "shares in DARCH vest in people but are non-transferrable, non-assignable and can't be pledged as collateral for loans so certain people can't buy them all up in after market transactions."

Ellen is now looking at Angelo too. She didn't know this.

"We provide a valuable service—"

"Save it, Angelo. I read Occupy Grassel," Damien says.

"What's that, D?" Ellen asks.

"Occupy Grassel is something Angelo wrote almost 100 years ago."

"Didn't know it was on the Internet," Angelo says.

"It's not. It's in DARCH though." DARCH stands for Data Archive. The overarching mission of their World LLC is to collect all information produced by human and quantum people and store it in three virtual and physical locations—one on each of the Earth, Moon and Mars.

Physical copies are made out of very thin gold plates that are perforated and can be played like old optical discs at high speed to retrieve data encoded on them. Their information density is low compared to modern data cubes but they figure they'll last somewhere between 500,000 and one million years as long as they are kept in pristine environments—like Yucca Mountain in Nevada where their Earth-based data archive is located.

Any and all data recorded in virtual space has proven to be perishable—almost none of it is accessible as internment and retrieval systems change from vacuum tubes, reel to reel tape recorders, film, eight track, cassettes, video tape, integrated circuits, floppy discs, CDs, DVDs, hard drives, optical discs to data cubes. Much of it is being lost. The heritage of humankind is being lost. Even cave paintings, archaeological artifacts and analogue media (things like books, paintings and music scores printed on acid-free paper and old films on celluloid, cellulose acetate and triacetate that Ellen likes so much) are disappearing due to age or vandalism.

No one, not even Damien or Jag, know if information they are storing in Q-space will be perishable too so they are taking no chances. Physically storing the data the way they are, is their answer. It's good for at least 500,000 years. It's the best they can do.

People can access DARCH through the Internet and now through QE mindlink as well. Better yet, everyone has the ability to upload directly to DARCH in their own personal part of the data archive. So it's become possible to curate the world and everything and everyone in it together with a cool GIS layer that Oper1s adds. Since people have physical form and can be placed exactly in terms of their geography, everything can be searched and indexed using spatial coordinates. This is not so easy to do with Quantum Entities because these days they can not only be in a gazillion parallel locations at any one time, they can be in different states too—anything from the virtual to physical and metaphysical. There is one more state they can achieve but it'll take Commonwealth scientists nearly two more decades to solve that set of equations—the Paul Dirac ones found beneath the tri-pyramids at Marco Gonzalez.

People can upload every single thought they will ever have to DARCH simply by instructing their QEs to transfer them there but hardly anyone actually takes advantage of that. It's way too embarrassing since there is no privacy or paywalls in DARCH. That is exactly the way Damien designed the system to work—to build an enormous public domain for the benefit of all people.

While they don't allow any advertising or sponsorship, they do permit people to build tools and apps based on DARCH—they can access their information and everyone else's for free. If they have a Q-phone they can do that with close to infinite speed so the uses it is being put to are amazing. The only thing they ask in return is, if you commercialize it, you pay an on-going semi-annual (and if it's a lot of money, quarterly) 1% royalty on revenues. It's the same royalty rate that Ellen and Damien had QCC (the original not the Angelo Keller more recent version) giveback to the University of Toronto for the assistance they received while they worked there. DARCH revenues from their new giveback program are growing fast along with real estate income from Moon and Mars property sales, land leases and percentage rents. All revenues (less what they need to operate it which is about 20 percent of income) are distributed tax free through the DARCH World Trust to human and QE shareholders equally so it's like a baby bonus—the more kids you have, the more you get at least if you are a woman of child-bearing age. The money goes to mothers until their child's 16th birthday. It's chauvinistic but it works on the same principle as the Hopi have used for thousands of years. Women are just that much less likely to blow it on crap. Why is DARCH like this? Cuz that's the way Damien set it up.

If he had his way, there would be zero property sales

on either Luna or Mars—DARCH would only issue land leases. He wants to follow the example of the Holy Roman Catholic Church which largely sustains itself for more than two millennia first by occupying choice real estate in thousands of villages, towns and cites across the globe and then never selling any of it—only leasing land for 49, 69 and 99 year terms. Church leadership take the position that their institution should have a planning horizon of centuries or longer instead of, say, a political cycle of three or four years or an entrepreneur's horizon which might be as long as their next payroll. The Church prefers a never ending (recurring) stream of revenues which works as long as you get your land back every half century or so. The House of Windsor and Emperor of Japan follow their example—the Windsors are the largest rentier in the (former) United Kingdom and the latter, well, the latter predates even the Catholics so there must be something to be said for their real estate strategy.

Oper1s does some work on this too—he reports back to Damien that of the 1,000 richest people in the Commonwealth, 54% of them have a substantial part of their wealth (substantial being more than two thirds) in real estate assets. This reinforces Damien's view so they restrict freehold land titles on Luna and Mars to no more than 20% of all DARCH lands there and only for qualified uses. Damien, with Ellen's support, makes sure that it's hard to qualify for this and that the 20% limit is embedded in DARCH's charter.

There's been an uneasy truce called between the Cartesian Powers and the Commonwealth in both colonies. It's a saw-off really. They have to cooperate when they inflate their lunar skin since Commonwealth presence on the Moon, both QE and human, is a fact. The Commonwealth builds their own space elevator on the Moon and then they are the first to complete one on Mars. Their space transports—Earth to LEO via spaceplane, LEO to space elevator station above Moon or Mars via spacebarge—are totally cutting edge in terms of what they can move (volume and weight), propulsion system, speed and comfort for human crew and passengers. And, of course, they have quantum-tunnels from various Earth gates to Moon and Mars as well as quite a few asteroids. They move huge amounts of raw materials, nutrients and manufactured products between all their origins and destinations. It's amazing how much you can hoover up using what amount to narrow diameter, low power straws if you are persistent and consistent in their use.

...

"What's Occupy Grassel all about?" Ellen can see that Damien's lost the thread. She is helping her husband snap back to reality.

"Angelo, would you like to tell them?"

"Not really."

"OK, I will." But then he has a better idea. "Pet3r, can you bring it up and display it?"

"Sure thing." This is what Angelo wrote when he was young—

The majority of the population of Grassel is made up of Grasshoppers, Squirrels and Ants. Mensa Ants account for 1% of the population. These are the groups that populate the World of Grassel, a place of 100 Rows x 100 Columns.

1. Grasshoppers are low wage earners who have to spend every cent they make just to survive. However, each Grasshopper starts life owning one square in Grassel with an asset value of $13,200. (All figures are in GD, Grassel Dollars.)

2. Squirrels are mid-income types and even though they have a lot more income than Grasshoppers, they somehow seem to spend all the Grassel Dollars they earn on current consumption. The amount they have left over each year for savings and investment? Zero. But they live on nicer squares in Grassel with an asset value of $19,800 each.

3. There is a minority population made up of Ants. They are an upper class volk who make many times what even Squirrels take home so they have some money left over for savings and investment! But these Ants are very cautious and

don't want to take any risks so they don't invest any of their hard earned money—they save it instead and put it in Grassel state-backed treasury bills that pay interest at 2% p.a.

4. Finally, we have a minority within a minority—Mensa Ants who make the same amount of money each year as the rest of the Ant class but they split their surplus cash between savings and investment. In fact, they place 90% of their surplus in investments; the balance they place in financial instruments. Since there is only one type of financial instrument in Grassel, they have some t-bills on which they get the princely sum of 2% p.a. in interest.

Grasshoppers and Squirrels are only too happy to sell the squares they own! Hell, they can use a boost to their current cashflow. However, they don't save any of the extra cash they get from selling their squares. And they don't invest any either! THEY SPEND IT ALL!

The Ants won't sell squares they own to Mensa Ants. They're into savings and they believe that owning a square is a form of savings for themselves and their volk.

The Land of Grassel is 100 rows by 100 columns; i.e., there are 10,000 squares of which Grasshoppers own 3,333, Squirrels own 6,234, Ants own 333 and Mensa Ants 100 at time, t = 0. The 10,000 squares represent a total asset value of $170,060,000.

Every Grasshopper, Squirrel, Ant and Mensa Ant starts out with one square of Grassel land each. But the gods of Grassel are wondering if they come back a generation later (20 years on), what will have happened?

Well, after just 11 years, none of the Grasshoppers own any property and after 17, the Squirrels get wiped out too! Of course, the Ants still own their properties since they refused to sell to Mensa Ants and they didn't need to so that they could maintain their lifestyle (like the Squirrels did) or just to pay for the necessities of life (like the Grasshoppers did). But they don't have much money either—their savings don't amount to much but at least they still have their squares. This proves that in Grassel, *you can't save your way to wealth, you have to invest your way there.*

However, Mensa Ants have done very well. They have some savings/financial assets (in the form of fairly liquid t-bills) but they own practically all Grassel property. In fact, although Mensa Ants only represent 1% of Grassel population, they own

95.5% of all assets (both squares and financial assets) after just 20 years. But what's even better for Mensa Ants is the fact that they have unearned rents practically pouring into their Mensa Ant suit pockets in Niagara Falls-like proportions. (They, being Mensa Ants, have heard of Niagara Falls in a parallel universe.)

Ants (333 of them) start off with assets of $8,800,000 and, after a hard slog, 20 years later they have increased their holdings via savings to $15,084,361.60 which works out to $45,253.08 per capita. Not bad but a lot of hard work has gone into this by resisting current consumption—including tasty treats like buying an iPhone.

But Mensa Ants (100 of them) who start with just $2,640,000 in assets, end up 20 years later with a humongous portfolio worth $320,262,657.24 or $3,202,626.57 per capita by investing 90% of their surplus income and saving 10%. What's even better is that their passive income from owning nearly all the squares in Grassel is providing them with unearned rents of $51,958,095.46 or $519,580.95 per capita per year by Year 20.

Investing has been a smart play for Mensa Ants, in part, because their Return on Investment (actually, their Return on Equity) is much higher than the interest rate on t-bills (22% p.a. versus 2%) and, in part, because they use leverage in acquiring squares—they are leveraging their equity (surplus cash) with a LTV (Loan to Value) ratio of 85%! Basically, they are borrowing from savers in Grassel to buy their squares from them or, put another way, savers are financing their own loss of property to Mensa Ants.

Their investment strategy has paid off so handsomely that, after 17 years, they have bought all the property they can in Grassel and must now look beyond their world for other opportunities. They have yet to figure out how to cross the border between Grassel and Niagara Falls but they're working on it.

What this shows is that without Grassel Government intervention in the form of effective redistribution, practically all the assets of Grassel end up in the hands of a tiny minority of Mensa Ants. The Government is also thinking of introducing a tax on consumption to encourage Grasshoppers and Squirrels to save and also some education programs to teach Grasshoppers, Squirrels and Ants how to invest too. The consumption tax is thought to be regressive but, in fact, may be the only way that the Grassel Government can get Mensa Ants to pay any taxes at all. Mensa Ants have such good tax accountants and tax attorneys that so-called progressive taxes on income are almost completely ineffective.

All of this is coming in response to the Occupy Grassel Movement which has seen Grasshoppers and Squirrels occupying squares they don't own anymore much to the consternation of Mensa Ants.

...

After reading this thing, Ellen is looking at Angelo in none too friendly a way. He is trying hard not to notice. "I suppose you're a Mensa Ant?" she asks pointlessly. "How many QCCII public interest shares have you bought, Angelo?"

"None."

"I don't believe you."

"It's true. I have purchased none at all." 'It's literally true; it's the smart truth,' Angelo is thinking.

"I believe the right question, honey, is how many QCCII public interest shares remain in the hands of their original shareholders?" Damien says. When he calls her 'honey' the General practically winces. Damien misses it but Angelo doesn't.

"Ah, I would have to look that up," Angelo says.

"Pet3r?" Damien says.

"I will ask Adu1us."

Moments later, he says, "Currently, the number is less than 50%." Pet3r has learned to summarize and simplify things for humans. This would be satisfactory for most of them but not Dr. Bell.

"May I have the exact number please?"

"48.749335%."

"So what happened to the other 51.25%, Angelo?" Ellen asks.

"They were bought by someone else," he says.

"Who?"

"Umm, actually QCCII Treasury repurchases shares in

public markets on a regular basis."

"I want you to stop that, Angelo and change the bylaws of the corporation to end that practice once and for all," Ellen says commandingly. The General approves.

"That will require a super majority to do that," Angelo says.

"What does that mean?"

"Ah, 90% of all shareholdings will have to vote in favor and a majority, 50% + 1, of all minority shareholdings too."

Ellen, of course, realizes that Angelo now controls more than 90% of the company (up from 80 originally when they set it up as a new form of World LLC instead of gradually heading down) so the first part won't be a problem—he'll simply vote his shares in favor.

"I expect you to be persuasive in the public arena to get 50% + 1 of minority shareholders to approve it too," she tells him forcefully.

"Yes, liebchen," he says to her as nicely as possible for an old crony like him.

...

Ellen and Naya are aboard Hortense. They are not exactly flying down the trail since Hortense is old even for a camel (in her 30s). Danny is there with his mother. He is a year older than Naya and hates riding with Ella. It's such a baby thing to do, sitting in a saddle in front of her while she keeps a death grip on him in case he falls off. He can jump off roofs and roll with it so he knows he won't hurt himself if their camel decides to scratch some fleas by rolling over on Ella and Dan. It's his over-protective Mom he'd be worried about.

He feels like screaming so he does.

"Oh shush," says pain-in-the-neck Naya to Danny. "Stop being such a baby. You're worse than my brothers!"

So Danny screams louder.

...

Damien and Nahuel are at the base of the canyon wall.

They can see dust rising, coming in their direction so they know the girls and the kids are heading back this way. Sabine and their three kids are also along for the ride. They're all older so they can ride on their own.

"Good business," Nahuel says companionably. "Many camel riders come."

Nahuel and his tribe are in the camel riding tourist racket. They take city dudes out on trails near Third Mesa and along the gorge. Hard to believe that dusty Third Mesa has become a tourist attraction but it has. A young Damien, if he decided to visit today, would find the place much changed. Folks want to come to the desert and have an authentic Native American/First Nations experience. Damien can't see anything authentic about camel riding.

"Naya good dancer," Nahuel says. She did a show in their Council Ring the night before. "Better than Nell even at same age."

"Really?"

"Yes. Look same."

"Yeah, she's been practicing to Nell's music and old videos," Damien says completely missing the point that Nahuel is making.

But then Damien says, "I can't figure it out."

Nahuel just waits knowing that Damien will spell things out eventually in over abundant detail.

"How come she, she talks about Nell the way she does, like she's real and," then he finally gets it out, something he's been thinking more and more about his daughter but has never said to anyone, "how come she is the spitting image of Nell, only Naya'll be taller?"

Nahuel looks at his brother-in-law like he's a fool which he is.

"What? You not know?"

"Know what?"

"How you not know?"

"Know what, Nahuel? How can I answer you about my not-knowing something if I don't know it?"

"You stupid like white man sometime. You marry same sister, twice."

...

He wants to get the whole story out of Nahuel but before he can do that, Ellen is there with Naya, Sabine, Ella, Danny and the rest of the kids.

Nahuel goes over and helps Sabine and the others get their camels sitting down. All the kids are ready for a swim in the stream nearby and Nahuel is like the pied piper, he leads a happy passel of them away. He's also really popular cuz he has a big pile of his special formula beef and turkey jerky for them to chew on after their swim. It's his own secret recipe. Ella hopes that there is nothing addictive about his recipe—Nahuel is tricky like his grandfather, Chief Dan of the Hopi.

...

Damien wants to either ask or tell Ellen about his last conversation with Nahuel but since he has no idea what Nahuel meant by his comment, he won't say anything yet. 'Sister' in a Hopi Chief's world might just be an all inclusive word.

Damien, as he walks silently next to his wife, can see that Farrar's recent visit and this trip back to Third Mesa have been good for her. She is more animated than he has seen her at any time in the last five years. At Naya's show last night, Ellen was laughing and clapping with everyone else—Naya is not only a terrific dancer, she's an unbelievable ham. Half her show is mime and she plays really well off her audience. Her brothers (shanghaied into her routine once more) are her straight men.

It also doesn't hurt that she is probably the cutest girl in the solar system. Even at five (nearly six she would tell you), she is a showstopper. Men and women stop Damien in the street in San Fran just to talk to her. He also knows that he will have to keep a close eye on his daughter. She is so outgoing and personable that she'll talk to strangers, to homeless people and everyone else to include them in

Naya's world which is a place of boundless possibilities, adventures and magic. He doesn't want to take any of that away from her so he just watches out for her.

Once when they are in a bookstore (which have made something of a comeback in the Commonwealth as people start collecting old things and authentic things again), Damien and Magellan are reading when he looks up, only seconds have gone by, and Naya is gone. Finn is picking his nose. Damien freaks. He and the boys start frantically searching the tall aisles for her.

But Naya isn't far—she's talking to one of the curators in this place asking him about his life.

But Damien is all shook up after that.

...

"Nahuel, please tell me what you mean by 'sisters'? Is that a euphemism?"

Nahuel thinks Damien is taking about Euphony.

"She make good Hopi wife."

"Who? You mean Ellen?" Damien can't see his point.

"You former girl. Nice hips." He draws Euphony's figure so Damien gets the message.

"No, I meant what is the relationship between Nell and Ellen? Why does Naya look so much like Nell? I need to know."

Nahuel looks at him much like Chief Dan did at this place almost two decades ago. It sends a chill through him.

"One day you come here always."

Seeing how much more alive Ellen is here, Damien thinks that is only too possible.

"Many year ago, Chief Dan, he have a brother—"

"You mean a blood brother or a genetically-related person?"

"You want story?" Nahuel is a chief and doesn't like being interrupted. So Damien clams up.

"Many year ago, Chief Dan brother die, young. I no remember how. Maybe he never tell me. Chief Dan take that white woman as sister-wife. They have baby, half white, half Hopi. That white woman run off with baby. Her family keep secret. Ashamed to have Great Spirit in family. They hide great grandfather. No talk to him."

Damien still doesn't see what this story has to do with Ellen.

Then Nahuel spells it out for him, "That baby is Ellen grandmother."

...

It's easy for Damien to check. It's true Ellen and Nell are related; they share 12.5% of their DNA from a single source. Chief Dan, trickster that he is over many years, is grandfather to Nell and great grandfather to Ellen.

Nahuel tells him that Chief Dan played another trick on them all. He convinces his brother's wife to call their baby 'Ellen' which is who, two generations later, Ellen is named after. 'Ellen' spelled backwards is, of course, Nelle.

It's been there right in front of his face the whole time. 'What a dope I am,' Damien thinks. 'I married the same girl twice. No wonder I love them both so much.'

Nahuel tells him there is a third sister but he won't say anything more about that other than, "She younger sister, Nell and Ellen."

...

When he tells Ellen, she does not act surprised because she isn't.

"Nell told me years ago, D. Before she died. You gonna get mad at me again?"

"No, never." That whole phase of their relationship is something that Damien is not proud of.

"I'm glad you know. It's a weight off my shoulders actually."

"I can see that." He smiles at her. He comes over to sit next to her, close to her but doesn't touch her. He can sense that she does not want to be touched.

They just sit there together, man and wife, watching the sun go down like thousands of human couples have before them from this vantage point high above Third

Mesa for at least the last 30,000 years. They are sitting in the lean-to he sat in with Nell almost 20 years ago. Damien has had it repaired but not altered.

...

Stockholm City Hall is built in the National Romantic Style on the eastern tip of Kungsholmen Island. Damien is there with his family (minus the twins back in Santa Cruz staying with Daniella and Micah) waiting as they all are for the Trumpeters cry by the King's Guard announcing that the King and Queen of Sweden are arriving. There are two traditional blue upholstered chairs waiting for the royal pair near the front of this gigantic Hall. It's an area exclusively reserved for them. Audience members are arrayed, Church-style, on either side in this post-religious society where secularity reigns supreme. After their arrival there will be a short concert by an artist selected by this year's recipient of the Nobel Prize in Physics, Dr. Damien Graham Bell.

This is the venue not only for the awarding of the prize but also for hosting the Nobel Prize banquet. It's the banquet that Naya is in a fever to get to. There will be dancing and JEL will be there. She can't wait til the boring stuff is over.

This sombre place took 12 years to build and its massive red brick exterior is dominated by a Monumental Tower topped by Three Crowns, Sweden's national symbol.

Naya and Ellen do matching dressup. They are both wearing near-identical floor length gowns and silver gloves that cover their forearms up to their elbows. Their evening dresses are silver beaded mermaid, trumpet darling floor-length numbers. Ellen's shoulders are bare and her dress shows an amazing amount of décolletage. Naya is frustrated that hers includes shoulders and quarter sleeves. Naya has the cutest beret ever sitting on her wild auburn hair at a dashing angle. Ellen is wearing her sterling silver Hopi lariat necklace with pendant shaped into Constantine's WE ARE ALL ONE symbol. It's the first time she's worn it since her sex tape experience with Damien in San Quentin, the second last time she was there before she had the place leveled to the ground. There isn't a man in the room that remains unaffected by this pair and a few women as well.

It's December 10th, the day these prizes (all except the Nobel Peace Prize which is given out in Oslo at its own ceremony) are traditionally awarded. It's exactly two weeks to Naya's sixth birthday. She is counting down. Sitting on the other side of her is Su7e looking a tad awkward in a chair. She is wearing a bright blue robe that looks rather like an ugly grad gown. It keeps slipping off her practically non existent shoulders. She has to keep propping it up with her long dexterous fingers. Pet3r is sitting nearby and Ash3r as well just as awkwardly.

Sunny Michaud and his wife, Traian and Dakota, José-Luis (their son), Dafne, Elsu, Tony Reznik, Nahuel, Sabine, their kids, Damien's Uncle, Dekka, Javier and Mica (Dakota's parents), Mary O'Regan, Caleb and his boy Tane, Aziz, Anthony, Sayed, Jerom Van Der Hout, Dr. Luis, Sally Thornton, Ellen's brother, Jon and his wife, Natalie, Mike Cronkey, Jay, Henry Linnert, Jagad Durai (but not his wife—Cady is expecting and is on their own personal no-fly list at the moment), Chuck Wong, Farrar Staubach, Jonesy, Zora (but not Euphony), Salem Bouazizi, Bob Schultz, Dr. Shelby Zewyki and Evan Salazar are among the 1,300 people in attendance. It includes 250 science students who bring a lot of energy to this audience. Attending via media wall are Angelo Keller, Daniella and Micah and Mr. Owen as well as several hundred thousand human viewers and every QE in the solar system, now numbering more than five billion.

Everyone stands as Sweden's King and Queen finally enter. Once they are seated, everyone else may sit as well. There is a single grand piano on stage and then he is there. No announcement precedes him. It is Carl Bray come to perform again for President Brooks (this time she is not in a basement at UBC having wild sex with Damien and making a baby) as well as the Royal Pair. This is Damien's surprise for Ellen. He looks over at her and can see she is captivated by his music and performance as is every other person in attendance.

For Carl, this is an opportunity to make up for a miss early in his career. More than 60 years ago, he is asked to play for another Royal Couple, a young Will and Kate, at a reception to be given in their honour at Rideau Hall in Ottawa. But he declines! No one says 'no' to their Head of State (the GG) but Carl does—his ethics are involved. He's already accepted a gig at Toronto's Jazz Festival and he always keep his commitments in the order in which he accepts them so he turns them down, flat. Today he finally gets to play for royalty.

His last piece is Talk of Hands—Ellen looks first at Naya, the baby they made the last time Carl played this (unknowingly) for them, next at Damien and then she reaches out and gives her husband's hand a light caress.

...

"JEL! JEL! Over here, over here!" José-Luis can't see Naya but he can hear her. She is hidden by useless adults taking up valuable, playable real estate in this humongous banquet hall.

She runs over to where he is, more than a head taller than her. She hugs him so hard it looks like her beret is gonna come off her head. One long glove is unraveling too. Her head only comes to his chest. Like most football players, even nine year old ones, JEL is very lean. He has long lean muscles, long brown hair, hazel eyes and a light brown complexion like his mother. Naya is the person who first calls him, JEL. When she is a baby, she has trouble pronouncing his name so she pronounces him JEL and it sticks. It is a derivative of his initials J.L. which Naya can read cuz like her brother, Magellan, Naya has always been able to read. Always. Mind you a mindlink with Su7e since she is a day old doesn't hurt because if she ever gets stuck on a word or, for that matter, any question, she just has to think it and the answer is there in her mind. So it's kinda hard to know where Naya ends and Su7e begins and vice versa. They both like it that way and neither of them can imagine life any other way. It's like breathing only way more fun.

JEL is embarrassed by this prolonged hugging thing that Naya is doing. Girls! But he likes his little friend. She can move like anything and isn't afraid of hanging with JEL and his amigos as they tear around every summer either in Third Mesa or at his family's farm near Bucharest. JEL speaks English, Romanian, Spanish, German and some Russian. Naya speaks only English. He's been attending every one of Naya's dance recitals since she was three and she's been at all his important football matches also for the last three years—via media wall.

"Hey, Naya, want to get out of here?" he asks.

"In a minute."

"Why in a minute? What's wrong with now?"

"I promised Da a dance! Then we'll go."

'Dance? Boring!' he thinks.

Now that she's greeted JEL properly like a lady she believes, she looks for Damien as a student orchestra bolstered by a cadre of professionals strikes up a nice Swedish waltz—lots of violins and lots of Scandinavian angst.

Naya knew it would be a waltz! She and Su7e checked out this part of the agenda (the only part other than hanging with JEL that is important). They don't do a lot (well any) waltzing at Meeza Elite Danse Academy, so she and Su7e have been practicing. Naya has to lead because Su7e is, frankly, terrible. But that's OK with Miss Bossy Boots because she knows her Da will be even worse with his tin ear and bad leg and she will have to lead him. She finds him in a huge circle of adoring fans; she bursts right on through and takes him by a reluctant hand. He knows what's coming and been dreading it. "Come on Da, this is our number!"

Then she is on her tippy toes trying to help Damien master a box step. She does the guy thing—left foot forward, then right foot forward just slightly more than shoulder width apart, bring feet together, step back with the right, next back with the left, then bring both feet together. It's easy! She counts for Da, it's a 3/4 beat—an international waltz. All he has to do is follow and listen to her count!

Just about everyone in the room is watching a newly minted Nobel Laureate perform ineptly but charmingly. But what they are really looking at are spectacular, smoothly flowing progressive movements by his dance partner, a tiny girl who is obviously going places. Naya supposes it wouldn't do to try a butterfly twist in her long evening gown.

...

After his dance lesson from Naya, Damien finally has a few minutes to spend with Traian.

"Long time, Tray."

"Too long, D. I was hoping you'd bring the twins." Traian is partial to boys and takes a huge amount of pride in his son's success on the field and in school. He's José-Luis' biggest fan after Naya.

"I thought it'd be too much for Ellen given the amount of time I have to spend on speechifying and PR here."

"She looks beautiful, Damien."

"Dakota too."

"We're both lucky guys," Tray says but then realizes he's had it easy by comparison—no prison time, no torture and no bankruptcy. "At least you brought Naya."

"We couldn't very well leave her at home, Tray. It's been JEL this and JEL that for the last six weeks. He's her superhero."

They both smile and are quiet for a moment, contemplating what a marvelous thing it is to have families that they both adore. They are immediately comfortable with each other; it's like they've never been separated at all. Neither of them notices that JEL and Naya are not in the ballroom any longer. It's a mistake of colossal proportions.

"I heard about the pressure they put on you. Thanks for not putting me in the soup." When Damien says 'they' he means the Russian mob and their pet government.

"Well, I wasn't going to tell them I didn't have the Key. But it wasn't entirely unselfish of me, Damien."

"Come again?"

"It was bad enough that you already had the US leaning on you. If I told them you are the only guy who has the Quantum Key then you'd have every crazy Ruskie gunning for you and they have people inside San Quentin so that wasn't going to work. On the other hand, if I had told them that then they'd have no further use for me and those guys are capable of *anything*."

"Did they threaten your family?"

Traian nods.

"So what did you do?"

"I gave them a counterfeit Key."

"What?"

"Yeah, they've been working with it for the last two years trying to produce their own QEs. I gave them a matryoshka doll—there is an endless nest inside the algorithm—it'll never work but they don't know that yet."

They both laugh but Damien looks at Traian—this is a dangerous game he is playing. But what Traian's son is doing right now is worse.

...

"This is spooky," one of the kids in their group is saying.

"I think we should turn back," says another.

JEL is leading, Naya right behind him. They pay no nevermind to any kid who is chicken.

"I read it's 365 steps. One for every day of the year.

This part of the building has been closed for renovations for the last eight years. But the real reason it's closed is cuz Swedish people get depressed and come here to die."

"How do they die, JEL?" Naya asks not a bit afraid to see dead Swedish people. "Is there someone at the top that like cuts their heads off for them if they ask?"

"Naw, they jump. It's 106 metres. They go splat on their nice steps. It takes like a week or something to mop them up."

"How big is 106 metres?" Naya asks.

"It's like taking one of our football pitches and standing it straight up."

That's really big if you are Naya's current size.

They are headed to the top of the Monumental Tower that is part of this structure built 150 years ago.

JEL scoped it out earlier in the day. He was inside the stairwell when workers were here. He sabotages the lock in the simplest way imaginable—he stuffs gum in the mortise (the recess in a door jamb that interacts with a door lock's tongue) so even though the guys think they've locked the place tight, a slight push from a healthy nine year old boy's shoulder and they're in.

...

Naya fully expects they'll have to fight an ogre when they reach the top of the tower. She can't imagine any princess needing rescue there because, well, she's the princess.

She's disappointed to find the balcony at the top is empty. But the view of the water (Riddarfjärden Bay), the city and the heavens above is spectacular. All the other kids turn back except Naya and JEL and one tubby kid whose name she has forgotten. He's out of breath but Naya and JEL could easily climb another 365 steps and never huff and puff like that.

"What ya doing?"

"You stay here. You're too little."

"Am not."

"Are too. Stay here, Naya, I mean it."

JEL is climbing over the copper railings onto the bronze metal roof that flares out from near vertical to a mere 30 degree slope at its edges.

"This is where depressed people come, Naya!" JEL is going to go to the edge to look down to see where they've been hitting the pavement. Maybe there'll be some left over remains or something. He's brought a couple of oranges with him too. They've been in his pants pockets, one on each side, since he swiped them from the banquet—he's planning to deploy his own experiment momentarily.

It's a clear night with a full moon. It's colder than anything Naya has ever experienced. She is standing there in her little shear evening gown. It's worse even than the Giant's Garden—which is cold and snowy but this is way, way colder she thinks and the sun never comes here. No wonder Swedish people all want to die. It's horrible here. She wishes she hadn't taken off her long silver gloves. Like most dancers, Naya is well organized and neat. She rolls them up and stuffs one inside the other before shoving them into the tiny matching purse her Mom gave her for this evening. Only thing is she can't remember where she put it or her beret at the moment. Her teeth begin to chatter.

Naya decides that she's not too little. She climbs over the railing. She's going to go join JEL but when she gets to the other side, she knows straight away that he is right. She's too short to reach the flatter part of the roof. Her black patent NoNo Bonit dress shoes are slippery too so she can't get any purchase to either climb back up or slide safely onto the part of the roof that is 30 degrees instead of nearly 90.

"Help, JEL, help me!"

JEL turns around and his eyes go wide with fear. He's a very active guy and he knows right away that his little friend is in real trouble. If she lets go, she's going to fall more than a metre, hit the roof at its steepest point and slide right off. 'SHE IS GOING TO DIE AND IT'S GOING TO BE MY FAULT.' JEL is nine not six. He knows the score. He lunges for her at the exact moment that her tiny frozen hands come unstuck from the railing.

He misses her but catches her dress as she goes whizzing past him. But he won't let go of her dress. In an instant he knows they are both going over but he's not letting go of her.

The fat kid is hysterical. He's blubbering like a baby.

It's a good thing that José-Luis is built like he is with unearthly reflexes because when she goes over the edge pulling him with her he is able to grab one of the huge lightning rods that are positioned at each of the four corners of the eaves of this mansard roof. He gets his left arm hooked around the thing; with his right he's got her dress in his fist. Little Naya is dangling horizontal to the ground 106 metres above very cold and very hard street brickwork below. He hears her dress begin to rip.

"Climb up, Naya! Climb!"

Naya has a terrific power to weight ratio. So she spins about in the air, rights herself and reaches up; then she shimmies up his arm like she does ropes at Meeza Elite Danse Academy. She can climb 2 inch diameter hemp ropes, 20 feet high faster than *any* girl at the Academy. By the time big girls have boobs and hips and stuff, they are pretty useless at it—so Naya instinctively knows there's an optimum age range for this sort of adventure. She's right there.

With a final push on her tiny rump, JEL has her back on the 30 degree part of the roof. He keeps his right hand on her tummy pressing her flat making sure she can't go anywhere. With Naya, expect the unexpected. He rests for a few seconds.

"Take off your shoes, Naya."

"No. These are my nicest pair."

"Naya, please? You can't get any traction in those.

You've got to help me get you over that." He's pointing at the railings leading back to safety which, from this vantage point, do seem kinda huge to Naya.

"OK," she says.

...

When Damien gets a look at his half frozen, shoeless daughter with her ripped dress, his face goes white with fear. He knows what happened to Nell at 16. But his daughter is two weeks shy of her sixth birthday. This is beyond his worst nightmare. He's been looking for Naya and Su7e (who has bugged out for some reason) for the last half hour. Then Naya just wanders back into the Banquet Hall. Ellen went back to their hotel earlier. She is tired.

JEL is with Naya. He's pretty messed up too but nothing like her.

Damien goes over to his daughter.

"Da," she says and faints into his arms.

...

The Royal Swedish Academy of Sciences awards the Nobel prizes in Physics and Chemistry as well as the Nobel Memorial Prize in Economic Sciences. But without a doubt, the hardest one to win is Physics. They still snail mail 4,000 individual forms—3,000 to human scientists and 1,000 to Quantum People who are tuned to science, specifically physics. It is a long and rigorous process and they use snail mail, in part, because it is tradition and, in part, to convey a sense of the importance of the matter at hand. The Academy will take 200 names and narrow it down to a list of 15. The process including who has been nominated is secret. A maximum of three nominees can win but this year it's only one—Dr. Bell.

Unlike the Nobel Peace Prize, Laureates do not give a speech at their award ceremonies. Instead, they are invited to give a Nobel Lecture prior to their award. For Damien, it's an opportunity to speak to the world on matters that are important to him. He asks for Ellen's advice but she tells him her days of speech making are thankfully behind her. "You'll do fine, Dear."

But he doesn't feel fine as he is getting ready to take the stage. The introduction is painfully long and is accompanied by video footage of his life, much of it recorded or made available by Pet3r. It's really embarrassing. But then there is loud applause and he is on.

...

"Good evening, Your Royal Highnesses, Your Excellencies, Ladies and Gentlemen.

"I am humbled to be here tonight. I am thinking about the men and women and now quantum people who have made it possible for me to be here. The contributions of my colleagues and friends, Dr. Luis Castagino, Mr. Traian Vasilescu, Dr. Charles Wong and Dr. Jagad Durai as well as our quantum partners Pet3r and Vl4d are immeasurable both in terms of the work we do together and the support they've given me over the years through some difficult and harsh times.

"I have to recognize the contributions of all scientists and all physicists who have gone before who make it possible for all of us to do the exhilarating work we do and to solve unimaginable problems in a Cosmos as strange and wondrous as what we see and observe all around us at macro and quantum scales. There are many mysteries yet to be unraveled so we must go on boldly to complete a never ending mission—to expand the boundaries of knowledge and the public domain that we are building through the efforts of all humankind and quantum people.

"I want to recognize above all others, the person who has made my life worth something in every way that is meaningful—we have shared an adventure together that has taken us from student life to corporate life to life in prison to revolution in the streets to renewal and now family life, my wife, President Ellen Brooks." Ellen blushes but she waves and there is a lovely round of applause and many appreciative looks especially from the male part of this audience.

Euphony is watching this back home and feels like puking when Damien says this. She tells herself the only reason she is watching is cuz Zora is there. Zora and Damien are friends. That friendship has survived the end of Euph's relationship with him.

"I want to use some of my time with you this evening to speak to you of the importance of the individual. Individuals count. It is never acceptable for any society to stop counting people as individuals, to view them instead as a mass. The calculus of death must end. We need leaders. And where do we find them?"

As he says this, he stops and smiles at his wife.

"Are leaders born or does their environment shape them? It is undoubtedly a combination of both. Leaders project confidence. They understand the 'way the world works'. They have a mental map of it against which they can quickly test their theories in what Albert Einstein called thought experiments.

"Leaders form plans. They react quickly to changes in their environment. They know when to press forward, when to retreat and when to wait. They bargain. They act. They change their personalities to suit circumstances. They inspire, cajole, uplift and face down evil in all its forms. They know in their souls that human and quantum people are more productive and happier when arrayed and deployed in teams—when they feel part of something bigger than themselves. In a crisis, they instantly organize people around them to save as many and as much as possible. If circumstances require it, they know how to get across a chasm that opens suddenly before them as quickly and safely as possible. They put round pegs in round holes and square pegs in square holes effortlessly to get the most out of any team. They set goals, let everyone know what those are and then make sure they achieve them.

Bruce M Firestone

"Characteristics you expect to find in a leader include great training, intellect and education, physical courage and prowess, wiliness and toughness and above all—broad experience.

"You cannot find great leadership where expectations are that leaders must be perfect without every having been imperfect first. That is called experience—to have a solid map of the way the world works you need experience. To gain it, you must first make mistakes. You cannot have it both ways—a leader cannot be authentic if she or he has no real world experience, no testing of their mettle, no mistakes made on the way. Be careful what you wish for—ask for perfection and you just might get it.

"If you want to do great things, it requires a total commitment of mind and body and soul. And it's going to require leadership.

"I am not recommending a reckless, fearless approach to life but maybe that's what it takes to be a leader, formed by the crucible of life's pressures and crises.

"Scott Adams once said humorously that leadership is about getting people to do things they know are not in their best interests. This is absolutely *not* what leaders do, at least, not successful ones.

"Instead, let me share with you my definition of what a real leader is—a leader is a person who chooses from among many alternatives, some of which s/he has generated and some of which come from elsewhere—either inside or perhaps from outside their organization or nation-state—the right path for his or her team getting buy-in from their whole tribe as well as their entire stakeholder group and making sure that all their resources are deployed optimally to achieve common objectives that are serving not only to further the interests of individual tribal members and the organization or nation but also a broader purpose for humankind and quantum people.

"My message here tonight is to be trustworthy as well as bold, to seek truth, to uphold the principles of justice, freedom and scientific method, to tolerate failure, to seek success, to embrace the journey with a boiling passion for discovery that knows no bounds, to lead by example and to look for leadership amongst individuals that count and who will stand up to be counted."

Next he says, "We Are All ONE," and then, in complete breach of Nobel protocol, etiquette and tradition, he makes the sign of Constantine I holding his right hand aloft, his thumb in support of his index finger. He is looking at Ellen when he does this. He did not die in prison. Why? Because she wouldn't let him. She faced down an entire corrupted empire to free him and her people.

It is totally quiet in the Hall. Even Naya is still while watching her Da make a silly gesture with his hand.

Damien is looking out over the audience and then Pet3r first, next Vl4d, Traian, Ellen, Jag, Sunny, Dakota, Aziz, Anthony, Sayed, Jerom, Chuck, Farrar, Jonesy, Zora, Salem and Evan all rise up and salute with him. They raise their hands together in complete silence. Pretty soon the entire audience is up including the royal pair who rise but do not join in the salute—this is as much as Swedish decorum can stand. It's quite a moment. Even Naya is making the salute now but she gets it wrong. She's doing the NBA's, 'I'm No. 1' thing with her little right hand. Then everyone is clapping. Life begins anew.

...

Dakota is so furious with her son, she cannot speak and when she does, she is hysterical. She cusses him out in Spanish but doesn't hit him. She would never strike her child. Then she pulls him to her and nearly crushes him, sturdy guy that he is and all. While she is alternately hugging him and berating him, she incongruously detects a strong smell of oranges. For some reason, her wild son has two crushed oranges that have burst in his suit pants pockets and ruined them. There is one on each side.

"I think it would be best, Damien, if José-Luis is told to stay away from Naya. That they see each other no longer." Traian is almost completely lost for words. There is no apology he can say to his friend that will convey his feelings at the moment.

"I agree," Damien says. He plans to block José-Luis from having any further contact with his daughter now or in the foreseeable future. He has the technical skills to ensure a total blackout. What he can't do is wipe out the horrible memories that Naya will carry with her the rest of her life.

When she wakes up later in their hotel room, she is fighting to keep from falling. She is flailing her little kid arms wildly. She is screaming. "Da, help me! Help me, I'm falling. I'm falling! Oh, Da, where are you? Why aren't you here?"

He goes to her and calms her down and she falls asleep again. She has mild hypothermia (which Damien knows how to treat). Also a few cuts and bruises and a red pressure welt around her tummy where José-Luis had her dress bunched up in his fist. Every time she wakes up, she starts flailing away and repeats her 'Da, help me' routine. It will last for years and will develop into insomnia so bad that Naya will think that she has no way out; she should have gone over the edge to her death.

They all miss something though. When Naya loses her grip on the railing, she automatically turns her head to the right to see where JEL is and also to avoid whacking her face on the roof when she makes contact with it. She hits the side of her head instead just above her left temple hard on its ribbed metal surface. The blow is hidden from view by her thick hair and she doesn't swell up on the outside of her brainpan. Inside, it's a different story.

...

Ellen, Damien and Naya are expected to go to Bucharest after Stockholm. They intend to go to another wedding—Traian has kept his promise to himself. He won't marry Dakota until his pal is there to back him up, to be his best man. But this is out of the question at the present time.

...

Damien will also notice within a matter of weeks that Su7e is sick—she is showing signs of psychosis.

...

Ellen is not surprised to hear that Angelo has relocated to the Moon. He apparently owns a retirement residence there—a whole chain of them actually. They are very successful emphasizing in their advertising that rich dudes like him can come to Luna and live at least 30 years longer in 1/6th of a G.

The only thing that does surprise her is that the chain is located in that part of the Moon claimed by Germania. Angelo Keller returns to his roots. When she thinks about it for a few more moments, she isn't surprised after all. No, not at all.

...

END PART V

Part VI—Naya

"Any one can hold the helm when the sea is calm," Publilius Syrus.

Chapter 12 Jam

"Da, I have to see him."

Damien's already come to the same conclusion. Naya's insomnia is, if anything, worsening. He's put a couch in the hallway outside his and Ellen's bedroom and Naya is there—every night. As soon as the sun goes down, she's unsettled. Bedtime is a nightmare. Anxiety peaks when the house goes quiet. Damien is beside himself with worry for his daughter. He's been home schooling her for the last year and a half. Ellen's at the point where she is just as desperate but her reaction is to withdraw from this situation—she's spending more time with the boys who are incomparably easier to deal with.

Damien's not willing to give up on Naya, not ever.

He's learned that his daughter would have died in Stockholm if not for what José-Luis did there. Banning contact between him and Naya is exactly the wrong thing to do, he realizes. His talk about 'Leadership' was all BS. It's one thing to talk about the value of leadership and experience but it's another thing to watch it happen to someone you love, especially when the consequences are highly negative.

...

"Hey, Naya."

"Oh, oh, you're here!"

Naya goes running over to JEL and hugs him just like she did when she was six (almost). She's not yet 13 (she's four months short of her 13th birthday) but she is already 5'11". Even so, she is still half a head shorter than her friend. JEL is three months shy of his 16th birthday and is already 192.5 cm tall. He's the premier footballer in Germania and will sign his new contract with Bundesliga FC Bayern Munich when he comes of age—at 16. He's at Revival House to see her; it'll be his last period of freedom for a long time. His contract calls for him not only to be a striker for Bayern Munich but also the face of the franchise for the next decade and a half.

His shaggy beach bum look and incredible genetic combination of Belizean Goddess and Romanian stud make him irresistible to a global marketing machine but then, fundamentally, he's a heck of a nice guy. Everyone wants to be his friend but he only cares about Naya who's been in trouble since frozen, Godforsaken Stockholm. He feels responsible. He should never have taken her up that damn Tower.

"How you doing?"

"I'm fine, better now that you're here," echoing Nell of years ago.

Still, she does not look well. She has bags under her eyes—he should ask her if he can carry them for her, they're so bad. Her Dad has told him a bit about what gives.

"How is dance coming?"

"Super! We're going to Orpheum in a couple of weeks. If we're top three, and we will be (!), we get to go to World Jam in San Antonio. Can you come? Can you get the time off from your club?"

Orpheum Theatre, built in 1927, is an historical site in Vancouver and seats 2,688 people. It'll be packed to capacity and beyond for Regionals; it's a huge deal just to qualify. Naya is lead dancer even though she's not yet 13. She'll head up her danse troupe from Meeza that numbers 45 that do stuff no one else has even thought of. Naya is operating on less than two hours of sleep per day. She can't fall asleep before dawn and then only manages a fitful rest for 90 minutes before their house comes alive.

Even though he's supposed to report in ten days, JEL says, "For sure, Naya, I'll be there." There is no way now that Dr. Bell has allowed him to see her again that he'll disappoint her. As long as he is not yet of age of majority, what can they do? He'll talk to his agent. He'll get it or, what the Hell, he'll get a new one.

...

"Da, can we go please?"

Seeing how much Naya has improved since José-Luis has been here, he's reluctant to say no.

"We'll catch the Skybus, Dr. Bell. I'll have her back here in two days," José-Luis says.

"Naya, can I talk to José-Luis for a few minutes, please?"

"Sure, Da. As long as you say 'yes'!"

"Naya!"

"OK." Naya quietly leaves the room.

"José-Luis, what's the plan?"

"I have to see my agent in LA. Naya wants to come. I think she should."

"She's a little girl, you understand?"

"I know that, Dr. Bell. I will look out for her... I've, like, done that before you know, Sir."

"Naya thinks the world is a fairy tale, made for her. But I think you know that's not true."

"Ah, actually, I think it is kinda like that for her, Dr. Bell. I mean everyone likes her and she makes people around her better because she, she expects them to be better and so they are. Does that make any sense, Sir?"

Damien is thinking that Nell was exactly the same.

"Yeah, it does. Can I think about it for a day or so?"

"IMG doesn't need me in LA til Tuesday so we've got three days. No problem, Dr. Bell."

...

#'You have to let her go, D.'

#'She's not even a teenager yet, Nell.'

#'I know that. But you can see the changes in her just since he's been here. They are friends in the most fundamental sense of the word and you should not have cut them off.'

#'I know that now, sweetheart.'

#'So what's the problem?'

#'I can't forget about what happened to you.'

#'You think José-Luis would hurt Naya?'

#'Never.'

#'But…'

#'But nothing. Your children don't belong to you. They belong to themselves. You have to let her go.'

#'Will you look out for her?'

#'She's my Goddaughter. Of course, I will. We talk regularly anyway.'

#'You talk with Naya?'

#'From the day she was born, D.'

#'Through Su7e, right?' Damien says in a sudden burst of illumination.

#'Yes, of course.'

#'What's wrong with Ellen?' he asks her next.

Nell looks away.

#'Nell?'

#'I can help you with Naya, D. But Ellen is your wife. That you must deal with on your own.'

#'I miss you, Nell.'

Nell looks away again thinking, 'One day.'

...

"Surf's up."

"Huh?"

"Surf's up. Reports are 6 to 8 foot swells with southeasterly winds. It'll be awesome."

JEL's not so sure. Naya is like this fish person and JEL is, well, Romanian. His power to weight ratio is fantastic and his density is awesome if you are a tall striker headed for the Federal League. He's very hard to knock down and can leap like Michael Jordan. He's seen video of the former great—the one where you just see his shoes in slow motion going past heads of opposition players. MJ takes off from the three point line. He's gotta be at least six feet in the air for 19.75 feet before the video returns to normal speed and Jordan dunks the ball. José-Luis can out jump defenders by nearly a metre so his wingers have to centre the ball way higher than for anyone else. Of his 35 goals last season, 14 are headers.

"We're going to Hermosa Beach. Come on JEL, it'll be stupendous. Waves are huge and they're breaking just perfectly with So'easterlies! We're going! But there's a shop we gotta stop at on the Strand first, come on!"

They've come down on Skybus from San Fran. Skybus is faster than those humongous airships out of SFA and even cheaper. Naya won't let JEL pay—she insists on paying for them both—he's her guest in California after all!

She's been saving up. She does some cleaning and shelf stocking for Green Stop in their neighborhood. They hire 12 year olds. She even gets her Mom to come teach a Yoga class in this little common room they reserve for community meetings. The place is packed. It's not often people get to see their former President; she's a bit of a recluse these days.

...

"What you doing?"

"Hold still."

Naya is applying a bead of nanosites to his sides and under each arm. He is already wearing Oz Viper swim fins and matching webbed gloves that do this weird thing. When he flexes the ends of his fingers they shoot out these Freddy Krueger extrusions that through some kind of metal memory promise to propel him through the ocean. He feels like a freak. She's already forced him to take a pill. It's supposed to coat him with nanosites that provide perfect UV protection. It's not chemical, she tells him. They're like a zillion little deflectors that coat his skin and prevent him from getting horrible sunburn which, for a Northern or Eastern European in Socal, is all too likely.

"You shed them or pee them out in 48 hours," Naya tells him.

"Do I really need all this crap?"

"Well, here's the choice—you can burn like a barbecue or go over the waterfall and separate your shoulder, Mr. Vasilescu, and miss the first two months of training camp or shut up!"

"My Dad's Worry Doll looks like this."

"My Da has one of those too. Two actually."

"What's with that?"

"I dunno," says Naya. "Da believes in that sort of thing. He talks to my Godmother. So do I."

"Why wouldn't you?"

"Well, she's dead."

"Oh, you mean you talk to dead people?" When it comes to Naya, nothing surprises JEL.

"Yup. Hold still."

...

"OK, so when I dive, you dive too."

"OK."

"Under the waves. We gotta get you out there, beyond the break. Alright?"

"Sure," he says dubiously. Being the world's no. 1 soccer prospect means nothing to the ocean off Los Angeles and now that he's up close, the waves look really big. But he's not going to be shown up by a girl!

"You gotta follow me, right? When we get out there, when I tell you to swim, you put your head down and go like heck. Just keep your head down. That's the key. Your head, especially your head, JEL, which is beyond big, will pull you into the wave. Then put your arms behind you, by your sides. As soon as you do that, your nanosites will bind together and give you water wings. Look, watch me."

Naya is doing dry land training with JEL. When she puts her arms together, she activates the nanosites beaded under her arms and along her sides. She looks Heavenly to JEL with these angel wings suddenly forming between her arms and body. They'll allow her to plane on huge waveforms. When she puts her arms together again, the nanosites automatically release so she can swim back out again.

When Naya finally gets JEL out beyond the surf break,

he looks at her like she is from another world which she is. She smiles back at him.

"When I start my front crawl, you too. OK?"

"Alright," he says anxiously.

"Push off the bottom too. Extra velocity. It's a vector as my Da would say!"

"Sure." JEL can't wait to hit the beach and watch bodysurfers, kitesurfers, windsurfers and surfers from the safety of the shoreline.

A monster set is coming their way. Naya waits until the last possible moment and launches herself perfectly into a wave. Her waterwings form spontaneously exactly on cue, her Freddy Krueger extensions act like retractable cat's claws and propel her forward. Her Oz Viper fins flip back and forth feverishly and she fearlessly bodysurfs a huge wave, zigzagging across its face for more than 150 feet. She extends one arm out in front of her and twists her body more than 90 degrees first in one direction then the other—she is planing on the wave front.

JEL watches as her perfectly formed, pink bottom encased in a Brazilian hipster bikini disappears from view propelled by a nearly ten foot wave. He can't help but notice that Naya sure has changed from the little kid he once knew.

JEL goes over the waterfall a few times, unceremoniously washing up on shore each time looking abashed that he is so hopelessly outclassed by Naya.

But now that he's involved, he tries again and again. While he doesn't separate his shoulder, he can't get the hang of this bodysurfing thing.

"Mr. Vasilescu. You are useless!" Naya calls out to him. He is half drowned. But still not deterred! They are back outside once more.

"Come on. Look, when I put my head down, you too. Keep it down. You're raising it too soon. OK? You watching? Here it comes! Now! Go JEL!"

They both swim like Hell. At exactly the right moment,

JEL kinks his fingertips and his Freddy Krueger fingers with metallic pico carbon tube memory propulsion extend and work like a charm. He remembers finally to keep his head down and to put his arms behind him and let the nanosites activate; his waterwings form between his body and his arms. He kicks like heck with his fins still keeping his big head down which pulls him further down the wave. The next thing he knows, he can lift his head and shoulders and surf this amazing force of nature. Two dolphins are suddenly there next to him jumping in and out of the surf like it's as simple as adding 2+2. They squawk at him, high pitched caws of pure joy. He raises his head and howls back at them. Wowza~~~!

When he cruises into shore, Naya is there waiting for him. She looks great in her Calatrava performance bikini. Its straps are crossed in front and back and filled with non elastic material so that they don't stretch and, like guy's board shorts, they remain tight even if their strings come undone. These bikinis have been field tested in Costa Rica, Brazil and Belize—they don't fail, ever. Her bottoms are red and black checks on her right side and all black on her left, same as on her right breast—a check pattern. Her left breast is all black. She's by far the prettiest girl on the beach and that is saying a lot.

JEL is pleased with himself, another sport mastered, sort of. Naya is there in knee deep surf. Caught up in the moment, JEL grabs her up, all 5'11" of her, and spins her 360 degrees. It only takes a second and a half to spin her around. But in that time, his world changes. Boys change to men. Men remember when. After he puts her down and he sees her there, she has gone from being his little friend, to the person who gets him, the human being he would do anything for to this magical presence that without which his life is meaningless. In short, he's addicted to her. Wowza!

...

"Jamal, I'm not going to report next month."

"Huh?

"I'm going to Vancity."

"Ah, no you're not."

"Yes, I am."

"Mr. Vasilescu, you have a $16.5 million QED signing bonus that says you are."

"That's when I'm 16. It's not for another nearly three months. So, like, what's the big deal?"

"They need you in Paris, for a shoot. What's preventing you from going?"

"I just need some time for some personal stuff."

"Would this have something to do with a girl?" Jamal Ugo is an IMG agent in charge of what could be/will be their next big meal ticket. Jamal runs IMG's Basketball Academy before becoming head of IMG Sports Academies. These are live-in sports schools and they coach people, 'not just to better their skills, but to make them better people.' At least that's what their ads say about them. Now he is worried about this kid.

"She's here."

"Well, I suppose we better meet her then."

A few minutes later, this incredible Amazon enters their conference room. Jamal and all the other agents in the room, including head of IMG Sports Group, sit up, some of them gulp audibly. José-Luis says, "Mr. Ugo, gentlemen, lady. This is Naya."

...

"Miss Naya."

"Hi!"

"Naya. Welcome to IMG," says Head of IMG's sports group.

"Thanks. It's nice to be here," she says looking at JEL. Her eyes are shining.

"I, I was wondering if, are you folks hungry?"

"Starving! We were bodysurfing at Hermosa. JEL you hungry?"

"You bet, Naya."

Head of Sports looks at Jamal like she just caught him surreptitiously scratching his balls. Where are his manners? These kids are hungry! Jamal orders in sushi, enough for everyone. Vegetarian for Naya.

...

Meanwhile Head of Sports asks Head of IMG Fashion to join them for a few moments; she is just as struck by these kids as they all are. The two department chiefs don't need to exchange any words—they simply look at each other—their no. 1 future sports property has somehow shown up with this fabulous creature; she's beyond anything they have ever seen. An unspoiled woman-child.

"Ah, Miss Naya, do you mind if I ask how old you are?" IMG Fashion asks.

"Sure, I, umm, I'm 15," Naya lies. JEL just looks at her open mouthed when she says this.

"When do you turn sixteen?" Jamal asks.

"Christmas Eve. I was born Christmas Eve."

'Can it get any better than this?' Fashion and Sports think looking at each other.

"Hey, would you consider an Mtv test?" IMG Fashion asks. She knows that even the prettiest girls can look like shit on modern scanner TV. It's like an old fashioned screen test to the power of ten. Media walls and television have migrated to scanned copies of everything at whatever scale consumers demand. At any angle or size, these are not holographs but fully formed images that can interact with viewers no different than actors on stage but even better cuz these are in your living room.

Mtv stands for 'materiality' TV. It's a medium made for people 25 years of age or less. When they say 'people', they mean women. Women in that age group glow with an essence that cannot be described. It just is.

...

When Naya's Mtv test comes back, they are blown away again. She can not only move and strut, she can dance, sing and act. She's funny too. They've just won the

Melbourne Cup, the Kentucky Derby, the Royal Ascot, the Grand National, the Preakness and the Breeders Cup—all IMG properties now along with the Nobel Foundation where apparently Naya's Dad won a prize or something.

"Miss Naya. We need to talk to your parents about this."

"About what?"

"Well your Mtv test is pretty good."

"Nice! We're staying at the H Hostel. You can find us there."

"We can find you a better place to stay, Miss Naya."

"That's OK. JEL and I will be fine there. We're gonna go bodysurfing again early tomorrow! H is right on Hermosa Beach. Duh!" Since she is paying for this trip, a youth hostel is all she can afford. JEL of course has access to practically unlimited funds but no way is he paying for them on this trip.

"Ah, yeah, we know where it is. Can we talk to your parents, Naya?"

"What for?"

"About your screen test."

"I don't think that would be a good idea."

"Why not?" Jamal asks.

"My Da thinks I should focus on school. My mother doesn't even know I exist."

"We think you could do something special—with modeling, maybe acting, singing and dancing."

"Super! I love dancing!"

"We could offer you a contract."

"Huh? A contract? JEL, what do you think?"

"It's up to you, Naya. What do you want to do?"

"I wanna dance!"

"Well, Miss Naya, we could offer you a signing bonus," Jamal looks at his bosses and says, "of $250,000 QED, I think. You could initial it now then come back in four months when you turn 16 and sign it."

"When would I get the money?" Naya asks, ever

practical.

"Would you like it in cash or check?"

Since Naya is really 12 and has no bank account of her own (her Da has signing authority over the account they open for her Green Stop paychecks), so she says, "Cash is fine."

JEL just looks at her in total amazement.

...

"You can't keep it."

"Why not?"

"For Christsakes, Naya, you're 12!"

Naya looks incredibly hurt when he says this.

"I mean, like, you have to ask your Dad. You just can't take their money; what if your parents say no?"

"My mother won't care."

"What are you talking about? They both care about you."

"My mother only cares about her image—her being President and all."

"That was like forever ago, Naya. What's that got to do with the price of rice?"

...

"I think I love him, Zora."

"You have to give it some time, Naya. How does he feel about you?"

They're in Euphony's foundry on Granville Island. Euph has retired to one of the Gulf Islands (Gabriola to be precise) and her daughter, recent Berkeley grad in English Lit, has taken over everything except illegal production of Wrecked Brew. She leaves that to her mother on Gabriola.

"I think he likes me."

"That's easy to understand. Look, Naya, I don't want you to do anything you'll regret later. Can you be cool about this?"

"I don't think so."

"How are you sleeping?"

"Better now that he's here."

"Did you talk about Stockholm?"

"A bit."

"What did he say?"

"He would never let go of me. He was going over with me if he couldn't stop me."

"Here's the thing, Naya. You're both alive. You didn't go over the edge. That's not love, it's, it's survival."

"Have you ever loved anyone, Zora?"

She sighs. She wishes Naya hadn't asked that question.

"Once."

"What happened?"

"He doesn't even know I exist."

"Why didn't you tell him?"

"Are you going to tell José-Luis?"

"Never! He'd just think it's yucky girl stuff."

"Exactly."

...

"Welcome to Orpheum. Top three finalists here get to go to World Jam in San Antonio. Who is it going to be? We have 17 of the best dance groups from the northwest here in Vancity with us today. What'll they do to get to Texas? Everything! Anything!" their MC says unctuously. It's a full house with a few hundred people sitting in the aisles or standing in the back row. If the Fire Marshal shows up, she'll shut them down—they're way beyond capacity.

"Who is going to blow up? Who'll go harder? Who will take chances? Is there a sleeper crew out there? Who will be the Mount Rushmore of Dance?" It's obvious that their MC is an American because no Canadian would use that analogy. There are a few groans from their audience.

"OK, this is how it'll go. Each group performs and our judges will score them and then all of our Mtv viewers will get their turn—50% of team scores come from our audience and 50% from our judges. The final five survive until tomorrow when the top three are chosen. Who is it gonna be? Stay tuned!"

Orpheum has been turned into Kosmic for this event by second year architecture students from nearby Emily Carr School of Architecture and Design. They're allowed into this special place to work their design and construction magic. It's an annual thing they do—they announce a theme and then change the building's interior to match. It's a fundraiser for them—they use the money they raise to pay for their DSA (Directed Studies Abroad) term. It also keeps the competition fresh and makes a place in it even more coveted.

...

"Is he your boyfriend?"

Naya thinks, 'Boyfriend?' The way she feels about JEL is not like that.

One of the girls in her troupe, a beautiful blond 16-year old, is asking. Everyone in Vancity is clamoring for his autograph. When she brings JEL to her dance classes, all the girls (and a few of the guys) shriek with delight and gather round him.

"No, he's not," she says simply.

"Would you mind if I take a run at him?"

Now that she thinks about it for a moment, she does mind. This girl is way prettier than Naya, Naya thinks. And lots more experienced. JEL will never look at Naya again if this girl even so much as shows off her beautifully formed ass at him which she'll have ample opportunity to do since they are all heading over to a blocko shortly. But it turns out JEL only has eyes for one girl and she isn't a blond.

...

They all put their hands in. Naya leads them in prayer.

"We're here to compete to do the things God put us here to do. We've worked hard and we deserve to be here. We're here for our family, our friends but mostly for ourselves, to be better than we ever thought we could be. I am glad for the company of my brothers and sisters and for the years of preparation at Meeza. Please, God, bless our efforts and, if we are deserving, may we win today.

Amen."

"Amen," they all repeat.

"How you doing, Naya?" Joe Jaime asks. He takes her aside. Joe 'Ya Ya' Jaime is Naya's revered dance teacher and choreographer for the last four, almost five years. From the first moment he meets her, when she is eight, he has that feeling that teachers seldom get that this is the ONE. Sometimes, not always, you get to teach a person who will define your career and your life. Someone who will so exceed what you have been able to do that it will be your defining moment to say that you once taught her or him. Ya Ya has known this about Naya from Day 1. Of course, he never tells her this.

"Good, Mr. Jaime. Hey, I slept nine hours last night!"

He knows about her troubles and her insomnia. He's spoken with her Dad about it. They've all been worried about her but lately she seems better. They rejoin the team.

"U2's Bono once said that the difference between good and great," Ya Ya pauses for emphasis as he prepares his group, "is huge. What that means is we are going to be great tonight and tomorrow. Do you know why? To be great, you need to be a professional. Being a professional means knowing your stuff, never giving up and always showing up."

On cue, Naya asks all 56 of them to put their hands in again—45 dancers, one instructor, two assistants and eight QEs. She asks, "So what are we going to do?" They all shout in unison, "SHOW UP! BLOW UP!" Then they turn about, ready for whatever may lie ahead.

...

Their troupe will do the expected—incredible, artistic, acrobatic, creative tribal dance. But then, they'll do the unexpected. Here's Ya Ya's (highly secret) plan—

• We start with an unusual aquatic effect featuring our QEs.

• They materialize in RL (in the tank).

• They have a physical presence and change color.
• They may be rudimentary dancers but they do interesting (although basic) stuff.
• We transition to fast paced, athletic, hip-hop/break dance/dub step.
• Naya is in the middle of our crew, slightly in front, so it is clear she is lead.
• Our stage is in the round (360°).
• It's on top of a large water tank 9 feet high which continues below main stage level with two submersible platforms—one is a small circle in the center and then there is a larger one surrounding the smaller circle which creates a solid floor when both are raised together.
• We finish with Maori Fire Poi—Naya does it very fast with lots of sexy, wriggling hips.

...

Theater lights dim and stage lights come on; all other lights are turned off. Their music begins—it's a mixture of violins and urban, hip-hop bass lines. People rudely continue talking about the last group who've just left the stage. This is pretty typical at these competitions—etiquette is not exactly at Vienna State Opera House levels.

Their Show Producer cues a loud explosion—it's the sound of a generator blowing up and their lights go out, their music fizzles. Some people in the audience start complaining and booing. Others are laughing. Some smart-ass teenagers yell things like 'Retire', 'You're busted' and 'Next'. But then inside the water tank, quantum entities suddenly appear. First all the audience can see are their huge expressive eyes—some are bright yellow, some are blue—QEs are moving about in the water. There are eight pairs of eyes, all moving around, staring quietly at the audience.

People are beginning to take notice, a few who were cutting up a short while ago start yelling at people to look in the water! As the audience really starts to take notice, QEs more fully materialize until they are beautiful beings of light.

So far all this has taken place in a total of 52 seconds. Now their audience is quiet as they watch these wonderful multi-colored beings move about underneath the stage in the water. They are moving in unison; they assemble into a four point formation in pairs. Imagine for a moment a '+' sign and at each tip there are two QEs one behind the other, facing the audience. They are the only thing emitting light at this moment in the theatre (other than safety lamps). As the front QE in each pair moves, the back one does also. Front QEs shoot their arms straight out in parallel to the floor and the ones behind open their arms like an Egyptian.

Then they change with each QE in the rear opening their arms in a diagonal line with their right arms up at a 45° angle and left arm down at a 45° angle, creating a perfectly straight line with their arms. Front QEs are doing the same but in reverse, that is, with their left arm up at 45° and their right arm down at 45°. They continue doing this in an alternating fashion, changing the leading arm each cycle. These are fast, snapping movements— clean, clear, sharp and calculated. All of them move at exactly the same time creating a spectacular display of light with their arms, which change to solid colors as they snap from Egyptian to diagonal and back. They do this a few more times and then all their arms point up and to the center of the stage. Then their bodies fade out, leaving only their eyes and their arms pointing to center stage.

As the break beat comes on, there is a back-break in their music which makes it sound like it is slowing down into a grave note and possibly silence. Then there is silence. Naya is finally lit up by centre stage lights. She is wearing a black baggy outfit, white gloves, white hat and white sneakers. She is standing still, feet shoulder width apart, legs straight out like an upside down Y. Elbows are straight out to her sides, perpendicular to the ground, nads together as if praying in a ZEN-like pose.

Their Show Producer cues more sound and light effects. It is now a winter blizzard. Lights on stage go to a very cool white/bluish color giving an impression that is cold. They can hear the sound of a freezing, rushing wind. At this point, eight perfectly positioned industrial fans start blowing, creating a circular rush of air around the entire theatre and through their audience.

While these effects are taking place, they can see four other dancers highlighted with individual spotlights pointed at them, descending onto the stage. While they are descending, they are spinning rapidly and since they are dressed the same as Naya, all the audience can see is this blur of their white gloves, hats and sneakers. They slow down as they touch the platform. 'Cold' lights remain on and now the audience sees snow falling from above.

Naya rubs her hands together while maintaining her pose. There is a strong, four-beat bass kick, to which her hands open and close in a robotic-like clap. On the 5th beat, her hands light up on fire and open up to the sides, parallel to the ground. Her dancers also open up their arms, all now with straight arms, parallel to the stage, touching palms. For four beats following each of her claps, the audience hears the sounds of industrial lights flickering on and off as if they are in a factory. While these sound 'flickers' are ongoing, each dancer's hands light up on fire so that the fire is spreading from Naya to her dancers' hands.

The music switches again. This part is to the beat of Naz-Nazty. Sound the alarm! People are starting to feel the choreo now. Dancers have their arms out, gloves still on fire. Stagelights change to orange then a reddish tint and their water tank lights go off. They use Shaolin style arms—hands perpendicular to arms at 90°. Arms remain opposite to create an illusion of straight line from hand to hand.

There are two and a half outside circles of dancers, each with their left hands leading with left foot following on the first circle, right foot following on the second circle. They stop midway and their arms come in again towards the center. This is followed by a 'hands in a box' chore, where only their hands are moving in straight angles, inside an imaginary 'box' which is marked by the core (chest and stomach) of each dancer. There is more fancy 'hands in a box' choreo for the next 12 seconds.

They finish with two complete full circles (front & back) and end it by hitting the ground so that while one hand is on the floor, the other one is straight up in the air. The arm on the floor is perpendicular to the arm that is straight up. Spotlights are synchronized and go from outer dancers to inner dancers, ending with Naya. They use 10 seconds on each set of dancers so this takes 30 seconds total. As hands hit the floor again, stage lights go blue. The fire on their dancers' hands goes out. Then there is another short silence for two seconds.

When hands next hit the platform, four dancers dive from the outer circle which has been lowered while their lights were off close to the water tank. They hit the water just as the fire on their dancers' hands winks out (that coincides with the two second period of silence.)

The four dancers (the ones who are now in the water tank) are each equipped with 'in-mouth' respirators that allow them to breathe. They are wearing makeup that makes their eyes and mouths look like they are glowing in neon colors once the lights come back up. They have matching gloves. Their shoes stick to the bottom of the tank, where a '+' shaped clear platform has been placed for them to walk on.

Internal lamps in the water tank are now switched on; they are bright red. The water dancers' shoes and gloves light up and the audience can see the outline of their eyes and lips but they are not so bright that they take attention away from dancers still on top. Both land and water dancers are in the exact same formation.

As this part reaches the 1:24 mark, there is a break-beat, something like a DJ scratching vinyl, which leads into the hip-hop portion of their choreography. Things are just starting to get really interesting.

Their music starts again but with a strong new beat. As it begins, four co-lead land dancers begin break-dancing. It's basic uprock, leading into some floor rocking then into a hand glide, ending with a hand-glide freeze. Simultaneously, water dancers are pretending to talk to each other, 'mocking' the dancers up on land.

The water dancers now start to shine brighter while lights on top go dim, except for Naya who still has a spotlight on her. Focus is shifting back to their water dancers. There is a back-break effect on the music and it changes to a dub step beat. Zillerexx—Bangerong is now playing. Water dancers do a complete set made up of popping and locking and some Memphis Jukin.

They begin by pretending to walk around the bottom of the tank with high knees extending into leg extensions—they land on their toes. They are doing this to the beat of music they can't actually hear very well (since they are underwater) which is pretty amazing. The whole while they are looking up and smiling. They transition from this funky knee-popping walk into a very 'liquid' form of Memphis Juk (Jook). They begin gliding around on the floor of the tank while pantomiming as if they were going to go up and battle the land dancers. They end up with arms crossed and they give a defiant look up at Naya.

But Naya is not deterred! Still she does not like this, she is displeased. Four of her dancers in a V formation jump into a nike-elbow freeze. And then it's time for BREAKDANCE NAYA!

She begins with a basic uprock and then does some floor rock before backing up into a Latin rock. She then does a combo consisting of a helicopter which leads into a hand glide, next a hand-glide freeze then she pops to an elbow chair then back to an elbow freeze and does up some windmills ending with a nike-elbow freeze. It doesn't look to the audience like Naya wants to leave it at that so she decides to get some of her own jook and glides in there! She glides around and in-between her dancers. She stops between each one only to pop & lock using some shaolin-style 'hand in a box' patterns.

The audience is really into it now. When Naya reaches the last dancer at the front of the stage, she turns and runs to the back of the stage where she stops, grabs a grey knit beanie with a visor sitting incongruously on the head of a waiting QE that she slaps on her own head at an oblique angle and then runs forward down the middle and does a stiff-body head glide forward, from the middle of their platform to the tip of its V. As she glides on her head, she arches her back and angles her body forward so that her legs simultaneously shift forward while her dancers go into a straight arm freeze. As her music ends, Naya propels her body straight up into the air and both Naya and her top four dancers drop flat on the ground, as if in a coffin. QEs reappear in the water below with sad faces as if to show they are downcast that it is ending.

JEL has never seen anything like it before. This is a really impressive solo performance by Naya and an amazing display by her whole team. He knows she is good but this? It's flabbergasting. He's floored. What he doesn't know is that female dancers between ages 11 and 14 are the best in the world—they make Vegas showgirls look like, well, girls who show their stuff but can't really dance.

There is a ton of cheering and some lights come on. Their water dancers exit the water, and they give a bow. Is it finally over?

No!

...

Naya will end their routine with Fire Poi this time to *Beat and the Pulse* by ancient Canadian Indie band, Austra. Aunt Zora turns her onto them; they're like this Wiccan group who dress in dark girly-girl stuff and pant while reaching into the souls of their audience.

Ellen sends Naya at 11 to New Zealand's North Island to study Poi. Aggie was a Poi dancer and Ellen wants Naya to study Maori dance. Mary is there in Rotorua.

Even at 11, Naya is taller than all the women in Rotorua some of whom remember Aggie. Naya never meets her grandmother but Kat, who is more than 90 years old now, remembers Agnes well. Kat greets Naya.

She sniffs her then holds her at arm's length. Then says, "Agnes came here once. You are here now."

"Thank you for taking me on, M'am," Naya says politely.

"You were born in daylight like your grandmother?"

"I think so, yes, M'am."

"So you white on the outside? Maybe, Maori on the inside?"

"I'd like to find that out, M'am."

"Did you know Aggie?"

"No, M'am."

"Before you leave here, you will."

...

A bright ring of light is switched on in the middle circle of their platform accompanied by a new electrical buzzing sound. From within this ring, Naya reemerges but her audience cannot see her yet because she is wearing (almost) all black. She is however holding a pair of short Poi. They have green and purple lights at the end of short ropes. The front of her costume is cut so that it narrows between her breasts showing completely age inappropriate cleavage as well as a bare midriff. It's not actually bare—her dress is held together by a skin-colored mesh that is nearly transparent. It is very low cut in back as well. They use the same trompe l'oeil trick there as in front. She is wearing a hairband that produces a mesmerizing light show that is proportional to and reflective of the speed of her Poi.

Her Poi move, slowly at first and, then as their speed

increases, they change color—from green to blue and from purple to red. Her long evening dress costume and crèche cape begin to glow too—they luminesce. Her lighting package (including hairband) is designed by her Da.

Their Sound Engineer cues Austra.

Feel it break
Feel it break
Nothing's a mistake, or you
Feel it break

During this scene, all the audience can see so far is Fire Poi; there is no Naya (or not much) yet—everything is dark except the middle ring of light, her Fire Poi and soon QEs will be performing on their cues. She begins with some three beat weaves, moves onto some fancier five beat weaves then does a butterfly, a combo of five beat weaves and more butterflies. She finishes off with a very fancy anti-spin flower, creating a four-petal anti-spin one. While this is happening, QEs rematerialize—now they are floating and moving around the ring of light, approximately 14 feet above Naya. Every 8th accent beat (16 counts), QEs light up, each time changing their arm formation and their colors.

Naya is spinning her lights faster than anyone has ever done. She does interior loops, leaning backwards and spinning her Poi in reverse so that they are impossibly close to her body. Her hips wiggle and her body undulates, now tantalizingly outlined by Damien's light show. Meeza dancers, invisible beforehand, explode with their own Fire Poi that light up suddenly. They begin to pulse and move in unison with Naya. Their outlines are rediscovered by the audience via the same evanescent lights that Damien is using to outline Naya. Austra continues—

Capture something read
Paste it to the edge of your bed

Someone will be there
Someone who will know what it says

Right at the end, Naya seems to split into two. Su7e materializes on stage behind her. Her QE doesn't actually have to dance which is good because she can't. But she matches Naya's size, runs her own light show and does arm movements which exactly mirror what Naya's doing at this point. It's another cool effect.

The combination of Jam Dance and Maori Fire Poi from Meeza certainly throws down big challenges to their top competitors—Stop Motion, The Furie, Mazehem, Evolution, netfuzion, Invyncybles and GoneGone Brothers. By the end of their routine, they appear to have won over both their audience and the judges; it seems like they're really into it and feeling the beat. People watching on the Internet can see Naya (via Mtv) as if she is in their homes which she is. She can be at any scale. It's enough to drive guys crazy. Girls want to be her.

Damien, Ya Ya, Naya, Su7e, other QEs, the entire group of dancers, their Show Producer, Sound Engineer, Stagehands and Costume Designers have worked on their technology, sets, costumes, choreo and music for almost eight months. They've got something even better planned for tomorrow if they make it to the dance-off which they are almost surely going to be able to do after today's performance.

Damien is in the audience. Finn and Magellan are there to support their sister. Ellen is back in San Fran. She hates crowds so rarely attends Naya's recitals or competitions. Zora is sitting with the two boys and she's as excited watching Naya as if she is her own kid of which she has none. JEL is watching from a wing of the Theatre (Naya gets him backstage with her by telling Security he is a part of their crew which in a way he is, at least from Naya's point of view). By the end, he is clapping so hard he'll notice later on that his hands hurt.

...

Bruce M Firestone

Naya and Meeza rank first going into the finals. They have a great shot at going to San Antonio's World Jam with its fabulous top prize of $500,000 QED (shared amongst the dancers) plus another $100,000 for their studio. But the real money for the studio is the PR hype that comes with winning World Jam.

For the dancers, money is cool but even better—Top Three at World Jam qualify for Solar Jam—Moon, Mars, Earth dance off. This year it's being held on Mars. All expenses paid to Mars. How can you improve on that? Ellen has told Naya that, if they qualify, she'll go with her. Naya looks at her Mom. She's surprised but pleased. Mom won't come to Vancouver but she'll go to Mars? What's so special about Mars?

If they do get to go to Mars, Naya and her team will spend months training for it in specially equipped rooms that mimic either Luna's gravity or Mars'. They use ceiling mounted, thirty-two foot long elastic bands tied to a harness strapped around their waists to simulate either gravitational force, Luna's being the weakest. Once they're on Mars, they'll have ten days to get acclimated then it's time to GET IT ON.

Solar Jam can only be held on Moon or Mars because kids there can't come to Earth's deep gravity well—it'll flatten them like pancakes.

...

"Naya, how you doing?" JEL asks afterward, backstage. She's still wearing her cute beanie on her head set at a rakish angle. JEL thinks she looks really pretty but she's still a bit out of breath and he thinks maybe a bit tired. No wonder.

"Fine. I've got a bit of a headache. No problem."

"You were terrific."

"Wait til you see what we're gonna do tomorrow!"

"It can't be better than today!"

"Wanna bet?"

"Nope," he smiles at her.

"I'm glad you are here, José-Luis."

She never calls him José-Luis.

"You sure you're OK?" He is worried about Naya. She pushes herself way too hard. And this is coming from a guy who practices harder than he plays.

"Yep. Da, Zora and the boys are waiting. Come on, let's go."

There is a team dinner at Hogtown Vegan. Naya can't bear to eat any animals; she's been vegan like forever. JEL's OK with that. It's Naya!

...

There is a lot of excited chatter and after everyone (blonds included) get over the fact that José-Luis is still there with them, things settle down. The cash only restaurant has a lot to cope with—45 dancers plus parentals, coaches, friends, roadies and helpers are a challenge but they manage it somehow.

Naya isn't eating much.

"Is the food OK, honey?" Damien asks.

"Terrific Da," Naya says.

But she doesn't touch her unchicken dish. It just sorta sits there looking at her unappetizingly.

"Da. Da?" Naya says before slumping off her chair onto the floor.

JEL is there before Damien can move.

"Naya? What's happening?" Zora asks standing over a prone Naya and a crouching JEL.

But Naya doesn't respond. She begins to tremble. Then she has a seizure.

JEL has never seen anything like this before. But it doesn't matter. He is completely calm. But the whole restaurant is bedlam. People are screaming. Zora is calling out Naya's name, over and over. For José-Luis it's like on the tower in Stockholm. Time slows down. He tunes out everything. His focus is on his friend. She's in trouble, again.

Her face is turning purple. Now why would that be?

Bruce M Firestone

José-Luis turns her on her side. Her beanie falls off her head from another violent spasm. He studies her but does nothing for what to everyone standing around them seems like an eternity. She is obviously choking. She's turning blue. She's dying. No fucking way, he's going to let her die. What's wrong?

He pries open her mouth. That's not easy to do when someone is having a Grand Mal seizure. He looks down her throat. Ah, ha. She's swallowed her tongue. He reaches in and pulls it forward. She hiccups twice then catches her breath. Her normal pink color begins to return. Her violent convulsive movements begin to subside. He places his hand in her mouth to stop her from swallowing her tongue again—there is nothing else handy to put in there instead so his hand has to suffice. She bites down, hard. His hand begins to bleed. He doesn't feel a thing.

Then she's at rest. Her convulsions cease. She looks up at him and smiles a beautiful Naya smile, then her green eyes close. Naya is asleep.

...

"Dr. Bell, Mr. Vasilescu, Miss Zora, we have induced a coma to prevent further brain damage and we have reduced her body temp by ten degrees. We need to decide what's next."

"Doctor, will she be able to compete tomorrow and in San Antonio next month?" Zora asks stupidly. She's stunned and not thinking too clearly at the moment.

"Ah, Miss Zora, umm, Dr. Bell, we have to worry about your daughter being able to walk again." The Doctor thinks Zora is Naya's mother. "The whole right side of her body has been compromised."

Damien looks away, goes to the nearest wall and leans his forehead against it. Zora goes over to him and puts her head on his back. She cries silently. Her chest is heaving with suppressed sobs.

"Doctor, what's wrong with Naya?" José-Luis asks.

"We're not entirely sure yet but our scans show she

suffered a blow to the left side of her temporal lobe. There are multiple lesions there and they are apparently growing and affecting Miss Naya."

"Do you know when the injury occurred?"

"We can't be sure but they appear to predate puberty. Maybe five to seven years?"

'Puberty?' Damien didn't know about that either.

...

A worried looking Jamal Ugo walks in. "JEL, I came as soon as I heard. How is she doing?"

"Not too good, Mr. Ugo. Can I introduce you to her Dad and Zora?"

Damien and Zora are looking at a formidable former NBA bench warmer well over 7 feet tall. They shake hands.

"Mr. Ugo's my agent, Dr. Bell."

"Hers too," Jamal says pointing at Naya's unconscious form on her hospital bed nearby. José-Luis was hoping he would not say this.

"What, what did you say?"

"I am with IMG, Dr. Bell. We're the largest—"

"I know who you are. What did you say about my daughter?"

"We represent her or will after Christmas."

"What are you talking about?"

"We agreed with Naya to be her agency of record after she turns 16 next month."

"You'll do nothing of the sort, Mr. Ugo," Damien says looking first at José-Luis then at Jamal.

José-Luis goes beet red and looks at the floor. Zora who knows about this is looking out the window on another rainy, misty Vancouver day.

"Excuse me, Dr. Bell but don't you think we should talk about this another time?"

"No I do not. There is no way you are turning my daughter into some kind of marketing product. Not while I have anything to say about it."

"We think that she should be judge of that, Dr. Bell

after her 16th birthday."

"That's not for another three years, Mr. Ugo."

...

Jamal is headed back to LA. He takes the news of Naya's real age surprisingly well. IMG makes investments in all sorts of kids worldwide and the fact that they might have to wait three years for her doesn't bother him much. It'll give her time to get her health thing worked out while he works on her parents. He'll bring them round.

What he can't figure out is how they were deceived in the first place. They checked her out of course with her QE, Su7e. He's never heard of a QE being wrong before. She produces documents that show Naya is 15. Could she have been lying to them? The girl, certainly. That's not unusual but her QE? 'Is that even possible for a Quantum Entity?' he silently asks himself.

...

Zora needn't have worried about San Antonio. Without their lead dancer, Meeza falls out of contention finishing fourth in Regionals.

"It's my fault, Damien."

"No, it's not, José-Luis."

"How do you think she got this way? The insomnia? Now this? I did it. She's hurt because of what I did. What am I going to do now? What is she going to do now if she can't dance anymore? She lives to dance!"

"You have to report to your team, José-Luis. It's no joke if you don't. You're 16 soon. They'll sue you into oblivion if you fail to show up."

"I don't care, Dr. Bell." José-Luis wants to die. He should have died up there with Naya on the Monumental Tower. "I know exactly what happened. I can see it in super slow motion, Dr. Bell, like it was a few hours ago. She turned to look for me and her head bounced off the roof. If I'd been faster I would have grabbed her before she fell. It's my fault."

"JEL, we all know Naya—"

"That's exactly my point, Dr. Bell. I know her. She does brave stuff like that. I shoulda known. I shoulda figured it out before we went up there."

"No one could have foreseen this. You were nine, José-Luis," Zora says.

"I'm staying. Until she's better."

"No, you're not," Damien says. "That's a process that's going to take weeks maybe months." (It'll actually take years although Damien can't know that.) "Your Dad wants you back home before you report."

"Like I said, Dr. Bell, I don't care."

"We do. Naya does. Go back to Europe, JEL. We'll watch out for Naya. You come visit in your offseason, alright?"

...

José-Luis does go back to Europe. As planned, he's Bundesliga's biggest star ever. His plan though to visit Naya regularly goes awry. In fact, he won't see her again for nine, nearly ten years. After he leaves Vancity, he decides to never let himself care about anyone ever again. What for?

He'll knock over the prettiest girls in Europe and quite a few beauties in Asia and Africa but he makes sure he never feels a thing. That's for suckers.

One more thing—he shaves his head. That shaggy haired, surfer dude look is for losers.

...

"Who wants to fuck me?" Naya is standing in front of a bonfire on her grandfather's property in Northern Ontario. She's quite an intimidating 15 year old creature now fully grown at 6'2" tall. They're having a bush bash and there are nearly 80 locals listening to music and getting drunk or stoned.

Half a dozen girls are dancing (badly, Naya thinks) around the campfire. They're only wearing their panties. Guys are egging them on. Naya would join them but she doesn't dance anymore. She's not allowed to get her heart rate up too high. Pulsing lights are out of the question and her meds interfere with her coordination. Not that she is too worried about her meds since she stopped taking them almost two years ago. She told Damien that she couldn't connect with the real Naya—they were interfering with her thought processes. And anyway, she is self medicating. She's found alcohol. Big time.

Naya's fed up with being the only virgin at these parties so she's decided to do something about it. Tonight. More precisely this morning. But no one is stepping forward to do the job. So she repeats her question, "Who wants to fuck me?"

Two guys, a short, hairy Italian whose name she thinks is Sal (he's 17) and his tall friend Barry (who is 18) are nervously shifting back and forth. Looks like she has found some local volunteers. She takes them both with her deeper into the bush. She is so drunk (but not stoned since if she takes any drugs she risks another seizure) she forgets to take the blanket she brought for this purpose. It's a crappy old Indian blanket. Something out of that shitty place her Dad used to drag her to in Arizona— BORING. Naya is just being ignorant. It's a Hopi wedding blanket. And it used to belong to Agnes not Nell. It was in her attic when they went to clean out Aggie's place after she dies. Damien knows exactly what it is the moment he sees it and it's the only thing of Aggie's he wants. He is not sure why but then a miracle happens—Naya happens and then he understands—it's meant for her.

...

It's close to daybreak. Naya is wandering aimlessly on Pops' land. Her face is soot covered. Her hair is a mess and she's sore. She doesn't know what the big deal is about sex. It's like everything else—a BIG disappointment. While one of the guys is plugging away, the other sticks his thing in her mouth. It's really small. She thinks it was Sal's. Not that she has anything to compare it to but she's seen tons of Mtv sex and all those guys seem to have really big wangers. You can blow up the actors to life size (or twice life size or whatever). She's done it and tried to wrap her long fingers around one of these humongous appendages like the girls do in those productions.

They seem to enjoy having sex but Naya is just sore. One of the guys musta had pubic hair like barb wire because her inner thighs are all scratched. Other than that, she didn't feel a thing.

...

She is walking carelessly under tall ferns and there are lots of junky cedars around too; she doesn't care if she pokes an eye out on a low hanging branch. Then she'll only hafta see half a shitty world. Maybe she'll get lucky and do both her eyes.

Naya quits high school and runs away from home, twice. Both times, Damien finds her—the first time three days later on the streets of San Francisco. The second time, he finds her passed out in East Hastings with an empty Imperial Gallon of Wrecked Brew next to her. He talks to Zora about that. He's not mad at her and isn't surprised to find out that Naya was staying there before taking off with her Mead.

Ellen has no patience with Naya and they rarely speak to each other. As far as Ellen is concerned, Naya is so disruptive to their family life that she *should* leave and stay gone. Finally, after another huge blowup between mother and daughter, Damien, in desperation, sends her to Pops' place. Sunny Michaud is there. He takes care of their property and is living with his wife of 25 years in Pops' old cabin now greatly expanded. Naya can have the cabin Sunny stayed in when he was a Corporal.

Naya spends her days drinking. She has no friends and doesn't want any. Her $250,000 QED IMG signing bonus is down to about $50k. Her plan is to drink that too then kill herself if the booze doesn't do it first.

...

"What the fuck?" Naya sees this pale bluish light

Bruce M Firestone

emanating from up ahead. She is starting to get a headache. She needs another drink.

She wanders over and sees it's a gravesite. She must be hallucinating because the light is coming out of the earth. It's weird but not scary. She is really getting a splitting headache. It's like when she's about to have a seizure, something that hasn't happened in more than a year. The last set of nanosites they injected her with seems to have eaten most of the lesions in her brain and she's been symptom-free, until now.

She's having trouble seeing out of her right eye. There is a shadow there, right in her middle view, obscuring her vision. Then it spreads to her left side, her good side. She is getting very tired. Maybe she should head back to her cabin. It's a mess. She never bothers to put anything away but at least the bugs don't eat her at night.

But she can't back away. She tries but the only direction she can go is forward. She staggers over to the grave. It's like someone has remote control over her body. She hovers over the grave for a few moments and then something forces her to her knees. The next thing she knows she is lying face down on the grave mound. She's pinned there and can't move a muscle. She has to work hard just to breathe. Then her eyes close and Naya is unconscious.

...

Three other guys at the campfire have heard from Sal that there is some great stuff available for free in the bush. They've come looking for Naya. These guys, all in their 20s, are to Sal and Barry what Attila the Hun is to Mother Teresa. They aren't going to let her off so easy.

They find her, passed out. This is no fun. They'll have to slap her awake. As they close in on Naya, a growl comes out of the bush. A huge black lab comes forward, its belly close to the ground. It is uncharacteristically baring its teeth and growling.

One of the guys pulls out a wicked looking hunting knife. "Come here motherfucker. I'm going to gut you."

But then a crazed blue-eyed, copper-red Siberian Husky that is faster than any wolf comes at him from an oblique angle and rips his hand taking two fingers off effortlessly; his knife falls uselessly to the ground.

"Motherfucker! My freaking hand."

He stupidly puts it between his legs, blood pouring out of him. His two pals laugh. One of them aims a kick at the Husky and misses. That's too bad because the dog has him by the crotch and, if not for his tightly woven jeans, he would be speaking with a high pitch for the rest of his life. As it is, the dog manages to pull one testicle out of his scrotum. This guy isn't too keen on fucking Naya anymore.

The other one backs off.

The first guy is trying to pick up his two chewed off fingers but the fucking retriever, doing what they've always done, swoops in and takes them first. He disappears into the bush with them.

The Husky lunges at them again but does not attack as long as they back away. He follows them out of the forest. He comes back to see his buddy, the big black lab, lying next to Naya, sharing his warmth with the troubled girl. The guy's fingers are missing.

...

"Uncle Sunny, can I speak with you?"

Naya is there. She looks terrible but at least she is clean. Her thick auburn hair is tied back with a piece of string. She must have washed up in the Lake since the only shower is at his place and she hasn't used that since Spring came to this part of the world, earlier it seems every year.

"Come on in, Naya. Would you like some lemonade?"

"Uh, no and no. Can we talk out here?"

Sunny comes out and they go over to a beat up wooden bench which sits on an old raft—beached after it starts to leak and sink years ago. It makes a nice platform for their bench though. They watch the loons fishing on the Lake for a few minutes. They dive for minutes at a time before surfacing with a meal. Naya is shaking all over.

Sunny knows better than to ask if she is OK. She is definitely not OK. He went over to the bush bash with his dogs, Lennie, his black lab, and Squiggy, last night. Not to talk to Naya—she was way too drunk for that. He spoke with a couple of the young lads he knows. He told them again no swimming in the Lake. It's bad enough that he has these drunk and stoned teens (and a few others he hasn't seen before—an older crew he thinks) on the property. If they swim, they'll drown. The thermal isocline in the Lake is very dangerous.

They promise him not to and thank him again for letting them have their party at his place. Of course he didn't let them—Naya did.

"I'm leaving. Today."

"I don't know if that's a good idea, Naya. You can stay here you know. It's safe," he says naively.

But he does kinda want her to leave. It's been really difficult having her around—it's a big responsibility. And it isn't his place—it's Damien's—and while he promises to look out for Naya while she's here, that's proven to be impossible. The only people who will miss her aren't people. Lennie and Squiggy spend a lot of their time hanging out with Naya; she plays with them when she's sober. For some reason, his dogs aren't doing much today though. Normally, they'd be all over her by now. But they're pooped—both of them are sleeping in the shade under the deck.

"I appreciate that, I really do. But I'm going home."

Sunny breathes a huge sigh of relief. He says nicely, "You know you don't have to go." But both he and Naya know it for what it is—it's the minimum he has to say to be polite.

"What'll you do?"

"I'm going to Berkeley."

"Huh?" he says wishing he could take it back the moment it involuntarily escapes his lips. The last thing he wants to do is dump on this poor kid. She's delusional. Berkeley is not in the habit of accepting 15 year old, alcoholic high school drop outs.

"I'm going to get my GED. Then I'll ace the SATs, Uncle Sunny. I'll get in."

This is a new Naya. One with a new purpose.

He smiles, this time the genuine article. "What you gonna study?"

"Agronomy."

"Agronomy?"

"Yep. I'm going to change the world."

...

She didn't exactly lie to her adopted Uncle. But she is not going home to Revival House. She knows that no one, except possibly Damien, wants her back. She's talked to Su7e (first time in nearly two years). She'll be staying at St Jo's. They'll help her with her addiction problem and be a support group for her.

They'll take her in just like they did her mother. Sally isn't there any longer. She passed away last year.

Naya's seen Hell open beneath her. She's hit bottom but she won't be staying there much longer.

...

"OK guys, you are voluntolds on this." Naya is talking to her brothers about her latest project. "You need 80 volunteer hours to graduate." She hears them groan. "So look at it this way, I'm helping you."

Naya has been intricating the twins in her schemes since she is five and they are three so this is nothing new to either Finn or Magellan. What's new is that her 14 year old brothers (now in High School) actually need to do the hours so they're more than voluntolds, willing participants even. Plus they have some plans of their own.

Although the boys would never say it, they're glad their older sister is back. She's not exactly all the way back but Magellan can see she's getting there. On her sweet 16 birthday, they're the only guests along with Dad, Mom and Zora. Magellan asks José-Luis to come but his team is involved in a friendly at Luna Colony so he begs off.

Soccer on the Moon is really cool. Nets are much bigger because goalies can leap so far and the entire field is enclosed in a clear pen so that the ball is always in play. You can bounce the ball off the end or side walls, even the invisible ceiling set at a standard 60 meters.

José-Luis is polite but distant. Magellan can't figure out what gives. He knows that Naya would like to see him.

"We are going to stage SKIP-AID here. It'll be a benefit for St Jo's, the Salvos, San Francisco Food Bank and Make A Wish Foundation Greater Bay Area. Also, we're going to raise money for Da's not-for-profit Belizean Leadership Institute but don't tell him that, OK? Let's surprise him."

Damien has turned Nell's ridiculously huge home, Maya Fair, into BLI, Belizean Leadership Institute. It's a place where post grads and some promising undergrads can go to do research and take a few courses, all expenses paid.

"How much we aiming to raise?" Finn asks.

"$600,000 in net proceeds."

Both boys whistle. This isn't your average neighborhood lemonade stand.

"Do we get to, like, keep any of it?" Finn asks her.

Naya just stands there disapprovingly with her hands on her hips. They're reversed just like her Mom. Magellan thinks about telling her that she looks like Ellen at the moment but stops himself just in time.

...

SKIP-AID is not a new concept. It's new to the Valley but not North America. In fact, it's an event Naya is borrowing from the Northern Ontario Muskoka town of Huntsville where they've been doing it for nearly 50 years. It's the one thing she did with Ray Michaud and his wife while staying at Pops' place that she remembers clearly because it's the one day she wasn't completely blotto.

They invite senior executives from the area (mainly Toronto) to come to Fairy Lake and skip stones. But there's a catch—they pair them with kids from families that use local food banks and with other kids who are in trouble. Everyone, anyone can skip a stone. They bring special skipping stones in from a local quarry, every hand size is accommodated.

So if a CEO, COO, CTO or VP can skip a stone say 11 times and their kid just 3, their combined score is 14. Execs can buy a mulligan for more dough. If they flub it or their kid does, no problemo, buy another rock.

It costs $350 QED for an executive to enter and $50 QED for each stone they buy extra. But the big money is from pledges. Naya hopes to get 1,000 bigwigs entering and that each of them can get pledges of $10 per skip so if they throw 14 times (combined score) that's $140 per donor. She tells her brothers she wants to raise $600k but privately she thinks they'll raise over a million.

Her Dad's friend, Dr. Durai, is letting her use his quantum bubble generator. Hers will be the first event to use it. She knows he thinks it's frivolous but SKIP-AID sponsors are gonna love it. SKIP-AID is being held at Spreckels Lake in Golden Gate Park. The entire Park will be enclosed in a quantum bubble which is invisible but can be tuned to anything they want. Wanna reduce solar irradiation to zero? No problem. Which means they can turn day into night, show Mtv on the bubble's surface or run slow motion relays of stone skipping (if, say, someone wants to challenge a referee's call that it skipped 15 times not 16.)

Jagad Durai is working with General of the Army (Retired) and CEO of DARCH Farrar Staubach on wrapping Mars in a quantum bubble which will eclipse the technology Imperial China used to wrap Luna by a factor of, well, infinity. So working on Naya's little project is pretty pedestrian but Jag is powerless to resist anything that she wants him to do.

Mixed Media Collective run by Darryl Hnatyshyn is one of the prime beneficiaries of this new technology. Darryl is a pal of Naya's, a recovering alcoholic like her and an event producer who at 37 has found a soulmate in Naya. She meets him in Vancouver while she is living on the streets there. One of the first things she does when she comes back to San Francisco is go looking for him. He's been living with her at St Jo's, in one of their sheds out back like the one that Dekka used long ago, for the last year. He is in awe of her and would do anything for Naya. He loves her for saving him from the scrapheap.

Their main setup area is gonna be at Golden Gate Equestrian Center. Naya has to argue with their admin people to get their permission but when she tells them she'll be bringing Make A Wish kids and women from the shelter she is staying at plus most of San Fran's liberal media to protest the fact that their Center is good enough for horses but not for kids, they crater.

What they can't figure out is how a 16 year old girl gets so politically savvy. First of all, they don't know that her Mom is the person who disposed of the old Republic, her Dad's a Nobel winner and she's been to Hell. Naya hasn't had a drink in almost a year and every day is a battle so going to war with patsies like Golden Gate Equestrian Center's admin people is a lay up for her.

She's added music (by Nell Enterprises of course) and crafts to her event. Her Da is bringing his crazy medallions and Worry People to the fair and her bros are gonna teach people how to play Street Paddle Tennis. It's a game that her grandfather, Pops, invented. In Naya's family nothing stays secret for long so she knows that Damien's grandfather is actually his Dad which means he's really her grandfather. Da doesn't talk about him much but she's pretty sure she woulda liked him—he was fucked up just like Naya.

Anywho, Street Paddle Tennis is probably the

cheapest sport you can do other than Ultimate. You got sneakers, some street chalk, a couple of wooden rackets and some tennis balls or whiffle balls, you in business!

The court is laid out by pacing it—its 54 feet long and 24 feet wide. You put a chalk line down the middle and a service line 8 feet either side of the center line. Any asphalt surface will do.

The court looks like this—

Official Street Paddle Tennis Court

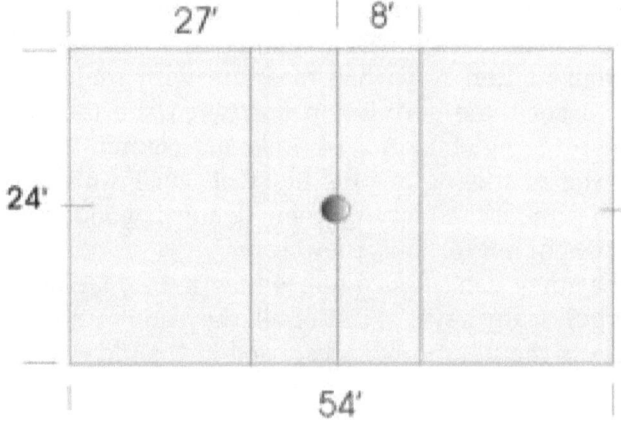

The boys will show people how to play and explain its rules which are:

Rules for a Serve—

1. Serve must be underhand.
2. Serve can be out of hand or bounced once.
3. Serve must go over the serve lines (it may land anywhere in the court past the serve line).
4. Person who is serving must stand on backline.
5. Receiving person must also be standing on their backline.
6. Both people must be standing within two feet of the

back centerlines.

7. Whoever has a ball, serves.

8. Once the person who is serving hits the ball both players can move.

Rules for rallying—

1. Players must hit ball on first bounce (or you may volley it out of the air except on a serve).

2. Ball must pass the center of the court (except on the serve, when the ball must go past the serve line).

3. Ball must land inside the court or on back lines or sidelines.

4. No overhand smashing (you may hit the ball overhand, except on a serve, as long as you stop at the vertical; i.e., no follow through on overhand hits—the idea is to promote longer rallies.)

5. Paddle or player cannot cross centerline.

Points—

1. If serve does not go over (or touch) serve lines, it is a point for the other player.

2. If ball lands out of bounds (before a bounce), a point is awarded to other player.

3. If ball dose not make it over the centerline then point is awarded to other player.

4. If ball bounces twice on a side then point is awarded to other player.

5. First player to seven points wins. (You do not have to win by two points.)

6. Point is awarded on every play except a let (the players play the point over).

Refereeing—

1. Players who are playing referee themselves.

2. If both players are not sure about a point then it is a let.

Spirit of the Game—

1. In a Street Paddle Tennis competition or tournament, scores are recorded after each match.

2. Each player also reports a 'Spirit of the Game' score for the other player(s)—this is a score that measures sportspersonship.

3. A score of 10 indicates a very high standard of fair play. A score of 5 or less indicates very poor sportspersonship. Individuals with consistent scores of 5 or less may not be asked to return for tournament play. Fair play is always encouraged.

Doubles—

1. Doubles are played like singles.
2. Both players have to start at their back line on the serve.

Safety + Suggestions—

1. Never play in traffic.

2. Any asphalt surface will do—such as a parking lot at work or school.

3. Chalk as many courts as you have room for and have a tournament amongst all your friends.

4. If sun or wind or other factors make a difference in the game, switch sides from time to time.

5. Each set is best of five games—first to three games, wins the set.

6. Each match is best of three sets—first to two sets wins.

7. Always play fair and, if in doubt, call a let.

8. You may use spray-on chalk to lay out a court on grass—street paddle tennis on a grass court is a different game but just as much fun; you can pretend you are playing at Wimbledon. You will have to make sure that the grass is fairly short.

Keys to Competitive Street Paddle Tennis/Handicapping the Game—

1. Rush the Centerline—it is a good strategy if your opponent does not have a good passing shot.

2. Move Your Opponent Back and Forth, Up and Down the Court.

3. Spin the Ball.

Bruce M Firestone

4. Get lots of competition with players better than you.

5. Organize Tournaments and Clinics.

6. Make holes in your racket for a faster racket. Before drilling the holes, take duct tape and place it around where you want to drill. Be sure not to make the holes too big so they won't affect your shot. After drilling the holes remove the tape, you should be left with a smooth hole. (Adam, age 13 discovered this).

7. Handicap the games so that everyone can play with everyone.

8. That means that better players can play with others who aren't as good and it can still be competitive.

9. The maximum handicap allowed under Street Paddle Tennis rules is 5. That means that a better player starts the game with a '0' while his or her opponent starts with 5 points. So the weaker player has to win just two points to win the game while the stronger player has to get seven!

10. Create your own ladder of competition with a handicap like golf only the inverse of it. For example, on our block we have the following rankings:

a. Finn Handicap 5

b. Adam Handicap 5

c. Magellan Handicap 4

d. Damien Handicap 3

e. Dekka Handicap 2

f. Naya Handicap 1

g. Ellen Handicap 0

11. Obviously, Street Paddle Tennis handicaps are the opposite of golf—the higher the handicap, the better the player!

12. In the above ladder, if, for example, Finn plays Naya, the score starts off Naya 4, Finn 0.

Naya's business model (she did learn something from her mother after all) calls for celebrity endorsement. This is what her model looks like so far—

Skip-AID 2070 Business Model

She can't ask JEL to endorse her event since he seems to be not talking to her for some reason. So she goes after someone closer to home—Tor Haden, star QB for the San Francisco 49ers. His nickname is (rather unimaginatively) 'Thor' because he can throw like anything; even better, he's a local boy from San Mateo County.

She could call Jamal and ask him for an intro to Thor but she doesn't need to—she'll just go over to their practice facility and ask him.

She's done 12 covers for IMG since coming back to San Fran, one of which her Dad does not approve of. It's her latest one where she is butt naked with only strategically placed quarry stones covering her most private parts with a headline, WOULD YOU SKIP A DATE WITH THIS GIRL?

Naya has to be completely shaved for this shot to work which is OK because she's been doing that since before her days bodysurfing with José-Luis. Calatrava bikinis just fit better and perform better when there's no pubic hair to get in the way. For her Vanity World shot, they attach really thin quarry stones with nanosite connectors that release when ordered to so no messy glue needed and therefore there is no pain when removing them either. The two stones they use on her breasts barely cover her areola; in fact, they purposely fall just short. Her breasts are now Nell-sized (although on her much taller frame they are not quite so dominant as Nell's are).

Like most dancers (retired), she doesn't care a hoot about naked bodies least of all her own. If it'll help SKIP-AID (and it sure does), Naya'd pose completely naked upside down on a trapeze.

She's the 'It' girl of the moment after release of Vanity World's updated app with Naya in it. She knows her Mom doesn't approve either but it's kind of hard for Ellen to be critical of her since the sex tape she made with Da is still the single most viewed video on the Internet.

Jamal keeps sending her scripts—several Directors want her to do a film but Naya is resisting. She has to be careful not to work too much and she needs to nap for an hour every day. She gets tired and she knows that's when she's most in danger from two things—another seizure or falling down a rabbit hole paved with alcohol. She can't even let herself smell the stuff—the craving becomes so intense it's scary. So no parties, no dinner dates, no sitting around campfires drinking wine, no weeks on a film set with enablers all round her plying her with drugs (which Naya couldn't be less interested in) and drinks (which she certainly is damnably interested in). She has no friends her own age but is really close with Zora and Daniella both in their 30s now. Daniella has four kids; the youngest is a red-haired, blue-eyed, vanilla colored girl of six who Naya adores. Her older brother, Danny, about Naya's age, is still the biggest, most juvenile pain-in-the-arse you can imagine. Finn loves hanging out with him. Magellan, not so much.

She has also rediscovered Third Mesa, camel riding, swimming (in the stream that runs along the gorge) and visiting Nell's grave. She feels safe there for a bunch of reasons not least of which Chief Nahuel, like Chief Dan before him, does not permit any alcohol in the place. She's not sure what her Uncle would do if anyone brought it into Third Mesa but she thinks the reaction would be swift and merciless. Nahuel has a great sense of humor but Naya can tell there's a toughness there too—much tougher than his grandfather she's been told.

The magazine calls itself a fashion, music, film, business and entertainment social catalyst which Naya thinks is just political cover for running titillating photos of nearly naked girls. But her story does pretty much cover the waterfront for them—she talks fashion and social enterprise with them. They also really like her backstory. Naya doesn't try to hide anything—her illness, addiction, recovery or even where she is living (in a women's shelter.) Their reporter can't understand why a girl who is the President's daughter, who has the resources to send Naya to a much more upscale retreat to get help, doesn't do that. It's the one question she doesn't ask Naya—she pulls her punches, once. The other question she should have asked but didn't was what caused Naya's illness.

This is the one subject Naya does not want to discuss because she knows it will hurt José-Luis' image and possibly his career if he gets blamed for what happened to her in Stockholm. He's already got a bad image as Germania's Playboy Princeling (they actually call him that.)

But Erik Renke doesn't miss either element. His story leads with NEGLECTED PRESIDENT'S DAUGHTER LEFT TO FEND FOR HERSELF over a picture of a destitute woman living in a cardboard box (not in San Fran but on a Toronto street) who is obviously not Naya. Inside there is an interview with a kid (still fat) who gives him the scoop on what really happened on Monumental Tower—how

Bruce M Firestone

José-Luis forces five year old Naya into the abandoned stairwell, tears her dress (the kid actually has a photo of little Naya like that on one of his fake social media profiles—he sells it to Toronto Chronicle Tab along with his version of the story), rapes her, then tries to cover it up, nearly killing her when he 'accidentally' pushes her off the Mansard roof of the place where Swedes have been coming for decades to commit suicide. Her head bounces off the roof which is what sends Naya crazy. It's the fat kid who finally pulls her back over the railing and delivers her to an uninterested mother (the President) who is too busy partying with Swedish Royals (here they publish an unflattering photo of the Queen with her mouth open and full of hors d'oeuvres) to even watch out for her only daughter. The photo also shows the Queen with a wine glass in her hand. If anyone actually takes the time to look closely at it, they would notice her glass has sparkling water in it. These days apps and Materiality TV (Mtv) are so good you can see if a guy missed anything while shaving this morning and the lines between television, film, journalism, magazines, documentaries, books, music, newspapers are meaningless.

When Farrar sees/reads/watches/hears this story (the background music they add is so moving that when he gets to the rape part and he sees Ellen's beautiful daughter with her tiny full length ripped dress, Farrar is stirred even though he knows the whole story is crap), it's a reminder that he still has some unfinished business on Earth, not that he needs to be reminded.

José-Luis loses four of his main sponsors when the story breaks. None of the tabloids bother to report that José-Luis was nine when all this went down preferring to run images of a fully grown, fiercely competitive, bullet-headed man next to the picture of little Naya with her torn dress, fainting into the arms of her Dad. It's a killer set of images. Raping five year old girls looks believable given his Germania's Playboy Princeling backstory.

Only a shoe company and an alcohol one stand by him. The latter is exceptionally pleased with the story. Hey, life's a party and what's a party without booze and pretty girls? This story has everything they're looking for. Bonanza time!

José-Luis cannot believe how Naya has sold him out. He's been hurting for years and now this? The story is everywhere. She must have done it to get even with him or for money, probably both. Fans whistle now when his name is announced even when they play at home. Every time he touches the ball, the whistling starts and doesn't stop until he lays if off or shoots on goal. As a result, José-Luis who has always wanted the ball on his foot when the game is on the line, starts to shy away. His game is changing. Not for the better.

...

Thor is heading to his car. He's got a date with his fiancée. He's got a Germania hybrid that is the fastest (legal) vehicle you are allowed to own in Nocal. He doesn't have to purchase it—he never has to spend anything. It's ironic that even though he's the highest paid sports guy in California, he can't actually spend his money—people just want to give him stuff. His car is part of his endorsement PACKAGE—cars, fast food, clothing, airship airline, shoes, soda pop, tablet, alcohol and marijuana (now legal in the Commonwealth). The only endorsement he's missing is a smart phone. Those guys at Quantum Computing Corp II are such miserly bastards.

From a 100 feet away, his car knows he's there. His driver's side door opens and his AC switches on. Wouldn't do for a 49ers QB to sweat anywhere but on the field or in the gym.

Then this girl pops up—she's this tall (almost as tall as he is) cutie. Barely legal. Probably come for a celebrity fuck.

Involuntarily, he checks his $650,000 Rolex (another gift) on his right wrist (he's a south paw) to see if he has time to accommodate her before meeting up with his fiancée.

The closer he gets, the better she looks. In fact, she is vaguely familiar. He's seen her somewhere. This looks tasty, mighty tasty.

"Mr. Haden, Mr. Haden, can I talk to you for a minute?"

When she speaks he realizes she's even younger than he thought. He's gotta make sure she's legal. You can get in real trouble these days for fucking 5 year olds. Look what happened to that German soccer player. Shit, he'd better watch out.

"Sure babe. What's up?"

"I work for SKIP-AID and we were wondering if you wanted to come to our event. Like endorse it?"

"All my endorsements go through my IMG agent, honey. You've gotta talk to them. But maybe there is something else I can help you with?" He looks at his Rolex again.

Then a couple of guys, boys really, and a QE pop up out of nowhere.

"These are my brothers, Magellan and Finn, and my QE, Su7e."

"Can I have your autograph?" Finn asks. Magellan rolls his eyes.

'Who brings their brothers and a QE to a fuck fest?' Thor is thinking as he signs Finn's t-shirt. Maybe this girl is kinky, he hopes.

Magellan can see as Thor reaches out to sign Finn's shirt that his forearm is running an NSM tattoo—it's a video loop of highlights from Thor's NFL career so far.

"We don't have time to go through your agency, Mr. Haden. Our event is happening next month. It'd be great if you could come," Naya says.

"We're still in training camp next month. Maybe I can do it. Like I said, ask IMG. Do you want to give me your quantum number, like, so I could call you or something but I've gotta get going?"

"How is Tulip?" Naya asks.

"Huh, what's that you say?"

"How is Tulip?" Naya repeats.

"I have no idea what you saying, girl. I gotta run. Sorry." Thor makes like to leave.

"I think he looks good in his red apron but better in his butterfly suit."

Her brothers have no idea what she is talking about and are looking at her kinda like Thor is at the moment.

"I don't know what you saying. You don't know what you saying. I'm outta here."

"Mr. Haden would you like Su7e to play the video. It's outstanding quality." She is referring not to Thor's penis size but his lover's. It's still not accepted by NFL players and it's not going to exactly help Thor's career if the fact that he is bi-sexual comes out.

Naya, like her mother, believes in being prepared for all eventualities. She'd really like the 49ers QB to endorse her event.

She leaves with his promise to message a SKIP-AID endorsement and to show up on the day. His agent at IMG is pissed at him for agreeing to this without his input until he finds out that his agreement is with another IMG prodigy, Miss Naya Brooks Bell. At IMG, Naya is their second most important client after football great, José-Luis Vasilescu, that is, until it is disclosed that Mr. Vasilescu and Miss Naya had a hitherto unknown but considerably one-sided relationship that is now cratering his career.

In a way, Naya would probably have eclipsed him anyway since she only does a tiny number of assignments each year and scarcity breeds value. It also doesn't hurt that Jamal leans on the guy. The reason he makes the NBA? He isn't afraid to go inside and mix it up with 7'6", 395 pound monsters who can run, jump, dunk and viciously elbow almost anyone out of the way. Mixing it up with

IMG agents is incomparably easier.

...

Naya's done her GED and her SATs. Her scores aren't as good as Jagad Durai's but then she doesn't cheat. They have quantum scanners now anyway in all their exam halls so if you do ask your QE for help, it's observed right away. Then they unceremoniously yank your tablet and kick you out a few seconds later. It takes effort to not ask your QE for help. Naya knows this since she cuts off Su7e for almost two years which makes both of them sicker. Since reestablishing her relationship with her partner, Su7e is getting better too.

Now all she needs is to complete her volunteer hours (she'll have way more than 80 after SKIP-AID is done) and she'll be at Berkeley come Fall; kind of on schedule (with a few detours)—she'll be 17 in December.

...

SKIP-AID is a free event to attend and they are expecting about 20,000 people to come. It's as nice an August day in San Francisco as you can expect in a mostly chilly place. Naya has over 150 volunteers working with her mostly from the Salvos, Food Bank and Make A Wish but there are a few from St Jo's as well—women that Naya has come to know though her support group. She's been there for nearly a year.

Over 1,100 Bay Area executives have signed up; after her Vanity World story comes out, registrations nearly triple. At the last moment, Naya adds a family team competition which is a pay-what-you-can-afford category. Her mother suggests it after looking over her business model.

"Most of your money will come from corporate types, Naya, and your sponsors but a family category will bring people out en masse which will please your sponsors. Plus everyone likes an audience, the larger the better," Ellen finishes.

So they add families and have to cap entries when it

reaches 5,000. It doesn't matter how big your family is or how small—they average scores so a family size of two or six, doesn't matter. What surprises Naya is the first family to register is hers. Ellen has added them as the *Brooks-Bell Team of Destiny*, a preposterous poser of a name, Naya thinks.

The twins are excited—they've been practicing but they groan when they see that Su7e is part of their team. (Ash3r and Pet3r both decline Ellen's invite as lacking in the gravitas and dignity that Quantum Numbers 3 and 1 deserve.) The boys know that Su7e will be horrible at skipping stones and their average will suffer. They want to win.

Naya doesn't know how she will find time today to participate on their family's team but she will—just seeing her Mom at the event is really something. People still want to come up to her, touch her and thank her for what she did for the Commonwealth. She and Da look really happy. Da is back to using a cane but only when he expects it to be a long day of standing which this one promises to be. He looks very handsome. He comes to visit Naya every week at St Jo's. They drink tea and talk about nothing for hours.

...

They have to close the grounds when their attendance count reaches 32,000; there just isn't room for anyone else. It can be dangerous to put that many people in a confined area.

The day (Saturday) begins at 9:30 am and is supposed to complete by 5 pm but it is almost certain that they will run overtime. They have just over 6,100 people going to 32 stone skipping stations set up around Spreckels Lake which means about 200 people have to be processed throwing three stones each (and more if rich guys buy mulligans). They expect it will take two minutes per person to get them into position, record their individual (heroic of course) performances for their posterity, kibitz a bit with them and send them on their way. That's about 6 hours and 45 minutes if nothing goes wrong.

They were going to do a playoff of the best corporate and family teams but this is out of the question. Dr. Bell points this out for Naya fairly early in her planning cycle. Maybe next year they can bring back top teams for a SKIP-OFF on Sunday. Naya'll raise even more money in year 2!

Her brothers are getting lots of traction at their Street Paddle Tennis demo. Finn is selling their wooden (Canadian pine) rackets made in Pops' old barn for them by Sunny Michaud. At $20 QED apiece, he'll run out of supply before 2 pm. He asks Magellan to boot up Pay Pal and they take reservations after that.

Damien is not doing as well with his Siberian Cedar Medallions and Worry Dolls. He's dumped the responsibility for running his booth at the craft fair on Pet3r who is not particularly good at sales. Still whenever Damien has time, he shows kids how to paint medallions, tracing images of their favorite characters or sports and music heroes on the wood and then coloring them in. He can't help but notice how many of the little girls want to trace then paint Naya on theirs. He also tells them the mythology of Worry Dolls/People.

They've got face painting, inflatable toys (waterslides, bouncers, obstacle courses, dry slides, castles), puppet stage and main stage for singalongs and dance demos. Meeza agrees to bring a troupe out and reprise some of their top numbers. Food and beverage covers all tastes but there is special emphasis on vegan, organic and local.

Clifford Hexham, the really good looking, tall, hipster-skinny heir to inner city chain of c-stores called 24/7 that sells alcohol, guns, chips and pop visits Naya and wants to present her with a big sponsorship check. He's seen her Vanity World spread and decides to check her out personally. It's a short meeting. Her answer is, 'No.' Green Stop sponsors her event instead although for less money than what Clifford offers her.

Wherever Naya goes, she has a troupe of little girls seeking her autograph, asking questions, telling stories—there's a lot of excited chatter. Naya is wearing a short forest green tunic over practical (matching) leggings that Zora helps her choose. She is wearing green and gold bejeweled, open-toed walking sandals and no other jewelry except a pair of tear drop shaped silver earrings just over a centimeter in diameter and a matching ankle bracelet. Inside each teardrop earring is a beautiful angel with her water wings spread wide over an incoming wave. These are earrings JEL had made for her after their visit to LA which he gives her before her life goes into the dumpster. Her ankle bracelet, she has had made recently to match. But inside its single teardrop is their new SKIP-AID logo.

Exactly at 1 pm, Naya has to go into a private tent she's had pitched near Middle Lake in an area off limits to the public. Dekka drives her over in a golf cart. After Naya lives at St Jo's for about a month, Dekka just somehow shows up. He's back to living in a shed behind the Women's Shelter. It's been winterized/insulated and has an (illegal) wood burning stove in it too so it's nice and toasty. Naya lies on a single cot and falls fast asleep. Su7e wakes her an hour later—it's time for the *Brooks-Bell Team of Destiny* to do its thing.

...

Finn is leading his family down to Spreckels Lake. He holds up both arms as if he is MMA Heavyweight Champion of the Universe. Magellan meanwhile is their flag carrier. The boys have made a fake family coat of arms—they're now the Order of the Bird or, to be more precise, the Order of the Heron. They have a big male Blue Heron set on a golden shield against a pure white silk background with a red cross on its breast. It's quite beautiful actually—Magellan designs it. It now flutters in a light breeze with 'Eam Numerare' (Latin for *Make It Count*) written in a lovely script on top in a flowing ribbon of a masthead.

There is a lot of local media there and quite a bit of national/international as well. They're a well known family and recent publicity involving Naya and her now disclosed (famous) attacker, José-Luis Vasilescu, have brought them out here in force.

The *Brooks-Bell Team of Destiny* is made up of Ellen and Damien, Naya, Finn, Magellan, Su7e and Dekka. Dekka is about as thrilled to be included in this as he was participating in a Nell singalong at the Ingersoll Homestead on the Salmon River a generation ago. But he's been coming down to Spreckels with the boys—all three of them have been practicing. Finn has even coerced Su7e into practicing with them a couple of times and she can now run a routine that lets her skip a rock maybe a horrible four or five times.

They each get three skips and can always get a mulligan if they want—it's free for family entries. Their high scores are:

Finn, 41
Damien, 23
Magellan, 22
Naya, 14
Dekka, a pathetic 11
Ellen, 8
Su7e, a surprising 6

Finn is proud of his old Dad. Turns out he didn't entirely waste his childhood at Pops' Lake after all. Their average score is a respectable 17.857142 which puts them in the top 1,000. Next year, Finn's plan is for just the three amigos to enter as a 'family'. Then they'll be top 100 for sure.

Naya's invited the world record holder to demo his skills at 3 pm. Finn's eyes bulge out of his head when he sees the guy (he's really skinny) skip a rock 54 times. And he's not even trying. His record is 62 skips. Hmm.

Damien is quite sure that 62 skips must be pretty near the limit that physics and human anatomy will permit.

Other demos in the afternoon include a California Golden Bears Women's Volleyball team friendly against a competitive boys (High School) team. Cal whips them three sets to nil.

Thor Haden makes his appearance as scheduled. Naya has had her roadies set up circular targets on Spreckels Lake at 20, 40, 60 and 80 yards. The diameter of each target is about three feet and they float about a foot off the surface of the water. They're anchored to the bottom of the Lake so they don't drift off.

There is a stack of NFL footballs and across from it a stack of perfect skipping stones. An Oregon quarry has donated all skipping stones and they enter their own corporate team—not made up of C-level executives though—three of their drivers decide to stick around for the event and participate.

Thor has to throw a football through each hoop but here's the catch—he has to do it before the little guy, the world stone skipping champ, can skip stones through his own set of equidistant targets.

It's a best of three. It's nolo contendere. Thor loses badly. He hates to lose especially to a midget. But then Naya is there laughing and he finally gets it; it was a setup. He laughs too.

He looks around and asks one of her flunkies to get him a beer but the guy says there is no alcohol anywhere in the Park. Come to think of it, Thor didn't see any beer or alcohol sponsor signs anywhere. What kinda party is this?

...

Finn has one more gag he wants to play. He's organized a group of Cub Scouts (six sixes so 36 in all) ages 7 to 10. These sturdy little guys are split into two teams and they do a demonstration tug-of-war, 18 a side.

There is a pit of mud, two feet deep and 14 feet in diameter that a backhoe digs for Finn. He fills it with a nice mix of water and Leda clay. That's the kind that has an internal structure that under a microscope looks like it is made up of a bunch of tiny paper leaves stacked and standing vertically but when any vibration is applied to it, this structure collapses. That is, losers get coated in sticky, bluish mud. It's fun, at least for the winners.

But this isn't his whole plan. He's got a Quantum megaphone and he's lined up six of the biggest guys he can find. Fat ones, tall ones, guys who look like all they do is hit the gym all day, every day.

The winning Cub Scout squad is gonna challenge these adults.

The guys are telling each other to take it easy on the kids. They limber up.

"All ready?" yells Finn. "Go!"

It's surprisingly even for the first minute or so but then, inexorably, the men are being dragged into the pit. They redouble their efforts and momentarily their position improves before it starts to deteriorate again. All the men get dragged into the pit. Huh?

"You see," Finn says to a rapt audience of kids and surprised adults. "Six big guys weigh about the same as 18 munchkins. But 18 little guys have 36 feet on the ground and the area under their shoes is way bigger than the total area under the men's feet. My Dad told me that friction is developed by and is proportional to Mass times Area. Dad also says that while friction coefficients play a role, I don't have to know what that value is since it is obviously the same for both teams. So the Cubs have way more friction going for them than the men which means that victory by the boys is as predictable as Naya acing her SATs and getting into Berkeley! Congrats, Naya!"

...

As the day draws to a close, they end their silent auction and accountants from all four charities start to tally up what they've raised—it's being split five ways although Naya has still not told her Da that she has cut his Institute in on her action. When they give her a preliminary number her eyebrows lift in surpise—they've raised net proceeds of just under $2 million QED. She's gonna have a lot of thank you messages to compose.

...

"Naya, we have something for you," Magellan says.

"What is it?"

"It's a surprise. But you have to come back to the Equestrian Center."

Naya's getting tired and Dekka has her golf cart ready so he takes her over. Magellan rides on the back fender.

When they get over there, Finn comes over and helps his sister out of the cart and he sits her down in a lawn chair they have for her. Her family is there and quite a few of the volunteers as well as representatives from all four charities. Their volunteers are dressed nicely—girls get cute purple pinafores they wear over black jeans; guys also wear black jeans but they get purple t-shirts. Pinafores and t-shirts all have a Bay Area SKIP-AID crest over their heart. Their word logo is stamped on an image of a young girl and boy, seen from behind holding hands watching a sunrise. To Magellan, the girl and boy look suspiciously like Naya and JEL.

Everyone is there to say thanks to Naya. They make a huge fuss over her. It's embarrassing but nice.

Then she hears a big whoosh. The boys have mixed water, little strips of Aluminum foil and Lye (Sodium Hydroxide) with which they fill a nearly eight foot tall lantern with byproduct gas. As it inflates, everyone can see that it has an incredible image of Naya hand drawn and painted on it by Magellan. The lantern's made out of the same pure white silk he uses for their new family flag. It is running another one of Damien's lighting packages so it glows with a shimmering warm internal light.

Magellan is on clear com to Darryl Hnatyshyn from

Mixed Media Collective. At his signal, Darryl opens a hole in the quantum bubble over them and (mercifully) stops running sponsor promos. Finn removes the anchor bolts and the lantern takes off. Naya's spirit is moving Heavenward with her image.

Normally the boys add a slow fuse (a cigarette butt works just fine) to their lanterns and a mix that is 75% potassium nitrate (salt peter used for pickling is a convenient source which they get when they visit Zora's place), 15% sulfur (from first aid kits) and 10% charcoal (grab it out of any fireplace). This is, of course, a recipe for gunpowder. They put it in a tin can (makes a heck of an explosion) and blow their lanterns to bits—around 500 feet up give or take 100 feet. But not Naya's lantern. Damien has added a tracking device and the guys are going to go find it wherever it lands and give it to Naya on Christmas Eve, her birthday.

Then Magellan asks Darryl to close their quantum bubble again. They play a tape of Naya doing her Fire Poi at Orpheum at age 12 over the entire sky above Golden Gate Park. Darryl's created day for night conditions. When he gets a minute or so into Naya's video, he suddenly splits his massive semicircular sky screen into two—the other half plays Nell doing The Successors. Even the thickest member of their audience has to realize now that these two are somehow intrinsically linked, i.e., they're related. Damien looks at his daughter now almost all the way back from oblivion. Next he looks at Ellen who returns his smile then he glances at Nell in the Heavens above and thinks, 'Thank you, Nell, for returning her safely to us.' Damien knows that even though the grave Naya lies on belongs to Pops, it's Nell who talks to her. What they talk about and what Naya is going to do, he doesn't know because neither girl will tell him. He's tried asking Su7e but she is just as involved in this cabal and says nothing.

They all clap and Naya's eyes fill with tears. They

want a speech but she is too overcome by the moment and too tired so Ellen steps up and thanks everyone on behalf of her daughter and congratulates the whole team.

Dekka takes Naya back to her shelter and she collapses into her bed. Dekka covers her with the Hopi wedding blanket he finds there. It's Aggie's. Naya remembers to bring it back with her from Pops' place to San Fran.

Her 80 hours of community service are (more than) fulfilled so it's off to Berkeley, soon.

...

Chapter 13 Berkeley

"Will not."

"Will too."

Magellan is telling Finn that there is no way he and Sean can set a new wind assisted world record for distance using a crappy old recipe for a flying disc they found last year when they visited Pops' old place in Canada. The three guys are living together on campus. Finn is in second year Business, Magellan is in his third year for Fine Art. He's heading towards a Masters in Fine Art also at Berkeley. The twins are 18; the reason Magellan is a year ahead is that his brother majored in girls, partying and dropped courses in his first year before getting a lecture from Ellen that it is either going to change or he will get zero support from his parents henceforth.

Naya is doing post grad work. She's been cooking up something but there's been a real effort not only by her and her Profs but also by the College of Natural Resources at Berkeley to suppress information about her work except to say that it is in the field of agronomy, whatever that means. Magellan has more information—Naya's told him their internal code name for her project is Farm-in-a-Box but what its functions are, she won't say.

Sean Ruane, their roommate, is the shortest of the three guys—Finn is tallest (even taller that his Dad who is shrinking anyway as he gets older), Magellan's next. Sean is 6'1", short for a guy these days and he's probably not going to grow anymore—he's a year older than the boys. Sean's also a grad student. He works with nanosite tech. He's some kind of whiz at it but you would never guess it by looking at him. He's a typical, thick, hairy, powerful, stocky troglodyte Irish Catholic—dark haired and dark eyed with a temper that is hard to raise but vicious when it is.

His family's originally from the poorest, toughest, meanest part of Catholic Belfast (near Antrim Road where the Troubles were worst) via Boston (Southie). His family probably would have stayed in Belfast except the UDA (Ulster Defence Association) decides to terminate as many suspected IRA members and possible collaborators as they could reasonably manage which means, among other things, killing as many Ruanes as possible. Then they would have stayed in Southie except first his grandmother dies in the Pennsylvania Incident and then his father, radicalized by her sacrifice, ends up dead along with his wife (Sean's Mom) in a revivalist domestic terrorist bombing of Commonwealth Ambassador Headquarters where both his parents are volunteers.

His grandmother, son in tow, buses to DC to gather in front of SCOTUS (the Supreme Court of the (now former) United States) with a hundred thousand other protesters. They are there to support human rights for Quantum people. Then the Army National Guard guns down protesters (including his grandmother but thankfully not his Dad) for no apparent reason. His Dad (and consequently Sean) hates the old Republic with a fierce passion that if you know anything about the Irish, is beyond scary. Irishmen are crazy, worse than any Hatfield or McCoy.

17 years after the SCOTUS fiasco, remnants of the old Republic, in the name of local autonomy, bomb Commonwealth Ambassador HQ in Massachusetts where Sean's Mom and Dad happen to be doing concurrent shifts. They are collateral damage in a continuing low level war between old elements of the Republican Guard seeking to reinstate their position of privilege and the Commonwealth trying to establish a new era based on principles enunciated by their first President, Ellen Brooks. The Commonwealth Ambassador program, established by President Brooks, is a nationwide group of volunteers who fan out and work at the grassroots level to

promote education, economic development and social responsibility.

Sean's Uncle Des who runs a B+B in Alameda, California (on Lafayette Street) asks his nephew then 15 and niece, 5 to come out to join him after their parents are murdered.

Micky (that's what everyone calls Sean, naturally) has been taking care of his younger sister, Niamh (pronounced 'Neve') Ruane ever since. 'Mh' is Irish for 'v'. Niamh is the cutest redhead ever with very pale skin. Even though it's getting harder for her to remember her life in Boston, she refuses to give up her roots—she wears a Red Sox cap everywhere.

Practically no one calls her Niamh though. She's been saying things like 'Holy Jumpin' since she is three so somehow it has metamorphosed to 'Holly'. Holly is Sean's family. He adores her. So when Massachusetts Child Protection Services tells him that he is going into a foster home for a year and Holly is going to a separate one for ten, he and Holly decide to bug out for California—they accept Uncle Des' invitation; they've been fugitives ever since—for four years now.

There is a quasi kidnapping charge outstanding in Massachusetts for Micky. It would be a good idea if he never goes back to the East Coast. There's no chance that any of the Irish in Alameda would cooperate in any police investigation of this matter so Micky and Holly just get on with their west coast lives.

When Holly isn't hanging out at Robert W Crown Memorial State Beach off Shore Line Drive, she's at nearby St. Joseph Basilica. It's pretty much deserted these days in what is becoming a post-Christian California society so Holly has to climb through a broken basement casement window so she can get into the nave and say her own version of the sacrament of the Eucharist. She lights two candles and says a prayer for her Mom and Dad. She doesn't have any money so she does volunteer stuff for them—like cleaning up litter—plastic containers, fast food wrappers, addict refuse, shared needles, used condoms, discarded firearms, used ammo, human and animal feces, the detritus of an economy not yet fully recovered from the last years of a corrupt Republic.

"So what's the plan?" Magellan asks his brother who like his older sister and their Mom always has plans.

"The winds above Third Mesa will do it, I'm sure. They come out of the canyon during the right conditions at a vertical acceleration of 28 feet per second per second—"

"Right, sure. Where did you get that information?" Magellan asks his business minded brother.

"Duh, Dad and I looked at weather patterns for the last 40 years—"

"Which means that Dad did the work and you did what?"

"Look at 28 feet per second per second on a sunny, winter's day when ambient temp is less than 40 degrees and the density of the air is thicker, we should get buoyancy that almost offsets gravitational pull. Sean will wing it and with Pops' design, it's gonna work."

"Is Dad coming?"

"No, he's gotta work on stuff with Jag. They're getting ready to wrap Mars in a quantum bubble or something. It inflates in the next few months so he can't make it."

"Sean, what do you say?"

Ruane just stares at his two younger buddies—Finn is obsessed with setting a world record in distance and time aloft for a flying disc based on a design his grandfather cooked up sometime in the last century. Micky is trying to keep his head down and not get arrested, at least until he can bring up his little sister and she turns 16, seven years from now. After that, they can bust his ass, he doesn't care. He would not be the first Ruane to unjustly spend time in a State prison.

...

They've been testing a few of these golf ball textured flying discs. Micky whips them up—135, 145 and 175 gram prototypes using his nanosite generator to create them. Micky is an expert coder and designer. When it comes to fabrication using nanosites, he can do anything. Fabricating a few flying discs is something that'll take him a few hours to do—60 minutes or so for design and coding and a couple of hours for nanosites to fabricate the suckers. It's trivial really.

But his specialty, the area where he is really breaking new ground, is nanosite deconstruction. He can basically take the most toxic waste sites in the Commonwealth, piles of dirty fissionable materials, huge tracts of derelict Commonwealth cities and reduce them to inert particles, water and water vapor in hours, days, weeks or, at most, months. He is using quantum shaping to change existing nanosites from constructors to deconstructors. Governments and real estate developers are all over his research but he has to be careful. Nanosite deconstructors would make a heck of a weapon if it could, say, be tuned to reduce individual human beings to their basic chemistry and water vapor.

The twins often get Sean to play Street Paddle Tennis with them—doubles. The twins love that stupid game. Sean plays single against the boys and wipes the court with them. He is amazingly quick, has reflexes that are ramming-speed fast, can turn on a toothpick and then pound the ball when he arrives. Plus he can anticipate not only where his opponents are but where they will be so he puts the ball somewhere else.

"Hey, Naya, Naya, come play!" Finn yells at her as he spots her crossing campus. Finn isn't asking Naya over just to be nice to his sister. He wants Naya to play with Sean because then he and Magellan'll have a chance to win—they'll average down their opponent.

Naya comes over, introduces herself to Micky, picks up a racket and they play. The game is tied at 2-2 when

Naya joins and Finn intends to make sure they send every ball her way. But Sean is everywhere. If she flubs a shot, he's already behind her and whacks it. They establish an immediate rapport and switch sides, maddeningly confusing Magellan and Finn. Naya and Sean win 7-6. Finn challenges them to another game but Naya, who still has to be careful about her level of exertion, begs off with a wave and a 'Nice to meet you' directed at Sean.

Micky watches Naya as she disappears around a corner. Magellan is watching Sean watch Naya.

"That's your sister?"

"Yep," says Finn.

"How come you never introduced me before?"

"Protecting her virtue from a horny Irish Mickey," Finn replies.

"I've seen her films."

"Yeah. She's got another one coming out in November. They say it's an Academy candidate."

"How come she's here at Berkeley?"

"You got all night? The story of Naya is a long one."

"She's a student here?"

"Yeah, a grad like you."

"She can make a lot more money in films than being a research scholar here."

"Naya doesn't really want to do films," Magellan says inadvertently.

"Why not?"

"She finds them stressful, I guess."

"Why?"

Magellan is not comfortable talking about his sister even with Sean.

Finn pipes up, "She had a problem when she was a kid—with booze. She just doesn't like the lifestyle or maybe she's afraid of it?" Magellan is looking at his brother in a way that makes even a thick skinned Finn wary so he clams up.

"What's she studying?"

"Agronomy."

"What? She's going to be a farmer? She doesn't look like any farmer I've ever seen."

"Why you so interested, Sean?" asks Magellan.

"I don't know. She's really pretty."

"Forget about it, Micky. She's older than you by about a thousand years. You've as much chance with a girl like Naya as you do playing center in the NBA."

"Anyway, she's already got a boyfriend," Finn adds. "And he's a lot handsomer and a lot richer than you, you Irish dog."

The boys go back to playing Paddle Tennis. Micky whips them again 7-3.

Afterwards, they agree to go out to Third Mesa when weather conditions cooperate and try for the world record using Pops' design; Sean says they'll try a 145 gram flying disc first.

The theory is that its dimpled surface will bring to flying discs the same flight characteristics they do to golf balls. They'll create a turbulent layer over its upper surface which will act kind of like graphite or lubricant. Lift will be improved and drag reduced. To attempt the record, Sean will spin 360 degrees once before launching the thing backhand. The disc they will be using is apparently called a 'Superflyer'—that is Pops' name for it which they discover from his notes. He is the holder of an industrial design patent on it too.

Sean, without trying too hard, can fling it over 700 feet. He is impressed. With some help from updrafts at Third Mesa, maybe they can go after both time and distance records. One thing he will have to do is improve its stiffness. Even a small deformation in its Taco shell surface will significantly degrade its performance.

...

"Hey Magellan come here."

"No! I've a design project I'm working on. It's due Friday."

"Tough. Come here."

When Magellan goes into their common room, he sees both Finn and Sean stripped to the waist with deadly short Wakizashi swords in their hands. They're sweating heavily. They've bought a new Sinofighter unit and they are coordinating their attacks against the device but need a third hand to try to overcome the fighter.

Magellan picks up a sword—he can't very well leave his two brothers to die at the hands of this Imperial Chinese game player—and they attack ensemble and finally hack it to pieces. The Sinofighter reconstitutes itself and bows then politely asks, "Would you like to play Level 3?"

The boys say 'No' and Finn gets them all a beer. They drink Olympia 'Fix' beer (from Greece) not because it is especially good brew but because of its name. Everyone at Bezerkeley loves to order another 'Fix'.

"What do you think of their hack?"

"What hack?" Magellan asks.

Finn look at his bro like he lives under a rock, ignores his last comment and glances over at Sean.

"It's pretty cool."

"Have you tried it?"

"No but a friend of mine did. With his boyfriend."

"I'd like to try it with a girl I met five seconds ago. Like on Chat Roulette or something."

"Wouldn't suit me," Sean says.

"Me neither," adds Magellan.

"You guys are no fun. Look, you meet someone on the Internet, a minute later, she's in your room humping you and you're in her room fucking her. You feel EVERYTHING. You can't get any diseases and no commitment—you don't even have to know her name."

"What's the point?" Magellan asks.

Finn just rolls his eyes. "Why does there have to be any point. How about it if it feels good, do it?" Then he adds rhetorically, "Hey guys, do you want to know my

Bruce M Firestone

view of male-female relationships?"

"No," both Magellan and Sean say simultaneously.

Finn presses on regardless and oblivious, "See, women aren't really human—they're these eggs surrounded by 135 lbs of female flesh. The eggs control everything—get your hair done, color it, go for a manicure and, while you are at it, get a pedicure. Then go shopping for clothes, the skimpier, the better. Then the eggs take their flesh out for a walk. They have a plan! To interview sperm donors! The eggs use eyes which are conveniently located on a vertical axis that swivels—it's called a neck—so they can scan the horizon for healthy sperm. When they see likely candidates, they cause the body to strike provocative poses—shy, sexy, aggressive, pouty, sultry, legs together, legs crossed, legs apart and hands on hips, hands playing with hair, find a reason to bend over ass extended, adjust bra, tilt head one way, then the other, keep one leg straight with the other slightly bent, adjust skirt, smooth skirt, if they've got a dance background, put one foot next to the other at a 90 degree angle and—"

"Enough, bro, we get it," Magellan says exasperated by Finn's endless chauvinism.

"What's your view of men then, Finn?" Sean asks.

"For Chissakes, don't encourage him!" Magellan exclaims.

"Glad, you asked! Men aren't human either! They are sperm surrounded by 195 lbs of flesh. They fight other 195 lb creatures for resources so that they can be especially attractive to eggs. They can not only fertilize eggs but take care of the result too. They get hot cars so that they can take eggs for a drive and then date them—" ('Date' is a Finn euphemism for 'fuck'.)

"But Sinofighter sex can't result in fertilized eggs so your whole paradigm breaks down, Finnegan," Sean says with a smile.

"Exactly, sperm are fooling eggs. There is the promise of fertilization and resources without having to actually make good."

"That's another reason why I despise those things," Magellan says seriously. "You are breaking trust with another human being—someone who is giving herself to you in a way that is very special, it's like two souls communing..."

Finn just looks at his brother and shrugs, "You are such a loser in the Sperm Wars!"

But Sean is interested. "You said 'another reason', Magellan. There are more?"

But now Magellan doesn't want to say. He's afraid his brother will laugh at him some more.

"Well, at least one more," he says after a few moments.

"Which is?"

He says quite defensively, "I really like the way women smell and you can't experience that with Sinofighter sex."

Finn does laugh but Sean is looking at him with a surprised expression—it's one of recognition. While he is playing Paddle Tennis with Naya, he notices her smell as she crosses paths with him on the court—it's a wonderful smell, a combination of Naya's natural odors with some type of mystery perfume. Sean is not an expert in women's perfumes but if he was, he would know it is Nell Perfume, the kind with Ambergris in it. It's a love potion.

...

Chinese-made Sinofighters are everywhere these days; someone has hacked them and one of their main utilities now is simulated sex. These simulations as Arcady Valenzuela once reported are beyond good, they're really, really good. So in about a year, Sinofighter consoles are ubiquitous. They're so much fun that couples who've been married less than five years use them to spice up their sex lives, daring to do things with each other that they can't actually bring themselves to do face to face so to speak. So the hubbie goes into his study with his Sinofighter console and she goes into her boudoir with hers and you GET IT ON! It's way better than Sildenafil Citrate (the stuff that goes into blue ED pills).

Imperial China denounces misuse of their consoles as another example of western decadence—using heroic instruments of human betterment for debauchery is why Imperial China and its allies will prevail in a contest of cultures that has been going on for 3,000 years or more.

But it's a funny position for their government to take since this hack is intentionally released by National Revolutionary Army underground coders. They know that console sales will crossover from a young male demographic to, well, nearly everyone once people learn they can have guilt free sex that is nearly as good and, in some ways better, than the real thing. Console sales explode planet-wide.

Their hack derives, of course, from work done by Jag Durai in Shenyang. His excursions with Cady did not go unnoticed. It's the biggest, best sex toy ever.

What everyone misses at first is that if you can travel from Shenyang to Texas to have sex with your girlfriend in zero time (and vice versa), you can also use these consoles to have face time at business meetings, conferences, classes, dances, parties, study groups, tours, openings, concerts and galas. When techies in the Valley start equipping every office with Sinofighters so they can interact (with their clothes on) with colleagues in LA, Boston, Moscow, Bucharest, Lagos, Johannesburg, Sydney, Auckland, Mumbai, Rio or Buenos Aires, these things start spreading faster that facsimile machines in their day, email, messaging, social media and Q-phones. Quantum Computing Corporation II finally has some real competition.

...

The only reason Magellan plays these stupid games with his brother and his friend is that since he is 15, he discovers that if he does not get enough exercise, his world closes in on him and depression settles on his shoulders and neck for weeks at a time. After seeing what happens to his sister when she is told she might not walk again, let alone dance, he realizes that a predisposition to depression runs deep in their family and he'd better watch out.

...

Cliff is taking her to the opening of her (third) film in LA. She doesn't really want to go but it is part of her contract so she does. He is taking her from San Fran to LA in his private plane. It's a nice aircraft with a lovely bedroom on its upper deck. The skin of the aircraft can be made transparent over its king-sized bed so it is possible to fuck at 42,000 feet with stars seemingly nearby.

Cliff is a very tall man in his early 30s. He's hipster thin and mega rich. His family owns 24/7 and, despite Commonwealth efforts to curb sales of guns and booze in these corner stores, it's still rampant everywhere.

Cliff has laser hair removal done so he is completely hairless everywhere except his head where one side is shaved and the other folds over in a Hitlerian look. The only thing missing is the mustache. Cliff likes kinky sex but at least on this flight down, he spares her this.

She first meets him in the run up to SKIP-AID. That's when she turns down his ridiculously huge sponsorship deal in favor of a smaller package from Green Stop. But he keeps after her—asking her out on a date doesn't work, offering her money for her charities fails miserably but finally IMG intervenes. Cliff underwrites production of a film by a top Director who is experiencing some tough times. His last four movies have flopped badly and he needs a fresh face and an inspired script. He finds the latter in a small offbeat story about a kidnapping of a librarian who falls in love with her captor and tries to save him from himself and from a mad, mad, mad world. The Director refuses to make the film with anyone but Naya.

Bruce M Firestone

Cliff insists that he'll green light financing of the movie (almost all major studios lay off most of the financial risk of films on private investors) but only if the setting is changed from a library to a 24/7 c-store and the girl from a librarian to a c-store clerk. Naya only sees the script with the c-store clerk in it. It doesn't matter, her answer is the same, 'No.'

But Jamal visits her. He tells her this role is made for her and that she can reach millions of people with this story/her story. It's the kind of movie that the American Academy of Motion Picture Arts and Sciences loves and she is sure to get a nomination.

Naya doesn't care a fig about these self congratulatory types of awards but she cares a lot about the message—love can save people and people can turn back from their dark side to find something pure in themselves and others no matter how hopeless things may look.

In the film, Naya is kidnapped in a botched robbery at her c-store in Boise where she is alone on a nightshift. An off duty cop walks in for some cigarettes and this spooks the robber (a weirdly named Dr. ZinQ) who kills the cop with a single shot to his right eye. He grabs Naya and they escape in the cop's car. It is never explained as to why Dr. ZinQ would show up at a suburban c-store in frigging Idaho on foot.

He takes Naya back to a remote ranch that is owned by some rich easterners who come out a few weeks a year to pretend they're living a frontier life. He stuffs her into the wife's humongous clothes cupboard for a biblical 40 days and 40 nights. Her captor is a charming psychopath who alternately berates her and then shows pity on her. She can never know which Dr. ZinQ will show up.

Most of the next 50 minutes of film is shot in the closet. Naya's backstory comes out and she slowly gets Dr. ZinQ to unburden himself. The audience starts to identify with Dr. ZinQ who is now falling in love with his insurance policy. All their 'love' scenes are filmed in the closet with only the director, one cameraman, one lighting tech and one sound guy in attendance. They make Ellen's sex tape look as quaint as a Shirley Temple film. It's beyond graphic.

It seems that Naya is on the verge of convincing him to chuck his current life and run away with her to a new one when the unlucky easterners show up in a Land Cruiser of preposterous dimensions. They'll single handedly destroy the Earth's environment with their car.

The husband with his fake Cowboy hat and boots that have never seen the inside of a barn let alone stepped in any cow pies, sets off the worst chain of circumstances imaginable—both he and his wife die gruesomely at the hands of Dr. ZinQ.

Still Naya, now fully in the throes of Stockholm Syndrome, won't give up on her alternately charming and vicious lover. She can still save him!

Meanwhile the dead cop's partner has tracked them down (it's the car, stupid). As the film ends (it's done by Austrian Director Helmut Goetschl), the local SWAT Squad, intent on freeing the girl next door that everyone loves, wounds her instead because she takes a bullet meant for Dr. ZinQ. He holds her as she lies dying but her only thoughts are for him, to save him, the worthless piece of shit that he is. The SWAT Squad is closing in, he's sure to die too. But there is a safe room in the place and he activates it. Still he is cornered. The safe room has all kinds of tricky defenses and Dr. ZinQ manages to kill quite a few cops. The audience is not sure who to cheer for now.

Naya is dying but not yet dead. It's taking a long time but here is one thing you have to know about Hollywood scripts—once a girl is injured, she's gonna die, for sure. You see it's OK for a guy to have his looks mussed up a bit (and survive) but not the girl. So discerning filmgoers know Naya is finished.

Now the SWAT leader, who is fed up with losing men,

has to make a decision—call in a drone strike to blow the place up or fight crazy-ass Dr. ZinQ in this house of horrors, door-to-door. Of course, a drone strike will kill Naya too. What's a guy to do?

After seconds of suitable anguish, he calls for a drone strike finally finishing off Naya in a whale of a fire with great Foley effects. But little does he know that Dr. ZinQ has found a secret underground tunnel leading from the safe room to a nearby canyon where he escapes to wreak mayhem in Death House II.

...

When Naya sees the finished product at the opening, she is beyond appalled—it is the most worthless piece of garbage ever. More than half of her dialogue with Dr. ZinQ about turning back from the dark side never makes it to the final cut. There are plenty of successful murders and unsuccessful murder attempts, gun play, torture, explosions, criminality, police action and pulsating female flesh (aka Naya) to satisfy every teenage male in the solar system. It's without a doubt the biggest piece of shit since well every other piece of shit that Hollywood has produced since like forever.

Audience and critics love it. Those tense scenes in the cupboard are hailed as some of the best since sex fiend Alfred Hitchcock's work on Psycho, The Birds, Rear Window, Vertigo and North by Northwest and there is a lot of talk about Academies for Director, starlet, screenplay, sound effects, supporting actor (Dr. ZinQ) and cinematography.

Anyone who has a thimble of brains can see that Naya actually has talent even though screenwriter, producer, director and studio have done their best to bury it. The film is the sleeper hit of the Fall season. Naya is now the hottest young actress anywhere and can name her price for any future work she may want to do. Naya is sure that her acting career will match James Dean's for longevity and productivity—a total of three credited films.

...

Cliff and Naya live in his palatial SF home appropriately enough located in Sea Cliff. It is as ridiculous as it is ostentatious. She has her own room in this 34,000 square foot monstrosity that only has two bedrooms, one of which is hers. His bedroom is 3,400 square feet and includes a complete workout room. His personal trainer comes in six days a week. How do you think he can keep his hipster look after 30? Starvation and exercise.

Naya at 20 (last year) is lonely and vulnerable. She's never had a boyfriend other than her infatuation with José-Luis who has apparently forgotten all about her and then her seven minutes in the bush with Sal and Barry. Cliff is hip, rich, powerful, manipulative, confident. He's also had his security people do a full work up on her so he knows that she is an alcoholic and has basic insecurities like many young women forced to be thin, smart, career oriented, self sufficient, look like a porn star and then act like one. He is quite sure that if he keeps alternately pursuing her then spurning her, she'll fall over. And she does.

He treats her like she's special and then turns on her, belittling her looks and intelligence. It's part of his profile—he's used it many times to subdue even the prettiest, wealthiest, smartest, most independent women (the only ones he likes) and turn them into anything his vivid imagination can suggest. Cliff believes that Naya will be his greatest creation yet—the degradations that he will force her into—making her beg him for more—will be legend. And he records every second of these adventures for his pleasure and those of his colleagues in his private Club—Les de Sades. It's a Club made up of San Francisco's elite—judges, lawyers, businessmen, police, professionals—they trade in girl flesh, images, video and experiences and protect each other.

He also knows that like many battered or abused

Bruce M Firestone

women, Naya will blame herself when she finds herself ensnared by Cliff. She already blames herself for being an epileptic, for failing to achieve her goals as a dancer at Meeza, for falling into the abyss of alcohol, for disappointing her mother, for losing her first boyfriend then inadvertently ruining his career, for letting herself be fucked by a worthless pair of Canadians and now for making a deviant film under the watchful eye of Clifford Hexham that will only appeal to prurient interest. Once he has her, she'll come back again and again like a kicked dog. And when he tires of her, he'll throw a bone to one of his friends in the Club or, better yet, get their whole crew together and let them all taste her.

...

They are back in San Francisco. Cliff has just received a late night message from his Head of Security. He explodes, "What the fuck! Your brother is helping Green Stop raise capital? That's gotta stop,"

"Can we please go to bed," Naya says.

"No. Play music," Cliff says to his House Monitor. She plays Beethoven's Ninth. She also plays the video of the rape scene from A Clockwork Orange, one of his favorites.

"Can you please not play this?" Naya asks.

"Why not? You like it. Right?"

"Fuck you, Cliff."

"You already did that. Look, Finn cannot help our competition raise money. They're cutting into our market share those pissant Canadian Paisanos. You'll have to talk to him."

Naya just shrugs him off and starts to leave.

"Don't ever turn your back to me, you cunt."

"That's a low rent comment, Cliff," she says. Then she does leave. If they give her an Oscar for her latest film, she'll go back to drinking and kill herself for sure.

...

When Green Stop begins renovating what will be its new headquarters in San Francisco, the convenience store with real food (most of it sourced locally) cum meeting center and coffee shop turns to its community for additional funding. They establish a program called 'plant a seed,' whereby customers can buy gift cards in amounts varying between $250 and $1,000 to help local farmers and growers. A customer receives her or his money back in installments of *Green Stop Dollars* every six months over a three-year period. Customers receive a 20-per-cent bonus on the value of their investment.

This is the program that Finn is working on that Cliff objects to.

Green Stop customers have been asking for years, 'How do we support you?' so during one of his coop terms, Finn helps them launch this program. It is also an opportunity to generate buzz around the company's new HQ which, along with a Green Stop c-store and coffee house will include a new 28,000 square-foot roastery and a room for staff training and a larger space for community use.

The roastery will supply coffee to the company's shops in the northwest of the Commonwealth as well as western Canada when it opens, allowing for more frequent shipments and giving Green Stop more control over its products.

Raising money via script is a clever way to self-capitalize and, while it is not new, it is largely forgotten in the last years of the Republic when all the emphasis is on mega deal making via Wall Street.

Back in 1870, Reynolds Brothers Sawmill in the Adirondacks (established by Orson L. Reynolds) used this method to raise funds. They issued their own 'currency' called script. These are $5 promissory notes they can use to pay their bills and fund new ventures or additions to existing ones. Their script says it is, 'Due to the Bearer, In Trade At the Company Store' which means the bearer of the script cannot redeem it for a sovereign banknote of the nation, i.e., cash recognized by the now former United

States of America.

The fact that it is redeemable only 'In Trade' is key. Finn's research shows that Reynolds has a healthy margin (of 40%) on each trade so a $5 note with this kind of GPM (Gross Profit Margin) really costs them $5/(1 + .4) or $3.57. It's a great deal for Reynolds but is it a good deal for a supplier or laborer who accepts script instead of banknotes?

The answer is, 'It depends.' If you can't get any other work, $5 in credit at a Reynolds Company Store, $5 in cigarettes or candy from a Reynolds vendor (which you could then trade for other stuff) or $5 in Reynolds products (milled lumber) might be better than watching your family starve or having you join them in that unfortunate predicament circa 1876 even if you know in your heart of hearts that it's only really worth $3.57.

So Finn recommends this technique to Green Stop who don't have deep pockets but do have really loyal customers and suppliers. Further research turns up plenty of other examples. He finds out that Conn Smythe built Maple Leaf Gardens in Toronto (where Damien and his grandfather/father used to live) in a six-month period during the Great Depression (1931) at a cost of $1.5 million CAD. He funds it partly with script. If the 'Carlton Street Cashbox' as it is later called does not live up to its name, that script might have become valueless. Nevertheless, for an out-of-work ironworker back in the day, it sure beats unemployment. They could always find someone in the gray market to take script off their hands (at yet another discount) so they could eat today. It is what it is.

Why do Green Stop customers (and some suppliers) buy their script? Because—1. they love their coffee, cooking and yoga classes as well as artisanal products and services, 2. they love the ambiance of their stores, 3. they support local producers and are (mostly) able to compete/keep up with mega chains like 24/7, 4. they're an underdog, 5. they want to feel like they helped make it all happen and belong, in a way, to something bigger than themselves, 6. their stores are all in locations that people can actually walk to, 7. they have outdoor patios and provide more eyes on the street making the public room safer, 8. they like their inexpensive 4 pm 'blue plate' (smaller portion) specials for elders and 9. they trust Green Stop. Bundling is big these days and looking at each business model as a platform is essential. Green Stop is a *platform* for delivering a *bundle* of services. But there's another reason customers support their script issue—they get a 20% return (over three years)!

Green Stop gives them $1.20 worth of trade value on every Green Stop Dollar. That's a lot better than putting a $1,000 QED into a savings account and getting a .7% p.a. return. It's true, these days on a $1,000 CD (certificate of deposit) at your Bank, you get $7 in interest for a *year*. If you take off Bank fees, it's obvious you are *paying* your Bank to take your money from you.

Now what about Green Stop? Are they hurting because they give a 20% return? Not at all. Since their GPM is .6, their cost of $5 in script is 5 x 1.2/(1+.6) or $3.75 so you can see that Green Stop's cost of capital for expansion acquired this way is a *negative* $1.25 for every $5 raised. Negative perspiration for Green Stop! Now try getting that kind of deal from Wall Street where they raise money for you at interest rates less than zero. Not going to happen.

Finn gets an A+ (his first) on his coop term report. He also manages to help them raise more than $12 million QED. Not bad for a second year student. Ellen is the first to hear about his A+. She is so pleased.

...

"You are missing the point."
"I can't see what you are getting at."
"Look Miss Naya—
"Please don't call me that."

"Alright, then Naya, you are forgetting that people don't care about tech, they care about product. What does it do for me?"

"Our nutrient system is our Achilles. If we don't get that to work more efficiently, our whole project is compromised."

"That's because you're using the wrong approach. Go to the ocean for everything you need," Sean says.

They're in Naya's lab. Sean and Naya have been trading messages about his work (not hers) for the last few months and she has him sign an NDA before she'll bring him here.

"How would you do that?"

"I've been working mainly on nanosite deconstructors. But the same feed system I'm using will probably work with Farm-in-a-Box—"

"We just call her 'Roxie'."

"Her?"

"Well, our box will sit in a basement, a corner of an apartment or inside a one-room house and produce enough fruits, vegetables, grains (cereals, rice and pasta), nuts, beans, eggs, tofu, seeds, fats, oils, sweets, dairy (milk and cheese), even spices for a family of four. Since it is feeding people, we think of it as a her."

Their box certainly looks like a 'her' to Sean—its shell is created by one of the Valley's leading industrial design shops—it is pico scale carbon tube extruded stuff but it doesn't look like all the brown crap everyone else is producing. It's a deep blue and very curvaceous, has obvious teats for liquids, a mouth and series of valves for nutrient inputs and several other portals for outputs. There is a larger, human scale door for access and egress to get inside for maintenance and another smaller fitting—it's for fuel. Roxie can produce different types of fuel (kerosene, for example, which is highly portable and has a high energy density) or hydrogen gas to power external machines including cars, trucks and motorcycles like the new Kill-e-cycle that Sean has and loves. It has a fuel cell that produces lots of power (electric) from a hydrogen source. It's damnably fast with an acceleration (17.4 feet per second per second) that if he could keep it up for 35.1 minutes would produce Earth escape velocity (about 36,667 feet per second). It'll take three people on it—he knows because he gives both Naya and Holly rides—skinny Holly sits on a cheater seat he installs at the aft end of his rig; she is pressed against the cycle's backrest where he normally has his road-ready luggage.

Holly meets Naya when he and Naya's brothers go to Third Mesa to try to for the world record using a Pops' flying disc. They get a flight time of 22.1 seconds and a distance of 1,206 feet. Not bad but short of the world record by a few seconds and about 170 feet. Finn is discouraged but not Sean. He's going to reduce the weight of the disc in his next prototype, Superflyer XIV, and frig around with the golf ball pattern a bit. The dimples are set in ordered, concentric rows with smaller diameter dimples on the outer ring; they get larger as you travel towards the center of the disc. Micky feels that this is inherently right but he'll use a random walk instead to dimple the next iteration of these discs he fabricates.

The main reason Finn is disappointed? He wants to create a Personal Business for Life based on these old designs by his grandfather and setting the world record would help launch an artisanal business. He also wants to submit the accompanying business model he's built and guerrilla marketing plan for one of his seminar classes. Why not double end his work?

They do get some cool video though. Sean can throw the thing (it's very stiff) with a launch velocity exceeding 100 feet per second. They run a split screen video—on one side is the view from their Mtv scanner mounted on top of the Mesa and the other is from a tiny one Sean's added to the disc itself. The canyon walls, the stream at its base, their cornfields (maize) and pueblo, a beautiful

Bruce M Firestone

sunrise, it's all there.

Then Naya takes Holly out for a camel ride. After this, Holly has a Naya movie poster permanently displayed on her media wall in her bedroom at Uncle Des' place. She also vows never to wash her t-shirt (the one with Naya's autograph on it) EVER.

Roxie can also make any type of drug you might ever need—both the legal kind and illegal. Naya puts no constraints on that even though her University legal advisors tell her that she should. Naya says kids'll just hack around any limitations anyway. They tell her it will absolve them all of legal responsibility if a hacker does it and not Naya and her team. Naya doesn't care about what's legal. Roxie is designed to talk to people and she'll warn them and educate them if they are doing anything harmful. Roxie also produces prodigious amounts of electricity and heat.

Naya is also working with a group of Canadian engineers on how to use their waste heat. They've come up with a simple, elegant solution—pump the heat into the engineered fill (gravel) under existing structures during the summer and pull it out during winter time. It turns out gravel is a highly efficient thermal sink and it's really inexpensive in most parts of the world. They tell her, their calculations show it'll work even better in new structures if they'll add about 80 cubic meters of extra fill. It will improve stability of foundations anyway and it's cheap to do.

Naya's research is all about plant DNA—she focuses on getting the science right inside Roxie. She uses viruses known as bacteriophage to build materials inside Roxie that are the basis for any type of DNA-based product that she can design and some that are apparently not. Some of her work is based on self directed evolutionary techniques that are producing incredible outcomes. They can fold proteins, the workhorses of cells, into any shape and produce food and energy in prodigious amounts. But when they hook up beta copies of Roxie to existing commercial nutrient lines, their artifact is not efficient enough—she costs too much to run.

"Well Roxie should have her own tentacles. Commercial piped supply will be way too expensive and they're not available everywhere. So let's not use those pipes," Sean is saying. "The tentacles we use to deconstruct pretty much anything are more like long lines of tiny (nano sized) underground ants that can be as long as you want; they pass stuff on sort of mandible to mandible. But we could reverse the direction of flow and pass stuff back to Roxie. You go to the ocean with these and then you'd have an unlimited supply of every kind of nutrient, metal and chemistry. I think we go to hydrothermal vents—we can get every kind of mineral there in unlimited amounts. There are black and white smokers I've read about—they're near either underwater volcanoes or where tectonic plates meet—that are so big that a handful of them can supply all our energy needs and nutrient demand for a thousand years, I'd bet. As more of these things, sorry Roxies, get installed, our network of tentacles will get more efficient—hey neighbors will be able to trade back and forth—I need a cup of sugar and you need some salt. Except no one will know. We'll build intelligence into the tentacle system, it will self moderate, no problem."

As Sean is talking about his work, Naya notices that he's not as plain as her brothers make him out to be and he's only an inch shorter than she is. She can tell he's a solid guy and would make a good friend. Sean notices Naya noticing him and he stops.

"Did I leave you behind? Sorry." He's starting to get used to being in the same room with her but it is hard to reconcile her fame, her reputation for doing crazy shit with this white labcoated, basic researcher who seems really nice. Sean has seen her last film. Despite himself, he likes it. Naya is fantastic in it. Holly wants to go see it with him—that's absolutely not going to happen.

"No, I get what you are saying. But will it work for inland settlements too?"

Sean has a bigger vision. "Naya, it'll work on a continental scale, planetary even. We could get access to supplies of gold, copper, silver, platinum, palladium and every other kind of valuable mineral in the 100 million ton range and up. Hey, Naya, you could have gold reserves larger than India's! A jewelry collection bigger than the Queen of England's. Would you like that?" He'd like to see that!

She just laughs at his fantasy.

"Umm, have you thought of its economic implications?" he asks more seriously.

"I have."

"What'll farmers do?"

"Well, Roxie doesn't make meat, they'll ranch I suppose or use a version of Roxie for specialty foods that they design. Each Roxie comes with a Q-computer and simple user interface so everyone can tune theirs a little differently or program them to suit their tastes. Or they can just talk to them like they do to any QE."

"Have you made any wine with the thing? If you've got grapes coming out, you can do some cool things with fermentation."

"Uh, no. But I am sure a whole industry will form around that—people will put Roxie to uses we can't even imagine right now. Roxie's really a design for a platform for human ingenuity, Sean."

"You can also put municipal sewage treatment out of business, Naya."

"Huh?"

"Instead of shipping human wastes in sewer pipes to treatment plants and then dispersing it in bodies of water, just dump the excrement into a settlement tank. Our tentacle system will reduce it to its basic elements, water and water vapor. It'll be a closed system. Very efficient."

Naya wrinkles her nose at this.

"Hey, if our deconstructors can disassemble fissionable materials and make them safe, what's a little human waste?"

Naya laughs again.

Both Sean and Naya are vastly underestimating the economic implications of Roxie—it's not just farmers and waste treatment plants that will be impacted. Trucking, shipping, supermarkets, food manufacturers, big pharma, drug cartels and their delivery arms, motorcycle and local gangs, alcohol and tobacco companies, beverage companies, petroleum producers, miners, energy firms, even clothing companies are going to have to adapt to a new era. You can ask Roxie to produce bamboo, for example. Bamboo is an excellent material for athletic wear—stretchy, absorbent, heat shedding and, best of all, doesn't retain body odor after washing so smelly, hairy guys like Sean Ruane won't have to worry about BO after hanging out with the guys playing Ultimate, Paddle Tennis, pick up round ball and the other stuff they like to do in their spare time which is becoming scarcer as they all get busier with adult lives.

"Naya, do you mind if I ask how this got started?"

At first she thinks he is asking how did a Hollywood prostitot get involved with plant DNA coding but then she realizes she has to stop thinking of Sean as if he is part of Cliff's set of friends. He's just earnest and interested.

"It came to me when I was 15."

"What, one day you wake up and decide to build something like this?"

"Pretty much." She's not sure if Sean knows any of her history. She needn't worry. Her brothers would never tell anyone, even BFF Micky Ruane, what really happened to Naya as a teen.

"I'm not believing you."

"OK, let's make a deal. You tell me why every time a cop walks by you cringe—"

"You noticed that?"

"Pretty hard not to Mr. Ruane. You tell me what you are running from and I'll tell you how Roxie came to be."

"Deal," he says.

"OK, you first."

So he tells her his story and she realizes his family and hers are inextricably linked. It is SCOTUS' lack of courage and failure to act that gives the Republic the upper hand for a few more years keeping her Da in prison, nearly killing him. She hates all lawyers and judges just on principal.

Then after she finishes telling him her story (it's the first time she has ever told it to anyone, not even her Da knows the whole thing), he also realizes that they are connected. His grandmother indirectly died trying to get Damien out of San Quentin. It's the beginning of a relationship based on mutual trust. Naya is right—Sean makes a good friend.

Suddenly, Sean sits up straighter—like most guys, he slouches. "I just had another thought. What if we hook some of these tentacles to the ends of those quantum tunnels—the ones your Dad, Dr. Durai and DARCH have strung all over the solar system. Your Roxies would be really handy on Luna and on Mars, a lot better than what they have now to produce food there which mostly tastes like crap I hear."

"That's outstanding," Naya says placing her hand on his shoulder when she says this. Sean shivers when she makes contact with him. "I'll talk to my Da about it!"

Later, she tells him how she talks to her Godmother, Nell, since she is born and that it is Nell who saves her that night in the bush at Pops' place when Naya was at the bottom of a deep pit and about to exit this life prematurely.

"I'm glad you didn't die there, Naya."

"I had a vision," Naya continues as if she doesn't hear him, "not only about Roxie but about another trip we are all going to take. It's a voyage."

"Where, Naya, where?" Sean is completely spellbound now by her.

"It's a voyage to an Earth with human population of 1.2 billion souls instead of the 10 billion we have now. It's a place where 95% of all lands are returned to nature, where we won't need farmland or pulp or quarries or mines. We'll have a living of standard many times what we have right now with a much smaller environmental footprint and a lot more free time. If you want Rhino horns cuz you think it makes you more virile, you can get it out of Roxie instead of hunting them illegally. Want dolphin penis in your sushi, order it from Roxie. Leave our cousins in the sea alone, fuck you very much."

She's getting upset and she has to take a few breaths to calm herself down.

"There's more—

But before she can continue, Cliff is there to pick her up. He never goes anywhere without a large retinue of followers. He comes sweeping into her lab, says hi to the dumb shit working as some kind of wage slave lab tech he supposes and grabs her. They're heading to a company sponsored event—it marks their 13,000th store opening.

"Come on baby cakes," he says in his false retro hipster way, "it's time to make some history."

...

"I want you to entertain three of my suppliers," Cliff tells her later.

They don't look like suppliers more like financial types or lawyers. They're in their 30s or maybe 40s, it's hard to tell with these hipsters.

"I'm not going to do this anymore, Cliff. You'll have to get another girlfriend—"

He slaps her and then punches her sternum hard then grabs her right nipple and twists viciously. "Don't you ever talk to me like that, Naya. You'll do what I tell you to do like always or I'll hurt you and then your family. You're

472   Bruce M Firestone

a bad girl, Naya. You know it and so do I."

So she goes into the master bedroom and gives them all a blowjob. It doesn't take long—they're pretty het up about having infamous actress Miss Naya Brooks Bell on her knees in front of them.

Cliff sits in a nearby armchair. After she finishes with the other men, it's his turn to degrade her and he has many ingenious devices and methods he'll use tonight. The men all stare in wonder at his bravura performance, all recorded for Les de Sades.

...

While working alongside Naya the next day on their now combined project, it's obvious that something is wrong with her despite the ridiculous amount of makeup she is using. Sean, who is from Southie, knows a thing or two about abuse. She has a red welt on her face that is clearly the imprint of a large hand—a man's hand. He wants to ask her about it but he doesn't want to pry. With Naya, it's complicated. He understands that. Her brothers warned him about it but they clearly don't know what is really happening.

"What are you looking at?" she asks.

"Nothing."

"Well focus on your tablet not me."

"OK," he says mildly. Then she bursts into tears. She leaves the lab and Sean isn't sure whether he should follow her or not. He can't help himself. He follows her.

"Naya, do you want to tell me what's going on?"

"No."

"Don't you trust me?"

"I do. I just don't want you to get involved."

"But I am involved. Look at it this way—if it affects your work, it affects mine too. So tell me."

She smiles ruefully at him through her tears. "It's dangerous, I think."

"It can't be anything like Belfast or Southie?"

"It's worse, Sean." She never calls him 'Micky'. It's

degrading.

"I'm not afraid, Naya. I can handle myself."

She knows enough about him to know that this is a true statement. He is Irish Catholic tough. But she doesn't want to tell him, in part, because he'll think less of her. He has these hangdog eyes that practically worship her, she's not blind to that. But she doesn't deserve his respect or friendship. So she says nothing.

"Let me guess, that poof you are dating hits you. He looks like a moron with that stupid haircut of his and he minces about like a spastic shite on amphetamines which I'm sure he takes so he can stay up all night and party with his crew and he takes roids so he can lose weight and stay fit which makes him even more unpredictable. The roids are affecting his ability to get it up so he has to demand more and more weird sex—which he likes anyway—from his partner which is you. You put up with him because you don't think you deserve any better but you do Naya. You don't want to tell anyone because you do know better and you are ashamed to tell anyone and you can't reach out for help anymore than you could when you were 15 and in trouble. You are also afraid if you do, Cliff will hurt them like he is you. Did I sum it up OK or what?"

She has to smile at his acumen but then she realizes it makes no difference—wherever she goes, Cliff will find her, his people will come after her and everyone around her will suffer, maybe even die. She is sure that Cliff is capable of murder and may already have done a few snuff films.

"Look forget it. Let's just go back to the lab. I'm better now, really."

"Oh, shite on the lab, Naya. You have to get out of there."

"I can't, Sean. He'll, he'll kill me if I leave and you too and maybe Holly," she says 'Holly' really, really quietly.

When she says Holly's name, she sees a complete

change come over now 20-year old Sean's face. "He's had her followed?" he asks in a very low, hoarse tone.

"Yes, I think so. His security people like to know who is around me. They have files on everyone."

"Not for much longer," Sean says.

"Look Sean I don't want you to tell anyone or do anything. I'll be alright. You can't tell my Da or Dekka. It'll start a war."

"I won't tell a soul. I promise, Naya."

He gets up to leave then turns back. "Did he hit you anywhere else?"

She lifts her blouse. He can see bruises on her sternum where Cliff punched her and her right breast has been hurt somehow. He motions for her to turn around and he can see obvious manprints around her narrow waist where Cliff grabs her for rough anal sex.

"Did you check for hematuria?" he asks her.

"What?"

"Blood in your pee. Are you bleeding inside, Naya?"

"I'm OK, Sean."

"Naya, you've experienced blunt trauma. If you're bleeding inside, you won't know it until it renders you unconscious or dead. I want you to go pee in the toilet and don't flush. I'll check it. It's not always obvious."

"Alright." She turns to go to the Ladies.

"Wait a sec. Come here." He takes her pulse and looks for signs of anemia.

"You still have the heartbeat of a dancer, Naya. That's good." He smiles encouragingly at her.

"What is it?"

"52 beats per minute."

Since her heart rate is strong and steady and her face is not abnormally pale, he thinks she's probably in the clear on this account.

"Are you cold, Naya, or experiencing any numbness anywhere?"

"No, Sean."

"OK, go on then."

He checks the color of her toilet water—it appears to be clear and normal for her. This is a relief because if she is experiencing internal bleeding, no first aid will help her. He will have to take her either to a doctor or clinic and that will just bring them into contact with officialdom and police and Sean is sure this will lead back to Cliff. That guy's got connections.

So he tells her to wait for his Uncle Des to come by and get her. The Irish will hide her and Holly in Nocal for a few days. Then he'll come get both of them and take them to Nahuel in Third Mesa on his fast Kill-e-cycle.

"Where are you going?"

"I'm going to have a talk with Clifford."

"That's all you'll do, promise me, Sean?"

"Of course, Naya," he lies.

"Don't you think that maybe my brothers should go with you?"

"Absolutely, not. Don't tell Finn or Magellan anything, Naya. Promise me? Not a word to anyone, not even Des, OK?"

"Alright."

"Not a word," he tells her again making eye contact with her for extra emphasis.

They'd only get in his way. Before Sean visits Cliff, he has to stop by his place and get a few things.

...

"Hello, Mr. Mukono."

"Hello, Erik. Long time."

"What's so important that you have to come to Toronto from Lagos?" Renke can't figure this out. Aziz, former CFO of Quantum Computing Corp, wants to talk privately. All of Ellen's old crew hates him. The feeling is mutual.

"I have a proposal for you."

"Uh, huh?" This'll be good. Maybe Ellen will try to buy him off. No chance of that. She's gotten him a Pulitzer and paid for his Muskoka cottage, his downtown Toronto loft and his nice black, top of the line Benz.

"We're organizing a group of ten investors."

"Uh, huh. What type of investment?"

"A private one, a very private one," says Aziz.

"And what would this have to do with me?"

"Well, let's just say it's an opportunity of a lifetime."

"Yeah, I'll just bet it is."

"Mr. Renke, how would you like to be part of a group that takes control of QCC II?"

"Eh? Come again?"

"How would you like to be part of a group that takes over ownership and management of QCC II and finally put the boots to that bitch, Ellen Brooks? She kicked me out of QCC, swindled me out of most of my shares before their IPO. It's payback time."

"And I get this extraordinary opportunity because?"

"Because you are a prince of a guy, Erik."

"I am not buying what you are selling, Aziz."

"Because you stupid, fuck, you are our Ace in the Hole. You are going to have a ringside seat at the greatest corporate takeover in history. We're gonna yank QCC II out of the hands of ratfink Angelo Keller and Ellen and ruin both of them. I am going to be President and CEO of QCC II, which I should have been anyway during its first incarnation which would have prevented its immolation under Brooks and you are going to head up our media relations. We're going to assassinate both of them, media wise I mean, and profit immensely."

Aziz when he is talking about Ace in the Hole is referring to one of Ellen's favorite old films—the one with Kirk Douglas as a corrupt reporter offering his New York services at New Mexico prices. The character he plays, Chuck Tatum, is on the run after slander and adultery have made him persona non grata in NYC. A middle aged local Indian artifact hunter, a simple but nice guy, becomes trapped in a mine collapse and Tatum manipulates the speed of rescue efforts to keep his story in headlines all of which Chuck gets to write. It's his chance to get back to the show. The rescue becomes national news and everyone comes to know the trapped guy through interviews he is able to do with Tatum. The rescue takes too long and the guy dies. The reporter has caused his death in return for a story. The guy's wife (an unsavory character herself) stabs Chuck with a pair of scissors.

Erik has no understanding of the reference—too bad for him.

...

Here's their plan. Aziz has incorporated MMC, Mukono Management Corporation. Ten investors including Erik, Aziz and eight others capitalize MMC with $15 million QED, $1.5 million each. It is a bit of a stretch for Erik but he can manage it by mortgaging and pledging assets like his home, cottage and Benz. Lenders are standing by to loan him the dough.

MMC will in turn incorporate MMC2 which will be capitalized with a $15 million investment by MMC. MMC now owns 100% of MMC2. Bain Carruthers, who apparently has a big on-going beef with Bessemer Ventures and wants in on this plan to give them their comeuppance, raises third party funding from outside investors (i.e., not insiders like Erik and Aziz). A total of $14,411,760 will be raised this way which will give those outside investors 49% ownership in MMC2 which now has capital on hand in the amount of $29,411,760. MMC2 will incorporate MMC3 and capitalize it with $29,411,760. Bain will sell another 49% of MMC3. After which the process is repeated until they get to MMC10 whereupon they will have a total capitalization of $6,411,280,440 QED. This is their war chest with which to launch a hostile takeover bid for QCCII.

MMC through a cascading system of control (owning directly or indirectly) 51% of MMC2 to MMC10 now controls over $6 billion in cash with an initial investment of just $15 million—that is, 99.767% of all funding comes from someone else. They plan to split a success fee (just on capitalization) of 3.5% or nearly $225 million. If (when) their takeover of QCCII is successful, they'll pay themselves another ginormous success fee (8%) of the takeover value of the corporation which is almost certainly going to exceed $200 billion QED. All this to say that Erik's $1.5 million investment will bring him 10% of all these fees less whatever they pay Cain. He's guessing that he will net somewhere between $900 million and a billion. Plus he'll be reporting on this story from the inside this time. He is right about the latter.

...

On the settlement date (the day when an executed security trade must be settled), there is a crash on Wall and Bay Streets heard most clearly in Toronto. There is no cash available for settlement of the largest (purported) takeover of any publicly traded corporation in the last three years. MMC10 fails to perform and the whole MMC structure comes unraveled. Turns out the only funds in this bizarre corporate structure belong to none other than Erik Renke. But the treasury of MMC is nearly empty—they had some unavoidable costs along the way after all and someone had to pay for them.

It is a fraudulent transaction and the only corporate directors that the SEC and CSC can find are Aziz Mukono (safely back in Lagos which has no extradition treaties with either Canada or the Commonwealth) and one Erik Renke who conveniently has a Toronto address. The RCMP picks him up.

Renke is denied bail—he's a flight risk—maybe he'd go to Nigeria? He has to apply for legal aid because his lenders have applied for and been granted Power of Sale rights over his assets of which now he has none. Legal aid lawyers aren't exactly top notchers; Renke is given 20 years for perpetrating a massive fraud on a scale of some of the biggest Ponzi schemes of the last century.

His dumbass plan is apparently to kite the settlement and make off with a billion or so in fees. The presiding judge just shakes his head at the audacity of Renke's plan which is almost as audacious as it is stupid.

His lenders are controlled by a pair of Vanuatu corporations—the kind where the shares of one are owned by the other and vice versa. Such ownership structures are virtually impenetrable. But if one could ever see through this veil of corporate ownership, one would find that they are controlled by the head of DARCH, none other than General of the Army (Retired) Farrar Staubach currently resident of the Melas region of Mars.

Melas Chasma is part of giant 4,000 km long Valles Marineris that cuts into the middle of Mars; it's a canyon with 9 kilometer walls—making Earth's Grand Canyon a minnow by comparison. It shades settlers from massive solar irradiation and storms as well as planet-wide hurricanes that whip up from time to time. When they get their quantum bubble inflated (soon), they'll finally be able to settle the surface.

Farrar's Vanuatu companies somehow decide to donate proceeds from the sale of Erik's real estate assets (anonymously) to the next Bay Area SKIP-AID but not the Benz. That goes to Toronto Soup Kitchen. They use it to ferry homeless people in world class comfort from the streets of Toronto to the Kitchen on cold nights to make sure, if nothing else, they get a decent hot meal.

One last thing Farrar does. He calls in a favor from the warden; he makes sure that Erik bunks in with someone at New Kingston Penitentiary who appreciates a nice warm tight concave orifice that has never been used before for anything except excreting. But Renke won't be a virgin much longer.

...

"What may I ask are you doing here?"
"I've come to talk about Naya."

"Ah, you're the lab tech. By the way, how did you get in here?" Cliff has defense-in-depth systems that are the most modern available and they should make it impossible for anyone to enter without his permission. If he placed less emphasis on technology and more on instinct, he would be quite worried about Sean's uninvited presence here.

"Mr. Hexham, here's my final offer—you delete all the files you have on Naya, film, video, background reports, EVERYTHING plus what you have on my sister, Niamh, and then you give me your word that you'll leave them alone."

"And what pray tell me do I get in return?"

"I'll be your friend, Cliff."

"I have lots of friends—"

"No you don't, Clifford, you only think you do."

"I suppose you think you love her. But she's only going to hurt you. By the way, what's your name?"

"Sean."

"Ah, Micky. I've read something about you. The police are looking for you, I, ah, believe for kidnapping a girl. You like fucking 5 year olds? It's been done before, even younger." When Cliff says this it looks to Sean like he is remembering. Sean goes white.

"She'll come back to me you know. She thinks I'll chase after her but I won't," he lies. "She'll want what only I can give her. You'll just be a momentary dalliance. Have you fucked her yet?"

He can see from Sean's reaction, "Ah, so you haven't. You come here, apparently unarmed, are you armed? And she hasn't even given you a taste. Hmm, you are naïve. She's just using you."

For a moment, Sean wonders. But then he remembers who the source is. This guy leads a cult, sure he's persuasive. But he's a liar. He's Satan or one of his disciples. Without thinking about it, Sean draws the sign of the cross in front of him.

Then he says from Psalm 22,

"Be not far from me (Lord);
For trouble is near;
For there is none to help."

He's alone in Clifford's study face to face with the Devil.

...

"So what are we to do?"
"I already made you an offer."
"And if I refuse?"
"The rest of your life will happen."
Clifford Hexham just laughs. He draws a small pistol. It's a lovely deep concealment gun—a XIL-Tech Q32 which means it shoots a puny 32 caliber bullet and pops out of a clip attached to his belt. He has a license for it not that it will matter. One of his de Sades will dispose of the body for him.

...

"You know Mr. Hexham, you should never draw a gun on an Irishman from Southie." Guns don't frighten Sean. He's had one or two waved in his direction before.
"Is that right, Micky. But then I am standing here," he says waving his pussy weapon this way and that, "and you are sitting there and only one of us is armed, wouldn't that be right?" Sean is about ten feet away.
"In a manner of speaking, that would be true."
"You know you should never have come here uninvited. No one comes here uninvited. If they do, they never leave again… alive. I quite value my privacy, Micky."
"Is that so?" Sean says. Cliff is not sure whether he is referring to his comment about never leaving alive or valuing his privacy. Doubt fills his mind but only for a moment.
"You know after you are gone, I think I will hunt down Naya and your sister and party with them both."

Bruce M Firestone

"You'll never find them."

"You think you can hide them from me and my *compadres*? We have vast resources, *police resources*, Micky."

"They won't help you, Mr. Hexham."

"We'll see. Pray tell me why one should never pull a gun on an Irishman from Southie?"

But Sean doesn't answer this last question. He's been watching Clifford. He's got his finger on a double action trigger, held carelessly in one hand (his left) which means when Sean launches himself out of his chair to his left, the gun has to swing right. Cliff is so jumpy, he'll stupidly pull the trigger which he does. The gun spits once. By that time, Sean has moved to his right and the gun swings back, reversing its arc. An overconfident Cliff overcompensates and fires a second time missing by a mile. He won't get to fire a third time because by then Sean's cosh, which he has whipped out of his right pants' pocket, makes contact with Cliff's gun hand, breaking it in three places. Cliff howls and drops the gun. Then Sean swings around backhand like he is throwing a flying disc and makes contact with Cliff's right temple. He goes down like he's a piece of sugar cane cut off with a razor sharp cane knife. Sean takes something off his backswing so he won't kill Cliff with his cosh.

He picks up Cliff's piece of shit revolver and holds it to his right temple. Cliff is face down, stunned and Sean has one knee on his back. The guy is made of nothing. Sean is stocky, heavy and very strong. Keeping Clifford pinned down is easy. He leans forward and says quietly in Cliff's ear, "The reason you never pull a gun on an Irishman from Southie is that you've just escalated it from a discussion to a deathwatch." Then he blows Cliff's brains out the other side of his head making quite a mess on the guy's marble floors.

...

Sean is sitting calmly at Cliff's desk. Odri4n, Uncle

Des' QE, has materialized in the room and they are both busy hacking into the recently deceased Clifford Hexham's files and those of 24/7 too. Sean and Odri4n are going to eradicate every 24/7 server in the galaxy and all their cloud files. They don't have time to be selective so they decide to nuke them all. 24/7 will spend the next two years trying unsuccessfully to recover from a total data wipeout. Then in a much weakened financial state they'll fall victim to a takeover by Green Stop.

Sean and Odri4n want to make sure they get everything on Naya and Holly. Odri4n is named after St Odrian, one of the first bishops of Waterford where the Ruanes originally hail from before fleeing there to look for work in Belfast and then fleeing there, fearing for their lives, for the United States.

As they are going through Hexham's files, a recent playlist pops up—it's a loop of video on Naya. After watching less than five minutes, Sean presses delete and writes over these files with a random number generator he brings along for these purposes. Then he goes over to Cliff's body, pulls his cosh out once more and beats every part of his body to pulp until he is covered in blood, feces, partially digested foods, bone splinters, arteries, brain tissue, cerebrospinal fluid, heart muscle, kidney, spleen, pancreas and bits of other organs. You would never know that this pile of shite had been a human being because, in fact, it wasn't. But he is the Devil's disciple no more.

...

Sean enters Cliff's house by releasing a specially designed set of nanosite deconstructors, first on the house monitor then on his security system and finally on his door locks. Basically, they eat the brains of the home and then all of its physical defenses too. Now he uses a separate set of nanosite deconstructors to do a cleanup of the constituent parts of what was formerly Cliff Hexham. They will reduce him to his basic elements and dewater him as well. They will evaporate the water turning most of him into vapor. They crawl all over Sean too cleaning him up as well—anything that has a trace of Mr. Hexham's DNA will be toast. Then all Sean has to do is use a tiny shop vac he also brings with him that holds about eight pounds of dust. The detritus he vacuums up will make fine fishfood.

Sean plans to do what Lennie, Sunny's black lab, did with the two fingers of the guy who also wanted a piece of Naya. These are the fingers that Squiggy takes off. Lennie decides to feed them to Pops' largemouth bass in his Lake. The bass are highly appreciative. Mr. Ruane is going to go to the Bay and feed the remnants of Mr. Hexham to the fish there. Then if anyone ever asks him if he knows where Cliff is, he can honestly say, he has no idea, he could be in a thousand places and probably is.

...

Chapter 14 Return to Third Mesa

Naya and Holly are wearing matching blue cotton bibs that are cinched at the waist and flare out into practical skirt shorts. Underneath they both have lighter blue v-neck, long sleeve stretchy yoga wear shirts. Naya has braided her hair and Holly's (one's auburn, one's red) into quadruple-flipped ponytails.

She won't let Sean leave the Walmart Supercenter in Redding (on Dana Drive) until she has all the right equipment which includes—brushes, rat-tail comb, spray bottle, at least a dozen clear hair elastics, something called an Oopsie Tail tool, hairspray and other accessories. 'What is it with girls and their hair?' Sean is thinking. Every time Naya is nervous about something she starts to unconsciously play with her hair—alternately braiding it, combing it, twirling it, flipping it or fluffing it with her hands. Then for something different, she'll drape it first over one shoulder covering her left breast then, sometime later, repeat only this time on her right side. Now Niamh is doing it too—it's contagious or something but apparently only girls can catch it. Instead of stopping for 15 minutes like he plans, they're there for nearly 45. He pays for everything in cash.

They're in Oregon. He plans to head to Third Mesa but not by going east like anyone in a hurry leaving Nocal might do. He's gone north instead and will circle around eventually passing through Boise and Salt Lake City before hopping on practically deserted alternate US Route 89A whenever he can. They'll pass nearly a dozen National Parks including Kaibab National Forest before reaching Third Mesa from the north. He avoids Vegas, stays off the Interstate Highway system and avoids cops. Odri4n is with him and can scan for police at distances that are truly remarkable so this is easier than you might think. He knows where they are at all times, so hiding from them in a thousand bolt holes available on these back roads is a breeze.

There are four people on Sean's Kill-e-cycle although, conveniently, Odri4n is reduced to the size of Tom Thumb and is currently part of Sean's motorcycle's headsup display panel so he is not taking up any physical space other than some Mtv real estate. His cycle looks like he's part of a hillbilly clan, he's got so much packed on it, a lot of it girl infrastructure maintenance stuff.

Sean feels like a poor Okie sodbuster migrating from a dustbowl farm circa the 1930s for the false promise of California. He hopes for a better result than what most of those folks ended up with. He can't believe they got over the plains, the mountain passes and the desert in things like 1924 Model TT Ford flatbed Three Quarter Ton Trucks with three generations of people and all their goods packed on top of a rickety suspension. Their maximum speed and power when new were 43 mph and 27 hp but by the time Okies got a hold of most of them, it was probably half of that. Sean is a gearhead.

He is also, as cops like to say, armed and (highly) dangerous.

They are on their third day out and so far, there is no sign of any pursuit but Cliff Hexham's disappearance and 24/7's data implosion are national news Odri4n tells him. He hasn't told the girls anything other than they're headed to Third Mesa. Holly can't think of anything more fun than to be on a road trip with her two most favorite people in the whole world including the most glamorous and smartest actress anywhere wedged between her and her brother. Naya is trying not to think at all.

Sean knows cops will want to interview everyone close to Cliff and that will include Naya who they will find is missing too. Then what is currently a big national story will turn into a colossal international mess. Sean is also remembering Cliff saying, 'vast resources, *police* resources.' Whatever else, there is no way he'll ever give up Naya to cops. That's just not going to happen.

"Are we stopping somewhere?" Holly asks. "I'm getting hungry." She says this quietly into her quantum mike which is attached to her white helmet. Both she and Naya have half shell white helmets that look more like spelunking than motorcycle ones because, well, they are. They sit cutely on top of each head. They are also both wearing goggles that automatically tint as needed and will protect them from sun and dust. Sean does not wear a helmet.

Holly is having trouble adjusting to Sean's rhythm— he makes two, one-pot meals a day for them—at brekkie and before nightfall. During the day he eats very little— some fruit and occasionally some bread. He makes tea.

Naya doesn't cook (she never learns the first thing about food prep mostly having had someone around catering to her including, right now, Sean, so this proves to be a winning strategy for her). Holly can cook a bit, but nothing that Sean (or Naya) would actually be interested in eating.

Sean knows that Naya is vegan so he is doing his best to accommodate her. Holly has just announced she's gone vegetarian too—this is a recent conversion for her happening as it did on their second day out of San Fran.

"Sorry, Holly, you'll just have to hold on. Eat some of the trail mix in your pocket."

Apart from an hour each day when they have to stop for Naya to rest (Sean plunks her under any shady tree or bush he can find and spreads out a sleeping bag for her) and time spent avoiding the police, Sean keeps going.

At one rest stop, he settles Naya and goes off to do some routine maintenance on his cycle. When he comes back, he sees not only Naya fast asleep under a creosote bush but Niamh and a passel of Canadian geese as well. The long neck of one of the females (geese that is) is draped over Naya's side, womb high. The rest of the flock (another female, two ganders and at least half a dozen goslings) are asleep on either side of Naya and Niamh. Niamh's on her side with her back to Naya and her head on one of Naya's arms. Naya's other arm is wrapped around his sister—they're spooning and the female goose is sort of spooning Naya. Sean has never seen anything like it. He asks Odri4n to record it. After that, he gently prods Naya awake.

"Naya, can you see this?"

"Yes, Sean. When did they get here?"

"I dunno. I wasn't here. This ever happen to you before?"

"No. It's nice. I can feel their heat. And your sister's too."

They are both whispering.

"How are you feeling?" he asks.

"At peace."

"I'm glad."

But then everyone else starts to wake up. One of the females starts to sample Naya's arm then Niamh's. She doesn't bite; she samples them and obviously likes what she tastes. They're friends now. But then one of the ganders starts to get jealous; he threatens the girls—first hissing at them and then scaring them by spreading his large wings (which can inflict quite a blow). It looks like he is preparing to bite them next.

"Time to leave guys," Sean says. Sean backs up while the girls skip away, holding hands and giggling.

"What would you have done if the Gander had attacked, Sean?" Naya asks after her giggling fit finally ends.

"I would have hit him with a lawsuit."

"A class action lawsuit!" Naya adds hilariously.

"A class of three! I volunteer to write up the report for *class*!" Niamh says, that is, if she ever can get back to a school which doesn't seem likely to happen any time soon.

More seriously, Naya asks him, "Are you looking for some place in particular, Sean?" She's quite content to drift along on his motorcycle forever.

"Yes, but it may be hard to find now. I know it's not far. It'll be overgrown. It's been abandoned since the early 20s." (He's referring to the 2020s.)

"It's part of Umatilla National Forest. We're in the Blue Mountains, girls. We're looking for some property owned by Costa Levendakis' family."

"I thought all the lands around here are owned by the State," Naya says.

"Most but not all. Costa and I went to school together. His family owned a huge number of newspapers in the time before the Internet ate their homework. They went out of business and most of their assets were lost in the Great Reset. But they still own about 4,000 acres of Umatilla and, so far, they've resisted State expropriation. But they don't have the money they used to so the place is really run down. We're going to hole up there for awhile."

He would really like to press on to Third Mesa but two things—first, there is a rule when being hunted, stop every once in a while to see what your hunters are doing and, second, he's really worried about Naya. He knows that she is sick as a girl (with epilepsy) and that if he presses too hard, what with recent events and all, she could have a seizure and he doesn't have any hope of helping her much on the road nor will he take her to a hospital under any circumstances.

Human beings are really good at spotting movement, not so much stationary objects. You can be six feet away from a police officer in the bush in broad daylight or just lying down on the grass a few feet away from a cop with a flashlight at night, as long as you don't move, make a noise, swivel your eyes in your head, breathe noisily or, worst of all, lose your guts and run like a fool, you are safe. Sean knows because he's done both.

"We're going to hole up just like Bonnie and Clyde

did," Holly says. Hollywood's just made a third remake of this classic story which she's seen—Holy Jumpin thinks her older brother and Naya would make a really attractive pair of banditos—take that ya dirty rats.

...

There is no way anything other than Sean's Kill-e-cycle could possibly make it into Costa's place. It is so overgrown that it's become a labyrinth which suits the place—Costa's grandparents, infatuated with their home nation-state of Crete, decide, with the practically unlimited resources at their disposal at the time, to recreate the earliest palace at Phaistos circa 1900 BC in an Oregon forest.

It is a fairly faithful rendition of Minoan architecture with flagstone paved courtyards, beautiful monumental stone facades, lightwells, baths, lustral basins, magazines (for storage of wine, fruits, foods, grains and water), marble revetment, 'royal' apartments, banquet hall and their own amphitheater. The only thing it's missing is a room for human sacrifice. The Levendakis had to draw the line somewhere but it does have a Greek Orthodox chapel.

Sean's not going to have a chance to show the girls any early Minoan architecture tonight. By the time they get there, it's nightfall, it's chilly and they are all done in, even Sean. He decides not to cook anything (he can cook using a hydrogen burner hooked up to his cycle's fuel cell); he gives them each some yogurt and nuts with a few raisins mixed in and some herbal tea.

"When were you last here, Sean?" Naya asks.

"There was a group of us; it was my last year of High School. We flew out together from Boston. Our parents were still alive then," he says wistfully. He misses both his parents every day; he sometimes finds himself (whenever something good happens to him, like when he first met Naya), wanting to call his Da and tell him. He actually has to stop himself reaching out to make a call.

"Were you with a girl?" Naya asks. Like most women,

she's curious about the people she is close to and wants details.

Sean just shrugs. When she presses him for more info, he says simply, "It was just me and Costa and a bunch of guys." Since no girls are involved, Naya loses interest immediately which Sean figures will happen. He is fibbing to her—there was a girl, just not THIS girl.

They sleep in tents that Sean brings with them— these are modern, lightweight tents that self fold into amazingly small packages (suitable say for carrying in saddle bags on a bike) and they are incomparably more comfortable than a ruined estate no matter how grand it once might have been. He tells the tents to inflate and to set their internal temperature to 72 degrees Fahrenheit. It'll be nice and toasty. The girls sleep in one tent, Sean in the other. Odri4n stands guard (he's at macro scale mimicking Sean's height but not heft since his weight is equivalent to a Dirac-mechanism generated mass of a neutrino (around 0.04 eV, electron volts) times 10 to the power of minus 23) and wake Sean if anything is up. Nothing is.

...

Sean wakes before the girls. He's got several choices of fruit for them, more yogurt and more tea (Naya does not drink coffee—it's one of the stimulants on her banned list of substances because of her seizures and because she has an addictive personality). He's also got a surprise for Holy Jumpin—when the girls are deciding on which hair care products to purchase at Walmart, he buys a few baguettes and a large bar of semi-sweet Ghirardelli chocolate—so he can make Chocolate Panini for her. He's been doing it for her even before their parents are killed and it's a favorite.

He slices the crusty bread to about 3/4 of an inch thick, sandwiches a bit more than 1/2 an ounce of chocolate between two slices, butters the outside of the sandwich and then cooks 10 of them in his one frying pan until they are golden brown on each side, pressing down with his spatula from time to time. He wraps them in tinfoil to keep them warm.

Holy Jumpin can smell Panini from a hundred yards. She ignores everything else and chows down three of the suckers. Her mouth is all over chocolate and her nightshirt has chocolate finger marks on both sides where she wipes her hands before grabbing another one.

Naya eats one of them as well as some pineapple and orange slices; she smiles first at Holly and then at Sean. It's a really nice smile.

...

They spend the morning exploring the place; Sean's doing his best to be tour guide but some of it is pure guesswork on his part.

There is an actual labyrinth in the place that Holly solves way faster than either Naya or Sean can. Sean tells her the story of the Minotaur and the annual sacrifice of seven girls and boys (he does not use the term 'virgin' with her). Her eyes get big when she hears that parents agree to let their kids be slaughtered like that. 'How can that be?' she wonders.

"Why is almost everything here made out of stone, Sean? They didn't use much wood in those days, I guess," says Holly. They are standing on a part of the planet blessed with immense and abundant trees yet everywhere she goes, it's stone walls, flagstone steps and plazas, stone lintels, stone arches, stone columns, stone benches, stone porches and balconies, stone retaining walls. You name it, it's stone (except their roof which uses orangish brown clay roof tiles).

"Well, Niamh, Costa told me that the Greeks think that when the Gods went around the world giving places like Oregon wonderful soil with lots of nutrients in it, when they got to Greece they ran out so they just dumped the leftovers there—rocks. So Greeks being practical and inventive types, built roads, plazas, homes, squares, theaters, markets, palaces, towns, ports and jetties out of quarried stone—they've got an unlimited supply."

"If they're so inventive why didn't they invent a few new gods who could fix it?"

"Well, maybe that was beyond their technical capabilities but they invented lots of other things."

"Yeah, like what?" a dubious Holly asks.

"Democracy for one. Women's rights so people like you and Naya could own a place of your own, vote, choose who you marry—"

"What? Girls couldn't choose their own guy?" Niamh asks looking first at Naya and then at Sean.

"That's right. They were considered property and a valuable resource—"

"Like a slave?"

"Not exactly a slave, more like a trade good."

"I'd trade you, Sean!"

"For what?" he asks.

"More chocolate Panini!" Niamh says.

"You don't think much of me?"

"What would you trade him for, Naya?"

"I don't know. Maybe a car instead of a motorcycle?"

"A town car like the mafia used to drive?" adds Niamh helpfully.

"A limousine?" Naya suggests.

"A tour bus?" Niamh trumps her.

"A double decker London Bus!" Naya says.

"A train à grande vitesse," Niamh says having just learned about those a few months ago when she used to go to a school.

"An airship!" Naya says.

"You guys are really funny," Sean says. "Ha, ha."

"What else did the Greeks invent?" Naya asks to mollify him.

"Well, they developed the watermill, screw, the gear, winches, water clock, wheelbarrow, canal system for raising and lowering boats and wind vane. They did a lot with mathematics—they understood prime numbers, for example. They were big in surveying and cartography, that's map making, Holly and—"

But Holly loses interest all of a sudden—she runs over to an enormous clocktower (made out of stone with stone steps, of course).

"Come on, Naya. Race you to the top!"

It's no contest since Naya can't run and Holly can, like the wind. Sean suddenly feels like a fifth wheel.

...

The afternoon is warm and while Sean is preoccupied with some work he is doing with Odri4n, Naya plans to take Holly over to the swimming hole after her nap. Holly, who hasn't napped since she was like three, now decides that she needs to have a quiet time too because, well, that is what beautiful actresses do to enhance their beauty. Both girls retire to their tent. It's team nap time.

...

After finishing up with Odri4n, Sean goes looking for Naya and Holly. When he comes to the swimming hole, he isn't sure where to put his eyes. Both Naya and Holly are swimming after their nap. They're in monokinis. They are splashing each other and fooling around. When he looks at Holly, well that's too weird. Even though he's her brother, he can't help but notice that Holly (now ten) is starting to get those female s-curves. Looking at Naya, well that's a whole other story. He's only there a moment and decides to turn around and leave them to their private play when Holly, totally unselfconscious, yells at him, "Sean, come on in!"

Sean shakes his head, 'No.'

"Sean, get in!" yells Naya.

Then he has a thought. He goes back to his Kill-e-cycle and takes out something—it's a Pops Superflyer XIV.

He goes back to the water, strips off everything except his black briefs, dives in and surfaces holding his flying disc. He leaps out of the water and throws it 15 yards to Holly who is a top Ultimate player in her age group. She snaps it out of the air and with a single fluid motion uses a forehand throw to expertly send it Naya's way. Naya muffs the catch and then throws it vaguely in Sean's direction. Her throw is worse than her catch.

"You throw like a girl!" Holly says.

They play catch for a few more minutes getting closer to each other because anything beyond four or five yards is too far for Naya.

"Show me how to throw this thing, Sean," Naya commands. So he goes over to her to show her how to grip it properly for a backhand launch, how to let it go before it reaches the horizontal plane (so it flies level) and how to flick her wrist at the last second. He stands behind her, off to her right a bit to help her practice. Naya who is used to a lot of nudity (in dance and film) thinks nothing of this but Sean is profoundly affected standing next to the prettiest girl he has or will ever see wearing nothing but a red monokini that is a little bit more substantial (but not by much) than thong underwear.

After that, he has to take a break—he tells them he is going to do a few laps. While swimming, Sean mind's eye runs a movie of Naya playing in the water and laughing, how different from the Naya of Berkeley. He notices that the bruise on her sternum where Cliff punched her has faded but isn't entirely gone yet. When his mind runs that image, he wants to go back to Cliff's place and kill him again.

Naya notices that Sean has a very low percentage of body fat—he's just thick, broad but well proportioned and very strong. He has a light covering of manhair on his chest that unlike his head is a light reddish gold. She's not used to seeing body hair since most men her age now have hair removed everywhere including under their arms. It's all the rage but Sean apparently didn't get that memo or, if he did, paid no intention. Naya thinks it's a different look but not unattractive after all.

To call this a swimming hole is an injustice. The Levendakis take the stream from its original bed and run it into their palace to feed the public baths they have there. 'Public' refers to friends they invite to stay with them at Phaistos (Oregon not Crete); they often have upwards of two dozen guests staying with them, some of whom remain for an entire summer. Costa thinks they did things like party for days or weeks at a time and maybe trade partners but that could be rumor.

The swimming hole upstream from the palace where they play with their Superflyer XIV has sandy banks and large flagstone surfaces for outdoor picnics and dances.

When Sean's embarrassing reaction to Naya subsides, he turns around to see what the girls are doing. Naya is turning blue and is ready to get out. Both of them notice at the same moment that Holly is nowhere to be seen.

...

"Naya, where's Holly?" he shouts. He's about 25 yards away.

"I can't see her! She was just here!" The water is opaque three feet below the surface so finding Holly is going to be very difficult.

"Where?" Sean starts swimming over to her with powerful strokes but by the time he gets there, Niamh surfaces. She seems to be having trouble staying afloat.

"Holy Jumpin," she says. "I've got something. Help me Naya!" She is trying to swim holding onto a round object that is just less than six inches in diameter but it's heavy. Naya grabs ahold and the two girls swim ashore with it.

When he sees that she is OK, Sean yells at her, "Niamh, don't ever do that again! Always stay where I can see you!" But neither Niamh nor Naya are paying any attention to him. They're both looking at a reddish colored disc.

"What is it?" Naya asks.

"I dunno. Sean?" Niamh asks.

He has joined the girls by this time. Now that he has

something else to focus his fine mind on, he's not as bothered by their near nakedness. You can get used to anything he supposes.

He doesn't answer Holly right away. He takes the disc and looks at it—flipping it over then back again. He can see that there are unique symbols on both sides. They are hieroglyphs of some sort. There are 45 of them spiraling in a clockwise pattern to the disc's center. It is a tablet of fired clay with some kind of clear protective coating on it.

"Let's take it back to Odri4n and ask him."

"Hey, Sean?"

"Yes, Holly?"

"Can I keep it?"

"I don't know. It could be quite valuable."

"Well, I don't see why I can't."

"You can't because something that is unique has a lot of value. Potentially."

"It's not unique."

"How do you know?" he asks her.

"Cuz there are a ton more of them down there."

...

"This appears to be a copy of the Phaistos disc—a Minoan artifact dating from the Bronze Age. It has never been deciphered," Odri4n says. "The original is in a museum in the City of Iraklion."

"Where's that?" Niamh asks.

"In midwestern Crete—on the north shore," says Odri4n.

"But what does it say?" Niamh is full of questions.

"When Odri4n says 'It's never been deciphered' what does that mean, Niamh?" Sean can see that this is a teaching moment.

"Oh, d'oh. Sorry."

"When you say a copy, Odri4n, do you mean a modern copy?" Naya asks.

In an uncanny repetition of what Pet3r and Vl4d did years before, Odri4n says, "If I have your permission, I can use thermoluminescence to date this artifact."

"Will it destroy the disc?" Naya asks.

"No, but it may discolor a tiny fraction of it equivalent to about .013% of its surface area."

Naya and Sean glance at each other; they're in agreement. "Go ahead, Odri4n," Sean says for the two of them.

"Please back up and look away," Odri4n says as he generates an intense beam of radiation, heating a tiny portion of the disc. He calibrates the material for a few dozen seconds and then announces, "It appears to date from the Subminoan period, around 1100 BC."

"So it's not modern. How did it end up here?" Naya asks.

"That is unknown—there is no record of this artifact ever having been exported from Crete," Odri4n says.

"Legally," Sean adds.

"There is something else strange about this disc," Odri4n says.

"Don't hold out on us, Odri4n," Holly says rather rudely.

Odri4n stares at her with his large expressive yellow eyes. He says nothing for a few moments, an eternity as measured at his internal clock speed.

Sean is staring at Holy Jumpin too.

"Please ignore anyone under 20, Odri4n," he says.

"Well, there is a number here on what I take to be the reverse side that is not on the original." Odri4n is pointing at a number that is three horizontal bars with four dots on top.

"That's a number?" Holly asks unperturbed by the apparent rebuke from her bro.

"Yes, it represents the number 19 in base ten arithmetic, Niamh," Odri4n says.

"That's the decimal system we use," Sean adds for Holly's benefit.

"Who uses numbering like that?" Naya asks.

"It is Mayan arithmetic, I believe. They use base 20 instead of base 10. So 10 is 20, 100 is 400, 1,000 is 8,000, 10,000 is—"

"Wait a second, Odri4n. Holly if 1,000 is 8,000, what is 10,000 in base 20 arithmetic?" Sean asks. Another teaching moment arrives.

She thinks for a couple of seconds and says, a smidge less confident than her normal self, "160,000?"

"Very good, Niamh," Odri4n congratulates her. Naya smiles at Holly and then gives her brother a very warm look. He notices and blushes. All he can see in his mind's eye is that her smile looks a lot like her monokini seen from the back—her cute bottom, her cheeks there, smile at him whenever he looks at them; he tries hopelessly not to do that. He's got to stop running images like this in his head but he can't seem to help himself.

Sean says, "What do you suppose '19' means?"

"It's not the answer to everything," Holly says.

Naya says, "Huh?"

"The answer to the Ultimate Question of Life, the Universe and Everything according to Douglas Adams is 42," Sean explains in a way that is no explanation at all. "Niamh's reading my copy of the Hitchhiker's Guide to the Galaxy."

"Huh?" Naya repeats.

"You can read it with me, Naya! Then you'll get it!" Niamh says excitedly.

"OK. You're on, Holly." The girls smile at each other.

Odri4n takes this opportunity to say, "I conjecture that this is 19th in a series of these. There could be more—"

He is interrupted again. "There's way more of them! I saw them on the bottom!" Holly exclaims.

"Odri4n, has there ever been more than one Phaistos disc found?" Sean asks.

"There are no reports to that effect," he says.

"What I'd like to know," Naya says, "is—what is

Mayan arithmetic doing on a Minoan artifact?" Naya knows that Minoan civilization, even Subminoan culture predates the Maya by at least a thousand years probably two plus they're separated by more than 7,000 miles of tough terrain and ocean so there can't be a connection between a Minoan artifact and the Mayan numbering system, can there?

...

"Naya, do you want to tell me the rest of the story about Voyage to Earth? You never finished it."

She's pleased he remembers and even more so that he doesn't mention that it is Cliff who interrupts their convo. She shivers at the briefest recollection of Cliff and she is truly frightened for Sean and Holly, more so than for herself. She can imagine what Cliff will do to her, she's had lots of experience. But thinking about what he might do to Sean and Holly if he catches up to them is much, much worse.

Seeing her shiver, he asks, "You cold?" It's late afternoon and while it was above 80 at 2 pm, it's in the mid 60s now.

"No, I'm fine." She reaches for her sweater nearby and gives him a wan smile that says, 'See, all good.'

After a moment more to collect herself, she continues, "I don't think there really is such a thing as living in harmony with nature, Sean. We are part of nature and have always had an impact on our environment, just as all living species of plants and animals have had.

"So creating a sustainable economy is probably not possible if it means having no impacts on the environment. Perhaps we ought to be looking at a future where the impacts we do have on the planet are not so large as to cause other species to go extinct or cause permanent damage to oceans, rivers, streams and lakes as well as soils, the atmosphere and water table—damage that cannot be easily absorbed by the environment through dilution.

Bruce M Firestone

"If you think about North America, say 600 years ago, there were perhaps two million people living on this continent. When things got polluted and people started getting sick from their local environment, in those times, they could just move on. The environment could absorb their wastes fairly quickly and, a few years later, they could safely return.

"It is harder to do that today with more than 200 times as many people here and some of our wastes are likely to be around and be dangerous for at least 100,000 years. So what to do?"

"I don't know, Naya, maybe better tech will help mitigate the mess we are making. I know that I can deconstruct some of those waste sites and it won't take 100,000 years to do it."

"Tech will help, Sean, but then again, maybe not as much as we all think. Probably the only way to ensure we have a future is for us to take a Voyage to Earth, population 1.2 billion humans. I think we will have a planet with more Quantum Entities than humans, Mr. Ruane."

"How long will that take?"

"We won't see a world population of 1.2 billion until the year 2610 or thereabouts. It'll take 540 years, maybe more."

"You're kidding?"

"Nope. The reason is that when a society goes to a one child policy, their population tends to continue to increase simply because of the sheer number of females that can reproduce. Eventually, populations begin to fall. But even then, it falls slowly.

"Think about it this way. Say you have an isolated tribe of 100 people lost on a deserted desert island because of a recent plane crash. Miraculously, none of them suffer a scratch from the crash. Another miracle, they are a bunch of nice looking people who happen to be perfect breeding material needed to start a human colony.

Next assume that they are never rescued and they're on their own for all time. But they decide to be environmentally conscientious and only have one child per adult female. OK, so how long will it take until their population is down to say 50?"

"This sounds suspiciously like a television series, Naya."

"It was but answer my question."

"I don't know one or two generations—25 to 50 years?"

"Nope. OK, here's the score—let's assume out of our 100 crash survivors, 10 are kids and 10 are elders so there are 40 breeding couples. In the next 25 episodes (excuse me, 25 years), they each have one kid. But ten elders all die, either of natural or supernatural causes, we're not entirely sure. In any event, 25 years later, their population equals 100 + 40 - 10 or 130. So it's gone up not down!" Naya pauses and laughs at Sean's chagrinned face. "Hey demography isn't your field so cheer up!" She gives him a friendly nudge in his side. Even that brief contact with her warms Sean up again. He looks away for a few seconds.

"Pay attention, Mr. Ruane. It's just getting interesting. So even with a limit of one kid per adult female, 25 years later, the population is more not less. But wait a minute, the kids during that time (10 of them) have grown up and have formed 5 more breeding pairs. Again, another miracle happens—an equal number of males and females. Maybe all of those young couples have kids of their own as soon as they reach puberty or shortly thereafter. After all, it's a hot sweaty place with cute guys and girls running around without much in the way of clothes."

When she says this, images of Naya in her monokini come to Sean's mind.

"So maybe by 2093, the island has a population of 135 not 130. It's even higher than we thought!

"Now there are a total of 45 kids who have been born

504   Bruce M Firestone

on the island. Let's assume that 23 of them are women and 22 are men—that is pretty typical, women outnumber men anyway in the 'real world'. So over the next 25 years, each woman has one child, so there are 23 children in the next generation. And let's assume that 25% of the first generation (G1) breeding pairs die in the next 25 years after G2. Hey Odri4n, can you access my file LOST AND NOT FOUND and display the G1 to G4 results?"

That is trivial for him to do and he produces an Mtv display of it for them.

G1
Year: 2068
Pop.: 100

G2
Year: 2093
Pop.: 135

G3
Year: 2118
Pop: 135 + 23 - 20 = 138

"So even 50 years later, gosh, the population is still growing! Now in the next 25 years, the rest of the first breeding couples pass away. Now there are only 23 kids from G3 (again more females—12 of them), so there are 12 kids born in G4. So we have:

G4
Year: 2143
Pop.: 138 + 12 - 60 = 90

"Finally, the population is starting to fall. But it took 75 years before the Island's population started to show a meaningful decrease! So you can see, Mr. Ruane, it takes a long time. But if we don't do it, I think our planet is doomed or at least human people are. QEs can walk around a destroyed planet, rats and cockroaches will probably hang in as well but who would want to?"

"How long til your LOST AND NOT FOUND population dies out assuming they keep their one child policy in place? Did you run your model to a conclusion?" Sean asks.

"Yep."

"Can I see it?"

She's glad that Sean is interested in her work. Her previous boyfriend had no interest in it or really her except for what she could do for 24/7 and its PR machine and then again he had other uses for her too.

"Sure, read this." She asks Odri4n to call up the rest of her file so Sean can read the balance of her report for himself. She gets up to go check on Holly.

By Generation 5, you have:

G5
Year 2168
Pop.:
-10 (deaths)/Age 100
45 (living)/Age 75
23 (living)/Age 50
12 (living)/Age 25
6 (newborns)/Age 0
86 (people on the Island)

G6
Year 2193
Pop.:
-45 (deaths)/Age 100
23 (living)/Age 75
12 (living)/Age 50
6 (living)/Age 25
3 (newborns)/Age 0
44 (people on the Island)

It has taken 125 years for the population on the Island to fall by somewhat more than half!

G7
Year 2228

Bruce M Firestone

Pop.:
-23 (deaths)/Age 100
12 (living)/Age 75
6 (living)/Age 50
3 (living)/Age 25
2 (newborns)/Age 0
23 (people on the Island)

G8
Year 2243
Pop.:
-12 (deaths)/Age 100
6 (living)/Age 75
3 (living)/Age 50
2 (living)/Age 25
1 (newborns)/Age 0
12 (people on the Island)

G9
Year 2268
Pop.:
-6 (deaths)/Age 100
3 (living)/Age 75
2 (living)/Age 50
1 (living)/Age 25
0 (newborns)/Age 0
6 (people on the Island)

G10
Year 2293
Pop.:
-3 (deaths)/Age 100
2 (living)/Age 75
1 (living)/Age 50
0 (living)/Age 25
0 (newborns)/Age 0
3 (people on the Island)

G11
Year 2318
Pop.:

-2 (deaths)/Age 100
1 (living)/Age 75
0 (living)/Age 50
0 (living)/Age 25
0 (newborns)/Age 0
1 (people on the Island)

G12
Year 2343
Pop.:
-1 (deaths)/Age 100
0 (living)/Age 75
0 (living)/Age 50
0 (living)/Age 25
0 (newborns)/Age 0
0 (people on the Island)

This calculus of death is not very comforting to read about but what it tells you is that it takes a long time to reduce a human population to zero—in this case, 200 years pass before the Island loses its last (lonely) citizen.

This is why there are still a few people running around on Pitcairn Island today (one of the least populated places on the face of the Earth) who are descended from Bounty mutineers and their Tahitian companions, who settled there in 1790, almost 280 years ago, a similar time period to what we see above for our imaginary Island. Sound like coincidence? Demographers wouldn't think so. Of course, in the Pitcairn case, they wouldn't have had a 'one child' policy but disease, decadence, accident and other factors would have affected such an isolated population such that the effect might be similar to our Island.

The solution I provide for the Island is amenable to tracking individual age cohorts because we are looking at an isolated, simple world. It serves the purpose though of giving you some idea of how complex and tricky these calculations can be. Imagine if fertility rates change (as they almost certainly would) as the Island heads towards zero population. Or what if accident or disease rates varied or medical breakthroughs impact differently on different generations changing lifespans?

It also tells you why financial projections for things like

National Old Age Security Plans are so hard to do—they greatly depend on demographic trends, which can be hugely altered by small changes in either mortality rates or fertility rates or, indeed, immigration or emigration. For example, the number of working age people can quickly change by making small changes in any of these factors.

For the world population model, I use mortality rates and fertility rates to project population changes. Refer to the spreadsheet provided in Appendix I to this report.

After reading this part of her report (he asks Odri4n to bookmark the rest of it for him to read tomorrow), the question foremost in his mind is why this incredible female ever spent one nanosecond with an asshole like erstwhile 24/7 head honcho, Clifford Hexham?

...

They're in the large amphitheater and Naya is bundled up in two blankets. Sean, who appears immune to cold, has a long sleeved flannel shirt on and a vest. He's got a hydrogen powered lantern going.

Holy Jumpin is giving them a concert. She has a lovely voice and acoustics here are terrific. But they're about done for the night, Holly is getting tired. After her last song, she yawned so broadly, the top of her head nearly fell off. The sky above is clear (which is one of the reasons it's so cold—no cloud cover means no blanket in the sky to retain body heat for poor old mother Gaia).

"One more, please?" Naya demands.

"OK. Any requests?"

"I have one," Sean says putting up his hand politely.

"Uh huh?"

"Join the British Army!"

Holly loves this one. She starts to stamp her little foot (she is wearing clogs) and does a cute step dance. Sean starts slapping his knees keeping time with Holly so Naya does too. She can see that Holly would make a really good dancer if she and her brother ever get to stay in one place long enough for her to get decent training. They had to bolt Boston and now flee San Fran. Is that ever going to happen? Naya knows that none of them can ever return to Nocal, ever. It's all her fault. Her post grad work, her PhD? Gonzo. Then Holly starts to sing—

When I was young I used to be as fine a man as ever you'd see and The Prince of Wales, he said to me, "Come on join the British Army!"

Too ra loo ra loo ra loo, they're looking for monkeys up at the zoo. If I had a face like you, I'd join the British Army.

Sarah Comdon baked a cake; it's all for poor old Slattery's sake. So I threw meself into the lake, pretending I was balmy.

Too ra loo ra loo ra loo, I've made me mind up what to do

and I'll work me ticket home to you and fuck the British Army.

Sergeant Heeley went away and his wife got in the family way, And the only words that she could say was, 'Blame the British Army.'

Too ra loo ra loo ra loo, Me curse upon the Labour crew that took me darling boy from me to join the British army.

Corporal Duff's got such a drought, just give him a couple of jars of stout; He'll frighten the enemy with his mouth and save the British Army.

Too ra loo ra loo ra loo, I've made me mind up what to do

I'll work me ticket home to you and fuck the British Army.

Every Irishman loves this ballad especially the part that goes 'fuck the British Army.' Holly substitutes 'muck' for 'fuck'. Concert's over, everyone heads to bed. They'll be back on the road early tomorrow morning.

...

Sean is lying on his back in his tent with his hands behind his head thinking, 'This has been the best day for me and I am pretty sure for Niamh since our parents died.' He thanks God for this and turns on his side getting ready to go to sleep. But his day isn't over. It's about to get a lot nicer.

...

Bruce M Firestone

"Sean, you awake?"

"Yes. What is it Naya. Anything wrong?" He sits up immediately, alarmed.

"No, we're OK. I was wondering if I could come in?"

"Sure, of course."

He orders the tent to open and it unfastens its front flap.

Naya enters. She is wearing a heavy white cotton nightshirt that comes down to her knees.

Sean orders the tent to reseal itself to keep out the cold, damp night air.

"It's chilly," she says.

"Umm, I could get you an extra blanket from the cycle."

"Can we talk?"

"Sure. But—"

"Just budge over."

Naya climbs inside his sleeping bag. Sean is totally embarrassed now—he realizes he is naked—he never sleeps in any PJs.

"Ah, what did you want to talk about?" he says to make conversation.

"This," she says and leans over him and kisses him softly.

Without understanding how it happens, Naya removes her nightie and maneuvers herself under him. Sean is mad with desire for her.

"Slow down, Mr. Ruane," she says smilingly and then holds him at arm's length. He helps her by supporting his upper torso with his powerful arms.

Maddeningly, she won't allow him to enter her more than halfway and even then she makes him freeze in place. Then she takes her long left arm and fingers and starts to stroke the part of him that is not allowed to enter her. It feels like she is milking him. She alternately strokes him then reaches even further down and squeezes his scrotum gently kneading his testicles releasing huge amounts of endorphins into his blood stream. Then she goes back to milking him. Finally, she takes her right hand and begins to massage her clitoris but in a way that not only can she feel it but he can too.

She can stroke, squeeze, milk and massage with both hands in time and with a rhythm that gets faster and faster. She is looking up at him with a fierceness that is intense and might frighten other men. But not Sean because he is looking back at her with an intensity that matches hers—remember this is a crazed Irishman we are talking about here even if he is young and relatively inexperienced and she clearly is not inexperienced. Sean doesn't give a fig for who she may have slept with or how many since she has decided to sleep with him, that's all that matters to him. Finally she removes both her hands and lets him plunge fully into her. While he is doing this she kisses him—her tongue enters and exits his mouth exactly in time with his thrusts. Finally, she stops this and presses him fully to her. She is now concentrating on opening up as much as she can to him, accepting him as deeply as she can. Suddenly, she is also concentrating (her eyes now shut) on herself, her own needs and wants. This is a new experience for her. Sean explodes a few seconds after that. Interestingly so does she. It's the first time she has ever come with a man inside her.

…

"I should go. I don't want Holly to wake up and I'm not there."

"OK."

"I don't want to go."

"Tá grá agam duit," Sean says. It just comes out of his mouth.

"Don't say that to me, Sean."

"It's true. Do you know what it means?"

"I can guess. It's Irish, right?"

He's glad she knows that it's not Gaelic. It means, 'I have love for you.'

"Would you prefer if I said it in English?" he asks with a nice smile.

"No, just don't say it, ever."

"Why not, Naya?"

She just looks away. He knows enough about her to not touch her right at this moment.

"Tell me."

"Because I don't deserve it. I've gotten you and Holly into a complete mess."

He answers her now the only way possible—he kisses her and they make love again with her on top, mostly. Just before dawn, she does head back to her tent.

Sean knows that he can't tire her out so he lets her sleep in—they won't be making any miles today; it's raining.

...

Sean and Odri4n figure out the stream system that the Levendakis' have going here at Phaistos. They divert the stream into a secondary channel so there is no additional recharge into the pool. They turn valves and experiment but, without power, the pumps are useless. Sean brings over his Kill-e-cycle which produces a lot of juice and they macgyver it.

"I estimate it will take 8 hours and 42 minutes to drain this volume of water at current pump velocity, Sean."

"OK, let's find something else to do."

...

It keeps raining steadily all day and Holly is like a caged animal. Finally, he conjures up a makeshift poncho (a piece of blue tarp with a hole cut in it for her head) and sends her off with Naya in a light drizzle telling them to stay within earshot of him and the palace. Meanwhile, he asks Odri4n to show him the rest of Naya's report about Voyage to Earth—

We estimate that if our species were to act to reduce its

headcount to about 1.2 billion (around where it was in the year 1850), we would be able to—a) still have a post modern economy with all the bells and whistles (good health care, good economic prospects for ourselves and our children, cool tech, decent education, etc.), b) reserve 80% (possibly as high as 95%) of the planet for connected wilderness zones where people seldom or never go, c) achieve a sustainable economic equilibrium, d) maintain and improve our political and cultural institutions, e) make demands on the planet's resources and ecology that are responsible.

Humans may be suffering from a too-may-rats-in-a-cage psychosis. There isn't a square foot on this planet that is not claimed by one government or another (and often by many as in the case of Antarctica). What if we suddenly decided to somehow depopulate the planet from a total of nearly ten billion to one billion via war or disease (not quite like in the book, The World Without Us, where the hypothesis is that ALL of the people mysteriously disappear one night—possibly they get whisked away by aliens or go off to visit Jesus?)

I am afraid that power abhors a vacuum and that we would be more likely to end up like the survivors in Stephen King's The Stand, at war in no time at all.

So I decided to see what might happen if every nation adopted a one child policy (actually in my model I use 1.1 children per adult human female), how long would it take to go from a population of 10,000,000,000 to 1,200,000,000 souls?

The calculation is surprisingly difficult and I must apologize in advance to demographers for—a) the many assumptions I make and b) any errors in the calculations which are wholly my own.

Demographics is a complex subject where small changes in behavior can make huge differences in outcomes. What if men were to adopt the practices of post Civil War behavior and marry and father children in their later years? This type of thing can wreak havoc with forecasts. So you are welcome to question my assumptions and substitute your own. Nevertheless, I believe the broad sweep of my conclusions will stand up.

Here are some of the assumptions I made—

- World Population is now around 10 billion.
- Under certain assumptions, it will grow to 11.4 billion by

2110.

• Average life spans will continue to increase, eventually reaching 122 for men and 130 for women.

• The mortality rate will be around 0.92%.

• Females make up 50.5% of the population.

• Females will have on average 1.1 children during their lifetimes.

Unbelievably, with these assumptions in place, it will take more than 540 years to reduce the population from today's level to a point not seen since 1850 even with a universal 'one child' policy.

(Naya puts all of her calculations in an Appendix which Sean also reads.)

To me a future world with 1.2 billion souls is not very interesting if we have to go back to having short, brutish lives with economic and governmental systems based on, say, medieval practices. In a book by Bill Bryson, *Shakespeare: The World as Stage*, he describes conditions in England at the time of Will's birth (1564) this way: "But plague was only the beginning of England's deathly woes. The embattled populace (...which had fallen nationally by 6% in the decade before Shakespeare's birth...) also faced constant danger from tuberculosis, measles, rickets, scurvy, two types of smallpox..., scrofula, dysentery, and a vast, amorphous array of fluxes and fevers..."

Folks today have NO IDEA what conditions were like even in the last century. The Spanish Influenza pandemic of 1918/19 killed around 50 million people world-wide and as many as 40 percent of the world's population became infected. Anyone hankering after the 'good old days' and a return to nature have no clue as to what they are really wishing for.

So part of my calculations entailed asking a second question—what would the growth rate in personal productivity have to be so that by the year 2610, we not only had a population of 1.2 billion but that population was capable of producing the same volume of goods and services as we do today?

I used PPP (Purchasing Power Parity) to calculate the true state of welfare in the world today. It is not fair to compare, say, the welfare of someone living in a pricey state like Switzerland with someone living in a low cost/low wage country like

Namibia where one AU Dollar presumably buys more goods and services in Namibia than it would if converted to Swiss francs and used there.

Now understand, I am not saying that the world would produce the same goods and services in 2610 as it does today. I am saying the total value would be the same—but the mix of goods and services would be vastly different. Presumably, there would be a much lower energy and labor content and a much higher content of capital, management and QE input and it would be infinitely more environmentally friendly.

But it turns out that productivity over the next 500+ years would only have to increase by 0.4526% per year to maintain current volumes. Non-farm productivity growth in the old US from 1947 to 1973 grew at 2.88% per year. It slipped to 1.30% from 1973 to 1995 but accelerated to 2.8% from 1996 to 2001. It was much lower during the reset of the 2020s but still higher than 0.45% and it accelerated sharply with the advent of quantum economics which coincided with the arrival of quantum people on this planet. So for the world to produce the same volume of goods and services even with the population falling, we would only need to see less than a 0.5% increase in world productivity over the next 540 years. Easily achievable for super smart creatures like Homo Sapiens and quantum people.

And that would mean an incredible increase in the welfare for humans living on this planet in 2610—1.2 billion people would enjoy a lifestyle with more than 5.5 times the PPP of a person living in 2070.

Now I think that we are likely to see this happen even without government dictat. Reproduction rates are falling practically everywhere approaching the one child per adult female. So maybe the future isn't quite so bleak for our planet.

Here are a few things we might consider doing during our Voyage to Earth Population 1.2 Billion—

1. Cities can save us. In the latter part of the 20th Century, Khmer Rouge rousted over three million Cambodians out of Phnom Penh in a matter of a few days. The Khmers were enamored with the idea that the proletariat and the peasant were the ideal form of human culture. The forced evacuation of the capital of Cambodia killed millions of their citizens not to mention that it was also an environmental catastrophe due to

rapid deforestation as desperate people tried to live, cook and survive for the first time in a forest environment. Every nation in recorded history that has denuded its lands of tree cover has ended up destitute.

2. Preserve wilderness. Many urban planners like to think that an urban park is an environmental issue or that chopping down a diseased tree is also an environmental issue. An urban park is no oasis for wildlife. It is a place where cities apply various poisons to get rid of weed infestations, where our kids play in a soup of potentially harmful chemicals, where the only living creatures other than kids are rodents and other pests (squirrels, chipmunks, skunks, bats, mice, rats, raccoons, etc.) Do you know where wilderness truly exists—it exists only where humans are not allowed to enter. We should reserve at least 80% of the planet for connected wilderness areas where people NEVER or at most seldom go.

3. Reform agricultural practices. Our Roxie project can potentially free up vast tracts of land for a return to nature.

4. Produce more goods and services locally. Everywhere an artisanal movement of local production has taken off in the last 60 years so has their local economy.

I am sure there are hundreds more things that we can and should be doing. But one thing I am certain of is—we have to be careful. I have already said that for a thing to be environmentally sustainable it also has to economically sustainable.

The economic value of a thing reflects its inputs—capital, labor, energy, management, QE work. In principal, the higher the cost of a thing, the more capital, labor, energy, management and QE work went into producing that thing. Energy balance and eco balance calculations are fiendishly complicated, especially if you are doing whole lifecycle calculations that include decommissioning a product at the end of its economic life. What I am trying to get at here is that we cannot make assumptions based on hearsay evidence or because we happen to like the sound of one thing more than another. We could easily make things worse not better.

I completely understand the argument that economic calculations may not take into account all environmental impacts; but that doesn't mean we throw out 10,000 years of marketplace behavior. It does mean that we have to price-in the costs of decommissioning and the costs of using the natural environment, in my view…

After getting this far in her document, it's almost time for dinner which means Sean has to make it.

…

He's doing another one pot dinner meal (the only kind he makes, in part, because they only have one and, in part, because that's all he knows how to make). This one is a Basmati rice dish with fried onions, cardamom, cloves, a few sticks of cinnamon (broken up into pieces that are about an inch to an inch and a half long), turmeric and green peas. He usually finds a way to add some protein to these meals he is preparing for his group that now includes two vegetarians by throwing in some lentils or couscous but they would just muck up his Indian rice dish. So he'll give them cheese and nuts for desert and what's left of his supply of baguettes.

"It's Indian food that you are supposed to eat with your fingers. But only with your right hand."

"Let's eat with our fingers!" says Holy Jumpin.

"Why only your right hand, Sean?" Naya asks. All day, they've been looking at each other with longing but, not wanting to let Holly know anything has changed, Naya restrains the impulse to go over and put a big wet kiss on Sean's manly lips with her soft, luscious ones. He's been thinking similar thoughts all day.

"Well in India before they had TP (toilet paper) which they couldn't afford then, you washed your bottom off but only with your left hand. You kept the right one as your eating utensil."

"Eew, that's disgusting, Sean." Holly says.

Naya laughs and she and Sean exchange another smoldering look.

"Holy Jumpin, what gives?" says Holy Jumpin.

"What do you mean, Niamh?"

"You two look like girls in my class who have crushes

on each other, passing secret notes back and forth all day."

"We are not passing notes back and forth all day, Niamh," says Sean indignantly.

"Ah, yes you are."

Naya bursts out laughing.

"So, you guys getting married or what?" Holly asks in the direct manner of a child who gets right to the nub of the matter in seconds something that adults, especially ones as complicated as Naya, might take years to do.

...

Everyone is cold so pretty much right after their meal, they all turn in. Naya does not visit him but he sleeps like a baby anyway—Sean is pooped.

...

They are standing around the drained pool. It's early morning. There are exactly 400 discs that have been hidden there. Each one is different.

Odri4n has a complete scan of each disc. Sean holds them up one by one and then when Odri4n is done, he turns it over and Odri4n scans the other side. Sean asks him to peer inside the inner structure of each one as well. Good thing too because in the middle plane of each disc there is a whole other set of instructions. At least, Sean thinks they are instructions.

"I think that is the primer," Sean says.

"You mean like priming a pump or your cycle, Sean?" Holly Jumpin asks.

"No. It's something that teaches you how to decipher something else. It is either in a code you already know or possibly in another language you know or are supposed to know. It's like having a key to an apartment building, Holly, and then once you're inside, you need more keys to get inside each separate apartment. This is the key to the place that holds the other keys that lets you read the whole message."

"It's like *primary* school!" Holly Jumpin says.

"Right!" her brother looks at her proudly.

"Why would they put their primer in a place where you couldn't see it and, if you did, you would destroy these discs to read it?" Naya asks. "Not everyone has access to quantum scanning and certainly not anyone who lived before the quantum era began so what's the point?"

"It's kinda like they put them here so we would find them!" Niamh says.

"Yes but who are THEY?" Naya asks.

Sean and Odri4n both shrug.

"The numbers 381 to 400," Naya says pointing to a collection that is obviously placed in its own grouping. "What are those symbols, Sean?"

"That's Dirac notation."

"Paul Dirac?"

"Yes. How did you know that?"

She tells them the story of what her Da and Nell found below the tri-pyramid structure at Marco Gonzalez and how Damien has been working on deciphering it ever since with pitiable results so far. For some reason, she leaves out the fact that Traian and Dakota, JEL's Dad and Mom, are also there.

"Do you think these things could help Damien figure it out, Naya?" Holly asks her.

"I don't know. But he'll want to see this for sure. Odri4n, can you send a message to my Da and the data set to Pet3r too?"

"Absolutely."

She records her message and Odri4n sends both.

"Guys," Naya asks, "how could Paul Dirac's notation created by him in the early part of the 20th Century get inside something that dates from 1100 BC?"

Sean and Odri4n look at each other. Odri4n shrugs. "Maybe your Da, Naya, can tell us," Sean says.

...

Like the kid she still is, she is persistent. "So can I keep it?"

"No," Sean says putting the disc she found back

exactly where she found it. It's obvious where it goes—the shadow of where it has been pressed against the bottom of the pool for a long time tells him where it was.

At his signal, Odri4n diverts the stream back to the main channel and the pool starts to fill up once more. The discs are hidden by the water within half an hour. It's time to leave.

"You're mean Sean!" Holly says to him.

"Look, Niamh, it's my view that archeologists should dig up the past, examine what there is to be found, record it, then put everything back and rebury the stuff."

"What a waste of time! That'd be like digging ditches and filling them back in—make work stuff like my teachers always make me do!"

"It's not the same at all. They gain knowledge."

"But they don't get to keep the stuff, right?"

"Mostly, these days they just send it to a museum but some of it gets sold on the black market."

Holly knows what a black market is. She and her brother have been running from the police for a long time so there are lots of things they can't get legally like ID, medical insurance or even sometimes schooling for her.

"So if it goes to a museum, that's OK?"

"Nope."

"Nope?"

"Why not Sean?" Naya jumps in.

He doesn't really want to answer this question in front of his sister.

"Sean?" Naya repeats.

'Are all girls this relentless?' Sean asks himself. He takes a deep breath. "Well, look. Everything that's ever been dug out of the ground, I mean everything. Stuff that is thousands of years old. All of it, in museums, in private collections, is doomed. None of those institutions are gonna last. They are all temporary. Look at what happened to the old Republic of the United States! Totally dominant at the turn of the Century, broke, corrupt and finished off by your Mum, Naya, less than three generations later! This, this," he says pointing to imaginary museum buildings and to the ruined estate of Phaistos (Oregon), "is just temporary, ah, (he was at first tempted to say 'bullshit') crap that will go back into the Earth soon enough. Let Gaia protect what she has protected way better than humans ever could do and she's been doing it for eons. Stop lying to ourselves! We're not as smart as we think we are. It's just hubris to think that we can take care of things better than Mother Earth. Everything we build is going back into the ground over time through fire, flood, earthquake, war or other catastrophe."

By the time he's finished, he's really upset and breathing hard.

"OKAY, OKAY, I was just askin," Holy Jumpin says.

Naya goes over to him and puts one arm around him. As soon as she does this, Sean calms down, his breathing returns to normal and he feels better almost immediately. Just the smell of her is enough to trigger these reactions in him.

...

They get to Third Mesa on their tenth day out of San Fran. They have some close calls with State troopers but no real problems. They find that Ellen is there—she's been frantically looking for Naya—the news is breathlessly inventing stories, everything from Naya and the heir to the 24/7 empire have been kidnapped to tales that Cliff is seduced by soft-core porn actress Naya Brooks Bell and the two of them have apparently absconded with a fortune then wrecked 24/7's IT infrastructure to cover up their crime. There are rumors of weird sex, greed, intra-family struggle (between Cliff and his 100+ year-old father) and worse.

Ellen who is not normally demonstrative with her children hugs Naya and asks zero questions which for the former President of the Commonwealth and a mother is all but impossible.

She knows Sean and Naya introduces her to Holly. Ellen hugs Holy Jumpin and then Sean too for good measure. Ellen makes arrangements for the three of them but makes no comment when Holly moves her stuff out of Nell's old room into Sean's and Sean moves in with Naya.

Life is what it is when you are talking about Naya or, for that matter, anyone else.

...

Naya orders a sterling silver pendant from one of those service providers who promise overnight delivery even here to Third Mesa. It's easy for them actually because their fulfillment operations are not far away—they're in Lost Wages. It's the biggest industry in Nevada by far. Casino gambling is a distant second.

When Holly opens it up, she sees a beautiful 2 centimeter diameter Phaistos Disc on a delicate silver chain with a bevel mount. It is a faithful copy of the Phaistos disc that Niamh dragged from the water including the Mayan symbol for the number 19. The whole assembly is perfectly suited to Niamh's slender neck. This disc will save Niamh's life one day.

"Oh, Naya, this is the most beautiful thing I've ever seen! Oh, how can I thank you!" She runs over and gives Naya a huge hug. Naya gently strokes her long red hair. Then suddenly worried, she turns to her brother, "Can I keep it, Sean?"

"10-4."

"10-4?"

"Ah, that means, yes definitely!"

"OK, great!"

Sean looks over at Naya still hugging his sister and brushing her hair with her fingers. She looks back at him. 'God, I love this woman,' he is saying with his eyes. Hers are saying it too.

...

"They may come for her," Sean is saying.

"Yes, I think that possible."

"She cannot leave this place again. Naya must stay here, I think forever."

"You bring death here maybe. Hopi may die. We die before, we die now."

"Do you want us to leave?" Sean asks.

"She is daughter, sister, mother." Here Sean thinks he is referring, in part, to Ellen.

"Hopi live through spirit of woman. She stay."

"Thank you."

...

They do come for her on the seventh day after their arrival. 17 State troopers and a bevy of lawyers show up at the base of the canyon. They have a bunch of official looking California papers seeking to interview Ms. Naya Brooks Bell as a material witness in the matter of the disappearance of Mr. Clifford Hexham.

Nahuel, Hopi elders, four Hopi Marshals and Sean Ruane meet with them near the stream on the canyon floor. Sean looks at the group—some of them look like they would be right at home in Cliff's Club Les de Sades. The reason they look like that is because four members of their Central Committee (the innermost claque that runs Les de Sades) are there. Sean has to restrain himself from wading in and trying to kill them all on the spot.

The local Sheriff, looking mighty uncomfortable, says, "We have a court order to search your pueblo, Mr. Nahuel, for Ms. Bell who we have reasons to believe may be in the vicinity."

"What you want with girl?"

"We just want to talk to her. You saying she is here?"

"Why you want to talk?"

"We want to know if she is in possession of any information with respect to a missing persons report we have on a Mr. Clifford Hexham."

"She never come here. You find her, you tell us."

"OK, I'm alright with that Mr. Nahuel. Just let us

search your town and we'll be on our way."

"This Hopi land. You fuck off."

When Nahuel says this, the four Central Committee members move forward trying to surround Chief Nahuel. Sean steps in front of the Chief—he is a formidable presence. Everyone freezes.

"Now hold on there a minute everywho," says the Sheriff. "These here men have State papers that say they can search for Ms. Bell."

"You can wipe your ass with those papers, Sheriff," Sean says. "This is Federal land and California court orders count for less than these pieces of shite you've brought with you today." As he says this, he points at each of the four men he thinks are Cliff's people—he cocks his finger at each of them in turn like he is dry firing a handgun at them.

"Who might you be, son?"

"My name is Micky, ah, Micky Spillane." Near enough.

"You some kind of lawyer?"

"Yep."

"What type of lawyer are you son?"

"The frontier kind."

"Well, I think you should tell this here Chief that we are going to have to come in one way or another."

"I'm afraid Sheriff, it'll have to be another because there is no one in Third Mesa that has any clue as to the current whereabouts of Mr. Hexham."

...

By dawn of the following day, the number of State Troopers, Club Les de Sades members and private security forces has increased to well over 100, some of them on top of the Mesa, most of them in the Canyon below. The only way to get into or out of the Pueblo is via hand and toe holds—either down or up.

It is easy preventing access but also easy for them to prevent egress which means the men and women of Third Mesa can't easily get to their fields or jobs. They get hassled coming and going. Not too many tourists are coming for camel riding lessons either.

Nahuel has a force of nine Hopi Marshals, all of whom own hunting rifles but they have no real armaments. But Sean does.

...

"Nahuel, meet Odri4n."

"Hello."

"Nice to meet you Chief Nahuel."

"What you bring QE for?" Nahuel asks.

"Odri4n, tell him."

"I have scanned everyone at the base of the canyon and on the mesa above. We have a complete record of their DNA."

"How many?"

"There are currently 178 persons surrounding Third Mesa with another 15 in their supply chain providing them with coffee, nutrition and information as well as surveillance. We have a copy of their DNA as well."

"Nice. You tell what future illness they pass on to their children with DNA?"

"Yes, we can forecast what issues may come up with future progeny but DNA is remarkably resilient and we cannot be certain what those combinations and permutations will look like. Even for quantum computers, there are surprises."

"That's not the point, Chief. We have a record of their DNA which means, we, I, ah, can kill them all."

"You no do that, Mr. Ruane. You turn problem into war. They send more. They come next with bombs. Kill all Hopi." Nahuel is getting frustrated. The siege has been going on for almost three weeks. Everyone is jumpy. Their local economy is in the toilet and there are food and other shortages developing.

"I know that. I am not suggesting that at this time. We should cooperate with them to a point."

"You give up Naya to these...?" Nahuel can't find the

right word. 'Animals' would insult the animal kingdom.

"Never." When Sean says this Nahuel can see he means it.

"So what use DNA for? What cooperate mean?"

But Sean doesn't say.

...

The noise starts about an hour before sundown. It's fast paced rock 'n roll played at a level that overwhelms human senses. Human beings don't like having their hearing (in effect) taken away from them—it's one of their most effective defenses. In addition to economic pressure, the Les de Sades (that's who is obviously behind this whole show) decide to add psychological measures as well. They add random flashing lights too, not timed to the music so they are asynchronous and have maximum impact.

All night, the wail of monster electric guitar riffs, drum sets, head banger music of all sorts plays endlessly. Sean and Nahuel and the Marshals hand out cotton earplugs which do practically nothing to help but even a few seconds spent with each family seems to prop up morale.

Sean sets up a nutrient tentacle and fabricates quantum earbuds which cancel out all of the noise being thrown at them. But it takes him a few days to make several hundred pairs. By that time, people are really desperate.

Even with these new earbuds, they can still feel the pressure wave from the noise in their chests, sinuses and other body cavities so despite the fact that they can't hear it anymore, they know it is there—always.

...

International media have by now found Third Mesa again. It's this weird place in nowheresville Arizona with a bunch of Indians in it hiding a fugitive now thought to be directly implicated in the disappearance and possible murder of Clifford Hexham. Strangely, the daughter of the former President who herself was nearly assassinated in this place, has chosen this wretched spot to try to elude justice.

Interviews with the local Sheriff who says, "We are just trying to interview Ms. Naya Brooks Bell as a person of interest. She is not a suspect," are completely ignored. Obviously, she did it.

...

About an hour before sundown, the music finally ends. There is a blessed silence for two, then three, then ten minutes. People finally come out of their homes, taking out their quantum earbuds and asking each other, what's going on?

A few hundred people gather in the town square and along the lip of their wind cave to look out on the canyon floor below where media, cops, Les de Sades and by now 100s of other onlookers, curiosity and thrill seekers have gathered. Many of them are hoping for another Arizona massacre of Indians like the one in 1864 in Skull Valley. Soldiers lure a bunch of Yavapai families to a canyon west of Prescott and kill them all. They leave their bodies unburied. Others are hoping for something more telegenic like the 1993 burning of the Branch Davidian Ranch outside Waco where 55 adults and 28 children die in a holocaust after the ATF and FBI surround their compound and use tactics much like what the Les de Sades and their allies are using now. Maybe they'll get to see adults and children throwing themselves off the cliff either to escape fire or, better yet, actually on fire.

If Aziz could see the situation, he would immediately recognize it as a sort of repeat of Ace in the Hole.

...

People are starting to relax a bit—it's been more than an hour since the insane music stopped. It's just past sundown. But their ordeal is not over yet. It's movie time.

...

Bruce M Firestone

Images from Naya's latest (and what she hopes will prove to have been her last) film begin playing—at a scale more than 300 feet high. It is a marvelous Mtv production that can be seen clearly from all angles and from as far away as a half mile. Perfect for a desert setting like this one.

This is the film that Sean would not let Holly see. It's very graphic. But Les de Sades have edited back in much more explicit scenes that the studio had the Director and Film Editor take out so they could get an 'R' rating on their film instead of 'XXX'. These outtakes are bad but they've also added in random images from some other things that Cliff had Naya do which are much, much worse—Sean and Odri4n obviously did not get Cliff's entire library. Not surprisingly, Les de Sades have data caches that are not hooked up to the Internet and thus are much harder to detect and delete.

Sean is meeting with Nahuel when this all goes down. When he and Nahuel step outside to see what is going on, it doesn't take him long to react. He starts running for his room hoping to find both Naya and Holly before this goes on much longer.

When he gets to their rooms, neither girl is there. Now truly frantic, he runs east (the town square is west and he's just come from there) looking for them. He finds Holly at the far end of the wind cave. She is standing precipitously next to the lip of the canyon wall watching the horror unfold before her ten year old eyes. He calls out to her from 100 feet away but gets no reaction. He slows up, he doesn't want to spook her or run into her. Her toes are hanging over the edge.

"Holly," he says softly. "Niamh? Can you hear me?"

He gets no reaction. She's just staring at the film.

"Niamh, I need you to come over here. Can you back up a few inches, Niamh, please?"

Still no reaction. He eases a bit closer. She leans forward, away from him, perilously balancing over the precipice. She's in some type of catatonic state. He freezes. He is almost close enough to grab her. He is thinking, if nothing else, he can grab her long braid. It'll hurt if he has to pull her back by her hair but it's better than the alternative. It's hundreds of feet straight down to the canyon floor.

"Niamh, it's me, Sean. It's your brother. I am going to stand next to you but I am not going to touch you, OK?"

She doesn't say anything. Sean moves slowly sideways and comes to stand next to her with his toes also hanging over the ledge.

"You know mháthair and athair are watching over us right now. Ma and Da wanted us to go on. They love you, Niamh and so do I. There are some things in this world we are not meant to see—things that friends of ours—people like Naya—"

When he says Naya's name, Niamh flinches. He is reaching her.

Ellen has arrived on the scene. She is out of breath. Sean holds up his right hand and motions for her to stop about 20 feet away.

"Things that people who are friends of ours may have done, things that maybe they regret doing but which cannot be undone. Niamh, we are all flawed. We make mistakes. But it is not mistakes that define us but how we live our lives afterwards that does that. Do you understand? Now come away from the edge. Let's leave here. I'm going to reach out my hand, my left and I want you to take it with your right."

He reaches slowly for her hand and he feels the slightest back pressure from her little hand in his massive paw. Then he has her—he picks her up gently and brings her back from the ledge.

"Where's Naya?" he asks Ellen quietly. Ellen is watching the horror behind him. Her eyes go wide. "Ellen," he asks louder, "where's Naya?"

"I haven't seen her," she says still looking at the film

behind him where she can definitely see Naya.

"Ellen, turn away. Ellen!"

"Yes, yes, I'm OK."

"I need you to take Niamh back to her room. Wrap her up in a blanket, keep her warm and don't leave her til I get back. Not for one second, OK? Ellen! OK?"

"Alright. We'll wait for you."

Sean hands Holly to Ellen who has a bit of a hard time carrying her—Niamh is getting bigger by the minute but she manages it—at the end of the day Ellen is a Mum too and mothers can do whatever needs to be done when their kids need help.

"Where would she go?"

"I'm not sure, Sean. I ran over here when this, this abortion started playing. I don't know. Sean, you have to find her, please, right now."

Sean takes off.

...

It's hopeless. There are just too many rooms and possible hideaways in the pueblo for one man to search by himself. Odri4n is looking too but since there are few media walls in this place, he can't be everywhere at once.

Sean stops running. He can run PK (that's short for Parkour) efficiently and very fast around and over obstacles. He is the kind of kid who you could drop from a two story building or could come off his street skateboard onto harsh pavement at top speed, roll a couple of times, bound up and move on in one motion with zero injury not even a scrape. But this random search isn't going to work, at least not fast enough.

How is Naya going to react to having her people, the people of Third Mesa, hundreds of them, people who have known her since she was born, see her like this? She's going to want to put an end to it.

Sean slaps his forehead. He knows where she's gone.

...

Naya is on top of the Mesa in the lean-to where years

ago Nell brought her Da to experience what there was to experience that morning. Naya is frantic to get there, away from Third Mesa. She crawls inside. She can't see her movie from this vantage point but she can hear every scream, every grunt, every harsh command spoken in English and German (her Director being Austrian thought some of the dialogue, certain key parts of it, sounded better in that language. So he had his writers change Dr. ZinQ's character—they give him a German pedigree. She has to agree—he is right. Sadists do sound better in German.)

She can never go back to Third Mesa now. No one will ever look at her again and, if they do, it won't be the same. But Naya is underestimating the Hopi. They take Sean's view—it's not how many mistakes you make, it's what you learn from them that matters.

There is no place for her to go except back to the one place she belongs—Club Les de Sades. She drags herself off the floor. She's decided—she'll walk the Mesa til they pick her up. It won't take long.

...

Sean sticks his head in as Naya is getting up to leave.

"Go away, Sean."

"Nope."

"Please."

"Nope."

"I am not going to stay here. I'm leaving. I don't want you anymore."

"OK."

"OK, what?"

"You not wanting me anymore. Not the leaving part."

"Don't you want me anymore?"

"I didn't say that, you did."

"Well, I don't."

He just stands there calmly, implacably. He is smiling at her.

"What's so funny?"

"Nothing."

"Why are you smiling then?"

"It's always the girl who asks for a divorce."

"We're not married."

"That's true. Now why is that?"

"You wouldn't want to marry a whore, Sean. Didn't your father ever teach you anything?"

"Naya, never talk about me Da that way again." Naya has never seen Sean like this before. He's never talked to her like that either. Although she would never admit it, her respect for him just went up another notch. She was just being bitchy.

"I call my father, Da, too."

"That's nice."

"I'm closer to him than Ellen."

"You just have to give Ellen a chance, Naya. But mostly, you have to give yourself a chance."

"What are we going to do, Sean?"

"We are going back to the pueblo. It's dangerous up here on the Mesa. Those weirdoes are all over this place. We have to leave."

"Everyone hates me."

"No Naya. The only person who hates you is you. Everyone else knows that it's the people who make films like that who do Evil—they trade in flesh and slaves. Stop being a slave, Naya. Stop thinking like a slave grateful for a crumb from the table of your master. To Hell with that and them."

"But this can't go on. People here will starve. They might... die because of me."

"We'll think of a way, Naya, together." Actually, as he says this a new idea fully formed explodes in his head. He laughs—not a very nice laugh frankly especially if it's at your expense.

"Are you afraid?" she asks.

"Sometimes," he admits. He is really afraid for Holly but he can't say anything about Niamh to Naya. She'll only heap more blame upon her famous (now infamous) shoulders if he does.

"You don't show any fear."

"It's a front, Naya. But mostly I'm just mad."

"You're angry?"

"Pretty much all the time."

"Why?"

"Because we have all these school bullies running around this sacred ground pulling stunts like they did tonight and there is no way for me to get at them."

"You don't like bullies?" Now there's an understatement. Naya is talking to an Irishman; they've been bullied by the English—treated far worse than their dogs—for centuries.

"I can kill them all but Nahuel won't let me."

"I don't want you to do that either. Promise me, you won't do that? It'll make things worse not better. Sean?" She does not like the look on his face at the moment. It looks like he could really kill them. "Did you, did you kill Cliff?"

"He won't be bothering you anymore, Naya." As Sean says this, he has a faraway look in his eyes.

She can see he will never tell her anything else but in a way, he's told her what she has been thinking for a few weeks now anyway.

"I'll go back with you, Sean."

"Great."

"You know the part I said about not wanting to be your girlfriend anymore?"

"Yep."

"I didn't really mean it."

...

"Make love to me Sean." They are back in their room in the pueblo. Ellen is sleeping in Holly's room keeping an eye on his still catatonic sister.

He does not like the way Naya sounds. She reports earlier that she has a headache and right now she is standing a few feet from him. They've been back for about three hours and Sean has been asleep. Naya has not slept.

He can see that she's changed out of her warm white cotton nightie into a short skirt and halter top and she is wearing makeup for the first time in weeks. Naya does not need any makeup.

Then she turns around and pulls up her short skirt, moving her panties aside with her right hand. "I want you to have what other men have had."

"Naya, stop that. What are you doing?" He gets out of their narrow bed and comes over to her.

"Don't you want it?" When she says it, he realizes she is in some kind of trance. This is not good.

"Naya, I want you but not like this."

"They all want this. They want me like this. Don't you want to?" She starts moving her ass in lazy circles, first one way, then the other.

"We are never having sex like this, Naya, never."

"I knew it, you don't really like me."

He pulls her around so she is facing him once more.

"Naya, listen. Listen to me. He is gone. That life is gone. I am your friend, you can trust me. You don't need to do that. Not with me."

"But then you'll leave me if I don't do what you want me to do."

"I am not like those men, Naya. It's precisely because I'm not them, I don't want you to do that for me, ever."

Her trance seems to break, she folds to the floor, weeping into her hands. "Will you still like me even if I don't do that?"

"Yes, Naya," Sean says gently. "You are another beating heart in my family—now we are three." He gathers her up in his arms and sits on the bed with her in his lap and her head on his shoulder. She is shivering. She is a broken human being but he wants her soul even more than he wants her body.

...

Sean is fed up. Nahuel won't let him kill these people, at least not here, not now. But he has another idea.

He and Odri4n spend the next two days recalibrating and testing his nanosite deconstructors. They're going to turn things around on the Sheriff and his posse. Just for good measure, Sean has Odri4n sample everyone else's DNA on the canyon floor too—media and thrill seekers as well. Hey, welcome to the partay. Wouldn't want anyone feeling left out now would we? Sean and Odri4n smile at each other. Oh, those crazy Irish.

...

Using two quantum megaphones below and two above, a rebel Irish tune floods the canyon (it's Join the British Army) and the Mesa above with audio that makes the track they played with Naya's film sound like it was played on a single tinny mono speaker with just a few microwatts behind it. Join the British Army is followed immediately by a stirring Irish marching dirge with bagpipes playing in waltz time with a few variations in second and fourth verses. It reaches a crescendo moments before dawn. Everyone from their Pueblo comes out, sleepily. What gives?

...

Sean gives the order and Odri4n releases a plague of nanosites. They fly down into the valley and along the top of the Mesa. They start to eat everything. You can hear screams even over the blaring, stirring rebel march he is playing.

Naya is standing next to him looking better than she has for days. They are holding hands.

Even though he can't kill them, Nahuel says nothing about their equipment, clothes, weapons, vehicles, shoes—anything they touch will have traces of their DNA on it. His deconstructors eat everything that is inanimate. Pretty soon they are hundreds of men and quite a few women naked. It'll be a bitch walking back to town through the desert, shoeless and naked. The desert has

Bruce M Firestone

lots of ways to hurt you. It turns out they can't pick up anything either to hide their nakedness or protect them from the raging sun. As soon as they do, it turns to dust.

The Hopi are laughing at them, pointing at the fat ones, making fun of the men with small penises, the women from the media with fake boobs. Nanosites eat everything that is inanimate and that includes tattoos, jewelry, body candy, makeup, hair extensions and, of course, breast implants and all plastic surgery.

Naya just looks at Sean, smiling at him again. Her lovely green eyes are shining once more.

...

Les de Sades know one thing for sure—there is a wizard in this cave. They'll have to get him before they can get the girl.

...

"Yoga is a physical and spiritual journey that unites us with the primordial spirit of this planet, each other and ourselves," Ellen explains. She and Niamh are sitting on twin yoga mats in a flat part of the town square not far from their now shared apartment. Holly has moved in with Ellen. She hasn't spoken since Naya's film is shown but she is showing improvement each day; there's more animation in her face now and her body is moving in a more coordinated, less jerky fashion. When she sees her brother and Naya, she shies away from them and comes to Ellen. Ellen says to Naya and Sean to give it a few more days. Things will improve. They understand.

Ellen has decided to teach her the practice of Yoga and will do some basic things—Yoga for a (heretofore) active ten year old girl.

They start in a seated position, legs crossed with hands pressed together in prayer position.

"Niamh, breathe in with me, deep breath, breathe out—all the way out, hold, hold, now breathe in again, slowly. In and out slowly through your nose.

"That's good. Now on the next breath out, I want you

to make the sound of the Honey Bee. OK, deep breath in, hold, breathe out.

"Zzzzzzzzzzzzzzzzzzzzzzzzzzzzzzzzzzzzzzzzzzzzzzzzzz."

Ellen makes the sound but Niamh does not but she is following.

"OK, let's try again. In, hold, now a beautiful, smiling Honey Bee."

"Zzzzzzzzzzzzzzzzzzzzzzzzzzzzzzzzzzzzzzzzzzzzzzzzz."

Ellen can hear the faintest sound coming from Niamh.

"Very nice. One more time."

"Zzzzzzzzzzzzzzzzzzzzzzzzzzzzzzzzzzzzzzzzzzzzzzzzzz."

Louder, Niamh is definitely louder this time.

"OK, let's lie on our backs. Good. Now bring your knees up to your chest, grab your knees with your hands. Let's warm up our backs a little—six gentle circles, first counterclockwise. Right, that's it. Now breathe in for 180 degrees, breathe out for the last part of the circle. Go a bit deeper with each transit. Now the other direction. Very nice.

"Alright. Now lift your head and roll your neck, three times counterclockwise, good. Now the other direction.

"Nice. Now extend your legs in a Y and lift them slowly. Keep them straight. Breathe in as you lift them, now out as you slowly lower them. Don't let them touch the floor, Niamh. This strengthens your core. Alright, five more.

"Very nice. OK, relax here for two breaths.

"OK, now we are going to raise our bottoms up—six times. Breathe in, lift, hold, hold, breathe out and lower down. Now on our last one, I want you to hold it for four breaths and take your arms and clasp them together behind your back. Nice, Niamh! You're a natural! OK, breath out, lower down.

"Rest here for two breaths. Now roll on your right side and come to a seated position again. Cross your legs like me.

"OK, let's shrug our shoulders like as if your brother

just asked you a dumb question."

Niamh smiles.

"OK, five more shrugs. Nice. Breathe in when you raise your shoulders, then out as you lower them. Breathe through your nose, Niamh."

"Legs straight in front, Niamh. Hands to the floor. Right leg over left and hug it with your left arm. Now on the next inhale, put your right arm behind you and twist. Look behind you. Now close your eyes. We'll do two Honey Bees here."

"Zzzzzzzzzzzzzzzzzzzzzzzzzzzzzzzzzzzzzzzzzzzzzzzzz."

"Zzzzzzzzzzzzzzzzzzzzzzzzzzzzzzzzzzzzzzzzzzzzzzzzz."

"Now the other direction."

Ellen knows that with kids, you don't hold yoga poses very long—it's not good for their young bodies and they might get bored.

"OK, feet together in front of you. Grab your big toes with your hands. Now see how close you can bring that cute little nose of yours to your feet. OK, one Honey Bee here."

"Zzzzzzzzzzzzzzzzzzzzzzzzzzzzzzzzzzzzzzzzzzzzzzzzz."

"One more."

"Zzzzzzzzzzzzzzzzzzzzzzzzzzzzzzzzzzzzzzzzzzzzzzzzz."

"Do you know the bicycle, Niamh?"

Niamh nods.

"OK, so we are going to go over onto our backs with our bums in the air and our hands under them for support. It's called an inversion, Niamh."

They both roll effortlessly into this new position.

"Don't push too far—be gentle with your neck. OK, see if you can remove your hands from your bum and lay them flat on your mat."

Women often have trouble with this pose because, well, they have things like nice hips for carrying babies which Ellen certainly has but Niamh not so much, yet. Niamh has no trouble with it nor does Ellen. She's been doing Yoga since her late teens.

Then they roll back to a seated position where they do a half lotus. After that Ellen takes Niamh through some more basic movements including plank pose, cat cow, sun salutations (four cycles of them including one with a hip stretching pigeon position in it where they can rest each time for a few moments), downward dog, standing forward fold, warrior 1, warrior 2 and several more. Before they get ready for Shavasana (Corpse Pose, although Ellen will not call it that with Niamh in her class of one), she has Niamh lie on her back once more.

"OK, we are going to do happy baby pose. Grab your feet, Niamh, like you are a happy baby and move around like me."

"Funny."

"Did you say something, Niamh?"

"You look pretty funny pretending you're a baby."

"Well so do you, Miss, so do you." Ellen is so pleased. After her class, they walk back to their room. They both take a sponge bath using their tiny basin. Ellen combs out Niamh's long hair and then braids it. After that, Ellen reads to her. Niamh and Ellen hold hands. It's the Adventures of Huckleberry Finn. Hey, it worked before.

...

"Mr. Finnegan Bell?"

"Yes. Who are you?"

"Could you please come with us?"

"Ah, I don't think so."

But they grab him anyway and shove him into a waiting van. Finn is gone in seconds. His brother turns around to see him disappear into a van. He drops the Superflyer XIV they were playing with moments ago and runs toward the van. It's supposed to have its VIN (Vehicle ID number) displayed on its media wall exterior (both sides and rear) but there is nothing there—it's just dark.

...

Magellan calls his Dad—he's at Lawrence Livermore Lab. They're working with colleagues at UBC, in Houston and at Farrar's base on Mars pretty much round the clock getting ready to raise the planetary shield (which is what the PR guys have started calling it—sounds much warmer, friendlier, less scary than Quantum Bubble don't you think? Bubbles have been known to burst.)

Ellen has been keeping him abreast of matters at Third Mesa and she seems to have control over the situation until this.

After a few minutes, Damien tells Magellan to stay on campus. He'll arrange a flight for them and send someone to pick him up—they're heading to Third Mesa RFN.

"You're leaving, now?" Jag asks him as Damien heads for the exit. There are over 30 workstations set up in their control room, a smaller number in both Vancouver and Houston and dozens in Mission Control on Mars. It would be impossible to coordinate their efforts without quantum communicators—there can be no mistimed steps in what they are attempting. Simulations are one thing; this is envelopment of an entire gaseous atmosphere (Imperial China did not have to cope with that when they wrap Luna since it had no atmosphere) and fluid dynamics are tricky and often non-linear. Small changes could have big, catastrophic results for the 13 Colonies of Mars (most of which are DARCH ones although there are three that are not allied with DARCH—filled as they are with Germanians, Imperial Chinese and the last one—a tiny colony of Hippies. They're on Mars to find themselves but what they've found instead is a rough frontier society where one mistake, one letdown and you are deader than Abbie Hoffman, their patron saint who said things like, 'Avoid all needle drugs, the only dope worth shooting is Richard Nixon.')

Damien doesn't answer Jag just looks over his shoulder and says, "Pet3r, you're coming with me."

...

"They want you to surrender, Sean. They think you killed Mr. Hexham," Finn is saying to his friend who is just a year older but for some reason looks like he is way more experienced than when he last saw him—he's grown or something.

"They're offering some kind of deal, I presume?"

"Ah, yes. They'll remove, these are their words not mine, the noose around Third Mesa's neck, leave Naya alone and decamp. But they want you, Sean. So like, what are you going to do?"

...

"Sheriff, I think we can find someone who may have information that will help you with your missing person."

"Glad to hear that, Mr., uh, Spillane."

They are in the Sheriff's control center—a replacement trailer (the last one having been eaten and turned to dust) with massive communications and control equipment and the Sheriff, Nahuel, Sean, three Hopi marshals, two citified lawyers and now five Club Les de Sades members. They've learned from their last time here that they need protective layers so they don't leave their DNA all over the place. It's obvious that Third Mesa's wizard is doing some kind of reverse therapy with their DNA. Now they have airlocks everywhere and, when they are not sure, they just use old fashioned 30% by weight Hydrogen Peroxide lab solution (way more effective than bleach according to local Russian mobster Mikhail Andreeovich Zhukovsky who knows a thing or two about obliterating his tracks and advises Club Members on things like crime scene cover-ups) to clean surfaces they might have touched.

"First, you will have to withdraw every one of your people from the area. They cannot come closer than a 50 mile radius of this place. I will provide you with the coordinates. They must not, UNDER ANY CIRCUMSTANCES, come nearer and I mean by a factor of picometers which is a very, very small tolerance, Sheriff."

"Or what?" hisses one of the Les de Sades.

"Or they will be sorry. You've only seen the appetizer,

Bruce M Firestone

you don't want the main course, trust me."

They're assuming that, in addition to any smart booby traps that Sean may have rigged up, he is bragging about Hopi Marshal marksmanship with their rifles. These guys may be vicious sadists preying on women and girls, trading in their flesh but they're stupid—a circle with a 50-mile radius means they have a border perimeter of around 314.159 miles. Be pretty hard to establish an effective picket line that long with nine Marshals and Nahuel wouldn't you say?

...

Nahuel and Sean are sitting with three young Hopi Marshals. They can see that the pullout of State Troopers and others has begun. It will be complete within a couple of hours.

"Chief, you are clear? Only you can give the order to Odri4n? You understand?" Sean has been over this four times already with Nahuel. He gets it.

Sean's plan is to give himself up at noon. If they double cross the Hopi, Nahuel will order Odri4n to release nanosite deconstructors and this time they will kill (horribly) every one of the people who they have on a master file with their DNA signatures when and if they come within 50 miles of Third Mesa. If they send others, Odri4n will scan them too and Nahuel will order them dead.

"You afraid?" Nahuel asks. He's no fool. He can see that they will kill the young man. He will never make it back to SF for trial.

"No. Yes. I don't know." Sean hasn't said anything to Naya or Ellen. He can't even bear to think of what may happen to Holy Jumpin except Nahuel has promised to keep her safe.

"The Code Hero always die because we are all mortal. True measure is how we face Death. Man who lives correctly must have honor, courage, grace, self containment and endure through chaos. You are that man,

Ruane."

"I don't know, Chief. I don't think anyone can know how they will do until it is their time. I have always wanted to die with dignity. 'Code Hero' is that a First Nation's ideal?"

"No, Ernest Hemingway."

They wait for noon. Sean tries not to think about what may lie ahead or what he is leaving behind. His life has never really been his own. He kind of knew that by 15. He's just turned 21 (here at Third Mesa) and while Naya and Holly and Ellen make a fuss over him, he knows that his time is nearly up. When he makes love to Naya that night, it is the tenderest moment that either of them will experience, possibly for a long time, maybe forever.

...

At noon, they get up and head toward the hand and toe holds at the west end of the Pueblo that will take Sean up to the top of the Mesa. A car will take him outside the 50 mile no go area and he will give himself up. Nahuel and the three marshals will accompany him. No one else will know. Sean finds that he can walk although his legs are shaking. His hands are steady though and he feels that he can manage himself.

...

"Where do you think you two are going?" Ellen is standing there blocking their path with her hands on her hips reversed like she does when she is mad or fed up or just being stern. Behind her is Dekka. Ash3r's been watching Sean for the last few days. He and Ellen have been doing some research of their own and Ellen's been worried that Sean might do something stupid. Heroic but stupid which men do all the time, most of which doesn't even work. If he has made some type of deal with these people, the former President of the Commonwealth knows it is a worthless one since only one side can be trusted.

"Out of my way, Ellen," Sean says. He gently tries to

press forwards, he staggers a bit.

"You think I'm going to allow you to make my daughter a widow?"

"Please, Ellen, I have to go."

"NFW on that Sean. Dekka?"

Dekka steps up hesitantly. He is unsure where his loyalties lie—to save Naya or obey Ellen?

"Ellen, there is no other way. We can't start a war we will lose. They want someone and that someone is either Naya or me. Who is it going to be then?"

"Neither."

"I'm not running from those people anymore and neither is Naya. I am not hiding from them either. This is the only way, Ellen."

"You're wrong, Sean. There are always alternatives. Like you said, this is Federal land subject to Commonwealth law not State laws. There'll be 380 Army Rangers here by the end of the day today. They'll clear these people out. You are going nowhere except to see my daughter." Ellen has called in a few favors and so has General of the Army (Retired) Farrar Staubach. Enough is enough.

"Sean, there is something you don't know about these people."

"I know enough."

"No you don't. Ash3r has done a complete background workup on them. Club Les de Sades are allied with domestic terrorists—old Republican elements—the people who killed your parents, Sean! They never appeared before the Truth and Reconciliation Committee."

"So?" He tries to push by her but Ellen stands her ground.

"Listen to me! What, are you suddenly thick headed? If Republican Old Guard (the media have started calling them Rogues as domestic terrorism has become a persistent, low level threat and a big supplier of news minutes) don't appear before Truth and Rec, they automatically become outlaws and subject to immediate arrest. There is no statute of limitations on this. CPF will be here with the Rangers, they'll arrest every last motherfucking one of these SOBs." Ellen is referring to the Commonwealth's Police Force that replaces the disgraced and disbanded FBI.

He can't seem to stop his body. It's his time. He has to go! Ellen is not getting though to him!

But she needn't have said anything about going to see her daughter. Naya has known something is up with Sean since his 21st birthday party. Su7e, alerted by Ash3r, gives her the headsup that something is going down. She bounds along the rocky, broken path and flings herself into Sean's arms covering him with kisses and saying breathlessly, "Oh, Sean, Sean, Sean, I can't live without you! What were you thinking of? You can't leave me! Oh, Sean!"

Finally, it seems to sink in. "Naya?" He can hardly see anything. It's like it's dark everywhere instead of just after noon.

"Yes, Sean?"

"Ellen says I don't have to go."

"She's right. Listen to her! Oh Sean!"

"Alright. I'll stay. I'd like that better. Definitely, that'd be better." He's a bit shaky at his reprieve. "Hey Naya."

"Yes, Dear?"

"Do you think Holly would sing Join the British Army for us?"

"I think she might, Sean. Let's go ask her." Naya grabs Sean's hand and they head back to the pueblo.

Ellen watches them go—she is happy, something that is an anomalous state for her since like forever. The future is safe in the hands of these two. She is sure of it. Ellen is far more right than she can possibly know.

...

But when Holly finds out what he tries to do, she is so hurt she can't speak to him for two more days. 'What was he thinking? Boys are crazy!' Then she finally relents and sings his favorite for him.

By this time, Damien and Magellan arrive but Ellen, like always, has the situation under control. She and D sit with their entire family, now seemingly expanded by two—an Irishman and his younger sister who sits next to Ellen with her head on Ellen's shoulder when she is not singing—in their Council Ring.

Nahuel who rarely sings since his sister died brings out a Ukulele and plays Somewhere Over the Rainbow for them. He is accompanied by Israel 'Iz' Kamakawiwo'ole, the Hawaiian master musician who dies young like Nell— in his 30s too when he goes over the rainbow. Odri4n and Nahuel cook up this part of their show—all Odri4n has to do is project an Mtv image of the Hawaiian roughly on the same scale as Nahuel (which is harder to do than you might think since Iz is so much larger in every direction than Nahuel.) The two of them play in perfect harmony.

Ellen is remembering another time when Nahuel sings for them—it is in front of an audience of millions— Nell's words, All We Are Asking Is Give Us a Chance, set to a John and Yoko tune during the beginning of their protest movement that led to the founding of the Commonwealth. Now he sings—

Ooo ooo ooo
Ooo ooo ooo
Somewhere over the rainbow
Way up high
And the dreams that you dreamed of
Once in a lullaby

Oh somewhere over the rainbow
Bluebirds fly
And the dreams that you dreamed of
Dreams really do come true

Someday I'll wish upon a star
Wake up where the clouds are far behind me

Where trouble melts like lemon drops
High above the chimney tops
That's where you'll find me...

Oh somewhere over the rainbow
Way up high
And the dreams that you dare to
Why, oh why can't I, I?

Ooo ooo ooo
Ooo ooo ooo Ooo, ah ah

The sun is setting over Third Mesa. Naya takes Sean to the west side of the pueblo and she sits him down on a stone bench. Then she goes over to the setting sun. It is the perfect size to fit in the curved palm of her hand. Sean sees Naya silhouetted against the last of the sun's rays. She is beyond beautiful with the figure of a Goddess. The golden and reddish highlights in her hair glow. She says while holding the sun in her hand looking sideways back at Sean words she remembers from a Peter S. Quinn lyric—

The sun rays in your eye,
The love you're giving that I have found...

The love you gave from your heart;
What matter what we do or say,
Never let it depart...

Let there never be no bygones
Not today nor tomorrow...

This is the happiest, most complete moment they will ever experience. They just don't know it.

...

Between Army Rangers and the CPF, it takes several hours to round up and process these critters. They have to kill a few. They arrest all the ones who surrender. Only one of the five Club Les de Sades members gives up. The others manage to kill two rangers and one CPF agent plus wound three others. They are hard to kill. But CPF believes they have removed a critical Club domestic terrorist cell. The one member they catch thinks he is important. But really he isn't. The Club is made up of layers—cells within cells and what they got was an outer cell even though these particular cell members think they are important, actually, they're not.

...

Chapter 15 Storm Clouds

"She look strange."

"I think she looks really cute, don't you just want to hug her?" Holly is asking the Chief.

"I hug my wife plenty." He is talking about Sabine.

They've installed eight beta Roxies in Third Mesa, enough to supply the entire town with pretty much everything they need or could ever want.

"If those bhenchod ever come back here Chief, Third Mesa won't have any more shortages."

"What mean bhenchod?"

"It's a word Dr. Durai taught me," Holly says not wanting to tell the Chief what it means since it might shock the old guy. To Holly, anyone over 40 is really old and Nahuel must be what? Over 60. Egad.

"So, what it mean?"

"Ah, sisterfucker."

Nahuel just smiles at Holly. "That good word, bhenchod."

...

There have been no further intrusions into the 50-mile no go area that Sean and Odri4n establish and life has gone back to normal (sort of) for the pueblo. Finn and Magellan return to Berkeley with their Dad who is working crazy hours with Jag and their team of Mars planetary shield engineers. Ellen decides to stay on at Third Mesa. She is home schooling Holly and would certainly not be including words like bhenchod in the curriculum so Holly doesn't use her newly acquired killer word ammo when Ellen is around. Ellen has also taken on four other kids at Third Mesa who despite being super smart or maybe because of it are having trouble at the local public school they attend. So Holly has started to make friends her own age (and younger).

When Ellen isn't there, they trade swear words—recently bhenchod for diigis, Navajo for stupid. It is triply insulating because it's a Navajo word, ancient enemy of the Hopi. The Hopi don't have any swear words or at least that's what the other kids tell Holly. They've started calling her 'Kaya' which is Hopi for 'elder sister' so she acquires yet another nickname. Pretty soon she's going to need her own dictionary just for her collection of names (and swear words).

Her brother is happier than she has ever seen him. He whistles (softly and tunelessly) while he works. He doesn't even know he is doing it. It's his happy song although sometimes she hears bits of Irish marches in there before it goes back to being tuneless. He shuttles back and forth to Lawrence Livermore Labs and home to Third Mesa. Holly doesn't like it when he goes near San Fran but he tells her he is being careful.

He is getting ready to hook up his system of tentacles (that have just reached several hydrothermal plumes on mid-ocean ridges off the west coast of the Commonwealth) to beta Roxies they have at Third Mesa and elsewhere in various Western States and Canada. They've also transported Roxie components via Quantum Tunnel to Mars where these farm-in-a-box units have been welcome additions to what heretofore have been woeful Martian nutrition and culinary arts. Sean in a recent conversation with Damien and Jag asks, "Maybe this is a dumb question, but why not hook our Earthside tentacle system up to Roxie units on Mars too?"

"Huh?" Jag and Damien say in unison.

"I can deadhead in any, let's say all, our Earth-based labs. From those gates, we send nutrients via Quantum Tunnel to our network of tentacles on Mars. You get DARCH people on Mars to hook 'em up after that. You'll get way better results with an Earthside supply of nutrients, I think." Martian soils are just not as rich and varied as the bounty they are getting from the Pacific

Ocean nor is transportation via tentacle as efficient on Mars. They do expect some improvement after the Mars Shield goes up reducing incoming solar radiation to Earth levels.

Jag and Damien both glance at each other with a sort of 'Duh' look.

When they tell Farrar, he is pleased. Their crappy Martian diet has been bothering him; for one, it's bad for morale. For another, their foods are hard on the digestive system—Farrar is in top shape, enjoys Mars' low gravity (just over a 1/3 of Earth's so a bit more than twice Luna's) but, what the heck, he is 70. Change'll be good.

...

For Naya, there is no possibility she can go anywhere outside their 50 mile exclusion zone. The Paparrazzoids will hunt her down or, worse, Club Members will find her. But she is content. She is doing yoga with her Mom and Holly, working on Roxie 3.0 and also spending lots of time with Sean when he is home.

She's found that she really, really loves him. He is kind, gentle and, while maybe he doesn't have the emaciated modern American male look that Hollywood and magazine apps crave, Naya has come to appreciate the scruffy, dark, virile, hairy Irish look of her guy. There is strength to him—beyond his immense native physical power which comes from his working class roots not from gym workouts or fakery with roids—that goes to his core. He knows who is and what he is, he isn't searching for himself like, say, Naya is, her brothers are (OK, maybe not Magellan) and, Naya thinks, maybe even her mother is.

Naya's been spending more time with Ellen talking about business models, corporate structure, what went wrong with QCCII and what they did to fix those problems when they launched DARCH. Naya finally tells her mother the whole vision she has when she visits with Nell—the one that happens when she is lying on top of Pops' grave. Naya says it is Nell who shows her this new path both for

Earth and for herself. Ellen says she is glad that Naya talks to her Godmother and then smiles lovingly at her daughter.

They talk more about Voyage to Earth Population 1.2 Billion and her plans to launch a new organization with it to be called 'Voyager Foundation' in part to honor tiny spacecraft Voyager 1 which is the first human artifact (other than radio waves) to exit the heliosphere and enter interstellar space.

Then Ellen says, "I am still not clear on Voyager's mission, Naya? It's not like it was 100 years ago—today, any women who wants a BPI can get one. They cost a few cents so it's not an affordability issue."

When Ellen mentions BPI (Birth Prevention Insert), Naya's eyes slide away. Ellen doesn't notice that anything is amiss. After collecting herself, Naya says, "Well, for one thing I want to put all my Berkeley research into Voyager—I'm going to need your help with that by the way. The University wants 30 points and that is too much, I think."

When Naya asks for her mother's help, Ellen sits up straighter. She wants to put her arms around her daughter (something she has not been able to do very often since she runs away from home for the first time at 13) and hug her to bits. But she lets the urge pass because she does not want to break the intimacy that is developing between them, really for the first time. With Naya, it's little victories here and there.

"No problem with that. I know the Office of the President." The preposterously named 'Office of the President' is their systemwide HQ that covers all UC campuses. It's just another opaque bureaucracy. But Ellen knows their real President.

Naya reaches over and gives her Mom's hand a squeeze. Another little victory!

"That'd be great, Mom. What do you think would be fair?"

"Maximum 20 points, Naya."

"Thought so."

"So, Voyager's mission?" Ellen prompts.

"It's to develop the Roxie system so food and energy security are not issues for families anywhere. Roxie'll lift all boats and free up millions of acres of farmland to go back to nature. Voyager will have a separate charity arm—a land conservancy that will accept donations of land and will also, as sponsor funding permits, buy land and add them to Voyager's land bank. These properties will have development rights suspended for all time and will join other conservancy lands—the objective is to turn at least 80% of this planet's surface back to nature."

"Wow," says Ellen mostly to encourage Naya. She likes the plan since they had a similar goal for the Commonwealth when they first establish their new nation. It turns out not to be practical to implement on the scale they hope for until, that is, Roxie shows up. It's also obvious now to Ellen that she and Naya have been channeling ideas back and forth without knowing it. Ash3r, Su7e and Nell are their intermediaries. It's weird and beautiful.

"We might be able to get the ratio up even higher, Mom, but only if humans give up farming, ranching and hunting. Roxie can make that technically possible. Education will do the rest like it's done with tobacco over the last few generations.

"Here's the thing, every year Voyager will auction off a limited number of permits for people who want to hike these lands—it'll be like those hunting licenses where dumbasses pay like a million dollars or something to bag a trophy but these permits will be just to walk the trails, observe and record. It'll be a huge revenue source. One quarter of the permits will be available at no cost to the general public—we'll do a random draw for those. Another quarter will go to schools across the planet for free and they can decide for themselves how to get kids in to do some forest bathing which is really important for children." (Nell also tells Naya about this during her vision but Nell is actually recycling Damien stories for his daughter, her Goddaughter since she learned it from Damien back in the day.)

"So once," Naya continues, "all our research is part of Voyager—"

"Hold on, if UC takes, say, 20 points, what are you doing with the other 80?" Ellen asks.

"Well, I thought we should support St Jos where you and I both stayed, Dad's Foundation (the one that has taken over Nell's old home, Maya Fair) and a few other charities..." Naya sort of peters out.

"That's a bit of a hodgepodge," Ellen says careful not to describe it for what it is—a mess.

"Well, here's the thing. I am going to keep 51% of this for our family. It's (mostly) a *for-profit* corporation (except for the land conservancy), Mom. You and Da have given so much to everyone else, you don't own anything! Quantum Computing Corp that nearly got Da dead and almost got you assassinated is owned by some rich creep (Naya's referring to Angelo Keller, of course), DARCH is owned by EVERYONE. Da didn't keep or even license any of the technology he's created which CHANGED THE WORLD! All you've got is your crappy pension as former President of the Commonwealth, ITS FIRST PRESIDENT, which you reduced in one of your final acts as President so as not to be a burden on a nation that owes you *everything* it has. Our country was going into the shitter before you went around making a million happy speeches (Naya has seen videos of a young, beautiful Ellen doing exactly that) and *willing* this country out of the deepest economic and political problems it has ever faced including a complete regime change and now you are living in one room in a cave, sharing it with my sister?" Here Naya is using the word 'sister' as a Hopi would—to describe Niamh.

Naya is breathing hard after this last impassioned speech. Ellen is proudly and silently watching her daughter—her mouth forms a big 'O' during this period. It stays on her face for quite a while before she realizes it isn't her most ladylike pose ever and she shuts it with a snap. The two women look at each other and then both guffaw hugely (at Ellen's expense.)

...

The albedo of the Moon has changed significantly in the last few years. Its albedo is much lower than Earth's to begin with—0.11 versus 0.306. These numbers (called Bond albedo, named after astronomer George Bond who lives in the early to mid part of the 19th Century) are a way of characterizing the reflectivity of a planet and speak to its energy balance. It is the fraction of electromagnetic radiation scattered back to space.

There is so much water on the Lunar surface now as well as tree cover that its Bond albedo has shrunk to 0.067 which means that Cosmo's Moon, a moon so big and bright that even old men want to have sex with their equally old wives, would be meaningless today. It's become a minor environmental issue, almost a cause célèbre amongst the wealthy airship set who want their old Moonshine back.

General Yao, Imperial China and Germania who dominate the Moon much as DARCH dominates Mars care not one whit about western ideas of romance. The General finds western preoccupation with love and sex to be self serving, decadent and weak.

A much bigger environmental concern is how much of Earth's water has been moved to Luna. It's one area where DARCH and the Cartesian Powers have cooperated although DARCH has kept both quantum tunnel and quantum bubble technology out of their reach so far. General Yao is not pleased that his two greatest scientists—Damien and Jag have somehow gotten away from him.

They have filled half of the Moon's mare with water to an average depth of eight meters which means they have moved around 2.419 times 10 the power of 13 cubic meters of ocean to the Moon. That sounds like a lot but represents only 0.00174% of Earth's oceans vamoosing to Luna.

Damien and Jag both think that a change in the mass of the Moon could be a bigger concern because even very small changes in Luna's gravity might cause subtle changes in orbital mechanics as well as larger tides back on Earth. Water is heavy. Still, even with all the H_2O they move to Luna, its mass has only increased by 0.0000329%.

Earth gets some of this water back—every day 150 tons or so of interstellar dust, meteoroids, meteorite fragments, small pieces of comets and asteroids impact Earth and a lot of it is water ice which melts and turns to water vapor as these things pierce the atmosphere. It isn't very much but over millions of years, it adds up.

But given the sensitivity of chattering classes to anything having to do with lifegiving water, DARCH wants to find an alternative source for Mars. So they are experimenting with Quantum Tunneling on Europa, one of Jupiter's moons. Europa's liquid water is under a skin of sea ice and holds almost three times the volume of all Earth's oceans combined plus there are no Europan journos or pseudo environmentalists creating needless panic about 'stolen' water there.

On Earth, they've been blogging about how Gaia is losing her oceans to rapacious corporate interests like DARCH ignoring the fact that DARCH is a World LLC (with proceeds shared equally between all human and quantum people) and also forgetting that they are talking about 0.00174%.

One of the other nice things about using Europa as a water source, is it comes with highly edible fish. It is now generally accepted as scientifically demonstrable that panspermia is a viable theory for the spread of life throughout the Milky Way Galaxy.

DARCH has not yet found any viable lifeforms on Mars (the absence of liquid water and too much solar radiation appear to have put the kybosh on this) but it is now abundantly clear that Mars did at one time support life. Those lifeforms have probably found their way to Earth and many other places, carried there in dirty snowballs kicked into orbit by asteroid or comet impacts (or possibly by stupendous volcanic explosions) with enough velocity to escape planetary gravity wells (it's a snap with Europa's gravity being so low—a bit less than the Moon's and not too hard with Mars either with its relatively low mass as well). So much as humans expend a lot of energy so they can exchange bodily fluids and DNA in an endless mating dance (the one that General Yao so disdains), planets and moons are promiscuous too. And not just in our solar system but across our entire Galaxy. Stuff just drifts along for a few eons and then falls to a planet and, hey, presto, shrimp kabob.

But intergalactic distances are too great for panspermia to work. It takes too damn long to cross intergalactic space. Just to get to the galaxy nearest the Milky Way (Andromeda) would take a Mars or Earth or Europan artifact teeming with active lifeforms kicked into space by some enormous event and traveling at speeds close to the fast solar wind (say, 700 kilometers per second) 1.086 billion earth-years just to get to the edge of Andromeda. Then by some huge stroke of luck, it intersects a planet in a stable orbit around a distant star in what is regarded as the habitable zone (where liquid water can exist). The artifact descends to the planet's surface or better yet plunks into an ocean, breaks open and Solar System organisms which are now more than a billion years old say, 'Howdy' and flourish there. Or the reverse happens and Andromeda sends life to the Milky Way. Since the Universe is 14.6 billion or so years old, we are talking about an appreciable fraction of the age of the

Universe so if there is life in at least one other Galaxy then it is likely that on two separate occasions, life somehow has arisen *independently*. Has lightning, in effect, struck twice or possibly more than twice? Now that would be really interesting to know.

...

Farrar is the first human to eat Europan fish, or more precisely Europan crustaceans. He uses a classic Texan Gulf Coast hot seasoning (a dry rub) on his shrimp, barbequing them and then eating them in front of Mtv scanners to show everyone they're safe. Human beings are stardust he figures and share a common ancestry with everything in the Galaxy so they should be able to eat just about anything (he hopes). After he doesn't die and reports they're yummy, Chefs everywhere in the Solar System are clamoring for E-shrimp.

They also find fish on Europa that sort of look like fully blind Goby; they visit Mars the same way their smaller buddies do—via Quantum Tunnel. But they are bony and don't make good eating no matter how much Texas Hot Sauce you add. DARCH scientists think they make excellent prey for larger fish which they haven't seen yet but suspect are there.

The Goby form symbiotic relationships with Europan Shrimp (the ones that Farrar hasn't eaten). The shrimp, like their Earth cousins, create burrows where both shrimp and Goby live. Goby are the watchmen, giving shrimp the headsup if predators are coming their way while shrimp give the Goby a nice place to lay their eggs. Of course, if a Quantum Tunnel comes anywhere near your neck of the sea, everything gets hoovered up the straw and then (ultimately) into the waiting mouths of the most inventive predator in the solar system—human beings.

All the fish are blind not only because Europa's ice crust is 19 kilometers thick but also because it's so far from the Sun—5.23 AU (astronomical units). Since Earth is by definition 1 AU from the Sun, light when it gets to Europa is pretty weak and has no chance to penetrate a vast crust of ice many kilometers thick.

These fish survive near thermal vents (much like the ones Sean is busy attaching tentacles to in Earth's oceans) where there is heat, chemicals and nutrients. Jupiter's huge presence nearby creates tides, earthquakes and tectonic shifts in the crust and core of Europa which turns out to be vital to the cycle of life there. Mars and Earth ejecta as well as cometary impacts are certainly of sufficient force to break through Europa's surface layer of ice and deposit lots of Martian, Earth and interstellar organisms into a beautiful, vibrant ocean just waiting to be explored, colonized and developed by these invading lifeforms. They've been playing a vicious Game of Thrones down here for billions of years with one Kingdom disposing of the other before being supplanted by yet others in an arms race without end. Of course, the reverse could have happened—Euopan ejecta could've ended up on Mars and Earth so maybe Europan shrimp are first. No one knows.

It turns out science has been asking the wrong question. What they should ask is—How could you not have life anywhere you have liquid water and a viable, longterm source of energy? Just try to produce liquid water and not have any life in it—it's really hard. Ask the scientists who try to produce pure heavy water for SNO (Sudbury's Neutrino Detector). Heavy water is their detection medium. It would be bad to say have bloodsuckers or for that matter ameba swimming around in the stuff. Might mistake a tadpole for the answer to the value of the Cosmological Constant. Or put another way, life finds a way.

Of course, panspermia just postpones having to answer the question where and how life began by answering it, 'Not here. Don't know.'

...

It is PS (Planetary Shield)

T-1:02:37.194901238551021576815324

which should be read as T minus 1 hour, 2 minutes and 37.194... seconds. The precision is absolutely critical to the mission. If the bubble goes up and it is misshaped, say it bulges where it shouldn't or contracts where it shouldn't, it could kick up a duststorm that will envelop the planet for a decade and kill everyone on Mars. Every colony is in lockdown. But lockdown won't do much good if they mistakenly release forces equivalent to say 53 quadrillion megatons of energy—enough to blow up Earth. Mars wouldn't need as much since its mass is about 1/10th of Earth's. But the energies involved today are huge and could wreck either planet and have some leftover for, say, Europa and Luna. Nevertheless, it is quite understandable that all scientists on Mars, at UBC, Lawrence Livermore and Houston are excited but worried. The ones on Mars are more worried and the ones on Earth are more excited.

Farrar talks it over with his people. Maybe they should evacuate all non-essential personnel from Mars? But there are too many settlers now and neither Imperial Chinese nor Germanians will leave their posts—they'd probably be stood up against Der Wal and shot if they abandon their colonies. Hippies won't leave either— they'll stay in the natural caves near the volcano Arsia Mons that they find and inhabit—maybe they'll drop some acid and hope that the second coming of Timothy O'Leary will save them. Who knows what those freaky but mostly nice people are thinking?

Farrar is not going and never planned to anyway. His science people and his army are staying put. That's already been bought and paid for. Now that he's 70, he is finally thinking he would like to get married and have a permanent partner but there is only one person he wants in that role and she is currently on Earth, married to a friend of his, that he works with on a daily basis and totally respects. He sighs.

An Aid asks him, "You nervous, Sir?"

Farrar gives him such a disapproving look that the Aid makes himself scarce for the next two days.

Exactly on time, generators start up at 129,600 substations on Mars. This is of course the product of 360 times 360 so each generator covers one full degree arc (in every direction) of Martian sky. They all have to work together and the only way to make this function is by letting QE pilots take over their operation. Farrar will give the order but QEs will do the work.

There is a lot of debate on how far out to go— troposphere, stratosphere or mesosphere. They know that they have to go further out than first principles would suggest. Their Quantum Bubble not only keeps nice stuff like an atmosphere in and bad stuff like too much UV out, it also captures a lot of the sun's energy that is currently missing Mars. They are going to refract some of that energy down onto the planet's surface and heat this sucker up.

The bigger the bubble's diameter, the more solar radiation they can capture but that leaves them with a bigger bag of gas to deal with which they can only learn to control through trial and error. Error, as already noted, can kill them all.

Still they decide to go bigger—to the top of the stratosphere which on Mars is 60 kilometers up.

"T-5 minutes and counting," says Capcom.

Farrar only has to sit and wait. There is nothing more for him to do now other than give the final 'Go' or 'No Go' at T-2 minutes, just under 3 minutes from now.

"Ah, Flight, we just lost two generators, one at each pole," says Booster.

They know they may have trouble in these regions— extreme cold can wreck their best machinery. They have two backups for each generator north of 60 degrees and south of 60 degrees latitude. Everywhere else, just one. Every generator has to work or their goose is cooked.

But Farrar's biggest worry isn't that their systems will fail; it's that terrorists will take this moment to whack Mars. 'Terrorist' on Mars is a Farrar euphemism for Imperial Chinese or Germanian agents. Both nations know that if DARCH is successful with the Planetary Shield, Mars will become the main economic engine of the Solar System for the next 100 years. DARCH and Commonwealth scientists have lapped Cartesian researchers who, to be fair, may not be giving it their all since they are slaves. It isn't just quantum tunneling and shielding as well as Q-phones that have given the Commonwealth a big lift. Their airship industries, space transit systems, mindlinked Internet (which powers a vast virtual economy made up of human, QE and data nodes which do huge amounts of work at hyper speeds), Mtv products and nanosite generators are cutting edge. Also in the R&D pipeline are Roxie and nanosites deconstructors although not too many people know about either of those yet. Of course, some members of Club Les de Sades can speak to the latter with personal knowledge. For some reason, they appear to be reluctant to tell this particular tale. Only in Sinofighter technology can Imperial China match the Commonwealth.

So if someone wants to sabotage their planetary shield, now would be the right time to do it. Although, Farrar's army is out on patrol and their QEs are monitoring everything simultaneously, they can't possibly defend 129,600 substations. So a few hardcore saboteurs could take down the shield before it goes up or worse as it is going up.

"Crossover complete," says EECOM. This means that their backups are working properly and have taken over operation from failed units.

Every generator is coming up to speed and noise

levels are beyond deafening. It's way worse than with quantum tunneling—there is a lot more power involved. Anyone not wearing quantum earbuds who is within 250 meters of these things, would instantly have their eardrums burst. After they get the shield in place, power requirements to maintain it are relatively puny.

"11 more generators are out, nine more at the pole (north where it is currently winter) and two, one at -20 degrees (this is in the southern hemisphere where it is summer) and one near the equator," Booster intones calmly.

"Crossover complete." EECOM again.

This is more worrisome because now there are two places where another individual failure means Farrar will have to shut it down.

Farrar looks as placid as he does at a Texas Hold'Em tourney.

"T-2 minutes and 45 seconds."

Farrar says, "Capcom, please give me a status report every 5 seconds." If Farrar doesn't stop it before T-2 minutes then it's gonna fly. After that, there is no known force that can prevent it.

"Status—nominal," Capcom says calmly.

Five seconds later, "Status—nominal."

Five more seconds later, "Status—nominal."

Five seconds later, "Status—nominal."

Five seconds later, "Three more generators down," Booster says with just a tiny amount of nervous energy in his voice.

"Crossover complete. Uh, we are go, Flight," EECOM says.

Five seconds later, "Status—nominal."

Five seconds later, "Status—nominal."

Five seconds later, "Status—nominal."

"Ah General? Your order?"

"By order of DARCH and on behalf of the 13 Colonies of Mars, I say, 'Go'." He can feel tension rise even higher in mission control. They are in the safest place on Mars—9 kilometers below the surface (in Valles Marineris) protected by the tough basaltic crust of the Tharis plain but they can still feel the ground shake violently beneath them. The entire planet is shaking hard enough so that walking across mission control's floor would be impossible.

They anticipated this and everyone is strapped into their chairs with thick padded shoulder straps crossed over their torsos and hooked into a lap belt. Chairs and lap belt are securely fastened to the floor (but separately—if one gives way, the other may hold them to the planet) and below that into the rock of the canyon— anchors go down more than 18 feet.

Then across Mars there is a huge whooshing sound followed by a thunderous planet-wide *ping*.

At least 1.7 Googol (that is a 1.7 followed by 100 zeroes) zettabytes of data are flooding in from all over which are being processed on Earth and on Mars, all of it passing through S4y3rs who is processing it in parallel. The General knows better than to ask his QE anything at this point. These are the fastest known creatures in the Universe but even so this bolos of data is taking time for him to digest.

Everyone at their labs on Earth and here on Mars in Mission Control is completely silent. They are all looking at S4y3rs. A few are praying silently.

Finally S4y3rs turns to Farrar and says, "Congratulations, General, we appear to have a stable planetary shield in place. All nominal."

Men and women in mission control and on Earth freak out. They are not the most demonstrative types to begin with but now there is lots of hugging and cheering. Farrar can hear, 'Thank God, gracias a dios, dieu merci, humdelallah' and a dozen more variations. QEs are walking around shaking hands too. The monkeys have come to Mars and now they're going to be able to run the zoo. How about that?

To Farrar this is way better than the Cowboys winning a Super Bowl. But even with all the high fiving going on, Farrar's thinking he would like to share the joy with someone but it's the same problem as before. That someone is a long way away and anyway, unattainable.

...

They turn on the taps full bore a few weeks after successfully getting the shield in place and are flooding Mars with a new atmosphere (with LOTS of nice oxygen and nitrogen) and megatons of lovely Europan seas. It'll take years but not decades, centuries or millennia. Even just a few months after they start, average temperatures have climbed from a mean of -63 degrees Celsius to -12 now which for Canucks here is a mild day back home. They had to slow it down (by tuning their shield to reduce the amount of light it is refracting to Mars surface) because they are kicking up some dust storms but overall it looks like it is manageable. A new profession that is uniquely Martian is being created—meteormorphologist or weather shapers. Human guesswork, intuition and luck combined with quantum persons' ability to process and manage vast amounts of data are allowing them to create a new Mars. It's pretty cool.

Imperial China claims meteormorphology as their own since they also have a large gas bag to deal with around Luna but it's puny compared to what they've done here on Mars and much less complicated in part because it is smaller but mostly because they share the same orbit around the Sun as Earth and don't have the same energy balance issues that Mars does.

Farrar is on the surface and looking around with nothing more than the equivalent of a decent pair of Earth sunglasses—their Quantum Bubble is reducing harmful solar irradiation to Earth levels so his retina won't burn in 90 seconds or less like they would have done about half a Martian year ago (a Mars year is about 1.88 Earth years).

He has to wear a pressure suit since they are still way below the Armstrong limit (61.8 mbar) at which point humans can survive without them. But atmospheric pressure has risen from around 6 mbar to 20 and it's 25% higher at the bottom of Valles Marineris so it's ironic that the first place on Mars where they will be able to walk around without pressure suits will also be the first colony they establish here—mission control.

He hasn't told anyone yet, not even S4y3rs, that his plan (if the shield is successful) is to call a national plebiscite to turn the 13 Colonies (all of them including Imperial China's, Germania's and the Hippie place) into a new country to be called Mars, populated by Martians not hyphenated Martians, like Imperial Chinese-Martians, Canadian-Martians, Germanian-Martians, Quantum-Martians, Commonwealth-Martians, French-Martians, Black-Martians, White-Martians, Indo-Martians, to heck with all that. We'll just be Martians. It's time for DARCH to evolve.

He has made up his mind—he is going to ask for help with his We Are All ONE (Mars) plebiscite campaign from someone who has done it before—the First President of the Commonwealth. What's he got to lose? She can always say, 'No.'

Ellen can help not only with the plebiscite he plans but also to solve another Mars problem—there is a shortage of women here. Travel to Mars exposes crew and passengers to increased levels of radiation which stats show increases the chance of cancer in men by 3.4% which is terrible but a whopping 19% for women with their larger glandular tissues. Having women in their 30s, 40s and 50s die unphotogenic deaths from cancer squelches a lot of female emigration to Mars.

But with recent adaptation by DARCH of quantum bubble tech to spacecraft like PTST (Phobos Transit Space Tug, the pride of their fleet with a revolutionary ion drive that can get people and freight to and from Mars in weeks instead of months), women can go outside in their bikinis and get some sun during their Earth-Mars transit with nothing between them and say a (previously deadly) solar proton event than the shield—the worst that can happen is they get a tan. It won't be quite as nice as travelling on the Princesa Agnes but almost.

Ellen's yoga trained body, now in its 50s, still looks good in a bikini. How does the General know that? Because he and Ellen share the same SM service and have been swapping photos of their lives as they move along. She posts photos of her babies, their holidays, grad photos, anniversary shots what have you. Farrar can't help it, he spends hours looking at them, especially more recent ones of her taken on an Aegean beach during their last family holiday there.

If he can convince her to help with their plebiscite and then get her to agree to post happy photos of her in space transit and then on a new, safer Mars, it'll open the floodgates to females from all over wanting to improve their prospects. There are (or soon will be) a lot of wealthy, lonely men on Mars, one of whom is the General. The real reason he never asks Ellen to join him on Mars isn't really because she is married to someone else. The General detests dishonesty and that includes being dishonest with himself. No, the real reason he hasn't asked her is that she might say, 'No.'

...

The albedo of Mars is changing, perhaps not by the day but weekly. The ratio of Mars' Bond albedo to Earth's is 0.817 but it is sinking. Vast new seas are forming, lichen are taking hold planet-wide to be followed by shrubs and trees and many plants, some of them Earth species and now some that are uniquely Martian strains.

Ellen is having a hard time getting to sleep. Holly sleeps curled on her side in her single bed a few feet from Ellen's. Ash3r is watching her. He asks her softly, "So what are you going to do?"

"I don't know," she answers quietly looking at Niamh again. "I don't know." She can't leave Holly or, for that matter, Naya, Sean, her twins and her faithful husband of more than 22 years, can she? He wasn't asking her to do that, was he?

...

After the fantastic success of the Mars Shield-Raising Project, there is a party at Lawrence Livermore, at UBC and in Houston to say nothing of the incredible three day holiday everyone takes on Mars. General Staubach says, "It'd be churlish for any Mars employer to ask his or her employees to come to work today so let's all take a day (the Martian day is conveniently very similar to Earth's— 24 hours 39 minutes and 35.244 seconds long) and have a beer." The General is echoing former Aussie PM Bob Hawke who after Alan Bond's syndicate finally wrests yachting's greatest prize (the America's Cup) away from the dreaded Yanks in 1983 after 132 years of trying declared the next day an unofficial holiday. Aussies head to their pubs en masse but former union boss now PM is there first. After this, it's impossible to buy any bumper stickers that say 'I'd Rather Be Sailing'—they're all sold out.

Sean's been pretty much a spectator at this event. His main job has been to monitor the stability and efficiency of their tentacle system on Mars which feeds more than 1,300 Roxies installed there so far. They supply nearly 30% of all food stuffs and domestic energy on the planet so it's important that there be no supply chain interruption.

His tentacle system comes through a planet-wide shaking with minor damage; a few virtual keystrokes and adjustments by Sean and Odri4n take care of that. They'll self repair in a few days.

He says 'Goodbye' to Damien and Jag and a few other people he knows well at Lawrence Livermore and hops on his Kill-e-cycle for the 851 mile trip back to Third Mesa.

This time he'll head back through Bakersfield, Barslow, Mohave Valley, Kingman, Flagstaff and Winslow before turning north to Third Mesa. He'll be avoiding Las Vegas as before—the Club Les de Sades have lots of friends there.

Without girl infrastructure aboard as well as the girls themselves, he can fly—over 160 mph for much of the trip—he can make it in less than eight hours. He can't wait to see Niamh, Ellen, his friends and most of all, his beautiful, mysterious girlfriend, Ms. Naya Brooks Bell who most incredibly of all loves HIM.

...

"What do you mean she's not here?" Sean is saying to Ellen. "She knows she can't leave Third Mesa!" Without realizing he is doing it, he grabs Ellen and shakes her. "Ellen, tell me!"

"You're hurting me, Sean."

He immediately stops. "Where is Niamh?"

"She's in our room."

"Where is Naya?"

"She's gone to Hearth House?"

"Huh, where's that?" He is incredibly worried.

"It's within the 50-mile exclusion zone you set up."

"OK. Alright. Where is it?" He's never heard about this place before.

"It's on top of the Mesa about 22 miles northeast. They're riding camels there."

"They?"

"Yes Naya went there."

"They?"

Ellen doesn't want to say anything else.

Sean just looks at her and waits.

Finally he says, "Give me a map, I'll find her."

She reaches out her hand, places it on his arm gently and says, "Ah, I don't think that is a good idea." She knows how much he loves her daughter but she also understands he is a proud Irishman and she doesn't want anything to happen to him but also not to Naya either.

"Why not Ellen? Why not?"

Finally, although she is dreading this for days, she says, "José-Luis is here. They've gone off... together."

The hurt look on Sean's face when she says this makes Ellen want to cry. She hates crying but not as much as she loves Sean and his sister. She turns away, then runs away. Not to her room. Anywhere but there or here. She is weeping hysterically. Then when she finally stops running, she asks herself, 'Oh Naya, why, why?'

...

Three days later, Sean comes to see Ellen. He's been waiting for Naya to come back, send word or even message him by having Su7e talk to Odri4n. Nothing, no 'Dear John' letter, no goodbye/it's been swell, just this total God-awful silence.

"We're leaving, Ellen."

"I don't want you to go, Sean."

"I understand but we're leaving TODAY."

"She'll come around, Sean, I know it."

"Mrs. Bell, I don't care. Clifford Hexham told me once that she would just use me and she has. I can't believe that a guy like that knows her better than I do." Even now, Sean is careful to use present tense when talking about Cliff—he has not and never will tell anyone he killed that bhenchod (a term he learns from Niamh which seems appropriate first to describe Cliff and second because Sean almost never swears at least not in English or Irish).

"There has to be a reason, Sean."

"Yeah, it's obvious. A rich soccer player from the Bundesliga shows up and she sees an opportunity for 'personal growth' and she dumps the dumb Irishman who would die for her."

"She's known José-Luis since she was a little girl."

"And that is supposed to comfort me how? Oh, what does it matter? She used me and now has decided to trade up. We're going."

"Sean, I think you should leave Niamh here with me." She does not like the way he looks or sounds. He might hurt himself which would be tragic but if anything happens to Niamh, it would be unforgiveable.

"That shite (there is a time for everything under Heaven) takes my girl and you want to take my sister, my only family now, away from me? Never! You people have done enough to us for 20 lifetimes!" He is yelling at her now.

"I think you should talk to Niamh, Sean. Just ask her, please."

...

His motorcycle is packed up. He's getting ready to go. Niamh is there, her head is down and her shoulders slump. "Sean, I don't want to go. I think we should wait for Naya. There's got to be an explanation." Niamh is desperate. This is her home now but she can't leave her brother alone either.

Sean's jaw clenches tight at her mention of Naya's name. There is no persuading him otherwise. To be a cuckold, to be disgraced in front of other men in the pueblo, to have his girl run out on him—he must not be a real man. Somehow he fails Naya and himself. He's totally disgusted with himself.

"Damien would like to speak with you for a few minutes before you go, Sean," Ellen says.

"Tell him I said 'Goodbye'."

"Please, Sean, a few minutes?"

Sean gets off his cycle and goes into what is Nahuel's office which Damien shares with him when he is at Third Mesa. They speak for about ten minutes with Sean shaking his head and saying 'No' a lot. Finally, he comes out. There is a bulge in his left jacket pocket from something Damien gives him, really almost forcing him to take.

Sean gets on, Niamh behind him. There is lots of room since Naya is not riding with them today or, as looks likely, ever again.

Sean accelerates away. Niamh looks back, reaches out her left hand and yells, "No, Ellen, no. I don't want to go! Mom! Mummy! Mummmmyyyy!"

Then they motor around a few creosote bushes and are out of sight in seconds.

Ellen sinks to her knees, weeping once more. Damien is there. He doesn't touch her. He just squats down and is a quiet companionable presence for the next twenty minutes.

There really are no words in any language for the way Ellen is feeling—the hurt that Naya is capable of inflicting on people who love her is nothing new. What is new is the scale and the fact that Ellen is quite sure it is her fault. She doesn't blame her daughter, she blames herself. She's a failure as a mother and now has failed to protect her newest child, Niamh 'Holly' Ruane. When this thought passes through her mind, her sobbing becomes uncontrollable. She is having a hard time catching her breath.

...

They're in Hearth House and have been there for nearly ten days. Naya's been taking José-Luis through the 14 steps of sweat lodge purification. One day per step.

When he comes to her at Third Mesa, she can hardly recognize the man he is. His addictions include alcohol, tobacco, cocaine, oxycodone, uppers to keep him awake, downers for sleeping and modern nanosite drugs for everything from inducing hallucinations, states of euphoria, erections that last for hours and other states she can't even begin to understand. What she does understand is her best friend is in terrible trouble.

She writes a quick note, one to Sean and one to her Mom, to tell them where they've gone, then in her hurry forgets to press 'send message', saddles up two camels and heads to Hearth House with JEL. He is in such bad shape that she has to tie him to his saddle and he is

Bruce M Firestone

unconscious for the last three hours of their journey. She is hoping he will not die before they get to the sweat lodge.

For the first two days, she has to force feed him water, opening his mouth, pouring in a miniscule amount, closing it, watching most of it spill out then doing it again. If she does not keep him hydrated in the elevated temperatures of the lodge, he will die. But if he does not sweat out the poisons in his system or otherwise excrete them, he will die. It's dicey.

The first couple of days or so he doesn't complain much—he's barely conscious—but after that he says he's OK and wants to leave. What he really wants is to find the satchel he came with—there is a whole pharmacy in there. It won't matter even if he could get up and try to find it—she dumped his whole arsenal into an old steel trash barrel and burned everything. She throws his leather satchel into the fire too for good measure—it's just another reminder of an old life he has to leave behind or he will leave this one behind forever. Naya knows cuz she almost exited the same way.

"Where's my bag, Naya?"

"It's not here, JEL."

"Can you get it for me?"

"No."

"Please, I need it."

"No, you don't."

"Naya, that's it I'm leaving."

"I don't think so."

"Who put you in charge?"

"You did by coming here."

"Well, fuck off. I am going right now."

He is so weak and Naya is so tall and strong that restraining what used to be the premier male football player in the solar system is de nada at the present moment. If she has to, she'll tie him up. She'll use bridles from their saddles. Hey, she's lodge leader here!

On their third day, José-Luis starts to shiver

uncontrollably and vomit profusely. She has given him nothing but water but today she has made him some creosote tea with sugar. It is this weak mixture that is spewing out of him at both ends and through all his pores. His pores are also extruding a green mixture of goo that smells worse than it looks.

This is good, Naya thinks.

She starts their water trickle system so the sweat lodge turns from a sauna into a steam room. Hearth House is an octagonal wooden structure in plan view—its walls are double planked (two layers made up of four inch wide strips of tongue and groove lumber offset from each other at a 30 degree angle) and airtight.

The steady jet of steam helps her clean his body (he is naked and she wears only her monokini and a t-shirt) and Hearth House every hour but still the odors are beyond belief. She thinks he is over the worst but on day five (or is it six, Naya's lost track) he thrashes about and it looks like he might hurt himself. So Naya presses herself to him and holds on. After each episode like that, she has to drag him outside to cool him off and let him catch his breath.

She doesn't think it can get any tougher and then it does and she has to tie him up but finally by day 10, the worst has definitely passed. He has deep shadows under his eyes, his skin is yellow, he has lost at least 15 kilograms, much of it muscle mass but he is alive.

...

"I have something for you, José-Luis."

"I don't need anything else from you, Naya. Just your company," he says with a wan smile. "I've missed you so much. I don't know why I stayed away for nine years. I think I was mad at you, at me. Mostly at me."

"This is a gift for you but you have to promise me that you will care for it and, when the time is right, give it to someone else who is deserving."

"I don't deserve anything."

"Oh shut up. Just promise me, OK?"

"Yes, Naya."

She comes back inside Hearth House (now reduced to a more normal temperature). She has with her an old Hopi drum—it's made of cottonwood and covered in rawhide. It stands about two feet high. It is priceless.

There is a short, thick padded drumstick that produces a deep sound that resonates in your chest and lungs and stomach and a longer, thinner drumstick with a small head on it that creates a sharp, higher pitched note.

"OK, here is what we are going to do. You choose which drumstick you want to use and you begin drumming. I'll use the other one. When you feel like switching, you reach for my stick and we switch."

"I don't know anything about drumming, Naya."

"Yes, you do, you just don't know it yet. Before we start, I want you to finish your tea and your soup."

"I'm not hungry, Naya, let's just start."

"No, you need to drink and eat before we start."

"Why is that?"

"Because once we do, you are going to tell your life story through the drum and you can't stop for anything until you finish."

"How long will that take?"

"Days, I think."

...

Sometimes, he pounds on the drum like a drug fiend (which he is until a few days ago), sometimes like a loser (which he is until a few days ago), other times like a lover (which is something that has entered his mind now that he is feeling better and sitting across from Naya) then those thoughts leave him as undignified and he plays from his heart, then his soul and then there is nothing but the beat of the drum for over 56 hours until his hands are raw and his arms are ready to fall off. Naya never flags or misses a beat—she follows him to the end.

Then she makes him more tea and a light meal. When he is asleep and she is sure he is OK, she finally lies down on the floor (he is on the only cot in this place), covers herself with a flannel blanket and sleeps like a baby.

...

She gets JEL outside on day 15. He is so out of shape and weak that she can only get him to walk a half mile from Hearth House. But by day 18, he can do some light jogging and he is eating more.

"JEL, I want you to do something for me."

"Yes, Naya." He says this a lot.

"I want you to grow your hair out. This fascist look you've got going isn't the real you."

"OK, Naya." He smiles at her. She smiles back.

She runs her hand over his head and says, "Look it's started already!"

He shivers when she touches him.

...

They are sitting on the verandah of Hearth House. The sun is going down.

"I have some tea I made for you, JEL."

"OK, Naya."

"But it isn't creosote tea."

"Thank God!"

"It's something else. I think you should take it but maybe you won't want to."

"What is it, Naya?" He would drink cyanide if she asked him to.

"It's something from my Aunt Zora and her Mom, Euphony. It's a natural product with dictamnus in it. It'll help you sleep." He still has trouble sleeping and has frequent nightmares.

"OK."

"But it may do something else."

"Uh, huh?"

"It may help you with, umm, astral projection—I think you have to go back, back to Stockholm, JEL."

"It's OK, Naya, I know it wasn't you that started those rumors about me, ah, hurting you. It was that fat asshole kid who sold me, us out."

"This has nothing to do with the tabloid press, JEL, and everything to do with you and me."

"OK, Naya, if you think so." He drinks Euph's potion.

...

He is hovering about four metres over a nine year old boy standing on top of Monumental Tower, part of Stockholm City Hall. He's a good looking kid who moves well, is muscular and controlled.

He is saying to a little girl, "You stay here. You're too little."

She says, "Am not."

The boy says, "Are too. Stay here, Naya, I mean it."

Then the little girl cries out, "Help, JEL, help me!"

He watches the whole scene play out—the little girl climbing over the balustrade, falling, conking her head on the steel roof, the boy missing her but at the last second catching her dress in his fist, the way he won't let her go even if it means he dies too, hearing it rip, the thought of losing her.

Now he is below them and he can hear the boy say, "Climb up, Naya! Climb!"

He is watching from the little girl's point of view as the two of them struggle together to save themselves and each other. Then the boy gets her back to safety and finally delivers her to her Dad 365 steps below.

José-Luis is crying when he wakes up. Naya is there. She holds his tired head in her arms and brings him to her breast and comforts him. "Did you see? Did you see it? It wasn't your fault. You saved me and now I've saved you."

...

"I have to go back, José-Luis."

"I know. I'll miss you."

"You'll always have my drum."

"You look nice, Naya." He thinks she must have put on a bit of weight in the three weeks they have been at Hearth House but given the state he arrived in, he can't really be sure. She has a lovely figure, well endowed in every sense but now she is just glowing.

"Thanks. Where are you going to go now, JEL?"

"I have a contract to play at Shackelton. It'll be easier playing at Luna colony for awhile, maybe I can make it back to Bundesliga or the English Premier League." When he says Shackelton, he is referring to Shacketon Crater which is a town nestled inside the old impact crater that is 21 km in diameter and 4.2 km deep. It's at the south pole of the Moon and has nearly continuous light at its rim which means it produces a lot of power for Germanian towns in the vicinity.

"If anyone can make it back, it's you JEL." Naya says simply. JEL is only 26, there is time. "I'm really glad you came to see me."

"Me too. I don't suppose you would want to come to Luna with me?" he asks shyly.

She knows what he is asking but she shakes her head, 'No.'

She comes over and kisses him on the lips and he starts to press her to him but she breaks it off before it can lead anywhere else.

"Sorry," he says. Now it is time for him to go, he doesn't want to. This is forever. "Naya, I should have told you something years ago, I am such a fool—I've loved you, always."

"I know that JEL. I love you too."

"But not that way, right?"

He has to hear her say it. "No, not that way."

"OK, OK, I can live with that."

He smiles, turns away and walks out of her life.

...

"Hi Mom. I'm back. Anyone?"

It's dark and quiet in Ellen's room. She can't see Niamh anywhere either. So she goes to her and Sean's room to drop off her things (she isn't carrying much except a single knapsack). Sean isn't there either.

She really wants to see him but she wants to tell Ellen first.

...

When she finds Ellen, Naya's shock is palpable. Her mother has three bottles of Gin, two of them finished and she is working on the third. Ellen is looped; she's a mess. Naya has to get her cleaned up right away and get rid of the Gin. If Nahuel sees it, there will be real trouble.

Naya has never seen her mother drink let alone drunk. But Naya suspends judgment of other people. Look at her wasted teen years. She shudders.

Even touching these bottles and smelling their contents is almost too much for Naya. She insanely thinks about taking a pull from the partially full one before she settles down and dumps it into the dirt. Then she picks up a large rock and repeatedly crushes all three glass bottles until they are unrecognizable and burns their labels.

Then she goes back to get Ellen out of there.

...

"Naya, ish that you?"

"Yes, Mom."

"How you doin?"

"Fine Mom."

They are in Ellen's room. She is giving Ellen a sponge bath and from time to time holding her still beautiful golden hair (which has a few grey hairs in it) out of the way while she pukes into another basin. Naya's been doing quite a bit of this lately.

"Where's Holly? Where's Sean? Mom, Mom?"

"Not here."

"I can see that. I can't see any of Holly's stuff. Did she move to another room?"

"Yesh."

"Oh, OK. Whose?"

"Her own."

"Mom, where is Sean?"

"I dunno."

"How come you don't know?" Naya is getting concerned.

"He left, they both left."

"Huh?"

"They're gone."

"I see. When are they coming back?"

"Never." Then Ellen starts crying again. Naya has never seen her Mom drunk and almost never cry. 'What gives?'

...

She can't get anything more out of Ellen until the morning.

"Mom, wake up." Naya hasn't slept at all.

"Yes?" Ellen says sickishly.

"Why did Sean leave?"

"Cuz of you."

"Because of me! I don't understand?"

"What do you mean, you don't understand? You run off with your old boyfriend for weeks, you don't say a word to anyone and you waltz back here like nothing's happened? You crushed your boyfriend who would do anything for you. You ruined that poor little girl's life, Naya! You ruined her life! When she left, she was crying for her Mom, for her Mummy, for me! I hate you, Naya, go away!"

"But Ellen, didn't you get my message?"

"Huh? What message?"

"I sent both you and Sean a message that I was taking José-Luis to Hearth House to detoxify him and I would be back at the end of the month which I am."

"You didn't fuck him?"

"No, Mom! I didn't fuck him. How can you say that?"

Ellen looks intently at Naya when she asks this. There is either no answer or a long one. She chooses no answer but there isn't any prevarication in Naya's face, manner or voice when she makes this statement. 'Can she be telling the truth?'

When they boot up Naya's personal page, they can both see messages there, one for Sean, with a lot of emoticons, and a cc to Ellen (without the emoticons), neither of them sent.

"Oh, God, Mom, what am I going to do now? I'm having a baby and he doesn't trust me enough, so he leaves me?"

"A baby, what's that you say?" A hungover Ellen is having a hard time keeping up with events.

"Yes, Mom, I'm preggers."

...

To Naya, it's clear. He didn't really love her. If he did, he would have waited for her, message or no message. What is there to live for now? Her baby, that's what.

...

To Sean, it's also clear—she never loves him. She trades him in first real opportunity that comes along. What is there to live for? His sister, until she is 16 and an adult. Then he'll throw his worthless self off his bike at 250 mph into a concrete abutment with no helmet.

...

"Empuje, Naya," Elsu is saying.

A few seconds later, "Otra vez."

Then another, "Otra vez!"

Ellen, Zora, Daniella and Su7e are also there acting as coaches. Ellen is holding Naya's hand and reminding her to breathe with each contraction. Naya has a determined look on her face and has never complained, not once, during her labor although there are a few more grunts lately. Her long auburn hair is wet with perspiration. Her labor is in its third hour, not that long as these things go. Zora is on towel and worry detail. She mops Naya's forehead from time to time and then worries. She is the only one in the room who is not a mother and that includes Su7e.

Dafne is outside Naya's room in the Pueblo pacing

like a nervous, expectant parent.

"Almost there, Naya," Daniella says. "I can see the head of your baby. Your baby is crowning, Naya!"

"Otra vez!"

"Push, Naya, push," says Daniella.

Moments later a healthy baby boy, 8 lbs 11 oz is born.

Elsu expertly cuts the umbilical cord, takes the baby over to a nearby table, suctions his nose, does a quick cleanup while doing an equally brief physical assessment and making sure he has an acceptable Apgar score (he does, his is 9), wraps him up, fits a cute little tuque on his head and then places a perfect package on Naya's tummy. She then helps Naya with her after birth which takes about another ten minutes then begins to massage her uterus to help it clamp down properly. She takes Naya's pulse, looks in each of her eyes and them smiles at her, "Bueno! Buen trabajo." Good, she is saying, nice job.

She thinks Naya is very strong in her body and in her mind and will recover fast. Whatever may have happened to her as a little girl, whatever is wrong with her mind, it is healed now. Elsu wonders why her nice young man isn't here but she knows all she has to do is ask her partner, Dafne, and she will get an inside scoop. Dafne knows this entire town's gossip.

"May I hold him, Naya?" Ellen asks.

"Sure, Mom."

Ellen only has to look at him for a few seconds to know that she is holding an Irishman's son. This is a Ruane. Thankfully not an execrable Hexham or even a multi cultural Vasilescu. It's Sean's boy, no doubt about it. His skin is very fair, he'll have red hair when he gets more of it on his little head and it looks like he'll have green eyes. He's super cute.

"What will you call him, have you picked out a name yet?" Ellen asks.

"His name is Michael Brooks Bell. Now may I have my baby back?"

"Care to make love to a grandmother?" Ellen asks Damien. He's been at Third Mesa on holiday from work for the last two days and plans to remain there for another eight days. It's a well needed break for many of the people at the Lab who have been going at it hard to get the planetary shield up around Mars and then monitor and learn how to maintain it and fine tune it. Men, even men nearing 60 like Damien, can still get undressed in zero time when they are going to have sex with a beautiful woman like Ellen.

...

"He's a cute baby but I can't honestly say he looks a lot like our side of the family."

Ellen laughs. "He sure is a Ruane."

"I would have liked to have met Sean's parents," Damien says.

"I miss him and his sister."

"I know, Ellen. I do too."

Damien wants to ask her for more details on what went wrong between Naya and Sean but hasn't been able to bring it up—when he gets close to that subject, Ellen gets uncharacteristically weepy and very upset. So he restrains himself but he is pretty sure that Ellen knows something important and is keeping it to herself. It probably has something to do with José-Luis. He can't help it—he resents José-Luis showing up like he did after dropping Naya for nearly ten years and then breaking up the one relationship that, as far as Damien knows, makes Naya stronger not weaker. 'Relationships are complicated,' he thinks. He is about to get some firsthand experience in this area, RFN.

...

"I am going to Mars, D."

"You are?"

"Yes."

"Ah when?"

"I'm leaving next week."

Damien sits up in bed, asks the lights to come on and looks at his wife.

"When are you coming back?"

"I'm not sure?"

"Are you coming back?"

Ellen doesn't answer. She gets up and pulls on a robe. She goes to sit in front of her mirror and puts her head in both hands. She would really like a drink.

"Haven't I been a good husband, Ellen? You know I love you."

"Yes, I know that. It's not you, it's me."

"Oh that's beneath you, Ellen. That's malarkey—'this isn't your fault, it's mine.' It's just female bullshit for 'I'm leaving you, go to Hell.'"

"Are you coming back?"

"Maybe."

'More bullshit,' Damien thinks.

"You're going to Farrar, right?"

"He's asked me to help with their We Are All ONE (Mars) campaign."

"Oh save it for the media, Ellen. I know the way you and Farrar create political cover for yourselves. That's your cover story, right? But the real one is you're running out on me, your boys, Naya and our grandson. You're a coward, Ellen."

As soon as he says this, he would do anything to take it back. She saves his life at San Quentin and almost loses hers here at Third Mesa. She is anything but a coward. He only said it because he is hurting.

"I'm sorry, Ellen. I should not have said that because it's untrue. I am grateful for our life together."

When he says this, Ellen starts to cry. She's been doing a lot of this lately.

Damien comes over and pulls her up gently. He holds her and she kisses him passionately and soon they are

Bruce M Firestone

making love again. Damien surprises himself by still being able to have sex with her twice in one day. 'Heck of a nice treat,' he thinks.

Ellen plans on making love to D as often as she can before she leaves because she knows that when she does leave, she is never coming back.

When he says 'Goodbye' at SFA, he can see it too. She never tells him it's forever but it's written all over her face.

Ellen looks at Damien once more thinking of their life together. She knows that she has gone as far as she can down this path of her life and that she has nothing more to give them. They will have to manage on their own now. If she stays now, it'll be toxic for her and thus for them.

Magellan understands this but not Finn, Damien or Naya. They just feel hurt and abandoned. Naya thinks her mother has the hots for the General and will get over it not realizing how long the General and Ellen have already had a mad pash for each other.

But it isn't just her family she is leaving. She's given everything to the Commonwealth and to Earth. There isn't anything left in the tank for any of them. It's empty—she's been running on fumes for years. If she stays, it'll just be downhill from here until eternity.

She takes one last look at Damien and the boys. Naya and baby Michael are still back at Third Mesa not because they can't travel but because it would be incredibly dangerous for Naya to be in San Francisco. Nyet to that.

She waves one last time and turns to board the spaceplane that will take her up to the joint DARCH/Commonwealth Bradbury Transit Station at L2. She does not weep. She's finished with that too.

Bradbury Station is in a small, low energy orbit around L2 (one of the five Lagrange points in the Sun-Earth-Moon system where gravitational effects of these three masses are (mostly) canceled out and are (mostly) stable). It's there she will transship to her Mars transit vehicle.

Farrar tries to book her on the Phobos or her sister ship, the Deimos, which are far larger and more comfortable than the HG Wells but Wells is available sooner. Neither the General nor Ellen is prepared to wait any longer than necessary. It's been nearly 24 years. That's enough of that.

The Wells is equipped with Quantum Shielding, of course, so Ellen will be safe even if not entirely comfortable during her six and half week transit.

When she finally comes down Mars Space Elevator and debarks, she looks as pretty to the General as the first day he met her—the one where he saluted her. So he decides, if it works, keep doing it. He marches smartly over to her (he's in his DARCH uniform and looks very handsome today), snaps a salute and says, "Welcome Madam President to Mars." Then he grabs her up and kisses her unashamedly. Paparrazzoids take photos (yes, they have those on Mars too). They are there because they got a tip off that the President of Earth (yep, they still make basic journo mistakes like that) is arriving on Mars. Apparently, she is bringing a secret weapon with her that the General plans to use in his plebiscite campaign to unify Mars but whatever it is, they can't see it. It must be in her luggage.

The tipster this time is none other than Farrar. He is through living with their secret.

"Madam President, I was wondering if you would like to marry me?"

"Never, Farrar, forever never," Ellen says with a fantastic smile. "I have something for you." She adds a small, delicate silver pin to his uniform. It is the image of Constantine I's hand superimposed on a beautiful artist's rendition of Mars and its two moons.

She is wearing one too and soon most Martians will be wearing them as well.

She does indeed bring two secret weapons—this pin and her indomitable self.

Later, she asks the other man in her life the same question, "Do you mind sleeping with a grandmother?"

He says (looking like a boy about to eat a really big candy bar), "I believe in miracles, you sexy thing." She laughs. She knows the corny tune he is referring to and they make love as passionately as they did on the Princesa Agnes. Farrar is just as good and Ellen is even better.

She and Farrar will live together for a long, long time on what will soon be a united Mars. United and independent in every way just like Farrar and Ellen are right about now.

...

"Damien, I want you to come out of there."

"Go away, Zora."

"I'm not going away til I know you are OK."

"I'm OK. Just go away. I'm fine, really."

Naya has asked Zora to come to Third Mesa and get Damien out of his room. Her sad sack Da has been moping since Ellen left. What a loser. Other than play with Michael a few minutes here and there, he just sits in his room feeling sorry for himself. Naya knows what that is like. She also knows Zora's secret.

She's had an itch for her Da (who knows why, Naya can't see it) like forever. So now that Ellen has conveniently taken herself out of the picture, what's the prob? Like most women, when it comes to the heart, Naya is crazy but when it comes to practical matters like having a baby, she's zeroes in like a suicidal, white scarfed Nipponese fighter pilot searching for an aircraft carrier to sink by crashing his plane into it circa the Pacific Theater in 1944 and 1945. Naya takes out her BPI herself using a laser scalpel, some disinfectant, artificial skin and makeup until the tiny incision heals and never tells anyone least of all Sean. Good thing too that she never tells that shiftless Irishman who drops her because he can't stand competition of which there is none. At least now she can bring up Michael without the burden of some needy adult male competing for her attention and affections, all of which go (unhealthily, although Naya does not know that) to her baby.

"I'm coming in, Dr. Bell." Zora opens his door. Damien is just sitting there looking at photos of his wife.

"Damien, do you want to go for a walk?"

"No thanks.

"You know I was just remembering how much she hated sailing and then how good she got at it. She was like that about everything. I wonder if she'll get to sail on Mars?" Damien could easily check that. The answer is, 'Yes.' Winds are strong enough and Mars atmosphere is already dense enough to propel lightweight boats with a lot of sail area like modified Mars Lasers. Waveforms are different in Mars gravity and atmosphere—it makes for a wild ride for the few brave souls who are testing these boats there now. They've passed the Armstrong limit so they don't need pressure suits. They are equipped with breathing apparatus that are really no more than nose plugs that make Mars atmosphere breathable and they estimate that within three Martian years, they'll be able to dispense with those too.

Still, if you capsize into Europan seas (now conveniently relocated to Mars), you'll die of hypothermia in no time if you are not wearing a really good full wetsuit. It takes a long time to heat up that much (salty and hence denser) water so it will be awhile before Ellen can put on her bikini and go to the seaside with Farrar. Damien bursts into tears at that thought. Zora goes over to comfort him.

"You're suffering from withdrawal, Damien. You have to stop looking at pictures of her. Every time you do that, you reinforce your addiction. It's a physical thing. I can give you something for that." Zora is not referring to what most people might think she means—i.e., sex with her. She has something from her mother, from Euphony, a kind of anti-love potion.

But Damien, just shakes his head, 'No.'

...

The next day, Damien does come out of his room. He sits there watching Naya breastfeed his grandson.

"Da, why don't you take Zora for a walk?"

"Huh? What did you say?"

Naya is talking into his right ear which is practically useless. He turns his head to the right so he can present her with his left one.

"Why don't you go for a walk? See if Zora wants to go too."

"OK."

...

"Where do you want to go, Damien?"

"Nowhere."

"Come on, I know a place. But it's a hike," she says looking at him with an appraising eye. He's still an appealing man, tall, thin, some gray hair, bright, highly motivated (that is until recently). He walks with a bit of a limp and can't go too far but she thinks he can manage this hike.

"OK. Where we going?" Not that it matters. Like Sean, he's just making conversation.

"You'll see."

...

"Uh, I don't think we should be here."

"You mean the two of us?"

"Yes. No. It's not right somehow."

"Dr. Bell, you loved Nell, right?" They are at Nell's graveside. Which was and still is an enduring shrine to her huge number of fans that, if anything, love her more now, in part, because of her tragic, untimely death as a young woman.

"Yes, very much. I, I think I still do."

"Then you loved Ellen, right?"

He doesn't remember ever admitting this to anyone

before not even to himself, "I think I loved them both—at the same time. Is that wrong? Was I wrong?"

"Did you love my mother?"

Damien is getting uncomfortable with the direction this conversation is taking.

"Euph took me in and made me whole again. There are no words I can use to describe how I feel about her but 'love' will have to do because I can't think of anything else so, yes, I loved her too."

"So you see, it is possible to live again, Dr. Bell, and love again."

Then she stands on her toes and kisses him.

"Don't do that, Zora."

"Why not?"

"Not here."

"So not here but somewhere else?"

"No, not here where Nell is buried and not anywhere else, Zora. Ever. This is so wrong, on so many levels, I can't even begin to enumerate them."

"That's why it's right, Damien." And she kisses him again. She is taller than Euphony, less hippy but still very womanly. Damien can feel every curve, every nuance and then he thinks, 'Oh God, Ellen is gone, Nell is gone, Euph is gone' and so the rest of his life happens...

While they are making love, a part of Damien is thinking that this is a shrine to Nell, people come here all the time. They will see a half naked couple doing what human beings (in one form or another) have been doing for about four million years. Will they think it is inappropriate? Will Nell think it is inappropriate?

But it isn't—it's a celebration of life and that is what Nell stands for anyway. Then Damien just stops thinking which is as it should be.

...

That is how Zora gets herself pregnant with Zachary. She's in her late 30s but women these days are having kids into their 50s so she figures she'll be fine and she is right.

When she tells Damien and Naya (not together but separately), Naya reacts with overwhelming joy. "That's great news! Baby Michael will have a BFF! Is it a girl or boy?"

"His name is Zachary."

Naya brings Michael over to feel Zora's womb. She says, "Michael, meet Zach, my brother and your Uncle who'll be a year younger than you!" The baby seems to like this and coos correctly. "See, they're already best friends, Zora!" Both women laugh at Naya's cleverness with her Uncle/Brother skit which is doubly funny because it is accurate. She pantomimes a topsy turvy world flying Michael around the room first like a fighter plane with wheels (Michael's face) down then inverted (with her hand supporting the back of her baby's head) and finally doing a forward then backward roll. The baby smiles for his Mom; he hasn't quite got the hang of laughing yet. He's a happy baby, a good sleeper and a prodigious eater. Then he comes in for a landing on Zora's tummy who by now is lying flat of the floor, it's too funny.

DNA has worked its magic, again!

...

Damien says soberly, "But what will your mother say?"

"Don't you want our baby?" Zora is incredibly hurt by his reaction.

"Zora, I will love this baby and you forever. But I don't want to hurt Euph."

But he needn't worry that it will be an issue between mother and daughter or, for that matter, between Damien and Euphony. The elder wiccan tells Zora (privately), "Wonderful. I am so pleased."

"Really Mom, for sure?"

"Yes, Zora. I never told you—do you know why he ended up with Ellen not us?"

"You never told me."

"Because I couldn't have his baby; something happened to my insides when you were born."

"I didn't know that! It's my fault then!"

Even now, Euph won't tell her that she had her tubes tied. It's something that she can't fathom, how could she have been so stupid?

"Not at all. It happened later, nothing to do with you. Anyway, Damien was a young man and wanted a family. So Ellen finagled the situation to her advantage—she was always really good at that."

"Mom, Ellen is a fine person."

"Humph. Anyway, here's the irony, I get the best part of the man anyway—his son, my grandson. You have to come to Gabriola to have the baby!"

"Can Damien come too?"

"Yes, of course! Please ask him and send him my regards. Wait, I've a better idea! Let me ask him myself."

"Would you, Mom?"

"You bet!"

But Euph is only partly right. She's going to end up with not one but two little Bells to take care of.

...

It's another big party on Mars. The plebiscite results are in—they need a kind of triple majority. More than half of the Colonies have to agree (that is 7 out of 13), more than half of all colonists have to agree and more than half of voters (16 and older and all QEs on the planet) in each colony have to agree. What that really means is that they need 13 out of 13 Colonies on board—they have to win them all.

It's Ellen who insists on this. "Farrar, this is forever. We have to start with a clear mandate and that means a super majority."

"I'd be OK with 50+1."

"Typical man. The big Kahuna." Ellen smiles at him and he smiles back at her. She wants to have sex with him right now but unfortunately there are 26 Senators in their conference room at Valles Marineris with them (two from each Colony). Some laugh at the exchange between them, others like Mandarin representatives from Imperial China just shift uncomfortably in their seats at this exchange which seems more properly suited to a private bedroom that a constitutional conference.

Ellen gets her way like she does so often in her life, supported by Mandarins, Germanians and Hippies. The six Senators from the latter three Colonies all feel that she has just signed a death sentence for their plebiscite since there is no way they can get a majority to vote YES in any of them.

But they are underestimating the President. She makes wonderful speeches in fluent Manadarin, Cantonese, German, French and many other languages. Ash3r helps her with that. She uses her new QCCII phone's mike which completely suppresses her speaking voice by exactly reproducing the negative of the sound waves coming out of her larynx and replacing them with her speaking voice at a slightly lower frequency (which amplifies the importance of what she is saying in most cultures where a deeper voice is often associated with wisdom, age and (unfortunately) maleness) that sounds just like Ellen (almost) but in the local language.

In Hippieville, she asks Ash3r to disp her voice to a higher frequency because the women there clearly run the show since most of their men have big manboobs from smoking way too much weed and not doing enough hard work.

It also helps their cause that folks in Imperial China Mars and Germania Mars are slaves and don't often get to vote (i.e., like never) so when they do (Farrar's armed forces make sure everyone who is eligible to vote does) and, since it's a secret ballot, every Colony votes in favor—in fact, Imperial China Mars and Germania Mars citizens are amongst the highest YES voters. The lowest YES vote is in Hippieville where the returns are 50.4%

YES, 48.2% NO with the rest being spoiled ballots. Some of the men there aren't entirely clear on the YES/NO concept Ellen thinks.

It's a narrow run affair but a new Mars era is about to begin.

...

Almost immediately, General Staubach receives a cordial message that the leader of Imperial China (Earth) wishes to speak with him and requests most humbly a few rudiments of time from the important leader of Mars.

General Yao is pissed. They are not prepared, he tells Farrar, to accept the results of the Mars Plebiscite. He accuses General Staubach of using coercion—his army apparently forces loyal servants of Imperial China and her 1,000 year ally, Germania, to vote YES in what is clearly a rigged election.

But in fact, Yao is delighted. It is the excuse he has been looking for. Having Mars out of the reach of Imperial China is unacceptable. He also intends to reel in the two scientists who got away so he will correct three losses of face in one master swoop. Oh yes, he's added a third name to his list—Sean Ruane. His allies in the Commonwealth include the Republican Old Guard (Rogues) and their economic engine, a terribly badly named group called the Club Les de Sades. It is the latter who finally inform General Yao of a new weapon developed by this young man who shows such promise and will soon be working happily (or not, Yao couldn't care less) for the cause of the greater good of Imperial China.

There are also millions of drogues poised and ready to work closely together with their secret weapon—a huge installed base of Sinofighters that will soon show a completely different capability to Gwailo.

General Yao has a few Club Members killed horribly as an example to the rest—withholding vital information will not be tolerated. They are the first to see Sinofighters in action, up very close. They are truly exceptional in their violence which, as a result, has a quite satisfactory outcome—even the Club Les de Sades are cowed as soon everyone else will be, General Yao is sure.

Finally, the time seems auspicious to achieve the three primary goals of Imperial China's long held secret '1,000 Year Maidenhair' plan named after a tree of that age found in south central Hunan Province where General Yao was born. The plan includes—

1. Capture key scientists and technology to bring Imperial China to the forefront of development.
2. Establish a new hegemony over the Moon-Mars-Earth axis led by Imperial China and Germania with, of course, General Yao at the head of the snake.
3. Acquire a complete DNA data base of everyone, everywhere and the technology to deploy nanosite deconstructors instantly to quell any dissatisfaction.

There will never again be a repeat of the Mars Plebiscite or disobedience to Mandarins ever. It will be a New World Order of tranquility, prosperity and obedience. Now what could be better than that?

...

Farrar isn't Mars Texas Hold'em champ for nothing. He says, "That smug (he was about to use the word' bastard' but replaces it at the last second with) bureaucrat has something up his sleeve. There is no way he would lay it out like that if he didn't. I just can't figure it out."

Ellen and another person walk out from under behind a screen; they've been observing Farrar and Yao talking via Mtv.

Jag Durai says, "I can guess."

Ellen finds Jag, his wife Arcadia, their kids and his now ancient Dad, Pal, practically hiding out on the HG Wells. They have decided to put maximum distance between themselves and General Yao and now this, Yao has come calling. Jag has seen enough of the inside of a workcamp for several lifetimes.

"Please, Dr. Durai?"

"Well, I'm not sure so maybe I shouldn't speculate."

"Jag, tell us what you know?" Ellen asks.

"Well, I don't know anything for sure."

As a scientist he has had a hard time just shooting the breeze especially about things that are kind of within the ambit of his profession.

"Well Nesha and I have scanned them and we think there is a very large data set that has not been activated in any of them."

"Dr. Durai, I, we," Farrar says looking over at Ellen who nods, "are not following you."

"Those games, you know, those Sinofighter consoles. I was the one who developed the hack so they could be used for long distance, uh, exchange—"

"You mean as sex toys?" Ellen interrupts.

Jag blushes, "Well that yes but also for visiting friends or colleagues in a way that was never before possible. They are in use everywhere now. But the thing is, I never leaked the, ah, sex hack. They said it was some kids in Californian but I researched that—that's bogus. Imperial Chinese agents working for the People's Liberation Army/National Revolutionary Army did that based on, ah, my work and experiences. They did it to spread Sinofighter technology across Moon-Mars-Earth; people liked it and then when they found they could use it for more than sex, for work and for tourism, it was irresistible. They're ubiquitous now."

"Dr. Durai, what could this bolus of unactivated data be used for? What's its purpose?"

"Ah, I could be wrong but I think," Jag says so quietly they have to strain forward to hear him, "I think they could be a weapon. A very dangerous weapon. That's why my family and I came to Mars. They're getting ready for something big and this place has the fewest number of those things. People are too busy to play games much here. But there's a lot of them over in Imperial China Mars and in Germania Mars. I know I checked market data and sales data for Sinofighter Corporation."

"I'm scared, Farrar," Ellen says. She's not frightened for herself. She thinks Damien could be in mortal danger. Her kids too especially Naya.

"Me too," adds Jag.

"We have to warn the Commonwealth and Damien right away, Farrar," says Ellen.

"Ah, sorry Ellen, no. We don't inform anyone. Imperial China and Germania will have agents inside the Commonwealth. What do you think Yao was for decades inside the old USA? We'll only precipitate the miasma we are trying to avoid if they find out or even think we are on to them. In any event our first duty is to Mars now." Farrar, of course, has many agents inside both Imperial China Mars and Germania Mars but there isn't a single hint about this. How come? Farrar will find out but not right now.

"Let me at least warn Damien?"

"Give me 48 hours, Ellen? Then you can tell Damien and the Commonwealth, OK?"

"Alright."

...

The General can think on many levels at the same time and deal with complex plans that always require adjustment on the fly. Farrar will never get old because, like all great military minds, he is always learning. As long as a person is open to new ideas, they'll never be old.

"Ah, Dr. Durai, out of curiosity, I was wondering if you know why, ah, your QE is female and Ellen's is male when almost everyone else's matches their gender?"

Ellen looks up, first surprised by his question then curious too. She and Ash3r have been teased about this endlessly and so they would like to know too, that is, if Jag can answer Farrar's question.

"Sure, isn't it obvious? Doesn't everyone already know?" Jag says.

"No," Ellen and Farrar say at the same time.

"Oh!"

"Well?" Ellen asks, hands now (reversed) on her hips facing Dr. Durai. She's impatient. She would really like to know.

"It's cuz we're both left handed. Left handed people and quantum people are always gender mismatches."

Farrar bursts out laughing and gives Ellen's cute ass a nice squeeze.

Jag is embarrassed at this intimate gesture by the General and tries to look away.

...

After this, the General asks, "S4y3rs, can you please come here?"

They are going to organize immediate roundup and destruction of every Sinofighter unit on Mars. They'll go out in force. This isn't a plebiscite. He's going to invoke Martial Law if he has to.

Even if Jag isn't sure, the General is. Texas Hold'em develops instincts for this sort of thing. Jag being here, the confab with that pompous bureaucrat, the coincidences and the probabilities all point to an attack. They are in peril.

But the General of the Army is not going to wait. He'll be personally leading this roundup. Yeehaw.

...

When Naya has Michael baptized, she surprises everyone—she asks Farrar to be his Godfather. Naya figures if Michael ever needs any help in this life and, Heaven help us we all do, he'll get it from that sneaky SOB of a General who's snagged Da's wife.

Farrar attends the baptism by media wall. Damien is polite. Ellen is watching Zora stand next to her husband. They are standing together as ONE couple. Ellen's eyes narrow as she watches them. 'He fucks the mother and then the daughter. Are you fucking kidding me?'

Watching Farrar and Ellen, Damien and Zora at the service is almost as awkward as the scene at Ellen's mother's funeral. All that's missing is Euphony but then again she attends also via media wall so then it gets really uncomfortable for everyone except Naya and her baby. Even the Minister can feel the tension. She is thinking, 'I thought baptisms were supposed to be happy, family affairs?' It's a family affair alright.

The General seems pressed for time and leaves immediately after this part of Michael's baptism—

"Naya, have you chosen Godparents for your child?" the Minister asks.

"Yes, I have," Naya answers.

"Please have them come forward."

Naya holds her baby up towards the General who'd normally hold the baby at this point but that is a might awkward since he is physically on Mars right now. And then she gives her baby to Su7e to hold. Su7e has agreed to be Godmother.

"Do you Godfather and Godmother," the Minister says nodding to first the General and then to Su7e, "with the help of God Almighty, swear that you will do all that you can to help and support Naya in the bringing up of her Child?

"I will," says the General somberly. It is frankly one of the proudest moments of his life. He wants to give Ellen's hand a squeeze but given Damien's attendance here that might be a trifle unseemly.

"We will," says Su7e on behalf of herself and another unseen presence.

The Minister looks at Su7e thinking, 'That was odd.' She shrugs and proceeds. She says these timeless words—

"Heavenly Father, we praise you for this Child's birth. Surround Michael with your blessings so that he may know your love, be protected from Evil and know your goodness though all of his days. May he learn to love all that is true, grow in wisdom and strength and come through faith to the fullness of your Grace.

"May God the Father of all bless Naya, Godfather Farrar and Godmother Su7e and give them the grace to love and care for this Child. May God give them wisdom, patience and faith, and help them to provide for this beloved Child's needs.

"Eternal Father, we thank you for the rich variety of the families you have created for us (*this is an understatement in the case of the Brooks, the Bells, the Hopi of Third Mesa and the as yet undiscovered relationship of Euphony and Zora to the whole kit and caboodle rats nest of interwoven family ties present (sort of) here today*), and for the relationships which we see and enjoy within them. Help us to respect and learn from each other. We thank you too for love that binds families that are here today and ask your blessing on them.

"Heavenly Father, whose blessed Son shared at Nazareth the life of an earthly home, bless the home of this Child. Lord provide shelter, warmth and security to the family and this Child and to all those who visit.

"All this we ask in Jesus' name, Amen."

They all say, 'Amen' and then skedaddle out of there. Some like Farrar have many battles ahead, others are just glad to get to get out of an awkward social situation that rivals telling your friends and family, after a really big buildup, the funniest joke you know and then you are the only person who laughs.

Naya would like to tell everyone a joke; it'd go something like this—

Question: 'What's the one thing an Irishman with Alzheimer's remembers?'

Answer: 'A grudge.'

But she restrains herself because, first of all, no one suffers from Alzheimer's anymore so some people won't even know it's a disease that steals your memories and hence won't get her joke and, second, because everyone will see that it's just a cheap and dumb way for her to get back at Sean. She's missing Michael's Da. She sighs.

Still, both Naya and baby Michael, who already likes being the center of attention, are pleased with his baptism.

Naya makes cut sandwiches for everyone afterward but only has a few customers—Zora, her Da and, of course, Michael. Damien notices but does not mention that despite the fact that Naya is the inventor of farm-in-a-box, her culinary skills haven't improved much. She's a better DNA coder than a cook. Her sandwiches taste like sawdust.

...

Sinofighters are led by Ti3-Gu41. Each Sinofighter freed from its console homebase appears larger than life. Most of them are just over two and a half metres tall with large square heads, rectangular mouths that appear to have metal teeth in them (it's an illusion designed to frighten and cow people) and powerful square bodies. They carry virtual Jiujiebian (nine section whips) that can destroy a person in as few as four strokes. They are also deadly in hand to hand combat since they have the ability to put their hand inside a living being and rip its organs out or otherwise disrupt living tissue. They are designed for maximum destructive power, up close and personal. None of this long distance fighting with rifles, mortar, artillery, cannon, howitzers, landmines, IEDs, missiles, bombers, WMD, EMP, lasers or information warfare.

Sinofighters have a command and control hierarchy. The taller the Sinofighter, the higher its rank. Ti3-Gu41 is three metres tall, exactly three.

They also have another weapon which is about to be demonstrated—they are capable of mass destruction but in a way that leaves property and the natural environment unharmed. They only kill people, en masse.

...

Sean has taught himself how to play the mouth organ. All he plays are these mournful Irish ballads (the Irish have an unlimited supply of depressing music). He is getting pretty good at it. Niamh asks him to play Join the British Army but he refuses her and goes back to playing funeral dirges.

Then he surprises her—he plays a ditty by an English group. It's a pop tune and she thinks maybe he is getting better (i.e., over Naya) until she hears—

Love, love me do.
You know I love you,
I'll always be true.
So please, love me do.
Whoa, love me do...

Niamh speaks up for the first time in more than an hour, "I think you should call up Mrs. Hunter."

"Huh?"

"I think you should call Mrs. Hunter, Sean."

"Why would I do that? Is something wrong at school, Kaya? And don't call me Sean. It's Micky."

"I don't like your nickname though."

"It's not my nickname anymore, it's my name so use it." They're in Port Isabel in Texas. It's a tiny harbor on the Gulf of Mexico not far from Matamoros. It's the place that Pet3r mentioned to Damien when they are in the caves below the tri-pyramid at Marco Gonzalez with Nell. It's where Damien wants Sean to go. He says wait there. But for what, Sean has no clue.

On their arrival, he tells Niamh she is Kaya 'Elder Sister' Spillane and he is Micky Spillane. Odri4n makes them fake ID.

"So like call her."

"What for?"

"I think she likes you."

"What?"

Mrs. Hunter is 23 or 24 and a petite, blond Texas cutie. She's only a couple of years older than Sean and every time he comes to a parent-teacher conference, Mrs. Hunter, her home room teacher, makes sure to spend

Bruce M Firestone

extra time with him. And it's not because Niamh is a bad student.

Mrs. Hunter has a five year old daughter (also a cute blond) from a teen romance gone bad, really bad. She is positive that Micky and his sister are in some kind of trouble and the names they are using are just ridiculous. But this strange, taciturn Irishman and his beautiful sister (her top student) are good people, she is sure of it.

She would like a boyfriend (husband really if she is honest about it) but only the right kind of man will do. Not any man. But maybe this one. There aren't a lot of choices in a place like Port Isabel.

She has practically every kind of sex toy that you can buy on the Internet but she'd really like the real thing. Micky looks like the real deal to her. She's just about ready to burst with desire and she is having very active daydreams about him. She even gives Kaya her quantum number saying, 'If you need anything, please call.' But she is really hoping Kaya'll give it to her brother and he'll call her.

"I have her number. You should call. You can't spend all your time in this stupid room."

Niamh and Sean live in a single room. The bathroom they share with three other roomers on this floor is down the hall. Sean has hung two bed sheets around her cot to give her some privacy.

Sean is stocky no more. He's lost interest in cooking so Niamh has to learn to cook for him and her. But he's also lost interest in eating. Food just doesn't taste like anything. Everywhere he goes, he feels that he is somehow 'outside' everything going on around him. It's like he is in a twilight zone—running slightly behind everyone else's clock. He can't taste anything or feel anything and he can't connect with anything or anyone. He hopes each day, he'll wake up and it'll be gone. Sean is depressed but doesn't know it.

He works in a motorcycle repair shop. They have lots

of work and he is paid in cash. It's not much but they're getting by.

"So you going to call her?"

"Sure. Give me her number."

Niamh gives him the number. He puts it on his night table and forgets it's there even before he can turn his head.

He has run the movie of his time with Naya a thousand times in his mind. 'Oh, Sean, Sean, Sean. I can't live without you!' Yeah, right. That is until, Mr. Right shows up. But it doesn't make any sense. How can it be that she doesn't love him? How can that be?

...

606   Bruce M Firestone

Chapter 16 Sinofighters

"Sean, wake up. Wake up!"

"What Kaya, what?"

"Listen."

He used to wake up fast but these days he can't seem to snap to like he used to. But he can clearly hear shrieking on the streets and in town. It's everywhere. It's freaky. There is distinct wailing and screaming, raised voices, some of them angry, very angry. Others are really scared.

They don't have any media walls or Mtv scanners in this place. Sean doesn't want any. He doesn't want to watch a Bundesliga game and maybe catch a glimpse of Naya and her new/old squeeze partying. Maybe they're the 'It' couple at Luna base by now. Nope not going to be watching any TV.

So they go outside. It's bedlam. It's about an hour after dawn and people are standing around weeping, some are shouting, others just crying loudly.

"Sean, I'm scared," Kaya says. She is holding his hand.

They go over to one group. One of the guys says, "I heard they're coming here next." When he says this, people begin to run in every direction.

Sean finally grabs hold of one guy and asks him what's going on. But the guy's eyes are just bulging out in blind panic. "Get out of here, man. We're all gonna die."

"Come with me, Kaya." Sean heads over to a more prosperous looking home. He knocks. In Texas you have to be careful. They can shoot you just for being on their property and they all have guns.

The back door is open and there are no cars in the garage so he chances it.

They go in and turn on one of the media walls.

"Again, reports tonight, sorry, this morning, if they are accurate, suggest casualty figures in the Dallas-Fort

Worth metroplex upwards of two million. We emphasize for viewers that these are unconfirmed reports that are nonetheless considered reliable.

"Apparently at 0100 hours Central Time this morning an invasion of Sinofighters released by unknown forces although Imperial powers are suspected swept through the area and caused the results we are going to show you now.

"We remind viewers that these images are graphic. They have been taken by drone cameras and while the images are sometimes shaky they are unmistakably clear. No human or QE reporters have been able to enter the area."

The images they show are of people walking around aimlessly. Bumping into things, falling off balconies, bridges, driving cars into walls or just toppling over and lying still, not dead but not really human anymore either.

"What happened to them all, Sean?"

"Shh. Listen."

A talking head scientist is being interviewed, "There is no way to be sure until we can get hold of one of these, ah, walking corpses but it looks like perhaps, this is speculation you understand, their higher brain functions have been, ah, wiped clean by some unknown force. They're still breathing, we can see that, but there is no one home."

"What do you mean, Dr.?"

"Their, their brains have been devolved we think."

"Will you be able to confirm this?"

"I think it's only a matter of time before one of these, ah, creatures, wanders out. We'll get hold of one and examine it. Then we'll know for sure."

But Sean already knows. They've used Dr. Durai's scanners on millions of innocent people in Dallas— they've scanned their brains until they've emptied them out. America's just had its Hiroshima and Nagasaki moments rolled into one times ten. Sean knows enough history to realize it's just a matter of time before an ultimatum arrives.

He turns around and sees that Holly has slumped to the floor.

...

He has Holly back in their room. She is looking pale but better. He has put a cold cloth on her forehead and he takes it off from time to time, goes down the hall to their shared w/c, wets it, squeezes it and puts it back on her head. She gives him a little smile.

People are fleeing town and it is getting quieter. Sean is baffled. Where do they think they can go?

Odri4n is sitting there. He is silent. "Ah, someone is trying to get through to you, Sean. Rather urgently. It is Ellen Brooks from Mars."

Since Odri4n is Uncle Des' QE pair bond, he and Sean are not mindlinked so he cannot connect with Ellen that way. But Odri4n can communicate with Ash3r who is mindlinked to Ellen and relay what she has to say.

"I'm not sure I want to talk to her, Odri4n."

"As you wish."

"It's Ellen, Sean. Ellen!"

"Hi Ellen, can you hear me. It's Niamh! I miss you so much!"

Odri4n in an uncanny rendition of Ellen's voice says, "Hi Niamh! I miss you too! Is your brother there? I need to talk to him right away."

"Sure, hold on, I'll get him. Sean? Sean!"

Sean sighs, "Hello, Ellen."

"Sean, there has been an attack here on Mars. There are many dead. Well, they're not dead. But they might as well be. Farrar is missing."

"Yeah. We've been attacked too."

"What? What did you say?"

"Dallas was wiped out. Reports are more than two million dead."

"Oh my God. Look Jag is here, he needs to talk to you,

OK?"

"Dr. Durai is on Mars?"

"Yes, he's right here. Can I put him on?"

By this she means that his QE G4nesha will do the same thing that Ash3r is doing a moment ago for Ellen.

Odri4n now sounding like Jagad Durai says, "Mr. Ruane, we believe these Sinofighters are being released from their consoles and using reverse scanning to inflict the type of damage we are seeing on people."

"Yes, that was my conclusion too."

"Well we need to do something about it. Right now. I think they mean to kill us all."

"What did you have in mind?" Sean who is not as sharp as he used to be has no ideas at all.

"Well, I've detected a unique data set that was inactive until the last Mars or Earth day and that gives us something—a marker. I think you could program a set of nanosite deconstructors to seek out and destroy their consoles, all of them—"

"But if you are wrong, Dr. Durai, we could wipe out the entire IT infrastructure of this planet and yours. And you are just as dead on Mars without it as you would be if these things take over. We'll be in plenty of trouble on Earth too without IT. People will die."

Strangely, Sean laughs.

"Did you say something, Mr. Ruane? Mr. Ruane?"

Sean is lost in thought. He is thinking of what he and Odri4n did to 24/7's IT infrastructure. It effectively ended the corporation. This is much, much bigger. Without IT, trucks don't run, trains stop, tractors stop (IT these days runs up to 24 tractors simultaneously with just one human or QE driver to within a centimeter so they don't go over even the most minute patch of ground twice), ships stay in port, airships don't fly, nothing moves, people will starve in days. People without Roxies that is. Naya's Voyager project is going to go into orbit if they survive this. Sean is glad for her. It's his first step in a long process of getting better. Of course, he doesn't know this.

"Mr. Ruane!"

"Ah, yes, I'm here."

"Will you do it?"

"Can you hang on for 15 minutes? I need to talk to someone."

"Can you make it 10? We're just not sure what our, ah, status is here."

"Roger that, 10." Then Sean makes a cutthroat hand motion and Odri4n severs his link to Mars.

...

"Holly, we need to make an important decision. I can't do this alone. I need to have someone else help me with this decision. That is you."

"OK."

"I'm sorry to ask you to do—"

"I'm OK, Sean. I can help."

He smiles at her. "I'm sure you can. Now they've asked me to reprogram my nanosite deconstructors to take down Sinofighter consoles. Dr. Durai thinks he has detected a unique marker that we can use so that nothing else is damaged. But we can't be sure. And we don't have time to test it. If he is wrong, millions, maybe billions will die here on Earth. I read somewhere that Earth's natural carrying capacity is about 1.2 billion humans—"

"Naya said that!"

Sean takes a breath, "That's right, she did. But that's about one tenth of what we have now. It won't take 540 years to get there, more like one or two. Nine out of ten people will die."

"But what's the alternative, Sean?" Ellen taught Holly, 'There are always alternatives, Niamh, always.'

Sean smiles at her again. She is the most precious thing in his Universe. He's got to do better by her. This is step two in Sean's eventual recovery from his disastrous relationship with Hollywood actress Naya Brooks Bell.

"We can give up. This attack has a purpose, Holly. It's

like when the old US dropped nuclear weapons on Japan there was—"

"I know about that. I studied it with Ellen. It was called a 'calculus of death'. Would more people die if the bombs are dropped or if they aren't?"

"Exactly. I'm not sure if more people will die if we do what they are asking us to do than if we don't. And I am certain that the Cartesian Powers are behind this. But to gain what, for what purpose? They've been falling behind the Commonwealth. This is about establishing a new pecking order or something like that. We could give up."

"If we do what'll happen?"

"They'll round up those that don't cooperate and kill them. Others will cooperate. Scientists will be rounded up for sure. It'll be like what Dr. Durai went through in Shenyang but for hundreds of thousands. But they'll be alive."

"They'll be slaves, right?"

"Yes, but alive."

"They'd take you, right?"

"Maybe," he says but he knows the correct answer is 'certainly'.

"Sean, what's the most important thing in life?"

He doesn't have to think long about that at all. He's thinking about Naya. "Trust."

"Do you trust, Dr. Durai?"

"I do."

"Then do what he asks. I don't want anyone to take you away from me."

So with this implacable logic behind him, Sean through Odri4n calls Jag back. "You're on, Dr. Durai. It will take Odri4n and me about eight or nine hours to reprogram our duplicator. We'll send you," Sean pauses for a moment. Once he releases his IP to Dr. Durai, the genie is out of the bottle. No one else has the source code to his work. Once it's on Mars, they'll have a powerful new weapon (even though it isn't designed that way, Club Les de Sades forces his hand in that direction) that heretofore was exclusively under the care and control of one Sean Ruane. "We'll send you the source code. You'll have to fabricate your own duplicator on Mars. I can't send it via Quantum Tunnel because the nearest one is at Houston and right now that might as well be the Moon."

"Where are you, Mr. Ruane?"

"Port Isabel. It's—"

"I know where it is. I'm from the area."

"You are?"

"Yes."

'Now why would one of the most promising young scientists of his day be in Port Isabel?' Jag wonders. But they're too busy to engage in needless chatter.

...

They release Decon Force simultaneously on Mars (from Valles Marianeris) and from Port Isabel in Texas. It takes more than four days to destroy every Sinofighter in the Commonwealth and its allied nations. Longer on Mars.

Sean confines Decon Force to the boundaries of the Commonwealth and her allies because he is afraid that the Cartesian Powers will reverse engineer what they are doing and find a way to counteract it. But this is a mistake. If you give your enemy a sanctuary to hole up in, to resupply, to recuperate and to rearm then you cannot beat them. If the General had been available to advise them, this would never happen because Farrar is an expert, a classical warrior and a student of history while Sean is just a smart kid who never finishes his post grad work at Berkeley because, well, stuff's been happening.

Ti3-Gu41 escapes back to mainland Imperial China. Millions of Sinofighters are terminated but what matter? There are millions, billions more.

After their defeat on Mars and setback in the Commonwealth, General Yao elevates Sean Ruane from the capture list to the kill list echoing what he recommended to that fool President Schwinn years ago with respect to Damien Bell. Yao would kill Bell too but there is unfinished business there. Yao has control over Drogues, Rogues, Sinofighters but not QEs. For that, he needs the Quantum Key.

He has no doubt that his scientists (as useless as they are) will be compelled to find a solution to this deconstructor problem and they will be able to return in force once more. But as to the Key, he still needs to capture Bell to get that. When they do, they won't pussyfoot around with the guy.

The lever he needs to finally pry loose the Key from Dr. Bell is conveniently provided by none other than Club Les de Sades. Dr. Bell apparently has a daughter and grandson now. How would he like to see Ti3-Gu41 rip his grandson's heart and lungs out with one powerful hand? He'll be most cooperative like sentimental Gwailo always are when facing these kinds of challenges. After he gives them the Key, he'll let Ti3-Gu41 eviscerate the baby anyway. He'll give the girl to Club Members. She apparently has economic value.

He can't see it though. She's much too tall (much taller than Yao Allitt), her breasts are ridiculously huge, her hair, an ugly reddish, yellow, brown mess, her eyes, an evil green instead of the pleasing brown of the Han. There is no accounting for taste.

...

Ellen is methodically searching each of the Colonies with Ash3r, S4y3rs and more than 400 officers and personnel of Mars Army. They are looking for Farrar. They've found more than half of his expeditionary force so far. All of them in the same condition—their minds wiped. It turns out people don't live long in that condition unless they are force fed which Ellen has expressly forbidden hospitals and medics on Mars from doing. They don't have the resources to keep these people alive endlessly and it would not be the right, human thing to do. She finally understands why Damien assisted Aggie in the way he did.

She silently asks him to forgive her for her earlier ignorance.

She believes that they'll either find Farrar walking around with his fine mind a blank or he will have wandered off into Mars wilderness like many of his force have already done and forgotten to put their respirators on or they'll have fallen out of their nasal cavities and they don't know how to put them back in. They'll be dead in less than two minutes. It's a blessing really.

When they get to Imperial China Mars, it's obvious that a pitched battle took place here. There are more than 300 dead Mandarins and dozens of Mars Army personnel. All traces of Sinofighters are obviously gone thanks to Sean. But no Farrar.

They finally find him at Hippieville. He's there with 18 survivors. Some of them are wounded from the few but intense firefights they engage in but they're reasonably intact and their minds are fine.

Ellen has seen this film before—at San Quentin—the two men she has loved both in mortal danger. Farrar marches forcefully up to her and says briskly, "Thanks for coming to get us."

"How did you—"

He cuts her off. There is no time for explanations and no time for personal talk to tell her how much he loves her which he does. He says simply, "We have to get back to Valles Marianeris, Ellen. I know what we have to do. I have to talk to Dr. Durai, right away. "

...

"Reports tonight come from Houston, London and San Francisco. We start at Lawrence Livermore National Laboratory.

"So Steve, can you tell us what we know so far?"

"Thanks, Walter. What we know is that today around 3:12 am Pacific Time, the Planet Mars disappeared from our Solar System. If you look at the media wall to my right, you can see Mars as it would normally appear in the night sky. Now watch this."

The monitor shows Mars is there one minute and gone the next.

"So Steve, are you saying, this is incredible, that Mars has *left* our Solar System?"

"Scientists are at odds over this. But one thing is emerging. Orbits of other planets are apparently unaffected so it appears that Mars gravity or mass is still there."

"Do you mean that Mars is somehow a black hole?"

"Walter, at this point, I don't think we can rule anything out."

"Does that mean that everyone on Mars is dead?"

"That is unknown at the present time."

...

"Sean! Sean! Did you hear the reports? Everyone on Mars may be dead. Oh, oh. What happened to Ellen?" Niamh is in anguish.

"Niamh, easy, easy. I don't think that's what's happened at all."

"What do you mean? They said the Planet just winked out."

"Naw. The information about the Planet winked out. It's still there. I'd bet you my motorcycle against a dollar that it's still there."

"I don't understand. Will I still be able to call Ellen?"

"Um, that may not be possible for awhile." Sean is fibbing to her again.

"So like when can I talk to her? It was so nice just to hear her voice even if it was kind of creepy hearing her that way through Odri4n."

"You know how they wrapped Mars in a Quantum Bubble?"

"Yes."

"Well that's just an information layer. Someone, I would guess Dr. Durai (it is actually Farrar), figured out that they could use it to embargo every kind of information across its boundary—keep everything in but also keep everything out. I think the keeping everything out was the more important part after recent events. They've cut off contact with the outside Universe."

"I guess that means no calls with Ellen then."

"Correct. They just burned the Bounty. They won't be leaving Pitcairn Island any time soon."

"You got that from Naya too!"

"So I did, so I did." He ruffles her hair.

"Stop that!"

She's getting too old and grownup for that.

"I miss her," Holly essays.

"Me too, me too."

Step 3.

...

"Let's head north next week," Zora says to Naya.

"OK. Do you want to go visit Aunty Euph, Mikey? Hey babykins? What do you say? Woadtrip?"

Ten month old Michael is in his playpen. He smiles at his mother and then goes back to work. Sometimes gnawing on them and sometimes using them for their intended purpose (building blocks—he has Nahuel's large wooden block set from when he was a baby). Michael's thinking, 'I'm busy here, Mom!'

He's learned quite a few words like Mama, Ra (for Zora), up, big, Da (Naya thinks Michael is saying this on account of Damien's frequent presence but that's not why Michael is using the term), bye, gimme, heh, num num, dum dum, wawa, ick, bottle, wiz, tum tum, and, interestingly, he can clearly pronounce the word 'broken'. He's a very active little boy and this is a useful term to describe the detritus he is already leaving behind in his so far short life outside his mother's womb. He hasn't learned 'woadtrip' yet having just heard it for the very first time recently while his mother is engaging in baby talk with him.

Naya is also teaching Michael sign language. She is

doing this to help his cognitive abilities and also to give him the ability to express more complicated concepts than his little tongue and larynx can produce so far.

Michael can say in baby sign language—give me (tapping his chest with both hands and then pointing to an object), thirsty (index finger of dominant hand pointed at chin), want milk (squeezing dominant hand in a milking fashion), want juice (baby finger of dominant hand to chin), hurts (both index fingers touching), cookie (dominant hand with fingers curled downward over the other hand), blankie (both arms parallel across chest about two inches apart with palms of hands facing down) and about ten more signs.

They also make their own sign for 'angry'. Michael has an Irish temper and Naya finds making the sign for anger helps her baby. Naya and Michael both raise their hands to either side of their heads, forearms held vertically parallel to each other and act crazy with their tongues hanging out and eyes moving around like mad. Michael starts laughing soon after they do it and so does Naya. Then they'll do airplane or read a book together.

Naya is spending equal parts of her time being a mother and on Voyager. As Sean predicted (not that Naya knows that), demand for Roxies (and yet more guns but what purpose these will serve against the terrible events of last year, Naya can't imagine) has ramped up. Bessemer Ventures (which now has an office in the Valley) has helped her with corporate organization and funding as well as management and manufacturing infrastructure. Naya has no executive role and doesn't want one.

Her only title (other than she is Chair of their Board of Directors and attends Board meetings via media wall) that she will accept is Senior Researcher. She refuses to use more modern methods of attending these meetings like using an Mtv scanner or a Sinofighter console. Of course, no one uses those consoles anymore—there is a complete ban on those things and it would be a life sentence for importing a single one of them. She won't allow a scan of herself ever again after the fiasco of events at Third Mesa and the showing of her last film there.

For Naya, there is a Before Michael and After Michael life and the two seem as separate as the gulf between the Cartesian Powers and, well, everyone else. She misses nothing from her BM life other than Sean. She's thought a lot about him and he's like this mythical force in her mind now. Whatever bad traits he has, she can't remember any. She supposes he has them like everyone else but she just can't seem to recall any. Maybe he snores or something? But he doesn't snore. Must be something else. She wants to still be mad at him but she isn't anymore. She just can't figure out why he didn't give her the benefit of the doubt or at least call her. She doesn't even know where to find him but she is pretty certain that Damien knows. She wants him to meet Michael. But to do that he would have to see her too. She would like that, she is thinking now.

"Mission control to Naya Brooks Bell. Come in Naya?"

"Huh, what did you say?"

Zora can tell when Naya spaces out like this that she is thinking about Michael's father. Zora is seven months pregnant with Zachary and is much larger than Naya is at full term. Damien thinks it's a nice look for her. He is coming out next week to drive them up to Gabriola. It'll be his first time seeing Euphony in more than two decades but Zora's reassured him again that Euphony is OK with everything and they talked at Michael's baptism and once more after that so some of the awkwardness is already gone. They'll take a BC Ferry from Horseshoe Bay to Nanaimo and continue on from there to Gabriola.

It'll be Naya's first trip outside Third Mesa since fleeing here with Sean. She wouldn't risk it except there has been no activity of any sort from Club Members since they are defeated at Third Mesa by Army Rangers and Commonwealth Police and declared a terrorist group by the Commonwealth. Many of their members have been rounded up and prosecuted. The rest have gone to ground.

CPF feels confident enough that they've withdrawn the last of their officers and agents from the area around Third Mesa.

Anyway, Damien is bringing Dekka with him. Naya always feels safer when he is around. Plus they're not going to head to Vancouver through San Francisco that's for sure.

Damien also reassures her that Ellen is almost certainly safe on Mars. Like Sean, he concludes that Mars is surrounded by an impermeable information barrier—Mars is cutoff for sure but Martians themselves should be just fine and comfy inside where nasty Imperial Chinese devices can't penetrate their defenses.

The lack of information is itself information, Damien tells Naya. Her son's Godfather (he can't bring himself to use Farrar's name) must have found a way to destroy all the Sinofighters on Mars and then seal off the planet otherwise, they'd all be dead and the barrier would have come down. Mars would now be a Cartesian Power colony like Luna.

The fact that Mars disappears and stays that way tells Damien that Ellen and all human and quantum people on Mars are safe but now on an isolationist path. Anyone who knows anything about DNA and evolution (including perhaps QE evolution which they have shown signs of) realizes that isolation often breeds unique changes. Martians are on their own and will evolve to who knows what, Damien explains. Naya is both comforted and concerned. But there is a certain amount of awe too at what the Martians have done. Wowza.

...

It's another lovely morning. Fog is burning off. Naya is doing yoga in the town square. She has a nice thick red yoga mat. The square has a stone floor and is uneven so it helps to have a decent mat. Michael is there on his blankie. He's doing yoga too at least the happy baby pose. He's got that one down pat. Zora is still sleeping in her room nearby.

When she practices yoga she knows she is supposed to empty her mind and she can kind of do that—at least she can empty her mind of everything except Sean. She finds that she misses him most in the morning not at night when she is tired. Juggling being a Mom and working with Voyager isn't easy. She and Michael both nap together every day at 1 pm because, well, they both need it.

This morning she is thinking of the last time they make love. Sean is a very giving lover and he works hard to find all her pleasure spots. She doesn't tell him where they all are—heck, a lady has to have some secrets. But he is a hard worker (like her Da!) and finds them one after another. Her most powerful spot is not where one might expect it to be. She has a sort of square head under her thick mane of auburn hair. When Sean takes his huge hand and places it right on top and massages her scalp deliciously, Naya can feel it right down to her toes and in strategic spots in between. When she can't stand it anymore (he can keep it up all day and night!), she pulls him to her. Sean's a smart man. He realizes right away the effect it has on her. But he doesn't do it all the time. He makes her wait. Oh, how the tables are turned! Oh, Sean!

Su7e materializes and breaks Naya out of her reverie. She never interrupts Naya when she is doing her yoga practice. But it's a call (mindlink) with Damien.

#'Naya, can you hear me?'

#'Of course, Da.' Now why would he ask her that? It's a mindlink!

#'Your brothers and I are sssssss Revival sssss fffff sss and you should fff out ss there sss.'

Naya is hearing intermittent 'hissing' sounds in her head—like a harsh white noise.

#'Da, I missed that last thought. Sss you please ffffff ssss?'

#'Naya, you have ff sssss Third Mesa sssss fff.'

#'Aren't you sssss to ffff ss up tomorrow?'
#'Ssss now, Naya! You've got to ff to **Ssss Isabel**!'
Then her connection to her Da breaks.

What's wrong with this link? Naya's never heard of anything that can interfere with quantum communications let alone mindlink. And who is Isabel? Naya is thinking hard and fast.

...

Damien is trying to tell her to go to Texas (Port Isabel to be precise) for some reason but this part of his message is garbled.

...

"Zora, get up."

"Ask me again in an hour."

"No, I mean it. Get up. We're leaving."

"Is Damien here?" Zora can't wait to see him. They've been able to make love despite the fact that Zora is humongous. Zora's plan is to keep doing this as long as practical which might only include this trip north. They've become quite experimental with Zora acting as Chief Scientist.

"No. I got a call (these days people don't distinguish between an old fashioned phone call and a mindlink, what's the point?) I think he wants us to go on ahead." Naya doesn't want to alarm Zora.

"I've asked Kele and Hania to saddle up two camels for us." Actually she's asked the boys to saddle their whole herd. Something is going on and it's best to be prepared.

"Oh, do I have to?" Zora can't imagine anything worse than camel riding to the bus station. But Naya can.

"Yes, you have to. And don't bring much."

...

While she waits for Zora to get ambulatory, Naya puts Michael back in his crib and then returns to the square. Something is up. She can just feel it.

...

Bruce M Firestone

The music starts less than five minutes later. It is loud and obnoxious. It echoes throughout Third Mesa and into the canyon below before ricocheting up to the plateau above them.

The music is awful but the lyrics are worse. Naya and Zora can both hear—

I'm dirty, mean and mighty unclean
I'm a Wanted man
Public Enemy Number One
Understand
So lock up your daughter
And lock up your wife
Lock up your back door
And run for your life...

TNT oi oi oi...

The Club Les de Sades have come for Naya and her baby. Over the music they are playing, she hears their amplified voices braying in a singsong, 'Naya. Michael. Naya. Michael. Where are you? Come out, Naya. Come out, come out, Michael. It's play time. Come to us, Nayaaaaaaaa. Nyaaaaaaaa.'

...

But it isn't the Club Les de Sades at least not in human form who have come to collect Naya and Michael. Sean's decon force is still around and would eat them if anything DNA-based comes within 50 miles. It is 14 Sinofighters who have materialized in the western part of their wind cave.

They are led by Ti3-Gu41 again and two other Sinofighters (one who is equally tall and the other just slightly shorter) that sort of look like General Yao and Clifford Hexham, respectively. Their consoles are at Shenyang so they can't be destroyed by decon force either. It takes a prodigious amount of power to materialize here, a huge distance from homebase, but they won't be staying long. And they don't need very many of them to subdue a bunch of Indians.

General Yao can't believe how inept Club Members are; they allowed a guy by the name of Nahuel and nine marshals with pissant hunting rifles to hold them off for a couple of months and then defeat them? That isn't going to happen today. Yao Allitt has come personally to ensure that this operation goes according to plan. Their other operation overnight is a big time waster—Club agents go to pick up Dr. Bell at Revival House but he must have had some advance warning because he is gone by the time they get there.

Damien and his two boys along with Dekka have disappeared.

It won't matter. When Dr. Bell learns they have his daughter and grandson, he'll come quite nicely to them. Naya's their honey pot.

The other tall Sinofighter that looks vaguely like Clifford Hexham II is actually Cliff's 100+ year-old father. He is the second wealthiest person on the Planet after Angelo Keller and since Angelo is now resident of Luna, he is number 1. He is quite proud of that achievement but has never allowed his interests to be disclosed publicly. If convicts like former Toronto Tab Chronicle reporter Erik Renke ever try any of their shit with Clifford Hexham, they will find themselves dead not incarcerated.

Mr. Hexham asks General Yao not to order Ti3-Gu41 to eviscerate Naya's baby, at least not today. Clifford explains to the General that, just likes he needs Naya alive (for now) as leverage on Damien, he needs her half Irish bastard (who should have been his grandson!) as leverage on the woman. He has plans for Naya. She is going to make another film—her fourth. Actually it'll be in two parts so you might say they will actually be films four and five in her repertoire. But unfortunately, there will never be a sixth. Definitely, five will be it.

...

Bruce M Firestone

The whole pueblo is up now, milling about. Nahuel and his Marshals are there. Nahuel knows what the score is—no asshole but these assholes would disturb his town with poisonous music like this. They have their hunting rifles with them expecting to see human beings. Instead, they see 14 tall creatures approach carrying what look like whips.

The people are running from them. Sinofighters use their Jiujiebian like this—

One, to wound
Two, to paralyze
Three, to inflict pain
Four, to kill

They count out loud in their booming creepy voices every time they lash out with their nine section whips. They never miss. They are killing the Hopi of Third Mesa, one at a time.

One, to wound
Two, to paralyze
Three, to inflict pain
Four, to kill

One, to wound
Two, to paralyze
Three, to inflict pain
Four, to kill

One, to wound
Two, to paralyze
Three, to inflict pain
Four, to kill

...

Nahuel and his small police force crouch low and begin to fire at the Sinofighters. All but one of the Sinofighters are running some kind of video on their massive chests—it's video of Naya from her latest film (Death House) with other degrading images randomly inserted not just of Naya but of others they have humiliated or killed.

Three of them immediately detach themselves from the main group and close in on the Chief and his tiny force. They kill all of them except Nahuel who is seized by the tallest Sinofighter, thrown over his shoulder as if he weighs no more than a Hopi blanket and held in place by one of the creatures powerful arms and dexterous six fingered hands (one thumb and five long fingers that can grasp (fold or curl) upwards as well as downwards—they are bi-directional unlike human hands). In the other hand, he has his whip. He continues to kill Hopi.

One, to wound
Two, to paralyze
Three, to inflict pain
Four, to kill

They are still calling for Naya and Michael in their spooky voices which sometimes sound like Club Les de Sades members not Mandarins from Imperial China which is more what might have been expected.

General Yao is generous. He allows the Club to select the music (a detestable piece, it's by an Australian band he learns) and participate in this raid. General Yao cannot fathom how Gwailo could like such music and their taste in female flesh is beyond him. Their appetite for filth is endless. Which is good. It allows Cartesians to exploit weak Gwailo economically and dominate them politically.

...

"Take Michael, Zora," Naya says calmly but forcefully as she lifts her baby out of his crib. She has seen what is coming and flees back to their rooms from the town square. She is out of breath although it's a distance of less than 60 yards. Zora has also gotten a glimpse of tall

Sinofighters in the square and she is beyond terrified. She can't seem to move. The noise and screaming of the dying is horrendous.

"Zora. Listen to me. You have to take Michael right now and run."

"I can't leave without you, Naya!"

"Yes, you can, Zora. I don't have time to argue with you. They will be here in minutes. They are looking for me. If I go with you, they will hunt you down and kill you and your baby too. Do you understand me?"

Zora's hands immediately go to protect her womb.

"You know I can't run very far, I'll tire. But you can run, Zora, I know it. And you won't tire. You have to save your baby and mine. You have run to the east end of town and go down to the gorge.

"Zora, pay attention! Look at me! You have to run east. Go the bottom of the gorge. Our camels are there. You get on Sammy. He's the fastest and has great stamina."

"How will I know which one is Sammy?"

"He is the largest one and has two humps, Zora. You'll know him. He's huge. Tell Kele and Hania. Zora, listen to me!"

"OK. Right."

"Tell Kele and Hania to take the rest of our herd and get out of here. Tell them not to leave any animals behind and not to let any of them go before they are at least two miles from here. Zora nod 'yes' please."

Zora's horrified eyes are locked onto Naya's now. She nods.

"They can't see any camels here because then they might figure it out and follow you. Tell the boys to leave this place and never come back here, never! Zora nod 'yes' again, please."

Another nod.

"How do they know about Michael?" Zora shouts over the hellacious racket. Naya never allows anyone to take a photo of her baby and she asks everyone to never post or message anything about him.

"I don't know." Naya's been thinking about that too. Maybe there's another traitor at Third Mesa or there's been a leak. She knows a baby is a fact and hard to keep secret. But she quickly calculates that even if they've been told about her baby or somehow it's leaked out that she has a baby (they even have his name), they still don't actually KNOW anything unless she or an eye witness confirms it. Traitors and leakers are highly unreliable—if they betray one side, it's just a matter of time before they'll betray the other.

"Here's the plan, Zora. We *never* admit Michael exists. Never. It'll leave room for doubt. Alright?" Naya says.

"OK."

"Change Mikey's name and stick to our original plan—go north. Go to your Mom, go to Euph, Zora. She'll protect you and the boys."

Another nod from Zora.

"Good, that's good Zora. You'll have to bring up Michael now," Naya says as she hands her baby over to the older woman.

Zora begins to cry.

"Stop that. That's for later," Naya says. "Now I need you to be brave. You are my sister and my auntie. I love you." She kisses Zora on the forehead and then they hug.

"One last thing, I want you to find Sean. Tell him about the baby. I'm such a fool. Find him, tell him, OK?"

"Yes."

"And tell him about the unsent messages and that I, I love—"

"I understand, Naya. I will, I promise."

She kisses her baby one last time and makes their sign of love (arms crossed in front of her, rocking an imaginary cradle side to side). Baby Michael signs this back to his Mom.

"Run Zora, run!"

Zora runs as Hopi women have run for generations

from men (or their creations) intent on committing war crimes, genocide and rape. She runs as fast as any seven month pregnant woman can run which is pretty fast when you have ten foot tall mutants chasing you.

From the moment that Naya runs into Zora's room with her baby until Zora runs away with Michael, the two women have exchanged 45 complete thought units— utterances that convey information about a single action or issue. Humans in extremis, like Naya and Zora are at this moment, can routinely reach information transfer rates of 30 thought units per minute, peaking at 50 or even 60. Body language, signing, tonality, eye movements and other signals (even taste and smell) bolster information flow further. They can innovate, plan, change plans, adapt, reconsider, experiment, test, alter, measure and calculate while communicating at these speeds. No matter what language they speak, they all convey about the same information density tuned to the human perceptual system.

Naya, Zora and Michael (signing) have said their 'Goodbyes' in 111 seconds.

...

Naya watches until Zora is out of sight and then calmly turns around and walks to the town square where she stands face to face with 14 savage Sinofighters who surround her. The time of her Death has come, she realizes.

They taunt her and call her a Hopi whore (Erik Renke's second last story before his incarceration discloses the genetic link between Ellen and Nell) and much worse. All around her are dead Hopi. The rest have fled east. They have lived here in this community continuously for more than a thousand years until this day. There are no more Hopi in Third Mesa and won't be for a long time, maybe ever.

...

"My name is Clifford Hexham," says Clifford Hexham.

"You're not aging too well, Cliff," Naya says.

He bristles when she says this. No one talks to him like that. He wants to strike her but in his current incarnation as a Sinofighter, he would probably take her head off with a single blow and that would put the kybosh on the films he is planning to release with her as star and him as Executive Producer.

"Where is your baby?" Clifford asks her.

"I don't have a baby. Does it look like I have had a baby?" Naya slips gracefully out of her yoga clothes and stands naked before them.

She does a pretty pirouette so they can see that the merchandise is unblemished. She knows these people are perverts so she is putting on a show. She is buying time for Zora and her baby.

"Please put your clothes back on," says another Sinofighter, a Mandarin looking one. 'This is the prettiest girl in the world?' Yao is thinking. She is just as ugly up close as the images he has examined of her.

"Well if ain't Yao Allitt, the chicken shit little puke who betrayed the United States, the country that provided for him and his family after being forced into exile by other Mandarins who wanted him dead."

"Ah, Ms. Bell, those other Mandarins have paid for their mistakes."

"I suppose you re-educated them to death?"

"You might say that."

"I just did you deaf Gobshite." That's a lovely Irish swearword that Niamh teaches her. Sean almost never swears.

Ti3-Gu41 heads toward her but General Yao holds up a hand to halt him. He needs her alive.

"Ms. Bell, we will only ask you nicely once more, where is your baby?"

Naya says nothing.

Yao nods to Ti3-Gu41 who lays Nahuel on the ground. He puts a large foot on his chest and presses down heavily.

Nahuel gasps and looks at Naya who looks back at him and he shakes his head 'No'.

Naya looks at General Yao and says, "What baby?"

With another nod from Yao, Ti3-Gu41 places his hand inside Nahuel's chest cavity and squeezes his heart muscle. Nahuel spasms with pain.

"Ms. Bell, the answer?"

Nahuel shakes his head again, pleading with her with his eyes. 'Save your baby,' he is clearly saying.

"Go fuck yourself, you dickless yob." 'Yob' is a word she learns from Sean.

Ti3-Gu41 rips Nahuel's heart from his chest.

Third Mesa, if it ever gets a new supply of Hopi, will need a new Chief too.

Nahuel's face is composed, at rest, at peace, serene even. General Yao, who has seen millions of death masks, cannot understand how this could be? It should show anguish. He feels cheated somehow.

That's because Nahuel's spirit leaves his body before his heart does. Nell comes for him in the nick of time.

...

Zora is on Sammy. They are about three miles east of Third Mesa. She is prodding him on as fast as she knows how. The ride is surprisingly smooth. In fact, the faster Sammy goes, the smoother it is.

Michael is in front and the wind is whipping through his fine red baby hair. 'This is amazing,' he thinks. The smells of the camel, the scenes flashing by, the clippity clop of the camel's hooves on the stoney floor of the gorge. But Michael can smell that something is wrong with Zora and he can hear her sobbing. She is sad and then suddenly Michael is too. He starts to cry. 'Where's Mama?' he asks himself. Then he signs for her but she does not come to him. She always comes for him! Where is she? Michael cries for his Mom.

Zora is startled to see a large, alpha male wolf running next to them on her right. She stops her blubbering when she sees this apparition. Whenever Sammy starts to think about slowing down, this large wolf nips at him, not biting him hard, just enough to spur Sammy on. 'Faster,' the wolf telegraphs Sammy, 'or I will eat you! Faster, you big oaf!'

Soon Zora, Michael, Zachary (in utero), Sammy and the wolf are flying. The world is turning under their feet, faster and faster.

...

"Captain, can you come to down to Main Deck for a moment please?"

"Now what appears to be the matter here?" the Captain of the Jack Shadbolt (the newest ship in the BC Ferry Fleet) asks.

There is an exhausted woman standing there carrying an infant and it looks like she is about to have her second at any moment.

"She refuses to come aboard, Sir, without her animal?"

"Where is her animal?"

"Over there, Sir." The Second Mate is pointing to an equally exhausted looking, salt streaked camel held by a nervous clerk at the far end of the dock.

"Ah, Madam, I regret to inform you that to bring such an animal onboard a BC Ferry will require an order form the Exotic Species Branch of the Ministry. Do you have such an order?" This, the Captain knows, is a rhetorical question. The woman is obviously impoverished and alone.

"I am not leaving Sammy behind."

"I assume that Sammy is that, ah, camel over there?"

"Yes. We've come a long way together."

"May I enquire as to where you and this animal have come from?"

"Arizona."

"You and your baby have come to Vancouver from Arizona on a camel?" the Captain asks incredulously.

Bruce M Firestone

"Yes, we had a wolf with us too but he turned back after we got to Vancity limits."

"So you are not proposing to take a wolf with you?" The Captain wonders if she is in her right mind.

The wolf takes care of his strange retinue while they are in the wilderness. In addition to pushing them (especially Sammy) along, he stands guard and, when not doing either of these, he hunts. They eat quail, grasshoppers, rabbit and chickens (he steals these from farmers and ranchers) while in the south; their diet improves as they get further north. There they get to snack on elk, deer and even (an elderly) moose. Michael gets nicely predigested meats disgorged from the wolf's stomach which, for pups or tiny children, are highly edible.

"No, Sir," says Zora.

"Umm, how long did this, ah, journey take you?"

"Almost 60 days, Sir."

"You've been in the wilderness for two months!"

"Yes, Captain."

"What in the world are we to do then?" he asks himself rhetorically.

"Captain, you take cars, vans, trucks. You can take Sammy and us. Please?"

For the first time, the Captain really sees the strain on her face and hears the pain in this woman's voice.

"Please, Captain. I'm begging you."

"Now Madam, please get up," he says reaching down to help her. She has gotten awkwardly, heavily down on her knees and is begging him reaching both her hands up to him in prayer position.

"Have mercy on us, Captain? Mercy, please."

Completely embarrassed now, he says, "Please do get up, Madam. Please. We'll see if we can't work something out for you."

"For all of us, Captain?"

"Yes. Quite."

She is allowed to bring Sammy onboard as long as

she remains below decks with him. She also has to sign a release form absolving BC Ferries of any legal responsibility with respect to herself and her camel. The Captain asks one of his female officers to take her baby topside. It is dangerous to ride a Ferry on its vehicle deck. If they come loose in big seas, they will crush her and her camel. But when they try to take her baby, the woman becomes almost feral. "You can't take my baby from me! Never!" They give up and just leave Zora, Michael and Sammy below decks. It's against orders but that's why he is Captain. Once at sea, he is a god and this god decides, he'll take this woman and her strange entourage to Gabriola.

When he looks at the release, he sees she signs it, 'Romulus and Remus' Mother.' From the back of his mind, he recalls something about the story of Romulus and Remus. Twin brothers brought up by wolves who later found Rome. The woman mentioned something about a wolf.

"First Mate?"

"Sir?"

"How far is it from Arizona to Vancouver?"

"Whereabouts in Arizona, Sir?"

"Try Flagstaff."

"Approximately, 2,400 kilometres, Captain."

'That woman traveled 2,400 kilometres in 60 days? On a camel? Whatever she is running from (it is obvious the woman is terrified of something), this is one for record books. She travels over 40 km per day. Amazing!'

Zora has actually traveled 2,424 kms in 58 days *and nights*. She is nine months pregnant give or take a couple of days when she arrives in Vancity. But then the Captain has no more time to think about creation myths or mythical camel rides; he has a Ferry to launch and run.

And that is how Zora, Zachary, Michael and Sammy finally come to Gabriola. Euphony takes them in and loves them all, hero camel included. Three days after her arrival,

Bruce M Firestone

Zora gives birth to a healthy baby boy—he's a load. More than 10 lbs of baby comes zooming down her birth canal to join his older nephew in a strange new world that is happening all around them.

...

Naya thinks that maybe they will take her to Shenyang but she is pretty sure that they never leave the Commonwealth. Her time sense is distorted because they offer her alcohol. When she refuses, a Germanian Doctor attends her and gives it to her intravenously. It's her first drink since she is 15.

She has feared this moment all her adult life—a relapse but for some reason it does not have the effect on her that they expect. They can make her sick but not dependant. The Doctor is replaced with another equally corrupt one but nothing seems to work well on her. Her addictive personality is just plain gone. They'll have to find some other way to make her more compliant.

...

In fact, Naya is being held in vast underground caverns that go from Clear Lake in the north under Mount Konocti all the way to San Francisco Bay—a distance of over 120 miles. Like Angelo Keller, Clifford Hexham believes in exploiting all his rights including subterranean rights. This enormous network of tunnels belongs to him.

"Hello, Naya."

"Hi Mister Hex-sham. What r the haps?" an obviously intoxicated Naya responds.

"Enjoying ourselves are we?"

"Laff a minute, Cliff."

"Would you like to know our plans for you?"

"Shure. Let me gesh first? We can play 20 kwestions. S'alright?"

"I would prefer to tell you."

"Shure, kweeks draw, shoot! El kabong me!" Naya laughs. Naya is thinking of a fast shooting anthropomorphic horse from an incredibly old, so-badly-animated-that-it-becomes-fashionable-again cartoon. The horse is sometimes a sheriff and sometimes transforms into a poorly disguised alter ego who whacks bad guys with his guitar. "His dishgize is worsh than Clark Kent's, did u know that, Mister Hex-sham?" She likes saying his last name like this so she repeats it three more times, "Hex-sham, *Hex*-sham, Hex-*sham*," with loud, obnoxious emphasis on different syllables each time.

This isn't going anywhere according to plan. Hexham walks out and fires her second Doctor. He does this by expediently killing him and having his body dumped into Clear Lake to join several hundred other former Hexham employees who displease the boss.

The third Doctor is told to sober her up fast or suffer the same fate as Doctors I and II.

...

"So Naya, feel like having a discussion about your future?"

"You bet, Cliff."

"You're going to be making a fourth film and then a fifth."

"Is that right, Cliff? I don't think so."

"Well, yes, that is so. They'll be my greatest films yet. Do you know what Film Four is all about?"

"Let me take a stab at that. Perverted sex?"

"That's a bingo!"

"You stole that line from a Tarantino film."

This girl is really getting under his skin.

"Fuck off, Naya."

"Happy to. Just open the gates and I'll be adiós, muchachos."

"I don't think we'll be doing that."

"Thought so."

"We appear to be at a stalemate, Ms. Bell."

"That we do."

"Perhaps we can make a deal?"

"What sort of deal?"

Bruce M Firestone

"I let your baby and your family live, you give me the performance of a lifetime?"

"Heck of a deal, Cliff. Except if you had any member of my family, you would be parading them in front of me before having Ti3-Gu41 or one of those other pets you keep around rip their faces off. I don't think so."

"You underestimate me, Ms. Bell."

"I don't think so, motherfucker. My boyfriend will find you and kill you just like he did your son."

As soon as Naya says this, she knows it's a mistake. How many times did Da tell her, 'When you want to keep something a secret, tell no one.'

"Yes, that is a crime that Mr. Ruane will pay for—believe me, many times over. You know that gives me another idea! Perhaps we should invite Mr. Ruane to the party after all? He can watch you perform for an army of Club Members in Film Four which will go into, as we used to say, General Theatrical Release. Then we will press on, so to speak, with Film Five. But Film Five is for special connoisseurs. Men who will pay billions to watch a film, your final film, Ms. Bell. One in which the ending is as predictable as it is delectable—one that can never be repeated for which, sadly for you, there are no sequels. A film like no other that snuffs out the hottest young Hollywood actress in our Solar System. It's tragic wouldn't you agree?"

...

There are days that are bad and there are days that are worse. Film Four is shooting and Naya is drugged to her gills and forced to perform. It is degradation heaped upon degradation—it's all a blur really.

When she is left alone (which is never—there is always someone watching her), she thinks about Michael and Zora and her family and Sean. She never admits to Hexham that Michael exists and she regrets her indiscretion about Sean and his role in Cliff's death. She prays a lot for the deliverance of her family, her baby,

Zora, Zachary, Niamh and Sean and then for her own deliverance into the hands of Death which will be soon she thinks.

She regrets nothing in her life other than those two unsent messages. She is sure now that Sean would understand a debt like the life she owes JEL. He saves her in Stockholm and she saves him at Hearth House. A life for a life. An Irishman would understand that, right?

If only she presses 'send'. How different life might be. For the first time in her captivity, she breaks down and cries.

Then she hears music. She isn't sure if it is in her mind or if it's coming from the walls of her cell. It is all around her and comforts her. It is Nell playing a cover of SONSOFDAY's Revolution.

Why are you searching in the oceans?
Are you searching in the cities?
Are you looking for love? ...

Why you've been walking in darkness?
Are you running out of mistakes while looking for truth? ...

Why, oh why, I don't know why, oh why won't you open your eyes?
If you'll open your heart.

Oh, Sean, open your eyes! Open your heart! Naya isn't misleading him. She tells him the truth when she says, 'I can't live without you!'

She never gives up hope that he will come for her but as days then weeks go by, her hope grows fainter. Finally, her distress overwhelms her and she shouts into her nearly empty dungeon, "Oh Sean, Sean, SEAN! WHERE ARE YOU?"

...

END PART VI

Epilogue

There is the fool, the greater fool and then there is the greatest fool. I am the latter.

Zora calls me. It is a welcome call because she is my friend. But when she finishes, I am at sea. I know the movie of our life together. I've run it thousands of times and it doesn't add up because it can't. She never betrays me. It is I who've betrayed her and my son.

His name is Michael. That's a nice Irish name. The Irish translation of Michael is 'Michael'. She knows that.

Zora shows me images of him. He looks like Niamh, I think. I guess it's his red hair. Which reminds me, I'll have to tell Holly, she's an Auntie.

Zora can't tell me where they are. No one trusts our communications system anymore. It's spotty worldwide and that can only mean someone, the Cartesian Powers everyone presumes, has hacked quantum communications somehow.

War is coming. It is here. I don't mean endless skirmishing between world powers. Total war. But that's nothing, NOTHING compared to what I am going to do to Club Les de Sades and Clifford Hexham (the first) for taking Naya from her baby and I guess from me. But actually when I think about it more, the fool that I am, I did that to myself. Irish pride got in our way.

Still they are on the Eve of Destruction. They just don't know it yet. I have lots of ideas flooding my head. With those, I will *end* them all.

I am pretty sure I know where Baby Michael is— either northern Ontario or BC. I would guess BC. Wherever Zora's Mom is, that's where I'll find him. I will find him.

But first I will find Naya. I know she is alive. How you may ask do I know that? Because they have released a movie, simply called 'Film Four'. Its Executive Producer is Clifford Hexham I. It's not often you get to kill a man more than once.

Film Four is more of their filth and I have watched every minute of it, many times. Naya is looking through the camera lens at me. She is asking where I am.

A song is running through my head. It's an American song.

> Every night, on my knees I pray
> Dear Lord, hear my plea
> Don't ever let another take her love from me
> Or I will surely die
>
> Oh, I tell you it was just my imagination
> Running away with me

But it is not my imagination. She does love me. She always did.

I am here in Port Isabel in the Free State of Texas. But not for very much longer. I am at the dock of the bay and it is hurricane season here. There is much lightning out at sea and thunder coming from there too—perhaps six or maybe eight miles offshore. It is raining there but not here.

There will be another shite storm soon, not here somewhere else. It'll be the Wrath of Sean. If Ellen was here she would probably compare it to the Wrath of Khan. But genetically enhanced Khan Noonien Singh is as nothing compared to what Sean Ruane is capable of.

I guess that they have her in an underground studio. Where? In California, yes. But where? LA? I think not. San Fran? I think yes. I will go there.

I will bring my own music. It will be the last thing they will ever hear. They like AC DC do they? I'll play this on quantum speakers tuned to their DNA so only they can hear it—

I was caught

In the middle of a railroad track, THUNDER
And I knew there was no turning back, THUNDER
My mind raced
And I thought what could I do? THUNDER
And I knew
There was no help, no help from you, THUNDER

Sound of the drums
Beatin' in my heart
The thunder of guns
Tore me apart
You've been—THUNDERSTRUCK

Oh, yes, I'll be bringing the thunder, my own.

I raise my arms which pulse in time as I shout over an offshore rumble, "Oh Naya, Naya, NAYA! WAIT FOR ME!"

...

Euphony is watching Romulus and Remus play in her garden. Romulus is two and Remus is one. But no one calls them that. The older one is 'Gus' and the younger one is 'Ray'. Gus is Ray's nephew. They are beautiful, sturdy little boys.

Gus is a redhead and Ray is dark haired like his Mom, Zora, and his Dad who is not here. He and his other two boys are hiding out somewhere in Northern Ontario. These days, you are either hiding out or you are fighting or you are already dead.

Gus teaches Ray sign language. Often they don't even need that. They look at each other and seem to understand each other's thoughts, instantly.

Ray is a nice name for Zora's son, her grandson. It goes nicely with their family name which she never uses because, as Damien would say, if you want to keep a secret, tell no one. But since Euphony is alone with her thoughts just now, she feels OK saying it quietly under her breath—their surname is Romaine. It's Euphony and Zora Romaine. They come from a long line of Romanian

Romaines. They are Wiccans for as many generations as DNA will allow humans to reliably trace their ancestry.

They are part of a clan that includes the Vasilescus. Oh yes, Euphony knows the story of Naya and José-Luis Vasilescu. José-Luis feels like he is an exile on Luna but it might comfort him to know (if he is still alive, more about that in a moment) that he is part of their extended family now—Naya's Dad is Ray's father. More importantly, Ray's Mom is part of the Romaine clan which includes the Vasilescus. They are the wealthy part of their extended family and look down on the Romaines but life has a way of turning. 'Anyway, José-Luis, welcome to the party,' Euphony says to herself. Gus and Ray will make fine Romaines and Wiccans, Euphony thinks. DNA is magic.

They change the boys' names because if they are ever discovered, Sinofighters, Rogues or various other Cartesian forces will kill them just on general principle. Su7e is here with them and she is just as much a mother to these boys as Zora and Euph.

It is total war now. A fight to the end. Millions are dead and millions more will die. It will either be the Commonwealth and her allies that are triumphant or the Cartesian Powers. No quarter is asked or given. Mars plays no role now—Mars has self quarantined and no one knows what is happening there. Ellen, her rival, is there (perhaps). It gives Euphony great, guilty pleasure to know that she gets the better of Ellen—Ellen has her General but Euphony has Gus and Ray. No comparison!

British Columbia has raised quantum shields over most of the Province and that includes Gabriola. Without those shields, the Cartesian Powers would send in their Sinofighters or Drogues or stormtroopers to kill or enslave them all. It means that towns and cities are isolated and on their own. Every nation is now Balkanized into dozens or hundreds of separate city-states. There are food shortages but not for people who bought a Roxie like Euphony did.

One of their main strategic worries (but just one of several) these days is Fifth Columnists made up of Rogues but there aren't any of those at Gabriola or, for that matter, in BC. It's a huge, huge problem in the Commonwealth though. Apparently, San Francisco is crawling with them and many of them are cruel sadists who make films, some of them for profit, some of them to frighten and cow, some to encourage collaboration and surrender—propaganda films that promise a peaceful, organized, ordered society with no crime under the aegis of Cartesian might.

Only 42 nations continue to resist the Cartesians. More than 220 others are 'allied' with Germania and Imperial China which means they agree to allow Cartesia to station stormtroopers and Sinofighters within their borders, to pass laws that bring them into conformity with Cartesian strictures, to institute a draft shanghaiing men between the ages of 16 and 22 into the newly renamed Sol Liberation Army as shock troops and to accept Central Commission for Discipline Inspection and Party Loyalty hegemony.

Sinofighters have apparently been redesigned to eliminate any common markers so their consoles can't be found so easily and then deconstructed. If the Commonwealth is to survive, they'll have to find some other way of dealing with these invaders. Stormtroopers are just well trained and well equipped modern soldiers who work efficiently and effectively with Sinofighters to subdue, kill or frighten Commonwealth citizens and soldiers. It's a new blitzkrieg with Sinofighters leading and destroying Allied command and control infrastructure and personnel as well as key weapon systems. Stormtroopers do a mop up after that. Their shock troop conscripts are expendables—human shields that precede even Sinofighters into battle.

It's just as well that Zora and Damien and their boy never settle at Revival House—Zora and Ray would be dead and Damien would be a prisoner again. San

Francisco might very well be the first Commonwealth city to voluntarily side with Imperial China and Germania. But there is street fighting there and resistance everywhere else—Americans (mostly) don't make very good slaves. They will die rather than submit. Commonwealth patriots may very well all die though. No one knows.

Roving squads of Imperial Chinese Sinofighters and Germanian stormtroopers kill anyone they find outside Quantum Shields unless they carry Cartesian papers.

The Cartesians have resettled Dallas with Han and Germanians but it is a hole in the donut—the rest of the Free State of Texas is resisting, fiercely. Cartesians clean up the Dallas-Fort Worth metroplex, expediently burning millions of Commonwealth citizens and then they resettle it. It's a repeat of Tibet from the last century although on a vast scale. Now they are showing images and endless video of happy Han and Germanians going about their business. But it's not business as usual. They all have to have implants like BPI inserts only these are not to prevent conception—they have to coat their skins with nanosites (it's called skin coating) that don't leak DNA signatures otherwise deconstructors will, well, deconstruct them to their elements in minutes.

The first Quantum Bubble to be erected on Earth (Mars is first obviously) covers the entire Free State of Texas (minus Dallas). It is really the horrible attacks on Dallas-Fort Worth that signal the start of what everyone now calls Sol War I. Euphony thinks that Damien has had something to do with the shield over Texas and that he's somehow been communicating with Gus' Da who is there. Zora is pretty sure about that. She's talked to both Damien and Gus' Da but just once each. After Gabriola's shield goes up, that's it. Nothing comes in or leaks out.

She also thinks Gus' Da may have had something to do with the takedown of the three Cartesian space elevators at Luna as well as the fact that their entire protective outer layer gets deconstructed releasing their atmosphere in a matter of hours and killing pretty near everyone on the Moon. Their seas vanish in a matter of a few days more. If anyone can free Gus' Mom, it is him.

The Moon's albedo has returned to its eon's old pattern and Cosmo's Moon is back to inspire Earth-bound lovers. That is, if anyone is so inclined. Birth rates in the Commonwealth and her allies that are also under siege like Canada have fallen to zero.

Ellen's old colleague, Angelo Keller, apparently escapes this latest holocaust having both an underground bolt hole to flee to as well as a private spaceplane for a safe return from Luna to Earth. Nevertheless, Gaia's gravitational force flattens the old guy and he will never get out of bed unless perhaps he can escape again, this time to Mars.

But they aren't talking to anyone at the moment and they're not taking any immigrants at the present time either. It's a closed union shop, in a manner of speaking. That'll irk that old fascist capitalist—he won't be able to buy, blackmail, bully or bribe his way in.

Euphony figures the General might not want someone like Angelo Keller on Mars even if one day they reopen to the outside Universe assuming Mars is even still there. Maybe they've whooshed off to another dimension and are never coming back, who knows?

Angelo would be declared an illegal alien and deported from Mars if he ever manages somehow to get in, Euphony is sure. The General has too much sense, except in his choice of women (well one in particular), to do otherwise. For all Euphony knows, Angelo could be in Germania and probably is. No one in their right mind would live in the Commonwealth as it is currently constituted.

A few others—those who have immediate access to old moonbase structures equipped for hard vacuum—survive the collapse of Luna's ecosystem. Who knows if José-Luis is alive? Euphony hopes he is.

See life has a way of turning, wouldn't you agree? It reminds her of a folk song her great grandfather used to play on his guitar for her when she was a little girl. It's mournful but somehow she feels right away on first hearing it that the poet who writes it understands the perverse nature of life and the concept of hubris; moments before you even reach the top, your luck has run out and you're headed back down—

> Come writers and critics
> Who prophesize with your pen
> And keep your eyes wide
> The chance won't come again
> And don't speak too soon
> For the wheel's still in spin
> And there's no tellin' who
> That it's namin'
> For the loser now
> Will be later to win
> For the times they are a-changin'...

Euphony, who in some strange way feels like a winner right about now, is clever enough to know that times will change again and that she has to plan not for herself or even Zora but for their successors.

She has seen the first ten minutes of Naya's new film, her fourth. It is unbearable to watch. Zora is sick for three days after this abbreviated viewing.

Euphony feels that Gus' Da better hurry or Gus' Mom will soon be no more.

...

END BOOK 2

Unanswered Questions From Book 2

As with Book 1, there are quite a few unanswered questions in Book 2. These include—

1. Who is Daniella's father and why does Elsu keep this a secret?

2. What are Mayan numbers doing on Minoan artifacts and, for that matter, what are Minoan artifacts doing at the bottom of a pond in Oregon where Niamh Ruane finds them?

3. How did 20th Century Bra-ket notation (Paul Dirac equations) get imprinted inside Subminoan discs?

4. How did General Farrar Staubach and 18 Mars Army personnel survive the Night of Sinofighter attacks in Hippieville?

5. What inspired the General to come up with that new use for their Planetary Shield (their Quantum Bubble)—the one that allows them to impose an impenetrable information layer around Mars?

6. Now that Mars is on an isolationist path, what new unique evolutionary steps might occur for humans, QEs and technology there?

7. How are the Cartesian Powers intercepting and interfering with Quantum Communications and mindlinks?

8. Did José-Luis survive the meltdown of Luna's ecosystem?

9. Who will win Sol War I and how?

10. Where have Damien, Finn and Magellan along with Dekka gone to ground?

11. Is there life in galaxies other than the Milky Way and, if panspermia is not the vector for establishing it there, has life arisen independently? That is, has lightning struck twice or perhaps more than twice?

12. Now that Sinofighters have been redesigned to

eliminate any common markers so their consoles can't be found so easily and then deconstructed, what if anything can be done to combat this plague?

13. What role are Drogues playing in the War?

14. Since Cartesians are now using implants that generate skin coats that prevent detection of their DNA, is there another weapon Sean can come up with to fight an ever widening group of enemies?

15. Can Sean rescue Naya from the Club Les de Sades before they force her to make her final film for them?

16. Can the Hopi regroup and where will they find a new Chief?

17. How did General Yao and the Club Les de Sades find out about Baby Michael? Was there another traitor at Third Mesa or did the info leak somehow?

18. How did Erik Renke find out about the genetic link between Ellen and Nell?

19. Who is the third sister of Nell and Ellen?

20. Who is recording and writing this history of the Quantum Era?

@ProfBruce

@Quantum_Entity

...

Quantum Entity |
The Successors

PROLOGUE

"You're going after her, aren't you?"

"Yep."

"I'm coming with you."

"Nope. You are staying here with Mrs. Hunter."

"You talked to her?"

"Yes. She's agreed to look after you 'til I get back."

"That's not going to work. I'll follow you. I can help. You need someone to watch your back. That someone is me."

"I work best alone."

"No you don't, you only think you do. I am smaller than you. I can go places you can't. They have her underground—you're gonna need me. Plus when you need advice, who do you turn to? Me. You'll make better decisions if I'm around. And I'm faster than you."

He looks at her—she's just a 12-year old kid. Lately, she's taken to wearing loose black pleated pants that have five folds in front (three on her right side and two on her left) and two in back. He doesn't know it but these pants are called Hakama—they're tied in the Warrior style with a simple square knot in front. They're made out of a durable silk fabric and allow for easy movement so she can kick the bejesus out of someone. The seven pleats either represent the seven virtues of Bushido or the seven colors of the rainbow, maybe both.

On top she wears a black and grey bodice over a white silk blouse that flatters her emerging figure and doesn't interfere with her ability to either breathe or move. Her bodice is tied using tough gold-colored leather laces.

She's grown a lot in the last year; she must be 5'10" or close to it. Maybe she'll be taller than him. Who knows? She's very strong and very fast but there's no way she's faster than him.

"You're not faster than me, no how, no way."

She doesn't say anything other than, "Comitay." Then she adopts her fighting stance and she deploys a pair of her nunchuks.

Her legs are shoulder-width apart and she is holding her nunchuks by their Kontei (handles), one in each hand in front of her. She does a fast figure eight, stopping first under one arm then another. After that she grabs them over her right shoulder then her left. Next she does a helicopter spin followed by several arm switches (where she flips one Kontei over her right shoulder then reaches across her body with her left and grabs it under her right arm before doing the same thing on the other side), hand rolls, more double Xes, thumb spin, Around the Neck, whip over, flip throw and finally, adding still more power, she does a three hit combo then L and X strikes. Somehow she produces and deploys a second set of nunchuks in her final move so she can deliver blows with both hands which she apparently can do independently. She has just doubled the number of opponents she can take out.

While she is doing her demo, he hasn't moved an inch. He can feel her nunchuks whiz by and sometimes make contact with him but her control is so good they just kiss him lightly on both sides of his head and in other vulnerable places.

"Let me see those things," is all he says. When he reaches for a pair, she ducks under his outstretched arm, slips behind him and wraps the Himo around his neck and threatens to garrote him. Her nunchuks are not connected by a chain—she uses a wire rope instead. It's quieter, faster, more durable and works really well if you want to strangle someone.

Bruce M Firestone

"May I see them please?" he asks again.

"They're called The Trods."

"Can I please see The Trods?"

She releases him and hands over a pair. They are very heavy—her Kontei are not made out of wood. They're a very dense form of pico carbon metal.

"Why do you call them 'The Trods'?"

"That's short for Trodaire saoirse, Freedom Fighter." He already knows what 'Trodaire saoirse' means.

"So you want to be a Freedom Fighter?" he asks her.

"Nope. I'm a Warrior Monk."

"You mean that's what you want to be when you grow up?"

Now she's getting mad at him. "Would you like a demonstration for real this time?" She is about to adopt her fighting position again but he holds up his hands motioning for her to calm down.

"Is this what you've been doing every Tuesday and Thursday?" She's been disappearing for four and a half hours after school twice a week. He's asked her before what's up but she won't tell him. He assumes she goes to Church or something but obviously not.

"Yes."

"Where do you go?"

"Matamoros. I've been studying with Gran Maestro Iridia del Rosario Villa. I take the bus." Even though Matamoros is only 27 miles away, it takes an hour each way.

"Does Iridia teach you anything other than nunchuks? Won't be too helpful if the other guys all have guns." He's just needling her. He knows that where he is going, guns aren't going to be any use at all.

"She teaches me Korean Mouhébong Taekwondo and I know how to use a Kama too." Sure enough, she produces twin Kamas (right and left handed small sickles that look like they are razor sharp). Her Kamas are strapped to her back and she draws them by crossing her arms over her shoulders and deploying them that way.

"You must be part bird. The kind that sees bi-directionally with no overlap in their fields of vision. How do you do that?" He isn't making fun of her any longer. He really wants to know how she can fight each hand (whether holding separate Kamas or nunchuks) independently.

"I don't know. Gran Maestro Villa says I'm the only student she has ever had who can do it." She doesn't say this like a blowhard; she's just stating a fact.

"That's pretty cool," he says. "I've never heard of Mouhébong Taekwondo."

"So?"

"So like tell me more about it, really."

She can see that he is genuinely interested so she says, "It originated during the time of the Lee dynasty in Korea in like 1790 or something. Mouhébong represents the seven colors of the rainbow—purity, beauty, harmony (with nature), creativity, defense, therapy and betterment."

If there is anyone who better represents these seven values than her, he'd be surprised. "So why do you want to be a Warrior Monk?"

"I already am."

"Who says?"

"Says me."

"Little young don't you think?"

"*Let not our proposal be disregarded on the score of our youth.*"

"Who said that?"

"Virgil 2,125 years ago."

"Where'd you learn it?"

"When I was home schooled by someone who helped start one of the great companies of the last generation—when she was 19 by the way."

"So 12 is the new 19?"

"Yep. I can handle myself."

"I can see that."

"My name is Yulsa."

"Don't you think you already have enough nicknames?"

"It's not a nickname, Wonder Man, it's my name."

"It's 'Wonder Boy'."

"No, Wonder Boy wouldn't be so stupid as to let her be captured by the Evil *men* who have her." She's being sarcastic—adults are just so painfully dumb. How could he ever have abandoned her?

"What does 'Yulsa' mean?"

"I'm named after Monk Jajangyulsa who built the Magoksa Temple in Korean Province Chungcheong which is where our Donghaksa Temple is—it's the only place in the world by the way that has a female monk sect."

"But why a Monk?"

"Because I am never going to let what happened to my sister happen to me or anyone else I care about EVER AGAIN."

He understands that she really means it.

"Couldn't you just be a freedom fighter instead of a Monk?"

"No. I have taken a vow of poverty and chastity so there will be no distractions in my life EVER—no husband, no kids, no property to tie me down and keep me from doing my work. I'm going to walk this planet and others engaging in prayer, meditation and good deeds. And before God, I *swear* I will help you bring her out of the dungeon they have her in."

...

He adds a quantum computer to both The Trods and her Kamas. They are now capable (on her command) of delivering DNA-specific poisons, deconstructors, electric shock and vacuum energy via Kontei and sickle blade in addition to stunning or lethal blows.

He has his own weapons and plan. But secretly, he's glad she's coming. She has good judgment and she really is *fast*. It'll just be three against untold numbers of enemy. But they won't be able to see them coming. Why is that?

Because he has a personal, portable quantum shield which will impose a total information blackout around each person. Their enemies will have to fight the invisible man and his two sidekicks—a QE and an invisible girl as well. Let's see how they like that.

It's brand new tech and no one knows about it except him and the physicist from Northern Ontario who designed it and sent it to him. How did he get it to him since every community is isolated behind their own town or State-sized shield? He did it via TV.

There are presently two vacuum energy TVs in existence—they are really no better than old black and white television sets with crappy signal strength and controls. They have very low data transmission rates so convos take time and design specs for something as complicated as a personal quantum shield take weeks to transmit. But here's the thing—the Cartesians and Club Les de Sades have nothing like it and can't intercept it. You disturb the vacuum energy where you are and a matched VE TV displays the same image wherever it is. And guess what? It is the only known thing that can breach the shields that everyone is using to hide from the Cartesians—whether it's the Free State of Texas or Mars, if they have paired VE TVs, they can talk.

But he has another use for vacuum energy. He's taken VE TV to another level. He's hacked their design so he can not only use it for com, he can deliver enormous amounts of energy (on the order of 10^{113} Joules per cubic meter of space) from the end of his cosh. She can do it too now—using her nunchuks or Kamas.

1,000 Joules will lift 100 kilograms about a meter so they are capable of delivering enough energy from the edges of their weapons to move 1.297×10^{70} Earths to the edge of the Universe. It's also equivalent to 1.593×10^{117} Little Boy Atomic bombs that flattened Hiroshima. It's more power than anyone has ever had access to before. And that's each time they use them. Plus they'll never run out of ammunition since there are a lot of cubic meters in all of space for them to use. It'll be enough to disrupt operations where they are going. Oh yes, plenty he figures to teach them a lesson—about the power of love.

...

Contents

Quantum Entity Book 3 The Successors (2014)

...

Bruce M Firestone

About the Author

Bruce M Firestone
B Eng (Civil), M Eng-Sci, PhD

Bruce applied to go to McGill University in Montreal at age 14, arrived after turning 15, and graduated as a civil engineer before legally becoming an adult (then, age 21). He was rejected in his first job search because he was considered a "child," not legally responsible for his actions. Three and a half weeks later, he was living in Sydney, Australia. A new and exciting labour government had just been elected. The first two things Prime Minister Gough Whitlam did were to recall Aussie troops from Vietnam and to lower the age of majority to 18.

Bruce worked for the New South Wales government, doing operations research and building mixed integer programming models while continuing his education at the University of New South Wales, where he obtained his Masters of Engineering-Science degree, and then at the Australian National University in Canberra, where he received his PhD in urban economics.

He was among the first group in Australia to fly hang-gliders and not die. He has travelled to and worked in Canada, Australia, the United States, Sri Lanka, New Zealand, India, and many other nations. He has been, at different times, an engineer, a real estate developer, a hockey executive (founder of NHL team the Ottawa Senators, Scotiabank Place, and the Senators

Foundation—a children's charity), a university prof, a consultant, an art collector and benefactor, a writer, a columnist, a futurist, and a novelist as well as Executive Director of not-for-profit Exploriem.org—an organization dedicated to assisting entrepreneurs, artpreneurs, and intrapreneurs everywhere. More recently, he has started his Learn By Doing school.

Bruce has taught and studied at McGill University, Laval University, the University of New South Wales, the Australian National University, Harvard University, the University of Western Ontario, Carleton University, and the University of Ottawa in subject areas that include entrepreneurship, business models, architecture, engineering, finance, urban planning, urban design, and development economics.

He has launched, or helped launch, more than 172 startups. Currently, he writes two blogs—EQJournal.org (about entrepreneurship) and DramatisPersonae.org (about artpreneurship and urban issues as well as life)—and moderates lively @ProfBruce and @Quantum_Entity communities on Twitter. He is also author of *Entrepreneurs Handbook II.* His upcoming novels include *Quantum Entity | The Successors* (the last book in his QE Trilogy) and *Urban Nirvana and the Peradventures of Maddy Henderson.*

He is married to a most wonderful girl, Dawn MacMillan. They have five great kids and one fine grandson.

...

"Entrepreneurs follow a moral path when they—first, take care of their business so that, second, the business can take care of their families so that, third, their families can take care of them so that, fourth, they don't become a burden on society or their fellow human beings so that, fifth, they can help others so that, sixth, others can help their business," Prof Bruce, 2013.

His current motto is *"Making each day count."*

...

Blogs: eqjournal.org and dramatispersonae.org
Twitter: @ProfBruce and @Quantum_Entity
LinkedIn: www.linkedin.com/in/profbruce
Facebook: https://www.facebook.com/QuantumEntityTrilogy
and https://www.facebook.com/Exploriem
YouTube: http://www.youtube.com/user/ProfBruce
and http://www.youtube.com/user/quantumentitytrilogy
Read or send friends first four chapters of Quantum Entity Trilogy
FREE: http://www.old.dramatispersonae.org/images/QuantumONE_C
S_Third_Edition_First_Four_Chapters.pdf
Books available from: http://www.brucemfirestone.com

Bruce M Firestone

Author's Note

I always wanted American Spring to be less about learning outcomes and more about storytelling. Whether I succeeded with the objectives of Book 1 and now Book 2, I don't know. That is up to the reader to judge for herself or himself.

One thing I am sure about is that Book 2 is about love, trust and redemption. It's about accepting the fact that we are all imperfect and, it's from those imperfections that we come to gain experience and it's from experience we can find a path to wisdom. I tell (or have told) the love stories of Nell and Damien, Dakota and Traian, Ellen and Damien, Farrar and Ellen, Mary and Caleb, Jag and Arcadia, Micah and Daniella, Damien and Euphony, Damien and Zora, Sabine and Nahuel and, of course, Sean and Naya. I also tell the anti-love story of Naya and Cliff. I have one more great love story to tell in Book 3. Am I overdoing it? Again, readers can make up their own minds about that. But love and the trust that goes with that are what make human life interesting and worthwhile. Without love and family, humans are nothing in my view. Perhaps that is old fashioned but I don't think so.

I also deal with the concept of Good and Evil. The scene between Sean and Cliff where Sean realizes he is in the presence of the Devil or one of his disciples might not find resonance with a modern audience but then again, it might. I realize that many westerners live in a post religious society and will find some of the concepts I introduce here and the exploration of various religions foreign to them. I accept that. But I think folks should also accept that not everyone today shares a modern sensibility that 'everything is beautiful in its own way.' That, my friends, is bullshit in my opinion.

People who think there is some good in all of us and that Evil is an outdated concept should look at the white slavery trade that is rampant in our world today. We still have slaves, millions of them and many are women and children. They often follow the same slave routes and are sold into the same slave markets as Slav women and children were in the Middle Ages.

In how many countries, do tiny children live in the bush, beside roadsides or in trash dumps who are completely on their own—who have to fend for themselves and are prey to every type of adult exploitation? Millions.

According to Mark MacKinnon (Globe and Mail, September 11, 2012), thousands of North Korean labourers are imported into Russia (to places like Vladivostok) to work 12 to 15 hours a day. After each workday, they return to apartments shared with a hundred others or live in underground bomb shelters lit by single bulbs. Political cadres from the government of Kim Jong-un accompany labour gangs from North Korea to Russia and take *all* of their earnings and remit them to Pyongyang. Political cadres do no manual labour themselves.

If you don't believe in Evil, you just aren't looking. Sorry if I offend you.

...

There is quite a bit of technology speculation in American Spring. One thing I am positive about is that we are not going to be able to explore or colonize our solar system unless the tech we have gets a lot better and I don't mean more of the same, just faster. That has gotten us a long way from simple computers that can do basic functions that fill whole buildings to smart phones today that we hold in the palms of our hands that are millions of times faster and more capable. Nice. But that isn't going to get us a terraformed Mars or Luna. We need completely new tech that becomes so cheap and ubiquitous that mining an asteroid (or moving it and then mining it) is ordinary course of business.

Bruce M Firestone

It is when the boundaries of tech move outwards—in quantum leaps so to speak—that real progress is made. If something requires heroic efforts to do (whether that is finding clients for your new enterprise or putting human beings on the Moon), it isn't sustainable. Just think about how long ago the (heroic) Apollo landings were on Luna and yet no one has been back since. Now that sucks. But the real reason (apart from the facts that the US is tending to look more inwards these days, that the great rivalry in space with the former USSR is over and that the US has lost some of its guts to chance new things and not just in space) is that it isn't economically or politically sustainable precisely because it is heroic.

So to make American Spring a bit more plausible I had to invent some new technology. Here is some of what you see in Book 2.

Technology of American Spring

Airship
BPI, Birth Prevention Insert
DNA marking
DNA scanning
Farm-in-a-box, aka Roxie
Mindlink/Quantum Entanglement
Mtv, Materiality Television
Mtv Test, similar to screen test
Nanosite Constructors and Deconstructors
Nanosite Generator and nutrients
Pico Carbon Tube materials
Quantum Bubble/Planetary Shield
Quantum Scanners
Quantum Shielding
Quantum Tunneling/Transport
Sinofighter
Sinofighter console
Skin coat or skin coating

Space Elevators on Luna and Mars

Tentacle Nutrient System attached to hydrothermal ocean vents

I hope you've enjoyed learning about the tech of American Spring. There will be more in the final book of this trilogy, The Successors. (You get a sneak peak at that in the Prologue for Book 3 that I have included at the end of Book 2.)

...

In Book 1, I did my best to keep control over my characters and their technology. I wanted Book 1 to be less about science fiction and more about business and politics. But I figured if I could suck you, dear reader, into a world of Quantum Entity which is near term and believable, I could relax that control somewhat in Book 2.

But one thing I did not want to do is make this trilogy a story about wizards or magicians or witches who can use their staff, wand or spell to make cool things happen. Other people have done that far better than I could ever hope to achieve. So if a character in this trilogy ever wrinkles her cute little nose to bewitch someone or rearrange her house cuz the boss is coming over for dinner and she doesn't have time to clean house before he does, you have my permission to throw your copy of Quantum Entity into the nearest recycle bin or delete it from your e-reader.

There are a few surprises in Book 2 for the Author—times when my characters took control of my keyboard and wrote their own part in this tale. Ellen's trip to Mars, for example, was never in the original storyboard. She just made up her mind that was what she had to do. When I read what she wrote, it had the ring of truth. I hope you will agree. The geography is much wider in Book 2 and it is a much larger cast of characters so I added a Cast of Characters and a Geography List to the front of this Book to help the reader keep up with not only their names and where they are from but also all their nicknames.

Bruce M Firestone

When Naya talks to dead people (well, one dead person) or someone sweeps in to take Nahuel's soul *before* he dies, there are good explanations for that and it isn't based in mysticism or magic. I just haven't told you how this happens. Be patient, I will (in Book 3).

Still there is a lot of spirituality in these books, frankly, more than I thought when I started out on this journey. At the end of the day, anyone who tells you there is no room for spirituality (or for that matter religion) because there is no proof that there is anything more than the plane of existence we see around us and experience via our five senses (hearing, touching, seeing, smelling and tasting) is not being scientific. Science is open (or should be) to things not yet proven. Keep an open mind, everyone!

I personally believe that we have more than five senses. At least one more—feeling. Feelings make up an important part of our decision making. You feel with your head, your heart and your gut. I tell my students that they should never start a new project unless all three are in alignment and in agreement.

You think with your head, for example, that doing SKIP-AID would be pretty cool? OK! But what if your heart isn't in it? Well, if you're not passionate about it, it won't happen or, if it does, it will suckatate. Do you think Naya was able to raise nearly $2 million in SF for SKIP-AID because she wasn't passionate about it? I don't think so.

Now what if your gut instinct is telling you, THIS IS A BAD IDEA. Well, you should listen to it. So are feelings a sense? If the definition of senses is that they help you interact with the world around you, gather data about it and make decisions, then I would answer, 'Yes.'

Readers will also know that I believe humans are, in fact, capable of quantum thought—making huge leaps forward with scant apparent preparation so maybe thinking itself and consciousness should be added to our list of senses. But perhaps I go too far.

The point is, I think there are more, (possibly) many more senses humans use they just don't know it.

...

I put a fair bit in here about urban economics, urban design and development economics because Ellen faces an immediate crisis after she overthrows the old Republic. Their economy is in the toilet for a lot of reasons and she has to apply some basic lessons we don't usually associate with western nations.

There is no doubt in my mind that city-state economies form the backbone of any modern economy. Fixing a national economy seems more likely to work if first we get the right national signals in place and then we get local city-state economies humming. Foremost at the national level would be confidence and that is what Ellen focuses on by making Happy Speeches all over the new Commonwealth.

Then she spends time talking with Daniella and a QE specifically tuned to urban and development issues, Oper1s. They educate Ellen about what the pre-conditions for economic takeoff are based on the work of two noted economists—Walt Rostow and Hernando de Soto. She also learns about what can be done at the urban level to prime the pump there.

There is no doubt in my mind that we are building cities in much of North America and, for that matter, in many parts of the world that follow North American urban planning principles (which is pretty much everywhere these days) that are junk. I recently spent some time in Crete* where small towns and villages thrive all over that island. Now why is it that Crete can save their villages from decay or renovate them and not have them become ghost towns?

(* Chapters 12 to 16 and the Epilogue were written while I was there so if you detect a certain Cretan influence in the last third of Book 2, hmm, don't be surprised. Chapter 14 in particular bears the hallmark of a

Bruce M Firestone

certain family—Costa Levendakis' family and their ridiculous Oregon palace to be precise.)

I would start with the role of the car and the regional shopping mall. In the tiny village of Episkopi where I stayed for a month, they have recently redone the town square in flagstones. It is a small, vaguely triangular public space (sometimes called a platea) roughly 45 metres long and perhaps 25 across. There is a café that spills into the town square, a taverna, several private homes and two Churches that border it (helping to enclose the public room) and three main roads that converge on it in a Y-pattern. There are several driveways, courtyards and two more minor roads that join the platea at strange and unpredictable angles. Remember all this in a TRIANGLE that has a base of 25 metres and a height of 45. Every square metre counts.

The square serves as a meeting place, a parking lot, a series of patios, a party place (more on that later), a playground for tiny kids and big ones too and a major transit route for cars and trucks. Huh? What's that you say? A major transit route for cars and trucks. Are you kidding me? Actually no.

You see in Crete kids have the right of way over cars and if a building intrudes into the right-of-way, they don't knock down the building and pave it over, they expect cars and trucks to motor around obstacles not run them over or into them. Buildings overlook and empty directly onto roadways—if you own a café across the road from me and your front door is open and mine is too then guess what? Cars can't pass. They have to wait until our conversation is finished and one of us closes our door.

If you walk the narrow roads of Crete and hike along them in the mountains like I do, you'd better learn to walk on the *right* side of the road like locals do. You see you have to pretend (as a pedestrian) that you are a car (they drive on the right hand side of their roadways like we do in North America). If, while in Crete, you walk on the left facing oncoming traffic like you are taught to do in NA, you will die. Cars naturally hug the right side of the road on these narrow trails and, if you happen to be there, kapow, you get to meet St. Peter and sprout angel wings early.

Greeks (not just Cretans) are independent people and don't like rules. They are always on the lookout for 'windows'—we would call them loopholes. There is freedom in Greece to succeed and freedom to be a fool and fail. The one National Road on Crete (on the north side, the Aegean side of the island) that vaguely resembles a North American highway but it has fruit vendors on it so, on a hot sunny day (and they have many of those) you can stop and have some melon pretty much anywhere. There are hundreds of driveways, minor roads and dirt trails that link to the National Road and still cars and trucks can travel safely at 90 kph because Cretan drivers are not lulled into a false sense of safety by traffic engineers who are relentlessly paving over huge swaths of this planet with super highways that have minimum safe distances, limited access and turning radii that would be satisfactory even to Vogons.

In mid-August each year, the clans that inhabit Episkopi organize a dinner in their village square. They clean the square, set long tables with white table cloths and lots of local wine, beautiful flowers, build a stage at the west end of the square and party. Every generation is there. They start at 8:30 pm and end when it ends—close to dawn the next day. For that one night, it would be unwise to drive through the middle of their party because even though these are lovely people, they are also a mountain people and both the Turks and the Nazis had a tough time suppressing them and taking away their traditional property rights as well as their human rights.

Their music is not out of a can—DJ supplied. Instead, it is live music that is powerful rizitika—rebel tunes and folk tunes played on medieval instruments. If you have not heard it live, felt it resonate in your chest, you cannot say you have experienced it. They play with the lyra, the Cretan laouto and askomandoura (a type of bagpipe) and they sing. Tunes last for 2 minutes and 30 seconds, perfect for commercial radio, right? Not on your life—they last for 12 minutes or more. People dance together not alone.

By 9 am, everyone is bleary eyed and at Church which is filled to overflowing.

OK, so am I suggesting that what's holding these tiny villages and towns together is partying, music, tradition and religion? Partly.

But there is also economic opportunity. Lots of it. A world-class development expert who was with us in Episkopi tells me that Crete would thrive even without their tourist industry and I believe him. I met a young woman with two beautiful children and a handsome husband. Anna (not her real name) has not one, not two but three jobs. She works in her family's quarry each morning (Greece has lots of stone buildings and lots of stone), cleans investment property she and her husband own in the afternoon and then works in the local taverna at night. Her kids can visit her wherever she goes at any time.

Cretan people are hard working not just hard partiers. Crete produces a prodigious amount of agricultural product—olives, oranges, citrons, goat cheese and specialty cheeses, yogurt, viticulture, mutton, olive oil, figs, flowers, dozens of varieties of fruits and vegetables and much more.

It is economic opportunity that allows Cretan villages and towns to keep their most important resource—young people like Anna and her family. But much of their economic opportunity would be lost if they rip down their traditional stone buildings, pave them over, put in four lane divided highways and drive to a big box store megamall. We build cities that are car zoos; they build towns and villages for people.

We can learn a lot from Crete and, indirectly, Ellen does.

...

I could go on for another 600 pages on the subject of urban design (I taught Design Economics and Urban Design and Development for 14 years to architects) but I will spare you that. But when architects gave over (circa the post WWII era) the design of cities, towns and villages to urban planners with their moronic monoculture zoning maps (big box stores here, office buildings there, ridiculously named 'industrial parks' here, single family homes there and, oh, we forgot to set aside some land for civic buildings like schools and our budgets are tight so let's build schools on cheap crap land no one else wants like under high tension power lines so we can irradiate our kids when they are most vulnerable (i.e., experiencing the fastest cell division of their lives)), we started to produce the worst urban blight, maybe ever. Right. Hell of a plan.

I blame the profession of architecture. Architects actually know something about design, delight, light, space, negative space, art, beauty, utility, form and function. Urban planners have fucking zoning codes that they think are the equivalent of the Ten (Million) Commandments. Cities are being planned by Vogon bureaucrats? Are you kidding me? No wonder everything built in the last 60 years is a piece of shite, as Sean would say. (It (or Gobshite) seems to be the only swear word he will use.)

So I will stop there but if this novel has added in any way to your understanding of these issues, I am glad.

...

As in Book 1, there is quite a bit of music referred to in American Spring. Some of it, like the tunes I refer to in Naya's appearance at Orpheum, is just invention. If I accidentally referred to any song title that actually exists of the same name, I apologize.

But there are many real tunes I refer to and I try to be sure I give credit not only here but in the text to the marvelous creators of this music and poetry—

A British Tar (Gilbert & Sullivan)
A Night in Tunisia (Art Blakey & the Jazz Messengers)
Beat and the Pulse (Austra)
Boot Scootin Boogie (Brooks and Dunn)
Dancing Cheek to Cheek (Irving Berlin)
Home (Edward Sharpe & The Magnetic Zeros)
I Believe in Miracles (Hot Chocolate)
Beethoven's Ninth Symphony from Stanley Kubrick's A Clockwork Orange
Join the British Army (Ewan McColl)
Just My Imagination (The Temptations)
Love Me Do (The Beatles)
Nell's Folly (Chris Brydges)
People Get Ready (Curtis Mayfield)
Poi E (Patea Māori Club)
Revolution (SONSOFDAY)
Somewhere Over the Rainbow (music by Harold Arlen, lyrics by E.Y. Harburg)
The Times They Are A-Changin' (Bob Dylan)
Thunderstruck (AC/DC)
TNT (AC/DC)
Travelin Soldier (Dixie Chicks)

Alfred Noyes (The Highwayman)
Peter S. Quinn (The Sun Rays, a lyric)

I tried to be judicious in quoting these artists, using just enough to give the reader a sense of what the people in this story were experiencing when they heard this music or poetry.

I can only imagine what it would have been like to be Naya and have 10 foot Sinofighters appear with AC/DC music blaring at maximum volume and hearing this—

I'm dirty, mean and mighty unclean
I'm a wanted man

Public enemy number one
Understand
So lock up your daughter
Lock up your wife
Lock up your back door
And run for your life

Now how would you react if you were a young mother and someone was threatening to kill you and your baby and you heard this song? I think it adds terror to the scene and gives a reader an extra dimension to hopefully better understand what these people are facing. Overwhelming sound can be debilitating. Sinofighters and their creators know this as do most armed forces and terror/anti-terror forces on this planet.

My apologies to AC/DC, I actually get their music— it's very alpha male. It's not that men don't have these desires, trust me they do. It's your ability to channel that into something other than aggression, war and rape that matters.

...

I have many people to thank but I will be brief this time. I thanked most of them in the Author's Note in Book 1. A few people though deserve special mention.

Joe Krenosky worked terribly hard with me and my youngest son, Matthew Firestone, on the Texas Hold'em scene between the General and the repulsive guy from Queensland. Joe is a former MBA student of mine and a hell of a card player. He, Matthew and I tried to outdo Casino Royale's Texas Hold'em game (from the 2006 film). If Joe played General Staubach, I'm not sure who would win. It'd be a toss up I think.

Special thanks to Jaime Farfan, a Zumba Education Specialist and an unbelievable choreographer who worked with me on Naya's dance scene at Orpheum. What you read there is a blend of what he did and I did with a significant contribution from Vancouver-based actress and poi dancer Barbara Kozicki.

Jaime was born in Cali, Columbia and this is how he describes himself:

"I am a 5'9, 27 year-old Latino, in fairly good physical shape. My best quality is probably that I am willing to just throw myself into innovative things. I thrive when I find something new—it gets me excited. I have a very addictive personality so when I like something, it usually takes over my mind and it becomes my main focus, many times not fully thinking things through—just going all the way. I would say I'm a doer more than a thinker.

I moved to Canada at age 13 with my parents and younger brother. After studying business finance for a few years and having a job in retail, I realized my true passion is working with people. I am now married and we have four great kids. I served almost ten years as a reservist in the infantry ending up in an office for two years at the time my first child was born. Being in a stifling office reinforced my desire to work with people—my passion for life drifted away while I was in that office.

In 2008, I began teaching Zumba® Fitness—I had been weight training since I was 15 and dancing all my life so it seemed right! I totally immersed myself in the world of dance and fitness. I travelled five continents, licensed thousands of instructors for Zumba® Fitness and have new friendships all over the world. Now wouldn't it be great to actually do Naya's dance scene for real. What do you think?"

I would also like to thank my EA, Alex Wolfe, for the work he has done on Book 2. I also asked for and received his permission so he has a cameo role in Book 2 as an… EA!

A big shout-out to Jean Luc Cooke too (from CertainKey.com, a crypto systems company) who is a fantastic cryptologist. Jean Luc helped me with the random distribution of failures that Damien, Jag and Chuck experience with quantum tunneling. The formulae you see there are his…

If there are any errors or omissions in this work, it is the fault of the author and none other.

…

I work a bit more in Book 2 with biz models and I went at it pretty hard with SKIP-AID less so with Voyager. As far as the latter goes, it just is a fact that circumstances intervened to prevent Naya from really developing her plan for Voyage to Earth Population 1.2 billion. Those bastards from Club Les de Sades just would not let go of her. I hate them for it and I hope you do too.

SKIP-AID didn't actually come from Huntsville (Ontario not Alabama). It came from my imagination. So if you think it's a dumb idea blame me not the Muskoka town.

Naya is the most complicated character I have ever attempted to describe and I think that she represents, at least for me, the dichotomy of the human condition. We are all attracted to the dark side. Just ask Luke. It is from our dark side and our daemons that we get a lot of our creativity and energy for art and accomplishment. It pushes us, it seduces us, it pulls us in.

Naya's journey may make some people squirm, it is truly terrible. But look at what she accomplishes— triumph over disease, alcohol, deviant behavior followed by success in higher education, research, civic projects and commercial endeavour. She also finds her way to motherhood and true love. And then she sacrifices herself to save her baby and her friend. Wowza.

You may have picked up in Book 2 that Damien's speech in Stockholm is at odds with respect to his actions after Naya is injured on the Monumental Tower. He is being a hypocrite and does eventually come to realize that. You cannot expect your children to be great leaders if you hover over them and insulate them from RL. Of course, as a parent (I have five great kids), you naturally want to protect them.

This is really what I am getting at—so much of life is about contradictions. That is why humans often cannot *know* what the right thing to do is. They cannot figure it out with just their five senses because they can never resolve these contradictions, never, without employing some other tricks like using their feelings, gut instincts, heart and quantum thought processor (our minds not QEs). The other thing we do is we experiment—we try something and if it works, we do more of it. If not, we stop.

This is Naya. She represents the best in all of us and the worst. It is from this intense cauldron of experience that come wisdom and leadership which Naya might have the opportunity to show us in Book 3. That is, if Sean can get her out of the hands of the evil people who hold her prisoner. Go Sean! Go Naya!

...

@ProfBruce

@Quantum_Entity

Crete, Greece

List of Learning Outcomes*

1 Dr. Carlton B. Goodlett Place
20 Questions
22nd Psalm
23rd Psalm
100-mile Lunch
1924 Model TT Ford flatbed Three Quarter Ton Truck
1967 UN Outer Space Treaty

A
Ace in the Hole
Active services
Acute stress reaction
Adams, Scott
Adventures of Huckleberry Finn
Aggie Bonfire
Agnes of Denmark
Agronomy
Air Force One
Airship
Ajiba, Ahmad ibn
All-in
ALS
Ambergris
American Academy of Motion Picture Arts and Sciences
America's Cup
Andromeda
Anemia
Anglosphere
Antarctica
Anti-spin flower
Antiemetic

Apgar score
Apple
Arab Spring
Archeologist
Armstrong limit
Art Blakey & the Jazz Messengers—A Night in Tunisia
Ash Wednesday
Ashkenazi Jews
Assisted suicide
Associate Professor
Astral projection
Arms like an Egyptian
Army Rangers oath
Arsia Mons
Auckland
Austin
Average work week

B
Babel
Baby sign language
Back to the Future
Bamboo athletic wear
Baptism
Barton Creek Wilderness Park
Base 20
BC Ferries
Beaufort wind force scale
Bedouin tent
Begbie Lamp
Ben Ali, Zine El Abidine
Bhenchod
Birth canal
Black and white smokers
Blocko

Blood quantum law
Blunt trauma
Body language
Body surfing
Boggs, Wade
Bond albedo
Bond, Alan
Bonnie and Clyde
Bono
Bouazizi, Mohamed
Box step
Break-beat
Brainpan
Branch Davidian Ranch
Brand
Brujo and espíritu
Bulleit Bourbon
Butterfly move
Butterfly twist
Bundesliga
Bush bash
Bushido
Business Model
Buy the blinds

C
Calculus of death
Camel mount
Camel ride
Camp Mabry
Campbell, Ken
Cane knife
Capitalize
Captain Picard
Carpenter effect
Carthage
Casa Poporului
Cat cow
Catatonic state
Catholic Belfast
Celebrity endorsement

Centenary College of
Louisiana
Center for Complex
Quantum Systems Cerebral
perfusion
Cervix
Chaebol
Cheap flop
Chernobyl
Chocolate Panini
Choreo/choreography
Christie, Agatha
Churchill, Sir Winston
CINC
Circulatory shock
City-state
Civic budget
Clear Lake
Clear title
Clockwork Orange
Code Hero
Coleman Slide
College Board
College of Natural
Resources, Berkeley
Colonel Sanders
Complainant
Coneheads
Connected wilderness
areas
Conservation subdivision
design
Cosmo's Moon
CPR
Creosote tea
Crete
Croquet
Crowning
CSIS

D
Dallas-Fort Worth
Data archive
De Soto, Hernando
Dean, James
Defibrillation
Deimos
Demography
Depression
Development Economics
Devil
Dictamnus
Dirac notation
Disney Company
DMZ
Domestic terrorist
Don't Ask, Don't Tell
Dodo Case
Dollars are democrats
Double bluffing
Douglass, Frederick
Downward dog
Dragomen
Drone attack
DSA (Directed Studies
Abroad)
Due to the Bearer
Duties of Heart

E
Eam Numerare
Earth escape velocity
El kabong
Elmira College
Elna
Emasculator
Emily Carr University of Art
and Design
Emoticons
Emperor of Japan
Encyclopedia Britannica

Energy density
Engineered fill
English Premier League
Environmentalism
Epilepsy
Equity lord
Eucharist
Europa
Even-stacked
Evolutionary behaviour
Extradition

F
Failure rate
Family of nations
Farm marketing board
Fat Tuesday
FDR
Female s-curves
Female sacral powers
Femtoscale
Ferengi
Fertility rate
Fifth Columnists
Financial risk
Fire Marshal
Fire Poi
First principles
Fiscal impact
Fishpond
Flat call
Flight risk
Flopped the nuts
Flying disc design
Forest bathing
Fornix
Fort Leavenworth
Frederick II
Friction coefficient
Frontier lawyer
Fuel cell

Fulfillment operation

G
Gabriola Island
Gated communities
GED
Geld
General of the Army
General Theatrical Release
Ghee-free curry
Ghirardelli chocolate
Ghost
Giger, HR
GIS overlay
Glandular tissue
Golden Age for television
Golden Gate Park
Goldman, William
Golf ball textured flying disc
Googol
GPM (Gross Profit Margin)
Grand Mal seizure
Granny flat
Great Reset
Green Stop
Green Stop Dollars
Gravity well
Groundhog Day
Gunpowder
Gwailo

H
Habitable orbit
Hackathon
Hakama
Hand-glide
Hand-glide freeze
Handie-Talkie
Hands in a box chore
Hang glider for

Snowboarding
Happy baby pose
Hawke, Bob
Headsup display panel
Hematuria
Hemingway, Ernest
Hermosa Beach
High speed rail
Hip-hop/break dance/dub step
Hitchcock, Alfred
Hog Town Vegan
Hoffman, Abbie
Holy Roman Catholic Church
Honey Bees
Hopi drum
Hopi Wedding
Hopi Wedding Blanket
Hopi Wedding Manta
Horned God
House of Windsor
Human traffickers
Hydrothermal vents
Hypothermia

I
Ideomotor effect
Illegal alien
IMG
IMG Sports Academies
In utero
Infanticide
Information density
Information Transfer Rates
Infotainment
Insomnia
Intracranial injury
Inversion
iPad
iPhone

IRA
Iraklion
Irish Catholic
It girl
IT infrastructure

J
Jasmine Revolution
Jefferson, Thomas
Jeld
Jesse H. Jones
Communications Center
Jibe
Jiujiebian
Jobs, Steve
Joinery
Jordan, Michael

K
Kama
Kennedy, John F
Khmer Rouge
Kids Sit Down Windsurfer
Kill list
Kim Jong-un
Kimono
Kingston Penitentiary
Kirby and Co
Kite the settlement
Kosmic
Kotatsu frame
Kowtow
Krishna
Khmer Rouge

L
Lagrange point
Lake Baikal
Lammas
Land conservancy
Land lease

Landed immigrant
Lani
Lateral thinking
Law of unintended
consequences
Lawrence Livermore
National Lab
Leadership
Lee Dynasty
Leet name
Lent
Lesions
Liberal Arts and Science
Academy High School of
Austin (LASA)
Limited Liability
Partnership or Corporation
Limbic system
Line dance
Little Boy Atomic bomb
Local ordinance
LOST AND NOT FOUND
Lotteries
LTV (Loan to Value) ratio
Lunar colonization
Lunar day
Lunar regolith

M
Mad River structure
Maidenhair
Male sex drive
Management Corporation
Manboobs
Mandarin
Mandela, Nelson
Maori
Maori Poi dance
Maple Leaf Gardens
Marcom solutions
Mardi Gras

Mare
Marketplace behavior
Mars
Mars Colonization
Mars day
Mars Gravity
Mars year
Martial law
Martyr
Mayan arithmetic
Mead
Melas Chasma
Memphis Jukin/Juk/Jook
Mensa Ants
Mere
Mesosphere
Messaging
Metacognition
Meteormorphology
Military-industrial complex
Milky Way
Minoan
Minoan architecture
Minotaur
Mithridates VI Eupator
Mithridatism
Mithradatium
Mixed use neighborhoods
Mohave people
Monokinis
Monumental Tower
Moon Goddess
Moraine
Mortality
Motorola
Mount Rushmore of Dance

N
Nation State
National priorities
Natural Philosophy

NBA
Negative Cost Marketing
Negative perspiration
Neuroscience and cognition
Nike-elbow freeze
Ngati Rangiwewehi
Nobel Memorial Prize in
Economic Sciences
Nobel Lecture
Nobel Prize in Physics
Nobel Peace Prize
Nollie
Non-farm productivity
growth
Norman MacKenzie House
North Korea
Novel—genre, literary,
mainstream, learning
outcome
Nunchuks

O
Occupy Grassel
Office of the President, UC
Okie sodbuster
Old-Fashioned cocktail
One child policy
Ordinance enforcement
officer
Organized Research Unit
Orpheum Theatre
Orwell, George
Oxycodone

P
P3
Pacific Heights
Panspermia
Paparrazzoid
Parkour
Part time Prof

Bruce M Firestone

Patea Māori Club
Patent protection
Pay-what-you-can-afford
Pentobarbital
Percentage rent
Performance bikini
Perseids
Personal Business for Life
Personal productivity
Phaistos palace
Phobos
Phratry grouping
Picket line
Picoscale
Pitcairn Island
Placenta Praevia
Plan view
Planchette
Planetary gravity well
PPP (Purchasing Power Parity)
Poker etiquette
Political cadre
Political cover
Ponzi scheme
Pop & lock
Population projections
Port Isabella
Post-Christian
POTUS
POW
Power of Sale
Power to weight ratio
Precedent
Preconditions for economic takeoff
Presidential Executive Order
Primer
Probability mass function
Product placement

Productivity, non farm
Professional
Property taxes
Prostitot
Psychological measure
PTSD
Public domain
Public room
Purchasing Power Parity
Punic Wars
Pyongyang

Q
QWERTY keyboard

R
Rabbit hunt
Rabbit stick
Rail stand
RCMP
Reed Richards aka Mr. Fantastic
Reincarnate
Release form
Reserve fund
Return on Equity
Return on Investment
Reverse marketing
Revised ALS Functional Rating Scale
Rex Ball
Reynolds Brothers Sawmill
Ricardo, David
Riluzole
Roquet
Romulus and Remus
Ross Media
Rostow, Walt
Royal Swedish Academy of Sciences
Royalty on revenues

S
Sadists
Safe room
San Quentin
Sanctuary
SAT
Savannah College of Art
and Design
Savings and investment
Scientific method
SCOTUS
Script
Settlement date
Sex toy
Shackelton Crater
Shadbolt, Jack
*Shakespeare: The World as
Stage*
Share buyback
Shark Tank
Shenyang
Shaolin style arms
Shavasana
Shock troops
Shuanggui
SIDS
Sisyphus
Situational syncope
Skateboarding
Skater
SKIP-AID
SKIP-OFF
Skull Valley
Slav women
Slow-rolling
Smith, Adam
SNL
SNO (Sudbury's Neutrino
Detector)
Social Media

Socialization of risk and
leisure
Solar proton event
Southie
Space shuttle
Spanish influenza
pandemic
Sperm
Sperm Wars
Spermatic chord
Spirit of the Game
Sponge bath
Spreckels Lake
St Odrian
Staging operations
Standards
Starfleet
Star Trek, TNG
Steam room
Strategic Defense System
Street trees
Stiff-body head glide
Stockholm
Stockholm City Hall
Stratosphere
Street Paddle Tennis
Subterranean rights
Success fee
Sufi mysticism
Sufism
Super majority
Superflyer
Sweat lodge
Swedish Royals
Swedish waltz
SXSW
Symbiosis
Symbiotic relationships
Syrus, Publilius

T
T-bills
T-maze
Tabloid press
Taekwondo, Korean
Mouhébong
Taiji shirt
Talk of Hands
Talking uphill
Television-with-personality
Tenure
Testbed market
Texas A&M
Texas Hold'em
The World Without Us
Thermal isocline
Thermal sink
The Book of Eli
Thought experiment
Thought units
Three Crowns
Three Laws of Robotics
Tice
Titanic
Tow-in surfing
Traitor
Treasury
Tribal dance
Troposphere
Truth and Reconciliation Committee
Tug-of-war
Tunisia
Tunisiana
Turkish coffee
Twain, Mark

U
U2
Ulster Defence Association

Ultimate
Ultimate Question of Life, the Universe and Everything
UCSC
Unchicken
UNESCO
Union scale
Union shop
University of California, Berkeley
University of Texas at Austin
Uprock
Urban design
Urban economics
Urban planning
UT Physics
Uterus

V
Vacuum Energy
Valles Marineris Vancouver
Vanuatu Corporation
VAT
Vegan
VIN (Vehicle ID number)
Virgil
Vladivostok
Volunteer hours
Voyage to Earth 1.2 billion souls
Voyager I

W
Walkie-Talkie
Walkover
Warrior 1
Warrior Monk
Waspie
Waste heat

* Please note page numbers are no longer included with the List of Learning Outcomes. We apologize but the number of editions and platforms in today's publishing world make it nearly impossible to have stable page numbers. In most e-editions, you can use ctl 'F' or a FIND function to locate a topic of interest to you.